Barbara Cardy founded and edited erotic imprints In The Buff and The Hot Spot. To date she has edited 25 erotic anthologies. She lives with her husband, children and a host of animals in a cosy cottage in the lush English countryside.

Also available

The Mammoth Book of 20th Century Science Fiction
The Mammoth Book of Best New Erotica 5
The Mammoth Book of Best New Horror 17
The Mammoth Book of Best New Manga
The Mammoth Book of Best New Science Fiction 19
The Mammoth Book of Celebrity Murder
The Mammoth Book of Comic Fantasy
The Mammoth Book of Comic Quotes
The Mammoth Book of Dirty, Sick X-Rated & Politically Incorrect Jokes
The Mammoth Book of Egyptian Whodunnits
The Mammoth Book of Erotic Photography
The Mammoth Book of Extreme Science Fiction
The Mammoth Book of Famous Trials
The Mammoth Book of Funniest Cartoons
The Mammoth Book of Great Detective Stories
The Mammoth Book of Great Inventions
The Mammoth Book of Hard Men
The Mammoth Book of Historical Whodunnits
The Mammoth Book of How It Happened: Ancient Egypt
The Mammoth Book of How It Happened: Ancient Rome
The Mammoth Book of How It Happened: Battles
The Mammoth Book of How It Happened: WWI
The Mammoth Book of How It Happened: WW II
The Mammoth Book of Illustrated True Crime
The Mammoth Book of International Erotica
The Mammoth Book of IQ Puzzles
The Mammoth Book of Jacobean Whodunnits
The Mammoth Book of Jokes
The Mammoth Book of Kakuro, Worduko and Super Sudoku
The Mammoth Book of New Terror
The Mammoth Book of On The Edge
The Mammoth Book of On the Road
The Mammoth Book of Perfect Crimes and Locked Room Mysteries
The Mammoth Book of Pirates
The Mammoth Book of Private Eye Stories
The Mammoth Book of Roaring Twenties Whodunnits
The Mammoth Book of Roman Whodunnits
The Mammoth Book of SAS & Special Forces
The Mammoth Book of Secret Codes and Cryptograms
The Mammoth Book of Sex, Drugs & Rock 'n' Roll
The Mammoth Book of Shipwrecks & Sea Disasters
The Mammoth Book of Short Erotic Novels
The Mammoth Book of Short Spy Novels
The Mammoth Book of Space Exploration and Disasters
The Mammoth Book of Special Ops
The Mammoth Book of Sudoku
The Mammoth Book of True Crime
The Mammoth Book of True War Stories
The Mammoth Book of Unsolved Crimes
The Mammoth Book of Vampires
The Mammoth Book of Vintage Whodunnits
The Mammoth Book of Wild Journeys
The Mammoth Book of Women's Fantasies
The Mammoth Encyclopedia of Unsolved Mysteries

THE MAMMOTH BOOK OF

Lesbian Erotica

Edited and with an Introduction by Barbara Cardy

ROBINSON
London

Constable & Robinson Ltd
3 The Lanchesters
162 Fulham Palace Road
London W6 9ER
www.constablerobinson.com

First published in the UK by Robinson,
an imprint of Constable & Robinson Ltd, 2007

A copy of the British Library Cataloguing in Publication Data
is available from the British Library.

ISBN 978-1-84529-477-9

Printed and bound in the EU

1 3 5 7 9 10 8 6 4 2

Contents

Contents

Acknowledgments

A TASTE FOR PAIN © 2007 by Sarah Veitch. A shorter version appeared in her collection *Different Strokes* (Nexus 1995, reprinted 2000). Reprinted by permission of the author.

TYNESIDE LADIES' NIGHT © 2006 by Charlotte Matthews. First appeared in *The Hot Spot 4*. Reprinted by permission of the author.

TAKING STOCK © 2007 by Susan Wallace. Printed by permission of the author.

"PLEASE" © 2007 by Linda Suzuki. Printed by permission of the author.

SWEET REVENGE © 2007 by Rececca Henderson. Printed by permission of the author.

LITTLE WOMEN © 2007 by Rosemary Williams. Printed by permission of the author.

EXOTIC MUSIC © 2004 by Teresa Noelle Roberts. First appeared on SatinSlippers.com Printed by permission of the author.

THE LAY OF THE GRECIAN URN © 2004 by Roxy Katt. First appeared in *The Hot Spot 2*. Reprinted by permission of the author.

OWN GAOL © 2004 by Vav Garnek. First appeared in *The Hot Spot 1* under a different title. Reprinted by permission of the author.

NEIGHBOURS © 2006 by Marie Gordon. Printed by permission of the author.

Introduction

Barbara Cardy

Not one for long-winded intros as I know you want to get on with reading the book . . . It has been a great privilege to put this collection of stories together. To sum it up, this book is a sizzling collection of compulsively readable sexy short stories with a lesbian theme. A book that will appeal not only to the lesbian community, but also to straight women and men – think "Girl on Girl" meets Bridget Jones!

The exceptionally high quality writers have their characters involved in all manner of sticky situations and the plots throughout are absolutely superb and original – aspects very often neglected within the field of erotica.

Frequently humorous, sometimes deeply touching, but always highly erotic! So let me now pass the pleasure over to you.

("Google" your favourite writers to find more of their stories in other books and on various websites too.)

A Taste for Pain

Sarah Veitch

Aha! Kay Reid sat up straighter in her chair as she heard the floorboards on the stairway creaking. Someone was obviously sneaking downstairs. Experience told her they'd be making their surreptitious way towards the kitchen, a kitchen which was out of bounds to everyone except the chef. For days now he'd been complaining that food was going missing. She'd been right to stay awake and on guard.

Leisurely, Kay stretched out her tennis-toned arms then tiptoed towards her bedroom door, the mirror showing her five-foot-eight frame in her favourite khaki shirt and matching army surplus trousers. Heart starting to beat harder, she flexed her firm, right spanking palm. As owner of Trim Camp, she'd found that keeping discipline sometimes involved more than an inspirational lecture. A sly slap to the back of some eighteen-year-old's thighs was usually enough to take the overeater's mind away from pasta. A shaming spank to a jean-clad rump usually shocked a young woman into more sensible snacking, the option being going to college in the Fall still looking fat.

Kay was there to see that they got slim. That's why they'd enrolled at Trim Camp, paid thousands of dollars to live on this campus near Los Angeles. Kay talked to them, watched over them and weighed them, was the British slimming leader who'd gotten first class results here in the States.

And would continue to do so. Kicking open the kitchen door and turning on the light in one co-ordinated move, she inhaled hard and got ready to shout at her failing teenage slimmer. Felt her mouth slacken as she saw who the culprit was. "Lynette!" Lynette, a fellow Brit, was her recently-appointed Junior Diet Lecturer. She'd already ticked the girl off for weighing more than she should have on Weigh-In Day.

Kay stared at her trainee, who stood clutching three thick slices of imported Scottish cheddar, meant to be doled out in small squares to successful slimmers. The large multi-grain loaf, pound of butter and jar of pickles on the kitchen worktop told of her plans.

"Sorry – sudden snack attack," she muttered, reddening.

"According to the chef, you've been having them every night."

"I've . . ." The girl rubbed one bare foot behind an equally bare suntanned leg. Her thigh-length nightie rose at the awkward movement, showing the lower half of her chubby buttocks. "Well, the dinners have been small recently."

"And I've told you to make a second trip to the Salad Bar," Kay reminded her. "What am I always telling the girls? Choose fibre over fat."

"Sorry, Miss Reid. I am – really." The girl turned to put the dairy products away.

"No – leave them out. I want you to look at them while you're being punished." She let the younger woman dwell for long seconds on the humiliating words. They reverberated around her own head, giving her an unmistakable frisson. This would be the first time she'd disciplined a staff member aged twenty-two . . .

She stared at the blonde girl's slightly rounded tummy and made her voice especially hard. "What happens if you get plump?"

The younger woman swallowed. "I . . . get sent home, Miss."

"So perhaps you should think about packing?" That image should make her think twice.

"But I don't want to go home!"

"Then what do you think we should do with you?"

"You could . . ." The girl played convulsively with her long hair, winding it around her right hand in nervous tendrils. "I won't do it again."

"But stealing and stealth still deserve chastisement."

"I know." The diet lecturer dipped her head.

"What you need is a good spanking," Kay added. She held her breath, watched the hot shame redden the girl's face and neck and stay there. Young women who were completely uninterested in punishment or in femme2femme always told her to go to hell or threatened to take her to a tribunal at this stage. But

Lynette merely stood there, blushing, waiting for further instruction. *It was time to go for it.*

Kay took hold of the wooden armless chair and pulled it out into the centre of the room. She sat down and patted her lap with obvious inference. "Now get that over-indulgent little bum over my knee."

Lynette blushed some more, moved from the ball of one bare foot to the other: "But what . . . what if another Camp member comes in?"

"The kitchen's out of bounds, so they'd be transgressing. I suppose I'd have to spank you both, or even make you take turns spanking each other. I'd quite like to watch – and direct – for a change."

"You mean you've done this before?" Lynette's eyes were wide and fixed and slightly glassy. She resembled a somewhat chunky Barbie doll, someone who wanted to be conventionally pretty but was unwilling to exercise or eat healthily to get in shape.

"Mmm, frequently. More often than I'd have liked."

That last sentence was a lie. Kay loved to feel a young, firm female bottom under her hands, adored making the flesh jerk and redden. Ached with desire as she found her rhythm and caused the owner of the bum to emit little squeals and louder cries. Enjoyed everything from the first moment when she pulled down their panties and told them what she was going to do to their silky-soft hemispheres, to the last seconds when she let them slide, whimpering, from her knee.

"I think I'll use the wooden spoon on you for taking so long to acquiesce to your punishment," Kay said, her vulva twitching at the thought of baring Lynette's nightdress-covered bottom, "That's after your spanking for breaking our kitchen rules, of course." She made eye contact with the younger girl. "If you don't come over here now I'll have to fetch you, and that equals an even sorer bum."

"If you'd lock the door?"

"No, bad girls have to take their chances." She patted her lap again. "All this procrastination is earning you the hottest arse."

Lynette glanced at the door. She stared at the food she'd removed from the fridge then reread the notice on the wall which warned slimmers that they'd lose privileges for dietary transgressions. Slowly she approached her superior, her feet dragging on the warm floor.

"There!" Kay took hold of the girl's nerveless wrists, "That wasn't so difficult." She started the controlling sideways pull that would win her this pouting blonde victim, get her positioned and held defencelessly in place.

Hauling the junior lecturer down, she manoeuvred her across her knees, caught sight of them both in the chrome panel of the cooker. Kay looked strong and slightly sturdy, her short auburn hair and large dark eyes giving her the appearance of control, of presence. The girl over her lap had a fair-haired, slender prettiness of a more traditional kind.

"Right, let's get that arse warmed," Kay said, looking down at the bum curves outlined by the thin, embroidered cotton. She slid a roving palm beneath the garment and stroked the girl's twitching rear. "How fortuitous – you aren't wearing any knickers. Maybe you secretly wanted to be caught and thrashed?" She squeezed more strongly at the still-hidden prize, watching the back of the blonde girl's neck pinken with embarrassment.

"God, no."

"You mean you wanted to eat forbidden food? To put on weight? To ruin my reputation? Oh dear, it's going to take me a long time to re-educate this recalcitrant backside."

She raised her hand and laid on a firm, centre-of-cheek spank over the nightdress.

"Ouch!" Lynette exhaled hard, and reached both hands back to cover her chastened orb.

"Bad girl. I didn't give you permission to touch your bum," Kay murmured, glad of the excuse to further discipline her subordinate. "You've left me no option but to tie these wicked hands out of the way."

Slowly she leaned back, enjoying the girl's nervous – or was it eroticized? – squirming, and unbuckled the calfskin belt from her waist. "Right, let's get these protective fingers held in front." She used the belt to bind the girl's wrists together, adding lightly, "You have to learn to take your punishment without complaint."

Lynette gave an experimental tug at her bonds. "But it stung. You did it so hard."

"Of course it stung – that's my intention. And it's going to sting much, much more." So saying, she edged the thin nightdress up the girl's slender back and tucked it under her armpits, then contemplated the bottom she'd just bared – a bottom that was full and taut and frenzied. The handprint she'd made on one golden cheek was already fading. Kay flexed her fingers then slapped smartly down on the other orb.

"Ow!" Lynette was halfway through another squeal when Kay doled out five full-force spanks on alternate buttocks. Buttocks which writhed and pushed forward and arched backwards and moved sideways and jerked. She knew that it was vital to exert her authority from the beginning, that Lynette would respect her more afterwards – and get more turned on if she had a secret submissive side.

"Save your histrionics till you feel the wooden spoon on your backside," Kay said, then stopped to fondle the glowing trophy. She noticed that Lynette breathed hard and fast during her ministrations. It was a safe bet that the little minx was starting to get wet.

"Is your bottom hot now?" she asked conversationally.

A humiliated whimper: "Yes, Miss."

"And I'll bet you're not hungry any more."

"No, Miss Reid." The girl sounded breathlessly eager to please.

"Which shows that spanking you is good therapy, don't you think?" There was a pause. Kay stroked the hot, pink globes some more. "Answer me girl, or you'll make my right arm even angrier."

"I suppose . . ." each syllable sounded dragged from her ". . . that you were right to spank me, Miss Reid."

Kay ran her left thumb pad over the backs of the girl's thighs. "Were right to spank you? That's past tense, suggests that I've finished. Believe me, my dear, I've hardly started yet."

She watched the girl's shoulder's tense, heard and felt the shuddering indrawn breath: "But my bottom's so sore, Miss."

"I can see that it is."

The Camp Leader caressed the well-warmed, fleshy sphere. "But I have to teach you discipline, and a few light slaps will hardly do that, sweetheart. I need to know you've learned total obedience and self respect."

The young lecturer swallowed. "I won't steal food again. I'll fill up on salad. I'll be obedient, Miss."

"A good walloping will make sure of that, will remind you of the penalty for breaking rank here at Camp Trim."

Kay had been in the army long before she'd made it to the top on Civvy Street. She knew how to re-educate a young recruit, how to mould her into snivelling subservience. "I have to administer a thrashing that will remain in your memory forever," she explained.

"But what if someone comes in?" Lynette asked again.

"They'll see me using the wooden spoon on your naughty bottom."

"You mean you're about to . . . ?"

"Only once I've finished spanking you," Kay explained. She ran a thoughtful hand over the blonde girl's squirming cheeks. "Now stop complaining and thank me for the warm-up spanks."

"Thank you for the warm-up spanks, Miss Reid," the younger woman mumbled.

"You're very welcome. And tell me you're looking forward to the main part of your spanking which will be starting any moment now."

Silence. She fondled the pinkened contours, enjoying the girl's aroused pants and sighs.

"Tell me," Kay repeated.

"I'm . . . oh please, Miss, I'm sorry I stole food from the Camp."

"Say it or I may have to fetch my hard-soled slippers – and I have such big feet."

The naughty grown-up girl quivered. "I'm looking forward to my main spanking, Miss."

"It'll make you wriggle like a landed eel," Kay said.

She slid her right hand between the girl's labial lips and her fingers came away coated with gelatinous pleasure. Lynette moaned with what Kay presumed was uncertainty and lust. It was amazing how often a spanking turned a girl on, each slap to the lower arse cheeks reverberating to her sweet spot. She'd pleasured many such miscreants who hadn't previously seen themselves as wanting girl-love. "Your cunt's getting ever so hot," she said crudely. Let her pussy beg a little. "But the only part I'm interested in roasting is your arse."

She smiled to herself as Lynette hung her head nearer the floor, clearly overwhelmed at the ignominy. The girl had given up tugging at her wrist bonds for now and seemed resigned to the remaining bare bottom spanks. Kay laid them on hard, but not as hard as she was capable of. She was pacing herself, pacing the naked flesh beneath her determined right palm. She wanted to leave some of the girl's spirit and energy intact for when she tasted the more focused discipline of the wooden spoon.

When Lynette's indrawn breaths grew close to sobs, Kay stopped. "Let's have a little talk about your diet. What does eating too much butter do to the female bottom?"

"It makes it bigger."

"And you want a small, high bum, don't you, Lynette, because you want to run a Trim Camp of your own one day?"

"Yes, Miss."

"Want a bum that both men and women will admire?"

The girl snivellingly agreed that this was the case.

"So put the butter back in the fridge then get your backside over the table and take your medicine." She untied the girl's wrist bonds and watched Lynette get up slowly from her lap. Her movements were stiff and uncoordinated – lust did that to a girl – as she returned the butter dish to the refrigerator. Then she walked to the table, her nightdress covering her punished backside.

"No – tuck your nightie under your arms. I only reprimand bare bottoms."

"But if someone comes in, they'll see!" Lynette kept her arms clamped mutinously at her sides.

Kay got up and strode purposefully across the room. "Lift it up now or I'll have you back in Leeds before you can say the words 'sacked for gross misconduct'."

With a defeated whimper, Lynette edged up the cotton to reveal her tummy and neatly-trimmed pubis. Slowly, Kay turned her to face the table, encouraged her to bend over it.

"Where were we? Ah yes, about to correct this recalcitrant backside." She caressed the waiting flesh. "I've found that the harder you thrash a troublemaker, the more she respects you. The more prolonged the lecture, the longer it remains in the naughty girl's mind."

"I won't forget – honest, I won't," Lynette mumbled into the mahogany surface."

"I'll make sure of that by giving you lots of time to reflect between strokes."

"I understand, Miss Reid."

Kay looked searchingly round the room. "Oh, dear, I seem to have lost the wooden spoon. I may have to fetch the cane from my room instead and it's much more biting."

"Let me find it!" Lynette jumped up and stared around the

huge kitchen with its numerous hanging tools and colanders and saucepan sets.

"I'm getting bored with waiting." Kay tapped her foot irritably and slapped one palm against the other.

Lynette's hands automatically flew to her bottom and she stared more fervently at the various cooking implements. Suddenly her eyes lit up and she raced towards the large, decorative wooden spoon which hung from one of the alcove walls. As she stood on tiptoe to reach it, her nightdress rose up again, showing her tenderized bottom. Kay's lower belly convulsed with lust.

"Back you come, dear. The table is waiting," she said in a deceptively casual voice. "Hand me the spoon."

Reluctantly, the blonde girl approached and held out the wooden punisher.

"I'll never over-eat again, Miss!"

"The spoon will make sure of that," Kay said. She admired Lynette's nipples, now pushing firmly through the embroidered nightdress. "Bend over the table and grasp the edge." She watched as the younger girl obeyed. "Good girl. Now stick out your arse as far as it will go."

Again, the twenty-two-year-old hesitated. "I'll exercise more in the gym. I'll give up sweets."

"Sounds somewhat unbalanced. Now present your naked cheeks for the rest of their reprimand, please."

She watched as the younger woman took a deep breath, then pushed her buttocks up and back, making a perfect target for the large, smooth spoon.

"There, that wasn't so hard." Kay fondled the bum, enjoying its new humiliated display. "Looks very tempting. Looks like it's just begging for this kitchen alternative to the cane."

Lynette whimpered. The sound seemed to come from very far away. It was from the head, of course, which was obviously feeling very sorry for itself and dreading what was coming. But Kay just wanted to concentrate on warming the arse. She knew that, though the girl would hate each searing stroke, it would make her pussy wetter and wetter, that she might ultimately want to pleasure Kay with her tongue and be pleasured in turn.

She lined up the spoon with the underswell of the girl's rump and swung the implement forward until it hit smartly home. The junior lecturer yelled and started to scramble upwards. "That's bad. That's very bad." Kay stepped forward and cupped the girl's buttocks, cradling them like she would a frightened animal. "You don't want me to have to start all over again?"

"Please, no." Lynette got obediently back in place, then reluctantly presented her bottom for further punishment.

Kay contemplated her handiwork: the lower curve of one spank-reddened cheek showed the first precise lash of the spoon. "Let's make these cheeks nice and symmetrical," she murmured gloatingly before laying on a second stroke.

"Aaah!" The young woman flinched and drove her belly closer against the wood. She drummed her toes on the floor. Kay could hear but not see the scrabbling noises made by her fingers. They obviously wanted to propel her away from this torment, to at least cover her punished posterior, whereas her brain was warning her to get the thrashing over with, to stay in place.

Her brain was obviously winning – at least for now. Kay moved the spoon up a centimetre, and got ready to paddle her would-be lover. She was more familiar with using her hand or a belt.

"My friend at a rival camp enjoys making each failed slimmer's bottom as striped as possible," she told Lynette,."She loves the distinction between the hot red cane marks and the cool white surrounding flesh. Sometimes we swap naughty grown-up girls if we feel that they're growing complacent, can benefit from a change of discipline."

She flicked the implement above the previous glowing stroke then immediately added a fourth parallel mark to the other buttock. Lynette gasped loudly but stayed in place, perhaps contemplating what it would be like to be corrected by a complete stranger. "Now where shall I put marks five and six? Oh, I know, up here where it's feeling neglected." Kay stepped forward to tauntingly stroke the expanse of spanked-but-not-yet-paddled flesh.

"Oh, it really stings!" Lynette wailed. Her sex lips were wetly swollen, obviously begging for liberation. So was her bare backside.

"Just a few more to go," Kay said. Part of her wanted to chastise this pert bum for ever, but the girl was more likely to acquiesce to future thrashings – and subsequent sex sessions – if her pain threshold wasn't over-reached.

She added lashes five and six where she'd indicated that she would and swiftly followed them up with seven and eight towards the top of the luckless girl's posterior, taking care to keep away from the delicate spine. Lynette cried out and ricocheted up. Holding her small crimson cheeks in both palms, face flushed and eyes downcast, she backed away.

"You've done well," Kay said. Lynette faltered, then looked over at her. Kay approached very slowly. "I'd almost finished, dear."

"I just couldn't bear . . ."

"I know. I know." She looked over at the sink as if the idea had just occurred to her. "Look there's that cold cream that the cleaning lady uses to soften her hands. I could use some to cool your toasted backside."

Lynette's hot face reddened further and Kay knew that she was bi-curious but still coming to terms with her sexual desires.

She stared at the floor and mumbled, "I should probably do it myself."

"Are you refusing my generous offer?"

The twenty-two-year-old swallowed hard. "It's just that . . . I've never had another woman touch my bottom before."

"Yet you were happy enough for me to spank you?"

"I . . . didn't want to be sent away."

"Of course you didn't," Kay said. "It's cold back in England compared to here. The food isn't as varied. And if you don't get a good reference from me, you'll find it harder to set up a British camp on your own."

The girl nodded, made brief eye contact then returned her shamed gaze to the floor.

"Which is why you want to stay here, want to please your Camp Leader. Are very grateful when she offers to soothe your punished bum." She patted the kitchen table. "Put your tummy over there, my love." Lynette looked at the table top then moved slowly towards it as if half-expecting to be rescued. Was just settling her belly obediently in place when Kay re-crossed the room with the cream.

For the umpteenth time, Kay lifted Lynette's nightdress out of the way and admired her handiwork.

"It's an awfully hot rump," she murmured, caressing the trembling, smooth globes. Lynette twitched in mute but vociferous agreement. "So you'll be very grateful to Auntie Kay for massaging in some coolness," the older woman continued, taking a golfball-sized globule of cream and starting to massage it in to the glowing flesh. She used slow but firm strokes – erotic strokes. Felt her own groin expand as the girl breathed fast and hard.

Kay kept using her right hand to knead the ointment into the girl's bum, slid her left digits between the girl's parted thighs: "This is just to hold you steady." Smiled in power and anticipation as her squirming victim started to buff her clit against Kay's hand. "Such a naughty bottom," she continued, rubbing the emollient between the writhing cheeks. "So wriggly. Especially when I massage this dividing crack."

"Mmm," Lynette muttered. Her voice tone was something alien and hoarse, almost feral.

"Did you say something?" Kay asked conversationally, feeling the girl move slicker, wilder, harder, "Say that you were ready to take the rest of that paddling on your arse?"

"Mm. Uh. Aah . . ." Lynette gasped out.

Kay scooped more cream into the sensitive crease and stroked on, and on and on, loving the way the girl's sore bum quivered, exulting in her little desperate moans.

"Need to . . ." Lynette mumbled, moving harder.

"Show control, my dear – you mustn't come without permission," Kay replied.

Suddenly the clit beneath her fingers was pushed even more frantically forward and its owner cried out long and gutturally: "Aaaaaah!" There was a ten-second pause till the next rush of rapture obviously took over her bared and shamed body, "Aaaaaaaaah! Aaaaaaaaaah! Aaaaaaaaah! Aaaaaaaah! Aaaaaaah!"

Screams over, she gave a series of little grunts, pushed her thighs tight together, then lay, prostrate, across the table. "Oh, dear," Kay murmured. "I give you a motherly respite from your much-needed rebuke and you repay me by indulging in an unnatural act."

"I . . . But your fingers were . . ." Lynette muttered into the table. Kay picked up the spoon and used it four times in quick succession on the girl's anointed rear to bring her flagging energy back. Lynette wailed and squirmed quickly away, leaving a sex-juice trail on the mahogany surface. Sheepishly she got up and took hold of her hem as if to pull her nightie down.

"No, leave it there so that I have access to your bum whilst you make amends."

"Make amends? I thought I'd . . ."

"It's hardly fair if only one of us orgasms," Kay said.

"I guess," Lynette muttered, licking her full, red lips.

"Good girl. Now get that pretty little tongue over here and put it to use."

Praying that the girl would bring her satisfaction, Kay undid her army surplus trousers and pulled them completely off. Still staring challengingly at Lynette, she did the same with her crotch thong. Then she sat down in the chair and spread her legs into an expectant V.

"I've never been with another woman before," Lynette stammered.

"Sweetheart, you just came against my fingers."

"But . . ."

"You know that you want to, deep down," Kay said.

With a half sob, Lynette knelt before Kay and used her fingers to open up her labial lips.

Kay smiled. "I like a fast light pressure. Put the tip of your tongue directly on my clit." She groaned as wet tissue met wet tissue: she was almost there already. Doling out that spanking and paddling on such a fair bum had been all the foreplay she needed. Just a few flickering licks . . .

"Up a bit, sweetheart. Make sure you get it right, or I'll have to teach you. Have you ever had a big studded belt lashing down on your poor bare bottom? No? It's not too late." She tensed her thighs as the pleasure built. "You'd never be able to bear if without restraint, of course. I'd have to tie your arms and legs over the tallest stool."

Her groin swelled at the image. "Have to prepare your bum first with a sound slippering, then gag you so that you couldn't beg for help or start squealing." The familiar signal in her sex told her that she was almost there. "Or I could take you outside to the woodshed, bend you over a log, get out the whippy cane . . ."

She heard her own half-strangled scream coming from somewhere above her head as the ecstasy flowed through her throbbing pubes in long, hot pulses. Moaning, she grabbed the blonde girl's head and held it there to make sure she kept licking, finally slumped back in her chair.

When she opened her eyes a moment later, Lynette was still crouching on the floor. "Stand up. Bend over. Let me look at your chastened arse, my fallen angel."

The girl's lids fluttered down in embarrassment, but she obeyed. Kay stared at the bent cheeks of pain, at the wet trails of pleasure. "You can go. Your punishment is over. Obviously I'm trusting you not to transgress again."

"I won't, Miss. I swear!"

"Good girl. Then go to bed and sleep on your tummy. Tomorrow life will go on as normal."

"Yes, Miss Reid." Lynette walked towards the door with unusually stiffened thighs.

"And you can pull your nightie down."

The girl gingerly smoothed the pale cotton over the crimson hemispheres, "Yes, Miss. And . . . thanks."

The door closed. The stairs creaked. After a moment Kay heard the girl go into her room. Then silence. Slowly she got to her feet and struggled her way into her thong and army trousers, her tissues still tender from Lynette's surprisingly eager tongue.

She fingered the wooden spoon. When would she have a chance to use it again? There was this particularly impish twenty-year-old redhead called Jo who'd just started at the Camp as Games Mistress and who always gobbled her meals and asked for seconds. She must use up lots of calories on the playing fields . . .

Kay smiled as she buffed the hard, punishing oval of the spoon against her spank-pinkened fingers. It was only a matter of time before Jo made an illicit midnight trip to the kitchen. She wondered how much of a thrashing a well-exercised bum could bear before it turned scarlet and its owner began to beg.

Tyneside Ladies' Night

Charlotte Matthews

It was the usual women-only night – the company doesn't allow mixed parties – and they'd asked me to bring the whole catalogue. Now they were looking at a blow-up doll.

"Eeh, it's disgustin'," said Irene, a tarty woman in a tight red dress. "All them holes!"

"Aye," said Jeanette, the hostess, whose skirt was too short to completely conceal the tops of her stockings. "It's even got a hole in the, you know, the back passage. What's that for then, Pauline?"

"Anal intercourse," I said.

"She means takin' it up the arse," said Irene's daughter, Karen, even tartier than her mother in the kind of micro-mini known locally as a fanny-pelmet.

"What?"said Kathy, the quietest of the group. "You mean they . . ." She looked shocked.

They all laughed and Rene, a rough looking woman who looked older than the rest, said, "Aye, Kathy pet, they stick their things up your bum!"

"Eeh, I've never heard o' that," said Jeanette. She looked so shocked that they all laughed again.

"Oh, it's quite common," said Karen. "Some people like it more than the other way," and she looked meaningfully at her friend, Sharon, who blushed bright red.

"Ah, come on," said Karen. "You're not so shy when you're out with the lasses on a Friday night."

"That's different," hissed Sharon.

"Eeh, Sharon pet," said Jeanette. "Is that right? You let them . . . you know . . . do it from the back?"

"Sometimes," said Sharon, glaring at Karen.

Kathy was fascinated. "And is it . . . does it . . . how does it feel?"

"It feels great," said Sharon defiantly.

I thought it was time to step in. "It is quite common," I said. "There's even a special range of vibrators if you like it that way."

I held up the Derrière Demon, popularly known as the Arse-Bandit, a long thin vibrator with a swollen end. I switched it on and handed it to Kathy. She felt it shuddering in her hand and quickly passed it on to Sharon, who tried to appear casual, but couldn't disguise the pink flush that appeared on her neck and chest.

"Well, what about them little nozzles on the boobies then?" said Jeanette.

There was a moment's silence. "Oh, yeah, sorry," I said. "The Doll. Forgot about her for a minute. The nozzles? They're for squirting milk."

Jeanette's mouth dropped. "Away, Pauline. You mean . . . never. I mean I know men are dirty buggers, but—"

Rene interrupted. "I don't know whether it's dirty or not, but my Tommy used to like it."

We all looked at her. She was wearing a blouse that fastened at the neck, but it couldn't hide her enormous chest. "Aye," she said, not embarrassed in the least. "The first time I was expectin', I had too much milk. I had to express it – that's what they call it. And Tommy came in while I was doing it one day and he couldn't take his eyes off us. An' I had plenty, so I thought, why not?"

"What? You mean you let him . . . ?"

"Oh aye, Jeanette pet. I let him all right. And you can take it from me – when you feed a man like that you get wet, and I don't mean from the milk."

"There's no need for that," said Irene sharply.

"An' every time I fell after that – an' I've had seven, you know – every time I fell, me an' Tommy would go up to the bedroom and lock the door an' I'd get them out an' let him suck away to his heart's content. No harm in it. It was just me an' him."

"Rene!" It was Irene again.

"When I was really full I used to squirt it into his mouth. From right across the room." She grabbed her enormous breasts and squeezed them. "Two jets, like little fire hoses."

There was silence as we all stared at Rene.

Then Jeanette said, "I'll put the kettle on."

We all relaxed.

While Jeanette was making the tea, I put the doll away, cleared the top of the low coffee-table, and got out my box of goodies. When the first one came out – an ivory-coloured Non-Doctor – they all looked at each other and giggled. The second one – a seven-inch flesh-coloured cock with realistic balls, produced an "Oh, My God," and some elbow-nudging. The third one, ten inches, with in-out rotating action, had Irene saying, "Eeh, never in the world," and clutching Rene's arm. And from then on it was a steadily mounting litany of disbelief.

"You're never supposed to—"

"Where's that thing supposed to—"

"Jesus Christ, that'd split you in half!"

One by one, I switched them all on and put them on the coffee-table. When Jeanette came back in, she nearly dropped the tray. Her table was covered in buzzing vibrators, all moving around under their own power, slowly converging on an enormous black dildo in the centre that hummed smoothly like a dynamo.

"Pauline! My God! What do you do with them?"

Everyone laughed. Jeanette blushed. "Well, you know what I mean."

"It's not such a daft question," I said. "It just needs to be put slightly differently."

I pressed the play button on the remote control to start the video I'd loaded earlier, and continued talking over the opening credits.

"You see, when most women ask what something like that's for, what they really mean is, 'Dare I use it?' Am I right, Jeanette?"

Jeanette blushed deeper. The others said nothing.

"That's why we always show this video at these parties. It's American, so it's a bit over the top, but basically it's just women – all ages, all shapes and sizes – using vibrators for the first time. If you still wonder whether you dare, just have a look at this."

I switched off the vibrators on the table and went to the back of the room to watch.

The video's not porn, it's actually quite serious, made by a sexologist who found that most of the women who came to him with sexual problems didn't have problems at all – their husbands did. And when he was able to get these women "in touch with their own sexuality" (I told you it was American) – usually through getting them to use a vibrator – they never looked back.

So he made the video to spread the gospel to women everywhere. I said it wasn't porn, and it isn't, but that doesn't mean it's not a turn-on. The first few minutes are a bit slow: he's explaining to this middle-aged woman – about forty, I'd say – all about his theories and how the use of vibrators is medically recommended. But then he leaves her alone in his office to try one out for the first time, and that's when the fun begins.

You could have heard a pin drop as they watched her look around to make sure she was completely alone, then pick up the vibrator he'd left with her. She found the little slider button straightaway and switched it on – and promptly dropped it when she felt it buzzing in her hands.

They laughed, almost with relief I thought, and Jeanette said, "Nobody's drunk their tea. Shall we have something a bit stronger, lasses?"

I put the video on pause while she got the gin and sherry and Babycham out, and then pressed play again.

The woman on the screen picked the vibrator up, and this time, after looking around again, she sat in a soft leather chair, a bit uncomfortable at first, but then relaxing and moving her backside forward so that her legs opened a bit. She took one last look at the closed door, pulled her dress up to expose her white cotton knickers, and then gingerly, as if afraid it might hurt, put the tip of the vibrator to her crotch.

She opened her eyes wide when it made contact. Then she closed them, sprawled further down in the chair and really began to use it. She pressed it hard against her, giving a little shimmy with her hips as she did so, and began to move it up and down, turning it in her hand. Soon the dress was up around her waist and she was half lying on the chair. She kept up this low level stuff for a minute or two, then stood up suddenly and went quickly over to the door and locked it. Hurriedly, she took off her dress and slip and then pulled down her knickers and stepped out of them, revealing a thick black bush.

Their eyes were glued to the screen as she hesitated, then removed her bra. Her breasts weren't firm, but they were big, and they could all see that her nipples were hard.

This was usually the moment when the tension disappeared. This woman was not young, not a model, just an ordinary housewife who'd had kids and was getting on. Her figure was good, but her body was that of a forty-year-old, and being alone, she made no attempt to try and make it look better than it was. It made them feel good. The older ones, anyway – she wasn't too different from them.

She went back to the chair, and this time she sprawled, lying almost flat, her hips well over the edge, her feet and knees wide apart. I heard Kathy gasp as the thick black hair parted to reveal pinky-purple lips that were clearly wet. Then they all gasped as she pressed the vibrator to those soft lips and kept pushing until the tip had disappeared. She spread her legs wider, threw her head back, and inch by inch, pushed the vibrator up inside her. When only the last inch was visible, she began to buck her hips, thrusting hard against it. Her breath was ragged now and she was really giving it six-nowt, as they say in these parts, her body moving in complete abandon. They could all see that this woman was really doing it, really pleasuring herself, not caring about anything but coming.

And when she did come they were right there with her. She closed her legs tight, toes pointed, and pressed both hands down hard on her mound, intensifying the thrill of the rod vibrating deep inside her. Little tremors began to sweep her body and she clutched herself tighter, bucking against her own hands, thrusting her hips again and again until she suddenly went rigid, heels on the carpet, head against the back of the chair, and, body trembling and twitching, came like an avalanche.

"Bloody Hell," said Irene, her voice a bit shaky.

They'd all been knocking back the drink while this had been going on. Now they got fill-ups and started on them like there was no tomorrow as they settled down to watch.

After that introductory scene, which it was explained had been secretly filmed but only used afterwards with "the subject's full permission", the rest of the video took place at one of the sexologist's workshops. In a large, thickly carpeted room, twenty naked women pleasured themselves with a variety of vibrators and other implements. There were old women with hanging tits and sparse grey bushes, and young women with tits like firm melons and hard round arses, and every other type of woman you could imagine in between. Some had shaven fannies, and the camera tended to concentrate on those, since there was no hair to obscure the detail of what they were doing to themselves.

And they all had different styles. Some just concentrated on their clits, with the vibrators standing almost upright; some slid their vibrators up and down their slits, turning them slowly as they did so; some shoved them up as far as they would go and kept on shoving; some stuck them onto hard surfaces with rubber suction cups and squatted on them, flexing their knees to move the hard cylinders up and down inside them. Some had their legs as wide apart as they'd go, some had their legs pressed tightly together. Some played with their nipples, twisting and tugging with one hand as the other controlled the vibrator, some concentrated entirely on their vaginas, using both hands. And when they came, some grunted, some panted, some squeaked and some screamed.

I surveyed my little audience. Nobody noticed. They were all fascinated. Jeanette had sat so far forward in her chair that her skirt had ridden right up – her stocking tops and suspender straps were clearly visible. Rene was sitting well back in her chair with her heavy legs open, moving her hips every now and then as if to get more comfortable. And Karen and Sharon were biting their lips. What they wore left nothing to the imagination and their nipples were very obvious, hard little spikes pressing against the material of their tops. When the screen went dark, I said, "Well, ladies, this is the time when I suggest you try some of the goods for sale. You've seen what they're for. All you've got to do now is pluck up your courage and try before buying." This was directly against company policy, but I always achieved high sales so no questions were asked; and it was rare for me to even have to do any cleaning, because what they used they usually bought. "I'm game," said Rene straightaway. "Takes no courage. I got off twice just watching."

"Rene!" said Jeanette.

"Well, it's true," said Rene. "My knickers are soakin'. Are yours not?"

Karen and Sharon giggled. Nobody answered.

"Jeanette's got plenty of rooms upstairs," I said. "So to make it easier, I've put a selection of stuff in each one. Nobody needs to know about what you do but you."

"They can all watch for what I care," said Rene, and rose heavily from her chair. "See youse upstairs." She went out and we heard her climbing the stairs.

The drink had done a lot to loosen their inhibitions. It wasn't long before they made their excuses – eeh, I need to go to the toilet anyway – and followed her, one by one, a little unsteady with the drink. Only Kathy, the quiet one, was left.

"If you don't mind, Pauline, I'd just like to see the video again."

"No problem, Kathy. We've got copies for sale if you like it that much." I rewound it for her.

About ten minutes later with Kathy watching fascinated as the woman in the sexologist's office moaned and writhed again on her chair, I went upstairs with my order book.

The door of the first room – Karen's bedroom – was ajar. I knocked and peeped round. It was Karen and Sharon, both naked. Sharon was lying on her front with her legs spread wide and Karen was kneeling between them, holding her hair out of her face with one hand and shoving an anal vibrator up Sharon's arse with the other.

"Eeh, no," said Sharon as she saw my face appear at the door. Karen laughed. "Come in," she said. "Why not?" and she pushed the vibrator up as far as it would go and switched the power up a level. Sharon went rigid and began to moan. Her arse cheeks started clenching and unclenching around the black rod that protruded from between them, and – the time for proper language was long since past – her cunt gaped wet below. Karen giggled and began to wiggle the vibrator, pulling it slowly out and then pushing it slowly back home.

"Hang on," she said, and leaving the black wand in Sharon's arse, lurched off the bed to pick up a flesh-feel vibrator moulded like a cock. She switched it on, said, "Hold on to your socks, pet," and slid it smoothly into Sharon's cunt. Sharon began to writhe as the two vibrators buzzed inside her. "Oh God," she said in a choked voice, and then her arse clenched tight and she stayed rigid like that for a full minute as we watched her come.

Karen signed my order form. As I left, she was strapping a butterfly vibrator around her hips. She switched it on and fell back on the bed beside Sharon, pressing the moulded shape against her cunt with both hands.

When I knocked on the next door, there was no answer. I opened it quietly. Irene lay on the bed fast asleep. Her red dress was pulled up around her waist and her legs were wide apart, knickers hanging off one ankle. Her hands were clasped loosely round the last two inches of a ten-inch black dildo – the rest of it was inside her. As I watched, she snored and almost woke up. Then, in her sleep, began to move the dildo as if it was a gear lever. Her legs opened wider and a smile spread across her face. I left an order form on the bed beside her.

My knock at the next door along was answered immediately. "Come in." It was Jeanette's voice. "Eeh, Pauline," she said, in some embarrassment. "I thought it was Irene."

She was naked except for a pair of thigh-high red PVC boots with spike heels and she was trying to buckle herself into a two-way strap-on dildo.

"Don't worry," I said. "Nothing I haven't seen before. Having trouble?"

"Oh, it's all right, pet." She made as if to put the strap-on down.

"No, here. Let me help you. Lie on the bed."

She hesitated, then lay down with her hands over her crotch. "Open up."

She hesitated again, then removed her hands and spread her legs. Her fanny was shaven bald. She was blushing.

I raised an eyebrow.

"It just feels a bit cooler that way," she said.

I picked up the dildo and put the head of one end against her smooth cunt lips. Jeanette closed her eyes. I worked it a bit, and with a wet slurpy sound, the head went in. Jeanette rolled her hips a little. I rotated it gently and pushed.

"It's a big one," I said. "You'll have to help."

She reached down, still with her eyes closed, grabbed the shaft of the dildo and started to work it up into her cunt. I pushed gently on the other end and all at once she gasped and it slid home, all the way. All that could be seen from the outside was the other end, curving up from between her legs like a big pink cock. I buckled the straps and she stood up, her breath catching as it moved inside her. "Where's Irene?" she said in a thick voice.

I led her to the room I'd just left. The black dildo was hanging half out of her, but Irene was still asleep.

"The dirty cow," said Jeanette drunkenly. She crawled up onto the bed, her own dildo swinging, and pulled Irene's out and threw it on the floor. Irene woke up with a start, but Jeanette was already locating the head of her strap-on between her friend's legs.

"Eeh, Jeanette," said Irene, but Jeanette ignored her, and with three hard thrusts, drove the shaft home. Now there was a dildo inside Irene and a dildo inside Jeanette and neither of them was visible. But they were joined, cunt to cunt, and only the slightest movement was necessary for them to fuck each other very effectively indeed.

Irene was so drunk she was still half asleep. She didn't open her eyes, just grabbed Jeanette's arse and started humping. Then she lifted her legs and clasped them round Jeanette's back. That was when they both started to come. I was fascinated, couldn't stop watching Jeanette's arse, couldn't take my eyes away until they'd finished. They were both past their prime. There wasn't much firmness. Their bodies showed few elegant lines. But I thought they were beautiful. They were certainly real.

Jeanette pulled herself free with a plopping sound and staggered to the door on wobbly legs.

The last door, at the end of the passage, was wide open. Standing upright on the floor, attached by a huge suction cup, was a twenty-inch electric dildo, so thick my hands wouldn't have met round it. Rene, all sixteen stone of her, was standing over it, and as I watched, she slowly squatted until the end was against her cunt. She shimmied a bit to get it located, and then she simply continued squatting, taking that massive thing up her like a piston sliding into its cylinder. When she'd gone down as far as she could, she sat back with her hands behind her, the dildo bending on its flexible base, then lay down on her back and shuffled herself forward onto the big shaft. It took her a while, but eventually, more than half of it had disappeared inside her and her cunt lips were stretched wide around it like elastic bands. She grunted and switched it on from the remote control beside her. A low smooth hum came from inside her. The dildo was so powerful it made the flesh of her thighs wobble.

"I'll have one of these, Pauline." she said. Then, "You can piss off now – I've got work to do."

As I closed the door I heard the electric motor start to work harder.

Downstairs, Kathy was watching the end of the video. "Eeh, Pauline," she said, hurriedly straightening the skirt of her dress. "You gave us a fright."

"Enjoy it?"

"Oh yes. It's been an eye-opener." She looked shy all of a sudden. "I've always liked women's bodies more than men's." She blushed. "I don't know if it means I'm queer, but I sometimes . . . like to look at my own body in the mirror."

She dropped her eyes. "But I don't think I could use one of those buzzy things, Pauline."

"No need to, Kathy," I said. I looked her in the eye. "If you're game?"

She nodded, almost imperceptibly, and stood up. I put my arms around her. She shivered, but then I felt her arms go round my back. I began to kiss her, gently, letting my tongue dart between her lips as she stiffened, then relaxed. "Oh, Pauline," she said, and began to kiss me hard.

I grabbed the back of her dress and pulled it up until I could get my hands down the back of her knickers. I squeezed her arse and pulled her against me. She was very excited and had to take her mouth away from mine to breathe.

I unzipped her dress and unfastened her bra, then pushed her away a little so that she could let them fall around her feet. Then I knelt and began to lick and suck her nipples. They went hard in my mouth and I felt a thrill go all the way down to my cunt. As I chewed at her, I pulled her knickers down. When she stepped out of them I pushed her gently over to the couch. She fell back and spread her legs, shyly – yes, it is possible to do that shyly, and it's a huge turn-on. I buried my face in her bush. It smelled fragrant, and when my tongue penetrated the coarse hair, I plunged it deep into her cunt, feeling her juices coat my mouth. I opened her wide with my fingers and then took as much of her into my mouth as I could, sucking almost the whole of her cunt, chewing and nibbling at it gently with my teeth.

She stiffened and I knew she was close. Not yet. I stood to take my own clothes off, and as I unbuttoned and unclipped, she lay there with her legs wide open for me, and began to pull at her nipples with a sly little grin on her face. Quick learner.

I pulled my top off over my head and, while I was blind, she stood and came up behind me. She pushed her wet cunt against my arse and took my tits in her hands. She stroked them and pulled at the nipples, then let one hand trail down my stomach and my bush until its middle finger was deep inside my cunt. I pushed back against her and bent over. She fumbled behind me and then her finger slid into me, then another finger, and another, until almost her whole hand was in me. She began to move it in and out, brushing the nipples of my hanging tits with the palm of her other hand.

It was time. I pulled her down to the floor and when she was lying flat, I moved round behind her until I was kneeling over her head. Her tongue licked my swollen lips, sucked at them, and then I moved along her body until my head was over her crotch. I put my arms around her thighs and slowly buried my face in her wet cunt, and at the same time, felt her arms go around my thighs and her face plunge into my own cunt. My tits were squashed against her belly as I sucked her and I could feel her nipples hard against my legs.

Our tongues went in and out, our lips gripped fleshier, more complicated lips, our teeth nibbled gently at our clits as we strained to open up for each other. When I came I pressed my fanny hard against her mouth and felt her doing the same. We ate each other up.

When we eventually pulled apart, Kathy lay back exhausted. Her face was wet with me and mine with her. We kissed.

It doesn't pay that well, my job. It's the perks that make it worthwhile.

Taking Stock

Susan Wallace

Sue gently rubbed her clitoris, sparks of pleasure making her body quiver and jump beneath the pale bed covers. Her eyes were tightly shut as she drew closer to orgasm and imagined her manageress cornering her in the basement stockroom of the stationers. Miss Sear's lips were pressed to hers in a heated embrace that filled her with longing. She was pinned to the wall by the older woman's body, held in place as hands explored her chest, toyed with her small breasts.

The movement of Sue's finger quickened and its pressure increased on her clitoris as her mind's eye was filled with the erotic scenes of fantasy. Her breathing grew with her lust, skin becoming flushed, back arching slightly as the orgasm built to a crescendo and then rolled warmly out through her body in intensely pleasing waves.

Her finger's movement slowed and a satisfied smile curled her thick lips. Sue's eyes opened and she stared up at the ceiling, the room coated with a soft orange glow from the streetlight outside. She savoured the sensations as her thoughts turned to the next time she'd see Miss Sear; at work the following day.

Slowly sleep came upon her, its peacefulness aided and abetted by the gentle tapping of rain upon the window pane.

The next day Sue stood at the till behind the white counter at the front of the shop. She'd been working at the stationer's for nearly three months and her staff assessment was due at any time. The other two shop-floor staff, Kerry and Clare, were down in the basement stockroom and Miss Sear was on her lunch break. Sue had been left alone, but didn't want to have to call the manageress down from the staff lounge, especially after she'd confidently told Sue that she'd fit in just fine. It wasn't that she couldn't handle the till, she was just worried about customer enquiries which she'd be unable to answer. As it turned out, this worry was well founded.

"Do you have any A4 address books in brown leather?" asked the elderly lady with a sour face cross-hatched by deep wrinkles, a white bobble hat covering most of her grey curls.

"Erm . . ." responded Sue awkwardly, glancing over at the door on the other side of the store which led to the stairwell and nervously toying with a length of jet black hair, hoping that one of her co-workers would appear.

"Well?" demanded the old lady impatiently.

Sue flushed, partly in annoyance and partly in frustration. She wasn't supposed to leave the till unattended and certainly wasn't supposed to leave the shop floor completely devoid of staff. If she was caught doing so then Miss Sear would soon take back her vote of confidence.

"I'll go and check for you," said Sue after a moment's thought.

She signed off the till and stepped around the counter, nearly tripping over the old woman's tartan shopping basket.

"Could you hurry up," said the old lady.

Sue strode down the aisle of envelopes to the rear of the shop and opened the white, "staff only" door.

"Kerry? Clare?" she called down the stairwell, hearing her voice echo slightly up the stairs to the first floor where the staff lounge and office were located and then back down to the basement door below.

There was no answer.

Sue looked back along the aisle as she held the door open. The old lady glared back at her and then glanced meaningfully at her watch.

Sue rolled her eyes and trotted down the stairs after quickly looking round the shop, seeing only two other customers on this dreary Wednesday morning.

When she reached the bottom Sue was confronted by lines of heavily stocked shelves. It was then, as she peered down the length of the stockroom trying to catch a glimpse of her co-workers, that Sue heard the faint sounds of Kerry moaning.

Sue quickly walked further into the depths of the long room and as she drew closer to the noises her pace slowed. The sounds were of pleasure, and deep pleasure if she was any judge.

The moans and groans were coming from around the next line of shelves. Sue wasn't brave enough to step round and come face to face with whatever was going on between the piles of box files and diaries so she quietly stepped down the aisle beside her.

With pulse quickening, Sue tried to find a gap in the piles of stock where she'd be able to spy what was happening on the other side of the shelving.

She suddenly went still. Between the piled reams of paper she saw them. Kerry was leaning against the shelves opposite, her head back as she continued to make sounds of pleasure, strands of long, strawberry blonde hair sticking to the sweat on her forehead. Her black trousers were nowhere in sight, her smooth, white hips and legs revealed.

Clare's head was buried between Kerry's parted legs and Sue could hear the sounds of her tongue lapping and probing greedily, her hands reaching up to fondle her friend's large breasts beneath the white blouse Kerry was still wearing. Kerry's fingers held Clare's bobbed brown hair as she let the sexual excitement consume her.

Sue felt the heat rise between her legs as she watched Clare's head rhythmically moving as she lapped at Kerry's moist lips. She longed to see the soft vagina with Clare's tongue parting it seductively.

She slid her right hand down the front of her black skirt and inside the lilac thong she was wearing. Her finger gently parted her already moist lips and softly ran their length as she continued her eager voyeurism.

The fingers of Clare's right hand held Kerry open and Sue glimpsed the glistening pink lips of the other woman before she moved her tongue to the wetness once again.

Sue's index finger slid inside her and she reached out to support herself with her left hand. The shelf before her creaked ever so slightly and Kerry's head lifted. The two women's gazes locked immediately and a thin smile appeared on Kerry's face as Sue blushed and quickly pulled her hand from her knickers and skirt.

"Lick me harder," said Kerry breathlessly, her eyes never leaving Sue's.

Sue turned and left the stockroom as quickly and quietly as possible, her cheeks burning. She reached the shop floor feeling very flustered and took a few deep breaths to calm herself as she made her way back to the till.

When she arrived at the till point she discovered the old woman had left the store. "Old bag," she mumbled under her breath as she looked at the monitor behind the counter which was linked to a recently installed security camera. It pictured the far corner of the shop, an area all but hidden from sight. A teenager was loitering, fingering the various stationery products before him. Sue watched him intently until he finally left the corner and then the shop.

By the time Clare and Kerry emerged from their special encounter in the stockroom Sue was serving a businessman in a pin-stripe suit and was completely over her previous embarrassment.

Miss Sear returned from lunch. She strode up to the till point while running her hand through her short brown hair. "How's it been down here?" she asked with a smile.

"Fine," replied Sue, keeping her gaze averted and feeling her cheeks flush slightly, like a little girl with a guilty secret.

"Are you sure everything is all right? You look a little flustered." Miss Sear studied Sue's face, noting the touch of colour upon her cheeks.

Sue nodded weakly, barely managing to make eye contact with her superior and the subject of her private fantasies.

Miss Sear placed her right hand on Sue's shoulder. "Don't worry, you're doing very well."

Sue looked into the older woman's dark eyes and forced a thin smile. "Thank you," she replied as she recalled the job interview which had been conducted in the small office upstairs. The room had been extremely tidy and the sun shone in through a small window to the right as Miss Sear had sat behind her desk. There had been a distinct impression of being assessed, more so than with previous job interviews. Miss Sear had come across as very perceptive, a watcher and a listener who took everything in.

Miss Sear gave Sue's shoulder a gentle squeeze and then walked away towards the rear of the shop. Sue watched her, appreciatively taking in her full figure while feeling relief that she hadn't taken her questioning any further.

The rest of the day passed without incident and Kerry didn't mention the fact she'd seen Sue watching the sexual exploits between the shelves of piled stationery. Sue had felt tense every time Kerry was near, though thankfully Miss Sear didn't seem to notice as they tidied up and switched off all the lights bar those in the window displays.

The following morning everything went as usual. The customers asked questions she could rarely answer and she had to keep asking for Kerry or Clare's assistance, Miss Sear spending much of her time up in the office doing a stock order. There were mothers looking for items for their children to use at school and business people stocking up on printer paper, copier paper, and ink cartridges. It was a run-of-the-mill job, all bar the slight blip the day before.

"Could you go downstairs and get a couple of green leather diaries?" asked Kerry after Sue came back from lunch and while Miss Sear was having hers. "There's a customer coming in for them later," she added as she served an elderly couple.

Sue went to the rear of the shop and headed downstairs. She didn't really know where the diaries were kept and so had to check down each aisle in turn.

She turned down an aisle halfway along the length of the stockroom and was confronted by Clare.

"Hi, Sue," she greeted.

Sue jumped, but quickly composed herself. "Hi," she replied, turning her attention back to the shelves.

"I hear you enjoyed watching us yesterday," she said with a grin.

Sue went still, feeling her cheeks flush, back turned to her co-worker. "I . . ." Sue was at a loss for words.

She felt the back of her skirt being raised and her knees went weak as Clare's fingertips brushed the crotch of her white panties. Then the underwear was pulled aside and fingers stroked her warm vagina, Sue letting out a slight gasp.

"I'm supposed to be fetching diaries for Kerry," she protested weakly, turning as Clare withdrew her hand temporarily and then moved it back up her skirt.

"Do you think she really wants those diaries?" she asked with a knowing smile.

"You mean . . . ?"

Clare nodded, her grey eyes sparkling. "You've been set up." Her index finger entered Sue slowly, finding her wet and waiting for attention.

"I can't,' she said, pulling away from Clare. "Sorry." Sue quickly walked away and went back up to the shop floor.

When she arrived at the till Kerry looked at her in surprise as she rang in the price of a padded envelope for a middle-aged man.

Sue tried to ignore the look and neatened the ink cartridge display behind the counter.

As the customer walked out of the shop Kerry turned to Sue. "Is everything all right?"

"Fine," replied Sue bluntly.

"We just thought . . ."

"You thought wrong," interrupted Sue as she turned sharply to Kerry, seeing Clare exiting the stairwell door in her peripheral vision.

"But I thought you enjoyed watching us yesterday."

"I did," said Sue pointedly.

Kerry stared at her for a moment and then the penny dropped. "You want to watch," she stated.

Sue forced a thin smile. "Yes," she said in a quiet voice. "At least to begin with," she added.

A smile graced Kerry's full lips. "I'm sure we can arrange a show in the not too distant future."

It was just before closing when Miss Sear walked over to the till point. "I'll be up in the office if anybody wants me," she announced.

"Okay." Sue nodded.

The tall manageress smiled at her. "See you tomorrow."

"Bye." Sue smiled back as she prepared to take the cash-tray out of the till.

When Miss Sear had disappeared through the "staff only" door Kerry approached Sue. "Downstairs in five minutes," she whispered before heading towards the back of the store.

"What about Miss Sear?" asked Sue worriedly.

"She'll be doing paperwork up in the office for at least an hour," replied Kerry, Clare waiting for her by the stairwell door.

Sue watched them disappear through the doorway, her heart-rate increasing as she thought about what she was going to see. Her vagina became moist, the heat rising with her pulse and her nipples stiffening against the cotton of her blouse.

She went downstairs with a growing sense of expectation. Her stomach was filled with butterflies and her hands trembled slightly with nerves. Sue could hear the sounds of Kerry's moans and licked her dry lips as she approached the place where she'd witnessed the previous day's erotic display.

She neared the gap in the stock and stared through with wide eyes.

Kerry and Clare were stripped naked, their uniforms discarded somewhere on the dusty floor out of sight. Clare's lips sucked gently on Kerry's pale nipples one at a time, her hands holding the other woman's hips as she glanced over at Sue and smiled warmly.

Clare's right hand slid between Kerry's legs. Kerry's blue eyes suddenly closed as two fingers entered between her soft lips and pushed in to the knuckles, exploring within her with slow and gentle movements.

Sue licked her lips again as her right hand slid inside her knickers. Soon her index finger was probing her moistness, parting her vagina with a delicacy and slowness which made her sigh, mouth opening, eyes closing momentarily.

She watched as Kerry lifted a pale strap-on into sight. It was double ended and with a quick glance towards Sue, she then knelt before Clare and gently pushed the smaller dildo into the other woman. Sue watched in captivated amazement as the length of the small dildo slipped into Clare and Kerry tied the strap-on in place around her friend's hips.

Kerry stood and, with another quick glance at Sue, turned her back and bent over, using the shelves before her for support. She reached round with her right hand and spread the petal-like lips of her vagina wide in readiness to receive the larger, thicker dildo.

Clare guided it in, its head pushing Kerry wide, her vagina glistening with expectant moisture as it pushed deeper and deeper. Kerry thrust back, the final length quickly vanishing into her as Sue rubbed herself and watched with eager eyes.

Clare's white buttocks clenched as she began to gyrate her hips and Sue imagined the pleasure rising within the other women as the dildoes moved within them.

Then Clare began to thrust in and out of Kerry, the large dildo glistening and slick with her wetness as the sounds of pleasure became more intense and her buttocks rippled seductively with the force of Clare movements.

The rhythm of Sue's finger echoed that of the thrusting, becoming faster and more urgent as the pleasure built. Her left hand groped her small breasts. She pinched her dark nipples between her thumb and forefinger, rolled and squeezed them, tongue running along her dry lips as she caught the scent of the two women.

Kerry let out a long, low moan as she came, the sound sending Sue into the rush of orgasm, the warm pulse spreading throughout her trembling body. She looked at the couple, having to blink a few times to clear her slightly blurred vision. Clare groaned and thrust one last time, the smaller dildo moving inside her finally bringing her to the pinnacle of pleasure.

Kerry opened her blue eyes and turned to look at Sue through the gap in the stock on the shelves. Clare pulled the large dildo out of her friend and followed her gaze.

"I think it's someone else's turn," she whispered.

Sue watched as the couple walked out of sight, shortly to appear at the end of the aisle down which she was standing, her hand still inside her underwear.

Kerry strode up to her confidently, her breasts bouncing slightly. She took Sue in her arms and kissed her.

For a moment Sue didn't respond, but then her arms rose and she held Kerry close. Her fingertips ran down Kerry's back, felt the soft warmth of her skin and then the curve of her ample buttocks. She squeezed them lustfully as Kerry kissed her neck, the caress of her breath sending a shiver down Sue's spine.

Clare knelt beside them, reached up and undid Sue's skirt, letting it fall to the concrete floor as Kerry grasped her breasts and then began to unbutton her blouse.

Sue stood in growing ecstasy as two pairs of attentive hands stripped her, revealing her neatly trimmed black pubes and her fleshy lips, Clare's fingers immediately parting them as she located her clitoris and rubbed it gently.

Kerry licked around Sue's nipples, her fingers stroking her pert breasts. Sue trembled and closed her eyes, the air chilling the trails of saliva Kerry left so delicately on her skin.

Sue felt a finger enter her, but didn't open her eyes in order to see whose it was. Then another entered her from behind as Kerry's mouth continued to work its slow magic on her breasts.

Raising her hands, Sue held Kerry's large breasts, rubbed the firm nipples and enjoyed the feel of the malleable flesh against her palms.

Kerry moved to her side, lips caressing Sue's shoulders as Clare stood.

"Guide the dildo in," whispered Clare.

Without opening her eyes, Sue reached down and took hold of the thick length as Kerry's hands stroked her stomach and then her inner thigh sensuously, gently scraping Sue's skin with her nails and sending more chills down Sue's spine.

Clare pushed into her with a seductive slowness that made Sue want to grasp her buttocks and pull the dildo into her roughly. She could feel the strap-on opening her wide as Clare kissed her neck and Kerry's attentions lingered on her breasts once again.

Sue's vagina throbbed as Clare began to move in and out of her, building a crescendo of pleasure as Kerry's lips and hands caressed her upper body. She bit her lower lip and stifled a yell as Clare suddenly thrust into her and then became still, her body expectant, crying out for her next thrilling movement.

Another sudden thrust and Sue couldn't stifle her yell this time, letting it issue from her open mouth as her knees weakened and every part of her tingled with erotic energy.

Clare paused again and then pushed in deep. The next pause was shorter and slowly the rhythm grew.

Sue moaned with every push, the dildo's thickness parting her with increasing force and speed as Kerry bit her gently on the shoulder. The trembling and tingling of her naked body increased with every passing moment. The heat grew and Sue glistened with sweat, stomach tensing, chest heaving as she breathed deeply.

Clare gasped as she came for a second time and Sue yelled at the top of her voice as the orgasm rushed through her, raised her up on the crest of a wave of pure, ecstatic joy. She tried to catch her breath as warmth spread from the epicentre of her pleasure where the strap-on still remained.

As Clare pulled out of her, Sue slowly sank to the dusty floor, her legs unable to support her weight and eyes still closed. Kerry crouched beside her and held Sue in her arms.

"Thank you," whispered Sue.

Kerry chuckled. "Our pleasure," she replied.

"No, the pleasure was all mine," smiled Sue, opening her eyes and taking a deep, steadying breath.

Clare walked round to the next aisle and got her and Kerry's clothes. "Well, I think it's been a pretty good day at work," she grinned as she returned and began to undo the strap-on, enjoying the sensations as the smaller dildo slipped from her still pulsating vagina.

"Good, but exhausting," agreed Sue as she gathered her clothes up and used her last reserves of energy to begin dressing.

Soon the three of them were back in their work uniforms, though the odd trace of dust here and there were clues as to their stockroom antics. They went to the stairs and headed up to the shop floor.

The next morning Sue was doing a stock take. She stood along one of the store's aisles holding a clipboard as she made a note of how many of each type of sketch pad were on the shop floor. She picked a piece of grey fluff from her black skirt and then looked at her watch, the time passing slowly.

"Sue, can you come up to the office, please?" called Miss Sear.

Sue turned to see the manageress standing at the back door with a serious look on her slightly tanned face.

"Call down to the stock-room and get one of the other girls to come up and look after the shop. It's time for your three-month assessment," she added before vanishing from sight, the sound of her black high heels audible on the concrete stairs as the door slowly swung shut.

Sue's pulse quickened slightly as she continued to stare at the rear of the shop. She'd been told about the three-month trial period and just hoped she'd made a good enough impression. She couldn't think of any reason Miss Sear would want to let her go.

Shaking her head to clear her thoughts, Sue quickly put the clipboard on the counter and went to the rear of the store.

"Kerry? Clare?" she called down the stairs.

After a slight pause the two women appeared from below, both brushing dust from their clothes and looking a little flushed.

"Miss Sear asked if one of you could watch the shop floor while I go up and see her."

"She wants you in the office?" asked Clare.

Sue nodded as her co-workers stopped before her. "It's my three-month assessment."

Kerry squeezed her arm. "You'll be fine."

Sue forced a smile and began to ascend to the next floor where the cloakroom, staffroom, and office were located. Reaching the short, bland corridor, she walked to the far end.

Standing before the door marked "Miss Sear, Manageress", Sue composed herself and took a deep breath before knocking three times.

"Enter," came the muffled response.

Sue took hold of the handle and opened the door, finding Miss Sear seated behind her desk with elbows resting on the top and fingers steepled before her slightly angular face.

"Please take a seat," instructed her superior.

Sue nervously sat on the black chair opposite Miss Sear.

"So, how are you finding it here?" Miss Sear studied her newest member of staff, leaning forward a little.

"Fine, thank you, Miss Sear," Sue replied after a slight hesitation.

"It's Vivienne," said the older woman, "and I think you should know I had more than one security camera installed." She paused for a moment, studying Sue's expression, and then turned to a small TV monitor to the left, pressing the 'play' button on a video recorder beneath it.

Sue swallowed hard as she saw the recording of her watching Kerry and Clare in the stock-room, hand down her knickers as she masturbated. Her cheeks became red and hot as Miss Sear continued to watch for a moment and then turned to her.

"I had it installed in the stock-room just in case a potential thief sneaked down while the staff were otherwise occupied."

"I . . . ," began Sue.

Miss Sear held up her right hand to silence her member of staff. "There's no need for explanations." She slowly stood and walked around the desk.

Sue's gaze followed the other woman's movements as she were hypnotized. She glanced back at the screen where the soundless images were now of her, Kerry, and Clare having sex with the double ended strap-on.

She looked up at Vivienne as the manageress undid her navy skirt and let it fall to the floor. Miss Sear wasn't wearing any underwear and Sue looked at the clean shaven lips protruding between her legs, the distinct smell of arousal in the air.

"Lick me," ordered Miss Sear, her voice hushed.

Sue looked up into the other woman's dark eyes, hesitating a moment before slowly leaning forward.

Vivienne felt Sue's breath on her skin and then the sensation of her tongue gently pushing between her lips. She closed her dark eyes, her spine tingling as she ran her fingers through Sue's long, black hair.

Sue breathed deeply the older woman's scent and felt herself becoming wet as she tasted Vivienne. Her tongue flicked the hooded clitoris and she felt the manageress quiver. She raised her right hand and held Vivienne open with her fingers, moving her tongue to the inviting hole as her thumb rubbed at the clitoris.

Tongue delving inside, she savoured the taste. Her left hand slid up Miss Sear's smooth and slightly rounded stomach, vanished beneath her cream blouse and sought out her breasts. She stroked their lower curves softly and then her fingertips circled the left nipple, finding it stiff and ready for her attentions.

Vivienne let out a sigh as Sue's tongue began to dart in and out of her, then circled within her with deliberate slowness, thumb continuously toying with her clitoris.

Moving so that she could sit on the edge of her desk, Vivienne opened her legs wide and Sue's tongue delved deeper, nose pressed against the fleshy lips, chin moist with her wetness.

As she once again pushed in and out of her manageress, Sue felt Vivienne tense and then tremble, a stifled moan escaping from the older woman's lips. She slowed the movements of her tongue, licking gently the length of Vivienne's vagina.

"Stand," ordered Sue's superior in a hoarse whisper.

Sue slowly rose and Vivienne slipped off the desk and stood before her. They embraced and their lips pressed tightly together, tongues writhing as lust and passion took over.

Their hands scrambled to undo buttons and soon their blouses were discarded. Vivienne reached behind Sue and undid the clasp of her bra, which fell away from her small breasts. Briefly looking deeply into Sue's eyes, Miss Sear bent forward and took an erect nipple between her lips, gently nipping it with her teeth as her right hand toyed roughly with the other breast.

Sue ran her fingertips down the older woman's back, her eyes closed as a hand slid down her stomach, muscles jumping beneath the soft touch. She inhaled sharply as two fingers entered her, probed as deeply as they could, touching interior walls and filling her with desire.

She bowed her head and kissed Vivienne's neck, bit her earlobes as her heart raced. Her fingers moved to explore the other woman and they masturbated each other with growing vigour.

Their lips met once again, bodies pressed close. Sue's palm pressed against the shaven mound between Vivienne's legs as her fingers pushed in and out, the older woman's fingers mirroring the same movements as they climbed towards the height and heat of ecstasy.

Breathing heavy, hands exploring, bodies close, and the air filled with their scent, Sue and Vivienne were caught up in the intensity of the moment. Their spare hands stroked and grasped with growing urgency, fingers of their other hands moving in and out, in and out.

Sue let out a long, low moan of intense pleasure as she came, Vivienne following only moments later. Their fingers slowing, they collapsed to the floor together and lay down in each other's arms.

When she opened her eyes, Sue found Vivienne staring at her. "Did I pass my staff assessment?" she asked quietly.

"With flying colours," replied Vivienne. "But I might have to give you another assessment tomorrow."

They chuckled as they held each other close and enjoyed the gently fading sensations of orgasm.

"I have something to admit," said Vivienne with a hint of nervousness.

Sue looked into her eyes with genuine concern. "What's wrong?"

"It wasn't just Kerry's idea to get you down into the stock-room for some extra fun. I saw your first encounter on the security monitor and talked to Kerry about it." Vivienne sighed. "It was a way to get you up here and . . ." She paused. "I'm sorry."

Sue stared at her as she took in her words. "I'm glad you did it. I've been fantasizing about this ever since I first met you."

"Really?" responded Vivienne in surprise.

"Really," replied Sue as she leant forward and kissed the older woman tenderly. "Anyway, I've always wanted to star in my own erotic movie," she added.

The two women smiled and laughed. They held each other close in the small office. Slowly their bodies became aroused once more and their lips pressed close. A beam of sunlight shone upon their nakedness as they entwined on the floor in the heat of passion, lost to the world, but found in each other.

"Please"

Linda Suzuki

I never liked teaching in spring. Classroom windows are open,
sounds of games played on the quad drift in with smells of new
mown grass and apple blossoms – no teacher has material to
compete with that. So when the dean invited me to teach a class
for the spring semester, I turned her down – saying (honestly
enough) that my research left me no time.

A week or so later, I was at a department happy hour,
standing with a group of colleagues when someone asked this
question: If you could teach any class – any subject, any
structure – what would you teach?

The answer came to me easily because I'd thought about it so
many times, and it came out of my mouth easily because I'd had
a few glasses of wine. "History of Erotic Fiction," I said, much
to the delight of the rest. Only then did I notice that the dean
had come up behind me in time to hear.

"How serious are you?" she asked, smiling. And before I
could answer, asked, "Serious enough to teach it this spring?"

She had called my bluff, called it in front of a half dozen other
professors, and everyone was looking at me, waiting for my
answer.

I restricted the class to seniors, on the theory that the students
would be over 21 and I would have to field fewer irate phone
calls from parents. I also restricted the class to language-arts
majors, to keep out the football players, frat boys, and other
voyeurs. On the first day of class, I had ten students – the
maximum number I had agreed to take.

The syllabus was straightforward. We began with cave paintings, then pulled back the curtains on successive eras, surveying
the erotic fiction that was one of the few human constants across
continents and cultures. Grades were based on weekly papers

that were due at the beginning of Monday's class. Each paper consisted of over one thousand words of erotic fiction written in the style of the culture we had studied the previous week. (With one exception: The week we studied cave paintings, I had the class create their own symbols and tell an erotic story with finger paints – flattened cardboard boxes standing in for our cave walls.)

It was hard to say who enjoyed the class more – the students or me. The debates were lively, the questions challenging. The students were all good writers, some even rising to excellent – and one was extraordinary.

Her name was Sloane. I had seen her around the department, but didn't remember having had her in a class before. And I would have remembered. Whenever she walked through the door, I always expected everyone in the room to stop talking. She was the most beautiful woman any of us was ever likely to see in person – who for some reason, had enrolled anonymously at our college, disguising herself behind nerdy glasses, her hair in a careless ponytail. But regardless of what disguises she wore, she could not hide those high cheekbones, green eyes gazing up at me from behind thick lashes, full lips that slipped into a daring smile at the slightest provocation. On the first day of class, she caught me staring at her – and looked so willing in return – that I had to make a conscious effort not to look in her direction at all, or else I'd lose track of what I was talking about.

Perhaps it was because she was so beautiful that I expected so little from her. But what I got – week after week – was easily the best work in the class.

Unique among her peers, Sloane wrote all her stories in the first person. There was no distance between the author and the actions of her protagonist as she fucked her way through the centuries. After the first few papers, Sloane's work began to read like a time-travelling novel, with breathtaking references to her heroine's past and future sexual encounters. With each successive chapter, Sloane gave herself completely to some new fetish – but despite her well documented orgasmic satisfaction, left no doubt that she had not found that special something she was looking for. By process of elimination, I began to get a clearer – and more arousing – picture of what that something might be.

At first, Sloane's heroine was fucked by both men and women, but as the weeks passed, she was taken increasingly by women alone. It began to dawn on me only then that Sloane might be queer. (Internalized homophobia, I chided myself, to assume that no woman as beautiful as Sloane could be a dyke.)

But it was not just that Sloane's fiction was well written, it was not just that she could write to any time or any style, it was that her work was truly erotic. After the first week, I started saving her paper until last and would grade it in bed, just before I switched off the light – letting her words intertwine with my own fantasies, barely able to scribble my critique before reaching between my legs to satisfy the need her words never failed to create.

I had been teaching then for about 15 years, and this was the first time I had ever read a student's work for my own pleasure. I delighted in handing out the graded papers each week, perpetually turned on by my secret, watching Sloane out of the corner of my eye. Did she have any idea how many times I'd gotten off on her words, or how often my fantasy as I came included her naked body, stretched beneath mine in total submission?

Whenever I handed back graded papers, I reminded the students to see me during office hours if they had questions about my critique. A number of them did, some just angling for a better grade, some genuinely interested in improving their writing. However, since Sloane consistently earned the highest marks in the class, I was surprised to find her waiting to see me during my office hours early one evening. She sat across the desk from me, on the edge of her seat, and handed me her paper from the previous week. I skimmed it quickly, as though to refresh my memory – although I had come often enough to those words that I could hardly forget them – then looked up. "Tell me what you want."

Perhaps I imagined it, but it seemed as though she blushed a little. She lowered her eyes to the desk. "Please tell me what you meant about remembering the reader's purpose."

I read over my words, then laid the paper on the desk and leaned back in my chair. "Why do people read?" I asked.

She hesitated. "To learn . . . to go places they . . . to experience . . ." her voice trailed off. She was embarrassed by the inadequacy of her answer.

"Why do people read erotica?"

Her eyes met mine and a small smile played at the corner of

her lips. "To . . ." She tried to gauge how far she could go with a full professor.

"Say it," I encouraged her.

"To get off," she said, and I could tell she was trying not to show how turned on she was by saying those words aloud.

I nodded. "Sometimes, it seems like you're a little ashamed of your readers – writing as though you want them to believe that you believe they have some intellectual purpose for reading erotica, writing as though you don't know what their hands are doing while they read your words."

She held her breath. "I know."

"Then you know something very powerful. You know what your reader wants. You can give it . . ." I waited for the words to sink in ". . . or not. But either way, you need to understand how power works."

The last paper of the semester was due the last day of class. I had given the students free rein to pick any era, any topic, any format – but reminded them that the paper would count for half the final grade. When the class ended, I stayed in the classroom, talking with students – and although Sloane stayed too, she hung back from the crowd as though waiting. Finally, she was the only one left, handing her paper to me, but not letting go of it until our fingers had brushed together under the pages. The sheaf of paper was thick, far thicker than a 1,000-word paper would be. Before I could ask her why, she said, "I graduate the day after tomorrow."

"Congratulations."

She went on as though she hadn't heard me. "But I'll be on campus through the summer. I've got an internship on this study that just got funded."

"Tell me what the study is about."

She waved impatiently, "It's over in the Speech Department. Something about diagnosing aphasia in pre-schoolers. I'm really just babysitting." She looked down at the floor, and spoke hesitantly. "But what I wanted to say is that I'll be here all summer, and if you want . . ."

The classroom door opened and the departmental secretary stuck her head in. "Sorry to interrupt, you've got a call from IT. Something about your security code." Then she just stood there until I realized she intended to wait and walk back to the office with me.

"Thank you," Sloane said to me. "I wish I could have taken more from you." And with that, she was gone. I walked with our secretary back to the office, and spent the next half hour on the phone with IT, straightening out a problem with my laptop, getting wet again each time I imagined what Sloane had been about to offer me.

At home, I stacked the papers on my desk, determined to critique them all at one sitting, turn in final grades in the morning, and get on with my summer.

The stories were all good, and the more pleased I was with the quality of the work, the more I looked forward to reading Sloane's paper which waited for me at the bottom of the pile.

By the time I settled into bed that night with my self-congratulatory whisky, Sloane's paper, and a red pen, I was tired, my eyes dry and my hand cramped from writing. Still, I didn't for a moment consider putting off reading her words until the next day. She was to be my reward.

The work was titled *Please* . . . and subtitled "A Play". She had excelled at the short story format all semester, so I was a bit surprised at the change in medium. However, another of my students had written a screenplay, and several had written poetry for their final assignments. I turned to the first page. Written carefully in the centre – in what I assumed must be Sloane's handwriting – were these words:

"Just as cave paintings should be seen, plays should be performed – not read. I promise you that I know my role."

The next page began with the word "CHARACTERS" printed in bold face, and underneath that, these words:

SLOANE
Sloane has always desired domination at the hands of another woman – someone older, stronger, more able to control her than lovers her own age. She keeps this fantasy to herself, sure that few understand her desire, but also sure that when the woman appears who can dominate Sloane the way she needs to be dominated – they will both know it. And then Sloane will need only to wait to be told what time, what place, how to please . . .

On the next page, the words "ACT I" were printed in bold face. The rest of the pages were blank.

The next morning, I left the critiqued papers with the department secretary – each paper sealed inside an envelope – and turned in my students' final grades. I was mostly packed, but finished a few last minute errands, locked up my apartment, and drove to the lake.

The lake house had been in my family for three generations, coming to me after the death of my parents. My grandfather had built the house and, even though it was meant only as a summer getaway, he designed it to withstand the storms that blew off the lake all winter. It still gave me a sense of strength.

I aired out the house, tended to the immediate chores, and fell asleep exhausted.

Graduation was the next morning. Sitting on the porch, looking out over the lake while I drank my first cup of coffee, I imagined the cap and gown parade, the incessant clicking of cameras, the faces of proud parents. I knew the ceremony would be over by noon, Sloane would no doubt have a celebratory lunch with her family, then drive the hour to the lake. In the instructions I had written on her paper, I told her to arrive no later than 4.

She was a few minutes early, on edge because she had sped the whole way out of fear of being late. I opened the front door and stood leaning against the frame, watching her pull a bag from the trunk and lock her car. She didn't realize I was watching until she started up the porch steps, then gasped when she saw me.

"I'm sorry," she said automatically, "you scared me." Then blushed when I only smiled at her nervousness.

I held out my hand and led her inside. When I had shut the door behind us, I took the bag from her, and told her to go to the bedroom upstairs, at the back of the house. She started to say something, but then turned and climbed the stairs, looking back at me over her shoulder for the first few steps.

The sauvignon blanc was so cold that it frosted the inside of my wine glass.

She was in the back bedroom, sitting at the foot of the bed, arms crossed as if to protect her from the cold, even though the room was warm. I lifted my glass to her lips and let her take a sip, while I tucked a few stray locks of hair behind her ear. I rested my fingers lightly against her neck then bent to kiss a drop of wine from her bottom lip. Her eyes were wide and bright with fear, desire, it didn't matter which. I resisted the urge to tell her so soon how well she was doing.

I crossed the room and made myself comfortable, sitting in the window seat so that the slanting sunlight blinded her when she looked toward me.

"Undress for me."

She hesitated. She could not see the smile that briefly crossed my lips. I was glad we were going to get past any reluctance early on.

"I won't ask again," I said, speaking more slowly.

She lowered her eyes and unbuttoned her blouse, then shrugged out of it and let it drop to the floor. She was wearing a white silk camisole, her nipples outlined clearly against the fabric, and I knew she had worn this specifically for giving me the pleasure of watching her take it off. She moved slowly, the silk shimmering as she lifted the camisole over her head, and let it drop to the floor as well. She shook her head to rearrange her tousled hair, then reached behind her for the zipper of her skirt.

"Not that."

She stopped. I took a slow sip of wine, my eyes fixed on her body. Watching me for confirmation, she reached behind and took off the half-bra that had been proffering up her breasts to me so wantonly. All defiance gone, her cheeks were red with the first blush of shame, and her eyes were on the floor.

I took another sip of wine, then set the glass down. "Turn around and kneel on the edge of the bed."

She did as I told her, teetering a bit to keep her balance on the deep, yielding mattress. I came up behind her and ran my hands across her belly, and then her breasts. My fingers were cold from the wine glass, but that wasn't the reason she shivered at my touch. She leaned back, her head resting on my shoulder.

"What was the name of the last woman who fucked you?"

"What?" She seemed genuinely surprised by the question.

My hands trailed from her breasts, over her hips, and slowly up her back to her shoulders, increasing the pressure until I bent her forward. She braced herself on the mattress with her hands.

"The name of the last woman who fucked you," I said, in a

tone that made clear she would pay later for making me repeat myself.

"Sylvia."

I bent over her, tangling my fingers in her hair, making my hands into fists that pulled hard and held tight. "So 'Sylvia' is going to be your safety word. Say it and I'll stop." I leaned in close to her ear and whispered, "But then you go back to Sylvia."

She nodded and I stood up behind her. "Feet on the floor, elbows on the bed," I said evenly, then turned away, confident that she would do as she was told. I went back to the window seat, which concealed a lid, opening to a large cubbyhole beneath.

I knew that she was curious. I had seen her looking around when I first came into the room, which was empty except for the bed – a large four-poster sitting high off the ground, affording no cover for anything to be hidden beneath. Other than that, there was nothing. No furniture, no art hung on the walls, no carpet over the hardwood floors – simply the bed, which faced two windows and a door leading out onto the captain's walk. Because of the heat, I had opened the heavy outside door, and from time to time, a breeze knocked the lighter screen door gently against the frame. Long, sheer, white curtains billowed around the windows.

I knew she had imagined I would take her in a dungeon of some sort, and I enjoyed her unease as she wondered what else she might have been wrong about.

I pulled out a riding crop – black, the whip made of dark purple leather, the thick handle of latex ridged to ensure a good grip – or a hard fuck.

I crossed the room to her. She had her feet on the floor, elbows on the bed. I held the riding crop so she could see it out of the corner of her eye. "Spread your legs wider."

She did, stretching them as far apart as her tight skirt would allow. I trailed my fingers lightly over the fabric as it followed the perfect curve of her ass. The first lash with the crop was hard, the sound like a firecracker in the still afternoon. She cried out, more from surprise than pain, and balled her hands into fists. I could feel the tension, her every muscle taut with the desire to flee. But she stayed. The next few lashes were lighter, just a sting on her ass, then I surprised her with faster, harder lashes, alternating from one ass cheek to the other. Her breathing changed, her gasps following the rhythm of the whip. When I stopped, she wiped away a tear with the back of her hand.

"Pull up your skirt."

She stayed bent over the bed but reached behind her with both hands and pulled up the skirt, bunching it around her waist. I smiled at her choice of a black thong, made mostly of lace, and so delicate that it begged to be torn. I ran the riding crop up between her legs and followed the thin string of the thong between her ass cheeks. I caught one string of the thong with the end of the whip and twisted, then tugged it. She understood and reached back with both hands to push the thong down. When she had pushed it just below her ass, I slapped her hand lightly with the whip to stop her. Her skin was already pink from the earlier lashes, but I spent a few minutes slowly whipping her bare ass until it was bright red, the thong around her thighs acting not as a restraint, merely as a reminder that she was not to move away from the pain.

Without any warning, I thrust a finger into her cunt. She was wet, as I knew she would be, but wetter than even I had imagined so soon into her submission. She whispered, "Please . . ."

"Are you still a virgin?"

She tried to laugh but it came out more as a sob. "No."

"But has anyone fucked you?" I asked quietly.

Her whole body froze, her "yes" barely a whisper.

"Are you sure?" I asked, letting her feel the thick riding crop handle parting the lips of her pussy so that she knew I wouldn't ask again before I fucked her. Her "yes" sounded even less convincing the second time. Slowly, I dragged my wet fingertips from her cunt up to her asshole. I let my fingers rest there a moment, enjoying the sensation of her sphincter muscles spasming in anticipation of pain.

"No," she whispered, and I could tell she was begging me not to ask.

"Has anyone fucked you up the ass?"

She just shook her head. I stood her up then, and told her to remove the rest of her clothes except her heels. I opened the window seat lid and pulled out everything I needed.

Bending her back over the bed, I drizzled a few drops of lube down the crack of her ass. "This is mine, then," I said making small circles around her asshole with the tip of one finger. "Do you understand? Mine to do with as I please."

"As you please," she echoed in acquiescence.

For a few minutes, I did nothing more than tease her asshole. But each time I felt her relax a little, I increased the pressure until I heard her first reluctant moan. "That's right," I murmured, pushing the first ring of the butt plug into her. There was a sharp intake of breath, and her knees buckled for a moment.

"Say it," I commanded her, my voice more stern than before.

"I don't know . . ." She hesitated, her voice muffled by the bed linens.

I pushed the butt plug in to the second ring and she lifted her head, her back arching, and cried out in pain. I waited. When she had caught her breath, she managed only another "Please . . ."

"Please what?" I replied, aroused by how sure I was of her answer.

"Please . . . fuck me."

I trailed my hands gently from her neck, down her back, then over her ass. "Say it."

"Please fuck me in the ass," she groaned.

I moved in close to stand against her, my body steadying hers. She took a deep breath, and released it raggedly between her clenched teeth as I pushed the butt plug in to the hilt.

"Oh, God," she shuddered in pain, and then said again, "Oh, God," with something more like surprise.

"Get on the bed, lie on your back."

She moved awkwardly, the butt plug still buried deep inside her. I grabbed her ankles and placed her high heels at the very edge of the bed, forcing her knees up and apart at a sharp angle that lifted her ass. I put a pillow beneath her so that her cunt was tilted up toward me.

I took a small vibrator, twisted it on, and put it in her hand. She reached for me, but I caught her wrist – hard – and slowly pushed her hand away from me, down the length of her body, and between her legs. She blushed, but I held my hand over hers until the vibrator settled in against her clit. She drew a long breath, her embarrassment giving way to excitement.

I took my hand away and watched her pleasure herself, watched her slowly bring her other hand up to play with her stiff nipples, while she followed my every move. I stepped out of my clothes and her eyes widened when she saw that I was wearing a double dildo, one end of which had been deep inside my own throbbing cunt since I'd walked into the room. I lubed the other end of the dildo slowly, enjoying her fear at the size of it. She knew it was too late to tell me she had never been fucked before.

Still standing at the foot of the bed, I grabbed her hips and pulled her toward me, then took hold of the end of the dildo and used it to spread the lips of her cunt. Her hips bucked involuntarily, and the dildo slipped a little way inside her. For a moment, her hand, which was holding the vibrator, fell away, but I brought it back to press against her clit.

Slowly, I pushed the dildo into her, her tight pussy resisting every inch.

A cry of protest escaped from deep in her throat. I stopped, waiting to hear the word, but she shook her head and did not say it, her free hand clutching a fistful of the sheet so hard that her knuckles were white. I pushed deeper into her, and she bit hard on her lower lip, deeper still and she let out a shuddering moan, then I was all the way inside her, my cunt pressed against hers. Before she could take a breath, I pulled all the way out, then entered her again, a little less gently. She gasped and again I stopped and waited for the word from her, but instead she begged, "Please . . ." and I entered her roughly, thrusting into her over and over, as deep as I could go, my clit reverberating every time it slammed into hers.

She came hard. Every muscle in her body tightened and she let out a long, slow scream of release, her words barely intelligible, "Fuck . . . me . . . let . . . me . . . come . . ." And then cries of, "Please . . . please . . . please . . ." as successive waves of pleasure rolled over her.

When she was spent, she lay completely still, breathing heavily, eyes closed, a soft sheen of sweat covering her body. I put away all the toys, then lay down on the bed, pulling her into my arms. A few tears slipped from her eyes, slid down her cheek, and dripped onto my breast. I kissed her very softly, and told her she had been a very good girl. She nestled closer, as though every inch of her body had to be touching mine. I held her tight and she fell at once into sleep.

Sweet Revenge

Rebecca Henderson

Sara and I were on dessert – a luscious chocolate-kahlua mousse that we were splitting, passing one spoon back and forth – before we realized we were dating the same man. That isn't as far-fetched as it sounds. Our town is pretty small, less than 25,000 people, and those that date do tend to get around. Apparently Michael did, anyway.

It was my turn with the spoon, and I took my time licking every bit of chocolate from it, savoring the knowledge that it had just been in Sara's mouth as much as the taste of the kalhua-kissed chocolate. *Just think, I thought, this could be my tongue sliding into her mouth instead of over the slick, cool stainless steel.*

I opened my eyes and found her watching me intently. I blushed and handed her the spoon.

"Was it your understanding that you and he were in a monogamous relationship?" I asked, negotiating my way carefully through a subject that could be loaded, and more importantly to me, could impact my more lascivious intentions downright negatively. I wanted Sara to want me – not want me dead. As for my stake in the equation, Michael and I had an open relationship, so it wasn't surprising or distressing to me that he was dating Sara. In fact I was applauding his taste in women right at that moment. Sara is a vivacious, plump, spiky-haired redhead with impossibly blue eyes, curves I would die for and the kind of flawless white skin sprinkled with freckles you only read about in books. Next to me, a pale, tomboyish blonde, she was as vibrant and warm as a tropical sunset in the Arctic. Oh, yes, I could definitely see what Michael liked about her.

"No," she said slowly, frowning. "I guess not. I mean, we never really discussed it much. I just assumed—" She broke off and took a deep breath that pushed her lovely full breasts against the fabric of her silk blouse in a way that had me thinking still more lascivious thoughts, which I probably shouldn't have been, since it looked like the girl I was hoping to seduce might be too straight – and too monogamous. "I just can't believe he would go behind my back like that," she finally said, looking at her hands, sounding miserable.

I felt sorry for her. Consensual non-monogamy is supposed to be just that: consensual, and by definition it couldn't be if one side doesn't know the other is being non-monogamous.

In the next instant it was *him* I felt sorry for.

"The bastard!" she said, raising her head. The old cliché about a woman being beautiful when she's angry didn't begin to do her justice. She was spectacular, eyes blazing and spots of colour in her cheeks. In that moment it crossed my mind that maybe I could use that passion to, well, further my own ends here. Revenge sex can be so good.

Just as quickly, I discarded that thought. I really *liked* this girl, liked her in a way I hadn't liked anyone in a while. I didn't want it to be a revenge fuck. Or at least not only that.

I took a swallow of my wine to give her time to calm herself. When I looked over at her again the anger had seemed to have gone out of her and she was watching me.

"You're not upset about this, are you?" she asked. I took another sip of my drink, considering what to say. I wasn't sure she'd made the connection between what he was doing – dating both of us – and what she and I were doing.

The first time I'd met Sara had been at the funeral of a mutual friend. Hardly an appropriate place to ask a girl on a date, but I'd noticed her, and thought I noticed her noticing me. The next time I saw her had been at a friend's gallery opening in the Central West End. Apparently we had some of the same friends, besides Michael. That time I had asked her out, to the play we'd just attended. I'd felt we were hitting it off splendidly, although I'd been careful not to come on too strong. At the time I hadn't been sure if she was straight, gay or bi, and although my interest in her was definitely more than friends, I also liked her enough not to want to scare her away as "just friends" material. Unfortunately, that was looking as if it may have been a good instinct on my part.

Then I thought about how her arm had brushed mine in the theatre, how she'd let her thigh rest against mine seemingly by accident; how she'd leaned over me to look out the window on the Metrolink on the way back to our cars, and all of a sudden I wasn't so sure. I remembered the feel of her soft, heavy breasts against my arm, the scent of her hair and skin in my nose and the way her eyes had seemed to linger on my mouth as she turned her head to say something to me just before pulling away. I'd wanted to kiss her then, and couldn't think now why I'd hesitated.

Damn, I wanted her. I'm not a saint. I wanted the fire her red hair hinted at, I wanted her anger; I wanted her pulling my hair and scratching me, even if it was just working out her rage at him. I wanted to turn that rage into another kind of heat, the kind that burned her from the inside out. I wanted to shove my fingers and my tongue and the sweet hard strap-on I had at home into her, to claim that fire and make it mine, to fuck her into insensibility, until she couldn't think about Michael or anyone else.

"Allie?" she said, and I realized I had been silent too long.

"No, I'm not upset," I said. What I was, was shaking. Shaking and flushed and ready to say anything if it'd make her come home with me.

I did the only thing I could under the circumstances. "I'll be right back," I said, standing abruptly, and fled to the restroom to cool off. I hoped she didn't think I was insane.

I threw myself into one of the bathroom stalls and closed the door behind me. Get a grip, I told myself. It'd been a long time since I'd felt this kind of . . . lust, that was the only word for it . . . for anyone. But mixed with it was this bittersweet tenderness, too, this desire not to use her as I wanted to, this desire to protect her, to protect what I suddenly wanted to be more than a one-night stand. I really liked this girl.

"Allie?" Sara's voice came through the stall door. "Are you all right?"

What could I say? *"Sure, I'm fine, I just need to get away from you before I throw you over the table and kiss you until you can't think straight?"*

"I'm fine," I said. "Just felt a little dizzy. Must be too much wine."

"Oh," she said, her voice doubtful. "Okay, then. If that's all." I heard the water turn on and then off; heard the door open, letting in the sound of Lucinda Williams singing "Steal Your Love" clearly for a moment before the door closed, muffling it once again.

"God," I groaned. I wasn't going to be able to do this.

I pushed the door open. Sara stood there, arms crossed over her chest. There was a look in her eyes I couldn't name. "You like this song too, huh?" she asked. I stood there stupidly, waiting for her to move, but she only stepped closer. "Is that what you want, Allie? To 'steal my love'?"

"Sara—" The word was a whisper, a plea, though I wasn't sure what I was asking for.

"Shhh," she said. She stepped closer still, until her mouth was a breath away from mine. Her breath was sweet, touched with kahlua and chocolate and wine. She brought her hands up and pulled my mouth down to hers, and I surrendered to her kiss, to the taste and scent of her, to the feel of her tongue sliding into my mouth, to the feel of her hands so soft and yet so insistent on my face and her warm softness pressing against me. Somehow she managed to manoeuvre me back against the sink. I ran my hands down her body, over the curve of her hips to cup her lovely round ass, pulling her into me, wanting to melt into her, wanting her to melt into me.

"Don't do this because of Michael," I managed, when we both came up for air.

She drew back to look me in the eyes. "What if I am?" she whispered, her voice hoarse. "So what if I am? Does it matter?"

I stared down at her. Why not give her the excuse, if she needed one, to step over that line? Why not take what she wanted to give, even if it was just to get back at him?

I groaned again. "Yes," I said, pulling away. I twisted away from her to face the sink and turned on the water. *Cold* water. "It matters. I want . . . damn, I want this, but not because of him. I want you to want this because of *me*."

I watched her in the mirror watching me. When she spoke, her voice was soft. "This doesn't have anything to do with Michael," she said. "I don't even know him."

I stopped soaping my hands. "What? But why?"

"I'm sorry," she said. "It was . . . stupid. A stupid idea. When I found out you were dating a guy, I got this crazy idea in my head. I thought, okay, maybe you were dating someone else, but if you got mad at him, maybe . . ." She trailed off and looked away.

I stared at her. I was incredulous, appalled, amazed – and utterly enthralled. She looked miserable.

"You thought maybe I'd turn to you? That maybe I'd want to

get back at him, by, say, fucking his girlfriend?" I couldn't help it, I started laughing. "But you realized that wouldn't work, when I told you I wasn't upset about him dating you," I continued. "So then you came in here, thinking you'd play the victim."

She groaned. "God, I'm such an idiot!" she said. "I'm sorry . . . I just really wanted to be with you. I'm not . . . I'm not good at this," she finished. She was a bright red from her neck to her ears. A bright, *adorable* red.

Slowly, deliberately, letting her stew a while, I rinsed and dried my hands. Then I turned to her and pushed her back against the sink, where she'd had me only moments before. "You are an idiot," I said, tangling my hands in her hair as I brought my mouth down to hers. "But you're *my* idiot."

And I found out that Sara didn't need anger to heat her. She burned with a fire all her own.

Little Women

Rosemary Williams

Natasha stopped by the roadside because she could go no further. Unable to secure even a horse, she had walked for a day and a night, keeping, wherever possible, out of sight. Where she had come from had been the next best thing to slavery – luxury laced with imprisonment. She had woken as if from a sickly, dizzy dream, and left whilst the palace slept, in the first lavender hour of dawn. At every step she had expected the hoofbeats of the Tsar's soldiers, come to bring her back, but so far she had met only farmers' wives and the occasional hen. Now her boots were split and her shins were scratched and she felt her flight to be over.

The coach came over the brow of the hill, silhouetted against a rapidly falling dusk. If this was her pursuers, she thought, then so be it. She sat on a milestone and waited.

The coach was drawn by four black horses, mares, she thought, her country girl's eyes spotting the difference. It slowed, showing a driver wrapped in an all-enveloping black surtout, muffled against the likelihood of snow. She could not tell if it were man, woman or child: just a hunched figure holding the reins in gloved fingers. The coach came to a standstill with a rearing of horses.

"You poor thing!" The voice came from inside the vehicle. It sounded like warm rain. It was not a soldier.

In the doorway stood a woman, clearly a woman by the way its capacious fur coat hugged its contours. The hood was up, but nestled in the folds was a face, luminous in the twilight, with eyes like the two lone candles in a church.

"You must be perished, my dear. Give me your hand." The hand was tapered and warm, the fingernails dyed a purply colour. Natasha stepped into the coach which, at a word from its owner, began to move once more.

Inside was deliciously warm, lit dimly by ornate lamps which swung on chains from the ceiling. It was so dim that she smelt the room at first, rather than saw it: a magnificent scent. The woman had been burning spices, rich aromas suggestive of old wood and the Far East.

"Sit down," invited her hostess. Natasha sat down, on what? It was hard to see in the gloom. This was a much bigger coach than any she had ever been in. It was like an omnibus, a private barouche. The couch she sat on was soft and springy. It had a silky covering. The dimensions of the space were unclear, but she was glad to be out of the cold wind and seated for the first time in two days. She could feel no wall behind her. The woman called out for the driver outside to slow and as the coach rolled along she lit a tiny stove and warmed some water. Whilst it heated, she sat by the cold, tired girl's side, making solicitous noises, brushing her tangled hair from her eyes. The woman questioned her and gradually, Natasha told her story. The woman's voice said she was appalled, but even in the gloom Natasha could see her eyes widen and her pupils dilate. In telling the tale of her captivity she had spared no detail.

"My name is Natasha," she volunteered. "What is yours?"

"I must bathe these cuts of yours," was the reply. "The water is ready."

"Where are we going? Is this coach yours?"

Her hostess made no answer but added to the water a scented oil which filled the cabin with a mouthwatering astringency. Natasha's eyes had adjusted to the dark well enough now. She was intrigued to discover that she was sitting on the end of a large bed. Her heart fluttered.

The stranger removed the ruined shoes and, raising the skirt, eased down the tattered stockings, revealing the torn and bruised limbs beneath. The woman's hands were firm and she plied the medicinal cloth with tenderness. Natasha listened to the wind outside and the crunch of the coach's wheels on the frosty earth below their bodies. Above these sounds she became aware of another noise. It was coming from the woman. A soft noise, a kind of gentle mewing. Her bedside manner was not as professional as it appeared. The "washing" crept further up her legs. The edge of her already rucked skirt was getting wet. She felt a kindling in her belly, a little like the moment when, blowing sparks on a handful of straw, it flickers into fire. She hid her hungry look and bit her lip.

"What are you doing?"

"Your poor legs," came the uneven reply. "Will you let me remove your skirt?"

"I, I don't know."

With a force that belied the caring in her voice the woman dragged the skirt down Natasha's thighs. The knickers came too. Natasha wondered if she noticed the pearly sheen on her underthings which had blossomed at the first touch of the woman's hands. Next Natasha's blouse was raised over her arms, her slip and underthings coming too, exposing her skin to the lips of the warm air around her.

"That's better," said the woman. Natasha sat further back on the bed, utterly naked in the half-light, her buttocks slithering on the shiny coverlet, aware of her own wetness and the rigidity of her nipples. She was still prepared to be coy if that was what was needed but, despite her empty stomach and her exhausted limbs, a deeper need was surfacing. The coach rattled on, its motion jiggling her breasts slightly, making her whole body experience an imperceptible state of flux, like the thrumming of a hummingbird's wings. Her stomach mimicked her body's tremors.

The stranger's ache was perceptible now. Still pretending to wash Natasha she knelt on the bed in front of her, rubbing her stomach with the cloth. The warm water ran down her belly and pooled in her lap, matting her pubic hair. The cloth cleaned her pubis, gently, dipped between her buttocks and down the backs of her legs. Natasha's lips parted. She never broke eye contact with her companion. Gradually the woman leaned further and further over until Natasha was forced to lean back. Gravity and the rocking of the coach took their course, and the two ladies reclined, the still fur-swathed stranger sprawling on top of Natasha, nestling between her open legs. The experience of having her nakedness covered in heavy, silky fur, fur which moved with the impatience of arousal, was entirely new to Natasha and entirely welcome. Without further pretence, their mouths met in a deep kiss. The woman's tongue crept over the threshold of Natasha's small mouth and her taste was dark, something like the very rich black cherry preserves Natasha had eaten as a girl, something like that, but behind it the bitterness of black coffee, or warm liquorice. The tang of Roubles. Natasha's thighs parted wider as the stranger ground down her furred hips into the throbbing bed.

"Can you pay the fare?" the woman asked.

"I don't have any money," replied Natasha, smiling.

The woman licked her lips. "Good."

"What is your name?" Natasha asked again.

"My name?" the woman breathed. The warm air filled Natasha's mouth. "For tonight you may call me Lara. Now. Answer my question. Can you pay the fare?"

"I hope so," replied the naked girl.

The woman smiled and stood, unfastening her coat, parting the glistening fur. Underneath, her skin shone with health and warmth, naked, as Natasha knew she would be, undulating like the steppe itself. Her small, neat triangle competed for glossiness with the tumbling mink on either side, and there were clear marks of dew on her ample thighs. Her nipples too were erect, tickled now by the tendrils of fur at their tips.

Stalking around the cabin, rocking her body expertly to keep her feet against the roll of the coach, Lara assembled a small group of objects.

Natasha lay on her front, her buttocks wobbling, watching the enchanting creature pick up a bottle here, a jar there, and last of all, a large Russian Doll, what Natasha's mother would have called a Babushka.

"What's that?" she asked, as, still furred, Lara kneeled beside her on the bed.

"Your fare," said Lara.

The Babushka was similar to others Natasha had seen, and yet somehow different. It was, as ever, a painted, wooden representation of a woman, hourglass shaped, but longer than usual, skilfully rounded at top and bottom like an Indian club. It was about ten inches long and as smooth as glass. She could not imagine it standing up very well.

Lara unscrewed it in the middle and brought out a second doll, perhaps eight inches long. This she opened to reveal a more peculiar specimen, dotted as it was with little wooden pips, like semi-circles. The third, bumpy one opened to reveal a small, perhaps four-inch doll, and inside this forth, a fifth, a tiny one, the smallest of all, long and curvy like the rest, a shy smile on its face.

Lara loomed over the girl, her hair trailing over her face. She kissed her neck and throat, leaving raised irregular flushing wherever her lips and teeth touched. She kissed Natasha's breasts, sucking softly at the nipples, making the girl grit her teeth and hum her approbation. The fur still rippling over her, Lara licked Natasha's belly, her underbelly and then tugged at her pubic hair with her teeth.

"Yes," she murmured, "there."

With her eyes closed Natasha heard a rattling sound, as if Lara were flicking her own teeth with her fingernails. The woman teased between her legs, licking her thighs, blowing maddeningly on her clit. Natasha's juices oozed from her cunt like a sweet syrup, trickling over her bottom. Lara's fingers dithered there, smoothing her perineum, stroking the lower vee of her slit. Natasha waited for the tongue on her cunt but, to her surprise, felt a warm, sudden mouth on her anus. She gasped and half-closed her legs. Lara was making a meal of Natasha's fundament, holding apart her twitching thighs and suddenly, the girl was intrigued to feel a small, hard object, being rolled by Lara's tongue. She raised her head and looked at Lara's face between her buttocks just as the woman eased, with a practised tongue, the smallest of the dolls from her mouth directly into Natasha's exquisite anus.

"Ah!" cried the girl, half sitting up, shocked at the sensation of hard, smooth wood in her rectum. Her anus had yielded surprisingly quickly. It was a tiny doll, only the size of a peanut in its shell, but still, there was that buzzing edge of pain in the pleasure which made any action in that particular region so interesting. It wasn't something Natasha was particularly used to, but it wasn't something she was against. In raising up her torso she sat down on the object. The doll popped entirely inside.

"Ah!" she gasped again.

Lara smiled like a cat and crawled across Natasha, pressing her to the coverlet. She kissed her once more. Natasha tasted the salt-and-cinnamon of her own loins. She lapped at the older lady's lips.

"Is the fare too much, my sweet?"

Natasha shook her head. The doll was within her, concrete, like an imminent need. Lara put her mouth to her pinioned victim's ear and whispered:

"I will eat you now. Work on that little dolly, and when you feel like the time is right, give it back to me."

Lara drew the fronds of her furs deliciously down Natasha's palpitating body and settled again between the girl's splayed legs. Natasha's knees, wide apart, swayed to the rhythm of the galloping coach. With two fingers she smeared aside her own slippery lips allowing her liquid pinkness to gape.

Lara began to lick – softly at first, like a breeze, up and down the vertical lines of Natasha's vulva, just tracing its shape. Natasha quivered and parted her legs further, her hands between her legs, holding tenderly Lara's sculptural cheekbones, feeling the woman's face muscles twitch as she feasted on her wetness. Natasha was maddeningly conscious of the velveteen luxury of Lara's fur-wrapped shoulders caressing her thighs. Lara lapped, an accomplished lap, a muscular, steady tongue, lathering Natasha's labia with her agile tip, laying down sparkling layers of saliva, drawing out an effulgent sheen of warm honey. Occasionally, Natasha heard her swallow. Each stroke was imperceptibly firmer than the last, opening the girl's cunt with coaxing and compliments.

Natasha revelled in the exceptional licking. She had never been licked so well. Those girls she had tried to teach at the palace. Amateurs. Ingénues. Cold-tongued and awkward. Eager but inept. Even when she had turned the tables and instructed, bringing the shivering young women to surprised, profane climaxes, she had not been able to transfer her ability. This was more like it. She held the backs of her knees and arched her spine.

The flowering of her vulva was having an effect on the muscles of her pelvis. As ever, she could feel her insides getting hot, aligning themselves, steeling themselves for orgasm. This was only too perceivable in her rear, where the muscles of her passage were clenching around the little intruder, getting a grip, all the more because Lara would occasionally target one of her licks to Natasha's small, sensitive, drawstring entrance. She recalled her cunnilinger's instructions. As she moaned and rocked her hips, she concentrated tentatively on manoeuvring the doll.

Lara reached Natasha's clitoris for the first time with a tremolo touch which sent molten streaks of pleasure to the girl's pointed toes. She screwed up her pretty face and bore down. It was a delicious feeling. She felt the sensation under her tongue, liberating and awful. With surprising ease the small wooden doll crept from her anus, bringing with it a heavenly ache. She cried aloud. Lara, who seemed to know the signs, met it with her mouth and pushed it in again.

"Eep!" gulped Natasha, who, reaching for her own clit,

pushed out once more. Again, the doll was intercepted at its delectable zenith and once more firmly inserted by Lara's clever mouth. They were playing chess with a single queen. Eventually, as her revolving finger worked to a frenzy, the little piece of wood popped free into Lara's smiling mouth. She firmly removed Natasha's hand and leaned over her once more. The doll dropped from her teeth, trailing spit, and landed on Natasha's lips. It tasted of plums and wood and her own darkness.

"The fare not too much, my love? You can get out if you want to."

"No." gasped Natasha, slightly bewildered from being so close to orgasm and from having just passed a small wooden toy into a stranger's mouth.

Lara told Natasha to sit up. "Oil for the pussy and cream for the rose," she purred, pouring drops of gold from a stoppered bottle onto Natasha's wide open cunt.

"Shouldn't it be the other way around?" asked Natasha, breathing deeply as the warm lubricant landed in blobs on her raised clit. Lara took a fingerful of snowy ointment from a blue-glass jar and anointed Natasha's anus with it, slipping a long-nailed finger inside. She lay Natasha face down and began to bathe her back, shoulders and buttocks with her limber tongue. Natasha had a desperately sensitive skin. The tonguing made her writhe like a snake, causing her to part once more her blushing, sticky thighs.

Lara bent scientifically between the girl's open legs, gazing at her upraised rump. Natasha resisted the temptation to masturbate. She dare not peak and miss what was ahead. She felt that sensation of fear and anticipation which is true desire, when the mind says: I don't know what you mean to do to me, but I want you to do it.

The first thing she felt was something pushing at her cunt. Her lips were parted by cold wood and she felt a carved Russian lady slip inside. It was the second doll, a good size and she gasped, contracting her vagina. It was pushed all the way in and she heaved her hips, thrilled at the sensation of being fucked by this beautiful woman. Then another blob of cold ointment landed just where she needed it. Her sensitive rear was again invaded by the tiniest doll, its passage easier now after its first intrusion. It felt good, slipping in there on its bed of cream. It slid all the way and she felt her asshole closing behind it. A lascivious smile played on her lips as the small doll in her back passage nestled up to the larger one in her front. Then, to her surprise, Lara's mouth returned. Another slightly larger Babushka, thick with cream, was nudged against her anus. Pressure was applied, the doll being pushed seemingly by Lara's clenched teeth. Natasha swore aloud as her anus was eased apart and the doll forced inside, pushing its partner in deeper. "Fuck," was all she could manage.

"Good girl," cooed Lara, working the doll in her vagina. That felt good. It slipped substantially in and out, its hippy contours stimulating beautifully. Natasha was now up on all fours, her hair hanging down, watching between her legs as the woman in furs slowly fucked her with a painted wooden toy, slick with oil and honey. She reached for her clit but her hand was grasped.

"Not yet," teased Lara, and before Natasha could even cry out, a third little doll, the middle sized one, was inserted halfway into her dark passage. This was much bigger and stretched her uncomfortably, stopping halfway at the nipped in waist of the saucy Russian lady, her hand-drawn smirk protruding. The pain flashed down her legs and into her stomach, her nerve endings sparking, processing the discomfort automatically into sheets of ecstasy. She groaned a long "ohhhh" and drooled slightly. She wiped her mouth. She wondered what the toy looked like, jutting between her peach-like buttocks, wagging like an ornate tail, her sensitive membrane stretched thinly around its modest bulk.

"Push out, my sweet," said Lara, before taking the little woman in her hand. Natasha pushed out, feeling her tightness stretch, and Lara slid home the greased implement, driving all the breath from the girl's lungs and making her, with three Babushkas of various sizes in her bottom and a big one in her cunt, feel fuller than she had ever felt before. Her tongue lolled out involuntarily and she moaned, the sounds beyond her control, a mixture of pain and deep, deep, chemical pleasure, as endorphins flooded her brain. The Babushka in her vagina was gently withdrawn and Natasha was laid gingerly on her back. The three dolls in her bottom clacked together. The thrum of the horses' hooves was having a peculiar effect on their position. They did not seem to be empty. Could one . . . Were there stones in one? The middle one? Or beads? They throbbed ever so slightly. It was new. It was not altogether bad.

"Fare not too much?" inquired the coated woman. "Can you afford it?"

Natasha panted an affirmative and parted once more her legs. She had utterly surrendered.

Lara resumed her licking. She fell upon the young woman's pussy and ate ravenously, sucking her clitoris as if it were a sweetmeat. As she licked, her left hand fingers toyed with the lower entry, just as the right hand beckoned at the entrance of her vagina, agitating the occupants of that dark hall. Natasha, now well into the game, pushed and clenched, pushed and clenched, easing out with difficulty the third doll, with which Lara fucked her at intervals, twisting it round, pushing it in. Expelling it gave her mouth a divine taste of copper coins. Soon all three were out, lying lacy with frothy cream on the bed. Natasha felt loosened and slightly crazed. She was cresting a wave of desire which shrieked to be satisfied but could not bear to be dissipated.

"Well done," cried Lara, coming alongside her mate and kissing her warmly. Their tongues played together. Natasha, in her wantonness bit Lara's full lips.

There were blotches of red on Lara's breast, her nipples were hard and a spider-web of silky threads was strung between her knees where her own juices had trickled and become enmeshed. Nevertheless, her briskness did not abate.

"Now we begin," she said. In front of the panting, supine Natasha, she laid out the five, gradated dolls. The first three were warm from her bottom, the second-biggest was slick from her cunt. She threw the smallest into the shadows of the cabin.

"We do not need her," she said. "These," she said, touching the next three, including the one with the whatevers inside, "these I am going to slide into your pretty arsehole. Is that too much?"

The last one of the three had just been in her pussy. It was quite big. Natasha bit the inside of her cheek in wonder.

"This," she said, holding up the longest and largest, the queen of the dolls, "this I will put up your cunt. Do you want me to fuck you in your cunt, until you come?"

Natasha moaned her permission.

"With this little lady doll?"

"Yes, please."

Lara set about her work. Natasha was bent over on all fours once more, her face on the covers, her arse in the air. Lara creamed the three dolls liberally and inserted them, in reverse order, into Natasha's well-worked rump, the biggest first, slathered with cream. The shapely mannequin made Natasha wince and puff out her breath like a train.

She yelled as Lara forced it in deep with two slippery fingers. Natasha felt the top of her head trying to come off. The next was easier but lumpy and full of beans, and the last, the little nut-shaped one, popped in like a button. Lara licked shut the full arsehole and stood up.

At the foot of the bed she dropped her coat and stood naked before Natasha for the first time. Natasha, splayed on her back, simply stared. The structure of the shoulders, the round belly, the glory of the breasts, swaying in time to the horses' gallop, overwhelmed her. Where were they by now, wondered Natasha, half mad with pleasure and crammed to capacity. Mongolia?

Lara took a series of straps from a trunk. Natasha wondered if she was to be flogged. She simply did not care. She felt that she would come, and come hard, if she were flung naked from the coach, such a state was she in. No. No flogging. Lara was passing the straps between her legs, fastening them behind her regal buttocks. She took the largest of the dolls, a pert madam with the decency at least to blush in two cherry-red drops of lacquer, and, filling each half with fine black sand, reconnected her, and slipped her into the straps. The little woman stood out from Lara's body like a beautiful, dark, painted horn, springing from the woman's luxuriant hair. She bobbed with her newfound weight. Lara looked terrifying in the shadows, the swinging lanterns casting umbrae and flames across her awesome, sculptural nudity. Natasha's eyes widened. She could feel her clitoris swelling.

"Be brave, my dear. My pretty little dolly is very big. I don't want to split your little cunt." She spread golden oil over the doll's bulging head then lay down on her back next to Natasha.

"Ride me now," whispered Lara. "Ride me for your fare!"

With difficulty, as she was very full, Natasha swung one leg over Lara, straddling her partner. She crouched over the curvy doll and lowered her craving cunt onto Lara's hips. Lara urged her on, cradling her buttocks from beneath, kneading and stroking. Natasha eased herself onto the doll, feeling the mouth of her passage stretch, feeling the honey ooze around the doll as she was filled to her utmost, front and back, arse and cunt, Lara kindly but firmly driving the doll in to the hilt from beneath.

Their private hair curled together. Natasha's breasts hung soft over Lara's neck and tears of sweetness fell onto the woman's eager face.

The horses plunged ahead. Every bump in the ground, every rut the wheel took askance sent a tremor up the doll and throbbed against Natasha's cervix. They caught the rhythm of the coach, Natasha raising and lowering herself onto the luscious woman beneath her, Lara still cradling Natasha's bottom in one hand, squeezing her swollen breasts with the other, rolling her hips gently, fucking the girl fully and certainly from beneath. Each thrust rattled the secreted Babushkas, vibrating the beads, making them roll and shift and fuck subtly her unspeakably beautiful arse.

Natasha rode Lara until she began to moan urgently. She was getting close to orgasm but knew she couldn't come with three Russian dolls in her rectum. "I'm close, L . . . Lara," she sobbed.

"Good girl. Now let me have it."

"Uh?"

"The first little woman? Hmn? Just the little one. Push her out."

Natasha kept up the fucking motion of her shaking thighs, but staggered into a crude squatting position and squeezed. The smallest doll was right at the head and slipped out easily, giving the girl a shudder of joy.

Lara changed their positions, rolling Natasha off her and then dragging her onto all fours. Again the two rear dolls moved, scraping with sweet discomfort. Lara mounted Natasha like a donkey, pushing once more into her sopping cunt. The girl moaned afresh as Lara began to fuck her in earnest from behind, again, again, fucking to the pounding rhythm of the coach. She was so full, front and back. Natasha's breasts grazed the silk of the bed. She bit the pillow and swung her hips to the rhythm of Lara's hammering. She could hear the kneeling woman grunting with the effort of driving the slippery doll in and out of her pussy and as the sounds reached her ears, her rectal muscles twitched involuntarily around their welcome intruders.

It did not take long for Natasha to reach the trembling, whimpering stage. As she looked round at her perspiring assailant, her face was a mask of appalled arousal. Lara said, her breath ragged:

"Okay, the next little woman. Show her to me."

Natasha groaned, maddened by the perversity of it, her mouth full of the burnt taste of desire. She knew her lover was looking between her buttocks – at her pleated little hole, she relaxed, felt it open, and the head of the doll peep out.

"Can you see it?" she gasped.

"I can see it," she purred, "come on now, give it to me. Give – me – my – doll!" With each word she fucked the shaking Natasha with a swing of her hips.

Natasha pushed, feeling her tight ring widen and stretch. She felt the itching, burning pleasure of that special stretching and the slippery caress of the doll's sinuous, substantial body passing out of her anal cavity. The bump, bump of Lara's belly knocked the doll, fucking her ever so slightly in the arse as she fucked her cunt, but Natasha fought it and expelled the intruder with a wave of triumph and a wash of terrible pleasure.

"Precious!" crooned Lara as the Babushka rolled past her pubis and onto the bed. She fucked Natasha extra hard as a reward, grabbing a fistful of her young flesh on each side and pulling her yawning cunt onto the stiff doll. Natasha wailed her joy, the bed beneath her soaked with her sweat, saliva and spots of pearly juice.

Lara withdrew and Natasha collapsed onto the bed. She was as close to coming as she was to a kind of delirious sleep. Lara sat in the middle of the bed, her strong back straight, and asked Natasha to straddle her lap. Once more Natasha lowered her pussy onto the doll, wrapping her legs around Lara's buttocks. Lara took the shaking girl in her arms and holding her haunches, raised and lowered her onto the doll. Natasha cried with pleasure as she felt Lara's strong arms take over, the doll fucking her cunt, the woman fucking her mind.

"Now when you come, give me the last doll. The big one. Only when you are about to come."

Natasha was seconds from coming. Her every sound was a warble of need. Lara pulled Natasha's arse cheeks apart and she rode and rode the doll, squeezing and releasing her anus until, as the storm gathered in her cunt, and the blood rushed to her head and her toes, she bore down on the last, large, bumpy doll, stretching her poor anal ring wide. It came out half way and Lara, minx-eyed and panting with exertion, took it in her hand and forced it back again.

"Ah! Ohhhh!" yelped Natasha, as Lara fucked her arse to the

same rhythm as she was fucking her cunt. The double assault had the desired effect.

"I'm coming. Oh, shit, I'm coming," howled Natasha, as Lara forced the doll deep in her tunnel once again. She bounced savagely on both the dolls, soaring impossibly high on wings of climax and then it hit her in a sweet wave: the orgasm. The rapture which starts as magma in the pit of the stomach and travels like the ripples in a pond, like the wrath of a typhoon, until it turns the hair to seaweed, caught in the current.

"I'm fucking coming," she screamed, holding Lara in a ferocious grip. She howled as her orgasm turned her inside out, wrapped her in oblivion, so strong she could not at that moment have told you her name. Lara released her hand and Natasha passed the last doll from her bottom. She rode and rode, wringing the pleasure from every inch of her body, feeling her very skin catch fire as her paroxysm slowly ebbed.

They held each other, drenched and drained. Lara licked the tears from Natasha's face and laid her gently on the coverlet, withdrawing from her vagina the immense, strapped-on Babushka. It was thick with opalescent come and steamed slightly in the already warm air of the cabin. The coach rolled on.

Natasha kissed her strange lover, her eyes closing. The swing and sway of the coach seemed a lullaby. Her nerve endings crackled with the almighty climax she had experienced, her heartbeat palpable in her engorged clitoris. With the room reeling about her she touched herself there, and turning circles on herself, and sleep took her to its deep violet waters.

Natasha dreamed. In her dreams a huge, life size Russian doll leered at her, its suggestive mouth half-open, its wooden surface glossy with varnish that could have been the glow of perspiring lust. She lay back in the dream, spreading her thighs, and allowed the doll to suck her with its motionless painted mouth. The sensation was like the good itch of an approaching sneeze. The doll reared above her. From its loins protruded an object, long and smooth, a tiny human, flesh and blood, with cat-like eyes and a sour-plum mouth. Dream Natasha, reclining on a couch of fur, raised her legs to her breasts and allowed the doll to come between them. It entered her, the little Lara between its legs smiling as she disappeared head first into Natasha's dripping cunt. In and out slid the woman, smiling as if it were her birthday.

Natasha awoke to dawn's shattered light in the coach. It was still moving. She sat in bed. Lara had gone. Natasha stepped gingerly down from the bed. Her body ached from its exertions. Her rear passage throbbed and her vagina felt stretched and raw. A quick inspection showed that not only had Lara gone but so had Natasha's clothes, despite the fact that they were nothing more than rags. Her worn boots, her laddered stockings, her knickers, slip and blouse were all gone. She was alone and the only stitch in the still moving cabin was the opulent fur, its front stiff with patches of oil, ointment and her own salty emissions. Smiling to herself, rocked by the endless motion of the carriage, she put it on.

Exotic Music

Teresa Noelle Roberts

Allison scooped up some baba ghanoush onto a piece of pita, then looked her friend Daniel in the eye. "Are you sure this is a good idea – introducing me to this belly dancer?"

"Don't say it in that tone, sweetie. She's not a stripper. She's a *dancer*, just as much as any of us."

Danny's boyfriend Raoul, his mouth full of stuffed grape leaf, nodded in agreement.

Allison flushed at being included in the *us*. She tried to cover her consternation by continuing the argument. "It's not that. I know Silvia's a good friend of yours and I'm sure you wouldn't introduce me to anyone trashy. It's just that belly dancing sounds so . . ."

"Fluffy?" Danny grinned. "You won't hang out with ballet dancers any more, except for my choreographer self, but you still think like one. You don't have any luck dating non-dancers. I figured this was worth a try. At worst, you'll see something new and I think you'll enjoy it. I know I was astonished."

"Besides," Raoul added, "even I think Silvia's a babe."

As the lights dimmed, she fingered the charm on her necklace, the charm in the shape of the satin toe shoes she could no longer wear. Even to Danny she couldn't admit her anxiety: that alien as non-dancers were, she was terrified that any professional dancer would be put off by her weight gain and the awkward stiffness she still suffered in damp weather. And every time she watched someone else dance, it filled her with conflicting emotion – joy in the artistry itself, bitterness that she was barred forever from it.

The band in the corner started: a heavy, unfamiliar rhythm on the drums, an odd, nasal-sounding flute, a violin, and an electronic keyboard reproducing the sound of several instruments Allison couldn't identify. The effect was exotic and sensual, yet lively. Then the dancer emerged. She probably entered from some place as mundane as a back room, but she did it with a panache that suggested she had materialized out of Aladdin's lamp.

For a few measures she stood poised, veil held like wings, the light catching the beading on her green and gold costume on fire. Allison was struck by Silvia's regal carriage and the energy invested into that stillness. It was the mark of a gifted performer, she knew, to say so much with so little motion – and it was much harder than a non-dancer could imagine. At the same time, she was slightly bewildered by Silvia's appearance. She had expected a Middle Eastern sylph, someone with an Arabic look and a long, lean body. Instead, Silvia was below average height and fair, with a mass of strawberry blond curls. She was also very curvy, not fat, but definitely heavier than what Allison, who had been studying ballet since she was four, thought of as a dancer's body. Her instinct was to be put off, but almost immediately old-fashioned accolades like "voluptuous" and "a real hour-glass figure" came to her mind, and she found herself wondering what all that lush flesh would feel like. Those breasts . . . Most of her lovers, like herself, hadn't had much in that department, and the soft weight of Silvia's cleavage, enhanced by the beaded bra top, looked like it would be marvellously fun to play with. But she couldn't help wondering how fit could Silvia really be if she had enough body fat for such attributes.

Then Silvia started to move and as she watched, Allison's world view shifted. This tiny, curvy lady projected a queenly strength that equalled anything she'd seen in a ballerina – partly spiritual, partly erotic. Even though the dance style was utterly different, she was reminded of the Alvin Ailey troupe, how they could touch your emotions and make you drool at the same time, without doing anything that would offend your grandmother. Silvia made eye contact with everyone, male and female, old and young, and to each she seemed to offer some secret. Her hips snapped in precise time to a beat so foreign that even Allison's trained ear found it hard to break down. The moves looked deceptively simple, but Allison could appreciate how much work lay behind making everything look so clean and precise. As for being fit, there was definitely muscle underneath those curves. Her back was exquisitely defined, and as for her abs . . . she might have a little pooch, but anyone who could make her belly undulate up and down *and* sideways had to have good abs.

"You know," Danny whispered, "this is all improv. And the musicians are improvizing too. Middle Eastern music's like jazz. Even if you know what tune they're starting from, there's no guarantee it's going to sound the same way it did last time."

Allison's growing respect turned into awe. This was all spontaneous? That spoke of skill – but also of a great soul. Even if you had all the skill in the world, it took something special to improvize and make it look wonderful instead of merely acceptable.

She watched with growing fascination through several changes in music. What really captured her was the slow, languorous section. Saying that Silvia undulated, or that the effect was sensual, was true, but inadequate. That quivering thing she did with her abs looked like a woman in the middle of a series of mind-blowing orgasms, yet her smile remained serene and innocent and her hands caressed the air with graceful, birdlike gestures, making the effect sexy but not vulgar. She moved, Allison thought, sometimes like fire and sometimes like water, and without doing anything lewd, she led Allison through fire and water as well, or at least left her hot and somewhat damp.

When the music ended, it was much too soon.

Eventually, Silvia joined them at the table and Danny introduced them. In a simple dress, with her curly hair pulled back and her stage make-up washed off, she looked less exotic, but no less pretty. Allison tried not to gush at her about how impressed she'd been, realized she was gushing anyway and decided to roll with it. To her surprise, Silvia blushed. "Thanks. I was a little nervous knowing you were out here. Danny told me you'd danced with the Boston Ballet."

"But Danny . . ."

"Has been my friend since high school. If I were a professional golfer or an economics professor, he'd still find a way to say he loved my work. You're an objective audience."

"Not any more," she blurted out. Then it was her turn to blush.

Needless to say, Silvia ended up giving her a card, saying, "Call me if you're interested in lessons."

Needless to say, Allison called, and not about lessons.

On their first date, they talked until two in the morning. On their second date, they made out like teenagers in the park at the end of Long Wharf, and discovered that they both had a fascination with light bondage.

On the third date, they bypassed the date part of the evening altogether, picked up a take-out and went to Allison's apartment. The take-out was still on the living room coffee table, where Allison's cat was probably enjoying it while nesting in Silvia's blouse. It occurred vaguely to Allison, as they fumbled towards the bedroom, that they probably would be hungry later after a dinner of about three crab Rangoons and a lot of kisses. Oh well, the pizza place up the street was open all night.

They stumbled toward the bed in a classic late-night-cable blind clinch. In the movies, though, the couple never actually steers into the bedpost, which they managed to do. Silvia broke the embrace to see what had whacked her on the head. "These toe shoes look practically new," she said, touching the virginal pink satin. "I thought you'd retired."

"Had to retire," she corrected. "They were the last pair I bought before . . ." she took a deep breath. "Before the accident."

"And you've left them hanging here where you see them first thing in the morning and last thing before you close your eyes for how long?"

Allison buried her face in her new girlfriend's magnificent cleavage, hoping to distract her. Silvia moaned as Allison teased and suckled, but she wriggled away before she lost her head. "How long has it been?"

"Six years."

"For God's sake, why? That's got to be painful."

Allison thought about it. She'd felt the need to have them there, but Silvia was right. She winced every time she saw them. "I guess," she said slowly, "it's because I needed a reminder that I wasn't always a has-been."

"Do you want to talk about it?"

For about two seconds, Allison thought about it, but the curvy, half-clothed body pressed against hers felt too good to stop for a heart-to-heart. "Later." She began nibbling on Silvia's ear.

Silvia caressed the long, soft ribbons attached to the toe shoes. "I can think of something more entertaining to do with these than staring at them and thinking about the past. Do you trust me?"

Silvia and Danny had been friends for years, and she trusted Danny implicitly, which was the rational reason for saying yes. Allison knew it had more to do with grey-green eyes and soft, creamy skin that looked even fairer against her own olive complexion, and an intense sexual curiosity that grew the more Silvia fondled those ribbons. "Yes," she repeated, and kissed her deeply.

"Then finish getting undressed and lie down on the bed."

She could feel Silvia's eyes on her as she stripped. In her last couple of abortive relationships, she had been inclined to hide under the sheets and keep the lights dim, ashamed she no longer had the body of a ballerina. It was ridiculous to feel that way in front of a woman whose very roundness was part of her beauty, but she couldn't help flinching a little as the last clothing dropped.

Silvia reached out and stroked the despised curve of Allison's belly. "Lovely," Silvia purred. "Such a pretty tummy." Then dropping to her knees – and it was a controlled drop, an obvious dance move that made Allison's knees ache in sympathy for the bruises she must have acquired learning it – she began kissing and caressing the little soft curve of olive flesh.

Her mouth was tender, persistent, ingratiating, and her hands stroked Allison's hips and thighs (other areas she was none too fond of since they'd lost the catlike leanness of a few years back) without straying between her legs. At first Allison's brain couldn't get past the oddness of it. Lovers had admired her long legs before, or her breasts, which were tiny, but exquisitely sensitive, with large, dark nipples. But her pot-belly? That was just . . .

Just sweet, her lizard-brain decided. All that tender, sensitive skin, generally ignored, was catching fire under Silvia's skilled touch. Her navel, in particular, seemed to respond to licking and kissing. Little tendrils of fire coiled through her, heating her muscles, melting her centre, spreading to her groin. If Silvia would just move her mouth lower . . .

She didn't, though, despite Allison's increasingly pathetic pleas. Finally, when Allison was trembling and moisture was starting to coat her upper thighs, Silvia rocked back on her heels and gently pushed her onto the bed. "Put your hands above your head," she said, and Allison, in a fog of sex, complied. She gasped and writhed as Silvia slowly and deliberately criss-crossed the ribbons of the toe shoes around her wrists, binding them together. A shoe ended up on each side, immobilizing her further.

"If you're going to be all tangled up in the ribbons of your toe shoes, this has to be a better way." She smiled lasciviously and took off her bra. A soft sway to those marvellous breasts – they were obviously a product of nature, not science – and small, erect, rosy nipples that Allison longed to taste. When she tried to sit up, Silvia pushed her back down, then undulated to some inner music as she removed her skirt. Clad only in a thong, the movements of the dance weren't innocent at all, and when Silvia rolled her belly, Allison felt her own muscles clench and quiver in response. "Pleasepleaseplease . . ." Silvia grinned, slipped up out of her panties, then ran them over Allison's nose and mouth. They were slick, slick as Allison's had been when she finally shed them, and she was frantic to lick the source of that moisture, to penetrate it with her fingers and feel Silvia clasp around her. Almost beyond speech, she licked at the panties to show what she wanted, but Silvia shook her head and tossed them aside, then lay down on top of her.

Taking a hard nipple in her mouth, Silvia arranged herself so one leg was between Allison's parted thighs, their groins pressed together. She'd been waxed bare and the feel of the bare mound, the exposed clit, was almost more than Allison could bear. Teeth scraped her nipple, just enough of a painful edge to add to the pleasure. "This is the advantage of belly dancing we don't talk about in the beginners' class," Silvia said as she began to move. "Shimmies and pelvic drops can be damn useful." Her mouth moved up from the eager nipples to meet equally eager lips.

Allison couldn't have done those hip isolations if she'd been thinking about, but her body instinctively echoed Silvia's as best she could, arching against her, grinding her clit against her lover's. Silvia was intent now, pressed against her, kissing her deeply. She felt so good, not just between her legs, but everywhere. Allison struggled against her bonds, yearning to touch her, but Silvia had done a good job. The ribbon held fast, and she couldn't even embrace her with bound arms without the risk of hitting one of them with the toe shoes. Satin or not, they had hard toes to support a dancer's weight, and that would be a definite mood breaker. But the bonds were not. It felt so good to fight against them as Silvia kissed her, stroked her, vibrated against her clit. The heat was building, and when Silvia pinched

her nipples and whispered, "Come now," she writhed frantically and obeyed. Silvia raised herself up on her arms, and when
Allison came back to herself a little, she saw those beautiful
green eyes watching her. "You," Silvia gasped, "are too damn
hot." Her hips began to buck with no art except lust. Her face
contorted. She threw her head back, closed her eyes, made a
noise that seemed too loud and animalistic to come from her
compact form, then collapsed bonelessly by Allison's side.

But not for long. "You're not done yet, are you?" Silvia
murmured when she'd caught her breath. "I don't think you're
quite ready to be free of those ribbons." She moved down
Allison's slender body, kissing and nibbling as she went. She
kissed all the way to her feet. No one had ever kissed her feet –
rubbed them as a kindness, yes, but not kissed them. Ballerinas
had ugly feet, and for the first time in six years Allison was glad
she had soft-skinned feet with a pretty pedicure, not the battered, painful, raw appendages that came from hours en pointe.

Then Silvia worked her way back up, and Allison stopped
thinking about anything except the fire in her pussy as Silvia
licked her. Then two fingers entered her.

She bucked so hard that she smacked herself in the head with
the toe shoes, but she didn't care. All she cared about was
coming . . . coming hard and repeatedly as her lover's skilled
tongue and hands released not only the sexual tension built up
from being alone for too long, but a spiritual tension she had
become so accustomed to that she only noticed it once it was
gone.

Silvia cradled her as she came down from the orgasm high,
telling her how beautiful and hot she was, and how she couldn't
wait to feel Allison inside her. As she tenderly untied the satin
slippers that bound her, Allison started to cry. Silvia looked
alarmed, but Allison smiled through the tears. "No, it's good.
It's just that . . . I feel beautiful and worthwhile for the first
time in years. It's like you brought me to life again."

Silvia raised an eyebrow, the exaggerated expression as controlled and elegant as those she used when she was dancing.
"Tell me who made you feel anything but beautiful and worthwhile and I'll kick them for you."

She shook her head, wiped her eyes. "No one but me. I'd
been training as a ballet dancer since I was four. I had a
promising career ahead of me, and a ready-made social circle.
When you're a ballerina, you don't really know anyone else –

there's no time. Between one heartbeat and the next, I lost it all."

"What happened, if I can ask?"

"Darling, right now, you can ask me anything!" Although she was smiling, her eyes were wistful. "It was stupid. I was walking across Boston Public Garden with another dancer and she stopped to flirt with a cop on a horse. The horse stepped on my foot."

Silvia winced in sympathy.

"It gets worse. I didn't realize that things were broken, not bruised. You get a ridiculous pain tolerance as a ballet dancer. Something always hurts and you just deal with it. I went to rehearsal anyway, and then walked around on it for the rest of the day. Danny finally made me see a doctor, and by that time I'd damaged it really badly. Then I pushed myself to dance again too soon and got a stress fracture. Things had to be pinned. If I hadn't been a ballerina they'd say I made a full recovery, but there was no way it would ever be strong enough to go en *pointe*." She shrugged. "So my career was over before I turned twenty-five."

"And you finished college and started a new one?"

"And gained weight and had no time to date and no idea how to meet anyone when I wasn't surrounded by lots of attractive women whom I got to see naked in the dressing room on a regular basis. Okay, so maybe I was spoiled, but I was pretty miserable when I lost that world. It all disappeared: my friends, my job, even the pleasure of moving my body to music, which was what I loved best in the world ever since I was a little girl."

"You know," Silvia said gently, "I know it wouldn't be the same, but you could still do Middle Eastern dance. You'd have to start from square one – it's very different from ballet and a lot of the things you've spent years learning, like turn-out, you'd have to unlearn. But you only go up on the balls of your feet for emphasis. You can do everything else flat-footed, so it wouldn't put stress on the bad foot."

Allison started to protest that nothing else would be the same, but then she actually made herself think. No, it wouldn't be the same. It would be an utterly different art form – not like taking up jazz dance or modern, which derived so much from ballet that it would be tantalizingly close without being the dance she had loved for most of her life. And while she'd probably never belly-dance professionally, at least she'd be dancing. "I might just do that," she said. "Thank you."

Then she found another way to thank her.

Lovely as Silvia's undulations were while she was dancing, they didn't hold a candle to her helpless rolls and contractions as she came. She liked to be filled, it turned out, probably could have taken Allison's whole slender hand if they'd had some lube, but settled blissfully for four fingers fucking her hard. Her pussy muscles seemed stronger than other women Allison had been with, her spasms harder. For the first time in her life Allison found herself wishing she had a cock – not for Silvia's sake, but her own, because if it made her fingers feel that good she could only dream how it would feel on a cock. But Silvia didn't want a man inside her, she wanted Allison, as much of Allison as she could cram in, and her body and her incoherent noises made that abundantly clear. Then Allison had a wicked inspiration. She grabbed one of the toe shoes and gently rubbed the satin of it across Silvia's clit.

She'd heard about female ejaculation. This was the first time she'd ever encountered it.

Exhausted, sweat-drenched and slick with each other's juices, they finally dozed off. When the cat, having finished the Chinese take-out, came in for attention and woke them, they found that the ribbons of the toe shoes were clinging to both of them.

"These are going to have some pretty funky stains," Silvia said, holding up a distressed-looking slipper gingerly. "I don't think you'll want to display them any more."

"Maybe not – but they'll find a happy home in the toy box. Come on, let's get some dinner and come back for round two."

A few days later, Allison went out to buy another pair of satin dance shoes: soft practice shoes to protect her feet in her first belly-dance class.

The Lay of the Grecian Urn

Roxy Katt

It was damned exasperating, really. Here Amanda had worked as assistant editor at a fashion magazine all these years without getting too hot and bothered by all the female supermodels that came by – most of them struck her as quite insipid, actually – and then the boss had to go and hire his niece and Amanda had been all hot and bothered since.

Tory was her name, short for Victoria. Businesslike, professional, industrious, earnest, she was very fashionable in a drastic sort of way without a trace of showiness or gaucherie. She brazened forth what Amanda inwardly called the "sophisto-punk" look: much more of an edge than some mere compromizing punk wannabe, and enough class to know exactly what she was doing. No simple profusion of multiple hair dyes and facial hardware would do for this young lady.

And it was about time, in Amanda's opinion, that there was someone a little more radical, more challenging than the countless blonde Britney Spears clones that had passed through the office one after another. In fact, there was something of the aggressively virginal air about Tory, a slight downward cast of her large dark eye on occasion which bespoke not the 'please don't touch me, I'm too precious' wimpiness Amanda so deplored whenever she saw it, but more the 'I'm a bit busy for that sort of thing, don't you think?' that inspired in Amanda not only a respect for the younger woman's professionalism but more than one evening in bed accompanied only by a trusty vibrator.

Tory was about average height, thin, and had a wide, gorgeous smile – which betrayed just enough insecurity to make her boldness more of a triumph – and the most marvellous big eyebrows. One side of her head was shaved completely bald. The rest of it was covered in long, witchy jet black hair, heavily moussed, with burgundy highlights. Dark make-up, but not overdone, and no piercings save at the ears, each of which had a large, gold hoop.

Amanda, on the other hand, was old enough to be Tory's mother, but looked good enough to pass for her older sister. She was much shorter than Tory, and had short dark hair. Amanda generally kept up a traditionally professional look: snug Chanel suits and such, stylishly cut but in conservative colours, such as the one she was wearing today, light grey.

The two were getting along just fine, but the bitch of it was this boss's niece could easily have got just as good a job without the nepotism, and saved Amanda the distraction. But no, she had to work here, where her presence constantly obtruded upon Amanda's concentration, distracting her from her work, making her snap at people on the phone, dulling her professional edge, causing her to stop off after work at the newsagents for vibrator batteries . . .

And Amanda knew that Tory had never really noticed how much Amanda liked her – and in what ways. Amanda had sometimes dared to hint to Tory that she found her attractive, but though Amanda was not usually the retiring kind, here she was stymied. Yes, everyone at the office knew Amanda was a lesbian, and that Tory on the other hand apparently had a boyfriend; but that had not precluded, from the mind of hopeful Amanda at least, that the younger woman might have other interests as well. Amanda's gay radar was not flawless and, though the readings here were not promising, they were not hopeless either. Amanda would sometimes try to tease out of Tory some hint that she just might be interested some time, but of course you had to do this sort of thing in a way that didn't make you fall flat on your face. "Hi, so, Tory, do you ever have any, you know, lesbian inclinations from time to time?" would have been hopelessly gauche, and of course, would have elicited an emphatic "No", no matter what the truth was. No, ordinarily straightforward with attractive women she knew were lesbian, Amanda had to fish carefully here, drop hints, look for signs, flirt in a comical way that could be seen simply as straight "girl stuff" on the one hand, or seen with more seriously erotic overtones in case the unforthcoming Tory did have lesbian inclinations after all.

So it was that today, as Tory walked into the photographic studio with her clipboard hugged to her chest, that Amanda greeted her with a comically conspiratorial wink and a, "Hi gorgeous, what's up?"

Though businesslike as usual, Tory had come to work looking sexier than ever, as far as Amanda was concerned. Tory was very good at this: she could dress so exquisitely and then just simply forget how chic she was as she sat at her desk and worked out schedules for photo shoots or talked on the phone to this or that potential advertiser. She dressed with care and flair, and then just lost herself in her work.

Tory sauntered over to where Amanda was at a desk taking some notes, and looked about her at the ersatz Greek ruins and props that had just been used in one shoot, and were to be used again later that afternoon.

Amanda, really, was undone.

For Tory was hot. She was ever so tightly sheathed in a pair of thick, black leather trousers – a soft leather that seemed to wrap around her legs like jealous rubber. The sturdy trousers were back-zipped and had, intriguingly enough, a kind of small version of a sailor flap, tightly fastened over her front with four sturdy snaps. Her blocky, high-heeled platform boots, lacing three-quarters of the way to the knee, were the perfect match for these trousers. It was just like Tory, furthermore, to soften the outfit with a large, baggy rust-coloured peasant shirt of thick cotton, tightly belted at the waist.

Only yesterday Amanda had made her most artful – but as usual unsuccessful – pass at the younger woman. It couldn't be that she was now teasing Amanda, for Tory had apparently been completely oblivious yesterday to the fact that Amanda had come on to her at all. And even before Amanda had made her pass, Tory had already mentioned that the next day she would likely be wearing her new leather boots and trousers. No, Amanda knew "her" woman better than that: teasing was the furthest thing from the mind of someone like Tory – at least consciously.

"Hi, Amanda," said Tory cheerfully, holding her clipboard to her chest, as if nothing had happened the previous day, and, from her point of view, it clearly hadn't.

"Goodness," said Amanda, trying not to sound too appreciative, "don't you look nice today."

Tory spun around once, smiling like the proverbial cat who had swallowed the proverbial canary.

"Where did you get those fabulous trousers?"

"A little shop just around the corner from where I live. It only takes ten minutes to get into them!"

"I'll bet. They look fabulous," she said in a low voice.

"Thanks. Now which of these invoices—"

"I really think that cotton and leather combination is perfect for you."

But Tory was already through with compliments, for she was immediately into her work now. "Mmm-hmm," she muttered in response, and began to take an inventory of the props, ticking things off her clipboard.

"Tory," Amanda said, easing up next to her, "can I confess something to you?"

"Sure. Why not?"

Tory bent over to look at the row of urns. They were all on their sides on a table by the wall and there was supposed to be, apparently, some sort of model number on the bottom inside each of them.

Amanda lost her nerve to make the pass she had been preparing, and retreated into idle conversation. "It really would have made more sense to put the model number on the outside, wouldn't it?"

"Yeah. Even in this light it's hard to tell." She peered in.

Her trousers creaked as she bent forward, peering into one urn after another, busily recording numbers on her board.

Amanda felt the strain. Not only a sympathetic strain for those overloaded trousers and their heavenly cargo, but the strain of her own libido, the confusion (rare for her) of not knowing what to say, exactly, or how to say it. She had to say something, but didn't know what. Finally, she went fishing.

"So, uh, Tory, how are things with what's his name?"

"Donald?"

"Yeah, that's it."

"It's over."

"Oh. That's too bad. What happened?"

Tory looked at her. "He said he wanted to tie me up and fuck me."

"How dreadful." Licking her lips, and suddenly remembering herself, she stopped.

"I know."

"Especially when a woman like me can do such things so much better. Er, I mean, uh . . ."

"Huh? You mean you'd like to hog-tie and fuck me too?"

"No, no. I mean—"

"What is it with everyone these days? It's the trousers, right? I wear leather trousers and suddenly everyone goes crazy?"

Amanda threw caution to the winds. "Oh, you bet! I mean yes, about the trousers, and yes about the tying, and . . . Oh, I'm sorry for being so blunt, dear, but you asked and . . ."

"Well, I've never done it with a woman before, but better you than Donald, I dare say."

"You mean I can?" Amanda was momentarily astonished by her unexpected good fortune and Tory's forthright response.

Tory snorted. "I'll believe that when I see it."

Amanda was confused, but still hopeful. "But I have your permission?"

"What?" she said, bending down again to the urns. "Oh, yeah. Sure," she said dismissively. "Hog tie me if you can, Amanda. You'd be fulfilling my wildest dreams." And she snorted again. "No disrespect to lesbianism, Amanda, but we both know a woman just can't . . ."

Throughout the studio resounded the thunderclap sound of firm human hand on leather. There was a sharp, brief cry, which was abruptly smothered as Tory's head disappeared inside an urn with a "foop" sound and her pen and clipboard clattered to the floor.

Amanda stood backed, shocked by herself. She had really let go. "Tory?" she said tentatively, and then smiled.

But Tory had not likely heard her. Staggering to an upright position, wobbling unsteadily on her mighty heels and rubbing her leather-clad arse, Tory then reached for the edge of the urn which now encircled her neck. At first she pushed upward gingerly, and then more forcefully as the urn refused to budge.

A smile crept over Amanda's face as Tory struggled more vigorously. "Unh!" came Tory's muffled voice, "What the hell?"

"Having trouble, dear?"

"Unh! You bitch," came the mutely echoing voice, "what gives you the right? . . ." Her long-fingered hands continued to struggle with the urn, grasping it in different places, as she tottered uncertainly on her heels, bumping into the table, her delicious trousers groaning and straining as one moment she arched backwards pushing at the urn, and another she bent forward still pushing and twisting.

Amanda smiled, looked at her nails and said nonchalantly,

"My dear, I do believe you are having a bit of a problem. Is there anything I can do for you?"

"Yes. Get me out of here!"

"Oh. You mean that urn? Are you sure you can't get it off yourself?"

"Amanda, I'm really stuck in here. I can't get out."

"Hmmm. Yes, it appears you are. What a silly thing to do, dear, I thought you were smarter than that."

"What?!"

Amanda walked up behind her, then reached in front and started to undo Tory's wide belt.

"Amanda, what are you doing?"

"You'll see." She pulled the belt behind, and tied Tory's wrists behind her. As Tory struggled with the belt, Amanda stepped in front of her, and let her hands play slowly over the leather-encased hips. "My, aren't you a sweet, helpless thing. Not so smart now, are you?"

"Amanda? What are you doing?"

"Amanda, what are you doing," mocked Amanda, as her hand slipped between Tory's leathered thighs and slowly but firmly began to knead her groin. "As if you didn't know. You are pretty full of yourself, aren't you, dearie, to suppose no woman could take an aggressive hand with you, aren't you?"

"Oh Amanda, this is, like, really . . . humiliating!"

"Shh, you silly little cow."

Slowly, Amanda popped each of the four snaps over Tory's groin, one by one. The lusty leather flap burst open, revealing the crotch of a pair of panties which read: "Serious Enquiries Only".

Amanda laughed out loud. "Really? Was that for Donald?"

"Huh?"

"Oh, you do look stupid with that jug on your head," she said, beginning to stroke Tory slowly and firmly through the panties. "Really, darling, a girl young enough to be my daughter should be able to knock my block off – especially in those big boots of yours. My, my."

"Ohhh," Tory groaned, her voice low with shame and pleasure.

"You do realize, darling, that if you change your mind and say no I'll just stop and let you go. Of course . . ." and here she reached behind Tory with her other hand, unzipped her bottom, and began slowly to insert her fingers between Tory's panties and her smooth white arse ". . . nothing can change the fact that I could finger-fuck you front and back as much as I liked, couldn't I?"

"Oh . . . oh yes," murmured Tory as a finger of Amanda's left hand pushed the crotch of the panty aside and slowly pushed its way up her already soaking vagina.

"Miss Power Trousers Girl isn't quite so invincible as she thinks, is she?" Amanda smiled. "You poor, dumb, helpless pussy. Say that for me, punk girl. Admit you're my poor, dumb, helpless pussy."

"I'm your poor, dumb—"

"Louder, honey. I can't hear you under that jar you've got your pretty little head stuck in."

"I'm your poor, dumb, helpless pussy. Oh, no! Oh! Oh, my arsehole? Oh, Amanda, my—"

"Yes, your precious arsehole dear. Let me guess," she said, as a finger of her left hand still played slowly inside Tory's vagina while a finger in the right lightly circled the edge of her anus, "no one's ever come in by the back door, have they?"

"Gnnnghhhh . . . unnnh . . ." Amanda could tell this would be a tight anus.

"I'll take that for a no. Well then, dear, this way, please." Amanda pulled her hand out the back of Tory's trousers and her finger from her vagina, but caught a firm grip on Tory's pubic hairs, which were very long and black. She led Tory by her fur across the room as the helpless younger woman awkwardly clumped after her in her heavy boots. They went to the refrigerator, where Amanda let go of her prey and commandeered a few supplies.

"Are you still there?" asked the helpless Tory.

"Yes, dear," she answered. "Now just hold still."

Amanda hauled Tory's super-tight trousers and panties down to her knees, totally immobilizing her. Carefully, with the greatest appreciation, she caressed the younger woman's thighs as Tory trembled.

"Aren't you going to fuck me?" she asked plaintively.

"Who's in charge here? Is it you, dear? Because, if it is, how about if I just stand back and you do whatever you think is best."

"My God, you're good. You're—"

"Shut up, pussy. Hey, wait a minute, is that someone knocking on the door?"

"Oh, my God!" squealed Tory desperately from within the urn, "didn't you lock the door?"

"Why no," said Amanda thoughtfully, "I really don't think I did. Funny, that. You'd think I would have."

Tory went hysterical, renewing her yanking at her bonds, making a pathetic attempt to shake the urn off, babbling about how she couldn't be seen that way et cetera, her white thighs swaying and tottering as she wobbled pathetically in her great boots, until Amanda interrupted her freakout with her own laughter and went and locked the door.

"Stupid bitch," she laughed, smacking the young woman on the arse as she came back from the door, "no one was knocking. You punk girls look pretty imposing but you panic easily, don't you? Now bend over."

Tory obeyed. "Now," said Amanda firmly, "beg for it."

"What are you—"

"Beg for it dear, and accept what I give you."

"Please?"

"Oh. I guess you don't want anything, then. All right. I'll just untie you then and—"

"Oh! Please fuck me, Amanda, I'm begging for it. Please? Please? I've never begged for it before, I've—"

"Shut up, cow. I hear you. Now bend over. All the way, yes, that's it, oh, you're such a flexible young thing. Mmm, now I'll just push one finger up your tight little quinny, there we go, feel nice? And for the other hole a lovely surprise!" Tory shuddered as Amanda slathered the crack of her arse with lots of cold mayonnaise. "A lovely big surprise . . ."

"OH! Oh Amanda, please! Oh please not quite so fast . . . oh, my fucking . . . oh, what the—"

"It's a carrot, dear – not particularly long, but nice and fat. Just hold still while I pump you up nicely. That's it. You're being fucked with a carrot, dear. Remember that next time you get a little full of yourself. Remember you were once full of carrot and mayonnaise instead. Mmm, yummy. Now just a minute while I pull up a chair for myself and tuck into a nice fat trout I caught just a little while ago in a jar. Now, what is this I'm fingering here?"

"A nice fat trout."

And Amanda did just what she said, pulling up a chair and, while still working Tory's arse with the carrot, began to push her unusually long tongue up Tory's cunt, licking, sucking, stopping on occasion to remark on the delectability of the meal, and continuing as Tory groaned louder and deeper, her now husky sobs reverberating from within the urn.

"Still feeling smug, my little fishy?"

"Oh no. Ohhhhh . . ."

Tory had just about been brought off when there was a knock on the door and men's voices outside. "Hey! Why is this door locked? Hello? Is there anyone inside?" There was a confused murmuring and then both women heard someone distinctly say, "I'll go get Stan. I think he's got the key."

"Shit!" the women whispered harshly in unison. Seeing Tory's tied hands begin to fumble in a panic with the carrot buried deep within her arse, Amanda nearly came.

"Amanda, please. I can't . . . can't get this carrot out!"

"No time for that, you idiot!" hissed Amanda. Swiftly and authoritatively, she hauled up Tory's trousers and panties, levering her arse back inside the leather and zipping it closed over the insolent carrot. With lightning speed she untied Tory's belt and handed it to her, then stooped to refasten the snaps between her legs.

"But, Amanda," bleated Tory, "I've got a carrot up my arse! And the jug!"

"No time. Damn, this pussy panel is tight. How the hell did you ever . . .?" she muttered as Tory hurriedly put the belt back on.

The door rattled and then came open. Three men, photographers of the magazine, walked in. "Amanda? Why didn't you open the door? Didn't you . . .? Is that Tory? Why does she have that urn on her head?"

"Because she's stuck in it, poor thing. Can't you see? Lord knows I told her to be careful, but somehow . . ."

"Really? You mean she can't get out?" The men asked incredulously. "How in the hell . . . ?"

"Amanda," whined Tory pathetically, "please! I can't be seen this way!"

"Please, gentlemen," said Amanda, suppressing a smile as she grabbed the mortified Tory by the shoulders and speedily piloted her to the door. "This is embarrassing enough for the poor girl without your impertinent questions. You needn't concern yourself about this incident or mention it to anyone. Rest assured that I will get her out at once."

Amanda wheeled Tory down the hall, and into the lift. As it

went up, Tory wailed, "Oh, my God. I can't believe that happened. I have never been so totally humiliated in all my . . . I mean they all saw me with this jug on my—"

Amanda pushed her into the corner of the lift and pressed her knee between Tory's legs.

"Still ready to come, my little bovine? I'm still in control, you know. If you don't think so, I'll just let you wander the hallways, mooing for help."

"Oh. Please, Amanda, whatever you do, finish me first, please."

When the elevator door opened, Amanda grabbed her firmly by the elbow and piloted her down the hallway. They passed a bewildered-looking secretary: "Don't worry, Amie," chirped Amanda, "I'm just taking Tory here to the caretaker for some help. Everything's just fine."

In Amanda's office, door locked, Amanda again tied Tory's hands behind her and peeled her trousers down to the knees.

Tory bent forward as commanded as Amanda again played with the carrot and tongued the depths of her womanhood in a most authoritative manner. Again groans and shudderings echoed from within the jug as this time Tory came, helplessly, in repeated waves of delighted transport.

Of course, the jug had to come off sooner or later, and nothing was more suited to the purpose than one of Amanda's heels, deftly wielded by a firm hand, smashing the urn in a thousand pieces. It was time, then, of course, for bewildered Tory's tongue to do some work of its own, for Amanda's own need by that time was, needless to say, quite intense.

Everyone around the office bought the story that Tory had become trapped in the urn through some strange "accident" – which neither she nor Amanda ever explained. Basically polite people, the workers all refrained from asking further embarrassing questions. They did notice, however, that it was not long afterwards that Amanda and Tory became an "item", as it were, and word went around that the romance had been sparked by Amanda's being so helpful to the trapped and humiliated woman in her hour of need.

Well, they probably weren't that far from the truth, after all.

Own Gaol

Vav Garnek

Vanessa Clarke took a lot of time and trouble getting ready.

She hadn't seen Steve for a couple of weeks and she knew he would have wanted her – expected her – to look her best.

She had a long leisurely bath, the water slick with a heavily scented oil that left her skin feeling silky smooth.

Then, pink-skinned and slightly damp, she sat, still naked, at her dressing table and did her make-up. Her hair was a dark, almost chestnut brown, naturally thick and curly, and she piled it up high on her head keeping it all together with a large, metal clip.

Her face was long, angular even, large hazel eyes set in skin that stopped just short of being olive. Lots of eye-make up – thick black lines on both lids – and shadow in a dark, bruised purple, blusher heightened her already prominent cheekbones and painted her lips scarlet. Scarlett O'Hara. Scarlet woman. Finally she chose "Obsession" as her perfume – because it was Steve's favourite – dabbing it behind her ears, at her throat, beneath her full breasts and finally along the crease of her sex. He'd like that.

Vanessa had carefully lain her clothes out on the bed before bathing: matching bra and briefs in thin black net, so fine and wispy it almost wasn't there at all. Black, wrap-around mini-skirt that split up one thigh, a transparent black blouse through which her bra was all too clearly visible, flesh-tone lace-topped stockings that shimmered as she walked, swayed, in her black stilettos and flattered long, toned legs that didn't really need any help.

Finally she slipped on a tight-fitting puffa jacket, padded in metallic silver, with "FCUK" in large letters emblazoned across the chest. Dispassionately she considered herself in the mirror and wasn't altogether sure she liked what she saw. The overall effect was striking right enough, but possibly a little too tarty for her tastes and not entirely appropriate for a woman of very nearly twenty-nine. But then it didn't matter what she thought, it was what Steve thought that counted.

She walked the short distance to the Tube, and at King's Cross caught the Cambridge train and from there to the small market town of Bury St Edmunds, before catching the bus for Sudbury.

Throughout the journey she'd been aware of sidelong glances from other passengers, mainly men, weighing her up and down. Well let them look, but several times she'd caught herself tugging her mini skirt down as if in the belief that it has somehow ridden up her thighs. And she'd blushed furiously when she'd noticed the men watching that as well.

At least on the bus there seemed to be a number of other women dressed at least as brassily as she was; most younger and several with small infants in tow.

When the bus finally stopped and she, and they, got off at Barnfield, saw the high fences topped with razor wire and the familiar forbidding sign "Her Majesty's Prison North Lodge", she realized why.

Steve was three years her senior and ran his own small jeweller's shop in the east London suburb where they lived. They had been married for three years and dated for a further three before that. Vanessa had liked him from the moment they had met. He was a bit of a Jack-the-Lad, all right, but he made her laugh. And she loved the way he was able to lavish jewellery, gold and silver, upon her and the way there always seemed to be a big wad of cash in his back pocket.

What she had genuinely not realized until the day her world collapsed with the policeman's knock at the door was that Steve had been "fencing" most of the stolen goods in the area for years.

He got four years' time for the crime and that was what she was doing stood there in the middle of a godforsaken spot in the Suffolk countryside.

By now she'd been "visiting" often enough that she knew the drill by heart. Friends and relatives gathered in a large reception area, you had to hand over your Visiting Order in exchange for your "number", produce your passport to have your identity checked and then your hand stamped with an ultra-violet marker.

You were only allowed to take a maximum of £20 into the prison visiting area. All other personal possessions – bags, phones, keys, papers – had to be put into a locker. Numbers were called out in batches: 1—10, 11—20, 21—30 and so on; and when your turn came you made your way through the electronically-operated sets of barred grilles and into the prison itself.

In the entrance to the visiting area coats and jackets were examined, you went through a metal detector and were given a pat-down body search. Finally you had to line up against a wall while a trained sniffer dog gave you a once-over for drugs and then it was in for the visit.

Except that day was different . . . The dog was a friendly, chocolate-brown spaniel that wove excitedly in and out of people's legs until it got to Vanessa, at which point it simply sat down in front of her and refused to move.

A female prison officer came across to her, took her numbered ticket and consulted her clipboard: "Sorry about this Mrs . . . Clarke, but I'm afraid I'll have to ask you to come with me."

Silently she followed the officer down a long corridor lined with what looked like steel, cell doors until they reached a room at the very end. It was large, white-tiled, brightly lit, although windowless, with an examination table in the middle beneath a large light. There was a full-length adjustable mirror on wheels, a small bench to one side, something that looked very much a shooting stick – a metal pole set into the floor – topped with some sort of canvas sling and what looked like a medicine cabinet up on one wall.

The officer virtually squared up to Vanessa. She was shorter by two or three inches, although Vanessa realised this was probably solely down to her stilettos. She had short blond hair framing her round, pale face and a solid, almost stocky build. She also had a natural air of authority, a "toughness" of presence that Vanessa found disconcerting.

"Right. We can do this the easy way or we can do this the hard way. Do you understand?"

Vanessa could only nod dumbly by way of a reply.

The officer lowered her clipboard and fixed Vanessa with a stare: "I asked you a question. Do you understand?"

"Yes, er, yes."

The officer continued to glare at her while the silence grew between them until it was almost painful: "Yes, what?"

"Oh, er, sorry. Yes, Miss. I mean, yes, Ma'am."

"Right, that's better. Now, Clarke, as you know, the drug dog picked you out at the line-up and they're never wrong. So I have to ask you the following two questions. Firstly, do you have any controlled substances, Class 1, 2 or 3, about your person?"

"No, Ma'am," Vanessa replied truthfully.

"Secondly have you eaten, smoked or injected any controlled substances or other substances such as solvents, glues or aerosols, within the last week?"

"No, Ma'am," Vanessa lied.

"Right, Clarke, fine. Now I'm afraid I'm going to have to carry out a strip search. Please remove all your clothing and place it on the bench over there."

Vanessa looked around herself in a mixture of desperation and horror for anything resembling a cubicle or even a screen.

"Well, get on with it!"

"But, but where do I change?"

"Right here, Clarke and I have to watch you do it. Don't worry, though, you've got nothing I haven't seen hundreds of times before."

"But that's disgusting. It's disgraceful! I'm not stripping off in front of you."

"Well, that is your right and your choice. But I'm afraid that if you want to see that husband of yours then you're going to have to. You could always ask for another officer to be present but, as I'm sure you're aware, we're very short staffed and there are no other female officers on duty on this wing so it would have to be a male officer. I'm sure you wouldn't want that . . . and even if you did, since you're a woman and he's a man, I'd still have to be present anyway. So I can't see that's much of an improvement, really."

Reluctantly, a highly embarrassed Vanessa realized the officer was right and wasn't joking. Having come all this way, she wasn't going to go back to London without seeing Steve. So she walked over to the bench, facing the wall with her back to the officer, and carefully undressed down to her underwear, stilettos and stockings before turning back.

The officer snorted in derision: "Very fetching, but not what the doctor ordered. When I said strip I meant just that. I want you bare-assed naked or you can just put it all back on again and go home."

Blinking back hot tears of shame, Vanessa shed the last of her clothes and vestiges of her modesty . . . although she still kept one arm across her breasts and the other covering her pubic mound.

"Over here, Clarke in the middle of the room!" the officer barked. "And you can cut all that 'Miss Innocent' crap for a start. Hands up, behind your neck and lock your fingers together. Turn your toes out and bend slightly from the knees. Do it! Now!

"I'm afraid I've got to go and search your clothes again now and see if I can find whatever it was our canine friend sniffed out. You stay right here and don't move a muscle. Understand?"

"Yes, Ma'am," and it was only as the officer moved away from in front of her and over to the bench that Vanessa realized she had been deliberately placed in front of the long mirror and had no choice but to gaze at her own humiliatingly naked reflection. It was acutely embarrassing but Vanessa realized with an almost physical jolt that she was actually enjoying being at the beck and call of this stern young blonde, subject to her every whim and helpless to resist because of the power and hold she had over her.

The officer seemed to be gone a long time and, when she got back, walked round and round Vanessa two or three times, stopping directly in front of her. Vanessa realized that without stilettos she was indeed the smaller of the two women, and lowered her eyes, unable to meet the other woman's steely gaze.

"Well, that's much more like it, isn't it, Clarke? Not quite the snotty bitch any more? It's amazing how much more obedient people get if you take their clothes and their dignity away from them. And you'd be a lot more obedient still if I had you in here for even a month or so.

"Now, remember I still have to do this body search, and if you want to see that old man of yours then you'll do exactly what you're told, speak and move only when you're told. Is that clear, Clarke?"

"Yes, Ma'am."

"First things first. I have to have a look inside your mouth. So open wide, tongue right out and say 'Ah' for me."

But when Vanessa shook her head, without another word, the officer took her right nipple between finger and thumb, lifting her breast up and away from her chest until it was stretched taut and then began to pinch the tender flesh with gradually increasing force.

At last Vanessa's legs began to quiver with the pain and she opened her mouth to draw a long, ragged gasp of breath: "Ahhhhh!"

The officer stopped immediately, but only to turn her attention to Vanessa's other nipple: "And again," until she had literally wrung another gasp of pain.

"Good. Well done. I think we understand one another. Right, Clarke, I want you bent over that stool arrangement. Legs spread and when you're comfortable clasp the back of your calves with your hands. Don't move until I tell you."

Dumbly Vanessa did as she was told. The humiliation was almost too much to bear, although she realized it was about to get worse. What an obscenely lewd spectacle she must present: buttocks forced up into the air and the plump slash of her sex peeping out from between her parted legs.

The officer stood in front of her, rolled up her sleeves and snapped on a pair of latex gloves: "I've got to examine you both anally and vaginally," she said, almost kindly. "I don't know whether you take it up the arse – doesn't do much for me, I have to say, although I understand some people seem to like it – but it's not the worst thing in the world and I'll use lots of KY jelly. Then we'll do the other side.

"I've searched your clothes and there's nothing there . . . but the dogs just don't pick on you if there's nothing to find."

Miserably Vanessa wondered if she should tell the officer about the joint she'd smoked the previous evening, but realized it was too late and nothing was going to stop the officer completing her search now.

Coming round to stand behind Vanessa, the officer squeezed a large portion of KY jelly from a tube onto her index finger and gently applied it to the whorl of Vanessa's anus. It felt cold and slightly clammy, but once she was lubricated the officer began caressing the taut, pink globes of Vanessa's buttocks through the latex gloves.

It felt good, and after a few minutes Vanessa felt herself starting to relax . . . and that was when the officer slipped her index finger into her sphincter and in right up to the knuckle. Vanessa grunted in surprise more than anything, since the feeling was strange but not exactly unpleasant. And she relaxed still further as the officer's finger began to slide backwards and forwards inside her, describing ever-increasing circles as it explored every inch of her back passage.

"Good girl. Well done," she murmured. "See, that wasn't so bad after all, was it? Nearly done now."

The finger was removed from her backside and Vanessa heard the officer snap on a fresh pair of the latex gloves and felt a finger very gently probe the entrance to her sex. "Do we need some more KY? No, I thought not."

Then the finger was up inside her. Vanessa could gauge her own heat and wetness against its relative chill and she gave a little moan of pleasure.

"My, my. We are getting a little hot under the collar, aren't we?" And this finger too began to make a thorough examination of her most intimate place.

"Don't suppose you've been getting much fun unless it's been on your own. Have you?"

"No, Ma'am."

"Like me to continue?" And the first finger was joined by a second.

"Yes. I mean yes, please, Ma'am."

And then the fingers were replaced by a thumb while they sought out Vanessa's clitoris and, slick with her own juices, they stroked and caressed and teased and squeezed at her hard little bud until they brought her to an expert climax.

"Ohhhhhh! Ooooooh! Oh, wow! Thank you, Ma'am."

"Well, well quite the randy little slut, aren't we?" And the officer gave her a resounding smack across each of her buttock cheeks, each one raising a livid red palm-print almost immediately.

"Right, that's it, young lady. Get yourself dressed and down to see that husband of yours before visiting time's over for the afternoon. You might find sitting down on our hard chairs a little uncomfortable but it'll give you something to think about, if not talk about. You're obviously clean but next time try and be a little more honest with me . . . it'll save us both a lot of time and trouble."

"Hi, doll, you look great. What kept you?" Steve joked as they hugged and kissed.

"Yeah, sorry I'm late, but you're never going to believe this. I got pulled by one of the sniffer dogs and they gave me a strip search. Nothing to find, of course, but I still can't understand why they picked me."

There were perhaps twenty or thirty round tables with four chairs at each spaced out around the large room, virtually all occupied, and Steve led her over to his allocated space, off to one corner and by a large square column.

There was a raised dais along one wall at which sat half a dozen prison officers monitoring proceedings: "It was that blond one, in the middle, who frisked me. Bitch," Vanessa whispered.

"That's Officer Todd, Pam. We call her 'Barbie' – when she's not around."

"Well, she doesn't look like much of a doll to me."

"No, silly, it's short for 'barbed wire knickers'. Some of the guys think she's a 'lez' but I'm not so sure, although she can be a bit rough at times. She didn't hurt you, did she?"

"Hurt me? No, not exactly. But it certainly wasn't much fun."

"What, the strip search? No, I suppose not, but it's part of the way of life in here. You just get used to it."

Physical contact between prisoners and relatives is prohibited, but North Lodge, like most other gaols, took a fairly relaxed view of what was and was not permissible.

Steve and Vanessa sat facing each other, her legs parted either side of his, and within a few minutes his hands had crept inside her puffa jacket and were tenderly caressing her breasts through the thin blouse and bra.

"You always did have great tits, babe. Christ, that feels good."

"Mmm, yes it does. I miss you so much," Vanessa murmured in reply. "You're making me so horny. You can see my nipples are stuck out like bullets. They're so hard, they're aching."

Steve leaned forward as if he was going to whisper something, but instead he took one of her ear lobes into his mouth, nibbling and sucking on the morsel of flesh. Then his hands were resting on the tops of her thighs, only to slide down the outside of each one – so slowly it almost seemed like an accident – and then up under her mini-skirt. He suddenly stiffened when his fingers found the ridge separating stocking-top from the creamy flesh of her thigh, and his eyes widened: "You're bloody marvellous, but if I'm not careful I'll spend the next fortnight going blind over you!"

Then those fingers continued their journey, tracing their path back up over the tops of her thighs – although now hidden beneath her skirt – and down into the hot valley between until they met at the plump mound of her sex. Her heat and arousal were obvious as he stroked her through the thin panties: "Looks like I'm not the only one who's gagging for it. You're soaking," he breathed into her ear.

And with a jolt Vanessa realized that not only was it true but she was acutely aware of the burning in her buttocks where Officer Todd had spanked her: so hot she was surprised Steve couldn't feel that as well. And she squirmed in discomfort on the hard wooden seat as Steve's fingers continued to torment and tease her.

Visiting time was over all too soon. The prisoners remained in their seats until all their friends and relatives had left and then were lined up and marched back to their wings.

"Not you, Clarke. Over here to one side," Officer Todd barked. "Don't think we didn't see what you two were getting up to over there in your corner. You know we had to strip-search your wife on the way in and, as a result, you know we're going to have to do the same to you now. You also know we didn't find anything but you might tell the silly little mare to lay off whatever it was she was taking for at least 48 hours the next time she's coming in to see you . . . unless of course she wants me to give her another going over."

Officer Todd escorted Steve to another examination room, identical to the first except it also contained a single wooden chair with a very high, straight back.

"OK, you know the drill better than I do. Strip off." Officer Todd put on another pair of latex gloves, lubricated a finger with KY and, with Steve bent over the stool, briskly carried out the rectal examination and expertly massaged his prostate until his cock was achingly hard . . . not that it took long or much doing in his obviously aroused state.

"And I'll tell you another thing, Clarke. The strip search wasn't the only thing I gave your wife. She also got a bloody good finger-fucking. Came all over my hand she did. Randy little slut, isn't she? I'll bet she's going to be tossing herself off under the covers tonight. Just don't know who she's going to be fantasizing about . . . you or me."

Neighbours

Marie Gordon

I was jobless and broke when I moved from the city to a low-rent cubby-hole in the county of Hinton. It was furnished in a sort of way, comfortable enough with one large room divided into lounge/bedroom/kitchen. I knew it wouldn't be long before word got around that they had a lesso in their midst, and curiosity would soon get the better of them.

Sure enough, one afternoon two weeks later there was a knock on my door. I opened it to a rather plump woman in her thirties, who stood there, holding a cake.

"Hi," she said. "I'm Amanda, live a few doors down. Baked you a cake."

"Lovely, thanks, Amanda." I took the cake. "The name's Jane and please come in."

She sat on my couch.

"Tea? Coffee? Or something stronger?"

"That one – the last."

"It's just sherry."

"That's fine."

I poured, sat beside her and we clicked glasses. "Cheers."

Amanda sipped, then said. "We don't waste too many words around here."

"Then spit it out." I could guess what was coming.

"You havta know, Jane, you've moved into a nest of hets."

"You have objections?"

"Not me, and probably not them."

"So?"

"We're curious. We seen you round and heard you talk, educated, like. What's your sort doing in a dump like this?"

"I'm broke. Flat. Sure, I'd rather be somewhere else but it's not on right now. Got the sack from my teaching job for calling a spade a fucking shovel."

"Come again?"

"I used four-letter words in my sex talks to my students. The principal called it 'filthy gutter talk' and gave me my marching orders. So, anything else?"

"Yeah. We want to know – we'd like to know – what do your sort do – in bed?"

I laughed. "Nothing like coming right out with it, Amanda."

"I'm like that. I don't—"

"—waste too many words?"

"No."

"Well, before we sleep we . . ." I stopped, making her wait. She leaned forward. "And?"

"We make love."

"I bleedin' know that, but – how?"

"Want to satisfy your curiosity?"

"I reckon. I think. Maybe."

"Okay."

"Okay, what?"

"You'll have to suck it and see."

"I hope you're speaking metaphoric-like?"

"What do you reckon? Want to give it a go? Then tell your mates about it?"

"Aw . . . aw . . . I don't know about that."

"I won't bite you – not unless you want me to."

"*Jesus Christ.*"

"Save that for later." I put a hand on her knee and she jumped. "I'm free this afternoon."

She was suddenly breathless. "Oh, oh. What time?"

"How about now?"

She swallowed the remains of her drink in a gulp. "Now?"

"Of course I'll have to be paid."

"I don't have any money, Jane. Least none I don't have to account for."

"To your husband? You don't have any money of your own?"

"Nup."

"Shit."

"Yeah. He's a bit of an old dog with money but . . . I know . . . I could buy you something. Something legit. My hubby's a builder – on again, off again one, and that's the way the money is. Look around – low-rent houses 'cos no one wants to live here."

"I could do with some sheets."

"Right. I'll buy you a set. No sweat."

"Okay. Let's hit the sheets."

"Wh . . . where's the bedroom?"

"Just behind this curtain." I led her to the bed, her eyes darting to the door looking for an escape hatch.

"I don't know if I—"

"Can do it? Piece of cake, Amanda, but first you have to remove your clothes. Race you." I whipped mine off, then hopped into bed and waited for my ambivalent bedmate to join me. "Think of it as an adventure. Now, just relax."

"How?"

"Three deep breaths should so it. Don't want you hyperventilating."

She took the three breaths, then said: "I'm scared."

"Switch your mind off. Lovemaking belongs to the senses. All you have to do is feel."

"I feel, all right. I feel like what I'm doing is a mortal sin."

"That's thinking, not feeling. Now, if I touch your breasts like this . . . you will feel something . . . there. How does that feel?"

"God." She took a gulping breath. "Yes . . . um . . . it feels good."

"Women make better lovers than men because they understand another woman's body." As I talked, I caressed her breasts, her beautiful breasts, with nipples already high and hard. Throughout she gave soft moans of pleasure. "Men don't really have a clue. I mean, how could they? They have no idea how a woman feels when her nipples are being caressed . . . or nibbled."

Louder groans from Amanda.

"You like that?"

She gave another groan of agonized delight.

"Or twisted."

"Oh, my God."

"Too early for God, Amanda. Now, if you'll just turn over on your tummy, then on hands and knees."

"Do you want me to bark, too?"

"You'll soon appreciate the necessity for this position. Very soon."

"Wh-what are you going to do?"

"Relax, Amanda. I'm now putting my fingers in your cunt and they'll stay there until I find – then activate – your G-spot."

"G-spot. There's no such thing."

"Oh, yes there is. It lies on the front wall – the top part of our cunt. Believe. Now, bear with me. I just have to fossick around a bit . . . I need to exert a fair amount of pressure until . . ."

Amanda gave small happy moans.

"Sounds like I've hit pay dirt. Now, I'll just keep up firm stroking of your magic spot."

Amanda's groans get louder.

"You hate it, I can tell. It's reacting by not becoming swollen and slippery. Good . . . better . . . that's great."

Amanda breathed heavily. "I . . . I've never ever felt anything like this before."

"Let go, Amanda. Go with the flow – and there sure is a flow down here, baby. Give yourself up to it. This is what you were meant for."

Amanda's moans gave way to louder and louder groans. "Oh, my God . . . oh . . . oh . . . ooooh. Shit, fuck, fuck, fuck, fuck, fuck . . . oh, my God. *Jesus bloody Christ*."

"The religious experience."

"Don't stop. Wh-what are you doing? Don't fer Christ's sake stop."

"You want me to go on?"

Amanda yelled, "Yes . . . yes . . . yes, yes yes."

"You're sure?"

"Yes, I'm fucking sure."

"Quite sure?"

"Quit torturing me."

"Okay."

Amanda's cries of pleasure resumed and carried on until . . . "Oh . . . Gooooooooooood. Oh, shit, the neighbours will h-hear me."

"Fuck the neighbours."

Amanda gave a strangled laugh. "Yeah . . . F-fuck the n-neighbours." Screamed, "Oh, my God."

"Yes, my child?"

"Oh . . . that's wonder . . . wonderfu . . . wonderful." With heavy panting and tortured groans, Amanda, with a final scream, was taken over by orgasm.

"Well done, Amanda. Now, roll on your back and let me hold you. Did you enjoy that?"

"Enjoy?" she caught her breath. "*Enjoy?* What do you reckon? My whole fucking body exploded. I've never, ever . . . never ever . . ."

"I know, I know. Now you can teach your old dog new tricks."

Amanda wafted off and I waited for repercussions. Didn't have to wait long. At two the next day there was a knock on my door. "Business, methinks." I opened the door to three women.

"My name is Sarah. May we come in?"

"Have you come to complain?"

"Oh, no."

"Good. Then come in, sit yourselves down. I'm Jane."

Two of them sat on my couch; Sarah sat on a chair next to me. She said: "We saw Amanda leave here yesterday in a state of bliss. Couldn't get any sense out of her. She never sings, but she was singing, 'Heaven, I'm in heaven.' I asked her what had got into her and she giggled, 'You mean, who?'

"Then she said, 'And it's going to happen again tomorrow.' So, to coin a phrase, 'I want what she's having.' "

The other two chimed in: "Me, too."

"Okay," I said, "but it doesn't come cheap."

All together they said: "We'll pay."

"How much?"

"Up to you."

"Twenty-five?"

"Twenty-five, plus you spread the word."

Sarah grinned. "If we're half as blissed out as Amanda, we'll tell the world. Well, the females. The men, as well – if they're lucky."

"No. Not the men. Show but don't tell. I don't want them knocking on my door accusing me of god knows what. If any of them do, I'll triple your bills. Agreed?"

They looked at each other and shrugged: "What's to tell?"

"Good. Who's on first?" They rolled their eyes, eager beavers but scared. "Come on, decide."

Sarah broke the ice, "Me. Tomorrow morning at ten okay?"

I grinned: "It's a date."

"What about us?" wailed the other two.

"You tell me."

"We'll come separately the day after tomorrow and the day after that. At ten."

"It's a date." I waved them out, poured a drink and drank a toast. "To women, god bless 'em. And to the birth of a nice little earner that makes everybody happy."

Ruth, Roses and Revolvers

Lori Selke

Ruth couched the roses, dark as bloodstains, in the great glass vase that filled out the center of her dark cherry-wood dining table. She'd received the vase, tinted to a shade of midnight blue, as a present at her second wedding. Her second of three, so far.

Ruth wore black every day, out of deference to her husbands, all deceased. It set off her honey-blonde hair, her lips rouged to match the roses perfectly.

Her current live-in lover, Lina, came out of the kitchen carrying two fine china plates. She smiled when she saw Ruth arranging the blossoms with her white-gloved fingers.

Lina was broad-shouldered, toffee-coloured, with thick black hair she kept pulled back and slicked down. Her heavy black brows always looked like they were halfway to a scowl, but her generous mouth and her eyes, always alert, offset that impression. She had stripped off her shirt, leaving exposed her ribbed white undershirt, but had stayed in her uniform pants, the ones with the stripe down the leg and the belt with its leather holster.

"Another admirer?" Lina asked, nodding at the bouquet on the table. "Isn't it a little soon?"

"The proper mourning period for a dead husband is a year," Ruth said, soft as silk.

"Not that that's stopped you before." Lina smirked. Ruth smiled and shook her head, but didn't reply further.

Ruth had met Lina at the funeral of her last husband; Lina had been working as a security guard at the cemetery. It had been a whirlwind affair; soon enough, they were making love every night in Ruth's marriage bed, and within three months, Lina was moving into the tasteful but richly appointed house Ruth had inherited in the will.

They never discussed Ruth's former spouses, or the circumstances of their deaths. The centrepiece of Ruth's dresser was a small display stand that held three diamond wedding rings, each stacked above the other. Her closet held nothing but the most tasteful of mourning clothes.

But Lina seemed no more than amused by the attentions that other men had attempted to pay Ruth since they'd met. The small gifts, the awkward, respectful gestures of flirting and wooing. The cool reception Ruth always responded with. Lina had never bought Ruth a ring, or any other jewel; her dresser was already strewn with tokens from her former husbands, and Lina's small salary could never approach the riches they'd endowed her with. But Ruth was anything but cool to the ministrations of Lina's strong, bold hands.

"There wasn't a card," Ruth confessed over dinner. "I don't know who sent them."

Lina nodded, her mouth full of garlicky pasta.

"But they're just lovely, aren't they?" Ruth continued, reaching up to stroke the petals with her fingertips. "Love's blood and baby's breath. It doesn't matter who sent them, I don't care."

"Your food's getting cold," Lina said. Ruth obediently lifted a forkful of the pasta and its fragrant tomato sauce to her mouth.

"This is delicious," she said.

"I made your favourite," Lina said with a wicked smile. "Pasta Puttanesca. Whore's delight." Both women chuckled.

"I'm no whore," Ruth said.

"There's no such thing, though, as Coquette's pasta," Lina replied, and Ruth giggled, hand demurely placed over her mouth.

A moment later, Ruth said, "You know, our anniversary is coming up."

Lina raised an eyebrow.

"Our half-year anniversary." Ruth dabbed at the corner of her mouth with her napkin. "It's been almost six months since you moved in."

Lina smiled. "How could I forget?" she said.

"I don't know," Ruth said, setting her lips in a mock-pout. "Maybe I should be concerned." She cocked her head and failed to suppress a small smile.

"About what?" Lina asked.

Ruth shrugged with a slow, fluid roll of her shoulders. "I don't know. Maybe you're having an affair."

"You're the one who's getting flowers," Lina said.

Ruth smirked. "Touché," she said. "So what are we going to do for our anniversary?"

"Whatever you like, baby," Lina said.

"Anything?" Ruth asked, coy.

Lina nodded. "Name it."

Ruth put a finger to her cheek, thinking. "So many choices. I'll have to get back to you on that. But remember," she said, aiming a finger at her lover, "you owe me."

"You're not eating," Lina said.

"It's delicious," Ruth assured her. "I'm not hungry. Not for food, anyway." And she stood to clear her plate, hips swaying in her black crepe dress as she stepped into the kitchen.

Lina left her plate on the table and followed Ruth upstairs to the bed.

Ruth arranged herself on the bed, still dressed. Lina sat on the edge of the bed, one arm braced between Ruth's parted thighs. She kissed Ruth once on the lips, then at the juncture of her neck and shoulder.

Ruth lifted her fine-boned hands to Lina's belt. Quickly, she pulled it free, taking the leather holster that Lina wore with it. She cupped this to her chest.

"What are you doing?" Lina asked.

Ruth smiled like a child with candy and unsnapped the holster. "I've never touched your gun before," she said. "Yet you wear it to bed every night." She hefted Lina's gun in her hand. Its barrel was narrower than she'd expected, the body heavier.

Lina had stopped undressing. "Put that down," she said quietly.

Ruth glanced up at her lover, wrapped her hand around the grip, and rubbed the black barrel along her own thigh. She rubbed the dark metal suggestively, wiggling her ass on the bed's comforter.

"I've never held an automatic," she said. "My first husband, Anthony, he owned the first gun I ever got a good look at. He was a collector. He liked old-fashioned guns, war relics, revolvers."

"Put that down," Lina said, more sternly.

"What's wrong?" Ruth asked, a mocking tone in her voice. "Scared for me? Don't trust me?" She giggled a little, to herself.

"Anthony didn't like it when I played with his toys, either." And she pointed the gun at Lina's chest.

"It's loaded," Lina said, still in the same soft tone. "It's not a toy."

Ruth laughed lightly and placed the butt of the gun in her crotch. "Do you like it better this way?" she said, wiggling her ass suggestively, stroking the barrel with her hand. "Don't you think it's sexy? What's it's name, baby?" she asked.

"It's a Beretta," Lina replied.

Ruth scowled down at the gun in her hand. "I thought Berettas were tiny ladies' guns," she said.

Lina shook her head and actually smiled. "Not this one. Now come on. Put it down."

"Come sit in my lap," Ruth said.

Lina said nothing. Instead, she reached out slowly, wrapped her hand around the barrel of the gun, and pulled. After a moment, Ruth's grip slackened. Lina placed the Beretta on the nightstand next to the bed. Before Ruth could close her legs, Lina replaced the piece with her hand, the heel of her palm pressed against Ruth's lace-concealed mons. Ruth gasped in surprise, clamped her legs shut, and leaned forward to kiss her lover on the forehead. Lina withdrew her hand, moving it slow enough to tantalize and no more. She pulled off her white ribbed undershirt and tossed it aside.

"You like it that I have secret admirers, don't you?" Ruth said, her fingers trailing along Lina's collarbone, circling her breast.

"Yeah, baby, it turns me on. All those men, wanting you. And I'm the one who's got you."

Ruth shifted, straightening her back and pushing her chest out. Lina began to unfasten the buttons of Ruth's dress, still nuzzling at her neck.

"You're not jealous?" Ruth asked.

"What's there to be jealous of?" Lina said, putting a hand on Ruth's collarbone.

Ruth smiled above Lina's black hair, and bent to kiss the crown of her head. "They're rich."

"You're rich," Lina said.

"We're rich," Ruth corrected, smiling, and nibbled at Lina's ear.

Lina kissed her way down into the cleavage of Ruth's bra.

"You know how I got rich, don't you?" Ruth whispered and buried her mouth in her lover's hair.

Lina reached up to cup Ruth's satin-covered breasts in her hands. "You fucked them to death?" She teased, and kissed Ruth without waiting for a reply, until both were breathless.

But when the kiss broke, Ruth shook her head, and pulled Lina's hands away from her breasts. Lina kissed her again, lightly and then slipped her hand under the hem of Ruth's skirt; Lina's palm slid along the curve of her thigh to the top of Ruth's stockings. Where it stopped. "I think I know," Lina said, looking Ruth in the eye. "I think I've always known." And she plunged her hand past the lace edge of Ruth's panties, into the hidden moistness beneath. Ruth gasped. Lina manipulated Ruth's clit roughly, mercilessly, but for only a moment before withdrawing.

"Do you want me to tell you?" Ruth said, almost in a whisper.

"Is it confession time?" Lina asked. "Do you need a priest?" She put her hands to Ruth's breast again, playing roughly with her nipples through the fabric.

"I'm not Catholic," Ruth panted.

"I am," Lina said, and Ruth giggled and put a hand over her mouth.

Lina peeled back each finger, one by one, kissing the tips. "If you won't tell me," she said, "Then I'll tell you. I know exactly what you did. I know exactly how wicked you are." She sat back on her haunches. "Take off your bra."

Ruth complied, slipping the black lace off her pale shoulders. "Now turn over."

Ruth drew up her knees and rolled over so that she crouched upon her knees. Lina reached up between her legs and roughly removed Ruth's panties. Ruth gasped and pushed her butt back toward Lina. Her pussy was pink and moist, haloed by hair just a shade darker than that which was still artfully arranged on Ruth's head.

Lina leaned into her lover, placing her knee against Ruth's groin. "I know all about you, don't I?" She whispered, putting a hand in Ruth's hair and pulling her head back. Ruth moaned, rubbing her crotch against Lina's knee.

Lina swiftly replaced her knee with a hand, plunging inside Ruth's ready cunt. She fucked Ruth hard and swift, all the time talking in her ear, wrapping her hand in her hair, speaking between clenched teeth.

"Your husbands all loved you; you were so dutiful, so devoted, so beautiful, such a good lay. A good fuck." Lina punctuated her words with a jerk of her hand. "So pretty, so demure. They never noticed that funny taste in their morning coffee. The erratic beat of their hearts was the result of lust's flush, not the poison you'd been slipping them for months."

Under Lina's insistent ministrations, Ruth began to make low, rough sounds of passion, of assent.

"You're a black widow, a professional mourner. Sweet like the sugar you used to hide the bitter taste of your calculated plots. Your husbands were old, in poor health; nobody would suspect. Am I right? Am I?"

Ruth's voice began to rise into one long, orgasmic wail.

"You can tell me. You can tell me anything. I don't mind. There's nothing for me to be afraid of. I'm not some rich sucker, I'm not in any danger." Lina bent her head to whisper right in Ruth's ear; her hand left Ruth's hair, now in utter disarray, and slipped to her white, unblemished neck, stroking it slowly. "I admire you, in fact. You're smart, and you're set for life. That's sexy. That turns me on." And Lina buried her hand in Ruth's eager cunt, braced her other hand against her shoulder, and pumped with all her might. Ruth was shaking her head, her cry broken into a series of full-throated pants as her cunt clutched at Lina's expert hand, dousing it with her juices.

"That's right," Lina cooed. "I know all your secrets. I know how you got your money, and I know how to make you come like none of those rich bastards ever could. Am I right?"

Ruth gasped out "Yes," and collapsed to the bed, pulling Lina on top of her, her hand still between them, lodged in Ruth's flush pussy.

"God," Ruth said after a moment.

"God's got nothing to do with it," Lina said. "You're not Catholic, remember?" She slipped her hand from between Ruth's thighs and wiped it on the pillowcase.

Ruth smiled sleepily. "But you are."

Lina shrugged and rolled off Ruth's back. Ruth , in response, turned over on her side and faced her lover. Lina kissed her on the forehead. "You're absolved," was all she said. Ruth's eyes were already drooping; she reached to Lina for one long, final kiss before slipping into a blissful post-coital doze.

Lina propped herself up on one elbow and watched her lover's breathing slow, until she was sure that Ruth was asleep. Carefully, she rolled off the bed and approached the nightstand.

She picked up her Beretta, hefted it once in her hand before wrapping both hands around the grip. She pointed the barrel at Ruth's sternum.

She turned her head before she fired.

Then she located her belt and re-holstered her weapon. Before leaving the bedroom, she reached into her back pants pocket and pulled out a small gift card. A dark red rose was embossed on its cover.

Lina read it out loud to Ruth's corpse.

"To Ruth," she said. "From your former husband's family business associates. Best wishes in the afterlife." She threw the card onto her lover's body. Ruth's blood began to seep onto the heavy paper. "I made sure the funeral could be open-casket, baby. I hope you appreciate the effort."

On her way out of the apartment, Lina tossed the bouquet of roses into the trash.

Flowers in the Garden

Antonia Nardellini

Rose swore under her breath as she realized her keys were still laying on the hall table where she had dropped them the night before. She caught the door before it closed and retrieved her keys. Steve would make an issue of it if I did that again, Rose thought to herself as she let herself out of the house again, making sure she had her purse with her. She'd left that behind a time or two lately.

She walked down to the corner, grateful the weather was decent and not rainy, because she wasn't sure how long a wait she had until the next bus came. Thankfully, there was no one else waiting yet, so she sat down on the bench.

As she settled herself on the seat she reached into her handbag and pulled out the crumpled piece of newspaper she had read and reread for the last two days.

Katherine Anne Peters, nee Weston, born . . . She followed the words down until almost the end. There it was. *Survived by* . . . Again she read the name.

Thirty years it had been. Amazing how the days and the years just flew by. Rose stood as she saw the bus she needed turn the corner and wheeze to a stop in front of her. Hiking up her dress just a bit to reach the first step, she pulled herself aboard the bus and deposited her token into the machine as the driver nodded at her and closed the door. She found a seat very near to the front and sat down next to the window.

Rose had been a newlywed then. She didn't even know how to cut a whole chicken into pieces for frying. That's where it began, then. With the chicken and rice. Funny how she had just remembered that.

She'd been married to Mike. The love of her life, she told everyone. The man of her dreams and her best friend. She chuckled to herself as the bus came to another stop and some teens got on and went to sit in the back of the bus.

But it was the chicken. Mike had told her he'd love it if she made chicken and rice in the oven and have it ready when he got home after working the second shift at General Motors.

She had told him she'd have it ready for him, and there she stood, with a whole chicken she didn't know how to cut up and no cookbooks in the entire apartment. It was nine o'clock at night and she didn't know who she could call for help. When the phone rang she was so startled she dropped the knife she was threatening the chicken with.

"Rose? It's me, Melody. Did I wake you up?"

Rose laughed. "No, you didn't. I'm wide awake and trying to guess how to cut a chicken into pieces for Mike's dinner."

Melody chuckled then, too. "Just start with the leg, Rose. Pull it out from the body and cut real close. It's not *that* hard."

"Right," she had replied. "My hands are shaking as it is. I'm going to butcher this thing so badly that Mike won't know what kind of animal he's eating!" The laughter took some of the tension Rose had been feeling from her body.

"Look, if you want, I'll come over and show you how to do it. It's not like I'm doing anything right now."

"I can't ask you to do that! It's nine o'clock. After, now," she said while turning and looking at the clock.

But she had come. And she had brought her own knife in a sheath. She had done the first leg, and made Rose do the second one. She had done the first wing and made Rose do the other. She split the breast and also showed Rose the special parts to clean out where leftover innards still clung. She helped her put together her chicken and rice for Mike, then they sat down cross-legged on the couch with glasses of white wine and began to talk.

Melody was Rose's brother-in-law's current girlfriend. She didn't much care for her brother-in-law, but Melody seemed to be crazy about him.

"Rose, I think Dan is going to break up with me," Melody told her.

"What? Don't be silly," Rose had replied. "If he was, I surely would have heard something and I haven't." She took a long drink of her wine then went to fetch the bottle from the kitchen counter where she'd left it.

As she made herself comfortable on the couch again she saw

that Melody really was upset. Tears spilled out of her green eyes and down her cheeks.

Rose remembered that moment now. All of a sudden she had seen Melody with new eyes. She was beautiful, with her long, chestnut-coloured-hair, and her perfect body. She made Rose feel fat and awkward.

Rose put her glass of wine on the coffee table and sat next to Melody and wrapped her arms around her. She remembered thinking that Melody was like a hurt doe and just needed to know that someone cared. As Melody sobbed into her shoulder, she stroked her hair and patted her back. The smell of her hair and her perfume wafted up and Rose unconsciously buried her nose deeper in Melody's hair. She took a deep breath and felt the softness of Melody's breasts brushing up against hers. She squeezed her tighter and let her right hand fall to Melody's side and she gently cupped a breast to see if it really was as soft as it felt against her chest. Melody made no movement to stop her. She dropped her hand down and under the blouse Melody was wearing and in a move she could never understand, unclasped her bra and took an unencumbered female breast that wasn't her own into her hand for the first time in her life.

That's when Melody raised her head and looked at Rose. Rose put her other hand underneath the shirt and took the other breast in her hand. She felt Melody's nipples harden underneath her palms and wasn't aware that her breathing was coming in short gasps. She leaned toward Melody and gave her a gentle kiss on the lips, and liking it, gave her another. They touched tongues and Rose felt as if her body was on fire. She pinched Melody's nipples just a bit and heard an answering gasp.

She stood up then and held out a hand to Melody. Without a word she took it, and Rose led her back to the bedroom. Melody stood there as Rose slowly undressed her, taking in every bit of her loveliness. In the half light from the kitchen, Rose laid her on the bed and ran her hands over every inch of Melody's body before leaning over and taking a nipple into her mouth and gently sucking on it.

Melody moaned. Rose's hand dropped down to caress her stomach, her belly button, and going further, she ran a hand up the inside of Melody's thighs just to feel the softness of her skin. She found the furry mound, and knowing her own, she quickly found the nub of pleasure and gently stroked that with a finger.

Melody grabbed Rose's head with her hands and brought their faces together for another kiss, an urgent kiss, and Melody was fumbling with the buttons on Rose's shirt and the bra and then they were naked together on the bed and their hands seemed to be everywhere at once.

Rose straddled her then, kissing her face, then her neck, moving to her breasts and down her stomach. She backed off the bed and, stroking Melody's inner thighs, got her to open her legs. She slid a finger inside, then two, then gently stroked her clitoris while Melody writhed and moaned. Pulling her fingers out, Rose then bent to take a taste, and then another and then another. Reaching up with her hands, she played with Melody's nipples while Melody's hands lay on top of hers. It was over too quickly. Melody came with a rushing force and Rose had to hold her hands to keep her from crushing her face into her crotch and drowning her.

Afterwards, Melody had brought Rose to orgasm with her fingers and then they had lain in the bed, talking in soft whispers while their hands roved over each other's body.

Later, they had taken a shower together, each backed into a corner of the shower and brought to orgasm again using soap and gentle rubbing. They washed each other's hair and dried each other off, stopping to nibble and taste and kiss.

Melody left and fifteen minutes later Mike was home to eat his slightly overdone chicken and rice.

The bus wheezed to another stop and Rose, shaken out of her daydream, realized her stop was a block before. She got up and made her way to the front of the bus and out on to the sidewalk.

Today she would see Melody for the first time in thirty years. She was scared, she realized. She sat down on the bench by the bus stop to gather her thoughts.

Melody had been correct; Dan did break up with her, but that only meant that they could steal more time together. They experimented with sex toys and vibrators and tasty body oils. They bought edible underwear and ate them off each other. They bought sexy lingerie for each other and wore it when they got together. They had whipped cream and shaving cream.

She remembered the weekend Mike went fishing with "the guys" and she and Melody had spent the weekend together. She remembered the way Melody's naked body looked in the moonlight as they lay on the living room floor in Melody's townhouse. She remembered holding her all night as they slept in each other's arms. She remembered being woken up by Melody's tongue playing songs across her bare skin.

Six months they had loved each other by then. Six months of pleasure and sharing with Melody while her marriage went down the tubes. Strangely, she never saw the end coming. She thought that she was maintaining her double life rather well. At least until Mike came home and packed a bag and said he'd "had it" and was leaving. That was two months after the weekend of fishing.

He had told her, "I knew you and Melody had a little something going on. I just didn't think you'd carry it on this long."

He hadn't gone fishing, it turned out. He'd spied on her and followed her and had even peeked into the windows and seen them making love on the floor.

Surprisingly, Rose felt devastated. She knew her parents would be disappointed in her and what could she tell them about the reasons her marriage came to an end? Surely not the truth.

Rose sighed. She wanted children – eventually. She wanted a little house with a white picket fence and a flower garden. She didn't want to settle for anything less than her dreams.

"I can give you most of that," Melody had said then, her deep, green eyes full of love and longing. "We can build a life together. I'll make you happy, Rose. You will be the most beautiful flower in my garden of life. Come live with me and be my love."

But Rose had been horrified. "I'm not a lesbian, Melody. I can't live with you! What would people say? What would my *family* say?"

And so, she had run. She had run so fast and so hard that thirty years had passed and here she sat, trying to work up the nerve to go see Melody one more time. Perhaps one last time.

"Are you all right, lady?"

Rose looked up to see a young man standing in front of her with a look of concern on his face. "Are you lost or something?"

Rose smiled. "No, I'm not lost. But thank you for asking. I'm just resting a bit before I go to church." She smiled again.

"OK, if you say so," the young man said. "But you looked a little lost and confused there for a couple of minutes."

"I'm fine. Really. Thank you for caring. I'll just be on my way before I'm late,' she said as she got up from the bench.

Katherine had battled leukaemia for over a year, her obituary said. *Time enough for family and friends to say their good-byes,* Rose thought. *But still too young. Still so many years taken away from her.*

She made her way to the corner, then turned left. Half way down the block on the right side of the street was Saint Matthew's. That's where Melody's sister was, lying in a coffin while priests said Mass concerning her eternal soul.

Rose wasn't sure she had made the right decision. Maybe coming to this funeral was a terrible idea.

But she had to *know*. She had to find out if the years had been kind to Melody. She needed to know that Melody had found love and had been happy. She needed to know that her leaving hadn't ruined Melody's life.

Rose crossed the street and went up the steps to the church and went inside before her courage failed her. She took a seat in a pew two rows behind the last person on the right hand side of the church and caught her breath while she looked around.

Her hand reached up to her neck and found the crucifix there. How funny that she still had it after all the years.

She had taken it from around Melody's neck one night and said, "This I will keep as something to remember you by," and they had both laughed because they really didn't believe it would ever end between them.

But it had. Rose had run and Melody had never called.

Rose had wondered in the intervening years what she would have done had Melody just called her once to ask her to reconsider. Would she have? Would she have defied her family and followed her heart?

Rose had married again. She had a son, Steven, who lived nearby, and a daughter, Patricia, who didn't. She had stayed married to their father for twenty-seven years until he had a heart attack driving to work and died. That was two years ago.

It wasn't until her husband died that Rose realized how unhappy she had been for most of her life.

The children brought a certain amount of joy to her life, for sure, and there had been happy moments and times along the way. But Rose realized she was just going through the motions of what she thought others expected her life to be and here she was, approaching the end of her and wishing she had done things differently.

I would have been happy with Melody, she thought to herself.

After all these years I can finally admit it to myself. I made the biggest mistake of my life thirty years ago. I wasted my whole life. I can never get that time back.

The priests began leaving their places and swinging their censers around the coffin that lay under flowers by the altar. Everyone stood and Rose did, too. She faced the aisle as the coffin was wheeled down it and ushers were standing at the end of the pews indicating that the people in those rows should join the procession.

I was just so afraid, Rose thought to herself. Afraid of what society would think and too afraid to confront what ever that would mean to my life. I gave up love and settled for something else.

She averted her eyes from the coffin as it passed her pew, looking at the floor and thinking, What if that was me in there? *What if this is the sum total of my life?*

Then the ushers were at her row and she joined the end of the procession back out into the bright sunshine of the day, to watch as they slid the casket into the back of the black hearse.

"Rose? It *is* you, isn't it?" Rose turned and there she was.

The years have been kind to her, Rose thought. Some grey in her chestnut hair, but not as much as Rose had, hidden as it was under the latest hair colouring. Still with the deep, green eyes that were bright and clear and sparkling.

Her hands reached out and grasped Rose's empty one, the one without the purse, and the world melted away in that moment.

"Melody," was all Rose could manage to say although there was much more she wanted to say. She wanted to ask for forgiveness, wanted to apologize for the death of Katherine but mostly, she wanted to apologize for settling for an unhappy life. She wanted to explain that she now knew that the cost to herself had been expensive. That settling for less costs more than anything else in the world. It had cost Rose thirty years of her life.

"Wait here," Melody said. She turned and walked over to a small group of huddled mourners, said a few hushed words, hugged a couple of people, then came back to where Rose stood, shivering, even in the heat of the day.

"Come with me. I have my car. We can go and talk somewhere." Rose nodded again, afraid that if she spoke even one word the tears would flow. "We can come back and get your car later."

"I don't have a car," Rose said.

She had one thirty years ago. She had gradually given up driving because Jack said they didn't need the extra expense of a second car, and besides, "The buses go where ever you need to go," he had told her.

She had acquiesced, of course, because by then, settling was in her nature and this was the lot in life she had chosen. She would make the best of it.

They had talked then, at a little coffee shop a couple of blocks away, and Rose brought out the old pictures of Steven and Patricia that she had in her wallet, and a picture of Jack she didn't realize she had in there.

Melody had shown Rose pictures of her cats and of nieces and nephews, and spoke of her job and her house and her flower garden.

But it was Melody who asked the question, "Have you been happy?" and Rose started crying.

It all spilled out then. The regret. The fear that her entire life had been a sham, filled with useless drivel that had only eaten time and not given her any sense of fullness. And her shaking hands had spilled a glass of water and they laughed then, because the diner was not a place to talk of the real things, the things that couldn't be said in a public booth, tender words and words of memories and longing.

All too soon it was over, and Melody was driving her home.

They had exchanged phone numbers and with yells of "Call me!" she watched Melody's car turn the corner and disappear. It was only then that she realized she had never asked the real question she wanted to ask. "Did you think of me as often as I thought about you?"

Many were the nights that Rose had laid in bed unfulfilled after lovemaking with Jack. She would listen to him gently snoring and she would silently get out of bed and, after checking the children, would sit in the dark living room with a glass of white wine and she would touch herself in her woman place and she would remember.

Rose realized, as she went to her room to change out of the skirt she had worn to the funeral, that she would probably never see Melody again. "Call me!" Sure. Why had she gone to the funeral at all? To see if the price, the settling, was justified? And was it?

Her dreams had been fulfilled. She had the children, the house, a white picket fence, and even the flower garden. But what a price she had paid.

"I want to go back again," she whispered aloud. "I want to live my life over and tell society to go take a hike. I want to realize that where there is love, true love, you can face all the troubles that come your way." She had looked at herself in the mirror and said, "I want to know *then* what I know *now.*"

The doorbell startled her. She had quickly pulled on some sweat pants and walked to the door and opened it.

Melody stood there, tears running down her face, and Rose had pulled her inside the house and shut the door and they held each other in the hallway, the tears on their cheeks mingling as they kissed.

And Melody's hair had smelled as sweet, and her breasts were still as soft, and Rose realized, that wherever you were, as long as you were alive, there was still time. There was still the rest of your life, however long that might be. That settling didn't mean forever.

She would never settle again.

Nose Dive

Jennifer J. Sowle

Nicki pulled her T-shirt over her head and stood in the middle of the living room.

Not bad – most of the dog hair had given up after a struggle and surrendered to the lint brush. Every once in a while her old compulsiveness surfaced, like it had this morning. She wanted the house "presentable for company", as her mother would say back in the fifties. She opened the fridge for a diet Pepsi and remembered she had put the litre bottle back with an inch of backwash on the bottom. She spotted a Corona behind the milk container – how long had that been in there? She popped the top and fell onto the sofa. The place looked pretty good after three hours of solid cleaning, a chore so abhorrent she had been in denial about how long it had been. There were definitely benefits to living exclusively with a dog and two cats. They never complained about how things looked and when you pushed them out of bed, they got over it. The sweat ran between her breasts and pooled in her belly button.

That was another thing – when you live alone you can be naked whenever you want, and never give it a second thought. If you're hot, you can take off your shirt. If your jeans are too tight, zip those suckers off and relax. She tipped back the beer and felt the prickly coolness fill her mouth.

The call from Corrine came out of the blue. They were the kind of friends who showed up at the same parties, played or sat in the stands at the same softball games, and, depending on who they were coupled up with, occasionally spent time at each other's houses. She always had liked Corrine; and when she hadn't been falling in love, or in the throes of love, she'd flirted with her a time or two. They hadn't been close enough for Nicki to touch base before she moved. In fact, after they caught up, she had asked Corrine where she got her number.

Not that she didn't want her to have it – just curious about who she got it from. Sometimes break-ups can be brutal – like hers was – and you couldn't be too careful about forwarding addresses. You might answer the door one day and find your old lover standing there with an axe in her hand. Her ex had made almost every other attempt to contact her – phone, fax, email and letters – who knows, next time she might just show up at the doorstep.

Now Corrine was coming up to Petoskey to visit her. They had chatted a bit – long enough to find out they were both single – and Nicki had invited her up. The drive was too long for a day trip, so she spent a good part of her morning clearing boxes and junk out of the spare bedroom and making up the bed. Now she sat back, her arms up over the back of the sofa, airing out her armpits and enjoying the cooling effect of the sweat evaporating on her chest, making her nipples stand up like little soldiers. The last couple of swigs in the bottle were warm, so she dumped it in the sink and put the bottle in the trash. It was only noon, she had plenty of time to relax and get cleaned up. Corrine's ETA was between 4:00 and 5:00.

A light rapping at the front door – Damn. Sadie the rottweiler thundered down the hall to the door, her butt wagging with excitement. Nicki ducked down and scooted into the bedroom like some kind of dwarf wind-up toy. She scanned her closet, and grabbed a pair of baggy shorts with an elastic waist and a tank top.

"Hey . . . how's it going?" It was the landlord – or, as Nicki referred to her, the Lesbian Landlord.

"Hey, BJ. You caught me cleaning," Nicki said.

"Too hot for that, girl," she laughed.

"Yeah, tell me about it."

Sadie rushed by her legs and twirled out onto the yard, reveling in the freedom.

"The dog is okay . . . she won't run. What's up?"

"Not much. I have to pick up a ladder and could use a hand. Would you mind?"

"Not at all. Let me slip on my shoes."

It was a heavy old wooden extension ladder – not a fancy lightweight aluminum one. They wrestled it out of the shed and hoisted it into the bed of the ratty pickup.

BJ was a strange mixture of butch and fem. She had long strawberry hair woven back into a single fat braid, with loose tendrils surrounding her face like a halo. She had millions of freckles sprayed everywhere. Nicki watched her muscles strain under the ladder.

"Hey, I got a cooler in the truck . . . beer?"

"Sure, why not." Nicki wanted to be polite. She didn't really know BJ that well, but she wanted to. She was new in town and needed friends. She'd been up north for six months, but spring was slow coming and it seemed that everybody stayed holed up during the winter. This summer she planned to get out more and meet other dykes. She was comfortable being alone, but her record showed that she didn't stay that way for long.

It felt good to be outside. BJ pulled a couple of lawn chairs from the shed, and shook them open.

"Might as well sit right here, huh?"

"Sounds good." Nicki popped open the beer and took a swig. Then she tipped her head back and raised her face to the sun – the warmth soothed away the stress of her cleaning frenzy – the beer helped too. They talked easily and laughed a lot. BJ had always seemed so serious; Nicki was pleasantly surprised that she could be so warm. They opened their second beers and the conversation turned – as it always does – to relationships. BJ had just been dumped by her wife of eight years, and Nicki could tell she was still pretty broken up about it. Her eyes glistened as she drank her beer silently, staring off into the yard. Nicki's eyes settled on her black SUV sitting in the driveway.

"Geez, I've got a friend coming up, and I just noticed how filthy my car is. I might have to wash it this afternoon." Her tolerance for relaxation was waning and her compulsivity was kicking in. She wanted to give the SUV a quick going over, although her legs felt like lead and her head was spinning a bit from the beer – she typically didn't drink much.

"I'll give you a hand."

"Really? Thanks."

They pulled out the hoses, and BJ hooked them together while Nicki ran into the house for the bucket, sponge, and brushes. They divided up the car by sections and started to work. Nicki was standing by the front bumper as BJ sprayed the top of the car.

"Hey, watch it with the hose!" She stood back with her arms outstretched, the front of her top and shorts stuck to her body.

"Sorry." BJ dropped the hose and came around to the front of the car. At first she was embarrassed to see Nicki so vulnerable – her wet top almost completely transparent, and the fabric clinging to her perky nipples like a second skin. She tried to focus her eyes anywhere but on Nicki's chest.

"I . . . ah . . . I'm sorry." She looked down at Nicki's shorts. They were plastered to her thighs and hugged her crotch. BJ could see she wasn't wearing underwear, a dark bolt of pubic hair revealed itself beneath the wet cotton. BJ's heart was pounding in her chest, tingling shocks shooting down through her body, briefly stopping at her nipples, and ending up in a wet sizzle between her legs. It had been way too long since she'd allowed herself to feel this way.

"God, you're gorgeous." She couldn't help herself. It was if her hand wasn't attached to her body as it swept up Nicki's arm and rested on her wet shoulder.

"Yeah, right." Nicki pulled her top away from her body with both hands.

"No, I mean it." BJ ran her hand to the back of Nicki's hair, took hold of it, and gave it a little tug. "I think you're beautiful, Nicki."

Nicki had seen that look before. It was the "I want you" look. A thought went through her head about the time, and the car being half-washed, and Corrine coming up – but it was transitory. She moved closer to BJ and put her hand on her waist. She lifted her head and willed a kiss with her eyes. BJ's lips were soft and urgent.

"God, that feels good," BJ said as she ran her hand under Nicki's shirt. She brought her other hand around and brushed the back of her thigh, slowly coming up under her shorts and grabbing her butt, pulling her close. "Oh, baby, baby." She ran her hand over Nicki's butt to the place where her thigh met it. She made circles with her hand, up onto her butt and waist, back down to her thigh, and closer and closer to her pussy.

Nicki was squirming and pushing into BJ's hand. She leaned into her and straddled her thigh. BJ yanked her own shorts up so that her bare leg was against Nicki's pussy. She could feel her warm wetness against her leg. They kissed as BJ rubbed her hand over Nicki's ass, gently tugging at her butt cheek with short gentle pinches. With each tug, Nicki arched her back and spread her pussy wider, her juices running onto BJ's leg as she slipped up and down on her thigh. She reached under BJ's T-shirt and shoved up her sports bra, freeing her breasts. She pulled at her nipples and swayed her breasts with her hand. BJ leaned back against the side window and moaned. Her fingers slid into Nicki's wet pussy just as she came, the soft walls tightening around her hand with rhythmic massage.

BJ was almost there herself. She tensed her legs and grabbed hold of Nicki's ass, sliding her slippery pussy up her thigh and onto her crotch. She had a fleeting thought of trying to pull her shorts aside, but they were too tight – it wouldn't work. But she knew what would work. She broke from the kiss and pulled Nicki's head back by her hair.

"Suck my tits," she said. Nicki's warm mouth latched on to her nipple, sucking it hard while she moaned softly. BJ's legs buckled against the car as she came, deep waves washed through her body, cleansing her from a million rejections, and giving her temporary respite from her grief.

"Holy shit," Nicki said as she threw her head back and laughed, letting her hands slide from BJ's breasts to her waist.

"Sweet Jesus." BJ looked her square in the eyes. "Thank you, God . . . and thank you, Nicki, Goddess of Love." She smiled broadly, her swollen lips sliding over even white teeth.

"You didn't plan that, did you?" Nicki said.

"Hell no. But if I'd known it would turn out like this, I would have."

They struggled with the awkwardness of coming down from ecstasy to the mundane happenings of the afternoon. They eventually finished the car, feeling weak and unmotivated and doing a half-assed job. They sat down on the chairs talking about the summer when BJ looked up. Nicki snapped her head around at the crunching of tires on the driveway. She stood up and looked, but didn't recognize the car. She squinted into the sun, until the figure was squarely in its path, revealing her face – Corrine. Nicki looked down at herself. Her tank top was dry, but it was filthy from rubbing against the car, her shorts were still damp and stuck in her butt crack when she stood up. She hadn't showered or even combed her hair. Fuck.

Corrine was radiant. Tan and trim and obviously spit and polished for the visit. Her short hair was bleached blond and spiked up with product – but not overdone. She wore a tailored blue chambray shirt, sleeves rolled up to mid forearm and tucked in Khaki shorts with crisp creases down the legs – and she'd just driven three hours.

"Corrine . . . welcome," Nicki said, dying inside.

"Hey. I didn't know if this was the place or not. But you gave good directions. How are you?" She walked toward Nicki with her arms extended for a hug.

"Are you sure you want to hug me? I'm a mess. Sorry, I didn't keep very good track of the time." They hugged warmly, like two old friends. Once Nicki got over her embarrassment, she felt her face flush with excitement at the thought of spending time with somebody from home.

"Corrine, this is my landlord, BJ. BJ, Corrine." BJ sprang to her feet and pumped Corrine's hand.

"Really nice to meet you. Yup, I'm the Slumlord," she laughed. "Well, you two have a great weekend. I've got to get this ladder over to my dad's." When she turned and walked to her truck, Nicki smiled to herself. She knew what was under that T-shirt. The truck fired up with a loud rattle and BJ stuck her arm out the side window and waved as she pulled away.

"Well, come on in," Nicki said as she grabbed Sadie's collar. They hadn't had many visitors lately, and the dog was a maniac, trying to jump on Corrine and lick her hands. "Sorry about the dog." She racked her brain trying to think how she was going to make this work – try to make it look like she was on top of things. Show her the house, and then what? She couldn't really excuse herself and take a shower and get cleaned up, how rude would that be?

"How would you like to go out to the beach, maybe take a little walk . . . Sadie is better behaved when she's exhausted."

"Sounds wonderful. I love the beach." Corrine also was trying to adjust.

The drive had been a long one, and now that she was here, it almost seemed as if Nicki wasn't expecting her. It felt like a risk to drive up for the weekend. It wasn't like her to just jump in the car and take off, but she was sick of being so conventional, so worried about appearances. Besides, she liked Nicki. Many times over the years they had run into each other. They hadn't had particularly deep conversations, but they shared a similar sense of humour and enjoyed matching wits. So what if she had lost track of time – things happen. It's more casual up here – less concern about time and being dolled up. Nicki had seemed happy to see her, she just needed to relax and enjoy herself.

"Let's go." Nicki had washed up, done something with her hair, and changed into different clothes. She looked good. Relaxed, needless to say, and happy. They rode out to the beach and talked all the way, discussing the latest gossip about mutual friends. Nicki knew a stretch of beach that was usually deserted – or close to deserted. They pulled up to find a couple of cars there, but nobody visible on the shoreline. The dog bolted from the back seat and twirled around expectantly.

"Okay, let's go." Nicki motioned her hand toward the water and Sadie took off down the beach, sand flying up behind her. The two women followed, slowly strolling and talking as Nicki tossed a stick to the dog.

There was an ease, a comfort that came from at least knowing *about* each other, even though they weren't close friends. There would be no surprises, like finding out your new lover had spent some time in jail, or was still married to a man, or had a reputation for affairs. They each had recently ended long-term relationships, and they had met years before that. At the same time, it was exciting to take it a bit further, really talk, find out more about what made the other tick. Before they knew it, Nicki looked down the beach to check on Sadie and could barely make her out in the distance – it was dusk.

"It's getting dark. Wow, that's hard to believe. Hungry?"

"Starving."

"There's a little bar just beyond the park. Great burgers and fresh fish."

"Sounds wonderful."

They sat in a booth and talked and laughed, sometimes to the point of tears. Nicki felt like the weight of the world was lifting, sitting here with an old friend cracking up over shared stories. The waitress brought the check and they each paid for their meal. Sadie was sound asleep in the back of the SUV when they came out.

The night was cool but clear, the stars thrown against the night sky like confetti. Nicki had a glass of local Pinot over dinner, but was more than capable of driving safely. Corrine had a Coors Light. They pulled in to the driveway and found the house pitch black. When they had left for the beach, it was daytime, and Nicki hadn't thought of turning on the lights. The small house was at the edge of the woods and, without lights, it was hard to see your hand in front of your face.

"I'll come around and get you." Nicki walked around to the passenger's side, opened the door, and reached for Corrine's hand.

"Here, give me your hand and I'll lead you in. I'm pretty good in the dark."

"I bet you are," Corrine said.

Did Nicki hear that right? Was that a flirt?

Corrine's hand was soft and warm. As she stood up outside the car, she pressed her shoulder into Nicki's to steady herself in the dark. They moved toward the doorway, and then squeezed together to make it through the entrance. Nicki put her arm around Corrine's back and guided her through. She could smell her perfume as she passed. She smoothed her hand over the wall until she bumped into the light switch. She snapped it on and got the dog settled while Corrine sat down on the couch.

"I don't have any beer, but would you like a glass of wine?"

"Yes. That sounds great." Corrine wondered what they would do with the rest of the evening. But that fear quickly passed as Nicki showed up with the wine and two glasses. She sat down on the other end of the sofa, turned sideways, and stretched her legs toward Corrine. They sat there talking and sipping wine until well past midnight.

"I hate to be the party-pooper, but I'm getting tired," Corrine said. "It's been a long day."

"Me too. And I didn't have to drive three hours to get here. There's a bathroom just outside your room. I have my own, so you have privacy."

"Thanks." Corrine moved closer for a hug, letting her cheek brush Nicki's. She could feel her soft breasts against hers. She pulled away slowly, hesitating slightly as she held on to Nicki's shoulders. She glanced up into her eyes.

"Well, good night," Nicki said, turning away.

"Night," Corrine said softly. She had started to feel a stirring earlier as she watched Nicki's mouth over dinner – had wondered what it would be like to kiss her. Walking into the house in the dark, with Nicki so close gave her a twinge – a sexual twinge. The feeling hadn't really left her. The wine and the laughter, both were aphrodisiacs. Her heart sunk as Nicki said goodnight. Maybe it was for the best.

Pretty soon she was scolding herself. For God sakes, were you driving up here for some kind of tryst? That wasn't her style, not what she was looking for. She had never done that in her life, always so practical, so sensible. She pulled down the quilt on the bed and arranged the pillows. She could hear the pipes bang in Nicki's bathroom. She closed her eyes and reviewed the night, thinking about Nicki's mouth, and then her body – what she might look like naked.

Nicki's muscles relaxed in the hot spray. Finally she could really take her time and get in all the nooks and crannies of her body, scrubbing away the afternoon indiscretion with BJ. Now all she felt was regret. She had invited Corrine up for the weekend and then, just as she was about to arrive, she had fucked BJ. What was she thinking? Her attraction for Corrine had been overwhelming, but she couldn't get past the guilt. How dare she think about Corrine in that way when just a few hours ago she was slipping all over BJ? She soaped up again at the thought of it and decided to wash her hair. The water was almost too hot, a kind of punishment. Nicki's skin was a mix of pink over her tan when she stepped out and reached for the towel. She pulled down the spread on her bed. It was too hot for clothes. She slipped under the cool sheets, hugged her pillow between her legs and thought of Corrine's sweet smell.

Corrine stopped in the doorway. Early dawn washed Nicki's bedroom in a soft yellow glow. Corrine's breath caught in her throat. Nicki was lying naked, her leg wrapped around her pillow, her hair wild with sleep. She breathed softly, rhythmically, her hands twitching from a dream. Corrine pulled the throw around her and moved silently through the door and around the bed, behind the sleeping beauty. She couldn't take her eyes off the pink between her legs, where her thigh lifted to clear the pillow. The arch of her tanned back curved down into an exquisite pale ass accentuated by a bikini bottom outline on her skin. Her legs were muscular, and her arms were svelte, like a ballerina's. Her lips were slightly parted, her face flushed in sleep.

Corrine sat on the edge of the bed, just below and behind Nicki's knees. She brought her face closer to that vee snuggled against the pillow, the smooth pink of Nicki's pussy. She couldn't take her eyes away as she brought her hand under the throw and down to her own lips. She knew she would be wet and slippery with longing. Her finger circled her clit, and moved down one side and back up the other, round and round. She had to be quiet. She didn't want to wake her – yet. She reached out for Nicki's calf and gently rested her hand on it. She pushed it forward and up, ever so carefully. As her leg slid higher on the pillow, her pussy spread, opening like a flower. Round and round Corrine's finger slipped, past her clitoris and down to her cave. She dipped into the river, and tried not to moan. She touched Nicki's ass ever so lightly. She moved in her sleep, bringing the leg closer to her elbow. Now Corrine could see everything, every part of her flower, the soft covering and the inner lips, the glistening opening. She had to stop the circles, keep herself at bay. She held her palm against her pubic hair and pressed lightly.

She stood up and took a few steps and then settled back down next to Nicki's back. She leaned forward and kissed her neck. Nicki sighed, but didn't wake. She kissed her hair and put her hand on her arm and caressed it gently. She whispered in her ear.

"Don't be afraid. It's just me."

Nicki moaned, but did not open her eyes. Corrine knew by her breathing that she was awake, and she also knew by her closed eyes that she didn't want her to stop. She dropped her throw and laid behind her, pressing her breasts into her back. She moved her hand everywhere, down her back to her ass, along her arms, up to her neck and through her hair. She reached down and took hold of the thigh that rested on the pillow. She pulled it up as far as it would stretch and laid it there. Nicki did not move it. She ran her hand down it and played outside Nicki's pussy for a long time, circling it and gently pulling on her lips, until she opened fully, and ran with glistening glide. She dipped her fingers and slid them in and out as Nicki worked her hips and moaned.

"Fuck me, baby, fuck me." Nicki's husky voice broke the silence.

Corrine stopped her hand and let her fingers rest just inside Nicki's pussy.

"Maybe I will, and maybe I won't," Corrine said teasingly.

"Please, baby, please . . . make me come," she pleaded.

"Turn over," Corrine said, her voice thick with lust. Nicki turned over and looked into Corrine's face. Her eyes were wild with desire and her lips swollen when they kissed. They pressed their bodies close and Corrine lowered herself on to Nicki and wrapped her in her arms. She moved down her body and laid against her pubic hair and reached down for her calves, she pulled them up and pushed them against the back of Nicki's thighs, her ruby lips spreading to expose her cave. Corrine slid down and put her mouth against her pussy. She licked her – hard – up and down the sides of her pussy and lightly around the top by her clit. She fucked her with her tongue.

"God, oh Jesus," Nicki screamed as her legs tensed and her body jerked.

Corrine lay on her pelvis kissing her stomach, until she relaxed. Then she lifted up on her knees and put one on each side of Nicki's body. She inched up, stopping to kiss Nicki's breasts and mouth on the way. When her thighs were on the sides of Nicki's head, she stopped and put her hands on the headboard. She lowered her pussy over Nicki's face and held it there, open and throbbing, inviting Nicki's tongue. Nicki grabbed her thighs and licked her from front to back, over and over, until she came.

When it was over, Corrine laid down next to Nicki and they kissed and touched for the longest time.

"I've never done that before," said Corrine

"Done what?"

"Took a risk like that and prayed you wanted me as much as I wanted you."

"I'm so glad you did."

They spent the rest of the weekend in bed, getting out occasionally to scrounge around the kitchen for food. They did drive to the beach once more before Corrine headed back down state. That weekend started a weekly pilgrimage for Corrine, leaving work early on Fridays, driving the interstate, and singing along with Anita Baker as her heart soared and her body ached. Almost always, Nicki would be out in front of the house, staring down the road for Corrine's car, except when she surprised her by not greeting her. Then she would be in the bedroom, either naked or whored up in a black garter belt and hose, smiling to herself with anticipation as she heard Corrine slam in the screen door. That September, on Corrine's fiftieth birthday, she packed up her belongings and moved north, settling in with Nicki in a house near the beach.

Even now, they delight in laughing about the courtship that lasted all of one day. When their friends preach about another couple bringing a moving van to their second date, they glance at each other and smile. It's their naughty little secret – that morning one June when they pulled out all the stops. Now they're an old married couple, but the passion still smolders under the surface of their comfortable life. They go to sleep every night in each other's arms – and wake up each morning, still together.

A to Z

Kristina Wright

I met Zoe in the library near the biography section. I was sitting in one of the big, overstuffed chairs by the window reading *People* when I looked up and saw her staring at me. She sat in the chair opposite me. She wore a long flowing dress the colour of a summer sky, her legs tucked under her, her brown leather sandals lined up neatly on the floor. Her eyes were the same colour as her dress and they watched me, unblinking. She held a book but I couldn't make out the title because she had it turned face down in her lap, as if watching me were infinitely more interesting than reading a book. I was flattered and annoyed. The library is my sanctuary. I don't go there to get cruised.

Funny thing is, I was never much of a reader before her. In fact, I'd only been going to the library for two or three months when I met her. I'd never been to the big Ft Lauderdale branch library, even though I grew up three miles away. One day I was paying a ticket at the courthouse down the street, so I thought I'd kill two birds with one stone and pick up some tax forms at the library. By then, it was already the middle of March. I'm a bit of a procrastinator.

I had no idea how wonderful the library was. Once I got out of high school, I made it a point to avoid all things academic. But that first visit made me a believer. I'd make a trip to the library once a week, maybe two, not for the books but for the silence, the utter sense of solitude. Everyone whispers in the library, everyone is deferential to your need for peace and quiet. It was so unlike my job as a waitress at one of the clubs on the strip , I couldn't help but return again and again. I'd have been happy to sit by the window on the second floor and watch the traffic go by, but the librarians gave me funny looks. Sometimes homeless people go to the library to cool off in the summer. I didn't think

I looked like a homeless person, but I figured if I had my nose stuck in a magazine, they'd leave me alone.

I looked up from an article about the summer blockbusters to see her still watching me, her finger stuck between the pages of the book, marking her place. Her hair was long and loose around her face, a halo of dark, wavy ringlets shot through with strands of silver. She was a few years older than me, I thought. It was hard to tell. She had an exotic look, maybe Indian or Saudi, all sharp angles and good bone structure. Her eyes threw me, though. They were blue as blue can be. I wondered how that recessive trait had popped out.

I realized I'd been staring at her and felt myself blush. I'm as fair as they come, pale skin, short spiky red hair, light green eyes the colour of sea glass. It was a funny joke God played on me, making me be born in a state that has sunshine three hundred and twenty days a year. I skulked about in long sleeve blouses, long pants, sun screen and sunglasses, protecting my pale flesh from the harsh rays that would turn my creamy skin into a mottled canvas of freckles. My last girlfriend, Maggie, used to bitch because I never wanted to go to the beach. But I never heard her complain when she explored every inch of my sun-free skin.

"Aren't you hot?" the woman across from me said finally.

I flinched. Her voice seemed to echo throughout the wing. No one else seemed to notice. I shrugged. "Not really."

"I'm hot." She hiked her dress up to mid-thigh and fanned her face with the hem. "It's usually forty degrees in here, but today if feels like they've got the heat on."

She was appealing, but I didn't want to talk about the heat. I wanted to read about the summer movies. I wanted to be left alone. I raised the magazine up and covered my face, hoping to discourage any further conversation. I didn't give in to the temptation to peek around the glossy page and see if she was still watching me. I finished reading about Jude Law's newest flick and moved on to a fascinating tale about liposuction in Hollywood.

I heard the swish of fabric and was almost disappointed that I'd run her off. I jumped when she pulled the magazine away from my face. "That shit will rot your brain," she said.

She dumped the book she'd been reading in my lap and then crouched by my chair. "A is for Austen," she whispered close to my ear.

I flipped it over. *Sense and Sensibility*. I shook my head and tried to hand it back to her. "It's not my style."

She pushed it back at me. "Try it, you'll like it."

"I don't have a library card," I blurted.

When she laughed, I shivered. "It's okay, I already checked it out. Just have it back in two weeks."

Then she was gone, her dress billowing out behind her like a blue cloud, her sandals slap-slapping across the floor. I watched her until she walked through the door. Then I remembered to close my mouth.

By the time two weeks had rolled around, I'd gotten through *Sense and Sensibility*. I still wasn't convinced I was cut out for that literary crap, but I was kind of surprised it wasn't as bad as I'd expected it to be. I dropped the book in the slot in the lobby of the library and headed for my favourite chair.

She was already there, looking resplendent in a sleeveless red sun dress with a gold Batik design scattered across it. She looked up at me from the book she was reading. Another book lay in her lap. "Did you like it?"

I shrugged. "It was all right. I'm not really into that high-brow English stuff."

She arched an eyebrow. "You're going to be a tough nut to crack, I can tell."

I played it cool. I sat down across from her and thumbed through the magazines on the table by my chair. I picked up Cosmo. She looked as if she was going to blow a gasket. I smirked over the top of the magazine. "I'm tougher than you might think."

It was part challenge, part bravado. I was intimidated by her exotic beauty and her obvious intellect.

She didn't disappoint. She glided from her chair and put both books on the arm of my chair. "B is for Bronte. Two books, two weeks."

There was no way I was going to read two books in two weeks. Before I could tell her that, she was gone. I looked at the books. *Jane Eyre* by Charlotte Bronte, *Wuthering Heights* by Emily Bronte. I vaguely remembered *Wuthering Heights* from high school. Actually, I remembered reading the Cliff's Notes.

Somehow, I got the books done in two weeks. More amazing, I really liked *Jane Eyre*. I showed up at the library, puffed up like a peacock, and returned the books. I grinned when I saw her sitting in her usual chair, dressed all in white. White shimmery blouse, white skirt with silver buttons up the front, white sandals showing off white toenails.

"Well?" she asked, looking up from the book open on her lap.

"I liked Jane. She had balls."

"Like you." She arched an eyebrow. "And Cathy?"

I wrinkled my nose. "Too whiny."

She nodded. "I'm Zoe, by the way."

I was surprised. I figured she'd go on being the mysterious woman from the library. "Amy," I said.

She studied me, her dark lashes blinking slowly, languidly. She stroked the pages of the book in her lap with a delicate white-tipped nail. I felt my nipples tighten as the pages fluttered softly. Her gaze never shifted from my face, but by her quiet smile I suspected she knew the effect she had on me. She stood and crossed the narrow expanse between our chairs. She knelt, placing the book in my lap with a gentle caress of my khaki clad thigh. "C is for cunt," she whispered, and I could have sworn her tongue slicked hotly against the rim of my ear.

When she straightened, I saw that several of the buttons on her skirt were unfastened. With a subtle adjustment, she parted the panels and revealed her cunt, with its dark, bare lips tucked up tightly and a silky black patch of hair on her mound. I wanted to look around to see if anyone else had noticed her display, but I was too mesmerized by the cunt before me.

It wasn't until she glided through the doors that I looked down and realized C was also for Agatha Christie.

I was still making a couple trips to the library each week, but I only saw Zoe every other week. I looked forward to our meetings and, if I was being honest, I'd have to say I was looking forward to the books she would choose for me. I'd expected something like Dostoyevsky for D, what I got instead was Daphne Du Maurier's *Rebecca*. She handed it over with a feral smile and a scratch of blood red nails against my wrist.

When I got home, I sucked the mark she left on me, imaging it was her skin. I read *Rebecca* in three days.

And so the weeks rolled by. Zoe gave me books: Zora Neale Hurston's *Their Eyes Were Watching God*, Susanna Kaysen's *Girl, Interrupted*, Anne Lamott's *Tender Mercies*, Toni Morrison's *Beloved*. The books were eclectic, unpredictable. Wonderful because she chose them, exciting because I enjoyed almost all of them. Our flirtations grew bolder, the brush of her face against my breast when she bent to give me a book , my lips pressing to her hand as she pulled away.

By the time she introduced me to Anais Nin's *Delta of Venus*, I was starving for her touch. I returned the book two weeks later, breathless with anticipation. Only Zoe wasn't there; her chair was empty. I waited for three hours and she never showed. I thought maybe I was a day early, but no, it had been two weeks to the day. I left the library angry and hurt, and with an insistent throb between my legs.

I spotted her at the back of the parking lot, leaning against my Honda. She was wearing a green sheath dress, darker than my eyes but lighter than my car. She didn't smile as I approached.

"Something wrong?" she asked, a lime green nail flicking at the corner of my mouth when I stopped in front of her. "Miss me?"

"Bitch."

She smiled at that. "Come on," she said. "Let's go for a ride."

She sat in the passenger seat, window rolled down halfway, watching me fidget as I pulled into traffic. I tried to play it cool. It wasn't as if we didn't both know what was going to happen. But, dumb as it sounds and as much as I wanted her, I was afraid if we got involved, if we fucked, things would change. The library would never be the same.

"Nervous?" she asked, watching me pick at the faux leather flaking off my steering wheel.

I shrugged. "Should I be?"

She leaned nearer, hiking my skirt up to my hips. "No, baby, you shouldn't be nervous." One lime green nail traced a figure eight on my pale thigh. "You should be wet."

I was soaked. I wasn't about to tell her that, though.

"Green light, Amy," she murmured, her fingers sliding up under my skirt as I belatedly let up on the brake and jolted into the intersection.

Her fingers were hot on my thigh. So close to my cunt I trembled. I kept driving, trying to focus on the street signs. Trying not to wreck the damn car. I felt her finger part my slick lips and I gasped. So much for playing it cool. I wanted to pull over and beg her to fuck me, but I didn't. I kept driving.

Her finger snaked into my cunt and I squeezed it with my muscles. She chuckled. "Hungry, baby?"

I didn't answer. I turned the corner. I was heading toward my apartment, I realized. My cunt quivered.

She finger-fucked me slowly, teasing me. Her thumb nail scraped my clit and I nearly ran over a little old lady crossing the street. "Careful, careful," Zoe chided. "Maybe it's time we headed back to the library."

I didn't question. I made the turn. The lights were against me, so it took a few minutes. By the time we pulled into the parking lot, she'd whipped my cunt to a froth.

Two fingers pumped me, she was half-leaning into my seat. I slammed on the brakes, jolting us both forward, and put the car into park. My thighs were shaking.

"Come on, baby."

It was all the encouragement I needed. With the shadow of the library shading us, I came with Zoe's fingers buried in my cunt, her lime green thumbnail flicking my clit. Rocking against her hand, my fingers wrapped tight around her wrist, I came with a moan. Months of pent-up lust had driven me to this, a quickie in a parking lot, but I didn't care. I didn't care because Zoe's fingers were inside me and she was whispering how good I was, how pretty, how wet. I came and I came. And when I was done, she pulled her fingers from my wet cunt and sucked them dry.

Before my heartbeat had returned to normal, she was gone.

The weeks went by in a blur. Books took on new meaning. I walked into the bookstore one day to buy a gift for my mother and had to go to the bathroom to get myself off. Just the smell of a book was enough to make me cream my panties. I wanted to tell Zoe but I figured she'd laugh. I also figured she already knew.

She introduced me to the poetry of Christina Rossetti and, even more appropriately, Sappho. The hypnotic words of the lesbian poet invaded my dreams, causing me to wake in a fever of lust, my fingers between my thighs massaging my clit even as I slept. I could feel my heart hammering in my chest when she walked through the door of the library two weeks later.

"Sappho get you hot?" she asked, settling in the chair across from me, her suede dress the colour of chocolate, her thick, curly hair wrapped in a bun at the nape of her neck.

I didn't answer. She stood up and took my hand. I resisted a moment, but at her insistent tug I followed her across the wing of the library to the bathrooms in the corner. She pulled me into a stall. Once inside, she slid the lock home and pushed me down on the lid of the toilet. She pulled her dress up and tugged her black panties to the side.

Within moments, my mouth was pressed to her bare cunt, sucking her as hard as I'd ever dreamed of sucking her.

"Oh, baby, that's it," she moaned, her voice soft and urgent. "You must have really liked Sappho."

Her sarcasm drove me on. I plunged a finger in her cunt and rubbed her G-spot roughly while I nipped her clit between my teeth, sucking it out, letting it go, sucking it back. Soon, she could barely breathe, much less talk. I jerked my jeans open and shoved my hand down my panties, rubbing my clit as roughly as I was sucking hers.

She came on my tongue in a gush of fluid that I lapped gently while I shuddered through my own orgasm.

The bathroom door opened and someone entered. We adjusted ourselves quietly, then she slipped out while I waited for the other woman to finish up. By the time I escaped the bathroom, Zoe was gone.

As we got near the end of the alphabet, I wondered what she would find for X and Z. I figured something by Malcolm X, but it didn't seem like her. I was right. Instead, she presented me with a fascinating little book called *There's a Whip in my Valise* by Greta X. I smirked, wondering if Zoe was trying to tell me something. I flipped to the back of the book, where the library's stamp should be. It was blank.

I looked up at her. "This didn't come from the library."

"I'll donate my copy when you're done with it."

She left me soaked. So did the book.

Y was a vampire tale by Chelsea Quinn Yarbro. I stayed up all night to finish it, I liked it that much. I'm still working on reading the others in the series.

When I returned the Yarbro, I found Zoe sitting in my chair for a change. The library was quiet that day, very few patrons perused the aisles. Maybe it was the weather, dark and unusually chilly for March in Florida. Maybe it was just wishful thinking on my part. When she beckoned to me and smiled, I didn't give a damn what anyone else thought. I settled on her knee, my head resting against her shoulder. She was wearing blue today, and I remembered this was the same dress she'd been wearing the first day I'd met her. I felt the softness of her breast pressing into my side and I ached to cup it, stroke it.

"You liked Yarbro," she said.

I nodded against the top of her head. "Yeah. I liked it a lot."

She turned her head so that her mouth was against my neck.

Instead of pulling away, I arched my neck. She nipped lightly at the stretched tendon, then pressed a wet kiss to my skin. "I want to fuck you right here," she said, louder than a whisper. I didn't care. I wanted the exact same thing.

This time, it was me pulling her toward the bathroom. I don't think the librarians noticed, but I would have knocked anyone who tried to stop us on their ass. I pulled Zoe into a stall, pushed her down on the seat and dry humped her thigh until I came with a whimper. When I tried to get under her skirt, she shook her head and pushed me off. "Not today."

We left the bathroom and the library. My heart thudded dully in my chest, partly from the after effects of the powerful orgasm I'd just had and partly in fear. Something felt different between us, something had changed.

I expected her to say something when we got to my car, but she didn't. Instead, she handed me a book. I knew this was Z. I was curious what she'd chosen, but at the moment I was more interested in the strange expression on her face. I saw a vulnerability I'd never seen before. It frightened me.

She turned and walked away without a word. I looked at the book in my hands. It wasn't a book from the library, it was a journal. Zoe's journal. I flipped to the first page and saw that Z was for Zoe Zimmerman and the date of the first entry was the day we'd met, just over a year ago.

Hot tears pricked my eyes even while wetness trickled down my thighs from my earlier orgasm. I read the book that night, cover to cover, then I stayed home from work the next day and read it again. Zoe wrote about herself, us, the books, the sex. It was the best of the books she'd given me.

I waited at the library two weeks later, but she never showed. Somehow I knew she wouldn't. I never saw her again at the library. Our alphabet game had come to an end. Still, I held out hope for five months that one day she'd stroll into the library and give me that little knowing smile. I stopped by more often and I even got a library card. She'd made me hunger for books as much as her body. I applied for a job as a library assistant and got it; I quit my waitressing job and enrolled in Broward Community College. I'd waited almost to the deadline to enroll, so when I finally got around to picking my classes, the only literature class left was something called "English: Special Topic." I signed up, figuring what the hell.

The first day of class I walked in to the full classroom and took a seat at the back. The instructor strode in several minutes later in a puff of lavender silk. She scrawled her name and the title of the class on the board. When she turned around, she saw me toward the back. There was a moment of startled recognition and then she grinned. I grinned back.

On the board, she'd written: Zoe Zimmerman, Women's Literature, A to Z.

I was pretty sure I was going to get both an A and a Z out of the class. After all I'd already completed the reading list.

Women at Work

Lynn Lake

Cherry Feliz dusted the door with her knuckles.

"What!?" the impatient voice of Nan Stewart came from within.

Cherry pushed the door open, stuck her head into the large, tastefully-appointed office. "Ms Stewart, I'm Cherry, from the payroll department, and—"

"It can wait!" Nan stated, waving a dismissive hand. She slammed a briefcase shut and stood up behind her huge expanse of mahogany desk. "Make an appointment to see me next week or something. Right now, I've got a date with a drink and a boat."

Cherry slipped inside the office, quietly closing the door and walking over to Nan's desk. "What I have to say won't wait until next week."

Nan looked up, her clear, blue eyes flashing angrily. She swatted a dangling strand of glossy blonde hair aside and demanded, "Just who do you think—?"

"I want to talk to you about the irregularities I've found on your expense claim forms." Cherry placed a file on the gleaming top of Nan's desk.

Nan swept it away. "Get out of my office! Now!"

Cherry didn't blink, big brown eyes locked on Nan's. "Part of my job is to enter all the executives expense claim forms into the system. Usually I only get totals for yours, but a while back I received a number of detailed forms. And I've been reviewing them, and I've found a number of irregularities. For instance—"

Nan banged a hand down on her briefcase. The office went quiet. She took a deep breath, large breasts straining the rich silk of her white blouse. "My expense reports are reviewed and signed by Mr Fielder, Chairman of the Board. No one else is allowed to see them. Now get out of here and consider yourself lucky to still have a job on Monday."

"Well, I guess Mr Fielder doesn't look at them too closely – being pretty old and all," Cherry persisted, tucking her shimmering, brown hair in behind her ears. She rubbed her tiny hands on the sides of her short, black skirt, licked her crimson lips. "Because you're missing a bunch of meal receipts from your trip to New York – expensive meals. And you filed a mileage claim for the trip when a plane would have been a lot cheaper."

Nan glared at the young woman, silver fingernails biting into the leather of her briefcase.

"And for your trip to Miami, you submitted all the receipts okay. But you've included expenses for some woman who, as far as I can tell, doesn't even work for the company."

Nan moved swiftly around her desk, slender, silk-sheathed legs whispering lethal. She was beside Cherry in an instant, looking down at the smaller woman from the end of her aristocratic nose. "Consider yourself terminated, effective immediately!"

Cherry looked up into the older woman's angry face. "And you were reimbursed for a trip to Mexico, even though the company doesn't do any—"

Nan slapped the girl across the face, the hot crack of flesh against flesh exploding obscenely inside the hushed, dignified confines of the business office.

Cherry touched her cheek, crimson finger polish flashing under the lights, diamond spider brooch on her scarlet top rising and falling in rhythm to her small breasts. "Even though the company doesn't do any business in—"

Nan slapped her again, even harder this time. Cherry's head jerked to the side, hair flying. She slowly brought her head back around, cheek burning, quiet smile on her pouty lips. Then she shot her hand up, as if to smack the CEO full in the face.

Nan staggered backwards on her spike heels, in fright and in realization that this was a girl to be reckoned with. Her face went deathly pale, her eyes wide. "W-what do you want?" she stammered.

"Bitch!" Cherry hissed, fists clenched with the effort to hold back, body quivering. "You think you can get away with anything! Treat this company and its employees like you own them!"

"N-no, that's not true," Nan gasped, staring into the girl's burning eyes. "I'll-I'll . . . treat you right."

"Too late," Cherry sneered. "Once I turn over what I've found to the Board of Directors, and the District Attorney, all your future expenses are going to be the State's responsibility."

Nan suddenly sagged to her knees, grabbing onto Cherry's skirt. She hugged Cherry's legs, pressing her face against the girl's brown, muscled thighs. "No-no, you don't want to do that," she whimpered.

Cherry looked down at the woman's bowed, blonde head, and laughed. "Why not?"

Nan jerked her head up, the shrewd businesswoman quickly conjuring up some tears, blinking them away so that they rolled down and over her high, haughty cheekbones, setting her mascara to running. "I'll give you whatever you want," she gushed, searching Cherry's eyes.

Cherry felt Nan's sharp fingernails digging into her plump buttocks, Nan's hot breath steaming against her skirt, pussy-level. She didn't say a word, even as the kneeling woman slowly unhooked her skirt with trembling fingers.

When Cherry made no move to stop her, Nan pulled the girl's skirt down, lifted her high heels out of the puddled garment. Then she ran her now tearless eyes up Cherry's gleaming, golden legs, to the tiny wet spot staining the red satin panties. "I know what you want," she breathed, inwardly and outwardly smiling. "And I know just how to give it to you."

Cherry grabbed Nan by the back of her $200 hairdo, jerking the woman's face up to meet her fiery eyes. "You think that's all there is to it?" she rasped.

"No, no!" Nan responded, sliding her hands up the back of Cherry's legs. "I'll make you my personal assistant – at any salary you name. And you'll go on all those trips with me from now on. Just you and me."

Nan's lips curled into a sly smile, as she brushed her fingers over the vulnerable backs of Cherry's knees, waiting for an answer. And when the girl's bare, bronze stems buckled, she had her answer. She moved her hands up and over the warm, firm swells of Cherry's buttocks, fingers sliding in under the girl's panties, nails biting into the soft, thick flesh there.

Cherry shivered, her body, her pussy surging with heat and moisture, tingling with the other woman's touch. She looked down into Nan's glittering eyes looking up at her. And the woman quickly brought her head in between Cherry's legs, lips bumping into the growing wet spot on the girl's panties, kissing it.

Cherry shuddered, Nan's tongue lunging out, licking the slick material that clung to her damp pussy. Nan tongue-stroked Cherry all the way from the narrow crotch in between her legs up to her waistband, over and over, long and hard. She painted the satin mound with her wet, dragging tongue, drinking in the intoxicating scent of the girl, reveling in it.

"You'll get what you want," she murmured. "And you'll forget all about those fraudulent expense reports, won't you?"

Cherry yanked the woman's head away from her sodden panties. Nan stared up at her, tongue hanging out. "Don't take anything for granted, bitch!" Cherry warned.

Nan smiled. Then she shook Cherry's hands free and pulled the girl's panties down. She gripped Cherry's clenched butt cheeks and without hesitation stuck her face into the damp, dark jungle of the girl's pussy.

"Oh!" Cherry yelped.

Nan dug her tongue into the girl's thatch, finding pussy lips and licking them. She lapped at Cherry's hairy snatch.

"Mmm!" Cherry moaned, little body vibrating, hands riding Nan's bobbing blonde head.

Nan licked and licked the girl's juicy slit, tasting, teasing, tonguing. Then she released Cherry's buttocks and dove her fingers into Cherry's fur, spreading the girl's pussy open. Wet, shiny pink was exposed, and Nan blew on it. Cherry jerked. Nan slurped the pink, chewed on the succulent cunt meat. Then she hardened her tongue into a blade and jabbed it into Cherry's opening, fucking the girl with her tongue. Cherry groaned with delight.

Nan withdrew her tongue and popped Cherry's swollen, cotton-candy clit out into the open with her fingers, jammed three more fingers deep into the girl's slit. She flogged Cherry's button with her tongue, fucked Cherry's twat with her fingers. Cherry clawed at Nan's hair, her body jumping, wet, wicked, unstoppable orgasm rising up from her worked-over pussy and engulfing her.

"Oh, God, yes!" Cherry wailed, riding the older woman's experienced tongue and fingers to ecstasy.

Nan quickly yanked her digits out of Cherry's gushing pussy and plugged her tongue in, throat working, swallowing the girl's hot, tangy juices. She only stopped when Cherry finally collapsed to her knees, too weak to stand any more. And then Nan devoured Cherry's mouth, swarming her tongue inside so that the girl could taste what Nan had done to her.

Nan stood up, licking her sticky lips with satisfaction, looking down at the cute, little woman still shaking with the aftershocks of her joy. Cherry clung to Nan's long, silky legs, the one in need of support now.

"Satisfied?" Nan asked rhetorically. "If you're a good girl – behave yourself – maybe I'll give you a little more every now and then. Maybe." She kneed Cherry in the chest, knocking the girl over onto her back. "Now get out of my office!"

Cherry rose to her feet, steadied herself. Then she grabbed the arrogant woman in her arms and mashed her mouth against Nan's open mouth. They kissed fiercely, tongues entwining, fighting an erotic duel.

Until Cherry licked the last of her come off the other woman's lips and shoved her backwards. "Thanks for the tongue-lashing," she said, grinning. "It'll be good practice for where you're going."

Nan stared into the girl's shining eyes, not understanding.

"I don't work here," Cherry explained. "But Mr Fielder just happens to be my great-grandfather. The sweet, slightly-confused old man who built this company from the ground up fifty years ago. The man I'd never let be taken advantage of by some scheming, conniving bitch like you.

"So when I heard rumours about all the extravagant business trips you were taking, from some people who work here, I decided to look into it. The records were sketchy, allright – you'd seen to that – so I decided my best bet was to confront you. With the hidden camera I'm wearing as a brooch rolling away." She tapped the diamond spider on her chest.

Nan's face went deathly pale, her eyes wide.

"I'll be turning the video of you confessing to your fraud, attempting to bribe me to cover things up, over to the District Attorney." Cherry smiled. "Well, not all of the video, of course." Her smile froze cold on her pretty face. "Now get out of this office! And consider yourself terminated, effective immediately."

Different Takes on a Shop Assistant's Uniform

Kay Jaybee

Take One

As uniforms went it was not the most attractive Mandie had come across. The pale blue blouse was stiff and shiny. It was made from such a cheap material that it reminded her of those worn by travel agents twenty years ago. The skirt was a navy A-line, with a short no-nonsense slit at the back, showing barely a glimpse of the regulation honey beige tights. Taking the shop assistant's job in the local bookshop and newsagents was definitely only a stop gap, but it would help keep a roof over her head and pay for what Mandie considered to be her real uniform: her large collection of expensive lingerie.

The shop manager, Martin, was very tall, very blonde, and very earnest. Mandie tried hard to concentrate as he showed her where the pens, paper, and folders were displayed. Plastering a willing to please smile on her face, she listened dully to the importance of customer service, pricing regulations and the layout of the shop.

It wasn't until she was shown into the store room that Mandie felt the first flicker of interest. One of her duties was to restock the books; a number of which were erotica. So here was the silver lining. Mandie silently vowed that she would ensure that this particular area of the shop would be thoroughly investigated and cared for.

As a present to herself for sticking out her new job for a whole week, Mandie bought an addition to her uniform that, although not regulation, made her feel much better, and far more confident. The honey beige tights had been replaced by honey cream stockings, secured by a beautiful ecru basque and knickers. Slipping them on under her drab clothes made Mandie feel as if she was living with a delicious secret. Now all she needed was someone to share it with.

Lost in a fantasy world as she stocked the selves, Mandie jumped suddenly as Martin tapped her on the shoulder. She was treating him to the "can I help you?" expression she had recently perfected, when she spotted the girl next to him. Mandie was vaguely aware that Martin was introducing her to a new member of staff, but she hardly heard him. Her eyes were fixed on the girl. The bloody uniform actually looked good on her; she even managed to look sexy. Definitely sexy.

Although she was nodding and smiling in all the right places, Mandie realized that she'd been operating entirely on autopilot and hadn't heard a word that Martin had said. She snapped to the present just in time to hear her boss say, ". . . so I hope you don't feel it's too soon for you to teach Harriet the ropes?"

"Of course not, no problem," Mandie spoke to his retreating back.

Harriet stood in front of her, a broad grin across her face. "Everyone calls me Harry, by the way."

"Oh, right." Mandie was robbed of her voice as she observed her new helper. She had bobbed shoulder-length red hair, remarkably pale green eyes, and a neatly shaped figure that even the nasty blue material couldn't disguise.

"Mandie, are you all right?"

"What? Oh, sorry, um, Harry. Right, well, I was just sorting these books out. What was I supposed to show you? I'm afraid I wasn't really listening."

"I bet this place does that to you. Don't worry, I'll liven things up a bit." Harry smiled with the flirtiest mouth Mandie had ever seen. If only she could engineer a situation where she could "accidentally" bump into Harry at a time when she wasn't wearing this hideous outfit. "You are supposed to be teaching me to use the till."

Gathering herself together, Mandie talked Harry through the finer points of till training. She had to dig her fingernails into her palms to stop herself putting her own hand over Harry's to guide her around the unfamiliar keyboard.

It was a relief when Martin came to take Harriet away for a tour of the stationery department. Mandie escaped to the sweet store, and took some deep breaths. This was ridiculous. No one had ever had such an immediate impact on her. Never before had she wanted to get a woman alone so badly.

As she hid in the ladies room with a suitably shaped chocolate bar and the latest erotic classic, Mandie realized that even her deliciously secret masturbation sessions suddenly felt like a consolation prize. Adjusting her suspenders and straightening her stockings, Mandie sighed out loud as she looked in the mirror. Even if Harry liked her when she wore her normal clothes, she'd probably read the signs wrong. Mandie touched up her dusky pink lipstick, pushed her shoulders back, pulled her stomach in, and headed to the store room.

Mandie had been up and down the paint-spattered ladder for over an hour, and her legs were beginning to ache. Why the excess novels had to be filed on the top shelf of the store room was anybody's guess. She had just got to the middle rung with a pile of chick-lits when she heard the squeak of the door. Unable to look down safely, Mandie called out, "Hi there. Can't move, I'm balancing books. Who's there?"

There was no reply, but Mandie could hear footsteps coming towards her. "Who's there?" Mandie nervously began jamming the remaining books in anywhere she could, before taking a step down the ladder.

A soft hand touched her ankle as it descended onto the next rung. Mandie stood stock still as an electric charge shot up her legs. Now she didn't want to look down, just in case it wasn't who she desperately hoped it was. The hand was stroking the back of her calf, slowly, methodically, as if it needed to discover every toned contour. A draught wafted over her arse, telling Mandie that the edge of her skirt had been lifted slightly, giving her silent companion the perfect view of her large firm arse encased in flimsy cream knickers.

Mandie held her breath as a finger traced the line from her heel up the back of her leg to the clip of her suspender belt. The touch was so gentle it was almost as if it wasn't really there, just a deliciously intoxicating daydream. Still she didn't look down as two small strong hands gently encouraged her to take one step further down the ladder. Mandie gripped the sides tightly to stop herself falling back against the head, which now held the skirt fully away from her legs. Someone was literally getting an eyeful.

Harry had known Mandie fancied her from the second they'd

laid eyes on each other. She couldn't believe her luck in finding her, and longed to see what lay under that wildly unflattering uniform. As Martin had dragged her through the routine of the day, Harry's mind had been full of stocking tops, lace, and sweet-smelling sweat. Now she really was examining at close range the delicately patterned tops of Mandie's stockings, she couldn't hide her delight.

"You're just so . . . well, you're fucking beautiful." She pulled her head away from the navy material to look up at her colleague.

Mandie blushed, "I didn't think you were interested."

"Are you kidding? You're bloody gorgeous." Harry's eyes shone as she commanded, "You stay there, young lady." Mandie watched in disbelief as Harry pushed a large stack of empty book crates against the door. "Just in case someone tries to come in, we'll have some warning."

Despite her rising excitement, Mandie paled slightly, "We can't! Not in here."

Harry's mouth twitched into a cheeky smile. "Why not? You've thought about it haven't you?"

"Well, yes, but you know . . ." Mandie's half hearted protests were cut short by Harry's return to the bottom of the ladder. Waiting, just as she had been instructed, Mandie shivered with desire as two hands ran up the back of her legs and over the round of her buttocks.

Each caress was like a kiss. Mandie feared she would come instantly under the gentle ministrations, and risk missing out on further delights, so she did her best to concentrate on making this experience last. When Harry finally pulled down the flimsy knickers, yanking them over the sensible shoes shop work demanded, Mandie trembled so violently that a single flick against her exposed clit broke her resolve, and sent her into preliminary rapture.

"What a hotty you are," Harry teased her as she ran a single sharp finger nail down Mandie's spine. "What do you think it will feel like in a minute when I run my wet tongue over your beautiful pussy?"

Mandie couldn't manage a coherent reply and simply moaned into the shelves of erotic fantasy, her eyes focusing on a suitably enticing photograph of a PVC-clad, whip-welding dominatrix. Her arms ached from the effort of not falling off the ladder as Harry kissed the exposed skin between her stockings and her arse. Mandie couldn't help but squirm, earning herself a hard smack from her new lover.

"Keep still, sweetheart. I'm going to treat you so good," Harry whispered as she pushed her neat head back up Mandie's skirt, grasped her thighs, and steadying herself on the bottom rung, took a long lingering lick from her clit to her velvety arsehole.

This time yesterday she'd never even heard of Harry. An hour ago she'd just been an exquisite fantasy. Mandie wasn't sure this was real. She felt faint; the throbbing need between her legs was being echoed by a feeling of neglect across her tingling breasts.

Mandie's juice leaked freely across the probing tongue. Her hands were weakening, and she knew she would have to come down the ladder soon. Harry withdrew her tongue and replaced it with two dainty fingers, one gently swirling inside Mandie's pussy, the other teasing her bud. It was too much.

Mandie let go of the ladder as her body rocked for the second time in five minutes. She fell, landing in a pleasingly undignified heap on top of Harry, who still had her head caught inside her skirt.

They burst out laughing, their hair strewn across their faces. Then, suddenly remembering the possibility of discovery, Harry stifled any sound by pressing her sticky lips against Mandie's mouth. As they lay there exploring each other, Mandie slid her hand beneath Harry's nylon blouse and gasped with pleasure to find that her tight little chest was already bare. Mandie delighted in trailing her fingers around Harry's neat tips, moving in a steady circular motion until she was rewarded with a deep groan from Harry's throat.

Mandie pulled her face away, smiling with joy, before plunging her free hand under Harry's skirt. "You dirty girl. Where are your knickers?"

"I didn't think I would need them!" Harry looked overwhelmingly endearing as she confessed, "I left them off when I popped to the bathroom earlier. I thought the wait to catch you out here alone was going to drive me mad."

"Oh, sweetie, why didn't you let me know? We could have gone home together after work."

"I wanted you here. You look so yummy in that uniform; I just had to have you in it. Well, for the first time, at least."

"So confident there will be a second!" Mandie nipped Harry's ear as she teased her. "Anyway, these uniforms are foul. I am very much looking forward to seeing you out of yours . . ."

Take Two

The look Harry gave her as she entered the shop made the heat rise within Mandie, filling her head with exotic possibilities. Just the mere thought of Harry's sweet nimble fingers holding her, her tongue flicking its way over her rounded body, sent jets of excitement down Mandie's spine.

When break time finally arrived, Harry's eyes twinkled wickedly. "I fancy a bar of chocolate. How about you?"

"Why not?" Mandie smiled as she recalled how these regular trips used to be conducted alone. They left the shop floor and headed through the sweet store. Harry grabbed a Flake, as they hurried on to the ladies' room.

"We have got to stop doing this," Mandie said with absolutely no conviction in her voice whatsoever, as Harry manoeuvred them into a cramped cubicle.

Mandie's skirt was already rucked up around her waist, her knickerless pussy exposed to Harry's skilful fingers. "Why, sweetie, you're wet. Perhaps there's no need to moisten you further?"

Mandie grabbed a handful of her lover's hair, and pushed her head down. "Oh, yes, there is."

Harry whispered, "Are you going to beg me?"

"I don't need to you, whore. You want to anyway."

Mandie shuddered with want as Harry silenced further comment by covering her mouth with her own, before sliding the unwrapped chocolate bar deep into her waiting cunt.

Coming swiftly, panting into Harry's shoulder, Mandie pulled out the sticky chocolate. Forcing it between Harry's lips, Mandie began to feed it to her, whilst teasing skilful fingers across her clit, bringing Harry to her own release.

Availing themselves of the facilities, the girls quickly smoothed down their uniforms, adjusted their lipstick and returned to the shop floor. Only three hours and they could go home.

Take Three

Mandie had prepared as carefully as she could. Slipping back into the toilets after her shift, she put on a pair of new, very delicate, plum-coloured French knickers, and a matching lace-up, which neatly encased her heavy chest. After replacing her stockings with clear hold ups, Mandie checked inside her bag to make sure the present she'd brought for Harry was still there. Her heart fluttered in her chest as she anticipated the evening ahead.

Harry's flat was only small, but it was neither cramped nor cluttered like Mandie's bedsit.

Together in the tiny kitchen they kissed long and hard before Harry broke away. "Will you do something for me?"

"Of course."

"Sit in the living room and wait. I won't be long, but I need to get something ready."

"Can't I help you?"

"No. This is for you. Please, just sit."

"Can't I at least change out of this foul outfit?"

"No," Harry shouted from the kitchen, "I like you in that. It's like taking off horrid wrapping paper and finding a pearl of a present inside."

Mandie left the kitchen reluctantly, subsiding into the living room's soft creamy sofa, cradling Harry's compliment like a prize.

Harry seldom bothered with underwear, but as Mandie adored it she had made the effort. The cream stockings that covered her slim legs, lead to a soft pair of cream silk briefs. Her neat breasts remained unfettered though, behind an almost transparent ecru blouse. The slightly crumpled material, draped seductively across her chest, had just enough buttons done up to suggest what delights might be found underneath. Slipping on her kitten-heeled strappy shoes to complete the effect, Harry took a deep breath, picked up the plate of food she'd prepared before work, and some wine, and headed for the living room.

Mandie stood up as soon as Harry entered the room, and wiped her lightly sweating hands down the side of her polyester skirt. "You look incredible."

"Good enough to eat?" Harry smiled mischievously indicating the plate in front of her. Mandie glanced at the neatly sliced, cleaned and conveniently shaped pieces of carrot, celery and cucumber.

"Well, that doesn't leave much to the imagination, does it?" Mandie kissed her as she took the plate out of Harry's hands and placed it on the unit behind her.

Harry pushed Mandie down, and lay on top of her, half on, half off the sofa. "I've been thinking about this all day. I want tonight to be for you. It's your present. There is only one rule."

Mandie slithered into a more comfortable position. "Which is?"

"You do what you are told. Okay?"

"Okay."

Harry led Mandie through to her small bedroom. They stood, holding hands at arms length. "Stand still," Harry commanded as she slipped the blue jacket off Mandie's shoulders.

Mandie reached out to remove Harry's blouse, only to have her arms gently restrained at her sides. "Not yet, honey. I said, stand still." Harry whispered.

Mandie stifled a sigh as Harry undid her despised work shirt instead, sliding the shiny material off, so that it joined the jacket on the floor. Harry's intake of breath at her first sight of her lover's lace up was worth waiting for. She stopped taking her time and yanked off the skirt, revealing Mandie in her beautiful new lingerie.

Forcing the basque's laces as wide open as possible, Harry pulled Mandie's tits out, so that they rested above the bindings. Falling on them with relish, a practised hand kneaded one, whilst Harry's mouth worked across the other. Squeezing, flicking, licking and biting until Mandie was utterly breathless. "Please, Harry, I'm gonna come."

Harry bit down hard on Mandie's nipple causing her to cry out in pain as she spasmed with longing.

Harry sounded insincere as she apologized. "Sorry, babe, I was going to make you wait, but for heaven's sake, you look so incredible."

"Don't be sorry," said Mandie as she dragged Harry back down on top of her. "I still promise to be a good girl and do exactly as I'm told, on one condition."

"Which is?"

"Let me unbutton your blouse. It's crying out to be taken off, and I can't concentrate. I need to see those neat little tits."

Granting Mandie's wish, Harry lay still as she savoured each button. Her light fingers trailed gently around each globe, rubbing the sensitive underside until Harry began to raise her hips in an automatic response to the feelings being aroused within her. Then, unexpectedly, Mandie let go. Harry moaned as the intense sensations were suddenly denied her.

"Well," teased Mandie as she twisted one of her lace-up's ties around her fingers, "you are supposed to be the decision maker tonight. Do I let you come or not?"

"Of course you bloody do!" Mandie grinned at Harry's hungry, lust-filled face. She locked her eyes into Harry's, licked her index finger, and almost in slow motion, lowered it on to the very tip of her right nipple. Harry bucked right then, the heat of the evening's expectations, and the attention to her chest tipping her over the edge.

"So much for seeing how long we could both wait! Come on, let's eat something; you're making me hungry." Once she'd caught her breath, Harry took Mandie back into the living room. "Now comes the part where you really have to do as you're told."

"Yes, Miss." Mandie looked demurely up through her eye lashes.

"That's a good girl." Harry patted the long thin coffee table which ran along one side of the room. "Hop on."

Mandie sat down on the edge of the cool brown surface, but Harry shook her head. "No. Lie down. Tonight you are going to be the fanciest tablecloth I have ever had. And as tablecloths don't speak, I don't think you should either."

Mandie lay on the hard, slim table, her discomfort relieved only slightly by two small silk cushions, which Harry slid underneath her head and bum, raising both slightly off the table. Still attempting to make herself comfortable, Mandie was taken by surprise when Harry pulled her left arm above her head and secured it to the table leg with a short leather strap. As Harry carefully manoeuvred her right arm into position Mandie's heart quickened and her head spun.

Leaving her ankles free, Harry stood back to admire her work. Words failed her as she examined the amazing sight she'd created.

The few minutes Harry took to decide where to begin felt like an eternity to Mandie. Her body was desperate to be fondled; she had to clamp her mouth shut to hold in the frustration that was building within her.

Well aware of the effect the delay must be having on Mandie, Harry took her time. She poured a glass of very cold white wine, and after a few sips, carefully balanced it on her new "table". Mandie gasped as the cool glass met her bare stomach; she hardly dared breathe, imagining how it would feel if the chilled liquid spilt across her body.

Picking up a handful of salted peanuts from a dish, Harry toyed with them a second before sprinkling them in and around Mandie's belly button. Holding the stem of the glass in place, Harry began to nibble them up, swirling the residual salt around the peach-coloured flesh with her tongue.

Mandie released a low moan as Harry finished her hors d'oeuvres. She didn't speak, but Harry knew she longed to. After a swig of wine, Harry removed the glass, and swung her leg over Mandie, so she was sat astride her stomach.

Mandie tried to lift her head towards Harry's clit; she was so sure that it was at last on offer.

"Patience," Harry admonished her with a light slap. "I thought you might like something moist to eat." She reached across to her tray and picked up a long thin slice of cucumber. Pushing her panties to one side, Harry slid the pale green wand up inside her own pussy. Moving forward, she stood over Mandie's face, offering her the contents of her snatch as a snack.

Mandie began to lick the end of the cucumber as if it were a tiny cock. Then she used her tongue to push it further up inside Harry, until it almost disappeared. Being unable to use her hands frustrated her madly. Mandie strained uselessly against her straps to get a better purchase on the treat that was being proffered.

Harry crouched down, until she was virtually sitting on Mandie's face. Struggling to keep herself still, as Mandie began to nibble the sticky baton from out of her, Harry felt a mewl building in her throat. Mandie's sensually slow tongue was driving her to distraction as the remaining morsel was twirled inside her body. She sat down abruptly on Mandie's chest, her climax overcoming her, causing the remains of the cucumber to escape.

"My turn, honey." A few seconds later Harry had recovered enough to move back down the table to collect a wand of carrot. Carefully, she teased the blunt end of the orange stick up and down Mandie's legs, causing her captive to writhe in her bonds.

Mandie was desperate to move now, to clasp Harry with both hands; but she lay as still as she could, waiting for the carrot to be stuffed into her neglected cunt. She bit her tongue in an effort not to speak, but as the teasing continued across her lower body; Mandie couldn't help but yell out. "Shove it in me Harry, please!"

Harry contorted her face in an effort to look cross. "Begging me already? I didn't even hear you ask for permission to speak."

"Please, Miss? I feel so empty."

Harry rammed the baton hard and deep, causing Mandie's backside to leap at the chilled invasion. It felt good, but was nowhere near thick enough to stem her rising need.

"I think it would be best if you weren't able to talk for the time being. Punishment for speaking out of turn." Harry disappeared from view as Mandie felt a sharp wave of panic sweep over her. She had been bound before, but never silenced. The perspiration prickled across her back against the hard table.

Harry returned with her hated work blouse, rolled up into a long thin gag. "Open wide." Mandie didn't move. "You promised you would do as you were told."

Mandie continued to hesitate until Harry leant down and began to suck her left breast. Automatically, Mandie opened her mouth to sigh, and Harry quickly filled it with the material, lifting her head to secure it in an uncomfortable knot beneath her. Mandie was still unsure, but Harry looked so deliciously triumphant and happy that she swallowed her fear.

"Now. Don't move." Picking up a small bowl of honey and mustard dressing, Harry took a long stick of celery and used it as a scoop to dribble some of the contents over each of Mandie's incredible tits. Mandie shivered as the cool sticky liquid trickled across her chest. Harry loosened the laced basque further, allowing the plum silk to fall to Mandie's sides, and watched the dressing run down towards the table, her tongue rescuing the drips before they hit the delicate material.

Mandie began to tremble again as Harry worked over her lush body, cleaning her up. By the time she had sucked all the dressing off Mandie's left tit, her right side was screaming out for attention and, her previous orgasm forgotten, her clit burned with need. The neglected carrot, too thin to have had any satisfying effect, fell out as she squirmed against the table. Mandie bit into the blouse, desperate to concentrate on anything other than the feelings that swelled with her.

Harry scooped up some more dressing. Refilling Mandie's belly button, she swirled sticks of food in and out of the mixture, before eating them in small neat, provocative mouthfuls. Mandie's legs began to twitch with the effort of keeping still. She began to wish that they had been tied down as well.

Aware of the effort Mandie was making to be good, Harry decided to reward her by jamming a large, thick, stick of celery into her soaking snatch. Even the gag could not totally suppress Mandie's cries, as her legs and hips leapt away from the hard table.

"You are gorgeous," Harry whispered into Mandie's ear, "I could look at you like this for ever." She turned back to the unit along the wall, "In fact, I think I will." Mandie was unable to protest as Harry produced a camera, and took picture after picture.

Finally, throwing the camera to one side, she laid full length on top of Mandie, pushing the exposed bit of celery in to her own body as if it were a double-headed dildo. She rubbed her whole body against Mandie, until she called out in ecstasy.

Pulling the gag away from Mandie's mouth, Harry kissed her long and hard. "I'm going to enjoy looking at those photos; they'll be the perfect souvenir of an incredible evening."

Mandie smiled up at her, "Permission to speak?"

"Yes?"

"Untie me. I want to take some snaps of you." Harry didn't hesitate, her fingers fumbling in her haste as she loosened the straps.

Mandie stretched her aching arms, before pushing Harry to the floor and sucking each of her small globes hard. "Stay there," Mandie commanded as she grabbed the camera and photographed Harry in her dishevelled heap upon the floor.

"I have a present for you." Mandie produced the little parcel from out of her bag.

Harry's eyes lit up as she carefully undid the pretty paper. Her lust-fuelled smile as she weighed the tiny silver vibrator in her hand said it all. It was the perfect size to be hidden at the bottom of the capacious pocket in her work skirt. "I have a feeling that tonight is going to get even better," she said as she pushed Mandie forward over the back of the sofa. "Come on you, I want to test this on your cute arse . . ."

The following day they sat in the staff room drinking coffee and eating biscuits. Mandie brushed some crumbs from her hated uniform, as Harry reached into her bag and produced a small packet of newly developed photographs.

They decided that today would be the perfect day to do some more work in the storeroom . . .

Another Fleeting Night

R. Greco

Erin's pretended schoolgirl-like innocence was wearing thin . . .
just as it always did. Although I had often seen my friend wear
this outfit – clunky heels; too short black and white dress; thong
underneath – right then the ensemble was only adding to her
petulance . . . and my desire to swat her ass.

"Over the edge of the bed," I demanded.

"Claire, I . . ." she tried, while turning to the soft bedspread.
"I . . ."

"Yes, you have been bad," I said to her unspoken protest.
"Now get."

Balancing her taut legs on those four-inch heels, Erin bent her
upper half across the high solid bed frame. Her short skirt just
covered her ass as she spread her legs slightly, bent at the knees
and looked to her side at me. I paid her no mind (or pretended
not to at least) stepping to the chair behind me to lift the leather
crop that lay across its cloth seat. Turning, I spied a slight smile
playing across my friend's angular features as she pushed her
cheek into her bedspread and regarded me through her fallen
hair.

"You know . . ." I began slicing the air between us.

Each "fick-swip" caused Erin's shoulders to twitch. She
peered up at me, her long straight hair falling across her left
shoulder, covering one eye. Once more she shifted her hips,
spreading her thin legs even wider.

". . . we go through this every time," I continued. "If you
just learned."

But I knew she wouldn't . . . and didn't want to. Erin's late-
night carousing, teasing and dancing were tempered well by
what we did here. And even though I had joined her on occasion
– I wasn't a nun after all and I liked to dance – Erin surpassed
me in frequency of her outings and phone numbers acquired . . .

numbers from men, even! She was a lesbian, as was I, but one who liked to tease whomever happened to be looking, so we often frequented dance clubs where she knew she could attract every eye in the place.

This all-out need for unlimited attention only fuelled the fire in me to beat her ass harder . . . and of course made me wetter at the same time!

"That dress is just too short," I said, closing the carpeted distance between us by taking another step.

"Well, I . . ." she attempted.

"No excuses," I said. Reaching down and across her, I fingered the hem of her dress and lifted it to the small of her bent back.

Erin's tight round ass was halved by a black thong. Although Erin and I were gay we had never been intimate, but God knew I dug her ass! I wasn't really sure if these spankings added to my longing for her, or quenched a thirst we could have built on; all I knew was that she looked and smelled hot as hell bending there! Would a time come when we'd finally risk the friendship and jump one another?

After she was sufficiently whipped, though, of course!

"I look good, don't I?" my friend snickered.

Christ she was cocky . . . but she did look good! Erin often took to spinning as she danced and I knew in this outfit everyone in the club had caught quite an eyeful. Regrets, my friend would never own, not now . . . not ever. So I reached back, flicked the long crop through the tight air of her bedroom and connected to Erin's bared cheeks.

As always, that first strike caused her to jump as she rode through the sting.

"Ah ha," she said. "I don't need it that hard!"

We both knew this wasn't true.

Erin had made me promise, some six months ago, that I would never, ever relent because of her protests. She trusted me to know what she needed and how hard; she might complain, cry out, growl and beg me to stop, but always afterward my dark-haired best friend smiled and thanked me for the beating.

Somehow, much to my own protests when first approached, I had learned to give Erin exactly what she needed. Hell, I loved looking at her ass anyway, that I loved making it red did come as a surprise to me at first, but . . .

*   *   *

"I need to stop this shit," Erin was confessing that late night as we sat huddled in the corner of the diner.

I had been only half listening as Erin bragged of her aching for some "new attention": wanting to rip up phone numbers in expectant faces; dance close with every girl her age in *Des Moines*! I smiled as I always did these Thursday night tirades; my friend was just feeling good about her lithe figure, a little buzzed and blowing off steam. But that particular evening, as we drove from club to club, finally settling at the diner at two, I did notice a tone of desperation in Erin's usually liquid voice. As we sat over ice-teas and fries with extra gravy I slowly began to listen as Erin confessed the plan she had been gestating for quite a long time, a plan she needed me to help her carry out!

"You are my best friend," she said and I nodded after another sip of my tea. "You know me better then anybody. We share so much."

This was true. It was so much easier avoiding people than making friends, especially when your lifestyle, as was mine and Erin's, didn't fit in to what was considered "normal" in our suburban town. We had found each other, realized we'd be better friends then lovers (after really only one night of some regulation heavy-petting) and then grew into being the best buds.

"I'm really out of control. I really need your help. I can't keep going partying like this," she continued, as always a bit over-dramatic.

"Just stop going out so much," I offered her slightly downcast gaze. "I mean it's no big deal. Just rest your ass for a couple weeks."

"But I don't want to," she said, smiling up at me then. "I really don't want to . . . but I know it's wrong," she continued, still smiling. "I'm staying out way too late. I've got a Lit. test tomorrow . . . later today, and I know I'm going to barely be able to drag myself to class."

"What do you want me to do?" I asked. "You know you shouldn't be goi—"

"—I know, I know," she interrupted, then looked long and hard across the table at me.

Damn, I knew that look well! When Erin levelled me with that stare I knew something heavy was coming!

"I'm going to ask you something, and no matter what, you've

got to promise not to laugh . . ." she said ". . . or think I'm weird."

"I already think you're weird."

"No, really, Claire," she pleaded and as I nodded, Erin explained her plan.

It was simple and perverse, much like Erin herself. In the five years of our friendship I knew my friend had indulged her sexual appetites plenty. Don't get me wrong, Erin was more tease and flirt than slut, but she had had her moments.

This was one of those moments!

Erin wanted to be whipped once a month! A quick, possibly week-night early evening that would probably only take an hour at most (or so she claimed). She said it would be penance for what she knew she couldn't stop; she had to pay for her carousing and a good beating across her bare ass would help her balance the wild abandon she felt when she did go out. At first I strained to understand; she wanted to be whipped? Beaten? But as Erin explained and I ordered another ice tea, the logic of her plan became clear. And what's more, I started to realize that I very much wanted to see her suffer in this way.

True, I loved my friend. True, I would do anything for her, but true I was jealous of her ease with other women and her flirtations. So when Erin asked and then explained that she had the crop, that she would have us meet in her apartment, that she would design the moment, that all I would have to do was show up and show her no mercy, I figured . . . what the hell? I guess we all have a bit of a sadistic streak in us if we can see the purpose it will serve.

I saw the purpose, and what's more, I was intrigued . . . and I must admit, even excited by the idea of whipping my friend's tight little behind for one evening each month. How Erin thought up this particular penance I had no idea, but I realized then, and came to learn later, that submitting to an ass-whipping had been a fantasy of hers for a very long time. With me spanking her for punishment Erin would "kill two birds with one stone"; fulfilled desire masked as constructive behaviour adjustment. And if anything this little "scenario" of Erin's would just deepen that ache we had for one another, an ache we never had acted on. An ache I wondered if we'd address, let alone do anything about.

What I couldn't have imagined was how the beatings would progress to the point where I would come to like them so much . . .

"I'm sorry, honey, but you need this," I said then, landing a third tight cut across Erin's cheeks. Again she easily inhaled through the connection, her little bottom circling slightly as she rode the sting.

"I . . ." Erin tried and I simply reached back and swat forward again. She yelped and arched her back on the connection.

"Now, tell me you're a bad girl," I coaxed.

"Nah, na," Erin resisted, pressing her chest further into the bedspread as if in defiance.

This was our usual ritual and would continue until my friend confessed her sins. I knew Erin had an iron will and could withstand quite the ass-whipping; we'd stay here all night if that was what it took to get her to finally confess.

"Tell me," I demanded and managed a look at the mirror to the side of Erin's bed. As usual at these times my blue eyes were alight with a flame I never really knew existed and my large chest was rising and falling as that little ass just lay in wait under me. God, she looked good, it was all I could do to keep from kneeling right there behind Erin and licking up her quivering thighs. I knew her pussy was as hot as mine; I'd be able to taste it even through her thong. With her tight, olive-coloured ass just beginning to show some deep square marks I was split, as usual, between continuing to beat Erin and kneeling to eat her from behind! This was the awful wonderful tease we both worked through these nights of Erin's whippings. And the more turned on I became and knew I wouldn't act on it, the more severe her beating. Had Erin planned it this way? God I hoped so?

"Swip-Pat. Swip-Pat." the crop said to her cheeks as I connected dead centre and Erin moaned aloud again.

"Tell me you are a bad girl," I demanded and again I brought the crop back, then forward to her waiting ass. This time I flicked the second hit upward; just the slightest bit and I heard the cut as it caused Erin to rise up on her hands.

"Well?" I prodded.

My friend looked over her shoulder; dammit, she was still smiling!

Had we come to that delicate point? Could Erin now endure every bit of pain I could muster? Had my effectiveness as her punisher been exhausted? This was exactly why I had brought with me the secret weapon I had for tonight's session.

"Have you been a bad girl?" I asked aloud, loud enough to be heard if one had been standing on the other side of the thin apartment door listening. And as Erin bent her head forward, preparing to lay her chest and face down once again, her apartment door swung open!

She felt the rush of cold air before Frankie came in. But before she could readjust, pull her skirt down; assimilate what in the hell was actually happening, Erin's neighbor was down Erin's hallway, in her bedroom, smiling down at us.

"Wow, you weren't kidding!" the lanky Asian man exclaimed, stroking his goatee.

"Cla . . ." Erin tried, nearly standing up off the bed. I leaned forward and sliced her ass my hardest yet to keep her bent in place.

"Frankie, Erin's been a bad girl," I chuckled, tapping the switch on my friend's bare ass. For her part Erin stayed bent, moaning, as she tried her damnedest not too look over her shoulder at smiling Frankie.

"She gets these once a month, but tonight she won't admit she's been a bad girl."

"Oh, I think she has been," Frankie added and we both chuckled.

I could see this attention, this matter-of-fact way we were talking over her was killing Erin. Frankie had been Erin's neighbour and a good friend for some three years. He was the type of guy a girl could come to when she had a problem, or just wanted to talk, with no fear of him misconstruing a quiet evening as anything more then just that. Frankie knew Erin was gay, as he knew I was, but he had the type of well-balanced ego that would never allow him to assume he and a gay woman would be anything more then friends; the very reason Erin had grown as close to him as she had, and why I had invited him over this night.

For her part, my friend was moaning ever so slightly. Shifting her hips, shucking back and forth, Erin afforded the attentive Frankie quite a view of her ass. I knew she so wanted to stand up, end this torture, but at the same time I knew if Erin was half as wet as I was she'd really want this to continue; her embarrassment all the more sweeter with Frankie ogling her and me readying the crop for what she knew would be her worst smacks yet. I knew when I asked her again Erin would admit to being bad. But she wouldn't get the chance without paying for it.

"Well," I said, still tapping her tight cheeks. "Have you been a naughty girl?"

"Yes," Erin whispered.

"Well, take down the thong, honey," I said.

I sensed Frankie halt in muted delight as Erin reached under herself, pulled the cotton thong out from between her cheeks and hammocked it mid-thigh. This last bit of humiliation was normal for us; I always liked to give Erin her last few with her ass completely bare, but with Frankie standing there I knew this moment held a new dread to it.

He and I both could see that thin glisten at the centre of Erin's winking chestnut.

"Tell Frankie and I that you have been a bad girl," I said, reaching the crop back as the tall man next to me offered a sharp inhale. "Say, 'I have been a bad girl'," I said and to both Frankie's delight and mine (and I'm sure a little bit of Erin's as well) Erin managed:

"Oh God, I . . . I have been a bad girl! Oh God, Claire! I've been a bad girl!"

"ZIP", "ZIP", "ZIP", "ZIP", I swatted my best friend, Frankie sighed and I grew so wet it was all I could do to keep standing!

Ten minutes later Erin and I stood at her lime green kitchen counter sharing a beer, while Frankie sat in her living room watching the last two innings of the game.

"That was really evil," my friend reminded me for the fourth time.

"A last resort," I said, passing across the cold bottle. "You left me no choice."

"I, ah . . ." she tried, but stopped to lift a long gulp from the frosty amber-colored glass. She had kept the dress on and I could see Erin's pinpoint nipples peeking through the thin material; there'd never be a question for me if she enjoyed these spankings!

"You want the punishment to count," I explained. "I have to bring in my own little ideas from time to time."

"To keep me honest, right?"

"Yes, to keep you honest," I agreed and as Erin walked from my side I halted her with my hand to her elbow. I smiled and turned her as to face me.

"Claire!" my best friend exclaimed as I reached under her dress.

I felt up between her thighs for the quaffed landing-strip between her legs. Erin had kept her thong off, as I had hoped she would when Frankie and I had left her to make her way off her bed and into the living room to meet us. I was being bolder then I had ever been with her, taking a liberty I never had – but wished I had – before.

"This night's full of new developments," I explained as Erin swooned there with her ass in my face as I sat under her and explored.

"Claire," Erin repeated, shuttering my name through her thin lips.

I opened her with my fingers, spreading her heavy wet lips, tickling her thick clit with my index finger. Laying herself almost back fully on my hand, Erin's dress swayed ever so slightly as I fingered her. She was so wet, so responsive, it was all I could do not to prolong my fingering, but the poor girl had suffered enough. As I heard cheers from the living room television I began to circle my finger quicker across Erin's thick clit.

"Claire," she sang and placed a hand back on my shoulder as I continued to look up at her and circle my finger.

"Cla . . . Cla," Erin said and I watched as her thighs began to quiver the slightest bit.

"Come for me," I simply said and Erin gulped and her whole body shook as my hand glopped with her wetness and she stood there.

During a few whippings Erin had got close to an orgasm, there had even been a time or two I allowed her a few seconds to circle her pelvis across her bedspread, but as far as I knew she had never come when I was with her. Maybe she released when she went into the bathroom to clean up afterwards (God knew when I usually got home I couldn't keep my hand from my pussy) but there in her kitchen we were being quite "obvious".

"Come, my naughty girl," I whispered and Erin looked down at me over her shoulder and then squatted hard on my hand. Arching her back she let loose right there in her kitchen!

"Shit . . ." she growled. I wasn't sure if Frankie had heard her, but then again I didn't much care!

Another hurtle jumped, I thought as I tickled Erin's silky lips and she moaned in submissive satisfaction. Could I fucking wait another month for another fleeting night?

Love is Blind

Alex Woolgrave and Jules Jones

There are disadvantages to living with a writer. You get woken up at four o'clock in the morning as they hunt down That Brilliant Idea That Won't Go Away.

You peer over their shoulder, and see the unexpected line: "Lilian's bosom was barely covered by the thin shift that was all he allowed her . . ."

You try to reason with them gently. "Now, Edith, there are times to write erotica, and then there's four o'clock in the morning, a time which exists *solely* to remind us of our own mortality."

Edith blinked at me slowly, eyes unfocused and hair sticking up all spiky from the pillow. "Not solely." And managed an unexpectedly coordinated grope.

"I s'pose one of the advantages of being a lesbian is that the other party can find the clitoris when she hasn't got her glasses on and isn't really awake," I said.

She grabbed the notepad and wrote that down.

". . . and one of the disadvantages is that a lesbian *writer* will probably reach for the notebook in mid-grope."

She put *that* down, too, then grinned and put her thumbs up. Judging by *where*, I wasn't going to complain, at least not more than by adding, "If I was shacked up with a bloke, at least I could rely on the cock overriding the brain."

"We multitask," she said.

"Yes, you multitask. I bet you'll be mentally taking notes even as you . . ."

"No, I'd rather try something out to see if it's actually feasible. I wouldn't have woken you up to try, but seeing as you're awake . . ."

I sighed and settled back. "Obviously I'm not going to be allowed to go back to sleep until you've worked out whatever it is." Especially not if she was doing that trick with the knuckle of her thumb pressing against my clit. That would keep me awake for some minutes.

She withdrew her fingers, and there was a lot of fiddling and rustling. *I ought to be getting suspicious right about now*, I thought, as something soft came round my wrists and was tucked carefully in, before my hands were pulled above my head.

"Er . . . Edith. We don't normally do this sort of thing, do we?" I mean, not that I was disgusted, or even averse; I'd just never thought about it. Going straight from not-even-talking-about-bondage to I-have-something-round-my-wrists was a little unsettling.

Especially as my little fluffy Edith, the mystery writer, was usually a little careful to keep a separation between life and art, and – hang on – wasn't known for her steamy erotic scenes. I said so.

"No, I haven't so far. But I have got this scene where the heroine is handcuffed to the bed – no, nothing kinky at all, the villain is trying to threaten her. I was going to say it wasn't erotica."

I opened my eyes. That must be why there was a set of handcuffs on the bedside table. Not fake leopardskin cuffs (not real leopardskin either), not leather or rubber (did people use rubber cuffs, if they had a . . . rubber kink?) – standard police-issue handcuffs.

The handcuffs she'd got for "Writing Purposes" on Thursday, when she'd realized the most straightforward way to acquire handcuffs was from a sex-shop, and she'd frogmarched me right down there because she was too shy to go in on her own. "Now, Sally, you go in and get me a set of handcuffs. Nothing kinky, mind."

It had flown right out of my mind because I'd picked up a couple of optional extras that we *did* like, but the handcuffs had come home to roost. On *my* wrists.

"You don't mind being a model?" she said anxiously. "I have padded your wrists so it shouldn't hurt."

"What happens to your heroine, in the end?"

"Alive, and happily married. I've got to pretend it's a bloke to sell the book, and he's got a touch of the Mr Darcy about him – which I have to keep playing up to boost the conflict – but the *nice* side of him is pretty much you with a moustache. Well, more of a moustache."

I was sensitive about the facial hair, which had *certainly not* reached the moustache stage. I pretended to scratch an itch on my cheek, and she tutted mildly, and pulled my hand back into place. "Even if I minded, Sally," she said, "it'll go away as soon as you're off that drug."

And that was why I'd lie here and let her handcuff me, if she so wished. She didn't care what I looked like, as long as I was me. She had no tact whatsoever, but she was warm-hearted, funny, and intelligent, and her bluntness was never malicious. And she'd just said I was her Mr Darcy only less of an arsehole.

I stopped trying to look daggers at her, and realized it had been wasted effort without her glasses.

She picked up the handcuffs and handcuffed me to the brass bed frame. We'd had this bed for years. "Edith, why did you get this bed six years ago?"

"Because we needed a bed after you broke the last one. Oh, I see – no, I certainly didn't get this bed because I wanted to put it in this mystery, I was doing a historical at the time, and I wanted to be convincing about sex in an old-fashioned bed."

I tried to work out whether that reassured me.

Edith managed to put the handcuffs on me without putting her glasses on first, which was a bit surprising. The way she was kneeling by the bed in an adorable state of rumpled myopia as she concentrated on it suggested it was a bit of an effort.

"Edith, is your villain short-sighted?" I asked, as she finished securing the handcuffs so that my hands were through the bars of the bedframe, with the handcuffs on one side of the bars and the rest of me on the other.

"Yes, about as much as I am. The heroine's managed to kick his glasses off—"

"While he was wearing them?"

"—oh, all right, *knock* his glasses off during the fight. That's one of the things I'm testing. Is he actually able to function as a villain in a state of extreme short-sightedness?"

"So that's why you wanted to test handcuffs in the middle of the night without wearing your glasses. Does it have to be four o'clock in the morning for plot reasons?"

"No, that's just when it occurred to me – could he get the handcuffs on her if he can't see what he's doing?"

"Yes. If he doesn't mind looking like a prat."

She sighed. "You're not taking this *seriously*, are you?"

"Sorry." She really did look adorable when she went into Authorial Fluster mode.

"You know," she said, "this villain has a beautiful woman at his mercy and he hasn't even twirled his moustaches at her yet. Do you think he'd get . . . interested?"

"She's knocked his glasses off. He can't see she's beautiful."

"He can remember what she looked like when he came in, can't he? And he can *feel* her." She smirked devilishly and began to fondle her helpless victim.

I wriggled uncomfortably. Of course, this was just a bit of fun with a woman I actually loved, it was just strange. We hadn't done much role-playing before, and I'd always thought Edith was naturally shy.

She didn't feel shy now. Maybe the role-playing made it easier for her to dress up in ideas she wouldn't normally try out, and Having A Good Reason always helped. Not that she was dressed up in anything at all, at present. "So he's grappling with her," she said, grappling. She tweaked a nipple, and said, "Aha, my pretty!"

"What's wrong with the other one, then?" I said.

"Nothing," she said, caressing it. "You're gorgeous in stereo."

"I don't believe any villain in the history of villainy since Bad King John lost his clothes in the wash has *ever* said 'you're gorgeous in stereo' to any heroine, however lovely."

"No, that was me. Can't you tell the difference between fiction and reality?"

"And was that you?" I asked, as she rubbed her fingertips round and round my nipples.

"Yes. But this is both of us," she said, as she bent down and licked at the left one.

Fine. So I was tied to the bed, while my girlfriend and the villain of her latest novel were molesting me at something-past-four in the morning.

"What's his name?"

"Kevin."

"*Kevin?*"

"Yes. He's had a lifelong complex because of his name and finally went to the bad." One hand traced down across my stomach. "I can't really be a Kevin if I can molest pretty girls like this," she (he) said.

Good thing I don't mind the occasional bloke, even if I really prefer girls, I thought, as she pressed her erection against me.

"Hey, that's *my* one," I complained, as she hit the ON switch.

"No, you can't emasculate me now," said Kevin.

I decided not to remind her that we'd actually bought a harness for a strap-on along with the handcuffs. Intrigued as I was by the sudden appearance of Kevin from whichever dark corner of her subconscious he inhabited, I decided I'd rather wait until a more sensible hour to be fucked by him.

Besides, the heroine *never* gets raped on the first date.

"Can't we just get on with it and go back to sleep? You can introduce me properly to Kevin in the morning."

"I told you not to emasculate me," she said, "but I'll settle for a quickie. I can't go back to sleep like this."

Come to think of it, neither could I. I could see she was excited; there was that pink flush rising up on my little fluffy fair blonde. As for me, 'Kevin's' erection was doing very nicely for me, even loosely pressed where it was as if she'd forgotten it. Edith knew exactly what speed setting kept me ticking over without quite getting me there.

"Ravish me now, sweetie," I said.

"That's supposed to happen later in the book – actually, that wasn't supposed to happen at all, but you've given me ideas. How am I *ever* going to sell this book if she runs off with the villain?"

"Kevin's a comic-Byronic anti-hero," I said.

"Nothing comic about *me*," Kevin said, pouncing on me.

I had to admit Kevin was a damn good kisser. He knew his way around a woman.

"You must have ravished *ever* such a lot of girls," I said, innocently.

"Lots and lots and lots – well, probably half a dozen before you."

"I know that's you, Edith. A bloke would never admit to being that inexperienced."

"But I do know what a woman likes." Grope, grope. She certainly did. I shouldn't be this hot this quickly – and certainly not at this time in the morning. Maybe there was something to this bondage lark after all. I didn't quite feel *helpless*, but I felt surprisingly vulnerable, and I couldn't quite tell whether it was the role-playing or just that we were doing something different.

Also, nobody had ever told me that you could have this much of a laugh in a bondage session. If they had, I wouldn't have believed them. I'd read a few rude books, and most of them had been distinctly po-faced about the whole thing.

Edith, and Kevin, had kissed their way right down to my clit, leaving me to discover that one of the . . . things, about this whole . . . thing, was that it was strange not to be able to move, or grab her hair, or touch her in return. I'd always felt that if I didn't reciprocate in some way it would feel awfully cold and strange for the poor thing, but she didn't actually seem to mind concentrating on me at all.

The handcuffs gave me permission to just lie back and enjoy it. In fact, they *insisted* that I just lie back and enjoy it. So I did. After all, it wasn't my fault. There wasn't a thing I could do except shut my eyes and just *feel*, every move seeming magnified, thrumming through me like the buzzing heat of the vibrator.

Just when I was right on the edge of orgasm, Edith stopped. I couldn't even protest, I was so caught up in it. All I could do was lie there and watch, as Edith lifted the vibrator between her own legs, and teased, and teased, and came, with a muffled shout, and collapsed on the bed.

I didn't even wonder until a moment later how the hell Kevin could get off by inverting his own cock.

"Now that Kevin has finished fucking himself, could he finish fucking me?" I asked politely. "After all, I'm a little tied up at the moment."

"Sorry," said Edith. It had to be Edith – Kevin wouldn't have said sorry. She levered herself to her knees with a ladylike half-sigh, half-groan. "I really feel like a bit of a sleep now, you know."

"You're a woman. Not a bloke. You don't go to sleep immediately you come. So perform your villainous duty."

So she picked up the vibrator, leered at me, and touched it to my clit, and damn me if I didn't come at once.

"Can't get the virgins these days," muttered Kevin. "Nowadays, they're *all* easy."

I was too busy enjoying coming to reply to that. *Something* about the scene, unconvincing male villain or bondage or not, had evidently got to me, because there was a hot glow all the way through me and I couldn't breathe. Until a moment or two later, when I could do nothing *but* breathe.

Both of us were lying there limply but happily.

"Actually, since I'm Edith as well as Kevin, I could probably manage to do it more than once. Where did we put that strap-on?" said my girlfriend, regaining a little more of her energy.

"Oh, over there somewhere," I said, pointing vaguely with my chin and forgetting what a dangerous thing this was to do when Edith couldn't see properly.

She set out, blithely enough, for 'over there somewhere', and promptly ran headlong into the little table her glasses were on.

"Fuck," said Edith, as her glasses folded gracefully to the carpet. She stopped dead, and I heard something else – something small – fall off the table as well. Small, like the key to the handcuffs I was wearing.

"Fuck," said I.

"Sorry," Edith said in a very small voice. That was definitely Edith and not Kevin.

"I want to cuddle you," I said, "but you're still a twit."

"Well, you can't cuddle me yet. If I move an *inch* I'm likely to tread on something very important."

"And if you break your glasses you won't be able to find the key." I strained, but I couldn't get into a position where I could see the glasses. I could see the *key*, though, which wasn't a fuck of a lot of use because the only person who could *reach* the key was Edith, and she couldn't.

"I could try talking you through it," I said.

"I still might stand on my glasses. And I don't know where my spare pair are. I mean, if I had my glasses I could find them."

Eventually, after very carefully inching forward, little step after little step, she nudged the glasses with her foot, retrieved them with a cry of triumph, and fell on the key.

She came back to me clutching the key in her hot little hand. I said, "*Don't* practise seeing whether the villain can get the handcuffs *un*done without his glasses."

She sighed. "Somehow I don't really feel like seeing if Kevin can get it up twice in one night. I think that's broken the mood slightly."

"And danced up and down on it," I said, as she released me. "But what has he got in mind for tomorrow? He has to throw the bound and gagged heroine out of sight into the wardrobe, because somebody might be coming."

Oh no, I thought. A gleam of authorial interest was sparkling in Edith's eyes. "Probably that big wardrobe over there – but it wouldn't be over there. For this story to work it would have to be in that other corner," she said.

If I didn't love you I'd swing for you, my girl, I thought, as I got up and helped her manhandle the wardrobe.

"OK, that will remind you," I said, panting. "Can we do the rest of this tomorrow?"

There are advantages to living with a writer. You get woken up at four o'clock in the morning while they want someone to block out a story idea, and they *really need* someone to help work out whether all the bits fit together, and it can go from mystery to steamy romance in an instant.

I'm very public-spirited, me.

The neighbours probably didn't appreciate us moving the wardrobe, but it was all in the cause of art. Honestly.

Peering Through the Crack

Eva Hore

"Hi, Sheila, it's just me," I said, bursting through the front door. I was running late for a dinner date with my sister, Christine.

I stopped dead in my tracks as I spied her coming out of the bathroom. I'd never seen her looking so hot. She nervously brushed a few wisps of hair that had escaped from beneath a towel that was twisted into a turban on her head, clearly unnerved that I'd seen what she was wearing.

"I . . . er . . . I didn't expect you home so early," she stuttered.

I couldn't keep my eyes off her stunning figure. She was wearing a red and black teddy underneath her robe. It was open, revealing her amazing body. She had beautiful ebony skin and the red complemented her, turning her into a vibrant vamp.

"I forgot something," I said, still staring at her breasts.

She pulled the robe tight around her body and rushed into her bedroom. I stood there looking after her. In the twelve months we'd shared this apartment, not once had I seen her go out on a date, yet these last five Fridays, whenever I got home, she was never here and didn't arrive back until Sunday morning.

When I'd asked her where she'd been, she just said she'd been out with some old schoolfriends. I suggested she bring them around here one Friday. I said I'd love to meet them but she just ignored me.

I was a snoop by nature and the fact that she had that sexy teddy on didn't fool me. Normally she dressed very conservatively. She was a librarian and, believe me, usually she looked the part. Hair pulled up in a bun, horn-rimmed glasses. She looked and acted like a mouse.

On the weekends prior she would just bum around in tracksuits and sloppy clothes. She always had her nose in a book. I must admit I didn't have much time for her, always busy with my own life. I had no idea she was so horny looking.

She was seeing someone, but who? And why the secrecy?

"See you," she yelled, as she passed my door.

I felt so alone when she left. I lay on my bed thinking about her. Dinner with Christine now seemed such a chore whereas before I was looking forward to it.

"Can we skip dinner?" I asked my sister Christine when she answered her phone.

"Yeah, why?" she said.

"Oh, I just don't feel like it that's all," I said.

"You okay?" she asked.

"Yeah, it's just that . . . it's . . ."

Christine knew I had a crush on Sheila. She'd already told me to either tell her or get over it.

"It's what?" she pried.

"It's Sheila. She's going out again tonight and I caught her coming out of the bathroom wearing a very sexy teddy," I blurted out.

"So what! Leave the girl alone. You have to get over this obsession you have with her," she said.

"I'm not obsessing. I'm just curious. Don't you think it's strange, her spending all those weekends away and not telling me anything?"

"I think you're strange. She doesn't have to tell you anything. You're not her mother. Don't bug her about it. It's her own business. I've got another call. I'll talk to you tomorrow," she said hanging up.

I rolled over burying my face in the pillow. I didn't care what she said. I wanted to know what she was up to. Many thoughts and scenarios rushed through my mind. I lay there thinking hard, wondering where she was and what she was up to.

I imagined that I'd followed her out, watched as she ran down the steps, her long hair trailing after her. She'd hop into a cab and her coat would ride up so I'd be able to see the tops of her stockings. Stockings meant suspenders and suspenders meant no ugly panty hose.

I'd keep my distance as the taxi sped through the quiet streets. It would stop in a seedy part of town where there were old warehouses. I'd cut my lights and idle along, just like in the movies. When she knocks on a door someone wearing a dark robe will answer it.

I can't see what the person looks like as the light from inside the room shadows his face. She slips inside and I'm left to wonder what to do next. I decide to cruise by slowly; my lights still off and park just around the corner of the building.

What would happen next?

Faint music would be coming from inside. There are windows but they are too high for me to see into. Skirting around the back I'd find an old milk crate. I take it with me back to a window and balance carefully on it. I'm able to peer inside, just between the crack of the curtain.

This room is a dinning room. A huge wooden table dominates the room with large ornate chairs that could seat about twenty people. Nothing at all mysterious about this room, quite boring actually and then I see someone walk past the room so I'd pull back on instinct, become more interested and grab my crate and go to the other side.

Can't have my fantasy too boring. I'd have to make it more exciting.

This room would be nothing like the other. This one is decked out with what looks like thick and luxurious carpet, with deep mahogany furniture and plush red velvet covers. There is a huge chair, more like a throne, placed at the centre of one of the walls. Small tables and armchairs are scattered about the room.

Large wooden posts are attached to the ceiling at the same end as the throne and there is a crate or cage with wooden bars nearby, an array of whips adorn the wall and in a glass cabinet I spy dildos, vibrators and other interesting toys.

Yes, that gives it a definite intriguing atmosphere.

Voices alert me to the doorway. Sheila is leading the way, wearing a long purple robe. As she walks the gown parts and underneath I see she is still wearing the sexy teddy and definitely stockings and suspenders. Her hair is draped around her like a shawl. Even from this distance I'll be able to see she has her face beautifully made up and as she heads for the throne, others will enter the room. All will be women.

Sheila will be the only one in purple. She'll stand out, look special. Some will be in black, some red and two girls will sit at Sheila's feet wearing white tunics, white see through tunics. I'll peer harder, nearly topple off the crate to see if either of them are wearing underwear.

They won't! Dark nipples will stand out like beacons as the

girls cross their legs to sit on the floor. Most of the armchairs will be taken up. Waitresses, dressed only in a short apron and nothing else, their breasts swaying as they walk will enter as well as two men wearing tight leather pants and no shirts. They'll stand on either side of the girls who are at Sheila's feet, their arms crossed, muscles flexed.

My pussy throbs as I plan which way to go from here.

I'd be intrigued for many reasons. Firstly, that Sheila would be the head of anything as she is normally such a mouse. Secondly, that women would dominate this room. They'd have to be part of some sort of association, which definitely has nothing to do with the library association. Thirdly, naked female waitresses will serve drinks to women who slap them on the arse or pinch their breasts. They'll be so submissive that they show no reaction.

My hand steals down to my pussy and I feel the heat emanating from there and I smile. This is the randiest I've felt for ages.

I can't hear what is being said, the walls would obviously be sound proofed to keep away nosy people like me and I can't even imagine what they would say anyway. The two men will walk from the room and minutes later come back, both holding the arm of a beautiful young woman who they stand her in front of Sheila.

I need to add some drama to this.

Some sort of heated argument will ensue and their body language will be tense. The woman will struggle to move away but the men will hold her firmly in their grasp. Sheila will approach the woman, look her up and down as though she is for sale. One of the girls who had been at her feet will hand her a cushion. Something will be resting on it.

It will be a knife.

Sheila will run the blunt edge of the knife down the side of the girl's face, over her neck and the swell of her breasts. Then down and under her shirt where with one quick upward motion she'll slice off the buttons and the shirt will fall open. The two men will rip it from her arms and discarded it onto the floor.

I really should get into this sort of stuff; it's definitely a turn on.

Now they'll hold her arms more firmly as she begins to struggle. I'll watch mesmerized, as the knife moves under her bra straps and slices through them. Her bra will fall forward exposing a luscious pair of breasts. Now Sheila will trace the knife around her nipples before lowering her head to suck one into her mouth.

She'll laugh while the girl struggles against the men. One of the girls in the white tunic will remove the woman's skirt until she is standing in only her panties and cut up bra. Her gorgeous breasts will be heaving as she continues to struggle.

Sheila will place the tip of the blade at the edge of her panties and slowly inch its way down to the crotch. She'll rip her panties off and with a quick slice into the centre of the bra the woman will stand before her naked.

The woman's body is beautiful. She has dark black hair that hangs over her face as she continues to struggle with the men. Her pubic hair is also dark and stands out against her pale white skin. She'll have a perky arse and long muscular legs.

If this fantasy was real I'd want to go in there and throw myself into the woman's pussy. With all those other women in the room watching me I'd let them rip off my clothes and have their way with me. That scenario will be for another fantasy though.

I'd be so hot watching that I'd carefully slip out of my panties and quickly stuff them into my bag. I'd run my hand over my mound and pussy before sliding a finger into my wet slit. That would feel so good. I'd throw my bag over my back to allow me the use of both hands as I pull back the hood of my clit, smearing some of my juices over it and begin to gently rub it.

My attention will be drawn back to the activities at hand and while fingering myself I'd watch as they lashed her to something on the floor. A waitress is on her knees in front of a woman whose black robe is open, revealing her nakedness underneath. The woman slings one leg over the arm of the chair and the waitress will use a vibrator to stimulate her. Then she'll lower her head; her tongue will flicker out to lick her. The woman will grab the back of her head and draw her in closer, before collapsing back on the chair to enjoy.

While this is going on the two guys will hoist their captive up to what looks like a rack after they have already spreadeagled and tied her to it. They hook the pulley ropes to one of the pillars and then move away.

Sheila will walk around her to admire her body, her fingers trailing over her skin. She'll have a small whip in her hand, and she'll stand in front of the girl, smacking it into the palm of her other hand as though to frighten her. Something is being said but I'll have no idea what. Then she'll lash at the girl's breasts while she begs for her to stop.

This is turning me on. I smear my juices over my clit and rub hard, enjoying the rawness of it all. I'd never been whipped or spanked – well, not like that – and I'm finding it quite a turn on, imagining what it would feel like.

Sheila will continue to whip the girl and I will see faint welts rising over her body before she falls to the floor in front of the girl and begins to lick her and I'll be so turned on just by thinking how my mousy flatmate would be into this sort of thing as I balance precariously on the crate.

Her tongue will roam over the girl's body before she stands and retrieves the whip. She'll take the handle and probe it into her pussy and I'll watch, licking my lips, as she inches it in and then begins to fuck her with it. This will all be too much for me and my juices will run down the inside of my thigh.

Now all the women in the black robes rise and come towards the girl on the rack. Their hands will be all over her, pawing at her breasts, fingers in her pussy and her hole, mouths licking every part of her. The men will not move from their position and from what I can see they certainly won't have hard ons. I'll assume them to be gay! How could you not be turned on by that display?

I can't see much; their bodies will block my view. I'd be so turned on that I'd lean my back against the wall and rub my clit harder, bring on a powerful orgasm and secretively hope that someone is watching me. I'd be as horny as hell. I'd want to go and see my girlfriend Louise but would be hesitant to leave.

An approaching car will make the decision for me. I'd jump from the crate and hide around the back. The car will drive past though, not even slow down. I'd be pretty sure that this is where Sheila has been going every Friday night and know I can always come back every Friday night to watch. I'd need some relief so I run back to my car to visit Louise.

The desire to be fucked and the thought of Louise wearing her big black dildo has me driving like a maniac. I don't tell her what I've witnessed but Louise is wondering why I'm so randy when I practically tear her clothes from her and demanded a good fucking.

The thought of fucking Louise right now nearly has me putting a stop to this fantasy but I want to continue on, to play it out to the end.

We'd spend the night and the next day locked in each other's arms but I make sure I'll be home early Saturday night so I'll be fresh for Sunday morning. I'll confront Sheila about her sexuality and I'll definitely want to see her naked so I'll have to come up with a plan.

I'd be nervous. Butterflies would flutter around my stomach as I bathe and make myself up. I wouldn't be quite sure how to go about it, and by the time Sheila does come home the thought of ravishing her body will be the only thing in my mind.

"Have a nice weekend?" I'd ask as she tries to sneak in.

"Oh, you're up," she'd say, stating the obvious.

"Yeah. Thought I'd get up early and welcome you home," I'd say.

"Why?" she'd ask.

I'd rise from the couch and walk towards her. Her eyes would be open wide; her tongue licking at her beautiful full lips. I'd lift my hand and release the clasp from her hair. It would fall around her shoulders and I'd remove her glasses and place them on the table. Slowly I'd unbutton her coat, slip it down her arms to reveal her sexy teddy that she'd still be wearing.

She'd stand there breathing hard as I soak in her beauty. I'd run my hand down the side of her face and grab the nape of her neck. I'd pull her back by the hair and kiss the hollow of her throat. She'd reward me with a low moan of pleasure.

My tongue will seek out a nipple as I pull her hair back harder. I'd flicker my tongue around, draw it into my mouth to suck on as my fingers roam her abdomen; her mound, and then I'd cup her pussy.

She'd grab at me, pull me into her body as her tongue kisses my mouth with such passion. My hands will be all over her, pulling at her stockings, tearing them in the process, while I try to undo her teddy. She'll laugh, push me away from her, and wiggle her way out of it.

She'll stand there before me only in her ripped stockings and stilettos. I'll lay her down on the white couch, her dark skin standing out beautifully against it. I'd run my hands over her body, cup her beautiful breasts, lick at her dark nipples, smother myself into her cleavage before my hands go down further, into her kinky pubic hair and down to her slit.

I'd open her up like a flower, her outer lips will be like soft petals, her scent intoxicating as my nose nuzzles against her clit. Her hands will massage my scalp, pull me closer to her as the tip of my tongue runs over a stud that will be pierced through her clit.

Her long legs will wrap themselves around my head, crushing me while I devour her. I'll pull back to feast my eyes on her while I quickly slip out of my own clothes. I'd lie on top of her in the sixty-nine position, my legs straddling her head.

I quickly remove my clothing so I can touch myself, massage my breasts, finger myself while I think about what I'd do to her if she was really here in my bed with me.

I'd be fascinated by the colour of her dark skin and hair against my own light complexion and blond hair. My hair would fall over her mound and for a moment the contrast of our colours would hypnotize me. She would pull at my hips, try to drag me down. Her scent would waft up to me, awaken me and I would grind my face into her, allow her juices to smear over my cheeks, lips, chin and mouth.

We'd ravish each other, pleasing, as only women know how. Later we'd lie on the couch locked in each other's arms.

"How did you know?" she'd ask.

"I didn't," I'd lie.

"I didn't want you to know," she'd say.

"Why?" I'd ask.

"Every time I live with a girl, their girlfriends always get jealous and I'm asked to leave. So I decided this time to play it cool, hide who I really was," she'd say.

"I can understand why people would get jealous of you. You're beautiful," I'd whisper into her hair, as I'd hold her tight.

"Come with me," she'd giggle. "I've got something to show you."

She'd lead me into her room and I'd watch her sexy arse sashaying provocatively before me. She'd lay me on her bed and retrieve a box from underneath.

"See anything in there that you like?" she'd ask.

It would be full of dildos and sex toys. Some I've never seen before. I'd pull out a huge black one with a tickler attached. I'd lift my eyebrows indicating I'm interested. She'd laugh and strap it on.

I'd lie back on her bed; my legs open and she'd kneel before me. She'd probe my outer lips, I'd reach up to pull her to me, kiss her hungrily on the mouth. I'd be able to taste myself on her lips and I'd grab her by the arse so the dildo could ram into me. She'd be amazing, having mastered the strokes so that in no time I'd be coming.

Oh, the thought of her and the dildo had me rubbing my clit wildly, my back arching as an orgasm builds up.

Then she'd roll me over, hoist up my hips and have me in the doggy position. This way the dildo would reach into the very depths of me, hitting my g-spot while the tickler tantalized my hole.

She'd be an amazing lover and we'd spend the whole day in bed together. Later, while lying in the bath I'd want to broach the subject of her weekends away.

"So does this mean your Friday nights will change?" I'd ask.

"I don't see why," she'd say, allowing soapy bubbles to slide over my breasts as her hands caress me.

"I just thought maybe we could spend more time together?" I'd ask.

"We have all week," she'd say evasively.

"Yeah I know," I'd say. "But what if I want to take you out somewhere?"

"We'll talk about it when the time arises," she'd say. "What about Louise?"

"What about her?"

"You'll still see her, won't you?"

"Of course." The thought of a threesome would be uppermost in my mind.

"Good," she'd say. "I don't want to spoil what we've got, either. Our living together has always been comfortable."

I'd wonder why she wouldn't mention the warehouse and the group she is involved with. I wouldn't care. I'd hope that one day she'd initiate me into their ways. The thought of being tied up and at her mercy would definitely appeal to me.

It would appeal to Louise too.

Louise . . . Still sexually aroused, I pulled myself away from this fantastic fantasy and decided to ring Louise.

"Hello," she said sleepily.

"Oh, sorry. Did I wake you?" I asked.

"What's wrong?" she wanted to know.

"Just wondering if you'd like some company. Thought we might pull out your box of toys and have some fun tonight."

"Do you know what time it is?"

"No, what?"

"It's four in the morning," she said.

"You're kidding," I said truly surprised.

I didn't realize my fantasy had gone on for so long.

"I'm feeling horny," I said.

"Obviously," she laughed. "Hurry up and get yourself over here then."

We had the best sex ever that night and from now on I intend to conjure up lots of fantasies, thought I might even write about them, see if I can get them published. Let other people enjoy them as much as I did inventing them.

Shiny Things

Elizabeth Cage

Business had been good so I'd decided to rent out my neat little ground floor flat in the quiet cul de sac I'd lived in for the past three years. It was a nice area, "desirable" according to the estate agents, so I knew I'd have no problems letting it. As soon as the ad appeared in the local paper I was inundated with phone calls. I wanted the new tenant to be female. I had this stereotypical idea that a woman would take better care of the place than a man. Not very logical, considering I was one of the untidiest people I knew. My excuse was I'd outgrown the space and that's why there was clutter and dust everywhere. Not today, however. I might live in a sought-after area, but I'd seen enough daytime TV to know you had to make an effort when you were showing people around. So the usually discarded clothes were scooped from the back of the sofa and shoved into the wardrobe, shoes and books were pushed into cupboards and kitchen surfaces were bleached.

Lisa was the first person to view. Lisa Steele. I liked the name. It sounded a mixture of feminine and masculine, vulnerable yet strong. We'd arranged a Saturday morning, not too early (I like my beauty sleep), 11 a.m. to be precise. The other prospective tenants were scheduled to view after lunch. Lisa only lived the other side of town, just a fifteen-minute hop by car, so when it got to 11.35 a.m. and she hadn't appeared I was surprised and a little irritated. Finally, at 11.45 a.m., the doorbell rang.

"I'm soooo sorry," she said sweetly. "Traffic was horrendous. A bus broke down on the roundabout. Hope I'm not too late?" Her voice was breathy and I could see she was flustered. It was a hot, sticky day, with the sun blazing, horrible weather to be stuck in town centre traffic. Her shoulder-length auburn hair was plastered to her forehead and tiny beads of sweat trickled down into the crevice of her luscious full breasts, pushed up to full effect by a plum red halter neck top.

"No worries," I replied. "I'm Kat. Come on in." I gestured her through the door, noticing her long slim legs, smooth and shapely under a short flared denim skirt.

"Glad you found it okay." My eyes continued to travel downwards, admiring her turquoise painted toenails. She had pretty feet. "Nice ankle bracelet, by the way."

She smiled, the silver bells jingling lightly in time with the sway of her hips when she walked. "Thanks. I like shiny things."

"As you can see, this is the kitchen. Small but functional."

The walls were painted white with a hint of pear, with light pine units. I pointed out the fixtures, my mind elsewhere. "Washing machine and fridge. Cooker. Sink. Microwave. All staying. The flat is let as fully furnished."

The window was wide open but the heat from the summer sun was still oppressive. "Would you like a drink?" I asked, feeling very thirsty.

"Mmm, yes please. Something cold."

I opened the fridge, the waft of chilled air very welcome. "Apple and mango juice?"

"Great."

"I'll put plenty of ice in it."

She took it gratefully and sipped. A drop of the golden juice ran down her mouth, and I traced its journey down her chin and graceful neck, onto her chest down to that deep crevice again. She noticed where I was looking and held me in her warm brown eyes for a while, giving a playful smile.

"So how long have you been here? And why are you moving? Not because of some creepy neighbour from hell?"

I laughed. "No, the neighbours are lovely and I'm not just saying that. An elderly lady lives one side and a young couple on the other. All pleasant people. I've been here three years and I shall miss the place, but needs must. What about you?"

"I've been sharing a house with a couple of friends, which was fun at first, but now it's time to find my own place." She'd finished her drink already and I downed mine, aware that I was still thirsty.

"Well, best show you the rest of the flat. The bathroom's there. Again, small but well designed. Power shower, sink, loo. Bath, of course."

"I like that it's all white. Clean and bright."

She was standing close enough to touch, the smell of her sweat mixed with a citrus scent, a heady mixture. I wondered if it was her shower gel – orange blossom, or satsuma or grapefruit. Ripe fruit. I was thinking of those damned breasts again. Stop it, Kat, I told myself.

"And this is the bedroom." My tongue lingered on the word and I hoped she didn't notice.

She seemed impressed. "It's very spacious."

"Big enough." I found myself imagining her spreadeagled on my queen-size bed. I felt like a bitch on heat.

She noticed the big framed photos on the wall immediately. "Is that you?"

I nodded, blushing slightly. "I used to do fetish modelling."

"They're gorgeous. You look so sexy. I love the shiny boots. Those killer heels!"

She looked at me, intrigued and I wondered what she was thinking.

"Through here is the lounge," I continued, sweating. "I think it's a good size."

Her eyes scanned the room, taking in the plasma screen TV, expensive hi-fi system, pink leather sofa, pink blinds, polished wooden floor, pink fluffy rug.

"I know pink isn't to everyone's taste, but it's my favourite colour," I explained.

"Hey, I like pink." She paused, considering her next sentence. "But I didn't expect to see one of those in here."

"I wondered when you'd say something. You can hardly miss it, I suppose. And no, it's not here to hold up the ceiling, as the gas man apparently thought."

She giggled. "I bet. It's very shiny."

"Don't worry, I'll take it down before I leave. If there are any marks on the ceiling they'll be made good."

"Are you a pole dancer then?"

"No. Yes. Sort of."

"Do you dance in clubs?"

"I have done, in the past. But I teach it mainly."

"Wow."

"I'm setting up a mini studio in my new house, with two new poles and mirrors. It'll look great. I have lots of clients."

"I can imagine. I bet you look amazing on that pole." She added, "You could show me."

I hesitated, not expecting this.

"I'd love to see you dance," she continued. "Go on. Please."

It was hard to refuse that sultry voice.

"I have to warm up first."

"Would have thought we were both hot enough already," she joked.

I put some music on and messed about round the pole, feeling unexpectedly self-conscious. I was wearing tiny shorts and a T-shirt, my feet bare.

"I want to see something spectacular," she said.

"Quite demanding, aren't you? So you want to see some pole tricks? Okay, I'll give you tricks." I slipped on my six-inch PVC platform heels and pulled my T-shirt over my head to reveal my cherry-red polka dot bikini top. I then grabbed the pole and deftly executed a sequence of spins before gracefully throwing myself upside down on the pole and hanging by one ankle, at which point my breasts fell out of my bikini top as I knew they would. We both laughed.

"Very impressive," she said and I wondered if she meant the tricks. "I wish I could do that."

"What, get your tits out?"

Now it was her turn to blush. "I meant the pole dancing."

"Anyone can learn, with practice."

"I doubt that."

"I'll show you."

Firmly, I took her right hand and placed it on the pole. "Feel how smooth it is. Now, place your left hand there, about chest height. Lift your outside leg and swing it round the pole, hooking on. Then bring your left leg round to meet it."

She looked dubious but followed my instructions and successfully managed to do a basic move. "Hey, I did it." She was thrilled.

"I told you, didn't I? Want to try it again? Imagine you have an audience."

"I don't have to imagine, do I?"

She repeated the spin, more confidently this time. The track had switched from upbeat house to haunting sexy Goldfrapp.

"That's very good. Shall I show you another trick?"

"I'd rather watch you instead," she replied, twisting a strand of auburn hair around her finger.

"A private dance then?"

She nodded.

I started to move sinuously around the pole, pivoting, circling, spinning, caressing the pole with my legs, my hands, rubbing my body against it, dancing for her. She was captivated as I climbed and inverted, the moves flowing seamlessly into each other. I ran my fingers through my long black hair, down my face, my body, pushing my firm breasts together, my hips snaking. Slowly and gradually, I slipped my bikini straps off my shoulders, keeping my breasts covered, teasing. Finally, while still sitting on the pole, I let my bikini top fall to my waist, revealing my brown nipples, which were already hard. All the time, I retained eye contact with Lisa, noting her expressions, her reactions to the impromptu show she was getting. I slid down the pole and continued the dance, unhooking my bikini top. But instead of tossing it to the floor, I stepped towards her and in a quick movement, wrapped it around Lisa's wrists, tying it securely. She gasped, and while she was deciding how to respond, I pinned them above her head and fastened them to the pole.

"What are you doing?" she murmured, her voice strangely distant.

"What does it look like?" I buried my mouth in her soft auburn hair. "I'm seducing you."

I could feel her heart beating faster, her breathing more rapid now. But she made no attempt to pull free. My fingers found the knot of her halter neck top and swiftly undid it, letting it drop on to the polished floor. She groaned as my hungry mouth found her erect nipples, licking and teasing and sucking while my right hand travelled down her satin skin and unzipped her skirt, letting that, too, fall to the floor.

"No knickers," I remarked. "You are a naughty girl."

My fingers hovered, tracing ever decreasing circles on her soft belly, down, inexorably, to her smooth, shaved pussy. Slowly. Very slowly, making her wait, teasing her. When, eventually, I exerted the lightest fingertip pressure on her clit, she cried out, as if it was a jolt of electricity. To stifle the sound, I covered her open mouth with mine, kissing her hard, using my tongue. At first, she let me kiss her, simply received the pleasure, but soon she was returning my attention, tentatively at first, then greedier until her passion matched my own. We consumed each other, our sweat mingling, our breasts glistening and sliding together, until we were melting. She pushed her eager wet pussy into my hand as far as she could, her body writhing, hands straining, but I wasn't ready to untie her. Yet. I continued to tantalize her helpless juicy clit, muffling her groans and whimpers with my left hand now, lowering my head to nibble and nip her exposed breasts as she wriggled and arched, so close to coming. When I felt her muscles tensing, I took my fingers away and she bit my hand, squealing with frustration.

"Bitch," she muttered, her eyes wide and needy.

I smiled. "Want more?" Before she could reply, I pushed her legs apart and knelt down between them, tonguing her delicious pussy, tasting her, breathing in her essence whilst tantalizing her clit with my right thumb and forefinger. Within seconds, she'd exploded, screaming and bucking, my mouth still clamped on her, my hands now clutching her lovely peachy bum cheeks.

She sighed. "About the pole," she murmured dreamily. "When I move in, you don't need to take it down."

"Why's that?" I replied, wondering whether to untie her before or after I made her come again.

She gave me a cheeky grin. "I like shiny things."

Vavoom

Jay Lawrence

"Oh, that does feel good. Please don't stop!"

Warm fingers massaged the nape of my neck, kneading and circling in small, firm movements. I felt my tension melt away. The girl laughed.

"Some people come here just for this alone."

"That wouldn't surprise me, Kara!"

Tepid water coursed over the crown of my head.

"Could you make it hotter?"

"I'll see what I can do."

"Thank you, sweetie."

Smooth, lightly scented skin brushed my cheek as the girl reached forward to adjust the faucet behind my head. It had to be at least six months since I'd been in for a haircut. I felt almost guilty, cringing inwardly as Kara raised a perfect eyebrow at my split ends. What a gorgeous girl she was, though. A perfect figure. Large, firm breasts and smooth, round hips. She usually wore skin-tight jeans and a loose-necked style of top, so that you could admire her cleavage when she bent to squirt the shampoo onto your hair. I envied her hair, a lush curling waist-length mass that varied in hue from dazzling auburn to jet black, depending on Kara's mood du jour.

"So, what can I do for you today, Mrs B?"

God, she made me feel like a senior citizen. OK, so I wasn't twenty-something like Kara, but I wasn't ready for the scrap-yard yet. I gave my usual response.

"Just trim it to shoulder length, cut me a wispy fringe and add as much volume as you can, please."

"You're sure you don't want to try something new?"

I stared longingly at the deep crevasse of golden skin before my eyes. Kara's breasts wobbled as she briskly massaged the shampoo through my saturated locks. I had an intense urge to reach up and squeeze them. Her fiancé was a lucky guy. I sighed softly.

"Any suggestions?"

It's not always wise to give your stylist free rein but I felt in the mood for taking a chance. Kara started to rinse off the suds, the water nice and hot, just the way I like it.

"Well, what about going a bit shorter than your regular style and adding some colour? It doesn't have to be permanent, so if you don't like it, it'll wash out over a few shampoos."

The young girl looked down at me with an appraising eye.

"You actually have quite a bit of red in your natural shade, so I'd suggest a light auburn tint. I think you'll love it and it'll really bring out those lovely blue eyes."

I blushed. God help me, I actually went as red as the hue the stylist proposed!

"Are you sure the water isn't too warm, Mrs B? You've gone rather pink."

"It's just perfect, thank you, Kara. And I think I'll go with your ideas."

The heat in my cheeks intensified as the girl applied a dollop of conditioner and smoothed it sensuously over my squeaky-clean tresses. I looked blissfully up into a rather concerned pair of green eyes.

"You're not having a hot flash, are you, Mrs B? Would you like a glass of water?"

I stiffened.

"I haven't reached that stage of life yet, Kara. I'm just fine."

It was the young girl's turn to colour.

"Oops! Foot in mouth disease. But it does happen to women in their thirties, you know. My cousin . . ."

"Light auburn, you say? Can I see a shade chart?"

It was rude of me to interrupt but I've battled raging hormones for nearly three decades and the novelty of the topic has long since worn off. Kara entered obedient servant mode and fetched me a chart. I sat up as she swathed my head and shoulders in a towel and vigorously rubbed me dry. A dizzying selection of coloured hair swatches greeted my curious eye. How on earth could I select the right one for me?

"I think I'm going to need some help. I don't want anything too bright."

We left the basin and headed for the big swivel chair in front of the gilt-edged mirror. As usual, I tried to avoid my reflection in the glass. It's not that I'm ugly – far from it, or so I've been told – but the bright overhead light is so unflattering. Kara flipped through the hair samples with a critical gaze. Finally, she selected one.

"I think we should try Vavoom!"

I laughed.

"Well, it certainly has a wonderful name. Let's have a look."

Kara laid the swatch against my cheek, nodded in satisfaction, then showed me the soft light auburn strands. Suddenly, I felt a surge of excitement, a sense of new and thrilling potentials opening up at the hint of a tint. A change of hair colour is like that, if it's a well selected choice.

"I think I'll take you in the back, Mrs B. The beautician doesn't have a client right now and it's much more relaxing than the main salon."

Slightly surprised, I let the stylist lead me, draped in my plastic cape and towel, through a warren of cubicles to a small pink room with a state of the art reclining chair. Kara closed the door and, to my vague concern, locked it behind us. She smiled reassuringly.

"Don't want us to be disturbed. You're rather tense, Mrs B. I'd like to offer you a special relaxing treatment free of charge. I'll do your hair too, of course. But first, I want to try out some special techniques I've been learning at home."

I realized my mouth was hanging open like a fish and promptly closed it. Kara handed me a thick towelling robe and gestured to a screen.

"If you'll just take off your clothes and put this robe on. This is all right with you, isn't it, Mrs B? You do have time?"

"Yes, I suppose so, but tell me – what does this treatment involve?"

The young woman smiled.

"If you don't mind, Mrs B, I'd like that to remain a surprise. I just know you'll find it very helpful. Relaxing."

Hmm. There was something about the way the girl was looking at me. Had she sensed my desire to lavish attention on her luscious boobs? Surely not. I was imagining things. I stepped behind the pretty floral screen and took off my clothes, feeling as nervy and awkward as a patient at a gynaecology clinic. The luxurious robe allayed my fears, however; super-thick, baby soft and lightly rose scented. Lovely. I crept out from behind the screen and lay down on the long leatherette chair. Kara appeared to be fiddling with some kind of electronic box. She turned off the bright overhead light, leaving just a soft pink glow from a silk shaded lamp. Mmm, I was already beginning to relax, with the comfortable seat and the gentle, perfumed atmosphere. The stylist leaned over me and I realized, with a sudden shock, that she was unwrapping the towelling robe.

"I just want to see. Don't worry, Mrs B. Please relax. This is going to be wonderful, I promise."

I held my breath as Kara exposed my naked torso. I have a very average kind of body, a bit plump around the tummy and hips. Quite large breasts of the soft and wobbly variety. Remembering that I had shaved my pussy the night before, I blushed again, glancing furtively down at my round pink Mound of Venus. The stylist turned to the little electronic box. A soft hum commenced as she turned a dial. Then she picked up what seemed to be a round-headed massaging device, attached to the box by a curly cord.

"You see, Mrs B, there is more than one kind of Vavoom. This is number two."

Kara leaned over me, her boobies bulging almost in my face. I relaxed, deciding to enjoy the joyous vista sans guilt. After all, what did I have left to hide? The young woman applied the vibrating massage head to my shoulders. The moment the soft rubber cushion met my flesh it was as if we were intimately connected, Kara and I. Her breasts jiggled perfectly in time with the tiny circular motions her hand performed upon my yielding skin. It felt divine and I told her so. She smiled in satisfaction.

"I just knew you'd love it, Mrs B."

Soft, springy curls of russet hair brushed my nipples and I felt a tiny drop of love-juice ease its way over my plump, nude labia. Kara was going to drive me crazy with this therapy of hers. I wanted to open my thighs to her. I was desperate for her to lower her crimson lips to nuzzle my clit. Suddenly, it occurred to me that she had asked me to lie face-up and, surely, such a massage would normally be done in the reverse position. Hmmm. Maybe there was more to the young lady than met the eye . . .

The whirring rubber cushion completed its shoulder-loosening task and headed south. I gasped as the buzzing sensation edged its way to the outer limits of my right breast. Was she really going to give me such an intimate massage?

"Breast massage is becoming quite popular these days. Stimulating the circulation seems to ease the symptoms of PMS. Would you like to try it, Mrs B?"

I swallowed hard and almost squeaked out an affirmative response. Would Kara gossip about me in the staff room? That lesbian pervert Mrs Bright. Well, too bad. She had started it! My right boob began to wobble outrageously, ecstatic sensations coursing through my blissed-out bod. It was too much. How could the girl keep a straight face; I wondered, as I watched the stylist carefully apply the massage-head to my large pink tits. It resembled a jelly in an earthquake. Carefully, Kara cupped my breast in her free hand, holding it gently as she moved the rubber cushion round and round. My nipples stood to attention, fully erect. My pussy was slick, creamy, juicy. I lay in an agony of ecstasy, a helpless victim to the pretty girl with the electronic box.

"I think I'll turn it up a bit. You do seem to be benefiting, Mrs B."

I bit my lip as the buzz intensified and Kara switched to my other breast. Instead of moving around the chair, she leaned further over me, almost tipping her bountiful cleavage into my face. I decided that she was a sadist and was on the verge of telling her so, when she paused to reach for a large pink bottle labelled "Crème de Aphrodite". With a flick of her wrist she squirted a copious dollop of divinely scented mousse onto my chest and began to massage it all over my tit. I couldn't help myself. I had an orgasm. I tried to suppress it, really I did, but I might as well have attempted to stop the tide. I glanced up at the stylist, feeling desperately guilty as the inner contractions ebbed away. Had she noticed? Smooth warm fingers kneaded my melony mounds, spreading the lovely moisturizing mousse. My boobs glistened. Kara looked pleased.

"I think you're going to see a big improvement, Mrs B. Now, just turn over and I'll do your other side."

I eased myself out of the loosened robe and lay back down on my front. The smooth warm fingers rested on the small of my back.

"Don't think I didn't notice what happened then, Mrs B."

I felt my face grow scarlet and was quite pleased that it was hidden from the girl. Her hand began to caress my buttocks and I moaned softly.

"I should spank you, shouldn't I? Would you like it if I did?"

I was hearing things. I had to be hallucinating. The electronic pulsing had fried my nervous system and addled my brain. I ground my hips against the warm soft surface of the leatherette chair. Almost involuntarily, I pushed my big plump bottom up towards the stylist's hand. I adore being spanked. But I'd never been spanked by another woman.

"Naughty, Mrs B!"

Kara's voice was mildly taunting, very amused. Suddenly, she brought the palm of her hand down smartly against the sensitive under-shelf of my naked rear. I yelped, more from surprise than pain. It was deliciously stingy.

"Having an orgasm in the beauty salon!"

The stingy sensation repeated itself. I squirmed, parting my thighs and beginning to make fucking motions on the chair. I desperately needed further release. Kara began to spank me quite hard, one hand on my back, the other slapping my wobbling buttocks fast and sharp.

"I'll expect a decent tip after this session!"

I mumbled promises of generosity into the chair. I was coming again. My bottom felt hot and happy. It was way too long since I'd last been spanked. As my second orgasm began to break, the young girl pushed her heated fingers deep inside my pulsing cunt.

"Is that better, Mrs B? I bet that feels good. Turn over again and we'll finish your treatment."

I let her take me to a third and final high, her deft, strong fingers spreading my copious juice around and about my swollen clit. I was like putty in the young woman's hands. She could do anything with me. This was therapy indeed. I lay well-oiled and gasping like a fish out of water, as Kara wrapped me in a heated towel.

"I trust I can put you down for a monthly session, Mrs B?"

The minx. We hadn't even started on my new hairstyle. I'd need to take out a loan to pay my salon bills if the girl kept this up. A monthly session? Why, I'd have a daily one if I could afford it . . .

"So, that was 'Vavoom 2'."

Kara laughed.

"Just wait 'til we do your hair. You're going to be a new woman!"

I eased myself up from the oily chair. I could have happily stayed there all day, so deep was my sense of relaxation.

"That's wonderful, Kara. Well, I suppose I did need a bit of a lift!"

The young woman gestured to the floral screen.

"Just get back into your clothes and we'll head into the salon for your colour and cut."

I limped over to the screen, having a bit of trouble regaining the use of my legs. She was potent stuff, Miss Kara. Stifling a giggle, I wondered if it would be safe to ask her for a bikini wax . . .

Flight Risk

Carmel Lockyer

The bar was so elegant I could have been in Manhattan or Paris. Only the monitors showing arrivals and departures revealed the truth.

Heads turned when I walked in. The Versace skirt – split to the thigh – was one reason. The shiny, black, stiletto-heels were another. I'd had my hair stubble cut and bleached platinum blonde, it was ultra-short with the design of a Celtic knot razored into the back above the nape. I looked dangerous and I knew it. I sat at a table, letting the skirt slide away from my hip, revealing my burgundy hold-up stockings. I smiled at a couple of men who clearly thought their airport wet dreams had come true, and something in my smile made them look away nervously.

I lifted my spritzer so I could watch a pretty girl over the top. A very pretty girl. She was wandering around the airport, introducing herself to upscale female travellers, talking to them for a few minutes, and then presenting them with an envelope. The whole process had a vaguely oriental feel to it – from the golden, Oriental-style tunic she was wearing, with its wide pale, green sash – to the deferential bow with which she said goodbye. She wasn't Oriental, though. She was small enough, and her long black hair could give that impression from the back, but her tiny, up-tilted nose and freckles destroyed the illusion. She had long legs, slender but well-muscled, the kind of legs that grip tenaciously.

I let her catch me looking at her, before lowering my eyes to her small, high breasts. She blushed.

I beckoned her over.

"You're selling something," I said.

She nodded.

"Why don't you try and sell it to me," I invited.

She went into her sales routine as if on auto-pilot. Had I heard of Venus Spas, she asked?

No, I hadn't.

They were the most exclusive, the most cosseting, the most female-centered experience available to a woman, she said.

I snorted, to let her know I doubted the accuracy of that claim. She faltered a second before recovering.

A visit to a Venus Spa would make any woman's holiday or business trip complete. The stress of flight delays could be eased away right here, in the mini-spa attached to the departure lounge. Alternatively, the Venus Spa at my destination or stopover point would soothe away travel weariness and send me out as fresh as a rose. She grinned at me, no doubt thinking I was the kind of rose that was mainly thorns. I grinned back. She raised an eyebrow. I shook my head.

"I'm not the spa type," I said, and watched her face become smooth and blank with disappointment. She was working on commission, I thought.

"But I'll buy you a drink in your lunch break," I added.

She blushed again. "I'm off for an hour at 12:30," she muttered, before skittering off to try and sell her spa experience to somebody else. I sat back – I had seventeen minutes to wait.

I saw her hand her envelopes to another kimono-wearing girl, so I stood, throwing back my drink and strode across the airport to gather her up. Her daffodil-yellow ballet pumps barely touched the ground, I moved so fast.

"Where are we going?" she asked. "Aren't we having a drink here?"

I replied by bundling her into a taxi. The journey was swift and silent. Several times she looked up and began to speak, but fell silent. I hustled her through the lobby of a chain hotel and pushed my card key into the bedroom door.

"Look . . ." she said, but I put my hand over her mouth and held it there while I eased her into the room.

She gave up all pretence of resistance. Her dark eyes got darker and she licked her lips invitingly. She swayed towards me, until her hips and breasts brushed mine. I felt tiny electric shocks where our flesh touched, and those little sparks moved through me like fire, making me hot, making me wet, making me want to come.

I put my arms round her, grabbing the ends of that stupid sash. "I'm wondering if this thing is long enough to tie you to the mattress," I said. Immediately, she lay down on the narrow single bed.

Decisions, decisions. Should I tie her hands and leave her legs free, or tie her legs and leave her hands free? If I tied her hands I would be able to push her legs open and tease her with my tongue – that would be great, but I'd only be able to see her up close. If I tied her legs though, I could pin her arms with one of mine while I hand-fucked her – and I would have a great full-length view as she came.

"Bev?" she said. "I've got to be back in an hour."

It broke the mood. I glared.

"Sorry!" she said. "Sorry, Bev. I mean – sorry."

I swatted at her with one end of the silk and she grabbed it, pulling me down to kiss me. I lifted her right arm above her head, tying the apple-colored material to her wrist, before reaching behind the headboard with the fabric, and knotting it round her left wrist.

"Now I'll teach you a lesson, Anna," I said.

I stepped back from the bed slowly, and turned in a circle, letting her get a good look at me.

"Do I look good?" I asked, knowing I did.

"You look gorgeous," she replied. "Where did you get those amazing clothes?"

"Dress agency – I hired the entire outfit," I said, kneeling on the bed, pushing her feet up and to one side, so she was curled like a baby. Under the kimono she was naked, and I paused to look at my favorite view.

Anna's slim hips hid a surprise – she had a lush vagina, with gorgeously ripe plum-shaded lips. And she was so receptive that if I brushed my hand over her thick pubes, she would moan and thrust her hips upwards. At first I'd thought she was faking it, but no, she really was so hair-trigger, the slightest touch would get her writhing and hot. A dirty girl, a very dirty girl indeed.

I held her ankles with one hand, and dragged the fingers of my other hand across her tight, high buttocks. She thrashed her head, her hands pulling on the silk bindings. She was going to pay dearly for breaking the spell of my carefully choreographed scenario. I glanced at my watch, letting her see me do it, before sliding one finger inside her.

She was slick and hot. She tried to spread her thighs but I held her ankles tight, keeping her feet pinned to the bed. It was an arousing picture. Her arms were tied crucifix style, her hair flowed across the pillow like ink, and her nipples showed sharply through the tunic. Her body twisted sharply at the waist, where the yellow fabric was rucked up to reveal her legs. Her knees were bent and almost touching her left arm and her feet, still in ballet pumps, were kicking against my hand.

"Please," she said.

I grinned and looked at my watch again, before taking her top ankle with my free hand. I separated her legs and pressed them to the bed. Immediately her hips lifted, just as I'd guessed they would. I ran my tongue along her slit, tasting her without opening her. She tasted sweet, an almond flavour. The first time I'd mouth-fucked her, I'd wondered if she used some kind of lube or lotion but that was simply how she was – her juices were addictively good.

Now my tongue probed her, feeling soft flesh, dipping deep and feeling her body responding, every muscle rising, like a flower turning to the sun. I held her on the edge of orgasm, pulling my mouth away whenever she got too close, before lowering it again to her keep her simmering. Soon she began to curse me, then she moved into begging and finally she became completely incoherent, moaning and shaking her head. She was so lost in pleasure that I envied her. I lifted my hands from her ankles and she didn't move, as though the need for orgasm had pinned her down. I took a final look at my watch, and stood up.

"Anna?"

She groaned. I bent and untied her hands.

"You've got five minutes to get dressed and down to the lobby for the shuttle bus to the airport. If you miss it, you'll be late for work – there isn't another one for half an hour."

She groaned again, reaching down to bring herself off. I stopped her by grabbing her wrist.

"Four minutes, or you'll be very late for work," I said. "And next time don't spoil things, Anna. Remember to stay in character."

Now she realized I was serious. She grabbed the sash and tried to tie it, but her hands shook too much, so she bundled it up and carried it. I pointed to the mirror and she saw the mess her hair was in. She was still trying to rake it into shape as we ran out of the lobby. I flagged down the shuttle and waved goodbye to her.

Did Anna truly have what it took? Okay she was a dirty-minded girl, wandering around the airport with a naked ass, and she loved to fuck, but real adventure took a wildness she hadn't shown yet. In fact, if I hadn't been asked to cover somebody else's holiday shifts last month, I'd never have noticed her. Working in her part of the airport for a fortnight had gradually brought her into focus. Low key, that's what she was, I decided.

I took a taxi back to the airport and sat in the bar again. Anna passed and re-passed, looking crumpled, never acknowledging me, until her break. She headed for the Calvin Klein shop. I threw down my drink and followed.

She waved at the girl behind the shop counter and went into a changing cubicle. I flashed my airport ID and followed. Anna was ready for me. As soon as I pulled the louver door shut, she pushed her hand under my skirt, grasping my pubes and tugging gently, before slipping two fingers into me. I turned her to face the mirror and pushed up the tunic, so I could watch as I hand-fucked her. It wasn't easy, both of us competing to make the other come first, and both watching in the mirror. Remaining silent was almost impossible. Anna was on tiptoe, like she always was when we fucked standing up, her leg muscles bunched up like a ballerina's. I was fighting to stay in control, but seeing her fingers jamming into me, while mine worked into her, was crazy. We were so different; she pushed her hips forward, her head whipped around, her free hand pushed hard on her mons, trying to feel my fingers inside her. I squeezed my thighs around her hand, my head tipped backwards as I got closer to coming, and with my free hand I tweaked my nipples, hard. When she came, she sank her teeth into my shoulder to stop yelling out. When I came, I bit my tongue for the same reason.

We must have both failed to be silent because the girl behind the counter was wide-eyed when we exited, giggling and rosy-faced. I swatted Anna on the backside and headed out of the mall.

Back at the hotel I laid out my toys – a CD player, a glass dildo, lubricant and some bondage tape. I used my master key-card to open the next room and stole its ice-bucket, checking the ice-machine in the hall was operational. Then I waited for Anna to finish her shift.

Her knock at the door was tentative. She must be worried about I had planned for her.

When she saw the dildo she gasped. It was a beautiful long, fat device, with seven ridged rings of coloured glass dividing the clear glass sections. Each ring was a different rainbow colour and with the tip and the final section, the whole device added up to nine and a half inches of elegant heaven. I stood behind her, tugging on the silk sash which by now was as crumpled as old wrapping paper. As soon as it was free, she began to unbutton the tunic. When it was open she tried to turn to face me, but I held her still and wound the silk sash around her eyes, making a blindfold, being careful to cover her ears with several layers of the cloth. I turned her gently and pushed the tunic away until she was naked. I slid my hands over her shoulders and high breasts, her slim waist and gently curving stomach before hooking my fingers into her vagina and feeling her wetness. She gasped. I pushed her onto the bed where she immediately spread her legs wide and held her labia open with both hands, inviting me to take her.

I picked up the dildo and put it down again. Anna was wet enough but I wanted her so slick that I could get the whole thing inside her as fast as blinking. I picked up the lubricant and began to coat her dark lips and inner contours with it. Her hands began to help, sliding over her flesh in time with mine. I moved my hands away and placed the dildo in the ice-bucket of warm water that stood ready. I pushed her hands over her head.

"If those hands move an inch, Anna, then I'm going to stop, and nothing in the world, no amount of begging and pleading, will make me start again. Understand?"

"Yes, whatever you say, anything you want. I understand."

She didn't of course, she had no idea what was coming next, but once she'd promised I knew she'd do what she'd said.

When I slid the glass shaft into her, she moaned with pleasure. I pumped her half a dozen times, just enough to get her hips bucking against its hot surface, then took it away again, circling her clitoris with my forefinger while I pushed the dildo deep into the ice in the other bucket. This time when the glass penetrated her she gasped – the cold was a total surprise – but the shape of it was what she craved, so she was perfectly balanced between pleasure and shock. She couldn't put her hands down to feel the dildo as it approached her, and so she was doubly agonized, the uncertainty and the need to keep to the promise she'd made. Delicious.

I alternated again and again, never letting her guess what was coming next. Sometimes it was cold twice in a row, sometimes heat. I was careful to make sure the music on my little CD player was loud enough to cover the sound of the ice crashing around, but between the silk over her ears and the moaning and begging she was doing, she probably wouldn't have heard anyway. Finally I let her come – this time she didn't have to stay quiet and she screamed her pleasure out loud.

I looked at the bondage tape, then at my watch. I was nearly out of time, but there were still just enough minutes left to drive her crazy. I lifted the blindfold to her forehead so she could see me, and kissed her briefly. Then I pulled her arms to her sides and rolled her one way and then the other, binding her wrists to her thighs and her upper arms to her shoulders. Her small breasts were pushed upwards by the tape to give her a tiny cleavage, into which I dripped lubricant. I slid the dildo into the narrow gap between her breasts, forcing them apart, and moved it gently against her as I straddled her, lowering my lips to her nipples and teasing them with my tongue and teeth. She began to whimper. I pushed her breasts closer together over the dildo, pinching and rolling her nipples between my fingers, then straightened up and pushed the dildo, heated by her skin, straight into my own cleft. I felt her head lift as she watched me begin to thrust the shaft deeper into myself, pumping it hard. Her vision was limited by the skirt, which fell across my body and hers, so what little she could see was dark – for example she couldn't know yet that I'd bleached my pubes too, so that they were the pure white of spun sugar. That was a surprise for later.

For now, all she knew was that she could see a little and touch nothing and that my orgasm was approaching so fast that in a few moments I would come. Just before I did, I reached out with my free hand and pulled down the blindfold again so that she couldn't see a thing. I heard her groan of disappointment mingle with my own moans of pleasure as the hot glass brought me to a peak of pleasure that left me panting and exhausted above her. Slowly I slid the dildo out of myself, feeling my vaginal walls contract around it, trying to hold on to the sheer slippery sides, unwilling to let go of this instrument of pleasure. But they had to. I had to. It was my turn to be due at work in thirty minutes.

I lifted the blindfold again and kissed her much more slowly, as I unpicked the bondage tape that had held her quiescent beneath me. She responded by digging her nails into my back, trying to pull me down on top of her. I was tempted, but I didn't have the time.

She sat up as I moved to the wardrobe. I knew she was watching, so I made a little show of taking off the designer gear and folding it into my briefcase before I pulled my work blues from the rail. I kept my back to her though, wanting those candy-floss blonde pubes to be a treat she hadn't been prepared for.

Anna loves a woman in uniform. She likes my security kit so much, she's managed to fuck herself with my extendable truncheon and the day I gave her a walkie-talkie tuned to the same frequency as mine, she talked so dirty to me at work, I locked myself in the custody room to masturbate.

She was biting her lip. I put on my cap and adjusted it, watching her in the mirror.

"I haven't forgotten our deal, Bev," she said. "Thank you for this amazing anniversary. I know next month it's my turn to help you celebrate our getting together."

I nodded. When I'm in uniform Anna likes me stern and silent. I could tell by her taut nipples that she was turned on all over again.

"I promise you, Bev, that when it's my turn to come up with an adventure, I'll do something totally outrageous."

I let her see doubt in my face. I really didn't think she'd got what it took to play this kind of game. It was a pity, but there it was. Real adventure requires a certain kind of spirit, a willingness to take risks, and I still didn't think Anna was equal to the kind of demands that would make on her.

I took the shuttle back to work. After a while I was called to a passenger who'd locked herself in a toilet cubicle. When I got there, one of my male colleagues was outside. Apparently he'd tried to help, but she'd yelled her head off about a man being in the "ladies". I grinned, mock-saluted and headed inside.

There were women all over the place, with bags and cases and duty-free shopping. I located the cubicle, and pushed the door. To my surprise it opened a little before being blocked by the soft pressure of a body.

"Hello?" I said.

"My hand is stuck in the toilet-roll dispenser," said a heavily accented voice. It didn't fool me though – the accent was good, but the voice was unmistakably Anna's.

I squeezed through the gap. She was standing with one foot on the closed toilet seat, tunic hiked up again. As soon as she saw me, she thrust her fingers deep into her slit, and began to yell and moan at full volume. I could hear the women crowding around the door.

"Anna, stop it!" I hissed.

She grinned. "Play along, it's a game," she said.

I couldn't help grinning back. So while she brought herself off loudly, I interjected comments like, "Nearly there madam, sorry about the pain," and, "Okay if you can just bend your fingers a bit I think we'll soon have you out of here," until she'd come.

I led her out, into a circle of awed, chattering women. She shook her hand as though it hurt and clutched at me.

"Thank you officer," she said. "I couldn't have done it without you." Then she winked.

I continued my rounds with a smile on my face. I'd misjudged her. I couldn't wait for my adventure in a month's time – Anna was well up for it!

Bringing Back the Light

Sophie Mouette

We were in the kitchen, lingering over empty bowls that had held minestrone, watching snowflakes waft promisingly downward and then evaporate upon hitting the muddy ground, when Gail asked, "So, are you coming to my parents' on Christmas?"

I shrugged, trying to look nonchalant. "Not sure, yet. I appreciate the invitation, but . . ."

Gail came around behind my chair and kissed the top of my head. "But the commercial holiday with the cast-of-thousands thing isn't to your taste? It's not really mine, either, but it's my parents and my three siblings and their spouses and their kids. That makes it a little easier."

She sighed. "Would you believe Brett's letter to Santa this year was three pages long?"

"Big handwriting?" Brett was her seven-year-old son.

"He used my dad's computer to make sure Santa could read it! And most of the stuff on it is either TV tie-ins or war toys." She shrugged. "What can you do? It's not like I can separate him from the world."

I leaned back against her. "Even if you did, it wouldn't help. When I was Brett's age, my parents were living off the grid up in the Cascades and home-schooling me." Which Gail probably had guessed, me having a name like Yarrow Dragonwind. "My grandmother sent me Barbies and I got hooked on them."

Gail roared with laughter. "Yarrow, admit it! You just loved those big Barbie breasts, even when you were little."

Relieved by the change of topic – and knowing she'd relish an opportunity for spontaneous sex while Brett was safely at a friend's house for the afternoon – I turned around my chair so I could cup her breasts. "If I liked Barbie breasts, it was because I didn't know how much fun real ones were. Especially yours." Gail's weren't exactly Barbie-proportioned, but they were lovely and full on her otherwise small frame. That was nice, but what I adored about them was their sensitivity, how even a light caress would distract her and anything more serious would turn her brains to mush.

It was always fun, and sometimes it was damn convenient. Right now I really didn't want to talk about Christmas with her family.

It's not for the reasons you might think. After Gail's disaster of a marriage, they were so delighted to see her with someone who made her happy that they'd have welcomed a fire-breathing three-headed Martian if it were good to Gail, let alone a harmless granola dyke. And all of Gail's relatives whom I'd met were genuinely nice and eager to make me feel like part of the family.

If anything, that made it worse. I could have handled a holiday soap opera in the role of The Queer Daughter's Dicey Girlfriend. But the idea of spending Christmas with a close family made me want to hide under my duvet with a pile of hankies and not come out until spring.

Concentrating on making Gail writhe in sexual ecstasy seemed like a much better plan than working myself up into a panic. But even that pleasure only took me so far.

Her hot, responsive body distracted me nicely for a while. I tongued her nipples until she begged for mercy, then pulled her jeans off, knelt between her legs and savoured the smoky, spicy delight of her until she cried out. She came, squirting as she often does, splashing onto the kitchen floor, and I laughed and used her shirt to wipe it up. But when she went to reciprocate, I couldn't lose myself in the sensation. Perched on the counter, I felt her clever hands and tongue doing things that would usually work like magic. Instead of getting all juiced up, though, I found myself getting more and more melancholy.

Finally, Gail noticed that, while I wasn't exactly crying, my eyes were at least as wet as my pussy. She stopped what she was doing and just held me. I wrapped my arms and legs around her, pressed my face against her shoulder and just shook. I couldn't really cry. It had been too many years and I had cried myself out. Crying would have been easier.

Finally I could talk. "I hate Christmas," was what came out.

"Something to do with your parents?"

I nodded. "Dying in that fire when I was in college, with my little brother. It was Christmas night – that's the part I don't usually tell people because it bothers them too much. And Oak was . . ."

Gail did the math. "He must have been about the same age as Brett. Okay, I can see why you hate Christmas, and why Christmas with my family is scary."

"It was never a holiday we celebrated, so I don't even have good memories to balance the horror. It's just the day my whole family died."

"You must have some good memories of this time of year. What about Winter Solstice – Yule?"

Gail hadn't been raised pagan as I had, but it was something she'd become interested in since we'd been together. She embraced the principles of it, but was still learning about the rituals and the history. Just yesterday we'd discussed the pagan origins of Christmas, agreeing that the Christian holiday itself had been almost buried in a snowstorm of commercialism.

I sighed. "That one's got too many good memories. My last Yule with my family was almost perfect. We did a beautiful ritual out in the snowy woods behind the house, and then came inside and lit candles everywhere and exchanged gifts – we never gave big presents, just some small thing that would be meaningful – and stayed up until dawn to praise the sun's return. Only I was a little distracted because I had a new girlfriend and was leaving the next day to spend the rest of break with her. The house burned down while I was digesting my first Christmas dinner."

She shook her head, kissed me again, and pulled away from me long enough to put on tea water and let us both get re-dressed. By the time we were snuggled on the living room couch, tea in hand, I was composed again, trying to pretend my meltdown didn't happen, and ready to apologize when it was clear that Gail wasn't going to let me ignore it. "It was almost fifteen years ago. I don't know why it's affecting me this much . . ."

She set down her cup and took my free hand between both of hers. "What did you do on the winter holidays until now?"

"Hid. Went to the movies, got takeout, found something to read that would engross me. For a few years I took extra shifts at work – they always need nurses on the holidays – but the ER turned out not to be the best place to be. Sometimes I went on vacation to someplace like Martinique or Jamaica, where it didn't feel like Yuletide. I'd like to try to be with your family, for your sake, but I'm afraid it'll dredge up memories."

She squeezed my hand. "What we need," she said, "is to make some holiday memories of our own. I'm going to go make some phone calls."

I must have made some confused noise, because she added, "The Winter Solstice is the twenty-first, right? I'm going to get a sitter and we're spending the night at your place. And while we're there, we're going to create a holiday celebration that's ours and ours alone."

The day of the Winter Solstice was cool and blessedly clear. Throughout the short day, I'd enjoyed catching glimpses of the mountains in the distance, unshrouded by rain or snow. I'd had to work, but Gail, a teacher, was off for the week and had spent the day at my house puttering. The sun was setting – a rare treat, in Seattle, to see a proper sunset instead of rose-tinged rain clouds – and a pale quarter moon was already hanging low at the horizon when I got home. Gail came to the door carrying a sprig of mistletoe and held it over my head as she pulled me close with the other arm. We didn't need mistletoe, but it made me smile.

When I walked into the house, I gasped. When I'd left in the morning I had a bare Scotch pine in the corner of the living room and that was it for decoration. Bought on Gail's instruction, it was the first tree I'd had in my orphaned adult life. Now pine branches and garlands of princess pine were festooned on the mantle and doorways, covering the tables, even strewn on the hardwood floor. The warmth of the house released their green, fresh-air fragrance. The room was full of unlit white candles – votives in protective glass holders, a nod to my uneasiness with fire. In the centre of the room sat the coffee-table altar we'd constructed over the last few days, a simple affair with cotton batting for the snow that would not coat the ground this year, holly and oak branches for the Holly King and the Oak King who battle for the love of the coming Spring, and a bunch of red roses in a gaudy peppermint-striped vase because Gail and I both love them and it just felt right. A picture of the two of us was propped against the vase.

On a table next to the altar was the ritual meal we had devised: pomegranate seeds, baked brie with apples, locally made smoked salmon, a bottle of Pinot Noir from a winery we had visited together over the summer, and, in honour of those boar's heads that turn up in the descriptions of old-time Christmas feasts, spareribs and pork wontons from our favourite Chinese place. A chocolate fondue simmered over a candle, the only one already lit in the house. Bright red and white candy canes decorated the areas not covered with plates. It wasn't like any holiday meal either of us ever had (my childhood memories involved a lot of home-canned vegetables), and that was the point. And it was all chosen so we could feed it to each other. The food added its own fragrances to the scent of pine and the faint honey-sweetness of beeswax candles.

"It's so beautiful!"

"No. It's just decorated. You're beautiful." She kissed me again, helping me slip out of my coat. "Go change into something comfortable," she suggested.

I stripped off my uniform and shoes and threw on a loose, comfortable caftan. When I returned, she had poured wine for both of us, as well as some in the chalice on the altar.

"Did you see the sunset?" she asked as we settled on the sofa. I nodded. "I spent some time meditating on it," she said. "About how short the day was, and how long the night would be. I can understand how our ancestors would have been frightened by the days getting shorter and shorter, and how they felt they needed to have a ritual to bring back the sun."

I nodded, savouring the smoke and berry flavours of the wine. "It made them feel in control."

"Now we have scientific proof of how it works, but ritual is still important in our lives," she said. "Which is why we're doing this, even now. Right?" She stood, extending her hand to me.

"You put it better than I could have, love." I smiled and thought about what she had said. "Because I was raised pagan, it sometimes becomes a reflex to me, like going to church might be for someone else. It's all fresh to you, and you remind me what it means. Thank you!"

Together, we lit all of the candles in the room, bringing light into the growing darkness. As we did, we talked and meditated on the wheel of the year. The Solstice heralded the birth of the sun and also the divine son, the saviour god. Whether you called him Jesus or something else, the sentiment was the same: a promise of renewal against the darkness and cold of winter.

Soon the room flickered with candlelight. Standing there, in the warm glow, I felt the stress melt away from me as the positive energy of the season coursed through me. This was *our* night, Gail's and mine. This was our ritual. It wouldn't cause the sun's return, but it celebrated the growing sunlight, the inevitable change from one season to the next.

We sat on the floor in front of the food, and fed each other bites: sweet pomegranate, smoky salmon, smooth brie, tangy Chinese, interspersed with sips of wine and luscious kisses.

"I think," Gail said, "we might be better off getting out of our clothes, so we don't drip chocolate on them."

I willingly let her help me out of my caftan, and then I returned the favour, noticing that she had also worn things that were easy to get off. I didn't usually do rituals sky-clad except in high summer – it wasn't practical in the Pacific Northwest and paganism is at heart a practical religion – but in a cozy house with only my beloved there, it seemed like a wonderful idea.

Make that an awesome idea, in the literal sense of the word. In that dimly lit room, rich with evergreen fragrance and illuminated only by candles, the beauty of her body stunned me. "You are Goddess," I whispered, and knelt to press my face between her thighs.

I felt her curl her fingers into my hair, fingers tightening reflexively as my tongue whispered over her clit. So I was surprised when she eased my head away.

"Not so fast," she whispered. "We have all night."

She pulled out the massage cushion and had me lie facedown on it. I purred as her fingers kneaded tension from my shoulders, as her palms lightly caressed my back. I shivered as she moved down to my ass, but alas, she didn't stop there. Her hands trailed to my feet, and I relaxed into her famed, delicate foot massage.

"Tonight's the longest night of the year," she said as her fingers pressed into the ball of my right foot with just the right amount of pressure not to tickle. "The night when we celebrate that, in fact, *it is* the longest night, and the nights will now start to get shorter, and the days longer. When we celebrate the return of the light while savouring the night's own joys."

Her voice was soft, hypnotic, lulling me into a trance.

"Imagine a ball of golden light," Gail continued. "It's surrounding your feet. It's safe and warm, bringing nothing but comfort and energy."

This was a basic meditation, but one I'd usually done alone. It took on a whole new dimension with her hands caressing me.

Those hands, coated in eucalyptus-scented oil, slid around to my ankles, then up to my calves. Gently she massaged the muscles there, all the while encouraging me to envision and feel the peaceful light.

And I did. Meditation has always come easily for me, probably because I learned it so young. It was a simple thing for me to slip into the mental state required, to blank my mind or to fill it with a particular thought or vision. I believed in the lines of energy that encircled the earth, and was able to tap into them. Now, that energy was golden light to me, moving up my body at the same rate as Gail's hands, relaxing and reinvigorating me.

When Gail reached my thighs, I started to tense with anticipation, but she crooned and stroked until I settled down again. It wasn't that I wasn't getting aroused, because I was – it was more that there was no urgency. My clit tingled, but I was more focused on the sensations of the intimate but not entirely sexual massage, and on the light that came with it.

Bit by bit, inch by inch, my muscles lost their tightness. I floated gently, only half-aware when Gail helped me turn over. She massaged my scalp, caressed my temples, worked her way back down. She reached my feet again and, like a good masseuse, didn't abruptly cease contact with me. One hand slid up my leg as she shifted, and I was dimly aware of her curling on her side next to me.

The caress of her lips against mine was blissful. I thought I heard her say "don't lose the light" before her tongue stroked against my bottom lip. Our kisses were soft, sensuous, rather than the almost-frantic quality they often took. How long had it been since we kissed this way, like new lovers exploring each other for the first time? I wondered dreamily. And why had we stopped?

She kissed my throat, tongued the warm sensitive hollow behind my left ear. Her hands, still soft from the oil, didn't miss an inch of skin on my torso, and her lips didn't miss much, either.

My right hipbone became the object of her worship. I had no idea of the nerve endings that existed there, and how directly linked they were to my pussy. She worked with excruciating, but wonderful slowness from there across my belly, teasing the hollow of my belly button until I would have sworn it was glowing from all the bright and loving attention. Then my ribcage enjoyed the same treatment, each usually unregarded inch kissed and stroked.

It certainly wasn't a disappointment when she closed her

mouth over my nipple, but it was almost a shock, this move from magical intimacy to something more pointedly sexual. But as she suckled the sensitive nub, I found the magical feeling growing rather than dissipating as I had feared. My whole body was filled with golden warmth, from my hair to my toes, but more and more it was focused between my legs. I was aroused, and my sense of need was increasing, but still I floated in a timeless, trancelike state.

My mind was lost in sensation, but I shifted my hips restlessly as the pressure in my cunt grew, like an expanding ball of light. Then her hand was there, warm and gentle, stroking my lips apart, exploring my wetness. "You are Goddess," she whispered, echoing my words from earlier, "Be thou light." She murmured in delight as she brought her fingers to her mouth, then brought her mouth to my moist core.

The golden glow bloomed within me, then exploded outwards as she brought me home.

"How're you doing?" she asked after sliding back up and spooning her body against mine, one leg thrown over my hips in warm possession.

"All glowy and tingly." Usually after an orgasm, I was happy but ready for round two (or three or . . .). This time, I felt languid, drifting, still feeling delicate aftershocks tremoring my clit.

"Good," she said, nuzzling her face into the hollow of my collarbone.

Lest you think I abandoned her, I did rouse myself after a long and delightful cuddle and treat her to the same attention that she'd lavished on me. I took the light energy that she'd given me and shared it back with her, massaging and caressing her until we were wrapped together in its glowing strands.

Sometime after that, I remember her pulling the quilt from the sofa over us. That was the last thing I knew until she was nudging me awake.

"Wah?"

"Look, Yarrow. We've brought back the light."

She was right. Through the sliding glass doors that led to the narrow deck, I saw the faintest glow on the eastern horizon. Pale orange tendrils of light parted the long night's gloom.

Something similar stirred within me. I still felt the residual golden glow, and I knew something had changed for me on that long, dark night. Tentatively I reached out and touched the memory of my parents, of my brother Oak, expecting a raw flash of grief. Instead, I found sadness, yes, but a sadness that glinted warmly with love. I missed my family terribly, but they lived on in my memory. Finally, I thought, I might be ready to admit another family into my heart.

Slowly, gently, the wheel of life had turned.

In the end, I went to Gail's family Christmas extravaganza. I chatted with her parents, laughed with her siblings, played with her son and nieces and nephews. They were kind enough to allow me to put a picture of my parents and Oak on the mantle, to be remembered.

I wish my parents and my brother could have met Gail. They would have loved her almost as much as I do. They would have thanked her, if they could, for bringing back the Solstice light in me.

The Instructress

Nicky B.

The smoke began to vanish with the light summer breeze; Sharon had a look of horror on her face and her hands gripped hard on the dashboard.

She sat back in her seat and looked at Suzie, her face went from shock to anger.

Suzie smiled in a hope of defusing the situation then decided that words would be better

"I love the smell of burning rubber in the morning!"

"Well, you have no problems regarding your emergency stop reaction time. How about you try not to skid next time?"

Driving instructor Sharon looked in her mirror to see the trails of tyre tracks still smoking a little on the road behind.

She had been teaching for a few years now and it was in danger of accelerating her ageing process.

Her blonde hair would disguise any grey easily but frown lines would be a different matter, though she did enjoy the job and the independence – and the chance to regularly meet new people.

Suzie felt like a naughty schoolgirl and shrank back in her seat; her humour had not gone down too well.

Her dark curly hair and low cut tops usually got her out of anything – or into it – but this driving instructor was a stern, hard nut to crack.

"Shall I drive on now?" Suzie asked sheepishly.

"Yes! Don't forget – mirror, signal and manoeuvre – rather than cardiology!"

Suzie giggled; she could tell that her stone-faced instructor was lightening up – and why not? Sharon had a date tonight and it was certainly going to end up in her bedroom.

Suzie checked her mirror, brought the car's clutch to biting point and peered back over her right shoulder. The engine stalled and Sharon rolled her eyes skyward.

"Airhead!" she said under her breath.

The small car finally moved off down the road. It was late afternoon and a cold chill was beginning to bite the air.

Apart from the odd hint as to which direction to drive, Sharon said nothing.

Suzie was sure she could feel herself being watched up and down but was never quite sure.

Sharon's mobile phone began to ring; she pulled it from her handbag and clicked off the musical ring tone.

Suzie noticed her face lighting up as she saw who it was and began to talk.

"Hi sweetheart!"

Suzie expressed a look of mock disgust and was seen doing so in the process.

"Just keep driving please!" she replied with a sarcastic smile to prove her bemusement.

Suzie kept driving and was soon aware that Sharon was not taking much notice of where she was actually going – her phone conversation was becoming quite heated too.

She decided to drive to a place she knew; it was an escape spot she rarely found herself in, what with having no car of her own.

It seemed like a good idea and, on arrival, she pulled up.

"Bitch! Never call me again and stay out of my way if you know what's good for you and your new fuck!" Sharon yelled loudly and it startled Suzie.

After sitting there for a few seconds with her head in her hands she finally looked up and remembered that she was not alone!

"Relationships, eh? More trouble than they are worth!" Suzie again tried to defuse Sharon's anger but should have known better from the first time.

"Mind your own fucking business!" she yelled and Suzie's jaw fell open. "Oh shit! I'm sorry, I didn't mean that. My, girlfriend has just dumped me and is rubbing my nose in it by sleeping with my ex-husband's new wife!" She calmed down as she spoke.

"Wow!" said Suzie. "That's about as complicated as these things can get! Wait a minute – girlfriend?"

"Yes. I'm bisexual and, just for your information, I'm not ashamed in any shape or form!"

"You've been with men *and* women? I've never been with a

woman but have always been a little curious!" Suzie said, as she looked Sharon up and down.

"Yes, isn't everyone until it comes to the crunch? And then they shy away when you try to kiss them!" Sharon looked around, having realized that the car had stopped. "Where are we?"

The car was in the middle of what seemed like nowhere; it had the appearance of a wide grassy ditch that blocked out the surrounding landscape – just the sky was in view and the feeling of isolation was strong.

The dusty track they had used left the car covered with a film of dirt.

"This is a place I come to whenever I can. It gives me space to think if I am on my own and if I'm not, well, you get the idea! It's also a good place to scream out frustrations at the top of my voice without anyone hearing."

"Well, surely someone must hear you?"

"No, and you'll find out why, soon!"

Sharon continued to look for a landmark to pinpoint her position. It was like a dried up river-bed, rife with weeds and overgrown grass.

It was peaceful and tranquil; Sharon could see how therapeutic it could be to spend time there.

She felt the weight of Suzie's stare and made eye contact.

"I wouldn't shy away if you kissed me. I know you've been eyeing me up all through these lessons so I'm afraid I shall have to give my gir-on-girl virginity to you!"

Sharon was aghast!

"You are sure you just are not doing it as a fashion thing? So many women do, you see, and it just spoils it for us genuine bisexuals!"

Suzie nervously took off her seatbelt and inched towards Sharon; her face was deadly serious.

"Fashion is for people who don't have the imagination to be individual!" said Suzie as she moved closer and beyond Sharon's personal space threshold.

Instinctively, she moved towards Suzie.

Their torsos rotated so they were lined up and they both sensed the combination of body heat and heavy breath; for a second Suzie was terrified.

Perfume and the scent of lipstick wafted under her nose; her heart raced and a hundred images went through her mind at the same time, but only for a fraction of a second.

As their lips met, Suzy felt as if a small weight had lifted inside her, the warmth of skin, the hands naturally lifting to slide around Sharon's back.

They embraced and held tight, their lips pressed hard together.

Suzy felt the pressure release as Sharon moved back and broke off the kiss; their lips smacked with the broken suction.

They were still embraced, as they looked deep into each other's eyes; another lifetime passed by.

Sharon moved herself closer and Suzy launched herself onto her.

Their mouths opened wide and tongues slid in deep, no more walking on eggshells – Suzie wanted all she could get, and Sharon gratefully presented likewise.

They wrestled as they French kissed – hands exploring each other's backs and legs sliding back and forth over the leather seats.

Sharon felt herself being pushed back into a forward facing position and Suzie's body seemed to rise up without losing contact.

Before she knew it, she was sat astride her on the passenger seat.

Her short skirt had ridden up and her shoes had already been kicked off.

She finally broke off the kiss and hung on to Sharon's shoulders, she was holding on to her hips in return and they made eye contact again.

Both of them sported huge smiles.

Sharon moved her hands from Suzie's hips and upwards, they eventually stopped on her breasts. She could already feel the stiffness of her nipples through the bra and material.

Suzie exhaled loudly and her eyes shut tightly.

"Oooohhhh!"

Slowly her hands massaged them as if she was kneading fresh dough, she curled her fingers up to hold them and her palms pressed against the swollen nipples.

Without thinking, Sharon moved away and slid her fingertips under the hem of Suzie's top.

The palms of her hands slid upwards over the smooth skin and around the back to the bra strap, as she fumbled with them she ran the tip of her tongue from the cleavage to under her chin.

As it passed over, Suzie looked down and extended her own tongue to meet it.

They both played as if they were sword-fighting, until the strap sprang free with a whip of elastic.

Sharon's hands moved back down and lifted up the skimpy top, the pert breasts were free and a cool breeze passed over them.

She took a stiff nipple between her lips and squeezed it lightly; as she did this her tongue flicked against the tip.

"Ooooh, my God!" Suzie said breathlessly and massaged Sharon's shoulders.

Slowly she moved her hands down to her breasts too.

Sharon breathed in sharply and broke her grip on the nipple; she grabbed Suzie's hand and pulled it downwards.

Before she knew it; she had her hand pressing against what should have been a drenched pair of panties.

To her excitement, she found that Sharon was not wearing any.

Suzie stroked her hand up and down over the drenched lips; Sharon's hips lifted slightly to increase the pressure a little.

They kept constant eye contact as they played with each other's body, until Suzie glanced up to see that all the car windows had steamed up and blocked out the outside world.

Their skin had a small sheen of perspiration too; it had become like a sauna.

"Shall we get some fresh air?" enquired Sharon,

"Yes, I want to see this wet pussy close up!"

Sharon opened the door and Suzie clambered out. The rush of the cool air invigorated her.

After fighting the temptation to bring herself to a climax, Sharon gracefully got out, walked straight past Suzie and lifted up her skirt to cool off a little.

As Suzie watched, she got up onto the bonnet of her car and lay back.

"Now give to me what you most like to receive!" She lifted up her skirt to reveal her pussy in all its glory.

Suzie leaned over and kissed Sharon full on the mouth again, when the kiss ended, they held each other's gaze for a second and Suzie knelt down on the soft grass.

The heat from the car's radiator warmed her bare breasts as she ran the tip of her tongue up the inside of Sharon's thigh.

The musty smell of a pussy that has been wet for a while

drifted under her nose, unable to resist any longer – she extended her tongue as far as it would go and pressed it against the pussy entrance.

Both women tingled with delight; Suzie slid her tongue up the full length of the wet opening and then let the tip follow a gentle path to the clit. As it made contact, Sharon had to reach up and cling on the car's windscreen seal as an anchor point.

This allowed her to thrust her hips upwards and make Suzie lick her harder, which she did with glee.

"Oooohhhh!" she cried as Suzy parted her wet lips with her thumbs and slid her tongue inside.

Sharon squealed as Suzie explored her inside, her thumbs were now pinching her swollen clit and her face was covered in the juices.

But then she stopped, Sharon looked down quizzically.

"Get this hot bum in the air!" They both smiled and Sharon rolled herself over and got onto all fours on the bonnet.

Instinctively, Suzie stood up behind her and kissed both cheeks in turn.

With no warning, she brought the palm of her hand down hard on one of her cheeks; it left a bright red mark.

"See what you have made me do? You are such a naughty little minx!" The hand struck the other cheek this time.

"Mmm, yes! Punish me some more, my student!"

Suzie slapped each cheek in turn and made them ripple with each strike. Sharon's face was pressing against the windscreen with her mouth wide open.

She massaged the smarting cheeks after each volley and then licked them in the hope of tasting the pain.

Sharon was panting loudly until she had no option but to scream as Suzie began to tickle her anus with the tip of her tongue.

Sharon thrust herself back and her cheeks knocked Suzie away, she slapped her hard once on each cheek as a sign of discontent and continued flicking her tongue against the forbidden hole.

She wanted to play with her own pussy but was struggling to manage, so she decided to try something out.

She got Sharon to get off the car bonnet and pulled down her own wringing wet G-string; after casting it aside she hugged Sharon and kissed her deep on the mouth to let her taste her own juices.

After savouring for a few seconds, they both got down on the floor.

The soft grass made Sharon's cheeks tingle as she watched to see what would happen next.

Suzie sat down and leaned back on her hands, Sharon did the same opposite her.

She moved closer and slid a leg underneath; eventually both of their pussies were touching as if they were kissing.

Both women began to move and gyrate their hips so both pussies stroked against each other; they were both very wet and slid around easily.

They were in heaven as they leaned back with their faces skyward and jaws wide open in ecstasy.

With time movements got more intense, Sharon watched Suzie's bare breasts and the stiff nipples as her chest heaved.

Suzie caught her eye and spoke up.

"Here's the reason I come here to scream without fear of detection!"

Sharon did not want the moment lost so she half ignored her – until she felt a movement.

A loud rumble seemed to come from all around; Suzie thrust herself harder than ever and both women could feel a climax rising.

Out of nowhere a very low-flying jumbo jet appeared directly above, the rumble passed right through them and the ground shook.

A high wind blew hard onto them for a second and made bird's nests of their hairstyles.

Like a mini earthquake, they were shook around and they closed legs as much as they could to retain contact. With the movement increased and their whole bodies shaking – climaxes tore through them like high current electricity.

Their screams were masked only by the thundering engines passing overhead. They stared wide eyed at each other until the noise died away along with their orgasms.

Both women fell back on the soft grass, laughing and catching their breath.

Time passed. Both women got up and brushed themselves down. Suzie looked around for her underwear but could not see it lying around anywhere, so she gave up and got into the car, where Sharon had already started the engine.

"I guess we are near the airport?" she asked.

"Well, the main runway at least!" Suzie was still shaking from her climax and needed to calm down some more.

She sat back on her seat and closed her eyes.

"Don't go to sleep. I still don't know how to get out of here!"

She opened them again and smiled; they both did as the car drove away over the bumpy ground.

The car returned to civilization and got caught up in some traffic. It had been market day and it was coming to an end. Nearby an elderly woman was walking by with her small dog when she let out a cry, a market trader came out to see what was wrong and he dropped his mug of coffee with the shock!

Sharon and Suzie looked on, confused, but then Sharon spotted her lipstick on the windscreen from before.

Leaning forward, she looked at the bonnet; there was a perfect reproduction of her cheeks, a small wet pool in between and almost certainly hand marks all over the roof.

They looked at each other in time for the traffic to ease up and make a sharp exit – complete with Suzie's G-string still hanging from the rear wiper!

First Time Play

Vicky Aston

"It's our first time together, right," Janet said. It was more of a statement than a question.

"Right. You and I. First time ever. Fine," Suzy acknowledged.

There was a rustling of sheets as Janet moved herself further between Suzy's opened knees. The room was cosy and dimly lit by a solitary bedside lamp that gave off a warm glow of pale rose. The scent of perfumed candles hung pleasantly in the air. Two empty wine glasses stood side by side on the bedside table. Both girls were entirely naked, their bodies glistening in the subdued light.

"Is it all right if . . . if . . . if I do *that*?" Janet asked hesitantly. Her voice was quiet, but it seemed somehow oddly loud in the expectant silence.

Suzy giggled, breaking the intimacy of the spell. "If you want to, Jan. I'm hardly going to stop you! After all, I'm lying back here, brazenly exhibiting my all to you! Hanging out the flags . . . for England!"

"Flags?" It was Janet's turn to chuckle. "More like *flaps*. Kitten-flaps, I'd say."

"No. Angels' wings . . . if you *please*, missy!"

"*Of course* you're an angel, Suz," Janet said absently, peering closer at the particular lobe of her scrutiny. "It's just that . . . that I find them so irresistible. Yours, that is. I mean, take this side for example. If I give it just a tiny tweaky-poo here . . ." At this, she gave a little shriek of amused delight. "Oh, my! It's already all moist . . . and slippery. But I'm persistent, Suz. I won't let it get away from me. Here we go. Gently does it. Yes, it's coming out of its cute little bud nicely. Pure magnificence! Ten out of ten for juicy lushness."

"Ooooah! You naughty vixen."

"Now for the other rim. Take it in forefinger and thumb . . . like so." Janet evidently liked to give a commentary as she worked. "I'll ignore its eel-like slipperiness. Now, gently stretch it out of that tight little bud. So far, so good. Jesus, Suz! It's like rippled elastic . . . and there's no end to it! Where's it bloody anchored to, for Chrisakes?"

"Probably somewhere where I know you're soon gonna get that cute little tongue of yours into, Jan."

"Hmmm. *Possibly*." They both laughed but Janet hadn't yet finished with her preliminaries. "I'd say it'd pull out a good two inches . . . maybe more, if I stretched it to its natural elongation."

"What, just *one* wing? Surely they must both be the same length?" Suzy sounded aggrieved. "I wouldn't want you to think I was a fucking freak, Jan! A girl has to have some symmetrical balance to her anatomy, after all."

"Well, let's see. I probably just need to . . . er . . . even them up. If I give this one another little tweaky-poo . . . and a teensy bit more. No, a *lot* more. Like so. And again on this side. Or perhaps I should pull them both together?"

Without waiting for Suzy's approval she brought the finger and thumb of her other hand into play now. "Take a firm hold of each of them," she murmured. "Don't let them slip away. We don't want them to be shy and scuttle back to hide away in their sweet little cocoon again, do we? No, we want them hanging out in all their full glory! And here they come! Both together."

"God, Jan, leave me with some of my stuffing intact . . . pleeease!" Suzy groaned. "You'll pull them off their bloody hinges, at this rate."

But Janet was evidently too engrossed in her tweaking task to take Suzy's pleadings into account. "Only a bit more. Stretch, stretch. It's good exercise for them, Suz. They'll get a good airing . . . and *eventually* something better. Hey presto. All systems go. Emerging butterflies from their chrysalis."

Then she gave a dramatic little gasp. "Fucking Jupiter! They're not butterfly-wings at all, Suz! They're more like piglets' ears . . . all floppy and rose-pink and . . . and fleshy-moist."

Suzy giggled again. "How many inches now then?" She was happy to indulge Janet in her rather saucy proclivities.

"Hmmm. I'd say *three* – on each side, that is. Jumping jelly-babies, Suz! You've got fucking monster-wings . . . not angels' wings! I've never seen anything like it. They're so huge you could almost bloody spread your wings and *fly* with them!"

Suzy thought that Janet's particular choice of vocabulary was rather on the crude side. However, not wanting to be out-gunned, she replied breezily, "Never mind the length, Jan. Feel the damned *quality* of the merchandise!"

"I am, too!"

Suzy grinned but made no further comment. Yet, feeling those soft membranes of her pubic lips being spread like that in such an admiring and attentive way sent a tiny shiver of anticipation down her spine. Not that Suzy had ever been promiscuous, but before Janet had come on the scene several other girls had also admired this particular part of her femininity. Although her labia were by no means unique, ever since she'd been a teenager they had always been unusually prominent, and the fact that Janet now enjoyed coaxing them out to their full glorious extent was quite flattering for Suzy – and even quite thrilling. However, Janet was by no means the first girlfriend to have admired Suzy's labia or who had been so attentive to them – not that this detracted at all from Suzy's sense of enjoyment. Besides, she was even secretly proud of them. And if Janet were enjoying the admiration, Suzy enjoyed just as much having her private parts being the focus of worship.

"Really, really *cute*! So damn cute that I could gobble them all up," Janet cooed from somewhere down between her friend's open thighs. "Mind you, Suz, they'd be a bit of a mouthful for lips and teeth as small as mine. It'd be like eating two rare fillet steaks in one go!"

Suzy snorted indignantly. "They're far too fine and delicate for that sort of crude comparison, Janet darling. And if you please . . . kindly treat them with a little more respect, yeah?"

"No disrespect intended, Suz. I adore fillet steak anyway . . . particularly when it's very succulent and juicy! And now . . . my sweet Madam Butterfly . . . I'm going to lick and suck each one of those pretty wings of yours . . . 'till I've extracted every last drop of juice and they become all dry and shrivelled up. After that, if I've got any breath left, I'll nibble all the bits until they're fucking raw!"

"What *are* you, Jan? A friggin' chipmunk?"

"No, just a randy rabbit that likes its lettuce leaves. Now open your knees wider so I've got room to work down here . . . and then I can get my lips into gear."

"Oooer! Promises, promises! So far, Jan, all you've used your lips for is to prattle on incessantly about *mine*. And here am I spreading my fucking thighs even wider, in the hope of all this promised action!"

"Patience is a virtue, Suz! Now where was I? Yes . . . once I've had a good nibble then I'm gonna immerse my whole face deep inside that magic tunnel and suck up every last silvery thread of your cum until my throat's sore and my lips swell up. And when I've finished doing that, I'll really get down to business!"

"And what sort of business might *that* be, may I ask?" Suzy chuckled, her thighs quivering slightly.

"Wait and see, Suz. Now . . . first off, I like to treat my nostrils to a bit of spicy scent."

Before Suzy could reply, Janet craned her neck forward, her face at once disappearing from view. As Suzy's line of vision was along the sweeping plain of her tummy and through the valley between her breasts, all that she could see of Janet now was the top of her head and its rich auburn hair.

There was a brief pause before she heard Janet inhale deeply. Then there was another longer silence while she held her breath for a few seconds before exhaling again with a deep lingering sigh.

"Oh Suz, you smell *heavenly* . . . really heavenly. My nostrils are simply drowning in your scent. What is that perfume stuff you use down here? I mean, it can't be all your natural scent, surely?"

"Just soap and water, Jan. Mind you, it's Roger & Gallet soap. Nothing but the best for my important parts! None of this vaginal spray crap for me."

"Divine."

With that, Janet submerged her face again into that so fragrant place, her nostrils drawing upon it greedily again so that her lungs and ribcage expanded visibly. A few seconds went by and then she uttered another of her long sighs.

"Oh, Suz, I'm gonna bloody die," she muttered plaintively.

"Not before you've bloody made me come, *pleeease*!"

"All right then. Keep your knickers on . . . I mean, off!"

Suzy didn't have a moment longer to wait now. She felt a wet tongue suddenly alight between the now gaping spread of her labia. A little frisson of erotic excitement travelled up inside her body, making her muscles freeze in a spasm of delightful rigidity.

"Oh, Jan," she gasped. "Oh, yes. More."

There was no verbal response from between her thighs now. Janet's lips were evidently fully occupied with other things. Suzy allowed herself to relax, her head resting on the pillow, her arms by her sides. She kept her feet planted wide apart on the bed with her knees tightly bent. Only her toes moved. They always had a tendency to wiggle whenever she was receiving oral sex.

She felt the first nibble at the bottom edge of her now profoundly extended left lobe. Janet's teeth and lips alternated with their gentle fondling, sometimes biting playfully but never harshly. At other times her lips were clamped in an airtight seal over the lobe before they vacuumed its generous flesh until the entire membrane had been sucked into her mouth.

"Oh God, that's n-nice," Suzy acknowledged, her voice a strained whisper.

By way of response, Janet's lips began to suck yet more greedily, stretching the membrane even further out from its tethering point. After some minutes of noisy slurping, she started on the other side, gently at first, then becoming progressively more forceful, tugging at rose-pink flesh that was perhaps reluctant to emerge so far from its cosy domain. At one point she took the cusp in her teeth, pulling it out and then holding it there as if to test whether its stretched elasticity would make it spring back into its natural repose when it was freed again.

"Oooh-er, Jan, you . . . you r-really *are* fucking eating me alive, you saucy vixen. Gently! Gently!"

Almost at once Janet let her go, suddenly coming up for air. Her face was damp and shiny, her cheeks flushed. She looked across Suzy's torso and grinned mischievously up at her, showing a row of sparkling white teeth.

"I am trying to be gentle, Suz! Promise. It's just that it's so, so . . . *scrummy* down there! My taste-buds are having a real treat and they don't want to stop!"

"I'm glad you like what's on the menu . . . but my nerves can't take any more, Jan. Neither can my wings!" Suzy giggled. "I just want you to make me come pretty soon, and I can't wait for that baby-serpent's tongue of yours to get stuck in there. Do I have to fucking beg, for *chrissakes*?"

But Janet ignored her, her attention focused once more on the place she'd temporarily vacated, her eyes fixed there as if in a trance.

"Suz, you know what?" She had that impish, almost childlike expression, and she spoke in a mock-serious tone. "I reckon it's a good four inches now . . . and it doesn't even bother to slither back into its bud anymore! It knows that it's *licked*! The elastic's finally gone, Suz! Zing, plop! And your labs are all sort of . . . well . . . wet, floppy and raw! All hung out like washing in the sun!"

Suzy uttered a deep sigh of what might have been tolerant exasperation.

"Oh, ha, bloody ha! For God's sake, girl, forget about the bloody size of my labia, will you? Most girls would be more interested in the size of my sodding boobs. Anyway, it's what lies between my wings that counts. Get stuck in there and stop tormenting me, yeah?"

Janet smiled wickedly. "Okay. You asked for it. Now you're gonna get it!"

With that, her face lunged down again. As it did so she kept her mouth open, as if to ensure that the full spread of her lips would be wide enough to cover the whole circumference of Suzy's breach. Although its outer perimeters stretched further than Janet's open mouth could accommodate, nonetheless her lips managed to form a tight enough seal over the actual area of her slit. Then at once she sucked deeply in, the muscles of her mouth and throat straining to make sufficient vacuum on all of that lush tissue that they encountered there.

"Jesus," Suzy muttered. "I'm being consumed by a human leach. All my bits are bloody gonna be sucked into your lungs. Jesus. Have mercy, Jan!"

But Janet had no intention of being merciful quite yet awhile. For some minutes she continued energetically, enjoying the texture of such vulnerable tissue in her mouth, feeling the silk-like softness of it and wanting more of it. Whatever gossamer threads of Suzy's passion-come had precipitated into the outer extremities of her vulva, these had long since been ingested, pleasingly so, the taste lingering evocatively around her teeth.

Then, almost abruptly, she stopped her vacuuming, letting the elasticity of all that succulent tissue recede back into its natural moulding. At that same moment all the released pressure from within that ribbed chamber was evacuated with a sort of gentle hiss of moist air.

"Oh, Jan." Suzy said it again, her voice dreamy. "Oh, Jan."

Not waiting even for a second, Janet brought her tongue to bear on the small heart-shaped web of glistening rose-pink tissue that joined the two seams of labia folds. At the apex she could see the tiny protrusion that nestled so delightfully there – a sort of shiny rounded button resembling a miniature penal head. At once she sought it out with the tip of her tongue; lapping around it; prodding and flicking at it; feeling how it seemed to swell slightly the more she agitated it. She felt Suzy's instantaneous reaction; her loins as though suddenly come alive.

"Oh, God, yes. Yes," Suzy announced in a voice that was strangely flat and emotionless – as if denying the ecstasy of the moment.

But Janet could already feel the first early flush that heralded Suzy's coming orgasm. There were those familiar telltale signs; the slight tremor to her body; the way the muscles and sinews in her thighs and legs seemed to flex and tauten in undulating ripples beneath her skin; those breathless little gasps; and the way her toes sort of bunched and squirmed around on the duvet-cover.

Yet if Suzy's rising climax had passed the point of no return, Janet was not quite ready to give her the release she so desperately wanted. She was totally in Janet's power; under a spell that was in her gifting alone. And this was a notion that Janet found oddly appealing. She, and only she, would choose the timing of her friend's deliverance. Until that moment of ecstasy, Janet intended to prolong the sublime torture. Cunningly so, she flicked her tongue several times more against that tiny glistening head, and then abruptly withdrew, knowing instinctively what suffering her mischief would bring.

"No! Please *no*. Don't f-fucking stop now, you . . . you cruel vixen!"

Janet laughed. "Turn over. On your hands and knees. Doggy style," she ordered.

"You sadistic bitch. I was in seventh heaven."

"You will be again . . . soon. Now get doggy-fied!"

Suzy complied, albeit reluctantly, cursing as she slowly turned over and put herself in that ungainly posture. Frankly, she preferred the more passive and relaxed style of lying on her back with her knees invitingly open, rather than to be on all-fours. Somehow it was a position that made her feel instinctively vulnerable and exposed. There was also the disadvantage of not being able to watch her lover at the same time – particularly at the point of orgasm. However, Janet evidently found this "on-all-fours" position to her liking. Therefore Suzy had no wish to disappoint her.

"Stick your bum out more. Knees wider apart," Janet commanded. "I want to get my face right inside that whole bloody chasm of yours!"

"Oh hell." At least Suzy could giggle now, despite her preference for a laid-back position. "I'm all sort of quivery. My knees have gone to jelly. Sadistic bitch!"

"I'm not gonna bloody *spank* you, Suz, if that's what you're worried about, for Chrissakes! I only want to *examine* you . . . and perhaps something more. That is, if you get lucky! Spanking can be postponed until another day."

From her doggy position Suzy turned her head round to give Janet a withering look of disapproval.

"Surely you don't *seriously* mean that, Jan? I'm not sure that I'm really into damned spanking capers!"

But Janet was too engrossed to answer, completely ignoring Suzy's look.

"Now, let me start at the top. North first, South later," she announced airily, putting her hands firmly on either side of Suzy's buttocks and sort of prising them wider apart. "Uh-ha. Nice spacious interior. Firm sweeping sides of the valley. Hmmm. Dark velvety sump down there." She was back to giving one of her commentaries again. "Everything nicely shaved thereabouts, I see. Just how I like it. I object to stray hairs getting in my mouth, you know. Now, let's see. Yes. Your sweet little backward-peeping pussy is showing all those crinkled up bits of juicy flesh! But it's all slunk back into its original place again . . . just as if I'd never pulled the bits out in the first place, you crafty moo!"

"I never touched them. Honest," a voice said from somewhere at the front of the bed. Suzy was getting into the spirit of things now.

Janet giggled. "You *are* a caution, Suz. But it's serious stuff now. Can't you bend forward a bit lower? Tits touching the duvet, please. And stick that pretty arse out more. Okay, that's fine. Here goes with my scent-ometer."

Before Suzy could utter another word Janet took a deep breath again and plunged her face between the cleft. This she still held open with both hands by applying pressure to each side of Suzy's buttocks. For a moment her nostrils exhaled in a gentle blow of air before inhaling again, this time in a long drawn out little moan of apparent appreciation as they drew in the aroma.

Then she emerged from the valley briefly to announce:

"Your scent there is just as *divine* as your pussy was, Suz. Full marks. You've passed my nose-ometer test with flying colours, girl!"

"Pleased to hear it. But what the fuck did you expect, Jan? I'm the Queen of Clean . . . not some hairy-arsed truck driver, for Christ's sake. I told you, I use Roger & Gallet soap."

Janet gave a little snort of amusement and returned again to her scrutiny.

"Superb view, Suz. You should see it. Two holes in one, each looking back at me from that Darkly Shaded Valley of Doom!"

"Crude bitch."

"Only stating a fact, Suz. Besides they're beautiful – the top one all sort of dark glistening crimson between those two curvaceous flanks. And the one peeping below is . . . let's see . . . like a tight mauve flower-bud again, enveloped in those little crinkled up petals."

"Oh, how poetic, I *don't* think. And I've got no wish to be discussed as if I were some bloody plant specimen on Gardeners' World, thanks awfully!"

Janet sniggered before returning to her task. "Now, here goes. Bum-hole gets it first. Once more into the breach, dear friend! Deep breath."

With her nose aimed just at the very top of the cleft – and just below the hard vertebra at the base of Suzy's spine – Janet's tongue went in deep and high, stretching to reach the velvety sump, wiggling in there at first, until finally it pushed down against the smooth fleshy resistance that it encountered there. For a second the wet tip of her tongue remained firmly wedged in that dimpled crimson velum. Then it began to tease around it with little jiggling motions, sometimes pausing to wipe along the sloping scarps before returning again to the tightly closed profundity.

All this had the effect of making Suzy arch her spine, her bottom thrusting out yet more acutely as if to make her cleft more accessible. Doggy style was not so bad, after all, she reflected. Her toes began to squirm on the duvet again, and she felt her buttocks quiver despite Janet's firm hold of them.

"Oh God. It's nice, Jan." Her voice was almost matter-of-fact. Then as an after-thought she added breezily, "Considering it's your first time in there, Jan, you certainly know your way around!"

But the lapping activity around her anal passage did not last. Janet had other distractions lower down, and her tongue descended South in a long wiping motion that left a trail of warm saliva in its wake. There was no sound now other than the occasional grunt or frantic intake of breath. Then Suzy felt her left buttock suddenly released from Janet's grip, and immediately the disengaged hand came under her, reaching up between her legs. Now searching fingers felt for her pudendal slit, finding it at once and beginning to fondle its backward-facing portals.

Suzy gasped, the cheeks of her rump suddenly contracting in a muscular spasm, her body held in a rigid seizure.

"Jeeezusss . . ."

Janet was concentrating too much to make any reply. Her tongue at once began to lap busily between the labia, the membranes of which her fingers had coaxed out from the shelter of their budded core. The synchronized action of tongue and fingers together went on with relentless abandon for several minutes, so that soon the labia were distended and swollen again, their elasticity stretched as never before. Occasionally Janet's fingers plucked at them, pulling them even further out, her tongue at the same time frantic to wiggle between every twist and knurl of soft tissue, foraging ever deeper in its eagerness.

"Oh Jan. Please . . . pl-please don't stop now. That's . . . oooer . . . heavenly. If I don't come soon I'm gonna fuckin' collapse. My legs are all weak."

Janet didn't stop. Not this time. Her friend had endured enough torture for one evening. Not to finish her would hardly be fair. Even though Janet felt her own wetness gathering, her already heightened plateau of lustful intrigue was perhaps enough reward for now. She revelled in the act of giving pleasure, enjoying the thrill that it gave her, knowing how it must thrill her partner even more. She did not really mind whether Suzy would make her come later or not. There was always tomorrow for her turn to be on the receiving end. For now, the act of being a simple benefactor of ecstasy was thrilling enough. First-time sex must always be selfless, dramatic and passionate, all inhibitions cast aside. She could savour every moment of their lovemaking, and afterwards sleep happily beside her new lover, knowing that tomorrow was another day. Freshly-served passion would be as delightful for the second time as it was for the first. Each new intimate discovery would make the relationship stronger; ever more fulfilling and passionate. Each lover would know the other's body and soul that much better. This was Janet's philosophy. She desired Suzy, wanting more of her, not wanting their relationship to fizzle out as many girl-girl relationships sometimes did.

"Oh fuck," Suzy moaned, her body quivering.

As if she had done it to her many times before, Janet knew the exact spot, her tongue working feverishly. She was oblivious to the awkwardness of her own posture, her neck straining to get her mouth deep enough between the open thighs and to reach the lower extremities of its lush interior. Now both her fingers and thumbs were holding the labia wide apart, needing to tauten the glistening web of crimson tissue and to fully expose its tiny heart. All the while her tongue lapped and teased, bringing Suzy further to the brink again.

"Jeez-usss! Oh . . . oooh . . . uuuh." Suzy was panting now, wanting but not wanting it to end.

Janet was skilled at her task, knowing precisely when the moment would come, the anticipation of it thrilling her to the core of her being. She wanted Suzy to cry out – loudly and without the slightest reservation. If she screamed the place down it would be even more thrilling. The knowledge that it would be Janet herself who had made it happen would surely be sublimely exhilarating. When it was over they could both collapse on the bed, laughing and happy, and lie together in a sweetly-sweaty embrace, two lovers enjoying the wake of such depleted passion.

And that was how it happened.

Suzy came with a final rigid shudder, the ecstasy of her climax such that it seemed to reverberate around the bedroom, her cries shattering the intimate silence of those few moments before.

Janet was herself panting from sheer exertion. Her face was flushed and shiny with perspiration as she quickly withdrew – just at the very moment before Suzy's knees and legs seemed almost to crumple beneath her.

"God . . . f-fucking hell, Jan. That was . . . pheweee . . . flaming bloody *mar-marvellous*," Suzy managed to utter breathlessly as she flopped face down on the bed.

"Glad you enjoyed it, Suz."

"Bloody right I enjoyed it, you rampant cow! But I'm knacker-rooed. It was . . . it was friggin' fantastic, Jan. No other word for it! *Fantastic!*"

"Well, if it hadn't been, I'd be really, really *cross*. I mean all that *effort* and so forth," Janet laughed, slumping down on the bed beside her.

Lying on her back she reached out and playfully ran her hand over Suzy's bottom, delighting at its smoothly-contoured peaks. The way they sloped so steeply down into her rift was fascinating – all the more so because it was a place that Janet knew so intimately and intrusively.

As if having read her mind, Suzy turned her head round on the pillow and grinned wickedly at her. "You've certainly got a fucking serpent's tongue on you, girl!"

"Uh-ha. Not bad . . . for my first time, was it?" Janet feigned seriousness, her eyes nonchalantly roaming the ceiling and deliberately avoiding her friend's penetrating gaze.

"First time, indeed!" Suzy snorted derisively. "Don't you think we could dispense with all this 'first time' crap? It's not that I don't enjoy our little 'pretend game', Jan. Really I do! But isn't it getting a teensy-weensy bit over the top, after all this time? I mean . . . we've only been *together* for the last *six* bleeding years, you daft moo!"

"Oh, really?" Janet mocked. "Well, that's strange. I can't seem to remember your wings being so big and meaty before! It felt like the first time I ever had them in my mouth . . . all *four* inches of them! If I'd had to have all *that* flesh half way down my throat every day for six years, surely I'd have bloody choked on it by now, yeah?"

"You rude bitch!"

Then they both lay back and rocked with laughter.

A while later Janet switched off the light. Under the duvet, and still naked and warm, the two lovers kissed, their bodies cuddling up close to one another. Suzy was quickly asleep, but Janet lay awake with a contented smile on her lips. Tomorrow was another day. Even if Suzy didn't wish to play their silly "first-time" game, at least Janet could pretend. Besides, this time it would be her turn to be on the receiving end.

The Escape

Helen Darvin

Amanda picked up a cushion and hurled it angrily against the wall.

What a day; what a sweaty, rushed off her feet, pandemonium of a day. It seemed that everyone in town had chosen that day to shop at the store, and to put the cap on it some of the staff had called in sick, and those who had turned up for work were hard put to cope. Things had reached rock bottom when two of the girls, tempers frayed and worn, had erupted into a blazing argument over some trivial matter and, while it might have amused the army of customers to watch the two red-faced assistants screaming and swearing at each other, Amanda, as the Department Supervisor, had been burdened with the unwelcome chore of stepping in to sort it out. She'd pacified the two contestants successfully, and restored a measure of calm, but by the end of the day she'd felt like she'd been fed through some kind of wringer. She was squeezed, she was drained.

She went over to the drinks cabinet, and made herself a large vodka and lime. She sipped at it gratefully.

No, if she was honest with herself, it wasn't just because of the work that she was feeling low. It was because things weren't too good in the pussy area.

Or, rather, because things were too good in the pussy area.

For the first time that day she felt a small, brief tug at the corners of her mouth. What an irony; to be down in the dumps because things were going well. Ridiculous, in fact; but that was the way it was.

And at the bottom of it was, of course, Denise. Full breasted, curvy, luscious Denise, who gave her some of the most glorious, most unforgettable comes of her life.

It had been all right before Amanda had met her. She'd been

having a good time, living a busy social life, and, as the phrase has it, getting her fair share.

Yes, certainly she'd had her share, her quim had been the recipient of more than enough attention to keep her, or anybody else, happy.

Warmed and relaxed by the vodka, she retrieved the cushion from the floor, replaced it on the sofa, and sat down, her thoughts drifting slowly back. Back to Gillian.

She'd been well-connected, had Gillian; she knew a lot of prominent people, had well-off friends.

Their first time together was when Gillian had invited her to a party held on a private beach on the south coast. It had all sounded fascinating, although Gillian had shruggingly referred to it as "you know, just a few girls getting away from it all for a while, sort of thing."

There'd been some people there that she'd recognized; a woman she'd seen playing a couple of supporting roles in television dramas, the lead singer of a new pop group, two models, and a newspaper columnist. There'd been champagne and good food on the hot golden sands by the calm blue sea, and she'd enjoyed the day.

Gillian had blonde hair, and friendly green eyes. She was quite short, but her body was as sinuous and winding as a country road, it seemed to Amanda. She was a pleasing sight in her minimalist bikini as she went off down to the water to swim a few strokes to cool off, or stretched out beside her, a bottle poised to refill their glasses.

After a day of her physical nearness and the sun bestowing its languid sensuality on her, Amanda was not sorry when, after a deep blue night had fallen, Gillian led her away to a quiet hollow nestling among the grass-topped sand dunes. From the way that the other women had been quietly pairing off and disappearing, she'd known what the interests of the guests had turned to.

She lay down without waiting for any prompting, and Gillian knelt beside her. Her fingers neatly undid the ties of Amanda's bikini bottom, and removed it. The cooler night air flowing in around her slit was a treat in itself.

She heard a whisper of cloth, and knew that Gillian was removing her own skimpy outfit. She smiled to herself; the silly woman had forgotten her top. She was bound to want to get to grips with Amanda's tits; better do her a favour, and get them out herself.

She wasn't mistaken. Gillian's first move was to come down on her now nude boobs. After kissing them all over, she sucked a nipple into her mouth, and gently bent it this way and that with her skilful, adept tongue. Amanda instinctively arched her back to push the nipple in deeper.

Gillian then enclosed the second tit in her hand. Amanda sighed her appreciation, massaging Gillian's tanned shoulders as Gillian tongued and thumbed the nipples.

Amanda pushed her groin into her to signal what she wanted next, and Gillian understood. She pressed her hand against Amanda's belly, then all the way down. As she approached her target, Amanda opened her legs to welcome her.

Gillian's hand arrived at Amanda's yearning cunt and cupped it. Then she began a slow, rhythmic kneading, each movement creating flares and sparks deep inside Amanda's joy tunnel.

Amanda had a sudden urge to get to know Gillian's fanny in her turn, and began to caress it lightly and delicately with her fingertips, running forwards and backwards along its rift. Gillian's breathing, already heavy, became a wind of passion at her ear.

Then Gillian brought her lips down again on Amanda's nipples, changing quickly from one to the other, and that, together with the insistent hand roaming freely all over her quim, brought her, almost sobbing with the incandescent pleasure of it all, to her own come time. She held on to Gillian like a life belt as she was tossed around on a turbulent ocean of delight, an ocean whipped into a storm by Gillian's gorgeous ministrations to that vital spot tucked between her thighs.

Their affair had been good while it lasted, but they'd drifted apart eventually. Gillian had gone off as one of a group sailing around the Mediterranean, and although they'd promised to get together again when she returned, somehow they never did. One solitary postcard from Cyprus was all Amanda ever heard from her. After that – nothing.

Amanda topped up her vodka and lime. Oh well; easy come – she smiled at the pun; it had been easy to come with Gillian – easy go. These things happened. And there were always other women out there, all with their own personal charms and tastes which she could sample as she wished, when she wished.

Girls like Karen. With tastes like Karen.

Karen was almost a direct opposite to Gillian. Where Gillian had been outgoing and keen on socializing, Karen was introverted and disliked large gatherings. She wrote poetry, but apart from a few which had passed the test of acceptance and been published, she refused to show her work to Amanda. Modest and unsure of herself, Amanda thought.

Physically, too, they were opposites. Karen was taller, with long curly black hair contrasting intriguingly with her eyes of washed out blue. She looked like the poet she was, wrapped in an aura of sensitivity.

There was one area, however, where she was very much the reverse of restrained . . .

It had begun simply enough.

They'd stayed behind at the badminton club for extra practice after the other members had left. The game over, they'd had a quick shower, and while they were drying off and chatting, Amanda had, in a fit of playfulness, flicked her towel across Karen's bare bum. It was only a light slap, but the look that passed over Karen's face had been unmistakable. And it inspired in Amanda a feeling she'd never known before.

It was one of those strange moments which occur in life when nothing needs to be said, when everything is understood as if by some form of telepathy.

Amanda rushed out to her locker, and collected the leather belt from her skirt. When she returned, Karen was already bent over, holding on to the edge of a sink to steady herself, her neat, tight rear poised expectantly for what was to come.

Amanda raised the belt and brought it down sharply across the two delicious half-moons of Karen's arse.

Karen squealed with delight as the belt lashed her.

Amanda applied the belt again. And again. And again. Each thrash squeezed a rapturous cry from Karen, and Amanda herself became more and more excited by the sight of that reddening bum.

Finally an especially vigorous stroke from Amanda brought Karen to a climax, and her shrieks echoing round the white tiles of the shower room testified amply just how much Amanda's treatment had worked her up.

Immediately, without thought, hardly knowing what she was doing, Amanda handed the belt to Karen, and replaced her at the sink, arse cocked, wondering what this new experience would be like.

She soon found out.

The belt whipped across her, bringing a stinging pain with it.

But a different sort of pain, dreamy, languorous, blossoming out from her lashed arse into her cunt and her swelling, hardening nipples.

As Karen continued to wield the belt, the warm languor grew ever more ripe, ever more engulfing, until, taking even herself by surprise, she orgasmed, a soft, lingering orgasm, which took its time, and gave her what seemed to be an age in which to savour all its subtle shades and flavours. A come for the connoisseur of comes.

Afterwards the two of them had stood, mutually red-butted, and stared at each other, Karen the knowing, experienced expert, Amanda the initiated pupil. But how willing a pupil she was going to be now.

And that was a good relationship also, when they met at one or other of their flats, and took their time with their pursuit. And no mere crude leather belt any more. Karen had just the thing already; a thin and pliable but strong cane which was simply ideal for its purpose. Ideal, thought Amanda, as it thrashed the lines of sexy fire across her willing bum cheeks.

But that, too, had petered out. Karen, she knew, had met someone else, some other ripe-arsed woman, and begun to drift away, until their meetings had stopped altogether.

Again, she wasn't too worried. All those other women were out there, with their dangling tits and their fulsome fannies. A whole world of them, laid out before her like sweets in a sweet shop.

And that's the way it had been. She'd be attracted to someone, they'd glut their appetites on each other for a time, then drift apart. It was all right, her cunt was contented, so how could there be any problem?

Then she'd bumped into Denise.

She'd landed a job, the one she had now, head of one department at one branch of a large national retail organisation. A responsible position. She'd slotted into the work well, and been a success. And she'd come across Denise.

Denise was in the transport section, helping to organize the vans which took orders out to those who preferred to have deliveries made to their homes.

Amanda was randy for her from the moment she saw her. She was of medium height with generous boobs and arse and a slender waist in between. Her hair was a luxuriant blonde – natural – and there was a smouldering look about the eyes. The lips were full and sensuous. When she spoke, her voice was low and intimate; it seemed to wrap itself around Amanda like a garment of fine silk, a caress to her whole body.

Amanda knew that Denise would only have to click her fingers at her, and she'd definitely come running, ready to part her helpless thighs in sweet submission.

It didn't take long, not long at all. One week, in fact, and at the end of that week they were in Amanda's bed, between her sheets, together.

It was every bit as good as she'd known it would be. Denise's body was well-tended, and vibrated with health and life. She had the proportions of a classical statue. Her tits were the best Amanda had ever encountered, perfectly balanced and formed. She felt almost privileged to hold them.

Denise, meanwhile, was doing her thing on Amanda's cunt, using her fingers with the skill of a surgeon to coax her into a growing avidity, and Amanda reciprocated the delightful favour.

The hands wanked each other lasciviously, until Denise, with a sudden, determined action, dived down to Amanda's groin, pushed her head between Amanda's legs, and rasped her tongue all along Amanda's slit.

"Aaaaah . . . !" Amanda couldn't keep in check the screech of unmitigated delight which burst from her at the touch of Denise's probing tongue.

And the screeches grew louder and more persistent as Denise pushed her tongue inside Amanda's love gate, and began to explore and caress her inner walls.

A compulsion gripped her; what else could she possibly do but again return the favour?

She made her own dive, and came face to face with Denise's aperture, an aperture which she quickly made sure was tongue plugged.

And that was how they detonated together, two tongues and two twats in fine tune, producing two writhing, almost impossible to bear, frenzies, which left them gasping and flapping like two fish stranded on a beach.

But not for long. The tide quickly returned, the two fish revived and regrouped their energies, then were at each other again, locked together in that sweet conjunction, sending each other wheeling up into the stratosphere of their desire for each other, and of the satisfaction that they eagerly brought each other with hands, lips and tongues.

That had been three years ago; and Amanda simply could not get enough of Denise. Denise could be ruthless and driving, but also, sometimes, tender and teasing. She could draw the encounter out to an exquisite age, she could make it fast, breathless and overwhelming. Sometimes Amanda felt as if she was no more than a slave to Denise's will, her own quim and tits merely Denise's possessions to use as she liked. How Denise did it all, Amanda didn't know; but she did it.

And now Amanda saw that she had come to live for nothing else; and she had slowly begun to resent this enthralment. Increasingly she recalled and dwelt upon those times when she'd been free and easy, at liberty to go for any female who made her fanny flare, and, when the time came, to part from her without regret. It wasn't like that now. Denise had begun to have power over her. And Amanda didn't like it.

And not only that; Denise, she knew, wasn't too much bothered with her. She knew that. Once, when they were lying side by side in bed, Amanda had asked, half-seriously, "Hey! What would you feel if I left you today?", and Denise hadn't even bothered to reply, just shrugging casually, and turning away to go to sleep.

Denise would merely find someone else to fuck.

In fact she was already involved with someone else. Amanda had accidentally overheard one of the female assistants say to Denise pleadingly, "You were fantastic when you tongued me off last night. Please – will you do it again soon? Oh, please . . ." So Denise was having her, obviously. And were there any others as well? Amanda was jealous, and she didn't like the unfamiliar emotion.

No, Denise didn't bother about her much. She even talked openly about a desire to move on, to go somewhere else. And she didn't talk of them going together.

Amanda replaced the cap on the bottle. She had no intention of going down that dead end road. That would solve nothing.

There was only one way she was going to escape from this chain that bound her to Denise, to recover the light-hearted, carefree existence she'd previously known. She'd get away, go some place where Denise wasn't. Do it cold turkey. The separation would hurt, but that would pass, then she'd be footloose and fancy free once more, able to take up and put down her pleasures when she chose.

She suddenly remembered the advert for the superstore an

American firm was opening in Leeds as its first venture into Britain. They were looking for all kinds of staff, including department supervisors, where her experience would surely give her an advantage. And she'd been to Leeds before and liked the place. She was sure it would be pleasant to live there full time. If she could get a job there, it would be the start of her new life, away from Denise.

Where was that advert?

She hunted among the pile of magazines in the rack until she found it. She took it over to the small writing desk in the corner. An old-fashioned hand-written letter, using her ultra-tidy script, would be best, she thought. A nice personal touch. Finding a pencil and paper, she scanned the ad and found the name of the Personnel Officer – a Mr Rowley – then began to prepare the rough draft . . .

"Well, now, you've met nearly everybody," Mr Rowley said cheerfully. "There's only one or two more to come. And in just one week's time we'll be open for business. Are you looking forward to it?"

"Very much," Amanda replied.

"So am I," Mr Rowley said. "And have you settled well into your new flat?" he went on.

"I'm very comfortable," Amanda told him. "It's quite spacious and nicely located, and—"

A knock at the door interrupted her.

"Excuse me one moment," Mr Rowley said apologetically. "Come in!" he called.

The door opened.

"Ah," said Mr Rowley. "Amanda, I'd like you to meet the person who'll be assisting me as Deputy Personnel Officer."

"Hello, Amanda," said Denise, with a smile.

Therapy

Helen Stevens

She lifted the hem on her uniform, fastened her suspenders and straightened the lace at the top of her silk stockings. One last check of her tight bun and soft makeup and she was ready for the day. If only they knew what she had on under her dress.

"Notes on the calendar for today say we have a visit from a new resident this afternoon. Mr Dunbar is an ex-serviceman in his late fifties, who recently had a stroke and now is in need of twenty-four-hour care. He will be moving in to the recently vacated single room in the Riverside Unit in two weeks time. Today he is coming for afternoon tea, a chance to look around again and meet his new key worker." Jo spoke confidently and openly to the group of nurses gathered around the large oak dining table sipping at much needed steaming mugs of coffee.

"I know it won't be the same as having Mrs Jessop here. I know we all miss her dearly, it was a difficult passing, but we all have to realize that she is no longer suffering. In this profession we have to be able to remove ourselves from our feelings for the residents and move on." The other nurses nodded in agreement.

"This morning's main duties are the usual mixture of routine tasks. All beds are to be stripped and remade, residents washed and dressed and into the breakfast room for eight am please. Mrs Mayfield in room nine is asking for another dressing for her pressure sore, so I shall be there should anyone need me. Please can we remember to turn her hourly, left to right to relieve the pressure, noting which side? Lastly, Abbie, please could you come to my office after the meeting? I would like to brief you on the new gentleman. You will be his key person."

A few moans went around the group. Jo continued ignoring the noises.

"Is there anything to report this morning from the night staff?" The nurses shook their collective heads.

"Good, then that concludes our meeting. Off you go, ladies." Jo stood from her seat and moved into her office whilst the other nurses proceeded to go about their duties. She heard the mumble of ill content, questions of favouritism and the usual moaning and groaning of a six a.m. breakfast shift as she filed away the meeting notes of the morning.

She was just closing the filing cabinet as there was a tap on the door.

"You wanted to see me, Matron?" A slender, pretty nurse stood meekly in the doorway, her soft auburn hair pulled tight into a French plait, her uniform starched to perfection.

"Come in, Abbie, and close the door behind you, please." Jo moved from the filing cabinet to stand behind her desk and sat down heavily in her faux leather office chair.

Abbie's regulation issue black, rubber-soled shoes squeaked as she shut the door and made her way towards one of the chairs on the nearside of the desk. Sitting demurely she crossed her legs and placed her hands in her lap, eager to listen and learn.

"I hate all this seriousness and pomposity," Jo said as she removed her clip from her hair. Her bun fell loose, letting her hair cascade around her shoulders.

"Oh, I don't know, I actually think it's quite funny, and in a way, it turns me on! I love you being all domineering. I've been working here for three months now and it's driving me insane seeing you be 'Matron' every morning." Jo pulled a smile as Abbie made a "tiger-pawing" motion and the growl to accompany it.

"So, what's this new chap like?" Abbie asked. Jo was glad for the change of subject – anything that distracted her from the urge to climb over the desk and ravish Abbie was good. Jo pulled a file from her desk drawer and handed the care plan over to her. She sat in silence, for about ten minutes, as Abbie flipped through the file and gathered some of the necessary details.

"Feel free to take it away with you for a while and have a good read. Are you free for lunch today?"

Abbie smiled coyly.

"Of course I am. You never rota me in for a lunch time shift."

"I'd never get to see you if I did," Jo interrupted.

"Melanie isn't in today and we've got an agency staff in, so I'll need to be floating about. What have you got in mind?" Abbie asked.

Jo stepped around the desk and leant in close to the nurse. Abbie could feel her warm, coffee-scented breath on her cheek.

"Just meet me in the treatment room at ten past one. I'll see you there once I've done the medication rounds. I'll let you in on a surprise."

Abbie smiled and then stood to leave the room.

"Speaking of surprises, you should see what I have in my lunch box today," she laughed. As her hand rested on the door handle Jo wrapped her arms around Abbie's shoulders and laid soft kisses on the nape of her neck. She opened the door slightly and then stopped.

"Um . . . Matron. Don't forget your bun!" Abbie giggled as she left the office, leaving Jo looking in the mirror, tying her hair back into the tight bun that she had had at the morning meeting.

Both nurses continued about their daily routines, not meeting again until the medication round at breakfast. Despite the distance across the busy breakfast room the desire between Jo and Abbie was palpable. The two nurses were engrossed in their illicit affair, and were excited by the danger of being caught conducting it directly under the noses of their employers, colleagues and partners. Both women continued to attend to the needs of the residents of the Albright Nursing Home for the Elderly and Infirm. Despite their distraction, their mutual profession tightened the bond between them. They truly understood each other's work-related stresses and didn't need to go into lengthy discussions in order to explain the day's events to each other, unlike when they went home to their partners.

Jo had been married for almost a year to Dave, who was a bricklayer. Jo had known about her bisexuality since she was about thirteen, when she had realized the feelings she had for a female friend were more physical than her feelings for her boyfriend of the time. Abbie had been in a relationship with Helena for six months, but they were still at the dating stage and neither was ready to commit any further. The nurses had embarked on their affair just a month after Abbie was employed at the home. After some serious drinking and flirting on a staff night out which resulted in them sneaking away early to Jo's apartment they had become engaged in the affair. Jo had returned home in the early hours of the morning, sexually exhausted and smelling like a brothel. She had spent an hour in the shower, scrubbing away the guilt of her adultery, before climbing into bed with Dave. Over the next few weeks she had tried to deny her feelings for Abbie. In the end she had given in. Since then the women had been meeting in secret whenever they were able.

Once the after breakfast medications were administered, Jo returned to her office and despite her growing pile of paperwork and medication charts, she allowed herself ten minutes of quiet contemplation. Of course her mind was focused on one subject – Abbie. And the thought of her bending over beds, tucking in sheets was making her more excited as the minutes ticked on. That vision was enough to keep her imagination occupied whilst she worked tirelessly through her duties until lunch.

Abbie too thought constantly about Jo, but the regular interactions with the residents were a pleasant distraction and assisted with her concentration as she continued about her morning duties. Lunchtime soon came around and once all the residents had been tended to, Abbie relaxed enough to feel the excitement of her tryst with Jo. It gathered in the pit of her stomach like a whirlwind of rampantly agitated butterflies.

Jo went about her medication rounds as Abbie cleared away the dishes into the kitchen. Once the agency staff had departed to the sitting room with the tea trolley Jo wheeled the medication chest back into her office, locked the door behind her, and slipped away silently along the corridor to the small treatment room next to the laundry store. They had chosen this location for their meetings as the laundry was only used by the night staff and it was in a secluded location away from the rest of the building. Also, Jo was the only member of staff who had the key apart, of course, from Abbie, who had been given a sneaky copy by Jo.

The treatment room was used for anything from alternative therapy to counselling and even though it was sparsely decorated, it was both comforting and relaxing. A sumptuous day bed occupied one corner of the room opposite a small sink unit. The indulgent cushions, pillows and bolsters scattered across its breadth clashed with the clinical nature of the therapy couch and overall décor of the room. Jo drew the vertical blinds; almost completely blocking out the midday sun and switched on a small table lamp which threw a pink hue across the room, softening its atmosphere.

Unable to find anything more appropriate than Mozart to put on the compact disc player, Jo hit the play button just as Abbie sidled in through the door, closing it softly as she came. Abbie stood with her back to the door, her hands still nervously clinging to the handle.

"Shouldn't you be changing Mr. Johnson's sheets at this precise moment?" Jo asked in her best "supervisor" voice, stifling a giggle.

"You know full well I would have been at this time. I've already done it. It was the fastest sheet change he's ever seen; might even have set a new world record. Who's minding the tea trolley?"

"Grace, the agency lady. I've nipped off to do paperwork if anyone asks her. We can be missing for a whole blissful hour and no one will notice."

Jo moved slowly across the room towards Abbie, the nervous excitement obvious in her movements. With a swift motion she placed her foot on the end of the therapy couch and swept back her navy blue starched uniform to reveal the deep lace of her sheer black stockings beneath. Abbie drew a sharp breath in. Jo was stunning. At a little over five foot nine and easily an extra large, her voluptuous curves oozed femininity and sex appeal. Her large hazelnut eyes were indeed windows to her soul, open and wanting and her blue-black hair shone like satin when it hung loose about her shoulders. It was all too much to resist. Abbie was turned on by her personality as well as her appearance and when she considered the two coupled together she almost exploded with desire.

"I bet Mr Davies in room eighteen just loved those this morning, didn't he?" Abbie spluttered.

"Almost had to call an ambulance. Thought he might have had a heart attack. At least I can be thankful he couldn't see the rest of my underwear beneath this uniform. If it had been white cotton not navy, I swear, he would have needed a defibrillator, not a bed bath."

Both women laughed softly. Abbie released the handle of the door and moved towards Jo, crossing the room eagerly.

"What exactly is holding those stockings up today? They're not regulation white hold-ups, are they, so what's supporting them?"

Abbie reached to the collar of Jo's uniform and began slowly undoing it, popper by popper, revealing the slightly padded cups and fine boning of a black lace basque. She reached down slowly and traced a line of kisses along each of Jo's collarbones. Jo moaned in delight, slipping her hands to Abbie's waist and releasing the butterfly clasp of her elastic belt. It fell to the floor with a clatter, which disguised the loud groan made by Jo as Abbie deftly removed her breast from its warm cup and gently took her large, already erect nipple into her mouth. She expertly caressed it with her tongue, her lips sucking greedily on her areola. Jo took Abbie by the forearms and guided her up to a full standing position so that they were nose to nose. The couple looked into each other's eyes, savouring the moment of closeness that drew them together for an eternity. Their lips met and the passion inside them, that they kept bottled up inside between rendezvous, exploded like a million fireworks going off at once.

The heat and the passion between them grew; their bodies writhed against each others as their tongues explored, hungrily searching for satisfaction. Abbie removed Jo's belt and peeled her uniform from her shoulders. The heavy starched material sat awkwardly at her feet, leaving her stood in her splendid basque for Abbie to admire. Jo shuddered with exhilaration as the cool breeze from the slightly open window and the excitement of the exposure caused her skin to erupt into millions of goose pimples.

At the sight of her lover's ravishing underwear, Abbie felt her own rigid nipples pressing tightly against the constraint of her uniform and with one deft pull, unfastened the poppers revealing her pert ample breasts heaving in her white, cut lace bra. She shrugged her dress from her shoulders and stepped out of it, kicking it to one side as she did so to divulge a matching pair of tight French knickers, a suspender belt and white lace top stockings.

"Wow," Jo whispered as she nestled into Abbie's shoulder. Their passion cooled for a moment as they treasured the ability to press semi-naked flesh against semi-naked flesh, their soft hands roaming freely over each other.

"Your body is amazing," Jo commented as she lowered her head to lay a trail of kisses across Abbie's chest. It was now the senior nurse's opportunity to release her lover's gorgeous breasts from their tight constraints. She gently fondled her in circular motions, breaking the pattern only slightly to take each nipple in turn and caress it with her mouth. The gentle approach was not what Abbie needed to satisfy a week's worth of lust and she pulled her breasts away from her lover. Taking her by her hands, Abbie led her to the plush day bed where she collapsed backwards, pulling Jo down on top of her. Their breasts crashed heavily into each other's and Abbie sighed deeply as Jo eagerly and passionately kissed her. The increase in intensity was exactly what Abbie had required and she let herself become lost in the hot blooded kisses. Jo rolled from on top of her, taking her weight from her body and giving her room to appreciate Abbie more fully.

Their kisses softened and Jo stroked her hand the length of Abbie's body. Her fingers fondling and caressing every inch of her torso. Abbie writhed with pleasure as her lover teased her. She was electrified as Jo allowed her fingers to circle Abbie's abdomen and pubic area with feather light touches.

"Touch me," Abbie whispered breathlessly.

"Be patient! Don't rush me," Jo giggled quietly but without hesitation she slipped her hand beneath the elastic of Abbie's French knickers and into the soft curly hair that covered her pubic mound. Abbie inhaled as with a stroking movement Jo ventured further into her warm dampness. She expertly slid her fingers between her labia, skimming her clitoris, fleetingly causing Abbie to shudder with delight.

"Don't be a tease, Jo," Abbie begged huskily.

With a slight hesitancy Jo pressed her fingers to Abbie's clitoris and began rhythmically rocking them backwards and forwards. As her fingers were busy she took her attention away from Abbie's lips and turned them instead to her pert nipples which were bobbing rhythmically near her face as Abbie's hips gyrated with Jo's fingers. She traced her tongue over the tip of the rosy pink nipple and teased her areola. With a swift movement she took the nipple between her teeth and pulled ever so gently on the end and Abbie bucked with pleasure at the slight pain coursing through her breast. Jo began to suck hard on it, returning a slight warming feeling as the sensation came back to her nipple. Jo's hand never stopped its movement all the time she was attending to Abbie's breasts, other than to change pace or direction, varying the sensations Abbie received. Within minutes she was writhing hard against the day bed. Moaning loudly as Jo continued to flick her fingers across her clitoris and suck at the nipple. With a small squeal of delight she clamped her thighs hard against Jo's hand, restricting her movement and gently placed her hand on Jo's arm. Jo's movements slowed to a stop and kissed Abbie firmly on her mouth to seal the intimacy.

"Unbelievable," was all Abbie could mumble as her vaginal

muscles throbbed deep inside her. Her breath was still heavy and Jo knew she must have begun what she had intended.

As Abbie recovered, Jo turned her attention to the therapy bed in the centre of the room. She used the control to raise the back upright and separate the legs apart, lifting the calf sections so that the bed resembled a couch in a gynaecologist's office, and opening up the foot rests that looked like stirrups. The foot rests were only normally used when the chiropodist was at the home, but today they would have a much more important function.

She returned to Abbie, whose breathing had slowed, and sensually removed her French knickers. Taking her hands and pulling her in to a sitting position, she squatted down to face her lover, who had a dazed, sleepy look on her beautiful face and again, kissed her gently on the mouth.

"Ready for more?" she asked softly. Abbie shook her head slowly and half-heartedly asked for a further break but she nevertheless allowed Jo to lead her over to the therapy couch. She assumed the position without question. Jo took her time to kiss the entire length of her slender legs, from toe to thigh, as she placed each leg in each stirrup. Jo raised the bed and pulled the stool from its position under the couch. The bed was at perfect height and Jo only needed to stretch her neck a little to run her tongue the full length of Abbie's succulent labia. Abbie groaned loudly as she thrust her hips softly towards Jo's face, eager for more.

"Are you ready?" she asked, but of course, it was a rhetorical question. Abbie placed her hands on her breasts and began to massage them firmly.

"Make me come!" she demanded in a whispered hush.

Jo needed no further commands, eagerly burying her face into Abbie's hot pussy. The muskiness excited Jo immensely. As she delved around Abbie's pussy with her tongue, she slipped her fingers in to her own tight lace thong and began to play with her own sopping pussy, rubbing herself with a much harsher ferocity than she used with her lover. Her tongue settled on Abbie's swollen clit and she slowed her pace a little, savouring the taste of her lover. Abbie's hand pressed firmly on Jo's head and encouraged her to increase her pace, but Jo had no intention of speeding up. With the very tip of her tongue she sent hard powerful single strokes across Abbie's clit, first from top to bottom and then from left to right. She alternated these with little sucks, pulling the clit out between the lips before delving back into the sticky loveliness. Abbie's thrusting increased and so Jo increased her pace ever so slightly. She was determined to make Abbie come more than once whilst she was down there.

She had not been lapping long before Abbie's hips bucked against Jo's head, almost forcing her backwards. Abbie screamed with ecstasy as she reached orgasm hard. Her pussy seeped sticky love juice, covering Jo's face and breasts.

"I love it when you scream like that," Jo whispered sultrily, running her tongue around her lips and over her breasts, lapping up Abbie's come. Jo waited for Abbie's breathing to subside just long enough before returning to her place firmly between Abbie's thighs.

This time she kissed her lover's soft mound, enjoying the sensation of her downy pubic hair on her nose and cheeks as she pressed her lips against the aromatic flesh. Abbie squealed with delight at the thought of more tonguing, but Jo had no intention of a repeat performance. Instead with her middle finger, she swept the tip around the tight muscled entrance to her velvety passage. Abbie shuddered with pleasure. Relishing the softness of her lover's pussy, Jo slipped her finger inside, feeling around with the tip for the holy grail of sex – the G-spot. A loud gasp from Abbie assured Jo that she had found what she was looking for and she didn't hesitate in inserting another finger inside her lover. She rubbed at the spot with slow circular movements at first but increased steadily in speed as Abbie's moans grew louder. With her spare hand she rubbed at Abbie's clit, bringing her to a sudden, crashing orgasm that Jo could feel as Abbie's tight hole squeezed around her fingers. Abbie reluctantly pushed her lover away from her, ignoring the complaints that Jo wasn't finished, in need of rest. She lay, spent, in her moment of absolute pleasure. She rested there for almost ten minutes, Jo tenderly kissing her feet and sucking her toes until Abbie had recovered.

"Now it's your turn. I've got a surprise for you!" Abbie said, gently removing her tingling legs from the stirrups and slowly moved to her bag near the day bed.

She took out a large Tupperware lunch box, which contained a smooth white plastic bag, which she removed and placed onto the therapy couch.

"What's in there?" Jo asked, her voice full of intrigue.

"I saw it on the Internet and couldn't resist it."

"It's not an inflatable fuckbuddy is it? I don't need one of those!" Her curiousness got the better of her, and Jo hastily picked up the plastic bag and ripped it open. Inside she pulled out what seemed to be a lilac leather G-string, but was very surprised, not to mention pleased and excited, when she turned it around and found a six-inch pink dildo attached to the leather. A huge, dirty smile spread across her lips and before she could say anything else, Abbie's hand slapped her arse with a ferocity that surprised her even more.

"Hey, we don't usually do punishment." Jo stood back, wondering where this side of Abbie's nature had come from.

"Just shut up!" Abbie commanded. "It's your turn to get on the couch! On to your hands and knees." As Jo put down the strap-on, Abbie's hand again met with her already tender rump, but this time she moaned with pleasure. Abbie raised the bed to a sitting position, so that Jo's large, round arse was lower to the floor than her head. Abbie eagerly stepped into the strap-on, altering the straps when it sat around her waist, to ensure that it wouldn't slip. Jo didn't move. Abbie fetched the tube of lubricant from her handbag and liberally applied it to the end of the phallus. Jo gave a giggle as Abbie searched around the therapy room for a towel or something to wipe her now sticky hand on. Instead, Abbie cupped the palm of her hand around Jo's mound and wiped the excess lubricant into her soft pubic hair.

"That's going to be sticky for the rest of the day." Jo exclaimed through whimpering lips as Abbie's fingers brushed between her labia, softly caressing her clitoris.

"That will give you a smile. Now shut up; I'm going to give you the fuck of your lifetime." Abbie stood close behind Jo, and with a gentle hand slipped the cock inside Jo's sopping wet pussy. Jo drew breath sharply and then moaned as the hard rubber buried deeper inside her. Abbie rested her body against Jo's back and reached around her torso to fondle her breasts. The dildo now fully inside her, Jo tried to rock her hips to begin the pleasure but with Abbie's weight against her back and her hands held firmly around her breasts, she could get no movement going.

"Wait!" Abbie ordered, as she gently kissed her way along Jo's spine. When she got as far as she could reach, she drew back her hips pulling the dildo from inside Jo and then slowly thrusting it back inside her. Jo's back arched as Abbie continued to glide the strap-on in and out of her lover's wet pussy. The squelching it made as it slipped in and out of the warm moist hole almost made Jo giggle, but she was focusing on the fantastic sensation that the knobbles on the cock were having on the inside of her pussy. Her G-spot was being stimulated like she had never experienced before. Abbie moved her hips from a slow gentle rock to a faster thrust as Jo bounced up and down towards Abbie, their sweaty bodies slapping as Jo's rump hit Abbie's stomach with quite a force.

Jo's breathing was becoming faster and she could feel the pleasure building in her pussy, her clitoris throbbing for attention.

"Turn me over," she breathed to Abbie, who withdrew far enough to allow Jo to turn onto her arse. Abbie pushed her lover's legs apart, Jo sticking her feet into the stirrups of the couch for more leverage. Abbie dived to her knees and eagerly began lapping at Jo's swollen clitoris with her tongue, Jo pushing Abbie's head into her pussy so hard that it was a miracle she could breathe let alone continue to suck and lick Jo's rock hard clit.

Jo's thrusting became wild as she continued towards the orgasm the dildo had started. Abbie anticipated the coming climax and, just as Jo was on the verge of the abyss, Abbie jumped to her feet and plunged the dildo into her mate, eagerly rubbing her clit with her thumb as she began to again pump the cock deep in and out of her lover's tightening pussy. Jo's moaning turned into screams as her orgasm spread through her body and her pussy juice squirted from inside her over Abbie's sweat glistening stomach.

As Abbie withdrew the cock, Jo collapsed back against the therapy couch. When her partner's hands fell from the bed to dangle limply at her side, Abbie played a tender kiss on Jo's forehead. Jo opened her eyes to look at her lover.

Whilst Jo recovered, Abbie moved to the sink and cleaned the dildo before returning it and the lube to her handbag.

"Oh, God!"

"What?"

"Unbelievable," was all Jo could mumble as she crept behind Abbie and placed her hands around her waist. She planted tender kisses on her neck affectionately.

"I'm glad you enjoyed it." Abbie smiled as she turned to face her partner.

The two women shared a deep passionate kiss and enjoyed the moment together.

As Abbie freshened up at the sink, Jo hunted around the room for her scattered underwear. When Abbie was finished, she and Jo returned the furnishings to their original condition and positions. For the last ten minutes of their lunch break, the women snuggled up on the daybed and basked in their respective after-sex glow.

The girls had just enough time to straighten their uniforms and tidy themselves up before they could hear another member of staff calling for Jo. Jo stepped out of the therapy room, trying to get the agency staff away from the door, leaving Abbie skulking behind it.

"There's a gentleman and his carer at the door. A Mr Dunbar? Says he has an appointment," Grace said, looking a little vague.

"Show me to him," Jo said, taking Grace by the arm and leading her off to the visitor's room where Mr Dunbar was waiting in his wheelchair.

"Good afternoon, Mr Dunbar. Do you remember me?" Mr Dunbar nodded. "Hello there, Miss Dunbar. I'm the Matron or you can call me Jo, if you prefer. Your key person will be Nurse Spencer, or Abbie. She is just finishing her lunch break, she will join us shortly." Just as Jo uttered the words, Abbie came into the visitor's room behind her.

"Abbie, you're just in time! Mr Dunbar, this is Abbie, Abbie, this is Mr James Dunbar and his daughter Rebecca."

The pleasantries were exchanged and Abbie sat directly in the seat to the left of the door. A brief chat and some paperwork completed, Abbie felt she had hit it off perfectly with James Dunbar or Jimmy as he preferred to be called. His daughter wasn't bad either, kind of pretty in a very innocent way. Abbie had noticed the glances Rebecca had been sending her and that Jo hadn't witnessed those, or indeed the looks she had been giving back. With an hour of exhausting and energetic sex, followed by an immediate return to arousal, Abbie felt she was in dire need of refreshment and was glad when Jo suggested she took the visitors into the conservatory for afternoon tea.

Jo excused herself first and headed off to her office to file the paperwork but was brought back to the corridor by a loud scream followed by a dirty-sounding laugh. When she turned the corner into the corridor she found Abbie pressed against the wall, Mr Dunbar rubbing his hands with delight and his daughter looking quite red.

"What's happened?" Jo asked, eager to get to the bottom of the problem.

"I'm going to like it here," Mr Dunbar exclaimed with glee, "especially if I'm going to get this welcome every day."

Jo looked on in bewilderment. Seeing their confusion, Rebecca made a twirling motion in the air, prompting Abbie to turn around and Mr Dunbar to again give the dirty laugh.

Much to Jo's arousal and Abbie's horror, in her hurry to dress Abbie had tucked her uniform into her suspender belt and her stockings and panties were on show at the back, and the smell of sex coming from her panties was overwhelming.

"Oh! How embarrassing! I'm terribly sorry." Abbie blushed profusely.

"Not a problem, my dear," smirked Mr Dunbar. "You dirty girl!" He patted his lap, adjusted his manhood and indicated for Abbie to hop on.

Queen High Flush

Pam Graham

Six players, actually four players and two con artists, sat at the number eight poker table. From the dealer's left they included the middle-aged blond guy with inflated muscles and a mechanic's fingernail woes, the Air Force lieutenant who surely chose to wear that uniform out of some misguided hope it might distract the other players, the cowboy who cleaned up real nice, the elegant blonde who had picked him up in the restaurant earlier, the grandfather wearing a blue silk shirt, and the warrior princess who stacked and re-stacked her chips to hide her fascination with the blonde.

Inwardly noting that this appeared to be a harmless bunch, the dealer settled on private names for them all. The men were a simple matter. They'd be Michelin Man, Fly Guy, Cowboy and Gramps. But the women. The blonde was all smooth coolness and light, and the sight of her made you hope for a creamy centre. Yes, she would be Cream. That left the tall and intense goddess who sat just to the dealer's right. Aphrodite might work.

The dealer shuffled the deck while going over the house rules and ended with, "So, this table features a variation of seven-card stud with no raise limit. You'll get your first card down, then four facing up, and finish the deal with two additional hole cards. Everybody gets to see four of your cards, but the privilege of looking at those other three is yours alone. Are we ready to begin, ladies and gentlemen? Okay then."

Cowboy took the first pot, and as he pulled in his winning chips, Fly Guy said, "Starting off right, I'd say."

Grinning at Cream, Cowboy said, "Already started off nice, before the game even got going." He'd told everybody how they'd just met that night and had dinner together.

It was against hotel policy to roll your eyes at the guests' comments, but the dealer really wanted to. Aphrodite did it for both of them. She sighed too, with an impatient grunt at the end.

The next hand got interesting as a battle of raises developed between Michelin Man and Gramps. By the fifth card they were the only two left in, which made way for Aphrodite to develop some brazen eye contact with Cream. To her credit, Cream weathered the barefaced come-on with an aplomb that Cowboy openly approved of.

Aphrodite got quite a nice hand and won the next pot, but she didn't capitalize enough on two tens in the hole to go with the one she had showing. Sitting on something like that, she should have done some moderate raising. The dealer diagnosed that lapse as Cream fever.

Half an hour later, Cream still hadn't won a pot. She didn't have much showing, but started raising on the fourth card. Everybody got wary since it was the first hand she'd put anything behind. When she pushed three hundred dollars to the center after getting a look at her fifth card, all but Aphrodite folded.

Aphrodite smiled as she slid her chips forward, and without another glance at her hole cards she winked at Cream and said, "Call you, and let's make it worth our while with three hundred more."

Cream peeked at her down card and stayed.

When she saw her sixth card, which was dealt face down, Cream seemed to be suppressing a smile. "Five hundred."

Aphrodite was wearing a matte black jumpsuit zipped to a level that showed little cleavage unless she leaned over. She laid her hole cards in front of her and placed an elbow on either side of them. Then she shifted forward until she was certain Cream had a good view and said from somewhere deep down in that jumpsuit, "I'm in."

The dealer marked this moment as a turning point in the dynamic. Cream was beginning to unravel.

The seventh card didn't seem to interest either woman. They'd apparently built their hands on the first six.

Cream continued to exhibit great faith in what she was holding. And her composure was back in place. She looked directly at Aphrodite. "One thousand."

As Aphrodite counted chips, she cordially said, "A bargain at any price – to get to see yours." Then she forwarded a second stack. "And how badly do you want to see mine? One thousand more."

Cream steadied herself by gripping Cowboy's forearm with one hand as she put in her thousand with the other, which was shaking, the dealer couldn't help but notice.

Aphrodite somehow transformed the act of turning up her cards into a sensual experience. Cream tried to dispel that effect by carelessly flinging hers to the middle of the table. Neither hand was much good. They had boosted the pot to over five thousand dollars on three nines and two pairs. Cream won it with the three nines.

Cream wasn't much of a force during the hand after that, and when it was over she excused herself for a few minutes.

Aphrodite stayed long enough to ante and look at three cards in the following hand before folding and getting up. She addressed herself to Cowboy. "Think I need to powder my nose, too."

At a discreet distance, Jacka followed Margaret to her room and, after checking that no one had tailed them, she slipped in the door.

Wide-eyed, Margaret said in the most controlled voice she could muster, "This is going to work, you know."

Jacka twirled her way to the bed and bounced on it hard. "Jesus Christ! It is."

"And not only that, my darling, it's turning out to be fun. I mean, I wasn't all that nervous once we got started, were you? And the patsies are just normal people." Margaret looked down at Jacka all kicked back on the bed, and then at her own dress and heels. "Next time I get to be the butch and you get to wear the dress."

Jacka hopped to her feet. "Be happy to, sweetheart. But let's not call them patsies. Isn't the term 'marks'? Aren't they our marks?"

"We'll have to look that up on the Net. Even if it is marks, though, I don't think we should call them that because of my brother Mark."

"Oh, right. Same thing with patsies for me, because of Patsy Cline."

"Didn't think about that. We'll look it up." Margaret checked her new fancy watch. "So, if we stick to our plan to be gone for twenty minutes, we've got fourteen left. Now, let's go over everything real quick."

Jacka laced her hands behind Margaret's back and swayed gently. "When we return to the table, you'll look flustered and uncertain. I'll look like the pussy that swallowed the canary."

"Yep. Then as soon as we both get a couple of barely worthwhile hands, we get into another unrealistic raising duel. That first one worked so perfectly. Did you see the looks on their faces when we showed our pitiful cards?"

"I was afraid to look at their faces. Okay, so we repeat that little operation. And I think everybody *will* be afraid to stay with us again, especially if we raise big enough and none of them has an extremely great hand. One more of those and we go in for the kill. The third time, when one of us is holding an actual first-class hand, they'll be so convinced we're playing with some organ other than our brains, a couple of them should stay right with us, no matter how high we raise." Jacka checked the time before slipping her hand under Margaret's dress and running it between her thighs. "Eleven minutes to worship the panty hose goddess."

Margaret opened her legs a little and Jacka traced figure eights around the crotch seam. "Tickle me just like that. Mmm." Margaret stepped backward so she could brace herself on the dresser and present herself better.

Jacka's fingers stopped. "Oh, no you don't. First day in our new careers and you want to take a chance on messing it up by fooling around?"

Margaret encouraged Jacka's hand back into action. "I'm supposed to look flustered, remember?"

"Flustered, not satisfied." Before resuming the lazy eights, Jacka delicately pinched at the silky material in the spot where it was getting damp.

"I won't come, promise."

A few minutes later, Margaret was ducking out the door, looking undone indeed. "Get to the table several seconds after me."

"Right." Jacka kissed her cheek. "Oh, wait, wanted to ask you something. What's your guess on the dealer? Lesbian?"

"Not a doubt in my mind."

Cream was all business as she took her seat. A quick survey told her that Michelin Man had enjoyed a streak of luck while they were away. She took the first pot and was raking it in as Aphrodite came back to the table radiating oneness with the universe. The moment Aphrodite was back on the scene,

Cream's composure went on a downward spiral. Between glancing uncertainly at Aphrodite every few seconds and the obvious effort of controlling the tremble of her hands, Cream did not seem to have her head in the game. Aphrodite just grinned.

Next hand, the dealer had to declare a misdeal after incorrectly distributing the third card face down. In keeping with house rules, the contents of that pot were carried over to the next one.

After enduring three deals under these edgy conditions, Cowboy asked Cream if she'd like to get some air.

"I just had some air. What I'd like is to play poker." She glanced at her hole cards again and said to Fly Guy, "See your fifty and raise one hundred."

Fly Guy called and laid down his three nines.

"That beats my," Cream fumbled to check her down cards again, "my pair of sevens."

Gramps, who had folded his pair of kings the first time Fly Guy raised, said, "Well for shit sakes," and glared at Aphrodite.

Fortunes waxed and waned over the next two hours until Cream and Aphrodite performed their battle of wills again in a raising contest that put almost six thousand dollars on the table after it was down to just the two of them. As had happened the first time, Cream won with a marginal hand.

Then Cream got a hand without much showing, but she started raising early in increments unevenly divisible by twenty-five dollars. That was the signal that she might be going for the kill.

By the time the fifth card was dealt, everybody was still in and raising hot and heavy.

When the bet came to her, Cream glowered at Aphrodite and said, "One thousand to stay."

Gramps was next, and he reflected a while before calling.

Aphrodite shoved her chips to the center without hesitation.

Michelin Man stayed.

Fly Guy eagerly got in on the action.

Cowboy stayed.

Everybody was in.

The pot held well over four thousand dollars profit and there were two more cards to be dealt.

Cream, seemingly unconcerned that the others were still alive, challenged Aphrodite to spend two thousand for the sixth card. Aphrodite did it smiling. Gramps got out that round, but the rest called. Ten thousand profit in the pot.

For the seventh card, Cream went to twenty-five hundred and Aphrodite raised that another thousand. After Michelin Man, Cowboy and Fly Guy were all in, the center of the table was piled high with over twenty thousand dollars more than Cream and Aphrodite had invested.

Turning up her hole cards for mainly Aphrodite to see, Cream proudly declared, "Queen high flush."

Grandpa was out, so Aphrodite was next. She shrugged as she displayed three twos.

Michelin Man moaned as he showed his three tens, and Fly Guy threw in his three kings so hard they almost scooted off the table. Cowboy was embarrassed to show the lousy two pair he'd stuck with too long, but after a certain point he'd have felt like a sissy for folding.

As Cream stacked her loot, their dealer broke the seal on a new deck and said, "Luck for the lady tonight."

Cream said, "Beginner's luck, I guess."

Aphrodite nodded solemnly once before aiming that smug grin at Cream and assuring her, "Beginners do get lucky. Sometime."

After playing conservatively for another half hour, Cream declared her intention to play one more hand and then cash in.

Aphrodite again excused herself from the table the first hand after Cream left.

Margaret had been in their room for over fifteen minutes when the phone rang.

"It's me, sweetheart."

"Jacka, what's taking so long? I thought we said you'd only stay for one more hand."

"I did, but there's a little complication. Your dinner date is following me."

"Crap. We didn't plan for that. We have some honing to do, but can you believe this? We're really going to make this work, Jacka."

"How much did we clear?"

"Eighteen thousand four hundred, plus or minus what you won or lost."

"I lost six hundred."

"Then that's a grand total of seventeen thousand and eight

hundred dollars for one night's work. And we're working *together*. And it was *fun*. Jacka, I'm so glad we quit our jobs to follow this dream."

Jacka checked the bar mirror to make sure he was still there. "Can't wait to get to the room and count it with you."

"No counting, darling, it's a cashier's check. This isn't the Old West, you know."

"Feels like it, though. Look, I'm going to try one more time to beat Sugar Pops Pete to an elevator."

"What do you mean, 'one more time?' Have you already tried that?"

"Yeah, but he stuck close and got right on with me. Didn't say a word."

"Jacka, this is an order, do not get on another elevator with that man. We don't know that he won't hurt you."

Jacka thought it over for a few seconds. "No, I think he's on some mission to preserve your honour. Deny me at your gate and all that."

"Whatever the case, we can't take a chance on him getting our room number."

Blowing out a long sigh, Jacka offered, "What if I hop in a cab and ride around for ten minutes, then get dropped off at the rear entrance and sneak through the other side of the lobby?"

"That would be smart. We'll figure out a way to avoid this in the future." Margaret's voice softened. "But a five-minute ride should do it, don't you think?"

Jacka laughed. "You've started without me, haven't you?"

"Maybe. I didn't think it would hurt to get back to where we left off earlier before going back to the game."

"So, what are you doing? Still wearing the hose?"

"Mmm hmm. I'm imitating what you were doing."

"Please don't come without me. Listen, it could take a couple of minutes to get the taxi. You have my permission to keep tickling yourself for ten more minutes. After that, I want you to lie back on the bed with your legs spread wide for me and imagine in great detail what I'm going to do when I get there. Keep your panty hose on, play with your breasts if you like, but do not touch anywhere near your cunt after that time is up."

"Hurry, darling."

Ages later, when Jacka's next call came in, Margaret forgot her telephone etiquette. "Where the hell are you?"

"You didn't come, did you?"

"No, but if you're deliberately—"

"It's not deliberate, believe me. I'm as hot to get there as you are to have me."

Margaret snickered. "Highly doubtable."

"So sorry, sweetheart. But the cab got caught in the gridlock from some accident and I don't know this city well enough to get out and walk, and I'm so sorry."

"Are you back now?"

"In the lobby. Just me, the clerk and your boyfriend. I don't think we should do the pick up a guy part next time."

"But it's essential to establishing the femme's straightness."

"We'll figure it out later. Anyway, do you have another idea?"

"Yes. First, let me make myself come. Then, you go to the desk and book another room. Tip the clerk to send a bellboy up to it with you. I don't want you on an elevator alone with the weirdo. He can't lurk around in a hallway like he can in the lobby. If he follows you up there, call security."

"Margaret, I know you're suffering, but please wait for me. And I think your condition is clouding your judgment here. We can't attract attention to ourselves by calling security."

"Then you think of something."

Jacka caught sight of their dealer walking toward the revolving doors, probably on her way home. "No time for details right now, baby, but I think the cavalry just rode in. Tell you what, you have exactly ten strokes to spend on yourself – anyplace you like. No more. I should be there soon."

The truth, or half of it, occasionally works as well as a lie. When Jacka explained that the cowboy was blocking her access to the blonde, and asked the dealer to distract him just long enough for an elevator door to close, she was happy to oblige.

Jacka walked in the room as Margaret was enjoying a well-earned orgasm. When it was over, Jacka commented, "Should have made that five strokes, I see."

Margaret propped herself on her elbows and said, "True. I couldn't have done it in five." She pushed her hair back and held out a hand to Jacka. "Hey, want to order something to eat and gawk at our cashier's check?"

"Not quite yet." Jacka lowered the zipper on her jumpsuit while saying, "Take off those hose. You haven't gotten your best hand of the night yet." When they were both stripped and snuggled under the blanket, Jacka squeezed three fingers together and pressed them into Margaret. "Nice preparation, sweetheart. I feel very welcome."

"I'm so ready for this."

Jacka used her knee to urge Margaret's thighs farther apart and pushed deeper as she added another finger. She pulled back until she was almost out and then thrust back in with just the right force to drive Margaret wild. Without breaking rhythm, Jacka whispered, "You get this for as long as you want before I come all the way in. Just tell me when to give you more."

"I want this for ever."

Jacka's voice was charged with the smile that swept over it. "Then I'll never quit." She twisted a little on the next entry so that her knuckles rolled across Margaret's most sensitive spot.

Margaret was clutching the sheets with all her might, groping for the strength to handle so much stimulation. Jacka lived for this part, for the ability to force Margaret into actually needing courage to deal with the pleasure she was giving her. Over and over, Jacka pierced her, varying the pressure, speeding up, slowing down and twisting, until Margaret implored, "All the way, darling."

For an unbearable moment, Jacka separated from her completely. Then, with her fist poised the way she knew Margaret could take it all in, she eased it just past the opening, holding there long enough to pick up on the strength of the pulse. She made four teaser attempts at full entry, rocking her fist as if to go in, but pulling back before really trying.

Her arms weak from clinging to the sheets, Margaret rammed her pelvis forward and made a faint effort to grab Jacka's wrist and force it in.

"Relax, Margaret. You've been so brave. Relax, and I promise to fuck you until you're done."

Margaret dropped her hand to her side and loosened her hips. Jacka whispered, "That's my girl," and penetrated smoothly until Margaret's cunt enfolded her fist. Jacka's hand pumped a gentle rhythm in time to Margaret's pulsing muscles until they gathered strength, stilled for a moment and erupted in wave after wave of release.

Later, when Margaret began to stir, Jacka asked, "So, did that beat your queen high flush?"

"Hands down."

Confessions After Midnight

L. C. Jordan

"Happy birthday to you!"

The familiar refrain rang out from a small group gathered around a table directly across from me. The restaurant was nearly empty; Thursdays were usually slow and I had commandeered a corner booth with my newspaper and tea.

Lowering the editorial section, I watched as my head waitress Gina carefully sat a cake down in front of an auburn haired woman seated at the table. It wasn't unusual for customers to include a request for a birthday cake in their reservations. I estimated that nearly eighty percent of the time the cakes were topped with an equally frightening and embarrassing amount of candles. This one however had a single candle flickering in the middle of the whitecaps of frosting.

The woman's face was slightly flushed, whether from laughter or nerves I didn't know. She looked around her circle of companions, spoke a handful of soft words that I couldn't hear, and in one quick breath extinguished the flame. Her friends applauded their approval and smiling, she glanced up in my direction and caught me staring. Startled at the unexpected eye contact, I could only shrug my shoulders, grin like an idiot and mouth happy birthday.

I was about to raise my paper again as an effective barrier when a voice close to my ear caused me to jump a good three inches off my bench.

"Whatcha looking at?" Gina whispered as she leaned over my shoulder. My eyes darted from Gina to the birthday girl, who judging from her wide smile was obviously amused by my antics.

Snapping my newspaper back in place, I raised one eyebrow at Gina. "Nothing," I replied.

"Musta been something. I asked you twice if you wanted me

to reheat your tea." Gina leaned one hip on my booth and looked utterly too pleased with herself.

"No, you didn't."

"Yes, I did."

"Want to do it now?" I slid the cup towards her.

"In a minute." She jerked her head to the left. "Know who she is?"

I sighed. Trust Gina to have come away with a name and social security number in exchange for that cake. I sometimes wondered if she was a former CIA operative from her ability to gather information. But she didn't look the part with her soulful brown eyes and five foot two frame. People just naturally opened up to her. If I owned a bar and Gina tended, we'd be rich.

Lowering my paper a fraction of an inch, I studied the woman in question as she stood slicing pieces of cake for her friends. She was slender but not thin, and a mint green sweater outlined the perfect swell of breasts and tapered down to the trim waist of her slacks. A few tendrils of copper hair fell forward and she absently reached up to push them back. Beautiful, I thought.

"Nice to see you're human after all," Gina said as she nudged my shoulder and brought me back to my senses. "Now, wanna know who she is?"

"You mean besides someone I'll probably never see again?" At that, Gina snatched a section of newspaper and whacked my leg.

"I swear, Kai, fate could be knocking and you'd stop to catch the rinse cycle to add softener before answering."

I had to laugh at that because it was pretty much the truth. Since my uncle retired eight months ago and sold Brody's to me, I had focused all of my energy here. Having my own restaurant was more work than managing one for someone else, but certainly worth it to me. Plus, how could I pass up the opportunity to see my last name in lights every night? Had to keep it in the family, I reasoned. Unfortunately it left little free time in the evenings and my social life had become less of a priority.

"Her name is Riley O'Fallon," Gina continued. "She's the host of that radio talk show I told you about. You know, Confessions After Midnight."

"Oh, you mean the station that has the 'alternative lifestyle format'? The one where women call in to see who has the most depressing love life?" I knew that would get Gina riled up. I braced myself for the inevitable paper slap but it never came. Instead, Gina tossed the newspaper onto the table and narrowed her eyes at me.

"It's a lot more than that, Kai. Don't knock something you don't understand. People call into that show just to have someone to talk to late at night when maybe there's no one else who'll listen."

"OK, OK," I held my hands up in surrender. A thought occurred to me then and I asked, "Have you ever called the show?"

"Yeah, I have," she answered, not meeting my eyes.

I reached out and tugged on her sleeve. "Hey, you know you can call me any time."

Gina met my eyes then and the corner of her mouth quirked up in a grin. "I know, but this was before I knew you were home every night. Now why don't you go do that thing you do and ask them how their meal was?" She pushed off the bench and strolled away.

Picking up my newspaper again, I tried to concentrate. After reading the same paragraph three times and not remembering a word, I gave up. Refusing to admit defeat, I stretched and unfolded myself from the booth. Slipping my charcoal blazer back on, I ran my hand through the black curls that just brushed the back of my collar and crossed the otherwise empty dining room to the only table left occupied. Four pairs of eyes, including two incredibly green orbs, all settled on me.

"How is everyone this evening?" I launched into my automatic speech. "We hope you enjoyed your meal and look forward to having you with us again."

"The fettuccini was excellent," a twenty something man replied enthusiastically. "Are you the chef?"

"No, that would be Stephen," I smiled. "My name is Kai Brody, I'm the owner. But I'll be sure to pass on the compliment." My gaze was drawn again to those green eyes as the woman whose name I already knew introduced herself.

"Nice to meet you Kai. Riley," she said as she offered her hand. "We really enjoyed ourselves."

As I took her hand in mine, the sensation was so acute I wondered if every nerve in my body had suddenly become hotwired to my palm. Dimly I realized I hadn't released her hand and I quickly broke contact. I gestured towards the remainder of the cake with my wayward digits.

"Gina can box up the rest of that for you when you're ready to leave." Disconcerted, I turned to go when Riley's voice stopped me.

"Would you like a piece?" Her question caused all eyes to once again focus on me. The unintentional double meaning to that simple question flashed across my mind and I was acutely embarrassed by my train of thought. I opened my mouth to decline, but Riley continued. "My friends need to call it a night but I actually start work in about an hour. I'd like another cup of coffee before I go if I could impose upon you to keep me company." She paused, then, "Or I could play the sympathy card since it's my birthday."

"There's the Riley we know and love," the fettuccini man chimed in as he picked up the check, accompanied by good natured laughter around the table. Everyone rose, taking turns to embrace Riley and then suddenly we were left standing in silence. I spied Gina and the busboy waiting in the kitchen doorway and I motioned them over.

"Why don't we sit over there?" I suggested, pointing to the next table. Automatically I pulled out a chair for Riley and a surprised expression briefly crossed her features.

Spinning back around to retrieve the remainder of the cake, I nearly collided with Gina.

To her credit she was trying to suppress a smile and didn't say a word, much to my relief. She simply handed me the leftover dessert and headed back to the kitchen. In a moment she returned with a fresh dish and silverware, a steaming cup of coffee for Riley and a carryout box. We both thanked her and she winked at me and followed the busboy's cart back out.

Suddenly nervous, I wiped my damp palms on my chinos and sat down. Riley had already cut a slice for me and was putting the rest into the cardboard container. The single candle stuck up just far enough to prevent the lid from closing. As I watched, she pulled it out and popped the icing-covered tip in her mouth, licking the bit of frosting from it. The innocent act suffused me with heat. Flustered, I said the first thing that came to mind.

"Did you make a wish?"

Riley's wide smile answered for her. "Yes, I did. But I don't think you're supposed to tell them to anyone or they won't come true."

"You have a point," I conceded.

She took a sip of coffee, studying me as I ate. "Kai," she said. "That's an unusual name for a woman."

I grimaced as I swallowed my last bite and Riley laughed at my pained expression. "I know for a fact that the food here is excellent, so it must have been the question that was sour."

Rolling my eyes, I repeated the same story I'd been repeating all my life. "It's a shortened form of the word kayak," I explained. "My parents had a twisted method for naming their children. Every summer they took a vacation and tried a new adventure sport. The year I was conceived, they paddled kayaks down the Colorado. Two years before that they learned to paraglide. My sister's name is Sky," I finished.

Riley snorted once in an effort to control her laughter. "I'm not laughing at you," she declared.

"Sure, I see that," I nodded in agreement.

"No, really I'm not. I like your name. Somehow it suits you," she said without any hint of sarcasm.

"Thanks. So Gina mentioned that you're on the radio." I wanted to steer the conversation away from myself.

Riley paused, then asked, "Do you listen to my show?"

Figuring honesty was safer, I replied, "No, not exactly. I've caught bits and pieces when I'm station-hopping in the car, but I'm afraid that's all."

"That's OK." Visibly relieved, Riley continued, "I'm actually glad you don't. I love what I do, talking to people about their hopes and dreams, their happy endings and their disappointments. Even with all the broken-hearted women out there this job is ten shades lighter than my last one. But I don't like to lead with it because people get a preconception." She grinned. "I'm far less entertaining in person than on the radio."

"So what did you do before?" I queried, then, "I'm sorry; that's a personal question."

"No, it's all right. I was a criminal psychologist. Don't ask," she warned in mock seriousness.

"You mean like a profiler?" I was intrigued. "Isn't that a bit of a leap in career paths?" I couldn't help teasing.

"Isn't it though?" There was that rich laughter again, but she didn't offer any further information. Glancing at her watch, she said apologetically, "I have to get going if I don't want to be late." Standing, she offered her hand again. "Thank you for extending the evening with me. I enjoyed your company." She hesitated, about to say more and then stopped.

"No thanks needed; it was a pleasure," I replied automatically, disappointed that it had come to an end but not having the courage to risk more. I watched Riley leave and was surprised at the vague sense of loss that followed. That lasted all of thirty seconds before Gina's voice behind me caused me to flinch again.

"What do you think?" she asked, hopeful.

"I think you need to stop sneaking up on me like that," I said, exasperated.

"You didn't used to be this jumpy. Too much stress. Need to do something about that. Why don't you ask her out?"

I rolled my eyes for the second time that night, hoping they wouldn't stick that way. "It's not that simple, Gina. I don't know if she's attached. Hell, I don't even know if she's gay," I pointed out logically.

Gina only took out her order pad and wrote something down. Tearing off the piece of paper, she slid it in my blazer pocket and asked, "Isn't it closing time?"

That night at home in my living room I sank into the deep cushions of the leather couch. Balancing a glass of blackberry wine in one hand and the remote in the other, I switched on the stereo. Gina's piece of paper lay on the coffee table. On it was scribbled the call letters WYXX and the digital number. Scanning until I found the station, I leaned back and looked at my watch. It was 11:58. The commercials finally ended and a voice I recognized came on the air.

"It's midnight ladies, and we know what that means. The kids are in bed and your parents aren't listening so it's time to confess what's on your mind. For tonight's topic I thought we'd explore birthdays. I just had one. Spent it with friends, did the whole blowing out the candle making a wish thing, and met a cute woman to boot."

At that, I choked on my wine and stared at the speakers as if they'd suddenly caught fire. Could she have been talking about me? No, I just didn't get that lucky. She must have meant somebody else. I focused on what she went on to say.

"So call in and tell us about that one birthday you spent with someone that you'll never forget. Or maybe you'd like to forget. Phone lines are open now."

I sat through the hour long program and saw how easily total strangers found it to talk to Riley. She never belittled, genuinely laughed when something someone said was hysterically funny, which it often was, and mostly just listened. And I figured that was the big draw for most of her listeners. I added WYXX to my favourites list and switched off the stereo at 1:00 a.m.

Friday at Brody's was always packed and a constant stream of customers kept me busy until closing. I didn't have time to think much about what, if anything, I was going to do with my infatuation. Gina did manage to ask me if I wanted to catch a late movie after closing with her and her partner, but I asked for a rain check. When she grinned and asked if I had a hot date at midnight, I did what any mature thirty-year-old would. I told her I had no idea what she was talking about.

11:45 p.m. Same couch, same radio station. I was a little early, but figured I could kill fifteen minutes opening my mail. When the familiar theme music came on, I tossed aside the envelope I was opening. Riley's voice came through the airwaves and I settled in to listen. The usual opening catch phrases aside, she gave the topic for tonight.

"It's Friday, people, so let's get a little wild. There's no full moon, but we can pretend there is. Haven't you ever met someone and fantasized about what would happen if you could take them on your own personal version of a perfect date? Would it be romantic or would it be steamy? I want details, ladies, but don't get us fined by the FCC. Call me later for that," she laughed.

I sat still, terrified of the idea that came to mind. No. I couldn't. I had never done anything nearly as crazy as what I was now considering. But I was seriously considering calling. What did I have to lose besides my dignity if it didn't work? I was already pretty sure that sitting at home listening to a woman on the radio every night was more pitiful than actually getting shot down by that same woman. I picked my cell up from the coffee table before I lost my nerve. I had to wait until Riley gave the station phone number again and then had to call twice before I got through, only to be put on hold. When a man's voice finally came back to me, he asked my name and told me I was caller five and to turn down my radio.

The room had gotten uncomfortably warm and I had trouble paying enough attention to what number caller Riley was up to as I listened to the show through my phone. When she said goodbye to caller number four, there was silence. Then her voice came back, but with a hint of uncertainty and she continued.

"Now we have caller number five and her name is Kai. So tell me Kai, what's your fantasy date?"

I didn't think; I couldn't or I would never be able to speak. I just said what came to mind without any filters.

"I hadn't really ever given much thought to what a perfect date would mean to me until tonight. If I had to pick a place, I could say a deserted beach, a blanket and seeing how beautiful her face looked in the moonlight. But honestly the location isn't important to me. Just being with her would be fantasy enough," I finished all in one breath and waited.

Riley didn't answer immediately and then said, "For not giving it much thought until tonight I'd say that's pretty good. It would work for me anyway." Pause again. "Is there anyone out there you're hoping is tuned in right now?" she asked.

"She heard every word," I replied, the idiocy of what I'd just done dawning on me.

"Well, then maybe you'll be calling us back with an update. For now though we have to break for one of our sponsors. Don't go anywhere," she ended as a commercial came on.

I wasn't sure if she meant me or her audience until I heard a click and the line was transferred to one without the program playing in the background. Then Riley's voice came back and she asked, "Kai, is that you?"

It was put up or shut up and I was already in deep, so I tried to sound more confident than I really was. "Hey Riley. Yeah, it's me. How many other women do you know by that name?" I tried to joke.

She wasn't having any of my nonsense though and stated, "I thought you didn't listen to my show."

"I don't. I mean I didn't until last night." Exasperated, I tried to explain. "Look, I know this was probably at the very best an inappropriate way to call you, but I didn't plan it; it just happened. I'm sorry if I overstepped," I finished, feeling more miserable and stupid by the minute.

"No. No, it isn't that. You just caught me off guard, is all. Listen, I have to get back. I'm off tomorrow night if you want to talk about this. What time can you leave the restaurant?"

Not expecting this, I stammered, "They can do without me any time after nine."

"Good enough. I'll see you then. Oh, and Kai?"

"Yes?"

"Turn off your radio. It's making me too damn nervous." And with that, she was gone.

The next day I alternated between mild panic and cautious excitement about seeing Riley. Gina kept giving me strange looks after I told her she was head honcho because I was leaving a little early. She basically ran things anyway even when I was here, so I knew I wouldn't be missed. She finally cornered me in the kitchen and wanted to know if I was sick. This of course triggered a fit of laughter on my part and I knew I really did need to try and get out more.

At ten minutes to nine I wondered how rude it would be to meet Riley out on the street and not have to let Gina see her. I didn't wonder for long because she was early. Gina spotted her the same instant I did but I got to her first.

Riley looked fantastic but maybe that was relative since I had only one other visual point of reference, but I didn't think so. She wore a white linen shirt tucked into black jeans and topped with a black leather blazer. "Ready?" was all she said and I nodded and followed her out.

We got into a mint condition sleek metallic blue corvette that I knew had to be at least a '56 or '57. She turned her head briefly and raised one eyebrow. "Do you always get into a strange car and not even ask where you're going?"

"No. Aren't you worried I'm some crazed fan stalking you?" I countered.

This got a laugh from her and she answered sensibly, "You don't fit any profile I've ever studied. And for the record, I never, ever would agree to meet any caller from the show. If I hadn't already known you from the other night this would not be happening."

She drove on in silence for several minutes and I realized that we were heading for the coast. You could already smell the salt from the ocean and the early March air already felt cooler. Pulling into a medium sized marina, she parked the vett and cut the engine.

Turning to face me, she said, "We could just sit here but the bucket seats are going to get old in a hurry. It isn't warm enough yet for the beach, but I think I have the next best thing." She grinned as she opened the car door and told me, "Come on."

I was beginning to realize that this wasn't your typical "let's get a cup of coffee and talk about it" kind of thing. She led the way down the docks to the third boat slip. I had never really gotten my sea legs, despite my auspicious name, and I hesitated as she climbed up the side of the yacht.

"I thought you liked the water," Riley cocked her head to one side as she stood on deck waiting for me to get on board.

"I like the water fine. Boats are another story," I admitted.

"I won't let you drown," she chuckled as she leaned down and held her hand out. I motioned her back and managed to climb up without ending up sprawled on the planks.

"Is this beast yours?" I asked as I took in my surroundings. The lights along the marina cast enough of a glow to see a blanket spread on the deck. There was a picnic basket, two Adirondack chairs and a bottle filled with sand. I could have sworn the tiny candle sticking out of it was the one from the birthday cake.

"She's mine. Not completely paid for, but mine and the bank's anyway." Her eyes followed mine and then she touched my sleeve. "Kai, maybe this looks a little presumptuous, but I honestly just wanted to talk. The whole thing you said last night . . . well, you seemed like you were sincere and I wanted to do this even if you laughed at me," she ended wistfully.

"No, this is great," I hurried to say. "I never expected, I mean, I'm the one who felt foolish for calling that way," I admitted.

"Why don't we call it a draw and just enjoy the night? There's no moon and I can't cook but I can order out with the best of them."

We sat on the blanket, forgoing the chairs and dug into the food she had picked up. From below deck she produced a bottle of cabernet and we each had a glass. As we ate, we talked about everything and nothing. The meal finished, I watched her gazing past the other boats out across the Pacific. I caught my breath at how lovely her profile was in the still of the night. Before I realized it, I had spoken.

"Good thing there isn't a moon because I don't think I could stand it if you were any more beautiful." Mentally slapping myself for sounding like a teenager trying out pickup lines, I waited for her reaction. She put her glass down and I sat with my eyes open as she leaned forward and her lips brushed mine. She pulled back and I felt her warm breath against my face as she spoke.

"From anybody else that would sound like a come on, but from you it just sounds sweet. You're just too damn cute, you know that?" Riley pulled back enough to search my eyes, her gaze dropping to my lips. My surprise wore off in that instant and I closed the short distance between us, my lips covering hers with a hunger that overwhelmed me. Riley threaded the fingers of both hands in my hair and pulled me closer. I braced one arm on the deck and wrapping the other around her waist, lowered her back onto the blanket.

The kiss deepened and I traced her lower lip with my tongue, silently asking for more. I felt her mouth open and the velvet softness welcomed me inside, making me shiver. Tasting the wine and something indescribably sweet that had to simply be Riley, I heard a moan and vaguely wondered if it was me. My hand slid up to cup her face as my lips moved lower, caressing her jaw line and then taking a delicate ear lobe between my teeth and gently tugging. Her whole body surged up against me and she gasped as my hand wandered inside the open collar of her shirt and my lips found her neck.

"Wait, Kai, wait." Her voice was strained and she gave a quick pull on my hair, raising my head back up. Immediately I stilled, confused.

"I'm so sorry," I began as I started to sit up. But Riley shifted and hooked one leg around mine, effectively stopping my retreat. Recognizing the uncertainty in my eyes, she reached up and kissed me tenderly.

"I said wait because even though I don't think anyone else is at the dock tonight I'd rather not chance having an unexpected audience. Besides," she broke into a sexy smile, "I'm overheated now but when this fifty-degree air hits my skin I'm not sure even you can keep me warm."

I couldn't help the grin that spread across my face. Riley released me and we got to our feet. She bent and picked up the glass bottle filled with sand supporting that miniature candle and wrapping her arm around my waist, led me below.

The flood lights of the marina cast enough of a glow through the portholes to see the steps descending to the cabin. Once we got inside, Riley sat the bottle down and picked a flashlight up off a small table, rummaging in a drawer until she found matches. There was an antique-looking lantern suspended from the low ceiling. She struck one of the wooden matches, the scratching noise loud in the room, and carefully raised the globe and lit the wick. Setting the globe back in place, she switched off the flashlight. The lantern cast a soft light over the small cabin, the flickering flame dancing off the dark wood walls. It wasn't a big space and every wall was flanked by some piece of furniture, including what appeared to be a twin sized bed on the side opposite from the stairs.

I sat down on the edge of the table, watching her. My throat went dry but I managed to speak. "Come here," I said softly. Riley crossed the short distance to reach me and then laying her palms flat on my thighs, she stepped into the vee of my legs. Our mouths met again, this time unhurried at first, simply discovering each other. I smoothed my hands across her back, rubbing circles lower and lower until I slid them into the back pockets of her jeans, pulling her against me. I could feel her nipples stiff against my own breasts and she was doing some incredibly crazy thing to my lower lip with her tongue. When she started rocking against me, my throbbing clit fired off a warning and I had to come up for air.

Riley leaned her forehead against my shoulder and said in wonder, "You're shaking?"

"Over-stimulated nervous system," I tried to laugh.

Without raising her head she started working the buttons of my shirt loose. "Just don't have a heart attack on me, OK? I'd nēver be able to carry you back up on deck to save my reputation," she teased.

"Worried about your reputation and not my cardiac health, eh?" I said in mock indignation. By the time she had freed the last button and was tugging my shirt from my pants, my desire outweighed my nervousness. In one quick move I scooped her up and sat her on the narrow bed.

Not relinquishing her hold on my shirtfront, she pulled me closer and then ran her hands down my arms, pushing the garment off my shoulders. I wasn't wearing a bra, but Riley didn't touch me. The heat in her gaze was enough to cause a flush to start at my neck and travel down to the hard tips of my breasts. Reaching for my belt, she unfastened the buckle and my hands covered hers as she started to unzip my chinos. I was feeling awfully exposed and more nervous than the first time I ever made love. Riley was still fully clothed and I needed to do something about that to even things up a bit.

Kicking off my shoes, I reached down and grasped her ankles, swinging her legs onto the bed and removed her boots. I stretched out beside her and wrapped my arms around her, maneuvering her on top of me while being careful not to knock us both off the narrow space. I nudged her up to straddle me and she did. Her linen shirt soon joined mine on the floor. I reached up and ran my finger along the upper edges of her bra. Her hands were gripping my forearms as I unhooked the front closure and the cups fell away. They were immediately replaced by my palms and Riley gripped me harder. Her body arched when I took a nipple between my fingers and rolled it.

Suddenly impatient, I reached for the waistband of her jeans. We both fumbled with the buttons and she finally had to stand up to get them off. I had never seen anything as stunning as Riley standing there with the shadows cast by the dim light outlining every curve. Her creamy breasts swayed as she moved and my gaze drifted lower to the triangle of dark red curls below her navel, evidence of her arousal making them even darker.

"I honestly could die happy right now," I whispered to her, totally serious.

"Don't even think you're getting off that easy," she warned as she crawled back up my body and began a series of mind numbing kisses. Her tongue trailed a wet path down my neck, stopping to nip at a pulse point and causing me to rise up against her. My hands were busy running from her shoulders to her hips, kneading the firm globes as I felt her mouth move close to my breast. She propped herself on one arm and with a wicked gleam in her eyes, took a nipple between her teeth and bit down lightly. The jolt ran straight to my groin. She released the tip and slowly licked it, soothing the slight ache before taking it into her mouth and sucking. She took each one in turn and then licked a path down my stomach, dipping into my belly button.

Her progress was impeded by my pants, and bunching up a handful of the material she jerked and demanded, "Off." I lifted my hips and then wondered how in the hell she got my pants and my briefs off in one swoop. But I didn't ponder that particular feat for long when she splayed her hands out on my inner thighs and coaxed me to open them farther.

She placed several lingering kisses on my legs, working her way closer to my center. I felt her fingers brushing the fine hair aside and gently parting my folds. I was wetter than I could ever remember being and she touched me slowly, massaging the swollen tissues. Only once did I open my eyes and look down at Riley. The visual was too much and I had to close them, but the image was forever burned into my brain.

As her stroking became more insistent, I had to have something to hold onto. Blindly reaching behind me, I grabbed the headboard. When she entered me with two fingers my back arched and the muscles in my arms strained with the effort of trying not to buck us off the bed. I had always been a quiet lover, but a deep groan tore from my throat. When I felt her tongue wash over my clit and then her mouth cover me as she sucked it in, I exploded. Riley curled her fingers deeper, finding the exact spot that finally wrenched a hoarse cry from me as I crashed over the edge.

My breathing slowly returned to normal along with my heart rate. Riley lay curled up against me, a quilt thrown over us to keep the chill air at bay. I had spent hours exploring her body, wanting to know her better than I knew myself and not relenting until she pleaded exhaustion.

Suddenly she sat up, throwing the cover off and causing goose bumps to pepper my skin. "What's wrong?" I demanded, concerned.

"Nothing," she answered. I watched, confused, as she struck another match and lit that tiny candle sticking out of the bottle of sand. The lantern had long since run out of oil and it was difficult to see clearly.

"Riley, what are you doing?" I was starting to get a bit worried. As quickly as she lit the candle, she closed her eyes and blew it out. Shivering, she jumped back in bed and pulled the quilt over us again.

"You want to tell me what that was about or do you just want me to use my imagination?" I asked into the darkness.

A slightly giddy chuckle sounded from the owner of the icy cold feet that just snuck over to my side of the bed. "Do you remember on my birthday when you asked me if I made a wish and I wouldn't tell you?"

"Yeah, I remember," I answered, still confused.

"Well, I have always made a wish on my birthday and if it comes true, I figure those candles or candle, as in this case, must be good ones. For wishes that is."

At this point I was glad for the dark so Riley couldn't see the skeptical look on my face. "And if the wish doesn't come true?"

"Defective candles," she answered.

"Ok, so I'm guessing that is what's left of your birthday candle that you just blew out again."

"Very good, Kai. Two points for you." She poked me in the side, making me squirm.

"At your restaurant, I saw you sitting there by yourself and then you looked so cute when Gina got you flustered, I wished for some way to meet you. I was this close to putting my own hair in my food just to have a reason to talk to you," she laughed.

I put my arms around her, holding her tight, and pressed my lips to the top of her head. "First," I stated, "I am not cute. Second, I do not get flustered." More laughter from Riley. "Lastly, are you going to tell me what you just wished for?"

She reached around behind me and pinched my cheek. "Are you insane?" she asked, disbelieving. "I'm not telling. That candle works!"

Hail Warning

Jean Roberta

KC dumped me in the rain, as though she wanted to wash me out of her life. Or maybe she did it then because she didn't want to see me cry, as if I would. Maybe she had some blood memory of her ancestors leaving their nearest and dearest in the Scottish mist as they boarded a ship bound for Canada. I had seen it coming, of course. KC had been on the rebound when she besieged me in the bar six months before after too many beers. In some sense, our whole relationship had been a long hangover on her side, while I had just been hanging on. Our soggy, muddy ending by the Victoria Street bridge was very predictable. Knowing this didn't make it easier to take.

"You know we don't have much in common, Jo," she told me diplomatically: no accusations or self-blame. "It wouldn't have worked." I choked back all the desperate words that sprang into my mind: *Relationships aren't just a matter of fate! You have to make them work! How can you say we have nothing in common? Have you forgotten my clit already? And my hungry cunt and my sensitive breasts and my eager fingers? They haven't forgotten you!* But I didn't say any of this to her in the rain, in the mud, under a vast grey prairie sky. "If you don't want to see me any more," I muttered, "then it can't work. If you want your freedom, I won't argue. It can't work if it's not mutual."

KC's eyes, which could pass for blue on good days, now looked as grey as the sky, and she couldn't look at me. "We had a good time while it lasted, didn't we?" she pleaded, fighting off her sense of guilt. "I'll see you around, Jo." In a small lesbian community, that was guaranteed, for better or worse. "We could have lunch sometime."

I couldn't resist a parting shot. "You're interested in someone else, aren't you?"

Her face gave her away. "Coral and I sort of want to get

together." This meant she was already courting Coral with flowers, perfume, coy love notes and invitations to dinner, movies, concerts, and the gay bar. Trying to be fair, I admitted to myself that KC had a talent for courtship, although she always floundered in the follow-up.

I was about to walk away, my face turned toward the rain so that it stung just enough, when KC threw her arms around me and pulled me to her with a strength born of guilt. That strength tempted me more than I wanted her to know. I like to think I'm not a weak woman, but rejection takes its toll. Against my common sense, I sighed and relaxed into her deceptively firm hug. She searched for my wet lips with hers, and gave me a kiss filled with the relief of knowing that her freedom had already been granted. I kissed back like an obsessed follower of lost causes. To complete the shame, tears filled my eyes and trembled in my lower lids, about to spill over.

She pulled away from me in the nick of time. "What are you doing this afternoon?" she asked as if my life still interested her. My mind shrieked a menu of answers: *Slash my wrists and write your name on my walls in blood! Ask around to find out where I can get a machine gun! And never mind why. Dig out all the old leather clothes I own and get ready to go to the bar so I can start a fight with a total stranger. Pick worms off the pavement and eat them with a flourish in front of a downtown department store.* Instead I answered, "I have errands to do," keeping it vague, aiming for a contemptuous monotone.

KC was giving me that patronizing look I sometimes get from other women in their thirties who think I'm cute because I look younger than they do: small and girlish. "I didn't want to hurt you," she crooned into my hair, tenderly lifting wet black strands off my face. "You probably shouldn't be alone today, honey," she had the gall to advise me. "Why don't you go see Ted? You haven't seen her for a while and she'd probably like to go for coffee. You two always have things to talk about."

I shivered slightly as an image of our friend Theodora sprang into my mind. I told myself this was caused by being drenched in cool rain after being dumped. KC's comment sounded like further evidence of how wrong she was about so many things, especially everything to do with me.

KC and all the shallow women we both knew seemed to think that Ted and I were friends. They saw only the obvious: I was rarely at a loss for words and Ted seemed like the kind of dyke who would never lose her cool, even in a natural disaster or the front lines of war. When we met, our conversations were usually witty and daring enough to entertain our audience, and we both liked to perform for a familiar crowd. I wondered if any of our friends had the faintest clue that I really didn't know Ted very well and wasn't sure if she would ever let me get past her public mask. Or vice versa.

"KC, don't tell me what to do," I told her. "I have a lot to do today. I'll see Ted when I see her."

I realized that I didn't have KC's attention when I noticed her looking over my shoulder in the direction Ted would come from if she were driving toward us from her apartment. The significance of this jumped into my stomach like a baby frog from the river. "Did you ask her to meet us?" I demanded.

KC reached for me, and I moved quickly out of her space. "At Java's across the street," she confessed. She looked at her watch. "I wanted to talk to you out here first, where we could be alone. We should go. I said we'd be there ten minutes ago."

"You can meet her," I instructed, deadpan with rage. "I have things to do. I'll see you later." I hoped my emphasis on the last word was unmistakable. I turned my back on the woman I hoped to forget as soon as possible and began walking into the rain toward my future as a lone wolf in the uncaring human pack.

Ted approached me head-on, hands in her slick vinyl jacket. Her short, assertive brown hair, almost a crewcut, looked unaffected by the rain that was running down my neck and chilling my nipples to hard points. "Hey, where you going?" she asked with rough sympathy. "I looked for you in Java's but you weren't there." The situation was getting unbearable. "Josephine, don't jam out on us. I promised KC I'd meet her for coffee because she said you'd be there." *Hold on tight,* I told my temper. *Some dykes are always cool, and I could be one of them.*

The self-talk didn't work. "KC doesn't fuckin' make my dates!" I yelled hysterically into Ted's faintly-twitching face, having to look up to do this. I took a deep breath, realizing that I had just made a fool of myself and probably couldn't undo the damage. "Look, Ted, I'm sorry and I'd like to see you some other time, but not now. I never agreed to this. I have things to do." KC stood discreetly to the side, looking as uncomfortable as a wet cat.

The sarcastic lift of Ted's thin, beautifully arched eyebrows hurt me like the sting of an insect, right in my heart. Somehow her pale olive skin colour enhanced the expressiveness of her features. "So you have things to do in the rain? Did you know the weather office has put out a hail warning? In about an hour, hailstones like golfballs are going to be bouncing off your head. Were you planning to go for a long walk in that?"

I hesitated for a moment too long. Ted's strong fingers, each a knuckle-length longer than mine, gripped my upper right arm while her other hand pressed firmly into the small of my back. She began pushing me toward the cross-walk which led across the street to Java's. She was doing it in such a way that she didn't appear to be using force, but I couldn't resist her without making a scene. Even the weather was on her side. "Come on, Josie," she cooed in my ear. "Come inside to get warm and have a coffee, then I'll drive you home." She was letting me save face by letting me appear to co-operate. I felt like the bride in an arranged marriage, like one of my ancestors whose submission had eventually led me to be here at this moment.

"Okay," I sulked. We were halfway there anyway. Ted smiled at me in a way that sent more shivers down my spine. This time I was sure this wasn't only a reaction to the rain.

The welcoming light and warmth of Java's made me feel better in spite of myself. A scattering of other customers showed various degrees of wetness, depending on how long they had been there, and they all looked reluctant to leave until the downpour let up. The three of us found a table in a corner.

KC's impatience was noticeable because it set her apart from everyone else in the place. "I can't stay long," she explained, looking away from me and Ted. "I sort of said I'd meet someone." Her whole plan was now blatantly exposed: she had invited me to go for a romantic walk in the rain so that she could break up with me as quickly as possible before assuaging her conscience by handing me over to Ted, who had agreed to babysit me so that KC could rush off to meet Coral somewhere.

"May you both be struck by lightning," I said quietly, with as much dignity as possible. "If you survive, may your car skid on wet asphalt and crash into a power line. May the roof cave in at your place and hers. May the hail kill all your tomatoes. Have a nice day, KC."

A waitress appeared at my elbow to hear the last few words.

"Small cappucino," I told her without changing my tone. Ted quietly ordered a French dark roast while KC chewed her lips.

My betrayer couldn't look at me. "Well, yeah, I'm sorry you feel that way, Jo. I'll phone you later. See you, Ted." She ducked her head, and faced the door as though she looked forward to the sting of rain after being pelted with my words. "Sorry about all this," she muttered vaguely. She left with speed, and I could see her breaking into a run as she headed back across the street toward her parked car.

Ted was watching me through narrowed eyes. "Famous last words," she remarked. Do you really want your good wishes to stick, Jo?"

This question had an adult-to-child tone, and I hated it. "Right now," I said, looking her in the eyes between damp strands of my hair, "like glue." Her mouth widened until she was giving me a smile that was like the hug of a conspirator, as though we shared a secret that tickled her immensely. When the waitress brought our coffees, she couldn't interrupt the silent bond that was building between us. Something about Ted's expression made me wonder what diabolical revenge she had carried out against any of her ex-girlfriends. Instead of feeling alarmed, I wanted to hear all the details.

I wasn't prepared when she casually reached across the table to stroke my face. "You're already wet," she remarked. She made it sound like a comment on the weather, which in a sense it was. "I think you need a drink, baby. How would you like to come to my place for a hot rum? It might prevent you from catching pneumonia, unless that's what you're pushing for. In that case, I could drop you off – but never mind. I could make sure you don't dry out." Her intentions (not to mention the way she was looking at my nipples, which must have been visible under my T-shirt) were now crystal-clear.

"Do you always try to pick up women who have just been dumped?" I demanded. "Your friends' leavings?" I knew I was only stalling for time.

She blew the air out between her lips in a "pffft" of contempt. "I pick up women who interest me," she told me as though I were a slow learner. "Sometimes I do it when they're vulnerable, or when I have a good chance. I don't always play fair, if that's what you're asking."

"If I say yes," I asked slowly, "can I expect you to lose interest by tomorrow? Or shoot the shit to everyone we know?"

Even as I spoke, I was vaguely aware that an untrustworthy date wouldn't answer such questions honestly while an honest one wouldn't need to be asked.

"Josephine," she explained, clearly wanting me to notice that she was more tolerant than I deserved, "we've seen each other a lot over the years, and we've shot the shit. How much do you know about my private life? Could you name the singer I was with in our home town when we were both teenagers, the one who went on to top the charts? Do you know who I've been with here? Do you even know what my first language was, or where my family came from?"

The full silences she could maintain in a conversation were exactly the point for me, I realized. Ted, I wanted to ask her, *who the hell are you, and what would it take to find out?* I took a deep breath and let it out slowly. "Okay," I answered, smiling my consent. "Let's go to your place."

As soon as we stood up, she wrapped a long arm around my shoulders. As we left the shelter of Java's, she squeezed me against the rain, which now pounded the pavement in sheets. Looking down, I saw that the ground was salted with little hailstones. I thought they looked like crystallized tears, visible signs of nature's own rage and grief.

In the passenger's seat of her little car, I was glad I wasn't driving. Like a fool, I trusted her competence or my own luck.

She pulled smoothly into the parking lot of an old brick building. Too soon, we had to leave the mobile shelter of her car and run through hail again. I hoped she would hold me as she had before, and she did.

Pulling me down a hall toward her apartment, Ted asked me something that sounded completely irrelevant: "Do you eat fish?"

"I'm one-quarter Japanese," I answered. I thought I should seize the chance to tell her this, since I look more-or-less white, and some people treat me differently once they find out, even if they're not WASP themselves and didn't seem racist before. You just never know. "I grew up on fish. I could eat it seven days a week."

"Then we have the same taste," she responded approvingly. The sexual implications of our taste in food must have seemed so obvious to her that she saw no need to make wisecracks. She unlocked her apartment door and announced, "Welcome to my lair, babe."

I got a brief glimpse of the leather sofa and glass coffee table in her living room before she wrapped herself around me, pushing me against the wall. She pressed her lips against mine, taking my breath away. When I opened my mouth slightly, her warm tongue pushed its way in. I felt as if I could melt into a soggy mass against her wiry, determined body. She radiated heat, and I craved it.

One arm at a time, she eased herself out of her jacket, which dropped onto the carpet. Without letting my mouth go, she began tugging the dripping denim off me, and I was relieved to be rid of it. Once my jacket had joined hers, she calmly unzipped my pants and pulled my T-shirt up so she could slide her hands underneath it to find my breasts. "Ummpf," I grunted in surprise.

"Come on, honey," she breathed into one of my ears. "You want it. Let me take them off, right here."

Being covered in cold, wet clothes didn't strengthen my ability to resist her assault. As meekly as she could have wanted, I pulled my arms out of my T-shirt sleeves and even unhooked my own bra for her. Then I stepped out of my drenched cotton pants and stood, dressed only in black silk panties (my little indulgence), for her inspection. "Ahh," she sighed, briefly looking me up and down. She looked amused. She kissed her way from my chin down to my collar-bone while she held me upright as though she were afraid I would fall down. I thought that was likely, since her attention was making me weak in the knees.

The nipples on my little breasts were pointed and puckered by the time her mouth approached them. I gasped when she sucked one hard, flicking it with her tongue. Both her hands slid up to support them, pushing them out. I wished I could produce milk for her.

She raised her head to look me in the face. "Sweet tits, Josephine," she told me. Somehow her use of my whole name made me feel more naked. "I want to bite them." No one before her had told me this so bluntly, but I wasn't surprised.

She pulled my left nipple into her mouth, pulling most of my breast in with it. Her strong sucking sent chills over my damp skin and sent a tingle to my awakening clit. She took her mouth off me for long enough to ask, "Let me?" At that moment, I wanted to grant her every wish.

"Mmm," I replied, spreading my legs slightly for the invasion I expected. Ted clamped her mouth on my right nipple.

Pain flashed through my flesh like the hard sting of rain. I yelped, realizing that she had bitten me.

Somehow she managed to say "Aww" while sucking my nipple as though she wanted to draw the pain out of me along with sweat, blood, any intimate fluid she could get. I wrapped my arms around Ted's head, running my hands over her thicket of hair. It felt to me like the fur of some exotic, powerful animal that I had never been close to before.

I shifted, subtly pushing my other breast toward her, to please her or to get it over with. She accepted my offer, pulling the point hard into her mouth, stretching it for the attention of her teeth. This time the pain reminded me of an electric shock from a needle-sized streak of lightning, as though the energy of an ancient storm goddess had come indoors with us.

Ted brought her mouth back to mine, kissing me possessively. She gave me the lightly salty taste of my own skin on her tongue, which had somehow picked up my two spurts of fear. Her hands held my breasts as if to protect them from predators like herself.

"I broke the skin, baby," she purred, nuzzling my neck. She sounded like a talking tiger. "Still feel it, don't you?"

"Yes," I sighed, shivering from the touch of her warm hands. One of them slid slowly under my panties and purposefully down my sensitive belly, which moved in response. She reached the hair that covered my lower lips. Two of her fingers slyly parted them, searching for my quivering clit. My legs were quivering too, but I knew she wanted me to stay on my feet as long as I could.

"Josephine," she breathed between kisses on my neck and cheeks, "do you want me?"

I wanted to cry. Not long before, lurid images of murder and ritual suicide had briefly filled the screen of my mind, setting off a mood that was fatalistic, desperate and calm at the same time. Ted's seduction of me had felt like the inevitable sequel to KC's casual dismissal. I felt like a leaf pounded by the hailstorm outdoors, and my own physical needs felt like part of the impersonal force that controlled me.

"Ted," I moaned, biting my lips. "I know you don't love me." I closed my eyes to keep the tears from escaping. "I've been around. I know what's happening. I made a choice." My clit was throbbing and my heart was breaking. "I want you. I just don't know how—"

"Ssh," she stopped me, kissing my eyes. "Don't think now, girl. I know the white assholes who've played with you, and I'm not them. I want to feel you, take you, leave my mark on you. You don't know me yet, but you will. You gotta have faith, honey. We're just getting started."

I quickly pulled my panties down my legs and lifted one foot out of them. I spread my legs apart for her, my arms around her neck. She slid down and entered me with three fingers. My cunt welcomed her as she searched, tickled, explored and demanded a response. She stroked my swollen button, gently insisting on surrender. I couldn't hold back, even though I felt as if I might faint when wave after wave of a wild orgasm rolled through my centre. Somehow I stayed on my feet. I felt the strength of my own blind hope, or maybe it was just my body's singing awareness that life is good, no matter what.

She held me for an endless moment as my shivering subsided. "You need a bath, puppy," she told me, brushing damp hair off my face. My hair stays wet for a long time.

Ted brought me to her bathroom, where she lit candles and set them on the counter. Light flickered on the blue walls, creating an underwater effect. When she turned on the taps and threw in a few bath beads, the sound of rushing water drowned out the sound of hail spattering the windows like gunfire.

This time she shrugged gracefully out of her own clothes and stood proudly naked, letting me see her as she was seeing me. When the water in the tub was as high as she wanted it and frothy with bubbles, she held my hips and pushed me forward. "Get in," she ordered.

She sat behind me in the tub, pulling me back against her breasts (heavier than I expected) and assertive shoulders. She began kneading mine, easing the remaining tension out of them. After a few minutes, she stood up and pulled me up by the waist.

"On all fours, babe," she told me. "You need it somewhere else, and I can clean you up right here." My hands and knees gripped the rubber mat on the floor of the tub as she playfully splashed water over my back and my ass. "Slippery when wet," she laughed, loudly slapping each of my butt cheeks.

I couldn't see what she was doing behind me, but I heard her blow out one of the candles.

"A little oil to help things along," she muttered, as though telling me a riddle. Then I felt her fingers at my anus, opening my smallest hole. The slippery wax of an oiled candle pushed against the resisting sphincter and then it was in, sliding further and further into my ass. My cunt reacted immediately, as though the possession of its neighbour had a direct effect on it. "That's it," she cooed, pumping gently, going deeper with each push, "don't fight it, baby." My excited ass clutched the hard thing that filled it, sending jolts to my clit. To my amazement, I seemed to come in the humble opening that had formerly only known how to push things out. I groaned loudly enough to be heard in the next apartment. "Oh, you like that. You were hungry for it," Ted snickered.

As my spasms subsided, she slowly pulled the candle out of me. Without thinking, I pushed my ass back toward her, loving the smooth wax as it withdrew like a receding wave. "You'll get it again sometime, honey," she promised. "If you're good."

After filling a puff with liquid soap, she washed me from face to bottom and from fingers to toes, making me sit and then stand so that she could reach every inch of my skin. As the water in the tub began to cool, she opened the hot tap, sending a steaming stream into the tepid lake. "Want to wash my back?" she asked me casually. I reached for the chance and the puff, eager to explore the surface of her body. I sensed that I would have to earn the right to explore her depths.

Feeling baptized, I finally stepped out of the tub at her command, pulled a thick towel off the rack and began rubbing her dry. She responded by holding my hands together with one of hers as she took the towel from me. She then dried me thoroughly, including my shampooed hair, touching me with an owner's pride. I realized that my clothes were still in a crumpled heap in the front room. "Warm enough now?" my keeper asked with concern.

"Yes," I sighed, knowing why she asked.

"Don't put your clothes back on," she told me. "I like to see you like this."

Ted pulled a royal blue cotton robe from the hook on the back of the bathroom door and put it on. I noticed that it flattered her willowy frame and her glowing pink skin, although she had always claimed to be bored by such trivial feminine concerns. Feeling her eyes on my bare curves, I was glad that she didn't find them trivial.

When we re-entered the front room, I could see the dark sky of evening through the windows, and it looked like the face of an exhausted child who has just recovered from a temper tantrum.

The sound of pounding hail had been replaced by the moan of wind.

"Will you dine with me, Josephine?" asked my hostess. "I just have to put this fish in the oven. While we wait, you can have the hot rum I promised." I was impressed to see that the dining table was already set with china and linen napkins that matched the tablecloth. I felt honoured, although I wouldn't have been surprised to learn that Ted sometimes made such an effort for herself alone.

The meal was delicious, and the best pieces of tender salmon were the ones that Ted fed me with her fingers. I was constantly aware of being exposed to her gaze. My skin stayed awake, as though a low level of electricity were flowing through me.

After the rum, the wine, the fish, the rice, the salad, the fruit, the crackers, the cheese and the coffee, Ted invited me into her bedroom. When I stood up, she pressed herself behind me, cupping my breasts. Rubbing the nipples, she asked, "Still sore?"

"Yes." I winced.

"Well then," she assured me, "I can't let you go until they're healed. And since I'm not planning to leave them alone, that might take awhile."

Despite my full stomach, the twinges in my nipples raced down to my clit, beginning to make me hungry again.

Ted pulled me by the hand to the doorway of her bedroom.

Glancing around the walls, I saw an old sepia-toned photo in a frame, showing two women in hats, jauntily posed with a bicycle in the cobblestoned street of a town that looked European, in the innocent sunlight of some pre-war era. I made a note to myself to ask her about it when the time was right.

Her hands began to move over me again, and my hunger for her touch felt inexhaustible. Even the surprises she had just sprung on me while my stomach was full couldn't dam the inner spring of my need. I wanted to know her in every sense.

She lifted me off my feet, testing my weight. "Uh," I gasped. "I'm not that light." Of course Ted took this as a challenge. She lifted me higher, then threw me onto her bed, where I bounced on her welcoming burgundy quilt.

The sudden change of position seemed to sharpen my senses. As I fell from Ted's arms, my eyes focussed on a white cloth on her dresser that was embroidered in a pattern I recognized from the blouses of some Hungarian dancers I had seen once. The image of their swirling skirts mixed in my mind with my sketchy knowledge of post-war (or post-atomic) history. The Soviets invaded Hungary in 1956, I remembered, and Ted's parents were probably in the resulting swarm of refugees. Ted must have been their seed of hope, planted in the new country. My quick thinking made me feel smug.

She had climbed atop me. Her lips pressed mine so insistently that mine spread open ever so slightly. Her hot tongue rushed in and begun exploring my mouth. I fervently hoped she enjoyed my taste as my other mouth watered, wanting her to feed me again.

I expected Ted's aggressive fingers, but instead, she slid down my body with a gentleness and subtlety that made me shiver. Running her nails over my belly, she looked up, teasing me with her eyes. "Spread your legs," she ordered softly. I did.

Her lips and tongue on my clit and my inner lips sent ripples all through me. I groaned, almost lifting my ass off the bed. Her long fingers grasped my hips, holding me in place to receive her true aim. The earlier electricity of her teeth on my nipples seemed to have flowed down to my centre, quickening my little button of flesh until it was ready to burst. I didn't understand why she was giving me so much pleasure without demanding my service in return. Her tongue and nibbling teeth wouldn't let me think clearly, though, and I realized that this was probably her point.

When two of Ted's fingers pushed into my very wet cunt and began probing a touchy spot near my womb in time to the pulling of her lips on my clit, I couldn't resist any longer. This time I came as though melting into a pool of hot wax, clutching her head with my knees. She seemed to forgive my lack of self-control.

She slid up and slid her arms around me as smoothly as a shark moving through water. I just wanted to lie still in her arms, feeling her warmth, but I couldn't rest. "Ted," I sighed into one of her ears, "do you want—."

"I want to know you're mine," she interrupted, stroking my back. "For now, I want you to let me. We have lots of time and I *will* want other things from you later, Josephine. You'll see." She exhaled in a silent laugh.

I was willing to believe in her promise. I nestled my head under her chin, feeling her heart beating close to mine. This duet seemed to be all the answer she needed.

Gunmetal

Roxy Katt

The scene is a university lecture theatre – or rather, just outside one. Students are filing into it. Lecture for the day. Post-revolutionary France and sexual dissidence, or something like that. Lecturer is Professor Frenesi Foxx: forty-two, no non-sense professor, brilliant, uncloseted lesbian, weird and won-derful in her taste in clothes, and specialist not only in gender theory but French history.

One of the undergraduate students in the throng is one Patricia, holding back from the crowd a little, waiting for her friend Felicia to appear.

She does, out of breath, chattering madly but half whisper-ingly into Patricia's ear as the two press through the thronged doorway and take seats right at the front of the hall.

"So," says Patricia, "you just saw her?"

"Yes, she's coming. And you've just gotta see . . ." Felicia here, obviously excited, like the impressionable young woman she is, by the impending arrival of some August personage. Patricia, for her part, is the same age, but less easily impressed. She is indeed that type: slow to make up her mind on anything, but quite definite once she does.

"See what?" asks the intelligent but ever so slightly morose Patricia.

"She's packed!"

"She is?" Patricia smiles. "Thatta girl." Smiling so brightens one's day. She leans back into her chair with the little armrest desk in front of it, opens a notebook. "This I gotta see. Foxx doesn't pack very often."

Well, you know who they are talking about now, but what is this "packed", you may well ask? Some freshman girls' argot no doubt, perhaps one that only the two of them share. All very cryptic, unless, of course, they really take a more than ordinary interest in professors packing their luggage or something, but that would be too stupid. Could it mean she's "packing heat" i.e. carrying a pistol? No, the good professor does not carry a pistol, though she is definitely sexy enough to make the odd student here and there well, more than the odd one feel as if he or she has been "shot" so to speak, through heart, balls, or beaver by her oh, so aloof and raven-haired beauty.

The professor was actually a model in her early twenties, but got bored. They said, as people do, that she would never have the brains for a prof, and if they are still watching, they have egg on their faces. Oh she has the brains all right: all the degrees on the wall and a curriculum vitae as long as a French swordsman's nose. All good stuff, too; not the finger-twiddling which so often usurps the name of postmodernism.

"So, you did see her packed, right? It's not just something you heard. If there's anything I can't stand it's a false rumour of packing!" says Patricia.

"Oh, she's packed, all right, I saw her myself. I just about dropped dead. My legs went weak. I had to sit down and fan myself with my miserable psychology paper."

"Cool. This should be good. Don't expect me to change my mind though; I still say she's a lipstick lesbian."

"You don't respect any lesbian unless she's a truck driver."

"Lighten up. I'm a lesbian and I drive a Suzuki."

"Well, I'm a lesbian and I drive a mountain bike."

"That's why you, my dear, are the lesser lesbian."

"Oh, fuck off!" says Felicia merrily, swatting her much larger friend with a notebook.

All the students are now in the room. A gleeful counterswat would be inevitable at this point except that at this moment the door at the front opens up. It is Frenesi Foxx. She takes the three steps up the lecture platform, puts her papers on the desk, moves the podium away because she never uses it, and proceeds to lecture: sure, confident, assuming full attention from her students and getting it – not an easy task with a room of fidgety undergrads, as any prof can tell you. This is what you need to know about sexual dissidence in post-revolutionary France she says in effect, and proceeds to tell them.

The room is filled with whirring pens and pencils.

This professor is actually pretty nice to look at, whether you are a straight male or a lesbian. She has lots of jet-black hair in a punkish style very obviously dyed, but that's the point, not so?

She's got a very white face and deep red lipstick. Well, if that makes a lipstick lesbian, she is one. Slightly on the tall side, slender, quite "well endowed" as the euphemism goes. She's wearing a tight long-sleeved sweater with one of those big, floppy, cowl collars. The sweater is black and goes over the pants, stopping just a little lower than the waist, hugging the top of the hip, held in close with a stretchy black belt.

Hmmm. Nice black leather boots. Tight. A high heel to them as well. They look quite fine as she slowly paces back and forth along the front of the lecture platform with the slow and unpredictable energy of a caged tiger.

Tiger, yes. Caged, no.

Pat and Felicia can't talk any more, so they exchange notes on half a piece of loose-leaf they pass surreptitiously back and forth.

– *what did i tell yu? is she packed?*
– *o she's packed alright*

But, you are asking, what the hell with this "packed" stuff? You can see for yourself: her pants. Sleek, gunmetal stretch leather pants with hidden seams, a thick, but very stretchy leather that forms about her like rubber and into which, yes folks, she is really "packed".

Do these pants make me look fat? A question the distinguished professor would never ask because she knows they don't. They make her look packed. They make her look tight, shoehorned, explosionary, but oh, so tastefully.

– *is she some packed, or what?*
– *she is*
– *packed and stacked*
– *yeah. stacked and almost pointy*
– *a fifties bra? a cantilever?*
– *a heavy underwire certainly*

Dirty-minded little things. Still, you can hardly blame them. How else is the lowly student to react to the inaccessible being? The scrap of paper is getting quite crowded with scribbles.

"The condition of post-revolutionary France is something which, at the time, had to be seen to be believed . . ." Yadda yadda yadda.

– *how do yu think she gets in?*
– *with great difficulty*
– *i mean seriously*
– *with serious great difficulty*

The professor steps down from the platform and paces about in the space between it and the front row of desks. She is lost in her own ideas. Back and forth, back and forth, in front of Pat and Felicia. They bury their heads in their notebooks, taking real notes now, but still hazarding the odd scribble to each other when the professor's back is turned.

– *she decided to show off today*
– *she shows off every day*
– *but not à la packe*
– *do yu think she can sit down?*

The professor passes by, talking about drag in Parisian bordellos. *Swit*! Ever so swiftly yet nonchalant, one would hardly notice she had done it, she nips the paper from Felicia's desk and begins to read it, not missing a beat, at the same time speaking out loud about the carnivalesque in 1820s Toulon, for all the world as if she were reading her lecture from the scrap itself.

Pat buries her head in her hands, as well she might.

Felicia stares ahead in white-faced terror. As well she might.

Flit flit flit go the professor's gorgeous green eyes (did we mention the big green eyes? The heavy mascara? Enormous eyelashes?) down one side of the scrap and then the other. She lectures flawlessly, her voice betraying no reaction to the scrap.

But she has also turned a deep crimson. The proverbial beet.

She folds the scrap and tucks it up the tight sleeve of her sweater. A tight sleeve is a useful thing to have when a woman has no pockets, and even if she had pockets in her gunmetal pants, they would just be for show anyway.

The lecture is over now: a big noise and the usual folderol as everyone picks up their books and lumbers out of the room. A deep red fingernail on the end of a crooked finger summons the two miscreants to the foot of the platform. Teacher's face is no longer red. She is very controlled (not unusual for her).

"Patricia, Felicia, I have another lecture to attend to immediately so I cannot talk to you right now. However, I will see the both of you in my office in exactly one hour. Understood?"

How can they say no?

The next hour is sheer hell. More for Felicia than Pat. Pat is scared too, but also angry. She gets surly, morose, we have said, when threatened by authorities.

"What business did that bitch have reading our note?"

"We shouldn't have been—"

"Ah, bullshit." These are two glum girls, sitting in the student lounge, downing coffee as if they needed anything more to make them edgy.

The hour passes. The girls are ushered into the great woman's office. It is a very big office with two plush chairs set far back from the front of her big desk. Off to the side there is even a coffee table and some more comfortable chairs. This prof must have some pull.

She barely looks at them; motions them to sit down, stands behind her desk bending over it, writing something during a half-finished lunch: a little bowl of salad, a fat salami, untouched, and an apple, in the non-writing hand, out of which she has already taken a bite. She has very big, white teeth, did we mention that?

"So," she says finally, putting down the apple and the pen. She comes around to the front of her desk and leans her leathered bottom against it, arms folded beneath her breasts, legs crossed. She smiles pleasantly. "Oh yes, of course." She pulls the note out of her sleeve, looks at it. "So what exactly, does 'packed' mean?"

Dead silence. They both look down. May as well answer the question. Pat is the bolder one so she raises her head.

"It means your pants are really tight," she says, looking the professor in the eye.

"Aaaah. Of course. That was the only part of the note I didn't understand. Yes, I guess they are rather tight, aren't they? 'Packed and stacked' as the note says. But then, I guess I was only showing off. I squeezed my fanny into the tightest pants I could find and hauled my boobs up to my neck with the uh, cantilever job you mentioned, in order to show off!"

There is an extremely long and painful pause. Painful to the students, that is.

"Girls – and I call you girls because your conduct hardly befits mature women – I cannot express my disappointment."

There is another pause, quite similar, actually, to the previous one.

"Do you think I spend years teaching history and theory only to have girls leer at me the way boys do?"

"We weren't leering, Professor Foxx," Pat speaks up. "That was a private note."

The professor is clearly unimpressed with this excuse. There begins a detailed private lecture, just for Pat and Felicia, during which the professor paces back and forth before them just as she did in the lecture hall. This lecture, however, has a considerable amount of what we might call moral indignation to it. The professor is clearly chewing them out.

The two sit there, staring down at the carpet they are being raked over.

The professor waxes quite eloquent, actually, even for her. There is a flash in her green eye, an extra little tilt of the lower spine (boosting the bottom in its confident thrust), a little more leather squeak in the thighs that pass and repass each other as she steps back and forth.

She stops to ask Felicia, now, what her feelings are on the matter.

Felicia gives the required response: submission, apology, etc. etc. She can't help it, really, the performance is far too impressive and she is just too embarrassed to begin with anyway.

The professor stands now before Pat, hands on hips, and addresses her thus: "Now, you, Patricia. What are your thoughts on what I have just said?"

Pat the Morose stares down at the carpet, clearly gathering herself for a response. She takes a deep breath, and then sighs, as if to say, oh what the hell, what's the use, or something to that effect. "My thoughts are, Professor Foxx, that I would very much like to take that salami on your desk and shove it up your ass."

The professor blinks. Once, twice, while her face turns scarlet. She still stands there, hands on leathered gunmetal hips, and stares at Pat. Clearly, she wasn't expecting this. But clearly, she isn't floored by it either.

"Very well," she says, turning, bending over her desk and picking up the big salami. She drops it in Pat's lap. "There you go. I've often found that when a person is challenged on an aggressive statement such as you have just made, she is unable to act on her desire even when given a golden opportunity."

Pat stares at the salami, wide-eyed. That got you, didn't it, dear? Morosity, if that's a word, is something a professor encounters often. She knows how to deal with it all right – insolence too.

"You are unable to comply, aren't you?" says the professor, brows lifted in mock surprise. "Rest assured, Patricia, statements such as yours are nothing more than a confession of impotence."

Advantage, Frenesi Foxx.

Pat mutters a confused apology.

The professor's face is white again, calm, self possessed. She tells Pat she can go now, but must write a one-thousand-word essay of suitable content (read, apology) on this manner and turn it in by nine a.m. tomorrow, or she is out of the course on her ass. She turns away from Pat, and talks to Felicia; this time, in a friendly and forgiving manner.

Ignored by the professor, Pat stands up as if to go, tail between her legs, and yadda yadda yadda. She puts the salami back on the desk.

Meanwhile, Felicia has been sniffling a little. Professor Foxx wants to reassure her she is back in her good graces. "There, there," she says, "I remember when I was nineteen . . ." She stands with her hands clasped behind her back, head tilted back a moment, eyes closed, as if to recapture a moment. The two students wait for her to finish, but she seems to be in no hurry.

"When I was nineteen . . ." Eyes still closed. Holy moly, are we going to have nostalgia time here?

A strange glint appears in Pat's eye. The professor continues: "I would have killed for a powerful, confident, older woman as a lover. In fact . . . Huh?"

Said "huh?" being occasioned by the professor's discovery that the cowl collar of her sweater has been hauled down to her waist somehow, pinning her elbows behind her, which are even now being more tightly secured together by her own belt!

Let us just say as this swift desweatering and elbow tying is completed that Frenesi Foxx is speechless with surprise, and that that open-mouthed look is actually quite becoming to her. Professor tugs at the belt that firmly binds her elbows behind her, hands flailing at her sides. These actions only draw attention to the tight, strapless, underwired D-cups now exposed – as if they could have been ignored in any case.

"Wh . . . what are you doing?" asks the professor.

A swift hand (Pat's of course) reaches for the hooks at the back of the professor's bra and deftly undoes them. The sturdy garment springs forth and flies across the room.

"Wha . . . ?" is the professor's eloquent comment.

She bends and writhes, tries to look back over her shoulder at the bonds that hold her. Oh she's certainly gone red again: one can hardly blame her, what with her big boobs bouncing all over the place. The really humiliating thing is, she can't help struggling against her bonds, but that's just what gives the other two such a fine show.

"Bouncy, bouncy," sings Pat. Felicia has stopped sniffling, and there's even a bit of a smile on her face.

The hooter show continues as the professor splutters her indignation: "This is the most unconscionable ... unforgivable ... what makes you think you can just ..."

Pat calmly reaches forward, and grabs the zipper at the front of the professor's pants. Zzzzipp! She's flying low. She gasps, shocked at the audacity, instinctually turns her back to them to zip up.

It's not an easy thing to do, in those pants. And with her elbows tied behind her, it's actually quite impossible. She futilely wiggles and twists, and a strange look comes to Pat's eye. Before Felicia can say, "Pat! No!" she gives the professor a resounding smack on the backside.

Open-mouthed with shock and disbelief, Frenesi Foxx turns to face her student. The apple comes in handy here – kershlorp! Pat wedges it deep in the older woman's gaping mouth.

"Pat?" asks Felicia.

Pat undoes the button at the waist of the professor's pants and hauls them halfway down her firm thighs.

"Glmmph?" says Professor Foxx, uncomprehending.

"Oh my God, Pat, you've humiliated the History department's most prestigious scholar!"

Well, that much is certainly true. Pat steps back to admire her handiwork. The professor totters about the office, unable to free her hands, unable to pull her pants up (lovely black panties by the way) and unable to spit the apple out. She stares at Pat, a huge question mark on her lovely face, and the question seems to be "this can't really be happening, can it?"

"Well," says Pat, "the packer unpacked." Calmly, she reaches forward and slowly pulls down the professor's panties, revealing a lovely dark bush.

"Glmmph?" responds the professor helplessly. The situation really seems to have detracted from her intelligence significantly.

Pat holds the salami before the professor's face and she stares at it, almost cross-eyed. Clamping her thighs tightly together, she tilts her hips forward as far she can to conceal her womanhood as much as possible. But this motion thrusts her posterior back to a ridiculously provocative extent.

Still holding the salami, Pat says, "I go thus far, and no further. I wouldn't do that to another woman. But I will leave your salami here on the desk to give you something to think about." Looking down, she smiles. Frenesi Foxx has been unable to hide the fact that she is actually a little wet.

Pat and Felicia turn towards the door. But can they leave the professor this way? Er, mmm, actually, yes, they can. She'll wiggle her way out of the belt soon anyhow.

And, not too many months later, when the professor puts on her usual Christmas party do, are Pat and Felicia invited? Oh, yes.

Funny How Things Turn Out

Mandy Scott

It was one of those relationships that was doomed from the start, but Paul and I had remained firm friends. To put it bluntly, in the bedroom department, it just didn't happen. We got on so well that we saw each other regularly for meals, or a take-away, and we chatted about current relationships, or problems at work. Quite often I would sleep over at his house after a couple of bottles of Merlot, and just drive home the next morning. We were mates, and on the odd occasions when he did get a bit frisky and try it on with the help of beer goggles, we reminded ourselves that we didn't really physically fancy each other, so what was the point? Nevertheless, he was tactile, and we still enjoyed a snuggle up on the couch, enjoying each other's company. It was a strange relationship, and neither of us had formed any lasting friendship with a member of the opposite sex since our own relationship had failed.

I had a busy work life, which left little time for a steady boyfriend, and it had been two years since there had been any "I think I'm in love" moments. Quite content with my life, I wasn't really looking; I had many good friends and an excellent social life, so I didn't feel desperate enough to settle for something that wasn't all that. There had definitely been that little something missing in all my relationships, and I could never put my finger on what it was.

On a cold Tuesday morning in March, my mobile phone bleeped, indicating that I had a text message. It was from Paul, inviting me over that night, and he said he had someone he wanted me to meet. Assuming it was another new girlfriend, I accepted the invitation and, since it was a more formal invitation than usual, requested a time for arrival. His second text said simply "8, B a B" which in our text-speak meant eight o'clock, and bring a bottle.

The taxi was late as usual, but I always booked early, so by the time I arrived at Paul's five-bedroomed townhouse, it was bang on eight. After greeting his nosey neighbour outside, I kicked off my shoes at the door and announced my arrival with a loud "yoo-hoo". Instantly, I detected the aroma of "Irresistible" perfume. She has better taste than the last one, I sniggered to myself as I made my way upstairs. The house had a strange layout; the kitchen was on the ground floor, the lounge on the first floor, and the bedrooms scattered all over. I didn't like it, but it was trendy and affordable, and overlooked a nice park. Paul kept it spotlessly clean, a trait I thought unusual for most blokes, but he was fussy about a lot of little things. Paul was thirty-six, tall, slim, smart, witty and fun to be around. He had introduced me to a string of prospective girlfriends of his lately, but I had never been overly impressed. Maybe it was because I cared about this man like a sister would for a brother, we chatted like best friends, and his slightly feminine attitude to life never failed to amuse me.

Sat in the lounge chair was my mate, and opposite him on the couch was the most beautiful creature I had ever seen. I remember thinking, how the hell has that ugly twat pulled her? We were formally introduced: "Abbie, this is Emily." I wasn't sure if I should shake Emily's hand, so I just smiled and we exchanged an acknowledging nod to each other. She was smart, and wore a fairly short skirt, which showed off her tanned legs. Not too skinny; I estimated a size fourteen, with an expensive taste in clothes, and nice bobbed hairstyle, which had obviously been well cut.

She looked sexy without looking like a tart, I thought, but she was definitely not Paul's type. Her cerise pink satin blouse was just a little tight, but it showed off her curves nicely. As the wine flowed, so did the conversation. It emerged that Paul had met Emily at the headquarters of the IT company he worked for. They had both been involved in developing some software for a Japanese car manufacturer. Boring, I thought, just get to the juicy stuff, how long have you been seeing each other, what's going on and why am I sitting here like a gooseberry?

After a couple of bottles of red and one pink champagne, we all sat on the floor for a game of "I Have Never . . .". A bottle of vodka was positioned in the tray on the big fluffy mat, and three shot glasses sat before it. Paul began the game by saying "I have never been shagged over the bonnet of a Ford Fiesta by Alan

Fremlin in Morrisons' car park". I objected that the statement was far too precise, but my protest fell on deaf ears, and I was forced to take a shot of vodka. I hated vodka. Needless to say I got him back. It was Emily's turn and she suggested that she had never had a threesome. Both Paul and I grabbed our glasses and burst into fits of laughter; of course we hadn't. As the vodka bottle drained, the suggestions got more explicit, and my last statement was "I have never had sex with a woman", knowing that Paul would have to take a shot, but never thinking that Emily would. My eyes must have bulged out of my head as Paul looked at me, smiled, and raised one eyebrow. She downed her drink, and Paul declared her the champion; then, realizing he had burnt the supper, jumped up and ran downstairs to rescue the pizza.

Emily and I sat back on the couch, complaining about our numb bums, and she turned to me and smiled. What a nice girl she was – attractive, intelligent, funny, just right for Paul. Like a mother hen, I quizzed her about her intentions toward my friend, and she stopped me in my tracks, insisting he was definitely not her type. I felt naïve, but the penny suddenly dropped – she batted for the other team. Not all lesbians were butch, I knew this, but she was gorgeous. The saying "don't knock it till you've tried it" came up in conversation, as Paul announced from the bottom of the stairs that he was nipping out to the shop for more supplies. I had been set up, that git had set me up with a fucking lesbian, for god's sake. No wonder he had nipped out for more bloody wine.

Emily's arm had been draped over the back of the couch, and as she began to tell me how beautiful and intelligent she thought I was, she touched my hair. It was strange but nice, and I felt a stirring between my legs. I had never experienced anything like this before but I felt sexy, and she was arousing me in a way that no man could ever do. Her gentle words and soft hands made me feel at ease; she was an extremely attractive girl. I could feel the wide smile starting to spread across my face as she touched my knee with her other hand. She drew my head towards hers and kissed me gently on the forehead.

Apparently Paul had told her so much about me, and had indicated that it was time I "woke up and smelt the coffee". I never was quick on the uptake, but as I tutted and shook my head in disbelief she turned her head to the side and kissed my lips. Part of me wanted to pull away and yell abuse at her for assuming that I would be susceptible to her charms, but the other part wanted to interrogate her, ask her what it was like to be a lesbian: what do you do in bed, how can you feel satisfied without a big hard cock inside you? I was curious and intrigued by this fascinating young woman, so I kissed her back, and the feeling between my legs got stronger and stronger.

Neither of us heard Paul come back in until he was halfway up the stairs. He must have known by the grin on my face that we were getting along just fine. He had been to the pizza shop around the corner and presented a chicken kiev pizza, his favourite – he never ever ordered anything else; he was a creature of habit. I sat on the floor with Paul, with my back to the chair. Emily remained on the couch as we tucked into our supper. Oblivious to the events only minutes before, Paul didn't notice Emily's legs open slightly; but then it was for my benefit, so why should he?

As she ate her slice of pizza, she licked her lips and at one stage slid her finger in her mouth, pursed her lips and indicated how very hungry she was, suggesting to Paul that the food was delicious, but insinuating something totally different to me. As her long pink tongue swept over her plump top lip, her lips pursed and she winked at me. My God, she was flirting with me.

What a strange situation it was. I had been transported to another plane, the night's events were unexpected and, as I prodded at my lukewarm pizza, my mind wandered off. I looked across the room at a grinning Emily, who commented on my lack of appetite. As she bent forward for another slice, I noticed the top button of her blouse was undone. It gaped open and her plump breasts were pushed together like two massive melon mountains. Paul tucked into his pizza and commented that we should definitely do this more often. Both Emily and I agreed with way too much enthusiasm. Emily suggested the following night, but Paul was due in London for a meeting, so Emily and I exchanged phone numbers and agreed that we would meet up the following night. It was obvious that Paul liked the idea of us both getting along so well. He yawned and declared it was past his bedtime, and my taxi was due any minute, so I bade my farewells to my friends and made my way downstairs. Emily followed me out to check the status of her taxi and, as we stood in the porch waiting, she pushed me up against the wall.

Astonished as I was to be kissed passionately by another

woman, I felt elated, excited, and boy oh boy was I turned on. In situations like that, it's always best to go with the flow, and my juices were certainly beginning to do just that. Her hand was on the back of my neck as she grabbed a fistful of hair and drew me closer. The other hand moved to my crotch and she rubbed the side of her forefinger up and down the crease between my legs. Through my linen trousers I could feel the warmth of her hand. She commented on how wet I was and she grabbed my hand and thrust it between her thighs. She was wet too; it was seeping through her silky pants, and it only made me want her more. This was amazing. I had never felt so turned on in all my life. Was it the alcohol? I wondered, or was this the feeling I had been missing out on all my life? Sex wasn't so overrated after all. God, this was amazing, I thought as she buried her head in my breasts.

The elasticized top I wore that night was now positioned underneath my large breasts; like a push-up bra, it held them in place while she caressed and fondled them. She was forceful and I liked that. I enjoyed being the sub in any relationship, and she played her part well. Her large blue eyes looked straight into mine as she sucked and squeezed both breasts, biting them as she snarled at me like a wild animal. In her eyes, I could see the passion, in her breathing I could feel the excitement, and I wanted her to fuck me. My God, how I wanted her to fuck me!

At precisely the wrong moment, the taxi turned the corner and the headlights shone into the dark porch. The sign on the top was not the rank I had booked. It was Emily's taxi, and she kissed me on the cheek and skipped off down the drive. As the car door opened, she bend forward and her G-string deliberately flashed underneath her denim skirt as she bounced into the seat. My taxi followed shortly afterwards and I yelled goodbye to Paul. There was no response; he must have been asleep. As I was climbing into bed that night, my mobile bleeped; the sender was Em, and the message read "X".

The following morning, I woke from what I thought was a dream, a very wet dream. I looked at my phone and realized it was 8.30 – I was late for work again. I ran into the bathroom and turned on the shower, tossed some clothes on the bed and had the quickest wash in history, then threw on my jeans and T-shirt, tripping over Bob my little border terrier on the way down the stairs. I threw my jacket over my bag and headed through the door, dog in arms. Bob came to work with me at the farm, where I was the bookkeeper for a local farmer. I loved my job, and my employer was so laid back; I worked hard for him, and was rewarded with a good salary and flexible working hours. Being allowed to take my dog to work was of course a bonus.

I tried all day to concentrate on finding the twenty-seven pence I had somehow mislaid in the books somewhere, but my mind was on the events of the previous evening and it was a fruitless exercise. During my tuna sandwich, I received another text message from Em suggesting we had dinner that evening at a nice little Italian close to where I lived. I agreed and told her I would meet her there at seven thirty. Rob, my boss commented a few times throughout the day how chirpy I seemed, and I had to agree. Surely it wasn't that obvious? I shook my head to rid myself of horny thoughts as I jumped into my little black MG that evening and headed for home.

The heating was roaring full blast when I got in, and I raced upstairs to light some candles and run a hot bath. As I poured myself a large glass of red, the back door opened; it was my friend Sandy from next door. The usual format for a Wednesday night was a few cups of coffee with Sandy, and discussions about plans for the weekend, but tonight I had my own plans. I explained that I had a date, which wasn't a good idea, because then she demanded to know more. What was his name, where did I meet him, was he hot? I made my apologies and escorted her to the door, promising I would fill her in on all the details the following evening. She smiled, and told me to enjoy myself. I fully intended to. I locked the door, grabbed my wine and headed up to my bath.

Relaxing in the bubbles, I picked up the soap and began to lather my breasts; I closed my eyes and took a deep breath. I thought about the previous evening, and Emily, and my reaction to her advances. I could not help myself; and my hands soon wandered further and I fondled myself while thinking of her. The thought of being all shrivelled up for my date forced me to jump out of the bath and get dried. I blew out the candles, all but one, which I carried into my bedroom. As I put it on the bedside cabinet, I looked at the clock; I had thirty minutes to spare, so I lay on the bed. It was hot, and I was flushed and wet; my hands began to wander again. I found my erect clit waiting for me and, as I imagined Emily's face buried deep within it, I became wetter and wetter. I reached over to the drawer and fished out my faithful rabbit. It fired up slowly and I made a mental note to buy some new batteries. It was nearly flat, I had used it so often. I pressed the revolving tip hard onto my clit as the little vibrating rabbit head wriggled about my lips. Then I turned it around and stuck the whole thing deep inside me, thrusting hard as the vibrator shivered against my clit. Next, I turned it around so the vibrating head just touched the tip of my arse while the cock was still deep inside me, swirling around, finding every crevice. As I closed my eyes tight, I imagined that it was Emily thrusting the huge member deep inside me while licking my clit. This of course made me climax immediately; a taste of things to come?

In the restaurant that evening, I waited in the bar area for Emily to arrive. I noticed the same taxi pull up outside, and knew it was her. She was blown in through the lobby by a strong gust of wind and her hair swept across her face as she acknowledged me with a little wave. She hung up her jacket on the coat stand and headed for the bar area, pecked me on the cheek and asked if I had enjoyed my day at work. I listened quietly as she told me about her day, and how much she had been looking forward to our evening together.

We ordered a main course only, and chatted as if we'd known each other for years; there were no long silent pauses, as you would expect on a first date, but then it wasn't really a date – or was it? I felt relaxed, and after the meal we retired to the soft couch in the bar for a Baileys on ice. She smiled as I told her of my past relationships, my first love, the tears, the heartache, the fun and the sex. She listened intently as I babbled on about my life, and anyone listening to our conversation would think we were new friends getting to know each other. We were, I suppose. It was exciting to think that people all around us didn't know the thoughts that were going through our minds.

Once or twice Emily touched me in a way that a friend would not, and I caught a fellow diner observing; she nearly choked on her garlic bread, and you could see it turned her on. It felt dangerous and exciting, and I liked the feeling I was experiencing. The woman didn't tell her husband what she had observed, that was clear; she wanted it to be her fantasy too, I could tell. But it was mine tonight. I was here, living it.

Our taxi pulled up; Emily and I got in it and headed for my place. I was proud of my little flat; it was cosy, compact, and tonight for a change it was tidy. Bob greeted us at the door.

Sometimes I thought his little tail would drop off, he was so pleased to see me.

Emily greeted Bob, telling me how much she loved animals, but it would be cruel to keep a dog locked up all day, so she couldn't have one. We sat in the living room and I turned on some music. The lighting in the room was not intentionally seductive, but appeared so that evening. We chatted some more and, as I put my feet up on the couch, she grabbed my ankle and positioned it on her lap, rubbing the ball of my foot. I had never had a foot massage, and Emily was obviously experienced in the art.

I was surprised that I felt no awkwardness at all in this alien situation – it felt right. She told me about her life, her loves and her past experiences with both men and women, and her understanding of what was going on inside my head. Thoughts were shared, ambitions disclosed, fantasies discovered, and events progressed until we passionately kissed again. She climbed over to my side of the couch and straddled my thighs as she unbuttoned my white blouse. Once again she cupped my breasts and sucked and licked them until my nipples were erect. My body was in submission as her tongue moved towards my mouth again, and her gentle hands teased my aching nipples. I moaned helplessly as her fingers traced their way to my already soaked knickers. As she fell to her knees she parted my legs and pushed my skirt up as far as it would go. I tried to speak, but my mouth could not form words; incapable of speech or thoughts, I was on that plane again.

As she gently held my thighs and pulled me towards her, I balanced on the edge of my couch and she slowly pulled my knickers to one side. I heard her utter her delight as she viewed my freshly shaven pussy. I moaned again as her fingers found my swollen lips, and parted them to my own ultimate delight. Her tongue traced the inside of my thigh and, like a precise missile, found the tip of my clit, right on target. With two fingers she wriggled inside me as she gently caressed me with her tongue. I shuddered as I felt an orgasm beginning to rise, and I cupped my hand under her chin to prevent an early climax to the evening.

I dropped onto the floor with her and lay her down on her back. It was my turn to please her. A little apprehensive, but actually the cliché "a woman knows what a woman wants" sprang to mind. If I did to her what I had wished men had done to me for the past twenty years, would I please her? Of course I would.

I lay on my side and stroked her hair; I cupped the back of her neck with my hand and pulled her face towards mine. I kissed her passionately, tracing a path down her neck to her large firm breasts. I had never sucked a woman's breasts before and it excited me. Never before had I felt more aroused that this night. I could have moved in to that void between her tits and lived happily ever after in there. Her golden tanned body reflected in the soft lighting of the room and she was glowing.

I unbuttoned the remainder of her cotton blouse and the top of her skirt as I positioned myself between her long gaping legs. Like a giant slug, my tongue made its way slowly from the ankles this time, up the inside of her legs, switching from one to another. When I reached the top, I roughly pulled her skirt up to around her waist. Every inch of her was real woman; soft and wonderful with curves like the Sahara desert. A little black G-string covered her neatly trimmed mound. I buried my head and licked through the satin patch until I could taste her juices through the fabric. I gently pulled the panties to one side and what a beautiful sight; large full lips which I blew on softly, then parted to reveal a proudly erect clit.

I had read once in a magazine that it was pleasurable for a woman to have her partner "tongue" the alphabet, so I thought I would try it. On her sodden clit, I flicked the shape of the letter A with my tongue, then B. It was good advice, for as I got to the letter "I", which I repeated a few times up and down quickly but gently, her buttocks began to rise and fall. I withdrew my tongue from her clit and buried my whole face in her gaping hole. My face was soaked in her juices. She smelt sweet and tasty as I thrust my tongue in and out of her hole, my nose rubbing her clit. My fingers, which held her lips apart moved in, like little soldiers on a military operation.

Two fingers entered her as my tongue found her clit again, and I thrust inside her searching for that beautiful spot. I flicked inside her with the same rhythm as my tongue flicked her clit. My other hand found its way around to her full arse and I grabbed it tight as she tensed her buttocks. My fingers were positioned just at the entrance of her anal passage and this aroused her; she was nearing orgasm. Her breathing was fast, her body flushed with colour and she moaned with delight as her come squirted over my face. She tasted delicious. I was in heaven; I had no idea sex with a woman was this good and was so in awe of her.

She pulled me towards her and kissed me passionately, licking her come from my lips; she was still in orgasm mode as she went down on me. Her right hand slid between the cheeks of my arse and fondled me while she nibbled on my inner thigh and made her way up to my clit. She formed a cone shape with her other hand and thrust it deep inside me. She sucked my clit and flicked it hard with her tongue and I could resist no more. I screamed with delight. I was in ecstasy, like the tide, a giant wave crashed onto the shore and broke, scattering its debris across the beach. Then another giant crash, and she surfed this one like a professional. I could hear her moaning with delight as she tasted me and shouted words of encouragement as I came into her mouth. She lapped it up with enthusiasm, smiling and moaning in ecstasy. It was the longest orgasm I had ever experienced, and the strongest.

She laid her head on my thigh, and sighed one word, "Wow." I took her by the hand into my bedroom, and lay her on my bed, lit a candle and lay beside her. I was naked, on my bed with another woman and I was content. I stroked her until she drifted off into a deep sleep. If this was the first and last time I fucked a woman, I would never forget it or regret it. Men would have to take a back seat in my life now. I had found what I really wanted in a lover, and it wasn't a big hard cock. It was a considerate, gentle, patient and beautifully formed female specimen – a hard act to follow.

The next morning, I awoke with a warm feeling between my legs, and a huge bulge in the duvet. She was under the sheets licking my pussy. It all started again; it was wonderful, and I would never tire of this. We sweated and rolled about, kissing every part of each other. She touched places nobody had touched, and aroused feelings I had never experienced before. She taught me moves and positions I had never dreamt of; it was like the first time, all over again.

We showered together and fucked again under the hot spray as we lathered each other's tits with lavender and camomile body wash, and I dried every inch of her like an obedient servant to an Egyptian princess.

Paul rang me the next morning from London to see if the night had been a success. I told him that we had had a very nice evening, and I thanked him. Although it was never discussed frankly, Paul knew what I was thanking him for. He went on to explain the reason for his trip to London, and it wasn't business. A "theatre trip with a new friend" was his description, and I knew what he meant. We had both experienced a life change, and it was for the best.

That Friday, Paul and I went out for dinner and laughed about recent events.

Funny how things turn out!

Shock Treatment

H. L. Berry

The club's hostess peered into the room. It was dark but for a single pool of light in the exact centre. Caught in that light was a naked woman, on her back, writhing in what looked like ecstasy. She was tied to the surface of a padded wooden table, arms and legs outstretched to its corners. Her prominent breasts were flattened due to her prone position, and they heaved as she breathed deeply. Her nipples were stiff and erect, their rosy colour matching the flush in her cheeks as an orgasm shook her. The hostess, known to everyone simply as "Q", smiled as she caught sight of the twin vibrators lodged in the woman's pussy and anus.

Q approached and leaned down so that her mouth was next to the bound woman's ear.

"Paige, Sarah just called," she whispered. "She's late again, but she'll be here in about half an hour. Do you want me to let you loose?"

Paige lifted her head and looked at the hostess, a humorous glint in her blue-grey eyes. "If you must. Duty calls, I suppose."

She couldn't suppress a sigh as Q eased the vibrators from her body and unfastened the cuffs around her wrists and ankles. Q helped her to her feet. Paige stood for a moment, panting. The hostess took her arm.

"Come along. You haven't got much time."

"Just a minute." Paige held back. "There must be time for this."

She turned Q so that they were facing each other, then leaned forward and kissed her on the lips. Q responded, opening her mouth and flicking her tongue out to touch Paige's. Their bodies pressed against each other. They held the embrace briefly then parted. Their eyes met.

"Come along," repeated Q, stroking Paige's cheek. "You're my chief guard. You want to look your best for this, don't you?"

They left the room arm in arm and made their way to Q's private office, where Q changed into her usual outfit, an all-in-one bodysuit that hid nothing of her figure. Shortly afterwards, three of the female guards dragged Sarah into the room. They positioned her so that she was facing the large mahogany desk. Q lounged behind it on a leather executive chair, her feet up on the top of the desk. In front of her stiletto heels was a large leather case, with the single word "Imperial" and a royal crest embossed on it in gold. Paige, now dressed in her brief guard's uniform, stood to one side of the desk, slightly behind Q. Sarah threw her a sheepish glance. Paige looked back sternly, giving nothing away.

"You know what to do," said the hostess. "Remove her clothes. Kelly, announce her punishment to our members and meet us in the treatment room."

Kelly left. Her voice came over the tannoy system, creating a buzz of interest outside. Angela and Jody, the two remaining guards, stripped Sarah of her skimpy attire. She was left to stand naked in the centre of the room. Angela cuffed her hands behind her back. Sarah squared her shoulders and stared at the hostess.

Q sighed. "Sarah, Sarah. Why do you get into trouble quite so often? If I didn't know better, I'd swear that you enjoy being publicly punished. Take her away!"

When she'd gone, Q turned to Paige. "Are you still confident?"

"About our wager?"

"Yes, of course. What time do I have to beat?"

"I managed fifty-seven minutes with you."

"Fine. The loser takes twelve strokes."

"Good luck."

Paige winked. "I don't need luck. You'd better get some ointment ready."

They led Sarah to a small room, where Kelly was waiting. It was like a cell, with green walls and stark overhead lighting. In the middle of each wall was a large, two-way mirror, through which the club's members could watch the punishment take place. The viewing rooms were already full.

"Look, Sarah," said Angela. "You've got quite an audience. I hope you're going to put on a good show."

There was a table against one wall with a typist's chair tucked under it. A hospital bed stood in the centre of the room, with a thin vinyl mattress and chrome rails down either side. Angela and Jody lifted Sarah onto the mattress and held her down while Kelly tied her to the rails with inch wide leather straps. Her arms lay underneath her, and one strap passed over them at the elbow, leaving her torso free. Another went across under her bottom, holding her wrists tightly but again leaving her pelvis free to move. From the lower end of the table, they could just see her hands as they stuck out from under her backside. Angela and Jody parted her legs, spreading them so that her knees were crooked over the side of the bed. More straps held her thighs firmly in this position. Her captors bent and tied her ankles together underneath the bed.

Kelly threaded another strap under Sarah's right arm, passing it up through her armpit, over her chest just above her pert breasts, and back down under her left arm. Finally, they clipped more straps to a collar around her neck and tied those to the rails as well.

Jody tweaked one of Sarah's nipples. "Can you move?"

Sarah gasped. "Bitch!"

"You've still got your attitude. Let's see how feisty you are once Paige has finished with you."

They left her in this uncomfortable position for some time. Because her knees were held down while her arms rested under her bottom, her pelvis was lifted up, exposing her vulnerable sex. As the uppermost strap also pinned down her shoulders, her back was arched and her torso described a gentle curve along the top, from which her breasts thrust upwards. Light reflected from her tanned skin, particularly along the succulent roundness of her straining thighs. Her blonde hair, usually immaculately cascading down around her shoulders, was now dishevelled. She could still move her head from side to side, and her blue eyes scanned the room fearfully.

The door opened and swung closed again behind Paige, pristine in a crisp white blouse and tight black leather mini skirt. Silk stockings gave her legs a soft sheen. With her dark hair gathered back into a long ponytail, she looked every inch the young professional secretary. Her patent leather stilettos clicked on the tiled floor as she approached the bound Sarah. She stood with hands on hips, legs parted, looking down at her captive. Her rouged lips parted in a delicate pout, and Sarah caught a waft of expensive perfume.

She opened her mouth to speak, but Paige quickly seized her jaw and forced a chrome ring between her teeth. A thin strap passed around her head, fixing it in place. With her mouth held wide open, Sarah could make no more than guttural sounds.

"First, I think I'd better shave you," said Paige. "It will make things so much easier later."

Sarah squirmed as Paige used a large brush to spread a generous quantity of shaving foam over her pubic hair. The dark-haired guard paused for a moment when she was satisfied with her efforts. She showed Sarah a shiny cut-throat razor.

"Now, this is very sharp, and I'd keep very still if I were you."

Sarah froze, trying desperately not to move as she felt the blade scraping across her sensitive skin. As the lather gathered on its steel surface, Paige flicked it into the corner of the room. It didn't take her long, and when she'd finished, she dried off the excess foam with a soft towel. She blew gently on the newly exposed skin, causing Sarah to shiver. Paige smoothed some moisturizing lotion into the area, lingering long enough for Sarah's body to respond. A tiny drop of liquid formed at the entrance to her pussy. Paige gathered it on her fingertip and licked it experimentally.

As Sarah looked over at her, Paige glanced at a two-way mirror on the other side of the room and signalled to an unseen observer. Seconds later the door opened, and Jody entered carrying the leather case from Q's office. She placed it on the table, winked at Paige and left.

With a flourish, Paige unclipped the locks and threw open the lid of the case. Inside was an old-fashioned typewriter. It had been immaculately restored, and certain extra features added by one of the club's technicians. Paige reached under the table and pulled out a bundle of wires, five red and one green. She plugged one end of each wire into a terminal mounted on the back of the typewriter.

Paige approached Sarah, holding the free ends of the four red wires. Each was tipped with a small but nasty looking spring loaded metal clip.

Sarah gulped.

Paige tweaked her right nipple until it was hard then snapped one of the clips around it, leaving a little pink bud protruding at the top. Sarah winced and cried out as the metal bit into her tender skin, not enough to puncture it but sufficient that it would not come off no matter what she did. Paige ignored her and repeated the process on her left nipple, forcing another whimper from the bound girl.

Sarah twisted her head away as one of Paige's hands approached. Undeterred, the chief guard took hold of a handful of blonde hair and forced her to look straight up at the ceiling. With her other hand, she reached thumb and forefinger through the chrome ring gag. She caught hold of Sarah's tongue and pulled it out. Sarah squealed. Paige let go of her hair and picked up another of the clips. She showed it to Sarah.

"Guess where this one's going."

Sarah knew what was coming, and gave an anguished wail as Paige snapped the clip onto the tip of her tongue and let go. Her tongue retreated back into her mouth. The wire trailed from it and brushed against her lower lip. The clip felt strange, and it dug into her flesh uncomfortably as her tongue brushed against her palate. In the end she was forced to allow it to stick out of her mouth.

Paige brandished the final red wire in front of her. Sarah rolled her eyes desperately as she tried to see where the other woman was going. With a gasp she felt warm air on her freshly shaved mound, followed by a gentle kiss. Paige lapped at her, teasing and flicking her clitoris. Sarah sighed, letting her head fall back to the mattress. She was totally unprepared for the sudden pain when Paige put the last clip onto her tender bud. Her whole body arched and she screeched out loud. Her toes and fingers clenched.

"Try to relax. You'll get used to it soon."

Sarah's breath hissed as she struggled against the tight restraints. Paige stroked her smooth skin, and after a few seconds her body fell limp.

Paige went back to her case and fiddled for a few moments out of Sarah's view. When she returned to Sarah's side she was holding a large vibrator, onto which she had fastened the green wire. The surface of the vibrator glistened with lubricant. Held open as she was, Sarah was unable to resist as Paige inserted it into her defenceless pussy. A narrow prong near the base of the implement wormed its way into her tightly clenched anus.

At last Paige stood back and folded her arms. She looked down at her helpless victim, smiling. Sarah's eyes pleaded with her, to no avail. She stroked Sarah's cheek once and sat down at the table.

"The wires link into the back of the typewriter. As I type, the keys complete connections, depending on which one I press, and that will send a current down one of the wires I've attached to you. The most common letters will activate the vibrator. I've no idea how it works, but believe me, it's very effective. Shall we give it a try?"

Paige turned to the typewriter and let her fingers dance over the keyboard.

My name is Paige. I'm British, 23 years old and I live in London.

Sarah gasped. A tingling sensation began deep in her pussy, followed by little pulses from each of the clips attached to her body. As Paige typed, she felt her nipples and clitoris respond to the gentle electrical stimulation, hardening beyond anything she thought possible. The vibrator inside her emitted a steady pulse. Its throbbing action was transmitted to the narrow probe in her anus, to her surprise and pleasure. Moisture started to gather around the part of the cylinder that was visible in her pussy. The pain when the clips were attached became a distant memory, banished by the pleasure of the moment.

"Nice, isn't it?" Paige's words broke into her rapture. "But feel what happens when I start to type a little faster. I'm going to write a story about life here at the club."

The keys clattered. *I'm single at the moment, well, sort of, but it's my choice. I get plenty of offers.*

Sarah stiffened, straining at her bonds as the sensations intensified. A whimper escaped her when the clip on her tongue brushed against her lips, causing a little jolt to pass through them. She tried desperately to hold it still. She felt the skin around her nipples tauten and her chest heaved. Vibrations flooded through her pussy and anus, the stimulation to her clit sending her nerve endings racing, as though she wanted to pee and come at the same time. Perspiration broke out on her body. Paige glanced at her and slowed down.

I'm about five foot eight, with long brown hair, blue-grey eyes and curves in all the right places. My ears are pierced, as is my left nipple.

"It's a shame, really," said Paige with a twinkle in her eyes, "that it's limited by my typing speed, so I can't do any real damage. It can deliver a fairly hefty jolt, though."

At that her fingers flew across the keys in a flurry of movement.

I have a degree in English Literature from a good university, and I'm an accomplished harpist. It's a very erotic instrument, I think. Quite apart from the evocative shape and the ethereal sound it makes, it's the suggestive way you play it, sitting down with it nestled in between your thighs. Sometimes, at home, I like to play in the nude. It's a wonderful feeling.

Sarah screamed in response, the pain that surged through her tongue, nipples and clit matched by an equal rush of pleasure delivered deep into her soaking pussy. Her fists clenched under her and her legs pulled at the unyielding cuffs. She curled her toes involuntarily.

"It's useful if I take you too close to your orgasm," said Paige. "It brings you right back down, fast."

Gradually the pain died away as Paige resumed a slow and steady pace, and Sarah settled back into the blissful daze caused by the multiple stimulations.

That's not what I do for a living, though. Instead, I work in a club in the heart of the city. You probably won't have heard of it. It's a somewhat unusual place Basically it's a sex club, catering to the wilder side of preferences, bondage and discipline, that sort of thing. You'd think it would be a really seedy place; many such clubs are, but this one's an exception, believe me. A woman owns it, for one thing, and for another the membership fees are absolutely astronomical. Discretion is its prime directive, and you'd be quite surprised at some of the names that appear on our membership list as a result. The press don't even know we exist. I don't know how much money is tied up in the place, but it must be considerable.

"The other problem, of course," said Paige, "is how long the operator can keep going before her fingers tire. I can do this speed indefinitely, but it's much more fun if I go faster. Q once kept me on edge for almost an hour before I came. I'm going to see if I can beat that."

I love my job. I've been working there for just over a year, as one of the "guards". We're all women, and effectively we're bouncers, though you wouldn't know it to look at us. Modesty aside, we're all pretty attractive (I've been told I resemble Liz Hurley), with good figures and above-average IQs. Despite the fact that we all sound very British, each of us speaks at least one other European language flawlessly. We know how to handle ourselves, though. All of us know at least two martial arts, and a regular part of our day is spent working out in a lavishly equipped gymnasium. It keeps us pretty well toned but not overtly muscle-bound.

She kept up a steady flow of words, typing faster only when she sensed that Sarah was on the verge of coming. The sudden stab of pain as she briefly increased the speed was enough to bring the blonde back down, just. After three such interludes, Sarah was soaked with sweat, her whole body gleaming under the harsh lights. Her hair was plastered to her scalp, and a pool of her juices had collected on the mattress between her legs. She was moaning constantly through the gag.

After an eternity Paige settled into a rhythm slightly faster than previously.

I tried to brace myself for what was about to happen, but still I shrieked when the first stroke landed across my buttocks. It hurt like blazes, but I remained bent over the desk, breasts squashed against its surface. I knew better than to try and escape. Before the sound had even died in my throat she lashed me again, harder than before. I began to cry. My knuckles turned white as I gripped the far edge of the desk tightly. After seven more carefully placed strokes my entire bum felt like it was on fire and I was wailing continuously, pleading with her to stop.

Sarah panted heavily, her breasts rising and falling almost in time with Paige's fingers. She closed her eyes and threw back her head. As her orgasm reached its crescendo, Paige cruelly accelerated her typing.

Q came and stood right in front of me. We're about the same height, and she looked straight into my eyes. I studied hers, which are dark brown, with little golden flecks in them. I find them fascinating. Without looking down, she untied the belt of my robe. She slowly slid the robe from my shoulders and down my back, caressing my skin as she did so. It dropped to the floor and I was as naked as she was. She rested her hands on either side of my waist and pulled my hips against hers. I went willingly. When our breasts touched it was like a little shock running through my body. My nipples were so hard. Her belly rubbed against mine. She tilted her head to one side and placed her mouth against mine, moving her lips delicately.

Sarah gave an ear-splitting shriek. Her back arched and her body was racked with spasms. She lost control of her bladder even as she came, a gush of hot liquid flooding out to pool on the mattress underneath her. Her pelvis pumped at the air as the orgasm shook her and the last vibrations died away inside her pussy. She gave a few small cries before collapsing back onto the bed like a punctured balloon.

When she came to moments later, Paige was standing over her. She looked as though she'd just stepped off a catwalk rather than having spent the last hour or so torturing Sarah. With a smile she reached down and removed the clip from Sarah's tongue and the gag from her mouth. Sarah worked her jaw in some relief, running her tongue around the inside of her dry mouth.

"Here, this should help," said Paige. She fed a straw into her mouth. Sarah sucked greedily at the chilled water. When she'd finished, Paige removed the clips from her nipples and clit. She sobbed as the blood returned painfully to their extremities.

"This had better come out too." Paige pulled the vibrator from Sarah's pussy. It made a sucking noise as it slipped free, and Sarah's hole gaped open. Paige batted her eyelashes at Sarah and licked the glistening device.

"You taste nice. Now, do you understand what you did wrong?"

Sarah nodded. "Yes, I do."

"And have you learned your lesson," asked Paige, "or will I have to carry on later?"

"No," whispered Sarah, "I promise I won't do it again."

"Good. And now, it's nearly closing time. We'd better get you into the reception area." Paige flicked a switch on the intercom. "Angela, Jody, will you both join me in here, please."

Jody and Angela brought sponges and soft, white towels with them, and used them to mop Sarah clean. Once she was dry, they gave her body a light coating of oil and wheeled the bed into the main entrance lobby of the club. Once in position, they locked the wheels in place, leaving Sarah on display for the gratification of the club's members. As they turned to leave, Sarah called out.

"Paige?"

Paige stopped. She dismissed the other two and swivelled round to look at Sarah, a half-questioning, half-smiling expression on her face.

"Yes, Sarah?"

"Thank you."

Paige leaned forward and kissed Sarah tenderly on the lips.

"You're welcome," she whispered. Straightening up, she walked across the lobby to where Q waited in the shadows.

"Very good, Paige. You beat my record, easily."

"So I win the bet?"

"You do indeed. Would you like to claim your reward now?"

"Of course," replied Paige. They linked arms and walked down the short hallway to Q's office. Inside, Q locked the door and removed her figure-hugging bodysuit. As usual she was wearing nothing underneath. Paige remained dressed, arms folded and an expectant smile on her face. The hostess leaned forward across her desk, reaching forward to hold the far edge.

"Did Sarah understand?" she asked.

"Oh yes," said Paige, picking up a supple cane and flexing it. "She won't borrow my Porsche again without asking. Now, the bet was twelve strokes, wasn't it? Are you ready?"

Q tightened her grip on the desk. "Yes."

Paige drew back her arm.

Gone Fishin'

Chrissie Bentley

"Okay, before we go any further, go back to my profile and have a look at my photograph. Do I look like the kind of girl who enjoys going fishing?"

There was a pause, then the beep of an incoming IM. I've cleaned up the spelling mistakes and abbreviations. "That photograph makes you look like you enjoy a lot of things. I was just hoping that fishing might be one of them."

I smiled and typed "goodnight"; hit Send, then fired off a line of kisses. Sheelagh was one of the first girls to e-mail me after I started posting erotic stories on a certain website and though her first letters were simply invitations to repeat the action at her place, they were written with a humor that made me curious to learn more about her . . . more, that is, than the admittedly impressive heights of horniness that she painted in another note. And over time, I did. She was an art dealer, she was single, and she travelled extensively – five foreign countries and 23 states in the last six months. I wondered whether mine was one of them?

Soon I was signing on at all hours of the day, just to see if she'd emailed me back, and she rarely disappointed. And one day, as she outlined her next scheduled trip, she asked where I lived. I told her the state; she mentioned a city. I sat and stared at the screen for a few moments. She was coming here? Careful not to give anything away, I typed, "When will you be there next?"

"This weekend. You?"

"I could probably make it. What are you doing there?"

"Fishing with some clients. And a reception Saturday night – a dozen or so people, out-of-towners like me, and some dear friends of mine, Debbie and Mandy, who just happen to own half the city. You should join us."

"I'll think about it."

I have one rule about online dating . . . don't do it. Hell, I won't even cyber with girls that I've slept with, let alone complete strangers. But did this really count as online dating? Okay, so we met online, but what if she'd written me via a magazine or a publisher? Then we'd be pen pals, and how harmless would that be? Plus, I'd have my own car, I'd let some friends know where I was going; and I did want to get to know her better. I hit the reply button. "Okay."

We made arrangements. Sheelagh would be flying in Friday, and driving out to the ocean the following afternoon. She mentioned the hotel where she was staying – of course I knew it . . . it was only 15 minutes from my apartment. But I was still impressed when she told me that she'd have her secretary book me a room, and charge it to expenses. "How about if we meet up in the dining room for lunch on Saturday?"

"Great. See you there." I signed off, and tried to decide what clothing would be the most appropriate for fishing in, but found myself spending more time in my underwear drawer instead. After all, if things did go well . . . surely I had at least one bra that screamed, "fuck me" from every fiber?

Yes, I did, but I don't think Sheelagh even noticed it, not when I walked into the dining room; not when we sat chatting at the bar; not when she waved a few friends off and told them she'd catch up with them later . . . not even when we went up to her room, stripped down in seconds, and fell onto the bed.

She was everything she'd described in her e-mails . . . mid-40s, good-looking, well-rounded, tall. Her voice was soft, as though every word was a precious commodity to be drawn out of her with the most exquisite tenderness . . . and that is how she fucked me (yes, *that* was everything she said it was, as well); calmly and deliberately, her face and her fingertips flowing across my body, everywhere at once and one place in particular, testing and teasing my flesh before settling down to one spot for a moment and then, tantalizingly, flying away to caress some place else.

Now I was crouching over her, my breasts just inches from her mouth. Sheelagh reached up, squeezed and then pinched each nipple, not hard, but just enough. Her tongue darted out and brushed them. I know what I was thinking, but I think I murmured it too, because she was sucking at it now, my nipple and a sizeable portion of my tit sinking into her mouth.

I held her to me, willing her to draw even more of me in,

feeling her hands shift to my ▓▓▓ and then down to my ass, stroking and squeezing my cheeks as a finger traced lightly between them. I felt the first stirrings of a distant orgasm, as she released my nipple from between her lips and we hung unmoving for a moment, as I wondered what next.

Sheelagh decided, grasping my hips and hauling me up, my pussy firm to her face. But I wasn't going to let her have all the fun. Deftly I flipped, parted her legs and gazed down at her slit. She'd shaved and I wished I had – although she didn't seem to care, as gentle fingers parted my lips and a tongue traced slowly up and down before nudging my clitoris for the first time, an electric shock that shook my entire frame.

I tried to concentrate on what lay before me, the sweet pink slit, the swollen clit that peeked out at me. But it was impossible. Her tongue was dancing between my legs and my body was completely out of my control. Her breathing was hard, her movements insistent and her rhythm was unchanging, even as I bucked my own hips, urging her to pick up the pace, bring me to the orgasm that was shuddering just on the other side of bunker-busting.

"Faster," I hissed, and she raised her head.

"Not yet. You've teased me with your stories for months. Now it's my turn." And she shortened her strokes, her hands pushing down on my hips until I could barely move them, but increasing the warm pressure of her tongue, so that every breath I took had a sharp, audible edge of pleasure; an edge that only heightened her determination to keep me dangling – which she did. I had never known anybody to be so painstaking, so patient, so totally in control of her own body that, even with a hellcat screaming seven shades of lust beneath her, she simply stretched the ecstasy out even further.

Finally I came . . . there wasn't a power on earth that could have stopped me; and as I writhed in the uncontrollable spasms of my own joy, I felt Sheelagh, too, pause . . . plunge . . . and then cry out as her lust blew up inside her.

We lay silent, shattered, sticky with sweat, and I think we must have slept. It looked darker when I opened my eyes, and Sheelagh now lay dead weight across me. I squirmed out from beneath her and crept to the bathroom. She hadn't moved when I returned and for a moment, I stood there, wondering what to do . . . which of the two or three thoughts that were now racing through my mind I should act on first? But before I could move, she opened her eyes and smiled. "We really need to make a move. I have that reception this evening, remember? You will come along, won't you?"

"Why not?" I threw on the clothes I'd arrived in, then headed back to my own room to shower and change. Half an hour later, she was guiding her hired car around the snaking bends that led towards the ocean, and the row of exclusive waterfront homes that were dotted along the coastline. "Dinner," she promised me, "alcohol, some tremendous people – you'll love Debbie and Mandy . . . and then, your choice. I can call you a cab back to the hotel . . . or else, we fish." I laughed. "I'll let you know."

The house . . . the mansion . . . was beautiful, more rooms than you could count; more *bath*rooms than you could count. I must have visited at least four different ones in the course of the evening, as the festivities shifted from wing to wing, while our hostess . . . Mandy, a startlingly pretty, middle-aged blonde, whose greying partner, Debbie, was a big wheel in computer programming . . . could not have been sweeter, even coming to my rescue when I took a wrong turn, and wound up in a room lined with wall-to-wall vintage erotica. Serious, no-holds-barred, vintage erotica. Some of those pictures must have been taken in the 1920s. Maybe even earlier.

For a moment, I must admit, I was shocked, both to encounter such a sight in such a palatial part of town and by the actual reality of what the pictures showed. We're all well aware that nothing we do with each other today has never been done before, but you really don't think about . . . I don't know, your grandparents, your great-grandparents . . . doing it as well. And then taking pictures to prove it. I've seen tamer photos on the Internet, and there were a couple that truly made me catch my breath.

"Oops!" A voice at the door made me spin around. Mandy stood there smiling. "As soon as Debbie told you to take the second door, not the third, I had a horrible feeling . . ."

"No, it's okay," I reassured her. "Just a little surprising, that's all."

"Everyone needs a hobby," she laughed, "and this is Debbie's . . . actually, it's both of ours'. Plus, it's a wonderful investment . . . 'cocks, not stocks,' as our accountant once put it." She continued chattering as I gazed around me, long sentences filled with the names of long-dead European porno-graphers, legendary modern collectors, auction prices that sounded like phone numbers, and well aware that the longer she talked, the longer I could spend looking, without actually appearing to do so. After all, how would you feel if a complete stranger caught you staring at their collection of lesbian porn? I had the feeling this happened to her a lot.

It was close to midnight before the party broke up, to reconvene at nine in the morning for the promised day of fishing. Mandy showed us to a room where we could sleep until then, but Sheelagh had other ideas. "Let's take a walk down to the beach first," she giggled as Mandy left the room. "It's such a lovely night."

Five minutes later, we were seated on the grassy sand, our backs against a large mossy rock, the ocean literally a stone's throw away, the sea breezes thick in our nostrils. Naturally it was our hosts' private beach . . . forget their house and guests, and there wasn't a soul, Sheelagh assured me, for miles. I scarcely cared. My pussy was still wet from my unexpected peep show, my mind racing with the notions that those photographs planted there. The moment we were settled, I threw myself at her.

We kissed, and I took her hand, placed it gently on my already-sopping slit and started to unbutton her dress, cupping her breasts through her flimsy bra, nipping the nipples with my teeth as I peeled the cups down, and then unfastened the clasp with one swift flick. My tongue swirled over one nipple, and I sucked the surrounding flesh deep into my mouth, as a long, contented "mmm" escaped the back of her throat.

Now I had my hand inside her panties, sliding my thumb against her slick slit and thrilling as her flesh sucked it deeper within. I raised myself a little, and began kissing down her body. But she halted me with an urgent whisper. "Don't stop. Keep doing what you're doing."

My hand was moving faster now, my fingers pressing against her outer lips, then gently parting them. Again, I shifted my weight. I had to taste her, I needed to taste her. But she moved too quickly for me, slipping from my grasp and scrambling to her knees. "Turn around."

Obediently, I did so, crouching on my hands and knees, my ass in the air, as she ran a hand gently down my buttocks and then slipped a long slender finger inside me. One finger, two . . . and then something else, longer, harder, firmer.

I lowered my head, tried to catch a glimpse of whatever it was that skewered me so unyieldingly. It remained just out of sight, but it felt heavenly, deeper and thicker than anything I had ever experienced, and so smooth, so gentle. Her hands clenched my sides and she began rocking me back and forth, as I closed my eyes, allowed her to control my every movement . . . sometimes fast, until my pussy felt as though it was turning inside out; sometimes so slow that I thought the dildo would never end; sometimes so deep that every thrust sent my innards lurching; and sometimes so shallow that I could feel the tip of the toy against my outer lips, and hear my hole sucking noisily at it.

Trusting one arm to hold both my weight and my balance, I reached the other behind me to caress her flesh. I touched her arm; she shifted a little and guided my hand to her pussy, warm, wet and soft. I imagined pressing my face to it, sucking at the pink before taking her lips, her clit, in my mouth. But she held me firm, merely groaning as a finger slipped inside her. "Keep doing that." I obeyed, all the while conscious of the ever-changing sensations that she was drilling into my pussy – and drilling faster now, her own hips finally joining the party, to roll against my rocking.

I clamped both hands into the sand beneath us, slowed my own motion . . . I caught my breath, then murmured insistently, "I want to feel you come on my face." I didn't give her a chance to react; she slipped the dildo out of me as I whirled around, crouched, and plunged between her legs, my tongue seeking out her rhythm and riding with her. One hand on her hips, the other reached for her breast, to tweak a nipple. I lapped at her pink, thrilling to the flavour of that delicious pussy, and her hand fell on my head, holding it still for a moment, before pushing me backwards.

Now she was on top, our bodies moving so seamlessly that I never lost her tantalizing taste for a moment and only when I was flat on my back once again did she shift, flipping herself around so that her mouth was at my pussy, as hers ground into my face.

I wriggled beneath her, gazed up at the beauty that hung just inches from my face, my mind flashing back to the photos I'd been looking at. I realized how dearly I love looking at a lover from this angle, seeing her cunt spread over my face as Sheelagh lowered herself down again and with her tongue wrapped warmly around my clitty, started fucking my mouth.

I could hear myself moaning as she lapped, little cries of shock and pleasure that accompanied every movement, and matched the motion of her tongue down below. I was coming quickly this time, and I hoped she would too – I wanted to hear her cry out at the precise moment my legs wrapped around her head, to hold her hard against my blazing cunt. And I wasn't disappointed, as a sudden twitch and a catch in her gyrations sent a telegraph ringing all the way down my spine, to explode in a flood of sensations in my pussy.

Sheelagh rose from her own juice-soaked paradise, her face streaked with the glorious glitter of my oils. But I wasn't finished with her yet. I pulled at her legs, drew her around so that she straddled my chest, and continued sucking and licking at her.

She looked down at me. "I never knew . . . I've dreamed about this so often," she breathed. "But I never realized just how beautiful you are until now . . ."

I was still sucking on her, relishing her taste and her texture. But I paused for a moment. "Well, I don't think I'll be going out in public like this, but I'm feeling pretty good, too," I whispered. I shifted my weight a little, and held her face in my cleavage, my breasts parted and pressing against her cheeks. I rubbed first one, then the other, against her, alternating circular motions that thrilled me as much . . . if that moan was anything to go by . . . as they excited her.

Our pussies were touching, rubbing together, slicking one another with their free flowing juices, then slowly, she began sliding up my body, slicking a warm path of pussy up my belly, between my tits, across my face, onto my lips.

My eyes were closed, my breathing heavy, hypnotized by the weight and warmth of her steady rocking, and the rhythmic sighs that escaped her lips. And when I heard her cry out her orgasm, and felt a sudden slap of salty wet against my cheek, I laughed before I opened my eyes – and saw that she was still riding me, her own eyes closed tight, her breath still coming in short, sharp gasps. Then who . . .

"Sorry, kids, but we couldn't help ourselves." Above and behind me, the voice startled me – shocked Sheelagh as well, as she halted her movements, gasped a stunned "What?"; and then relaxed, laughing. "Mandy. Debbie. Fancy seeing you here!"

"Well, it *is* our beach . . ."

Now I recognized Mandy's voice and as I craned my head

backwards, I could see her as well, standing totally naked on the rock above us.

I wasn't certain how I felt – furious? Violated? Or very, very excited? "How long have you been there?"

"We were here before you were," Debbie smiled. "For much the same reasons as well. Except, watching you guys go at it was even more exciting than what we were planning."

I smiled; Mandy knelt down and looked into my face. "Sorry if we startled you . . . to be honest, I never knew Debbie still had it in her." She kissed her partner. "She usually doesn't squirt past my wrist."

"Honey . . ." Debbie protested loudly but affectionately – I think she was actually feeling rather proud of herself. Measuring the distance with my eyes, even taking the trajectory into account, she'd sent a jet at least eight feet, and her aim could scarcely have been better. "Well, I'm impressed," I smiled; and then, remembering what they'd interrupted, "but I think Sheelagh here might be feeling a little left out of things."

Mandy's eyes flickered to my lover. "Yes, we did kind of spoil things, didn't we?" She scrambled down the rock; Debbie followed, and I saw a glance pass between them, before she settled herself in front of Sheelagh and kissed her firmly on the lips. I caught Sheelagh's eye and nodded; then walked over to Debbie and embraced her. She shook her head. "I'm going to sit this one out, thanks," she said quietly. "I've never been much more than a once-a-night gal myself. And besides, if I know Mandy, she's going to put on quite a show."

She was right. They lay flat on the sand, their pussies tight together and at first Mandy simply lay there, cooing encouragement to Sheelagh as she built up speed . . . whispers, at first, that I had to strain to hear; and then louder, more demanding, until she was almost screaming at her – "Fuck my . . . harder . . . faster . . . that's it, baby . . ." Until finally Sheelagh collapsed, spent at last.

"Debbie . . . are you certain that you're done for the night?"

"I'm sure, honey," she laughed. "But I do need a drink. Who's coming?"

Sheelagh groaned. "I'm not certain that I still have the use of my legs," she murmured. "But I'll give it a try. Who else wants a nightcap?"

Mandy shook her head. "Not me, I'm going to stay here for a while. How about you, Chrissie?"

"I'll stay here as well," I told her. Even though I lived so close, I rarely got out to the shore any more. And besides, I was curious about Mandy and Debbie . . . did they always do things like this?

Mandy shook her head. "To be honest, we've never done anything like this in our lives. I mean . . . We used to talk about it, as you do when you're heading towards another anniversary, and you've already exhausted every sex manual you can find. But we never did anything, and we probably never would have, if you two hadn't . . ." she paused. "You really didn't know we were there?"

"Didn't have a clue. You must have been very quiet."

She giggled. "I think we were so surprised when we heard you coming down the path that we stopped whatever we were doing . . . and then, once you got started, we really didn't want to say anything. But I'm not sorry that we did. I've often thought that, if I was free and single, I'd have snagged Sheelagh for myself years ago. I'm just glad she's found someone who's on the same wave-length as she is."

"Well, I don't know about 'found' . . . this is pretty much our first date; well, no, we've been e-mailing each other for a few months, but this is the first time we've ever met."

"Oh, I know that," Mandy laughed. "You're the story-teller. Debbie and I have read all your stuff . . . acted a few of them out, as well. In fact, it was us who first sent Sheelagh the link . . . remember the one where you said you looked a bit like the girl out of *Sex And The City*? Sheelagh adores her; so we had to let her know. And once you posted your photograph, I think it was love at first sight."

"So basically, you set the two of us up?" I laughed, squeezing her hand.

"You don't know the half of it." She leaned forward suddenly, and kissed my lips. I was surprised, but – hey, what's new about that, this evening? I kissed her back and she beamed at me. "We planned the whole thing. Even the wrong turn you made when you went to the bathroom. I mean, you write a good game, but you'd be surprised how many people that room has frightened off. You know Sheelagh found most of those pictures for us, don't you?"

Ah, so that's the kind of art dealer she is . . . I was about to say that, but Mandy's hands were on my thighs now, parting my legs a little more, to allow her finger to slide in deeper, and begin to gently fuck me. Instead I sighed, and she carried on talking. "And all that business about a fishing trip? To be honest, a few of the others may go out in the boat tomorrow, but the only fish that Sheelagh was interested in catching was you." She pushed me down on the sand, and her lips began grazing their way down my chest, my belly, to my thighs and beyond. "I'm just glad," she murmured, "that there's enough of you that we can all have a share." Then her words faded into an indistinct mumble, and I felt my puss being sucked into her mouth.

And if I wasn't already hooked, I certainly was now.

A Two-Way Street

Marie Gordon

Diana was known in lesbian circles as dominating, powerful, a woman who specialized in women like Sophie. "She's the answer to your prayers. Just what you need," said Sophie's ex. "Expensive but worthwhile, so I'm told."

Sophie would never allow herself to be dominated by such a woman. It was she, Sophie, who played the dominator, so, why was she driving to Diana's establishment? Sophie had never met a woman who didn't respond to her control-freak approach to love and sex but she didn't want to be in control; she needed to allow herself to be taken over. That's why she was going, well, that was one reason. That, and the photo she kept in the deepest pocket of her wallet.

She'd used a false name. To Diana, she was Sara. Not a good way to start but it had to be that way. For now.

Diana sized her up at once. "Don't be scared; I won't eat you, unless you want me to." Diana was in her early forties, with a strong face, high cheekbones, luxuriant hair and the assurance of a royal. "Come on." She took Sophie's hand in her own fragile one, and led her to a cubicle, "Slip into something more comfortable. I'll be with you in a moment."

The "something more comfortable" was a white satin nightshirt, with buttonholes piped in pink. By the time Sophie had shed her clothes for the satin gear, her heart was thumping loudly. She couldn't go through with this, not in a fit. She was—

At that moment Diana knocked on the cubicle door, blocking her escape route.

"Sara, are you ready?"

Ready? She'd never be ready. "I . . . I'm . . ." Words died in her throat.

Diana opened the door, took Sophie's arm. "I sense that you need a little encouragement. Come."

The guillotine awaits, thought Sophie, allowing Diana to lead her to a room large enough to hold a king-sized bed. Instead there was nothing in it but a single bed, a chair, table, wash-basin, plus lots of towels. The ceiling was completely mirrored.

"I don't like that." Sophie pointed upwards.

"Then you won't have it." Diana pressed a button on the wall and a false ceiling slid into place, covering the mirror.

"Thank you."

Diana pulled back the cover: "Now, just take the weight off your feet."

Sophie stared at her, mind so numb it couldn't take in the simplest instruction.

"Sit on the bed, then lie down."

That was better. Simple instructions, one by one. She could do that.

"You will soon be relaxed, I promise. Easy breaths now, while I wash my hands."

It's not too late. Sophie's mind was now racing. She could still go; Diana couldn't make her stay. She should never have come. What did she hope to achieve?

"The woman is a miracle-maker. Her hands are magic; she'll untie every single knot you have, or ever thought you had." That was friend Brenda, once frigid, now well on the way to being nympho.

"I'm not frigid."

"Of course you're not, but you do have trouble letting go – your words, not mine."

Sophie was well aware she had trouble. She couldn't hand over her power; didn't want to. Then what was she doing here?

Diana now stood beside her, smiling, reading her mind, no doubt, thought Sophie.

She was. "Still planning to escape?"

Sophie shrugged helplessly knowing it was already too late.

"You'll be glad you stayed." Diana sat on the side of the bed. "You're very beautiful, my dear. Why are you here?"

"I've been asking myself that question."

"And the answer?"

"I want to make love to women—"

"Of course."

"I'm very good as a giver, but I can't receive; can't surrender my power."

"You will receive from me. Love is a two-way street, honey."

"What can I learn from you?"

"You will learn how to let yourself to be taken over. To cry, to whimper, to beg for release, to be teased beyond your imagination."

"I can't do that." Sophie sat up, suddenly breathless. "I won't do that."

"You will, honey. Now, lie down, close your eyes and prepare for heaven."

Sophie did as she was told, but her body stayed tense as Diana caressed her first with her voice . . .

". . . forget for the moment where you are, think of something that makes you happy. Think of a place, a memory, a dream; something so good you want to live and relive it forever."

Her voice went on and on sending Sophie back in time to the sea and the first time she rode a wave to the shore.

"Very good. Your body is responding to your mind, as it is to my touch." Her oiled hands moved lightly over Sophie's body as she lay on her back. "There's nothing to be afraid of here. As they said in *Cabaret*, 'In here, life is beautiful.' *N'est-ce pas*?" Then, "Would you like music?"

Sophie shook her head. Diana's voice was all the music she needed.

"And now, it's time I think to remove your nightshirt. There, that's better. Now, if you will roll over on your side, I'll massage your back." As she drew soothing, sweeping strokes down and across Sophie's back, she said: "And now, for your butt. Stay relaxed while I massage and pummel it and draw it up and away from your cunt.

"Do you like that? Yes, it's good. Do you like your cunt? Germaine Greer says a woman should love her cunt. Two grunts if you don't, one if you do."

The single grunt from Sophie drew a deep, rich laugh from Diana. "I thought so, and why not?" In one movement she flipped Sophie on to her back and spread her legs. "What a beautiful cunt, and such a wet one."

"I'd like a mask for my eyes, face."

"Very well, just for your eyes, but believe me, soon you will rip it off, then ask for the shield to be removed from the mirror. Ah yes . . .

". . . our bodies are instruments to be played upon. Accept this, relish it. It is why you were made this way – for physical, mental and emotional satisfaction. Women have pleasure at their fingertips, and they don't know how to use it.

"I shall teach you, and you'll never want to get out of bed." Her rich laugh filled the room. "Of course, that's not true, but even when you're not pleasuring yourself or someone else, your body will be alive with the memory. You will walk, talk, look, smell like the sexy woman you are.

"Now, don't be alarmed, I am just touching your pussy ever so lightly. Do you know why women are afraid of growing old? Because they're scared of losing their femininity; their appeal. They're afraid it is the end of pleasure, of joy. If they only knew it is theirs for life. Partners may die, or turn to someone younger. No matter. Women are self-sufficient and they literally have the whole world in their hands – your beautiful cunt, my dear, is now voluptuous, so soft and receptive – they don't have to have a partner. Of course it's better if they do, but it's not the end of the world if they don't.

"We women are so lucky. Our entire bodies are there for our sensual delight. And we have a whole arsenal of caresses, fantasies, dildos, butt plugs at our disposal.

"Are you cold? No? Because if you are you will soon be warm, very warm. Now I am just lightly holding your breasts with one hand, while the other gently touches the lips of your vagina that is now so very enlarged.

"Soon – and I'm telling you this for two reasons – one, to prepare you and two, for you to prepare yourself. Anticipation, my dear, magnifies the moment of realization. Soon I will put my fist into your cunt and gently move it around. I note the anticipation pleases you.

"Where was I? Oh, yes. Women are a world unto themselves, and when they realize how autonomous they are, what a law they are unto themselves, they will walk, laugh, sing and dance with such *joie de vivre* they will never again fear age.

"Do you like that? My kneading your cunt? Just grunt, my dear. I'll understand. Of course you love it; it's what you are made for.

"Sometimes, when I'm feeling – oh, outrageous, I think I must invite men to see how a woman should be made love to. I tell them about the all-important G-spot, but I'm afraid it would go over their heads, just make them as randy as all hell and, thinking with their cocks, they'd learn nothing." Again her laughed filled the room.

"I am now paying a little attention to your clit. Just lightly – it is such a sensitive little thing, it prefers to hide behind its shield. Treat it roughly and it will reject all advances, and retreat.

"And now, what I have here is a dildo. I'm sure you are familiar with them. Like cocks, they come in all sizes. This is a medium size – not too fat, not too long, just right. I have lubricated it just a little but you are so wet, my love, it is not really necessary. Gently in and move it all about. Aah, you like that. Perhaps later you might like a longer one to reach your innermost recesses. Mmm?

"Groan and moan all you like, my dear. This room is sound-proof. Ah, the stories it could tell. Now, go easy, you mustn't come yet. We've a long way to go before I let you come. Oh, yes, it is I who am in control. You realize that now, don't you? I have taken control of your body. Do you like it? No, no. It's not time yet. We're not nearly done.

"You've not yet endured the exquisite agony of the butt plug. If you haven't had that, you are in for a taste of heaven. When it hits you, you can swear and scream all you want, honey, because that's what you'll feel like doing and your cunt will run like a river. But, even then, you can't go. Even then the game's not over. Now, a longer dildo? Yes?

"Uh huh. That's better, isn't it? It goes where no man has gone before." Again she laughed. "It's okay – moan and groan as much and as loudly as you want. It's your party. What's that? You want the butt plug. Are you sure?"

"Yes, yes. I'm sure."

"Quite sure?"

"I'm fucking well quite fucking sure."

"Very well. Roll on to your side while I oil the plug a little. There. Relax into it and enjoy. Well, I can see that you do. Now, I'll alternate. First in/out with the plug, then in/out with the dildo. I see that puts you in a spin. You can't stand it? I thought you were enjoying it. Just a joke, honey. You want to come?"

"Yes, yes, yeeeeeeeeees. Come, come, fucking well come."

"Not yet. Now for a little teasing. Just stay very still while your passion recedes a little. You are hyperventilating, and we can't have that. Just let your breath drop back to as close to normal as you can make it. That's better."

"Please. Please let me come. Make an end, Diana."

"You're sure that's what you want?"

"Yes, yes, *yes*." Sophie ripped the mask from her eyes.

"Very well. Now, instead of moving the plugs one after the other, I'll manipulate them both together. Ready? In, out; in, out. Two in, two out, two in, two out."

Sophie groaned in agony. "I can't take any more. Release me. Let me go."

"Do you want the mirror?"

"Yes, yes, *yes*."

"Good." Diana pressed the button and the shield rolled back. "Now you can watch yourself come. Ready?"

All Sophie could do was whimper, and then came the "Oh, my God, ooooh, my Go . . . o . . . od. I've never ever . . . never ever . . . never *ever* . . . felt . . . like . . . this . . ."

"Don't be scared. Your body is bucking like that because it's such a powerful orgasm, my love."

"Ss . . . sh . . . shattering."

When it was done Sophie let out a string of curses, before finally settling into a series of happy sighs.

At that point Diana pulled the cover over Sophie's depleted body. "A sleep is what you need, *mon amie*. I'll be back in 30 minutes."

When Diana returned Sophie was stretching like a cat.

"How do you feel now?"

"Wonderful, just wonderful. It's like I've been given a whole new body – mind."

"Shower and dress while I prepare coffee. The kitchen is to the left of the cubicle."

Sophie sipped her coffee in silence. She felt unreal, as if she was floating high above the world. "How can I thank you, Diana?" She shook her head. "Words – they're never there when you need them."

"You're free now to give and to receive."

"Back there I felt as if you were my lover."

"And for that time, I was."

Sophie sighed.

"I'm thinking of giving advanced sessions."

"There's more to learn?"

"Lots more, especially between two people."

"You mean . . . ?"

"Oh, yes. Definitely," she grinned, "a hands-on job. However, I'm only offering one place."

"Oh."

"Don't look so unhappy. I'm offering it to you. Would you like to become my lover?"

Sophie's spirits went from zero to the skies, and the quantum leap took with it the power to speak.

"One grunt for 'yes', and two for—"

At Sophie's single, definite grunt Diana's laugh exploded, filling the room, bringing tears. "With two people involved, the joy, the discoveries are endless." She stroked Sophie's hand. "Do you know what I'd like to do to you first, my love? I'd kiss your beautiful butt, and then . . ."

"Yes? And *then*?"

"You will see."

"Diana, you're teasing me – again."

"Occupational hazard. Now, when are you available?"

Suddenly, Sophie remembered the photo and all excitement went from her.

"What's wrong, Sophie – it is Sophie, isn't it?"

Sophie gasped. "How did you know?"

"You're so much like her."

"Who?" Sophie knew it for a silly question.

"Your mother."

"You knew all along?"

"No, not until a few minutes ago."

"Is that why you want me – because I'm like her?"

"No. I loved you long before that. I loved you the minute you came in the room looking so scared, so uncertain."

Sophie took the photo from her wallet – the photo of a much younger Diana in the arms of Sophie's mother. She gave it to Diana. "I found it among her things after she died. You can have it now; I don't need it any more."

"No, Sophie, you don't." Diana dropped the photo and held out her arms as Sophie snuggled safely into harbour.

Inside

Cheryl Moch

I like being inside. My least favourite phrase is "let's go". I don't like air blowing on my face. The wind alarms me. I like knowing that the air I am breathing is air I've already breathed.

As a child I studied peanuts, peapods, certain fruits, fascinated by how they were tucked so neatly inside their skin. I focused on the border between container and the contained, the inviting edge where things both come together and come apart. I admired clams and pitied butterflies as they left their cocoons to fly off to uncharted skies.

I liked to think of my body as an enclosure, my brain resting in the tidy capsule of my skull, my body the repository of so many busy organs.

I am happy only in my house, perched as it is on a cliff at the edge of the sea, the sea in which my parents perished. I am the master of my universe right here and if I want, Countess, Duchess, Empress, Queen. Small and insignificant in the world, I loom large in my own house. I venture no further than my own garden.

There's nothing I want that I don't have here: from the wall of glass in my living room I can check the ocean's many moods. Everyday is different and, though I have been here most of my life, I have never seen two days exactly alike. I do not want for company. The local bookseller stops by with some frequency, pleased to provide me with current titles so that together we might discuss them. The local grocer makes deliveries, bringing me the choicest of his produce. A neighbouring fisherman brings me the best of his catch, straight from the sea to my kitchen table.

My father, an artist of enduring reputation, built this house. It has become an icon of modernism, with its sleek lines and glass walls. My father's paintings of this house hang in museums around the world. It was at his knee that I learned to paint, but eventually I rejected slimy oils for hard enamels. I like the way the molten glass clings to the metal, forever bonded. In my studio I have a small kiln, and it's there I fire the miniatures that now command enormous sums. My dealer comes to me three or four times a year and eagerly scopes up each finished piece, each one a tiny cosmos no bigger than your palm, placed in gilded frames I've learned to build. Celebrities and CEOs collect them. My dealer brings with her all the juicy art world gossip I care to hear, and she would gladly sell the number of works I give her ten times over had I been able to create them more quickly. Each piece is slow, intensive work, demanding patience and a steady hand. Since demand exceeds supply, collectors vie for these pieces. They sometimes contact me asking to buy one, offering tremendous sums. I leave these matters to my dealer. Sometimes such collectors show up at my door, their expensive cars parked outside. I always let them in, glad to have their company for a while. I show them around my studio. I serve them champagne. They admire my home, the outstanding view of the sea, the paintings my father left behind. They flatter me, in their skilled way. But still, I sell them nothing. I'm an artist, not a businesswoman. I advise them to call my dealer.

It was a hot summer day when the first woman came to me. I don't know why this one came – she was not an art lover, or a collector. I first spotted her as she climbed the stairs leading up the cliff from the beach to my garden. The binoculars I keep at the window have superior optics and I watched as this woman climbed with ease. She was an athletic woman of no more than 30 – about my age at the time. But still, the climb is steep and strenuous and with the powerful magnification, I could see the beads of sweat collecting on her body as she climbed. She stopped once to wipe her brow but she continued on at once, at a brisk pace.

She was wearing a bikini.

People say I get my height and beauty from my mother and my fortune and talent from my father. This woman seemed to be about my height but the distribution of her taut flesh was different. Encased in her bikini top, shaped like twin clamshells, were large breasts.

My own breasts are quite small and I watched hers with interest as she climbed. They quivered slightly, and I felt an odd stirring as I watched them at a huge magnification. I'd felt this kind of stirring once before, when I was a teenager, for one of my father's young models. We furtively and passionately kissed in the bathroom one day, and I managed to slip my hand inside her panties. I had just wiggled a finger inside her when there was a knock on the door and she quickly pulled away.

There's a switchback at the top of the stairs leading from the beach, and I knew my view of this woman would cease until she emerged in the garden outside my studio window. I put the binoculars down and quickly went to my studio, stopping for a moment to look at myself in the mirror. I ran my fingers through my dark hair, cut short as a boy's.

The flower garden outside my studio was in full bloom. I'd had a hedge of sunflowers planted there that summer, a mammoth hybrid variety that grew to nearly seven feet tall. When I looked out, this woman was reaching up to one of these gigantic blooms perched on its curved stem. She was long-legged and trim. I didn't want to startle her as I quietly slid open the French doors that led out to the garden.

She must have heard the sound and turned to meet it.

"Is this your garden?"

I assured her that it was. I expected her to apologize for the invasion, but she didn't. She seemed a woman used to being welcome. Her gaze met mine and we looked at each other for a moment. She smiled.

"Would you like to come in? To see the house?"

My house, as I've said, is a visual icon. It appears on picture postcards sold in tourist shops on our island, on travel brochures and advertisements. My father's paintings have assured the immortality of this image. Yet this woman seemed to have no interest in the house whatsoever. One of my father's paintings of the house adorns a wall of my studio, a large work, still as he hung it some years ago. It's one of his best works and has never been seen outside of this room. Visiting collectors have offered millions for it. It drew no comment and barely a glance from this woman. She had no interest in my kiln, or the unusual magnification glass, framed with brass fittings, that I use to help me position the tracings of granulated glass that create my pictures.

I let her precede me as I showed her around. I wanted to see her from behind, the cheeks of her ass firm and muscular in their little crocheted bottom.

In the living room, she stood for a moment, admiring the sea from the wall of glass, then turned to face me.

"Where's your bedroom?" she asked me and when I didn't immediately respond she added, "Where you sleep," as if I did not comprehend the meaning of the word.

In my bedroom I've created my own cosmos. The room is small, barely larger than my king-sized bed. The walls are lacquered a deep plum, nearly brown. Blackout shades ensure round-the-clock darkness and the a/c is always on. I like to sleep cold and quiet. The ceiling of my room is thick with fairy lights, a private Aurora Borealis. They're on a dimmer to create a variety of moods. As we entered, I put them on just high enough to see the tanned glow of her skin.

"Nice," she said, climbing onto my bed, and sitting with her legs spread wide so that I could see a little curl of pubic hair escaping from her bikini.

I imagined deep holes, moist hidden passages.

Who made the first move? It's hard to say. She patted the bed next to her, inviting me to sit. Instead, I climbed on top of her, straddling her, my own legs spread. I pinned her beneath me and she did not protest as I pressed my cunt hard against hers, my linen clothes rough against her nearly naked flesh. I breathed in her salty smell, kissing her soft neck, thrusting my tongue into her eager mouth. I pulled at her silky hair and she groaned.

As I undid the buttons on my shirt, she watched me, stroking her own crotch. As I've said, my own breasts are small but they are shapely, my shoulders and arms strong and sinewy. She reached for me as I removed my clothes but I pushed her hands off and once again pinned her body under mine, spreading her legs with my knees, forcing them apart. I pressed my own small breasts against her firm substantial ones.

I removed the clamshell top and her breasts fell free for me. I felt their weight, before resting my face against them. I wanted my face all over them. She moaned as I opened my mouth wide and put one tit in, licking and sucking while the other nipple nuzzled the palm of my hand. I reached down and put my hand inside her bikini bottom. Her pubic hair was soft, her cunt already moist as my fingers stroked her lightly. She had invaded my garden, my house, my bed. I would invade her.

She moaned.

"Fuck me."

I knew just what to do. I'd lain in bed for so many nights, pleasuring myself and imagining this very scene. Slipping down the bed, I put my face to her cunt. With my artist's eye I took in the many colors of her labia, moist and shining, the sweet curls of her pubic hair trimmed short. With my face to her cunt, I spread her lips as I pressed my tongue against her clit. It was hard against my tongue as I licked and teased it gently, feeling my own rising excitement while tasting hers.

I am a steady and patient craftswoman. I took my time as I licked her pussy. I licked her slow and gently, slurping up her cunt juice like life's blood. I licked her hard and fast, pacing myself against her breathing.

My stroking tongue was encouraged by her hands gently pulling at my hair, her moans of pleasure, the steady flow of moisture, mixed with my saliva, wetting my face, my sheets. I was excited to feel the perfect fit as my tongue pushed against the inside of her pussy. Her moaning was getting louder. There was no one to hear us, and outside the sea raged. She was close to bucking up against my mouth, but I didn't want her to come, at least not yet, not that way. I would make her wait.

I pulled my slobbering mouth away.

I spread her legs and was face to face with the entrance to her perfect cave.

I knew my fist would fit entirely inside her. I had imagined such a portal for many years as I lay alone in bed. All I needed was a strategy for entrance. I pushed in one finger, then two, then three. She groaned as my fingers vibrated inside her. I pulled them out and shifted my angle slightly. I plunged back into her, pushing with quick thrusts. She squirmed, her cunt hungry to meet my fingers, to take them in. Her juices ran freely over my sopping hand. I stopped for a moment, this time to tease. She grunted, low and deep, " Please . . . fuck me, fuck me hard . . ." I pushed my fingers in again, harder this time, getting further in. She wrapped herself tight around my fingers as she adjusted to their presence.

When finally I plunged my entire fist up her cunt she gasped, and because she seemed to shudder with the intensity, I went slower and more gently as I pushed in further, feeling her pulsing energy as my fist spread her apart. I plunged in deeper and deeper, as far as I could go. When my fist was perfectly contained and the boundary between her and me unclear, I let go, pounding and grinding inside of her, my fist pulsating to her rhythm, to my rhythm, a wild sound emanating from us both. She rocked and bucked against my fist, as I pounded her wet cunt over and over again, her nails digging into me as she throbbed and screamed and climaxed. Oh Jesus, Oh Jesus, Oh Mary, she sang as we both collapsed, her body shuddering with wave upon wave of orgasm.

We lay there silently as our breathing steadied. The cool air was drying my dampened face. The sweet smell of pussy was everywhere. Reluctantly, I removed my hand and I shimmied up to place my cheek upon hers.

I knew I would soon fall asleep, but before I did I found, in the tumult of the bed sheets, her bikini top. Gently, I placed each breast back into its clamshell cup, but not before placing a tender kiss on each nipple. I felt a remarkable sense of well-being, knowing that her breasts were so encased, order returned to the universe.

Then I fell asleep. She was gone when I woke up. I went to the window of my studio to check the garden but it was empty. The sun was low in the sky but I could see that the high stems of two of my sunflowers drooped headless, their flowers gone.

Refreshed in every way, my senses sharpened, I worked all night, creating an erotic piece, the first I'd ever done. It was a close-up of two glistening cunts, painted in every shade of pinks and reds you might imagine. It became the first in an erotic series. My dealer did not wish to show this series, but when a young curator from a museum of contemporary art saw them, she paid a substantial sum for the entire series. They created a sensation. Now they are on permanent display, and scholars of queer theory have written dissertations about them. It is my hope they've inspired more than scholarship.

The flower thief must have told her friends about me. Soon a fairly steady stream of women began appearing in my garden. I watch from my window, as they make the strenuous climb from the beach. It's hard work, and they deserve the reward I always give them. And so do I.

The House of the Rising Sun

Alice Blue

Sunset: hot day melting into warm night. Amina stood, watching the shadows lengthen, feeling a heavy breeze pass her by – the hard iron balcony rail a stiff weight across her belly.

For a while she just looked at the people walking along the street below, calmly following their progress as they went wherever they were going. Not for the first time since Stanley had left her, she wanted to be one of them – any of them. A pair of Greek sailors; a young black man in threadbare jeans and a stained T-shirt, pedaling a wobbling, squeaking bicycle; a tourist couple in their pressed whites, standing out in their catalog-bought profiles; a fat man who didn't walk as much as slowly swim through the heavy sunset atmosphere, his legs seemingly linked by some internal arrangement to his fat arms swinging rhythmically by his side.

Many went by till the sun had dropped behind the filigreed rooftops, and the street lamps started to, at first, glow then burn brightly, but she sadly remained herself.

Finally the night touched, hinted at, becoming cool, so she turned away from the iron curlicues of the balcony and walked across the small boarding-house room to robotically turn the antique light switch by the door. Yellow light snapped down through a dirty, cracked ceiling fixture, bathing the room in harsh realism: sink stained with a rusty high-water mark, mirror above cracked with an angry bolt, wooden floorboards that had been worn not into a smooth sheen but rather a broken and splintered forest. Wallpaper covered the walls, a tawny rainbow of mildew, and where it didn't it curled away from the soft plaster in stiff tubes and torn twists.

"Bathroom's down the hall, girl; that's why you be gettin' this one so cheap," the manager had said. A polished noir Buddha, she'd sat, rocked back on a low stool by the front door. A simple white dress, all lace and tiny red stitching, covered her great body. She was a momma, like a primordial soft bosomy comfort made into a breathing person. As she spoke, she'd cooled herself with a fan lettered with a gospel hymnal – too slow to deliver a good breeze, but too fast for Amina to see what it said. "But you be gettin' a sink, so you ain't bein' completely uncivilized."

Amina hadn't argued, and yet hadn't agreed, either: the red-brick building across the street from the iron pickets of the cemetery had neither been her destination or even a way point. She been walking since dawn, a shocked sonombulation that had started with Stanley's note on the kitchen table, and ending with this big black woman calling to her: "Here, girl; rooms for a tired lookin' lady."

Money had been exchanged. How much Amina didn't care. Not many thoughts inhabited her mind during that long walk, and even after she'd climbed the stairs under the simply lettered sigh: Rising Sun. Only a few thoughts had managed to make themselves known to her as she'd leaned over the balcony – wishes to be anyone but Amina Robinson.

Then, as the sun set and the not-hot, but-warm night had started, she thought a few more. Not words, really, just a cool rationalization: she'd not brought anything with her. no razors, no gun, not even some pills. She was only two floors up, too low to jump. The ceiling fixture didn't look strong enough to support her, even if she had anything like a rope. The mirror was obvious, razor-edged cracks promising – even without a handy bathtub.

In the end, she retreated to the mildew-sink of the too-soft bed, old springs complaining as she settled into it: not avoiding the escape she so desperately wanted, but rather not wanting to face even her fractured reflection.

Amina sat on the bed for a long time. Listening with half an ear to the architectural mumblings of the old building: the hissing of water through pipes, the rolling creeks of footsteps next door and up above, the flapping of the shade in the open window.

Like a toothache she couldn't help tonguing, she replayed Stanley – hurting herself with his absence. Each act – the last fight, the daisies he'd brought home from work one day, the way he'd looked at her when she undressed in front of him, the colour of his nipples, his laughter – seemingly to press harder down on her shoulders. She cried, after a time, but her tears were long since used up.

She couldn't go on. She knew that, felt the truth of it somewhere down deep inside herself, but – still – she sat on the edge of that bed in the House of the Rising Sun and did nothing, except weep without tears.

Night: warm darkness pushed back by street lights, diluted by flickering advertisements. The sounds of passers by seemed louder, as if the sunlight of only a few hours before had done its own kind of pushing back, their volume increased by its absence. Now free, their voices and the sounds of their cars, bikes, and trucks echoed up into the small room.

Amina stood and went to the window, intending to close it. She stopped, though, in mid-stride. *What did it matter?* she thought to herself in sentiment if not in those exact words; *I won't be able to hear anything very soon.*

Then she did. Hear something, that is: a knock – thunderclap, pistol shot loud in the small room – and a voice: small, quavering, weak, helpless. "Hello?" someone said from the other side of her door. "Hello? Can you hear me?"

She didn't have to. Still, she did: turn, walk to the door, slip the cheap chain, turn the knob, and open it just so much.

"Thank God, I thought someone wasn't in here." She was small, young – maybe twenty to Amina's thirty, with hair as straight as dried pasta and as yellow as polished gold. Freckles dotted her pale cheeks, and her eyes were puffy and swollen from tears. "Please, can I come in – please?"

She didn't need to, but Amina did: open the door wider. Stumbling over the first words in many hours, "S-sure" sounded like gravel pouring out of a coffee can.

"Thank you, oh, thank you—" the young girl said, hunching down and moving quickly into the room. Then she turned, and before Amina could do anything, had wrapped her thin, surprisingly warm, arms around her.

Wet tears seeping through her dress, onto her shoulder, Amina's arms moved without her. The girl was so slight, so small, putting her arms around her was like hugging a doll.

"I just – I just didn't want to be alone," the girl said. Then she repeated, as much to herself as to Amina: "I just didn't want to be alone."

Amina patted her warm back, feeling – distantly – the knots of her spine and the planes of her shoulder blades. "I'm here," Amina said, without really feeling like she was.

"Can I . . . can I stay with you for a while?" the girl said, pushing herself back just enough to look up into Amina's eyes.

Amina still wanted to leave, just not be . . . there or anywhere else. But the girl's eyes, tugged at her, needed her. She didn't want to stay – in that room, in this world – but she also couldn't leave this sad, lonely girl, either.

Midnight: the darkness still warm, the sounds of sunset and early night chased away by the weight of hours. Twelve, it seemed was too deep, too back, to allow anything but a single wandering drunk who tried to sing – and failed – a song Amina didn't recognize.

Under the blankets they were warm. How they'd gotten there seemed so quick as to be part of a half-performed dance. One step then another: "I just don't want to be alone any more. Please, I just don't want to be alone." Then, "Thank you, thank you for opening the door. Thank you for being here." Her sobs had turned to shivers, and between her sobs she'd managed to slip, "Please, hold me close."

And so, in bed. Curled around each other under the thin blankets against a turgid breeze – shivering, ever so slightly until their mingled heat stilled the tremors.

Amina didn't speak. Instead, she stroked the young girl's yellow hair – a soothing motion that seemed to come from somewhere deep inside herself. She thought about saying something, the first real thoughts she'd had all day, but didn't. Words wouldn't have been enough – so, instead, she just stroked the young girl's hair.

The girl, though, spoke – or rather mumbled sleepily into her shoulder: "I don't want to be alone any more – don't want to be alone. Hold me, please, hold me. Don't want to be alone any more . . ."

Sleep started to tug at them, then pull in earnest. Before she was even aware of it, Amina's eyes closed and to the soft, rhythmic breathing of the young girl, she drifted off.

She dreamed of Stanley, of a time when the two of them had rolled around on their tiny bed in the back of their little house. It was like a slippery body memory, the touch of Stanley's rough hands on her thighs, the weight of his hips on hers, the slight tang of beer on his breath, the slight burning of his stubble as they kissed. The way his sharp toenails occasionally grazed her ankles.

From this she drifted up, floating away from the dream and back into that warm, dark room. The girl, invisible under the blankets, was molded on top of her – the gentle weight of her small body pressing lightly down, pushing Amina into the thin mattress. One of the girl's hands cupped Amina's right breast, her fingers calmly stroking the sides, delicately pinching her nipple.

Stanley had been a ferocious lover, a two-armed, two-legged thrust needing something to penetrate. When his lips found her nipples, Amina usually paid for this nurturing need of his with an even more vigorous than usual fuck – as if he was forcing his prick through herself and into his own weakness. A fuck like that was more a demonstration of his force than a need to come. After a time, Amina had feared his chapped, thin lips near her breasts and had taken to wearing at least a T-shirt to bed, and sometimes even a bra.

Sometime during the night the temperature had risen – and buttons had come unbuttoned. The girl's lips were too soft, too delicate: it was as if a hint, and not firm reality, was kissing – then sucking – Amina's nipples. The ghostly memory of Stanley's rough lips, flashed through her mind – then faded with a great surging wave of tingling pleasure. Even the deep reflexes of fear that usually accompanied any kind of contact with her nipples was stilled by the loving touch of the girl's gentle lips. With the wave, the swelling bloom of her body's response – nipples knotted, heart beating faster, breath shallower, muscles tightening, cunt liquefying – Amina found Stanley fading for the first time. A small tongue ringed her crinkled tips, and against her will, she found herself arching to meet the accompanying gentle suction.

It wasn't so much a girl's lips and tongue on her body – for Amina didn't really think of her in that way. In the darkness of the room, with the hole that Stanley's cruelty and departure had opened in her, it was just contact. Someone had looked down, saw the fragile, broken woman at the bottom, and had extended a hand down. Lips didn't matter as much as the though of being seen, and desired – who it was incidental to that fact.

Distantly, through the hot, heavy haze of the girl's breath between kisses, between sweet nibbles, between sucks, Amina caught the falling bass note of a ship's horn sounding on the river. The reminder of the heavy waters of the Mississippi, the still-turgid atmosphere of the night air, made it seem as if she were floating in bath water – buoyed by the girl's touches on her body. The sucking, yes, but also her thin fingers dancing along her sides, the curves of her heavy breasts, the tension of her thighs, the gentle quakes of her calves seemed to lift Amina up, hold her above the bed, above even the sad exterior of the House of the Rising Sun.

Squeezing her eyes shut against a sudden sharp peak of excitement, young teeth grazing her so-tight nipples as the girl's fingers playfully pinched at the underside of her tits, brought stars to Amina's eyes – completing the illusion of flight. Deep into a warm night, hanging above a vibrant tapestry of blue and purple starbursts, she floated on the girl's tender desire.

When those hands fell to the inside of her thighs, Amina parted them without a thought – save to be propelled higher into that starry canopy and away from the harsh earth, away from small rooms in run-down hotels, away from the pain of breathing, away from the pain of loneliness.

The first kiss was a lighting tear across that velvet darkness, a quick flash of desire that made Amina grit her teeth and whistle a breath. The first lick, the girl's tongue cautiously starting at the top of Amina's already wet cunt – just shy of her throbbing, pulsing clit – was a shivering rush through her body, a chiming that seemed to race through her. Toes to nose, Amina's body tensed and relaxed, tensed and relaxed to the accompanying strokes of the girl's strong, stiff tongue along her labia.

She crashed – down, down, down, through the ceiling, wham! into her body. Amina was a woman, on a smelly mattress, under a thin blanket, in a dive somewhere near the French Quarter, with a girl she'd didn't know. Her legs were spread, her nipples were hard, and her cunt was very wet. She almost brought those legs closed to keep the girl away from her and the shimmering pleasure she was delivering. She even tensed in preparation, lifting a hand – feeling it drag and catch at the scratchy blanket – to put it on the girl's head, and half-formed the words no, please. But she stopped, hand only raised, legs only slightly tensed, words completely unspoken.

At first she didn't know what it was. Later, in the morning and days beyond, Amina would look back at that moment with some sadness (too long) and much joy (looking forward to more)

– but there in that little hotel, in the middle of a warmish night, it was just good. It was the best kind of good, a whole, pure, brilliant, good.

The moan escaped Amina's lips without permission, escaping from tension and loneliness – a long struggle that made its release all the more intense. Soon, the moan turned to gasps, which evolved into sweet murmurs – cresting once, twice, and more, many more times in more sharp cries, more deep moans.

What the girl was doing was a mystery. But Amina didn't care. She was there, in that sad hotel, on that warm night, under that cheap blanket, and she didn't care. She was desired, and – best of all – she was loved.

They came even faster after that, as if the way had been opened and the coming flowed through that opening in herself. With each, her liberation released her body, and her hands rubbed the girl's head between her legs, stroked her tiny ears, and allowed her legs to squeeze – ever so slightly.

How many was a mystery – one of many. In the end, she slept – the opening and the outpouring exhausting her. As she slept she dreamed, but on waking she couldn't remember anything about it – except she hadn't been alone. Stanley hadn't been there, but she hadn't been alone.

When she awoke, hard morning sunlight beating through the open window, the girl was gone.

The front door was closed, but just barely: a narrow seam of hallway showed between the thin wood and the jamb.

Amina's dress was twisted and bunched. Standing quickly, she turned it, buttoned it, and smoothed it where it had crept up the cheeks of her ass.

Then she opened the door wider. The corridor was empty – quiet except for the muffled conversations of static-laced televisions talking to themselves. As she walked, then trotted, then ran towards the stairs, she wanted to call out, to cry the girl's name . . . and felt a deep tug down inside herself when she realized that she didn't know it.

The manager, the Buddha momma was outside, as if the black woman had not moved from her seat near the front door. As Amina trotted down the threadbare hall, the woman kept her rhythmic fanning – steady and undisturbed.

The street was just waking, slow pedestrians and the unearthly quickness of those used to the early hours. Faces approached and the silhouettes of bodies retreated but, standing on the narrow street, none of them was the girl.

"Excuse me," Amina panted, turning back to the big black woman, "but did you see a young woman go out? She was blonde, thin – blue eyes . . ."

"Ah, girl," momma said, smiling – a pure beaming light of cheekbones, bright eyes, and a shimmering smile, "she's gone, she is. Been here long enough, but she's had ta got back ta where she belongs."

"Please, I want to find her. Tell me where she is . . . ?" Amina said, hunger panting her words, making them sharp and forced.

"Girl, she be where she always be. She be where she come from," momma said, smile never wavering as she snapped her hymnal fan shut with a clap of rattan and paper. "She be where she be loved. You just be needin' to be shown that she there, is all. Sometimes you just be needin' to be shown how to be there for yerself, how ta love yerself." With the fan, momma leaned slowly forward and tapped – one, two, three – Amina between her breasts, over her rapidly beating heart.

"If the lonely be bitin', you just look down here –" tap, tap, tap "– and know that she be there. She always be there, girl, when you be needin' ta love yerself."

The day was starting. The city waking and starting to move around them. Smiling, leaning forward, Amina kissed the black woman on the forehead. Then she slowly walked off into the beginning of a day – the girl staying with her, keeping her company, loving her, with every step.

The Art

Lisette Ashton

Know the enemy and know yourself; in a hundred battles you will never be defeated.

—*Sun Tzu, The Art of War*

She put down the book and nodded agreement. The simplistic Chinese philosophy, originally written as a treatise on how to wage and win war, had been introduced to her when she first entered advertising. Its rules could be equally applied to any aspect of life. From politics to psychology and from sales to seduction; anywhere where there was a need to control a subordinate; Sun Tzu's wise words offered sage counsel and authoritative guidance. And this evening, once she had another conquest in her naked arms, she knew her victory would be a credit to Sun Tzu's teaching.

"This is more intimate than I expected."

"You were expecting some degree of intimacy?"

Toni arched an eyebrow. She looked like she was playing the role of the first female James Bond. Her dark hair and Hollywood smile made her seem exotic, striking and confident. Sally wanted to use the word "desirable" but she wouldn't let herself choose such a provocative description for another woman. Blushing, and hoping the cosy darkness that surrounded them would hide her embarrassment, she spoke hurriedly.

"I didn't mean I was expecting intimacy."

Sally used her wineglass to gesture at the single rose in the stem vase on the centre of the table. The movement of her pale fingers made the flames on the hand-carved candles tremble. Because the room was candlelit, the shadows around them broken only by the green eye of the background's whispering

CD player, the brightness flickered and fluctuated like the threat of a squalling tempest.

"I meant, I didn't expect . . ."

"I knew what you meant," Toni grinned. "I was only teasing."

Sally sighed with a moment's relief.

"I like to tease," Toni added. Her sumptuous full-lipped smile twisted mischievously. Her eyes, the mesmerizing brown of melted chocolate, shone with a wicked glint. "You don't mind being teased, do you?"

Sally deliberately avoided the question. Instead she asked, "Why did you invite me here this evening?"

Toni studied her in lingering silence and Sally got the distinct impression she was being appraised. In the depths of Toni's dark eyes she could see her slender frame, ash-blonde hair and porcelain complexion all met with the woman's salacious approval. Then Toni was shaking her head, tousling raven tresses across her brow, and Sally's reflection was blinked away.

"Maybe I thought we should celebrate your new position?"

Sally had been promoted to head of advertising as Toni's successor as Toni moved to a superior position in a different branch. Toni's excuse would have been plausible if she and Sally had been friends during their two-year working relationship. Instead, because they had only passed a handful of pleasantries, and a daily exchange of curious and speculative glances, Sally thought the woman was keeping something from her.

"This is a celebratory meal?"

"Maybe not," Toni allowed. "Maybe I wanted to say some things to you that couldn't be said when we were in the office?"

"What sort of things?"

"Things I could only say when we were alone together."

Sally's cheeks grew warm. She was briefly thankful for the candlelight that would disguise her blushes. Toni's voice was soft and seductive. It had grown mellower with each glass of wine. Now, with the remnants of their paella all but finished, and the bottle of chardonnay lying spent between their plates, her words were a velvet caress. The suggestive innuendo she imbued into every syllable was like the sultriest stroke of a tongue against bare flesh.

"I still don't understand." Sally sighed. "What sort of things?"

"In the office I can't talk freely about who to trust and who to watch," Toni began. "Tonight I can tell you about staff and clients with more honesty than if I was measuring my words in the office. Seeing you here I can openly warn you that Jenkins is a backstabber, Johnson is work-shy and Jamal is an eavesdropper. I can tell you, of the portfolios you'll be handling, the Wingate executive constantly tries to batter the price down, the Walker rep always asks for six more ideas – and then settles on the first one you gave him. And the CEO of Winston's expects sexual services as well as good advertising copy."

Sally blinked at this. She had been about to take a sip of wine but paused: shocked by the final revelation. "Winston expects sex from you?"

Toni's smile was smug with satisfaction. "Winston doesn't expect anything from me," she admitted. "Winston believes I'm a dyke."

This time Sally knew the candlelight wouldn't conceal her blushes.

Toni's ambiguous sexuality was common fodder for gossip amongst her colleagues. The fact that the woman dressed in power suits, blocky shoes and heavy, masculine overcoats only fuelled the speculation. Although no one had ever seen her linked with another woman she had never been seen with a man either. Her features were attractive and appealing – but better described as handsome than pretty. Also, in Sally's opinion, there was something about Toni that radiated a predatory sexual allure. Sally had suspected the woman's speculative interest each time they had been alone – exchanging innocent pleasantries. Hearing her most private thoughts put into words was acutely embarrassing. Struggling to remain calm and try to brush past Toni's remark, she asked, "Why would Winston believe you were a . . ."

She tried to use Toni's word but thought it was too strong.
Rude.
Insulting.

Starting again she asked, "Why would Winston think you're a *lesbian*?"

Toni shrugged and sipped at her chardonnay. "I don't know," she admitted airily. Fixing Sally with a challenging stare she asked, "Perhaps it's because I fuck women?"

A phrase from Sun Tzu came back to her. *For to win one hundred victories in one hundred battles is not the acme of skill. To subdue*

the enemy without fighting is the supreme excellence. The con-
notations of that sentiment, and how it could be applied to
seduction, resounded through her thoughts.

The CD player had been crooning a selection of light jazz
melodies. The sound of a sultry saxophone whispered from
the shadows and added a decadent ambience to the atmosphere.
As Toni made her shocking announcement, the disc switched
off and the two women were left in thickening silence.

Toni stood up and placed a hand on Sally's shoulder.

Sally struggled not to shrink from the long elegant fingers
with their blood-red manicure. She held her breath as Toni
stepped past her and disappeared into the shadows to replace or
replay the CD. Sally's heart hammered madly inside her chest.
A sheen of nervous perspiration sweated her palms and made
her brow glossy. When she was finally able to snatch a breath
she hid the gasp of amazement behind her wineglass.

Dulcet saxophone sounds swept from the shadows.

The soft whisper of Toni's stockinged feet, slipping against
the polished floor, warned Sally that her host was coming back
to the dining table. She caught the sensuous floral musk of
Toni's perfume and then realized the woman stood immediately
by her side. For an instant she felt sure, when she turned
around, Toni would be naked. She expected to discover that
the woman had undressed in the darkness and was coming back
to the table with her plump breasts bared and her slender body
exposed. It was too easy to imagine her presented as a stripped
and irresistible opportunity. Sally almost moaned with relief
when she saw Toni still wore her tight-fitting black dress. The
lightweight fabric clung to her hips, hung loose over her flat
stomach and stretched beneath the swell of her breasts.

"I didn't shock you, did I?" Toni asked.

"Shock?" Sally forced herself to laugh. The sound came out
as a nervous chatter; brittle against the smooth ambience of their
shared meal; discordant and unmelodic alongside the saxophone
solo. "Shock? Me? No. Of course not. Why would I be
shocked?"

Toni beamed at her.

And then stroked her fingers softly against Sally's cheek.

If the caress had been shown in a cartoon comic strip the artist
would have drawn the crackle of electricity that sparked between them. If the illustration had been in colour Sally ima-

gined it would have been recreated as a streak of blue-white lightning.

"It's sweet of you to say that," Toni murmured.

Sally barely heard the words. Her heartbeat pounded so loudly she could no longer make out the straining tone of the saxophone. She intuited that Toni had spoken before gliding back to her seat but her thoughts were still enchanted by the magical electricity that came from the subtle caress. Struggling to find a way of resuming the conversation, not wanting her thoughts to brood on the silence that stretched between them, Sally asked, "Does your being a . . . a lesbian . . . does that stop Winston's CEO from expecting sexual services?"

"He has the typical lurid interest of a man," Toni admitted, picking casually at the remnants of her meal. "And he's a persistent bastard." With a scornful smile she added, "He believes he can cure me. And he's offered to give tips if he was allowed to watch me with another woman. But my being a dyke allows me to rebuke him without him thinking it's too personal."

Sally digested this, aware the conversation was moving away from the frank sexuality that had come with Toni's revelation. "That's useful to know," she said with forced cheer. "Maybe you could give me some tips so I won't run the risk of losing his business?"

"Tips?" Toni pounced on the word. "I'd happily give you the full introductory lesson. But you'd need to know up front: it involves eating pussy."

Sally stared at her silently.

She knew she was being watched and weighed. When Toni had said she liked to tease, Sally hadn't realized the woman was making a genuine confession. She could see that Toni was having fun at her expense and she wondered how far the woman was prepared to go with this daunting game. Adamant that she wouldn't be intimated, deciding she could be as daring as her hostess, Sally took a deep breath and drained her wineglass. She put it down quickly, hoping the woman wouldn't see that her hands trembled. Fixing Toni with a firm stare, determined not to show any signs of hesitancy or weakness, Sally said, "Is that what the lesson would involve? It sounds like this evening could prove pleasantly educational."

The words were like a starting pistol.

Toni didn't bother confirming whether Sally was sure about

her decision. Acting with a haste that bordered on the unseemly
– as though she had planned the evening specifically for this
moment – Toni slipped from her chair and knelt by Sally's side.

The woman's mouth loomed close.

Disconcertingly close.

Sally could see the remnants of the white wine glossing Toni's
lips. The lustre was illuminated by the radiance of her Hollywood smile. When Sally raised her gaze the full force of Toni's
mesmerizing chocolate eyes stirred a sickening excitement in
her stomach. The muscles inside her sex, usually so quiet and
unobtrusive, began to clench and tighten like a grasping fist.
She was inordinately conscious of her sex. The smouldering
heat that tingled in her labia swelled to a ferocious temperature.
And then melted slickly into the crotch of her panties.

Warm.

Wet.

Obscenely excited.

Sally drew a faltering sigh.

"The first lesson should begin with the engagement of lips."

Toni was so close Sally felt the murmur of the words before
she heard them. The gentle warmth of the woman's breath
brushed her lips. Their mouths were already so close Toni's
striking face filled Sally's world.

And then they were kissing.

Feminine lips pressed gently against hers.

Lightly at first.

Then with more urgency.

Then with a tongue sliding into Sally's mouth.

Too much. Too quick. Too soon. Too irresistible.

Sally's hesitancy retreated as her tongue took battle with
Toni's. Their mouths were locked in an inseparable conflict.
Sucking. Kissing. Teasing. Tasting. Exciting. Toni broke the
moment, pulling her face away. Her chocolate eyes considered
Sally with such suggestive intent there was no longer a need for
words. She reached for the buttons on the front of Sally's blouse
and began to pluck them open.

Sally glanced down at herself and watched the pale flesh
being exposed. Her thoughts remained a turmoil of doubts and
hesitancy but she wouldn't let herself succumb to any of those
groundless fears. Sitting rigid as Toni toyed with the clothing,
she allowed the blouse to be pulled open and reveal the full
white bra that had been hidden beneath. Toni's fingers stroked

her skin, sliding swiftly beneath the upper arc of the bra's cup to explore the sensitive flesh inside.

Sally stiffened. She willed herself to smile, anxious in case Toni thought her rigid posture was caused by reluctance. But she felt certain her defensiveness and her attempts to hide it would be transparent to Toni's experienced eye.

Snippets from the book came to her. *All warfare is based on deception . . . When capable of attacking, feign incapacity . . . Hold out baits to lure the enemy . . .* Determined this evening would go as planned, she willed herself to focus on the importance of each remembered truism.

Sally sat naked on the chair. Her bra and blouse were strewn in the shadows of Toni's darkened lounge. Her skirt, shoes and panties were somewhere beneath the table. Every pore of her body tingled with mounting surges of desire. Toni had kissed her repeatedly as the clothes were removed. Her mouth pressed against Sally's lips. Then her throat. And then Sally's breasts. The woman's tongue stroked lovingly against the stiff bud of one nipple before she greedily suckled and nibbled. Sparkling rushes of energy fluttered from Sally's chest. The exquisite thrills were sharp and delicious.

"Open your legs a little," Toni suggested.

Sally nodded.

Turning on her seat, painfully aware that Toni was clothed while she was now naked, she forced her thighs apart. The movement made her aware of the muscles at the tops of her legs as they grew firm and the skin became taut. The knowledge that she was exposing her body's most intimate secrets made her heart pound faster. The excitement of revealing herself to Toni, and feeling sure the sight would be appreciated, sired a fresh surge of longing.

Toni's gaze dropped between Sally's legs.

Her eyes grew wide.

Her smile was appreciative.

She licked her lips hungrily.

And then she lowered her head.

Again, Sally urged her body not to stiffen. She tried to relax in the chair as Toni's head moved closer. The pressure of cool hands sliding against the warmth of her inner thighs was maddeningly exciting. The first tickle of Toni's fringe against her stomach warned her the inevitable moment of contact was getting nearer. Then the warmth of soft breath brushed her waxed mons pubis.

Toni's tongue stroked the flesh of Sally's sex.

It was nothing more than a feather-light caress. The simple sensation of a tongue slipping against her skin. Yet it inspired a reaction that pushed Sally to the brink of climax. She stiffened in her chair – amazed such sensations could be borne from so subtle a source. Tremors of raw ecstasy shivered from her loins. The inner muscles of her sex convulsed and twitched with avaricious greed. Gasping softly, desperate for Toni to continue, she wondered how much better the sensations would become when the woman properly began to excite her.

"You taste sweet," Toni murmured.

Sally didn't have the air in her lungs to accept the compliment. What little breath she did have was snatched away when Toni delivered another kiss to her sex. This time the woman attacked with more force. Her tongue pushed firm against the yielding split of Sally's labia and eased between the moist folds of flesh. The sense of penetration; the gentleness of Toni's mouth; the heat of her tongue; the breadth of it squirming inside her sex: all those sensations combined to take Sally to the brink of an explosion.

She gripped the sides of her chair and urged her legs further apart. If she had been more experienced with women, Sally believed she would be stroking the woman's head, gripping a fistful of hair and guiding her wherever she desired. But because this was her first time Sally forced herself to sit still and enjoy. She quivered in the seat as Toni delivered fresh kisses and teetered agonizingly on the brink of release. Her muscles ached from the exertion of sitting still and, when Toni's fingers pressed more firmly against her thighs and she finally touched her tongue to the tip of Sally's clitoris, her restraint was banished.

Sally bucked against the chair.

Her hands gripped the seat so tight she could have snapped the wood.

A jolt of raw pleasure flourished from her sex like the opening to a prestigious firework display. The surge of delight hurtled through her inner muscles before erupting into a cascade of dizzying splendour. With her eyes squeezed tightly shut she could see the startling illumination of pure joy as her body thrilled with satisfaction. Her sex clenched greedily against Toni's insistent kisses and her body melted with the fluid rush of orgasm.

She came back to the room as though she had been unconscious. She didn't think the pleasure had been extreme enough to make her pass out. But it had been sufficiently distracting to let her lose a moment or two. The first thing she saw was Toni's grin: moist and exciting.

"Are you going to undress?" Sally whispered.

"Would you want that?"

It took every ounce of Sally's self-possession not to hurl herself at the woman and wrench the slinky black dress from her body. Showing a degree of control that bordered on being heroic she drew a deep breath and nodded. There was a maddening pause as Toni eased herself from the floor. And then that moment was dragged out as the woman brushed her dress down and began to prepare herself for the slow process of a striptease. Sally watched with mounting impatience as Toni placed one stockinged foot between her legs, and then raised the hem of her skirt. She was allowed a glimpse of the woman's upper thigh as Toni reached for the lacy top of her stocking. And then she had to sit and squirm as the stocking was slowly rolled down to reveal one silky smooth leg.

The tease was not without its benefits.

Sally was able to admire Toni's commanding beauty and anticipate all the pleasure the night still had to offer. And she was able to catch the musk of the woman's arousal – a scent that was far more provocative than the heady perfume she wore. Sally studied Toni with forced patience as the woman shifted position and began to slide the second stocking slowly downwards. But her need for further satisfaction overruled her patience.

The prolonged tease of watching the second stocking sliding from Toni's thigh to her calf was too much. As soon as Toni had pulled it from her foot, Sally stood up and pressed herself against the woman. Toni's foot remained on the chair and Sally pressed herself against the roundness of her bare thigh. Her bare breasts were crushed against the sheer fabric of Toni's dress. And then both women were embracing each other.

Chilly fingers slipped against Sally's back, sliding down toward her buttocks. The scratch of Toni's manicure clawed lightly at bare flesh as Sally grew used to the idea that she was naked and embracing a woman. Raising her face to meet Toni's she studied the invitation of her moist lips for an instant, and then kissed her.

Aside from the exciting flavour of Toni's mouth she found the taste of her own sex still rested on the woman's lips. The forbidden flavour of her musk, warmed by Toni's kisses, fuelled a fresh urge for further intimacy. Taking a brief control of the moment she pushed the woman into the shadows toward the settee. They tumbled down together in a tight embrace.

A book was beneath them.

Sally pushed it aside without a second thought. Her interest was fixed only on undressing Toni and making full use of the woman's body. Urging the zipper at her back open; struggling to remove dark fabric and expose the pale flesh beneath; she gasped breathlessly as she stripped the woman bare.

Toni was naked beneath the dress.

Sally didn't bother to worry why the woman hadn't worn panties or a bra. If she had dwelt on the reasons she might have speculated that Toni had expected to seduce her this evening and was simply undressed and ready for action. But all Sally could think about was her need to taste and explore and again revisit the delight of having Toni's tongue against her sex.

Slender, chilly fingers teased at her cleft.

As Sally admired the beauty of Toni's exposed body, applying kisses to each firmly rounded breast, Toni touched the moist warmth of Sally's sex. The contact was formidable and frightening. Each time Toni teased a finger against her, Sally came close to shrieking with another orgasm. Determined she wouldn't simply succumb to the surge of satisfaction, adamant that she would properly enjoy Toni before that pleasure could take her, Sally pushed the hand aside and suckled against a breast.

Toni moaned.

The sound was the most rewarding exclamation Sally had ever heard.

The shadows of the room remained behind them, stretching darkness and accentuating their solitude. Sally suckled against Toni's left breast, and then her right, building herself up to the impending thrill of tasting the woman's sex. The prospect of another orgasm grew fat in her loins. Her movements and actions became urgent with greed. When Toni's hand returned between her legs, trying to force further contact with the dewy lips of her sex, Sally tried to brush the fingers away.

"I only want to touch you," Toni complained.

"I want to taste you first," Sally hissed.

"I want to see you come again," Toni countered.

They studied each other with mirrored expressions of determination.

Toni broke the silence. "Why don't we try a different position?"

Sally allowed her to resume control of the evening. Following Toni's guidance she lay on top, with her head between Toni's legs and her sex hovering over Toni's face. Her breasts pushed against the flat expanse of Toni's toned stomach. Her own lower ribs were treated to the pressure of the woman's nipples thrusting urgently against her flesh. But those sensations were merely peripheral distractions. Her true excitement came from the thrill of being so close to the neatly trimmed wetness of Toni's sex.

"We could never have done anything like this while we were working together," Toni marvelled.

When she spoke, Sally felt the breath from each syllable kiss at the split between her legs. Instead of allowing that pleasure to overwhelm her, Sally said, "I was just thinking the same thing." She could have gone on to add that the strictures of office protocol would have made any relationship between two women unbearable if not impossible. There was too much gossip and too many rules and regulations that frowned on personnel fraternization. Before this evening they would have run the risk of ruining their careers. After, they would be in different departments and unable to exchange speculative glances and sly, suggestive smiles. This evening – with Toni about to move up the corporate ladder and Sally about to take her role at the head of advertising – was the only opportunity that existed.

Rather than saying any of those things, Sally simply lowered her face to the split of Toni's sex. Lilac inner labia protruded gently from the tight split of the outer lips. Sally thought it looked as though the pussy was hungrily beseeching her for a kiss. She took a moment to drink the dizzying flavour of the woman's scent. The feral fragrance was rich, exciting and tempting. And then her mouth engulfed the lips as she sucked and licked with inexpert hunger.

At the same moment Toni pushed her tongue against Sally's sex.

The pressure of their naked bodies together was divine but

unimportant. The pleasure of tasting Toni's sex was a thrill Sally would remember for the rest of her days. But the true satisfaction came from the sensations of Toni's tongue pushing into the tight muscles of her sex.

Sally tried to inflict the same pleasure on the woman beneath her. She writhed against Toni's bare body with mounting impatience and urged her tongue between the wet, fleshy folds. Briefly she was able to dart her tongue against the pulsing bud of Toni's clitoris. The action was followed by a groan. Toni's hips squirmed and convulsed in a jerk of fluid satisfaction.

Sally barely had chance to acknowledge that she had caused Toni's orgasm. A tongue slipped against her sex and her clit was caught between frantically suckling lips. The cataclysmic explosion of pleasure flourished from Sally's sex. And this time, it was enough to make sure she lost consciousness for more than a few seconds.

Sally came back to herself, aware that Toni was asleep in the shadows by her side. She was shocked by what she had done and amazed by the way the evening had transpired. Snatching her clothes from the floor, dressing by the guttering candlelight that had illuminated their meal and their lovemaking, she realized her heart still raced each time her memory returned to all those things she and Toni had done. Dressing quickly, not bothering with her panties, stockings or bra, she simply pulled on her blouse and skirt and stepped into her shoes before reaching for her coat. Her fingers brushed against the cover of a book that had been pushed from the settee earlier. Anxious to look at anything that might distract her thoughts from all that she had just enjoyed, Sally brought it closer to the candlelight to read its title. Her pulse began to slow and her panic dwindled as she realized that Toni was also familiar with Sun Tzu. She wondered if, like her, Toni had also been reading Chinese philosophy prior to making plans for the evening.

In the Pink

Kristina Wright

"I fucking hate taffeta." My assertion was met by stares and silence from the other three bridesmaids who crowded into the country club powder room with me. I don't know what I was expecting. These girls were career bridesmaids while I was just the token dyke in the wedding party. My new sister-in-law Ginny was a wonderful girl, but it was an hour into this little shindig and I was ready to kick her ass for forcing me into a pink taffeta gown and matching underwear (a gift from the giddy bride). Then again, what did I know? If it wasn't jeans and a T-shirt, I hated it. And I hated the fucking pink taffeta dress so much, I was getting hives.

"But you look so pretty," cooed Melanie, one of the Stepford bridesmaids. She was dolled up in the exact same dress I was, but she somehow managed to look like she *belonged* in taffeta.

"I don't want to look pretty," I snarled, tugging at the neckline of the dress that barely covered the peekaboo lace of the matching pink bra I was wearing. "I want to get the hell out of this dress and into something that will let me breathe."

A collective gasp went up from the bridesmaids.

"Oh no, the reception has just started. You have to wear the dress for the reception pictures," scolded Victoria, the militant maid-of-honour. "And stop messing with your hair, you'll pull out the curls."

Me, with curls piled on top of my head. Me, in lace underwear. Me, in taffeta. It was some sort of wedding nightmare and I had agreed to this agony. "Shoot me now," I muttered. For the sake of my big brother's future happiness, I left the curls, the itchy lace underwear and the hideous dress alone.

The girls powdered their noses and we moseyed en masse back out to reception room of the Crystal River Country Club. Camera flashes blinded me as everyone but the waiters took my picture. I was trying to be a good sport, but I was stumbling around half-blind and unfortunately sober. I danced with the father of the bride, who said I looked lovely; I danced with my own father, who said he'd lost a fifty-dollar bet with my brother that I would actually keep the dress on through the reception and I smiled pretty for the endless amateur photographers who wanted just one more picture.

Finally, I'd had enough. I grabbed an open bottle of champagne from one of the tables, hiked up the miserable taffeta dress with my free hand and stalked outside before another wedding guest told me how pretty I was or another drunk guy asked for my phone number.

"Hey babe, where you running off to?"

The voice came from the shadows cast by the palatial white columns of the country club's entrance. I saw the flicker of a cigarette, but little else. At first I thought it was one more guy attempting to score at a wedding. "Some place where taffeta gowns and lace underwear don't exist," I muttered, stalking past my interrogator.

"Too bad. I was working up the nerve to ask you to dance."

The voice was deep, but not that deep. I paused mid-stride and turned. "What makes you think I'd want to dance with you?"

She stepped out of the shadows and leered at me, her tanned face bare of anything more than a glisten of perspiration from the steamy Florida heat. "Because I hear I'm your type."

Her hair looked like she spent a lot of time running her hands through it. It was short, red and tousled like she'd just climbed out of bed. My gut reaction was instant and surprising. I was turned on by her just-fucked hair. The rest of her wasn't so bad, either. She was tall and lean and dressed all in black – black shirt, black pants, black jacket, black shoes. The red hair above the unrelenting black was striking. It was also unmistakably a family trait because Ginny, the taffeta-happy bride, had the same colour hair, albeit longer and more fashionably styled.

"I'm Jae, Ginny's sister." I'd heard about Jae, the nature photographer who was currently living somewhere in the wilds of Australia. Heard of her, but in the two years my brother had been with Ginny, never met her. She was at least ten years older than me and sexy as hell in a confident, quiet way.

It figured I would be wearing taffeta when I met the dyke of my dreams.

"I just got in this afternoon, so I missed the rehearsal dinner," she went on, taking a drag off her cigarette before flicking it away. "I've been waiting all night for Ginny to introduce me to her hot new sister-in-law, but she's been a little preoccupied."

"I guess you know I'm Beth."

"Uh-huh."

The silence was awkward. I was actually nervous. Picking up chicks at weddings while wearing a gown is kind of outside my area of expertise.

Voices drifted to us from just inside the country club doors. Jae grabbed my arm and pulled me behind one of the columns. I was so startled, I nearly dropped the champagne.

"What — ?"

She put her fingertips over my mouth. "Sshh. They'll be looking for you to take more pictures."

With that, my mouth slammed shut and I nearly took her finger off at the knuckle. Sure enough, I heard someone call my name. One of the bridesmaids, it sounded like. I snuggled up against Jae and waited for the door to open again.

"Thanks," I murmured, suddenly aware of how close we were.

She kissed me, hard. Her breath tasted of wine and cigarettes. She slid her hands around the back of my dress as she hauled me up tight against her. She was several inches taller than me, but my heels took away some of that advantage, bringing us hip to hip. I pulled back slightly, laughing. Even through layers of taffeta, I could tell she was packing.

She gave a little tug that sent my curls tumbling in black ringlets down my back. "Let's get out of here."

I didn't attempt to play coy. She knew I wanted her as soon as she kissed me. Hard to argue otherwise when I'd just had her tongue down my throat. She grabbed my hand and I hung on to her as tightly as I was hanging on to the champagne bottle. We took off around the side of the country club, running full out for the golf course. I couldn't keep up with Jae while wearing heels, so I kicked them off and groaned as the blood rushed back into my toes. Jae just laughed and pulled me along, stumbling on the hem of my dress as we ran.

The rolling hills of the golf course were dark and silent and blissfully free of people with cameras. When we were a safe distance from the country club, we slowed to a walk. Somewhere around the ninth hole, we flopped down on the green, the pink taffeta billowing out around me like a puddle of Pepto-Bismol. I took a long drink from the champagne bottle and passed it to Jae.

"Whatcha got on under that dress?" she asked, leaning toward me on one elbow, her bottom lip glistening from the champagne. She looked predatory, like she wanted to eat me. I kind of hoped she did.

"Itchy lace underwear your sister made me wear."

"Poor little baby dyke." She made a tsking sound as she took another hit from the bottle and put it down beside us.

"Who you calling a baby?"

She was quick. She rolled me over onto my back in one swift move and pinned my arms above my head. "You, baby."

"Okay," I whispered, my voice sounding as shaky as I felt.

She kissed me again, sucking my bottom lip between her teeth and nipping it until I moaned. The rustle of my dress was the only noise for the next several minutes as she kissed me breathless. When we finally came up for air, we were both laughing. A bird sent up a startled cry of response from a stand of trees nearby and I giggled again, lightheaded from the champagne and lust.

Jae licked her bottom lip as if still tasting my mouth. "I've been wanting to do that all night."

I hadn't even known the legendary Jae was in town, but she'd been watching me all night. It made me grin like a fool. "If I'd known I had that to look forward to, I might have actually smiled for some of the wedding pictures."

"Well, if that makes you smile . . ." she said, letting the words trail off as she found the hem of my dress and slid her hand up the inside of my thigh.

I spread my legs for her, but she took her sweet time getting where I wanted her to be. She stroked my thighs softly while she kissed and sucked on my neck. I fumbled under her jacket and found her nipples through the thin fabric of her shirt. She was slim and small-breasted, but her nipples pebbled like diamonds under my fingers. I tugged them through her shirt and she bit down hard on my neck.

The dress was cut low and it didn't take much wiggling on my part for the neckline to slip even lower, baring my lace-covered breasts. She buried her face between my tits, nuzzling them through the itchy fabric until I reached up and tugged the cups of the bra away from me. She moaned softly as she licked my skin, sucking on the sensitive undersides of my breasts. She toyed with the lace waistband of my panties while she licked and nibbled her way across my chest.

"I'm going to die here if you don't touch me," I gasped when I couldn't stand her teasing any longer.

Her laughter was muffled against my chest but she didn't refuse me. She stroked down my stomach and then lower, running her fingers over my panty-covered mound. When she found the crotch of my panties wet and clinging to me, she whisked them away and tossed them on the grass beside the champagne bottle. By now, my dress was up around my waist and the cool grass was tickling me intimately, but I wasn't complaining.

Jae pulled away from me and I made a little whimper of protest, but she didn't go far. She knelt between my legs and stripped off her jacket, then rolled up the sleeves of her shirt as if she intended to go to work on me. I shivered as she used her thumbs to hold me open. She looked at my cunt like she was starving for a good meal.

"Baby, you're almost as pink inside as that damned dress."

I couldn't have given her a smart-assed retort if I wanted to, because at that moment she leaned forward and sucked my clit into her mouth just as hard as she'd sucked my bottom lip a few moments before. I let out a whimper, clamping my thighs around her head and burrowing my fingers in her short, silky hair.

She nursed on my clit, alternately lapping and nibbling at it until I was writhing beneath her. I felt her shift, her hands sliding away from my hips. I raised myself up on my elbows and watched her fumble with her pants. She dragged them down her thighs until I could see what she was packing. The dildo was tucked inside a pouch and she pulled it free.

"Want my dick, baby dyke?" she whispered, stretching out on top of me, one hand braced against the ground, the other guiding the dildo between my spread thighs.

"I want whatever you'll give me."

She drove it into me, deep and hard, and I screamed with the suddenness of it. Keeping up that hard, fast rhythm, she pressed her wet cunt against my thigh and moved with me. I clutched at her back, moaning as she fucked me, sending a couple more birds into frenzied flight.

"Keep your voice down or the police will be out here."

I yanked at her shirt until a button popped. I pulled it away from her body and bit down on her shoulder to keep from screaming again. I could feel her muscles tense and flex as she rode my thigh and fucked me with the dildo. She slid higher on my body, until her tits were in my face. I pulled one of her hard, rubbery nipples into my mouth and sucked it, feeling her grind even harder against my thigh.

"Oh, God, you're driving me crazy," I gasped as she dragged the dildo out of my cunt and thrust it back in. "You're gonna make me come on your big dick."

"That's the idea, baby."

I was incoherent after that. She fucked me hard and steady, and we were sliding across the grass, propelled by the slippery taffeta of my dress. I had visions of us splashing into a water hazard, but she drove that thought from my mind as she pummeled my throbbing cunt.

I sucked hard on her nipples until she was humping my thigh so hard I knew I would have a bruise in the morning. Despite her warning me to be quiet, her own moans wafted across the still golf course.

"Fuck me," I begged, every inch of my body straining for release. "Please."

She angled the dildo up high and hard and that was all it took. My body convulsed around the thickness of the dick inside me and I wrapped my arms and legs around her as if I would never let her go. She fucked me steadily, riding out my orgasm while I clung to her and panted her name.

I managed to roll her over as my orgasm faded to a gentle pulse. I was so weak I couldn't do much more for a few minutes than lie on top of her and kiss her. She was still moving against my thigh, leaving a trail of wetness on my skin.

I finished unbuttoning her shirt and kissed my way down her chest and across her stomach. Her cunt smelled like heaven, musky and sweet with arousal. I gave a quick swipe up the length of her slit and felt her jump. Sluggish from coming so hard, I settled between her legs, my dress still hiked up to my waist and the humid night air blowing a tepid breeze across my fevered cunt.

I nuzzled her damp thighs, wanting to take my time with her and knowing once I started I wouldn't be able to slow myself down.

"Eat me, baby," she growled, her hands reaching for my decimated curls. She gave a sharp tug and it was all the encouragement I needed. I buried my face between her thighs and feasted on her like an over-ripe fruit, reveling in the feel of her wetness on my cheeks and chin.

I sucked her clit between my lips and was rewarded with a soft, plaintive cry. I slid two fingers into her wet, clutching cunt and continued to suck her clit as it pulsed like a wild thing against my lips. She was so hot and ready, it didn't take long. A few more hard licks and she was coming in my mouth. I kept the flat of my tongue on her clit, feeling every ripple of her body as she alternately clutched at my hair and pressing at my shoulders.

Finally, I let her push me away. She pulled me up her body and I heard the distinct sound of fabric rending as my knee caught in the taffeta.

"Oh, shit," she muttered against my neck. I was draped across her body, too exhausted to move. "I think I ripped your dress."

"That's okay. It should go nicely with the grass stains."

"Sorry." She didn't sound sorry, she sounded like she was trying not to laugh.

"Please. I don't care if we torch the dress, just let me get out of it first," I said, groaning for an entirely different reason than the soreness in my well-used cunt. "On second thought, I might want to keep it as a souvenir."

"I'll take that as a compliment."

I suddenly had a thought. "You're the sister of the bride. So how the hell did you get spared the torture of being in the wedding party?"

Jae gave a little tug on my hair that was now spread across her bare tits like a shawl. "Don't ask."

"I'm serious. I want to know."

She chuckled softly, twirling a curl around her finger. "It's simple, baby dyke. I fucking hate taffeta."

Wuthering

L. S. Bell

"You're my servant, Nelly," Catherine ejaculated. "So get down on your knees and serve me."

Nelly glanced across at her mistress, not sure how to take the command. She carefully studied the woman's face, trying to discern some clue from her severe expression. The mane of unruly dark locks that framed Catherine's cheeks, and the solemn set of her large dark eyes, gave away nothing about her inner demeanour. Her lips, full, ripe and inviting, were set in a line that made her emotions inscrutable.

"Do you want a cup of tea?" Nelly asked.

"On your knees," Catherine said again. "Make me repeat the instruction and I'll be forced to use my horsewhip. Then you'll be sorry." To show the threat was not idle, she raised the leather shaft of the horsewhip and patted it lightly against her hand. The flicker of a cruel smile tugged at one corner of her mouth.

Obediently, but not obligingly, Nelly lowered herself to her knees.

It was clearly apparent that Catherine did not want a cup of tea.

It had been a strange couple of weeks at Thrushcross Grange. Nelly had found herself displaced from her former habitat at Wuthering Heights to reside with her newly married mistress amongst the hospitality of the Linton family. She had not thought the marriage between Catherine and Edgar was an appropriate match but, being a good servant and aware of her place in the order of things, she had kept her opinions confined to scurrilous gossip with other members of the house's staff. Yet, if she had been urged to guess fifty times a day for fifty years or more, she would never have imagined an instruction like this issuing from her mistress's lips.

"Stay down on your knees," Catherine said softly, "and crawl closer."

Nelly traced a pink tongue against her arid lips.

Catherine's smile blossomed with deviant delight. She settled herself on the side of her bed, pushing aside the curtains from the posts so she was framed by lace. Unladylike, she sat with her legs parted and her hands on her knees. Nelly had often enough seen her mistress go riding and knew the young woman was wont to straddle a horse in such a masculine and unbecoming manner, rather than opting for the more delicate and refined pose of side-saddle. The sight had previously stirred a rush of unfathomable desires in Nelly's loins. Warmth, moisture and general neediness had all risen in her gut like the onset of a pleasant fever. She didn't know why her mistress's posture should affect her in such a strong fashion but there had never been any denying the heat it always inflamed. This evening her mistress's pose continued to fan the embers of that same smouldering need and Nelly felt sick as she was consumed with sudden desire.

"Closer," Catherine encouraged. "How do you expect to kiss me from so far away?"

Nelly swallowed.

"Kiss you, mistress?" Again, she licked her lips. But this time, they did not need the extra moisture. As the agony of her lust grew stronger Nelly realized she was salivating like a hungry cur. Padding across the floor in the manner of Catherine's pet bitch, she crept closer and closer to the divine scent of her mistress's nearness.

Beyond the room the sounds of the house's industry whispered in perpetual clatter. The kitchens beneath them sang with the shrill cries of kettles and pot skittering together. Isabella, Catherine's new sister-in-law, could be heard practising her finger work on the parlour's virginal. Edgar was undoubtedly ensconced in his library and as silent as the breathless wind that swept across the brooding moors and down from Wuthering Heights.

But Nelly's attention was focused on her mistress. Her eyes grew large as she understood what was happening. Her heart beat faster as she realized she was on the verge of attaining a lifelong ambition. She tried to swallow and discovered her throat was choked with nervous anticipation.

Catherine was slowly drawing up the hem of her skirts. The

pale blue silk was worn over layers of crisp, white taffeta. Nelly could see the hem of the undergarments brushing against her mistress's boots. As the skirts were raised Nelly was treated to a glimpse of the boot top and then the mesmerizing vision of Catherine's bare calf.

"Mistress," she gasped.

"Closer," Catherine insisted. "And let's have less talk from you, shall we? I have other uses for your tongue and none of them involve you chattering." Clearly pleased with the remark, she released a salacious chuckle. Absently, she put the horse-whip by her side and pulled her skirt higher to reveal unclothed knees.

Nelly trembled before finding the strength to move forward. If she had been given a moment to collect her thoughts she would have pinched herself, to be sure this was the reality of Thrushcross Grange and not the product of her overactive desires and imagination. Knowing her mistress would not tolerate any further displays of hesitation, aware that she was needed with an urgency driven by understandable arousal, Nelly continued to creep closer across the bedroom floor.

Catherine inched the skirts higher. Her bare knees were completely exposed. Her thighs, as white as the moors in the depth of winter, were sinfully exciting. As Catherine shifted forward from the bed, pulling her skirts up to her waist, Nelly saw the thatch of thick dark curls covering her mistress's cleft. Not knowing whether to be more shocked by the display, or Catherine's lack of underwear, she resolved to move closer.

The tingling between her own thighs had turned to a clenching, animal need. The sight of Catherine's most intimate secrets inspired a yearning she had long tried to deny. But now, knowing the moment she had quietly coveted was almost upon her, she endeavoured to cross the final few feet of the room and do everything she was bidden.

"Hurry up, Nelly," Catherine insisted.

She parted her legs.

Rested back a little.

And reached for the horsewhip.

From her perspective at thigh-level Nelly had the clearest possible glimpse of Catherine's sex. Peeping from between the lush, dark curls were a pair of pink lips that looked flushed and ruddy with excitement. Nelly didn't know if it was an aspect of the light in the Thrushcross Grange bedrooms, or something peculiar to Catherine's mood. But she felt sure she could see a silvery glint of wetness coating the split of the woman's sex.

"You want me to kiss you, mistress?" Nelly breathed. She was close enough to touch Catherine now: if she had dared. She raised one hand, intending to place it on the woman's bare thigh while she brought her lips up to meet Catherine's face. Anxiety tightened knots inside her stomach. Her bowels clenched with the nervousness of not knowing if she was doing exactly as her superior wanted. Moving her mouth nearer to Catherine's jaw, marvelling at the all-consuming beauty of the woman, she asked again, "Do you really want me to kiss you?"

"Not on the mouth," Catherine snapped, pushing her down to the floor.

Nelly realized she had been forced to the same level as Catherine's parted thighs. The intoxicating scent of the woman's sex flooded her nostrils. The richness of the fragrance, a gamey perfume that suggested Catherine's arousal had been broiling for an age, struck Nelly like a slap across the face. She drank deeply on the intimate bouquet and tried to understand exactly what was required.

"You want me to kiss you?"

"Yes."

"But not on the mouth?"

Catherine groaned with impatience. Grabbing a fistful of Nelly's hair, pulling hard until she prompted a screech of pain, Catherine said, "Damn it, Nelly. Stop being such a tease. You know we both want this. You know we've both wanted this for a long time. Stop asking dumb questions and just fucking do it."

Nelly had no chance to respond.

Catherine had forced her face against the musky folds of flesh that protruded from the thatch of her pubic curls. The dewy split of her sex kissed at Nelly's face. The moment her mouth touched the sweet wine of Catherine's wetness, Nelly understood exactly what was wanted from her. She pushed her tongue through the gaping lips and savoured the warm, cloying flavour of her mistress's moisture.

"Fuck, yes," Catherine gasped.

Nelly wanted to pull away, and berate the young mistress from such a coarse turn of phrase. Such language and vulgarities were the fare of labourers and farm hands. Hearing profanities from her mistress's sweet and kissable lips was shocking to the point of blasphemy. But, instead of upbraiding Catherine for her expletives, Nelly could only do as her mistress insisted and devour the warm, wet flesh. She stroked her tongue against the musky folds of skin, savouring the tang of their saltiness, and then plunged it deep between them. Alternating between the tenderest of kisses and the most intrusive thrusts of her tongue, she was rewarded for her efforts by Catherine's mounting sighs of pleasure.

"Dearest Nelly," Catherine exclaimed. "Why on earth have you never done this for me before?"

Nelly moved her mouth to the apex of Catherine's hole. The thrust of a small nub of flesh pushed out at her, pulsing gently and glistening like a pearl in the bedroom's candlelight. Enchanted, Nelly watched it for an instant, sure she was on the verge of making another great discovery. She was already sweated with the strong desire that serving her mistress had awoken, and felt sure she would need to do something to exorcize the righteous arousal that now consumed her loins. But the sight of the throbbing bead of flesh inspired a hungry rush that was more animal than anything she had yet known. Daringly, she flicked her tongue against the pulse.

Catherine groaned.

She collapsed back on the bed, stuffing a fist into her mouth to conceal the ecstatic cry. Staring rigidly at the bed's lacy canopy she finally moved her hand. A beatific smile split her full, sensuous lips.

"Oh! Nelly," she murmured. "You can do that all night long."

Not sure if that was another instruction, or simply Catherine's way of urging her to continue, Nelly slid her tongue against the swollen flesh for a second time. She lapped until it grew to double its size. She moved closer, placing her hand on Catherine's thighs and marvelling at the lean, powerful musculature beneath the pale skin. Away from her sex there was still something about the perfection of Catherine's body that made Nelly believe she was in the presence of a divine creature. She had never known any creature – man or woman – able to awaken such profound desires in her body. Drinking Catherine's wetness, and basking in the warmth of the woman's satisfied groans, she wondered if she had finally found her true vocation as a servant at Thrushcross Grange.

"You're a good little servant, aren't you?" Catherine giggled.

Nelly moved her mouth away from the inviting split of pink

lips. The dark curls tickled her nose as she moved back. She stiffened in her attempts to suppress a sneeze.

"Am I doing everything to your satisfaction, Mistress Catherine?"

Catherine giggled and tried to pull Nelly's face back to her hole. Her sex was warm, musky and fragrant. The scent of her ripe lips threatened to engulf Nelly's nose and mouth. Nelly's face was lightly scoured by the scrub of Catherine's dark curls. The alabaster thighs pressed tight against Nelly's cheeks. But she resisted being dragged between Catherine's legs as she waited for an answer.

"Of course everything's all right," Catherine sighed. "You were tonguing me. What could be better than that?"

With an obvious effort, and no little reluctance, Nelly pulled her face further from Catherine's sex. She glanced meekly up and then wiped the back of her hand across her jaw. Her mouth was deliciously moistened by the excess of Catherine's wetness. The flavour was strong and inflamed the glowing coals of her desire. Touching her face reminded Nelly that she had been drinking deeply from her mistress's gloriously perfumed hole and the temptation to continue was almost overwhelming.

But she needed an answer before she surrendered.

Pausing to catch a breath, Nelly asked, "I need to know: is everything all right with your marriage?"

Catherine shrugged. "I'm not happy about being married to a dick. But we live in an age when only Edgar could propose to me. Isabella was never going to succumb to my feminine wiles, was she? So I'm getting on with my life as best as I can. And you're helping with that."

Nelly allowed these anachronistic comments to flow easily over her head. She remained convinced that something was amiss because her mistress had never before asked for this sort of treatment. Smiling with the dutiful ease of a pliant servant she pressed the issue of Catherine's happiness. "Are you unhappy with your new abode?"

"Thrushcross Grange?" Catherine shrugged again. "I'd be happier living somewhere that didn't have the word 'thrush' in its name," she said dismissively. "That can't bode well, can it? But Edgar will eventually change the name if he ever wants to get himself back where your tongue is currently going." With a frown she said, "Now get back to licking my hole, Nelly. Or I really shall switch your backside with my horsewhip."

The threat was daunting.

And, at the same time, luridly exciting.

Nelly was struck by a sudden mental picture of her bare bottom being presented beneath Catherine's whip hand. She could imagine the pale rounded cheeks of her own rear being striped and slashed by the cruel strap. In the mental picture Catherine was laughing with positive glee.

Driving the whip down harder.

Stripping herself naked.

Exposing her breasts and torso.

Rubbing her free hand against her own body and exciting her nipples to full erection. And still slicing the horsewhip repeatedly against Nelly's rear. The fantasy image was so vivid Nelly could hear the swish of the strap whistling through the air. She could smell the scent of her own overheated excitement. And she could feel the blistering sting from every painful kiss of the whip.

Fuelled by that fantasy, it was too easy to think of the mistress sliding two fingers into the velvety warmth of Nelly's wetness. Nelly could even believe Catherine would rub her thumb against the urgent ball of flesh that now throbbed at the top of her sex. The thought was enough to make her tremble on the verge of an explosion.

"Nelly," Catherine said. Her voice was sharp with impatience. "Get back to licking my hole. Or should I assume you want me to whip you?"

Blushing furiously, fearful her mistress would see the truth in her eyes regardless of how emphatically she made her denial, Nelly pushed her face against Catherine's sex. Squashing her mouth over the slippery lips; lapping, suckling and greedily devouring the woman's flavour; Nelly concentrated every effort on wringing satisfaction from her mistress's nether regions.

"That's more like it," Catherine sighed.

Glancing up at her, noticing the woman was about to recline on the bed, Nelly's gaze met the stark glare of Catherine's eye. The intimacy they had been sharing seemed to augment, like the moist and swollen lips that filled Nelly's mouth. Catherine's contented grin turned wicked and her eyes shone with the most devilish excitement.

"You *do* want me to horsewhip you, Nelly!"

"No, mistress."

Catherine was pushing her aside, standing up and reaching

for her horsewhip. "You do, Nelly. Don't deny it. I can see it in your face. You want to feel my switch brand your haunches. The truth is as plain as if you'd spoken the words aloud."

Nelly tried again to voice her protest but Catherine would hear none of it. With a swiftness that belied her bucolic disposition, Catherine hiked up her servant's skirts and pulled down the large cotton drawers. Nelly accepted the indignity without protest. The chill of the room's air touch the naked flesh of her bottom. She cringed with sudden shame. Her mortification was made complete when Catherine gasped loudly.

"Oh! Nelly!" she exclaimed. "You've been keeping secrets from me."

Shaking her head, nervous beyond words, Nelly stammered, "I would never keep secrets from you, mistress Catherine." She couldn't see the woman. Catherine had taken a position behind her and Nelly knew her buttocks and intimate secrets were being perused with clinical attention to detail. Her chest was so heavy the air couldn't reach her lungs. "I haven't been keeping secrets, mistress."

"That's not true," Catherine murmured.

Her tone was playful.

Teasing.

As she spoke she traced small, warm fingers against the mounds of Nelly's backside. "You've been keeping this glorious backside of yours a secret from me. How long have these gorgeous cheeks been hiding 'neath your skirts when they could have been presented for my entertainment?"

Nelly could think of no reply.

She remained rigid as Catherine's small hand fluttered from one cheek to the other and then nestled on the crevice between them. The pressure of the woman's fingers, deliciously light and maddeningly arousing, lingered for a moment on blushing flesh. Then, with a slow deliberation that suited the mood of arousal, Catherine's fingers slipped against Nelly's sex.

Both women gasped.

The shock of sensation was enough to make Nelly feel ill. She tried to stay still as Catherine continued to explore, not wanting to cause upset, or suffer the repercussions she knew would be waiting for her if she moved away. But the intrusion of the fingers between her legs, and the wondrous sensations inspired by Catherine's fingers against her heat, all plagued Nelly until she could no longer remain motionless. With a breathless shiver she tore herself away.

"Nelly," Catherine admonished. "You really do want to feel this horsewhip, don't you?"

Groaning with embarrassment, Nelly nodded.

She remained on the floor, facing away from Catherine and showing the woman her buttocks. Holding her breath, not sure if she was dreading or needing the sting of the horsewhip, Nelly trembled with mounting arousal. An agony of uncertainty clutched her heart as she waited to hear what Catherine would say. She was momentarily pained by the fear that her mistress would berate her for being so deviant and demanding.

The whip slashed through the air with the force of a winter tempest.

Nelly heard the hiss of the leather.

And then she was pierced by a brutal sting across both cheeks.

The switch landed with the sound of winter bracken breaking.

And Nelly howled from the sudden rush of agonising pleasure.

In the first instance it was almost as though her rear was ablaze. The heartiest fires that scorched the chimneys of Wuthering Heights had never produced as much heat as the inferno that currently branded her bare backside. She did not think her body had ever endured such a shocking heat. And it was only when the furious warmth bubbled into her sex that Nelly learnt she could suffer more intense temperatures.

Catherine slashed the horsewhip against her a second time.

Nelly's sex seared with the blistering heat of her rising need. Her upper thighs were sticky with the sudden overflow of her arousal. Her whole body had been reduced to a quivering convulsion. Gasping from the shock, pain and pleasure, Nelly remained motionless as Catherine continued to stripe her backside.

"That's it," Catherine laughed.

Her voice was rich with a merriment Nelly hadn't heard since they were growing up together as children.

"Suffer my whip, you impudent servant. Then get back to properly serving me."

"Yes, mistress."

She endured a dozen slashes from Catherine's horsewhip before her mistress tossed the instrument aside. When Nelly turned to see what the woman was doing she was amazed to find Catherine undressed and sprawled on the bed. The divine splendour of her naked body was an unspoken invitation. Putting her own craven urges aside, hurrying quickly to the bed, she hovered over her mistress and tried to discern where she should begin.

"Lick my hole," Catherine insisted. "Lick at it now and lick it well or you'll suffer another dozen stripes across your arse." She glanced up from her repose, her dark eyes shining with the most malicious glee. "Do it well, and I'll satisfy your needs. But if you don't do it right and soon, I'll simply make you do it again and again until you've properly learnt the skill."

Falling greedily between the woman's legs, Nelly didn't think that either of those alternatives sounded particularly unpleasant.

Two hours later – both naked, sated and wrapped in each other's arms – Catherine shifted position and stirred Nelly from the brink of a gentle slumber.

"Nelly," Catherine whispered. "I need to solicit a favour from you."

"A favour?"

"If ever . . ." Catherine's voice trailed off. She paused and frowned as though looking for correct words with which to compose her sentence. "You will keep these liaisons a secret, won't you, Nelly?"

"Only the taste of your kisses will ever pass my lips," Nelly sighed.

"You talk just like a gothic romance," Catherine laughed. Her smile was deliciously warming. She regained her composure with a shake of her head. Dark tousled curls brushed her face and brow. "I'm serious," she insisted. "You must tell no one of the passion we share. And, if it ever comes about that anyone should ask you the history of the mistress of Thrushcross Grange or Wuthering Heights . . ."

"I'll tell them nothing," Nelly said flatly. "And, if they insist on hearing something, I'll make up some bollocks about you being in love with that simpleton Heathcliff."

Catherine laughed. Taking Nelly's naked body into her arms she continued to giggle as she added, "Now, wouldn't that make for a great story?"

And Then She Kissed Me

Rita Winchester

I first saw her out my kitchen window. The kids were in school and I had a day of chores and cleaning ahead of me. Not very enticing or exciting. I was fighting my seemingly never-ending cycle of depression. Everything was blue, not just the sky. My mood, my emotions, my thoughts – all blue. A suddenly single mother. A soon-to-be divorcee. A husband who had found a twenty-something, gum-popping secretary more appealing than a happy married life. My happily ever after had ended.

The house behind us had been for sale forever. It sold the week Don packed up and left me. As he was moving out, the new neighbours were moving in. I soon found out it wasn't *they* but *she*. She was tall and lithe. Her hair was the colour of my favorite blouse. A deep mocha that had just a tinge of red here and there. She was also obviously pregnant. Beneath the sweep of her long graceful arms and above the length of her long slender legs, rode a swollen belly that made me smile and brought back memories.

When I would see her, I remembered the first swells of my pregnancy with Jacob and how it had seemed to take forever for me to show. I remembered the speedy bloom of my second pregnancy with Lacie. How quickly I had gone from a flat stomach to a shelf that would hold my dinner plate if I so chose. I also remembered the exhaustion, excitement and somehow mystical feeling of growing a life.

I introduced myself her third week in. Over the back fence, I shook her slender hand, told her that my name was Mary. She introduced herself as Holly and when I asked how far along she was, she told me six months.

"Big baby," I had laughed, looking at the bulk of her belly.

"They said he might end up around eight or nine pounds," she laughed. "Of course that scares me to death."

"First pregnancy?"

She nodded, a long swatch of dark hair covering her face for a moment. I had noticed that her eyes were the most amazing shade of cornflower blue. Added to the dark hair and her creamy white skin, she resembled a mythical creature of the woods. A fairy or a wood nymph. Her appearance was nearly otherworldly when you added the rosy glow of motherhood to the mix.

"You'll do fine," I assured her. "And once you've given birth, you'll feel like you can conquer the world."

"Until the insane cycle of two o'clock feeding, I hear."

Then I laughed for real. A deep belly laugh that lit me up from the inside. I had forgotten the physical release of laughter. It had been too long since a good laugh had lightened the dark things that had settled in me.

"Well, yes, until then. But cherish those feelings and those feedings. It feels as if the only people awake on earth are you and the baby. Do your best to remember because before you know it, it will be gone and he will be telling you he needs field trip money or new soccer cleats."

She nodded and smiled. Her lips were the shade of summer berries. "I'll try."

A tentative friendship had blossomed. I wasn't exactly sure why it made me feel so elated when I thought about it. I had plenty of girl friends. It wasn't as if I were starved for female attention. I had my mother, my sister, my best friend from high school. Other PTA moms and even a few teachers from school who I counted as friends. Holly felt special, though. A a slow rumble of excitement sounded in me every time I saw her outside. I never went to her house, but if I saw her in the yard, I watched her. I soaked up the sight of her. She made me smile. I tried not to analyze it.

The week the weather finally turned to Spring and the flowers started to bloom, I happened to walk out on the back deck and see her there. Holly was in her yard with another young woman. Younger than her it seemed but I was at a distance. They seemed to be fighting so I hung back, kept myself in the shadows by the sliding glass door. The younger woman was flinging her arms around and I thought she might be crying. I felt my hand go to my throat and then I felt my eyes prick with tears. It was so odd for me to emotionally identify with a stranger, but this scene looked familiar. It looked like a break up and my female instinct was to feel for this young girl.

Instinct told me to retreat into the house. I was witnessing something I shouldn't. I was a voyeur to their pain and that was simply wrong. I stood frozen.

Across the large expanse of my yard a few of their words were flung to me by the warm wind that rocked the large oak trees.

". . . love you!" The red headed stranger was sobbing in earnest now.

Holly went toward her. Her movements more motherly than those of a lover. Her emotions were already responding to the life growing inside of her. Her touch was not intimate but soothing.

"We can't be together. I . . ." and then the wind shifted and the words were lost to me.

I waited. I watched and when Holly embraced the woman, I sighed aloud. And then they kissed. It seemed to last an eternity.

Holly's ripe lips brushing the other woman's light pink ones. The kiss was full of sadness and love and tenderness. Tears pricked my eyes again. This time for several reasons. It was beautiful to watch but foreign to me. I had never *really* seen two women kiss. Not that way. Not the way I had kissed my husband a million times in our fifteen years of marriage. The other reason was the swift and intense flood of arousal that ripped through me. I felt my heartbeat between my legs as surely as it thrummed in my chest.

Two women kissing. I responded. What did that say about me?

I fled into the house. For the first time since the day Don left, I allowed myself an afternoon cocktail. I had settled my pulse and my emotions by the time the school bus arrived at three twenty. But through dinner and homework and baths, the kiss played over and over again in my mind. It was vividly playing in my head as I fell asleep that night.

I knew I was looking for an excuse. I knew it deep down in myself where the truth lives and refuses to be stifled. I put it out of my head. Every time my desperate brain tried to come up with a feasible reason to go visit Holly, I turned my attention elsewhere. School volunteering, chores, shopping, dealing with my lawyer. Anything to stop myself from confronting the fact that I was infatuated with Holly. That I wanted Holly to settle her delicate lips the way she had done with her former girl-friend.

I was not a lesbian. Was I? Was it normal to become

infatuated with another woman? Was it the stress of my divorce? Was it a latent tendency in my sexuality that I was unaware of? Or the worst, for some reason, was it Holly? Was it simply Holly who triggered this reaction in me?

My excuse arose on its own, without machinations from me. I was in the backyard transplanting my irises that had chosen to rise up in my dark, garden soil in a staggered formation. I had planted them years ago in a nice, orderly row. Each year they spread and each year their blooming was more chaotic. I was muttering to myself about garden soil and compost heaps when I heard Holly cry out.

I hadn't even realized that she had come out into the yard. When I heard her cry out a sizzle of fear shot through me. Was it the baby? It was way too early. She still had nearly two months to go.

"Holly?" I felt my face flood with colour. My voice was not only loud but panicked.

"I'm fine," she called.

When I popped my head over the fence, she was bent over clutching her belly. Her hair hung forward and the light spring dress she wore let me see just how big she had really gotten. She was either laughing or weeping. With her hair hanging in her face, I was positive which it was.

"I am a giant sissy," she wheezed and I let the breath rush out of me. She was laughing.

"Braxton Hicks?" I asked, removing my gardening gloves.

She nodded again and finally looked up at me. Those magical eyes full of warmth and kindness. "Yep. I have them all the time. It's that sometimes, when they catch me off guard, I go all . . . girly."

"Well, if I can remember correctly," I chuckled, "some of them can be pretty damn intense."

She nodded. "I'm getting scared, Mary," she said softly. "I'm not sure I can do this. I mean, I know I don't really have a choice." More laughter and she clutched her belly harder. "He is coming out one way or another, but as far as the bravery I had . . . it is failing me."

Oh, I remembered so well. The duelling emotions. Being ready to feel normal again, have your body back to yourself battling with the increasing fear that you simply did not have the strength to make it through the birth itself.

"Can I help?" I asked and then loathed myself at the thought of being alone with her. Of gaining access to her company under the guise of being helpful. But I did want to help, I reminded myself. I also had ulterior motives and that made me feel like a shit.

"Could you . . ." She trailed off, uncertain of her request most likely.

"What?" I prompted. Deep inside I was praying. Praying she would ask me to come over or if she could come over here.

"Come over?" she finished with a sigh. "I know I am being very juvenile, but sometimes being alone makes it even scarier. And you, well, you, have done this twice and maybe if we can just have a cup of tea and talk for a few minutes, I will remember that women do this all the time and live to tell the tale."

The flood of warmth and joy that radiated under my skin was overwhelming. I took a deep breath and reminded myself that she was simply looking for some company and reassurance. That this did not *mean* a damn thing. "Sure. Let me go wash up and I'll walk over."

"Thank you, Mary. I really appreciate it. I'm sure you think I'm silly . . ."

"Not at all," I said quickly. "In fact, I remember it well, what you're feeling. It's normal and it will pass." I waved my dirty hands at her and laughed a high nervous laugh. "I'll be right over once I've cleaned up."

I didn't let myself think about the fact that I scrubbed as if I were going into surgery or that I chose my most flattering floral dress to wear. I tried to recall the last time I had worn a dress during the day, I couldn't. Then I pushed it from my mind. After all, this did not mean a damn thing.

Her house was as inviting as her nature. Done in warm colours and eclectic furnishings. It made you feel welcome and safe the moment you entered. Holly already had a pot of tea and cookies on the battered mission-style coffee table.

I accepted my teacup and drank it plain. I didn't trust my shaking hands with the delicate cream pitcher or sugar bowl. I tried not to grimace at its natural bitter taste.

"How can I help you, Holly?" I asked and then wanted to kick myself for the pretentious tone in my voice. I was being so stilted because I was so nervous, but Holly didn't know that.

She shrugged, suddenly looking way too young for me to be so infatuated with her. I knew she was twenty-eight but at that moment she looked maybe sixteen. "I guess I'm just lonely. I want someone who's been there to listen to me for a few minutes."

"Family?"

"They don't approve." She dipped her head again and I let the subject drop. I wondered if they didn't approve of her pregnancy or what I assumed to be her sexuality. Did they find it offensive that she liked women?

"The father?" I deliberately kept my voice light and non-judgmental.

"We are very good friends," she said with a smile. "And he still treats me very well. He has his own life, though. This," she swept her hands over her swollen belly, "was nothing more than a mistake fueled by tequila and commiseration. He was having trouble with his girlfriend and . . . and so was I."

I nodded. "I understand. It happens. And the girlfriend." Then breathed and then felt stupid again. I was pretty sure I had seen *the girlfriend*.

"Donna was furious when she found out. She wanted me to give the baby up and then she would stay with me. I couldn't. I couldn't give him up," she said, her pale face flushing with colour. "It isn't Samuel's fault. That will be his name, Samuel. I can't give him up and she can't live with the consequences of my misjudgment."

Now I really was beginning to see. No wonder she was terrified. She had a family who didn't approve, a friend who was involved but not a partner, and a partner who had given her an ultimatum. A terrible one, at that.

"What can I do?" I asked, taking her hand. I rushed on before she could speak because the moment my skin touched hers, I started to burn all over. A heady, hot feeling of want that made me want to either clutch at her and kiss her, or flee the room. "I am always home. The kids are older. They have keys. If you need someone to take you to the hospital when it's time, or be your coach, or drive . . . whatever you need," I tapered off, dropping her hand because I was certain she could feel my attraction to her just from the contact.

Then she laughed in earnest. My nipples grew hard and I felt the blush in my cheeks re-ignite. I didn't know it was possible to grow so aroused by the sound of another person's laugh. This time, she took my hand. Her hand was pale and so thin. Delicate fingers that had somehow escaped the normal ravages of swelling from pregnancy hormones.

"Just coming over to sit with me is wonderful. I . . . like you, Mary. You're very nice and you've been where I am. Well, you had a husband and did it the right way, but you know what I mean." She put my hand on her swollen belly and at that moment, the baby shifted in her womb. The pulsing sensation and slow roll of fetal movement filled my palm and I smiled.

"A child is never a mistake," I said and pushed against her flesh. The baby inside of her responded and pushed back at me. I laughed. I couldn't help it. "Not if the baby is loved," I finished.

"Very loved. More than you'll ever know," she said.

"Oh, I know," I assured her. He moved again in there, little Samuel, and I was transported back to my own pregnancies. The cravings. The mood swings. Sitting and watching a foot press up from the inside, forcing my flesh out and pushing so hard that I could make out the tiny nubs of toes. "God, you must be horny," I blurted without thinking and then instantly snatched my hand away.

My God, I had gone insane.

Now Holly's laughter filled the house. She clutched her stomach and tears rolled down her cheeks as she laughed. I was too mortified to be aroused this time.

"Ah, God, Mary your face. No! Don't be upset. It is entirely true. True, true, true. I think I could hump the sofa."

Between her admission and my embarrassment, I started to wheeze laughter right along with her. She took my hand again, and put it right back on her stomach. I caressed the taut skin and hummed low in my throat.

Holly reached out and smoothed my hair off my face. An sizzle of electricity furled down the back of my neck. I wanted to say it but I was terrified.

"Mary?"

"Will you kiss me?" I asked, shame seething inside of me. I didn't care. "Would you kiss me the way that you kissed her?"

Her blue eyes searched my face and I had a brief hot stab of fear. I had fucked up. I should have kept my mouth shut.

"I saw you up there," she admitted and the shame became a roar in my ears.

"I didn't mean to . . . I wasn't expecting to see—"

And then she kissed me. Her lips were as sweet and intense as the color indicated. The first brush of her mouth over mine so soft I wasn't sure it was real. Perhaps I had imagined it, I wanted it that badly. Then her soft wet tongue parted my lips and swept into my mouth and I knew it was for real. Everything inside of me grew warm and soft. Everything inside of me rejoiced at the tea scented breath and the intense contact of her tongue on mine.

I smoothed my hands over her belly as she held my head and kissed me long and slow, I found the engorged peak of her breasts through her gauzy dress and rolled her nipples between my fingers. They stiffened instantly and I pinched firmly but lightly. She hummed into my mouth and stroked my jaw with her hand.

My head was buzzing, my body vibrating. She was as lovely to touch as she was to watch. I broke the kiss though I didn't want to and kissed down her throat and over her collar bone. The skin had grown rosy and splotchy from her arousal. I sucked her nipples through her dress, knowing from experience that the sensation would shoot straight to her pussy. An invisible line of pleasure from breast to cunt. In response she arched up against me as much as her burdened body would allow. I pressed the heel of my hand against her mound and let my middle finger trail the seam of her sex. I could feel that her panties were damp even through the cotton of her dress.

"Mary, you don't have to do this. I know that you . . ." She stopped talking when I pushed against the swollen nub of her clit with my fingertip.

"I want to do this," I said, kissing over the expanse of her belly and drawing her dress up as I moved.

I remembered it so well, the intense horniness of pregnancy. One day threatening anyone who tried to touch you with a swift, painful death. The next feeling like a mad woman, you craved sex and orgasm and human contact so much. I lifted the dress, taking her in with my eyes. Pale and big and sweet. She was ripe beyond words and her belly flickered and undulated under my gaze. He was moving. I didn't have any of the hesitation that a man might in this situation. I knew fully well that nothing we did would hurt him in any way. His mother, however, might find some pleasure. It was an effort to relieve her of her panties but we managed.

I slid my tongue down the darkened line from her belly button to her pubis and Holly ran her fingers into my hair, stopped, and clutched me there. My tongue parted her swollen labia, so dark raspberry from the hormones she looked ready to burst. I suckled at her, taking in the sweetness of her. Realizing that I had never tasted another woman besides the taste of myself on my husband's mouth. That I had never wanted to taste another woman until I met Holly.

"Mary, Mary," she simply said it over and over like a chant as I licked her. I paid careful attention to her clit, tiny and hard between my lips, as her juices coated my face. She painted my chin and my throat as I ate her and it was my intention to capture every last drop of what she gave me.

"Shh." I didn't want her worrying about me, I wanted her to worry about her. I pushed two fingers into her already clutching pussy and arched them as long and deep as I could. I increased the pressure of my tongue, lapping and swirling at her while she held my head and made soft sounds.

I flexed my fingers, searching deep inside of her, and finally finding the soft plush swatch of flesh, I stroked her G-spot gently at first. When her cunt flexed around me and seized my fingers tight, I increased the pressure and sucked hard on her clit.

Holly came undone crying out my name. It was the sweetest sound I had ever heard. I let my fingers play inside of her as flicker after flicker traveled her tight sex. She sobbed and a tiny bit of fluid slicked down over my thumb. Between the intensity of her orgasm and the attention to her G-spot, the tiniest trickle of urine had escaped.

"I'm sorry," she murmured, half laughing but blushing furiously. She gazed at me with one eye as if to decrease her embarrassment.

"It happens all the time. You have a large passenger on board," I said softly and winked. And to show her how little it bothered me I pressed that spot to my lips and licked it clean.

She blushed again but stroked my cheeks. I stayed between her legs, fingers deep in her, gazing up at her over the huge terrain of her pregnant stomach for a long time. When she drew me up to sit next to her, she handed me my tea and said matter-of-factly, "If you'll give me a few moments, I'd like to return the favour."

"It wasn't a favour," I said sipping my tea as if nothing had happened. The tea was cold but the bitterness gone. Now it was tinged with the sweetness of Holly still in my mouth.

"You know what I mean." She put her hand on my leg and just left it there. She didn't move at all but the warmth of her hand was enough to start a small flood in my own panties. Yet, I didn't want her to feel pressured.

"You don't have to return anything. I did it because I wanted to."

"And so do I," she said, moving her hand just an inch. "I've wanted to for a very long time."

Holly is due in two weeks. We are content to share our afternoons. Sometimes in my bed, sometimes in hers. She comes to dinner and plays games with me and the children. They adore her and cannot wait to meet Samuel. Neither can I.

Holly has made it clear that she is asking nothing of me. But there is so much that I want to give her. I have made it clear to Holly that I am asking nothing of her. But she has given me so much already.

We are okay with waiting to see how it turns out. Either way, Samuel is coming, and he will be very loved. By more than just Holly. No matter what the end result may be for us.

Butterflies and Stings

Angela Steele

The kids were playing some computer game and our husbands were watching a football match when Kerry first grasped the nettle.

Kerry was showing me round the garden and I recall she saw it first: the nettle growing among her flowers. Dear sweet Kerry, who spent so many hours pruning and planting and trimming, had finally let a mere weed escape her attention. I remember how embarrassed she looked that something had slipped through the garden fork as it were, that a wild plant had grown unsuspected among all the order and neatness.

I laughed when she made a fuss over it because I am not as diligent as her when it comes to such things. In fact, I knew it was a nettle but I didn't know what the plant that sheltered it was called, but it was one she liked. A shame that I should know so little of the natural world around us – but then I like to think I know the natural world within us. My friend even looked embarrassed about something that would sting amongst things that looked so pretty, as if that mattered.

Of course, it mattered to her. I could tell. But then I had known Kerry for ages – since before our kids were born – so I knew her better than most people did. That was why I said she should leave it. Let it be.

Oh she said, looking even more flustered, I couldn't do that. It had to come out, she said. That was when I said to Kerry she should grasp the nettle. No garden fork or trowel or even gardening gloves. Do it then and there and pull it out.

The look on her face was priceless. My good friend Kerry – Kez, she called herself – staring at me as if I as mad. But I wasn't: I simply knew it was time for her to do what I said.

Kerry is the kind of woman you would pass in the super-market and not notice. She's about average height, average build, average colour. Pretty when she wants to be, and she had made an effort today. Perhaps that's why I thought it was time for me to establish what I wanted, what I knew she needed.

I do know she hadn't noticed the many times when we had been together before that, when she had done what I'd said. Small things admittedly, but she had followed my suggestions. Or my orders, depending on how you see it. After all, when do hints become imperatives? In my mind, they had stopped being things in which she had a choice quite some time ago.

She was looking at me now as if slightly bewildered but that was because of what was going on in her. She was becoming aware of exactly how it was between us. Who gave the orders.

A brightly marked butterfly flew before us, landing on the nettle for a moment. Unsure if this was the right place for it, the creature's wings barely stilled before it flew on in the warm sunshine, fluttering in its zig-zag way. I was aware of Kerry watching it and then her gaze going back to the weed.

It was quite a moment when she did what I told her in the garden that afternoon. I even told Kerry to use her right hand to grasp the nettle. I have to confess here that I thought, should she masturbate later with that hand, the sting would remind her of my control.

I can recall her hesitating as she crouched by the nettle, taking a deep breath, steeling herself for the pain of grabbing the nettle. Oh, I know, people say by grasping it you don't get stung. Well, maybe they are right. But the purpose of my friend doing what I said wasn't to avoid pain.

So she was cautious and hesitant and she got stung. I think there must have been a goal in the match on TV because we heard the men shout just as she closed her hand on the nettle. A suitably dramatic moment, I suppose. Those lovely long fingers of hers enveloping something unpleasant. No, not unpleasant: something unexpected and sharp.

Then my friend stood up, looking utterly distressed, biting her lip and grimacing slightly. Oh, poor Kerry! She had tears glistening in her eyes as she stood there with that weed in her right hand. You see, even then she knew instinctively she hadn't been given permission to let go. Only when I said for Kerry to open her hand did she do so and there was the plant, rich green with spiked-edge leaves, slowly unfurling in her palm. A rash of little red and white blotches all over the woman's open hand. Perfect.

Kerry said that it hurt and I said yes, it would. That was when she looked at me and could have said something, that this was silly or childish or even crazy. Yet she didn't. She could have thrown the plant down, even got angry with me.

Again, she didn't. My friend stood waiting for my next instruction, blinking a little to get rid of the tears in her eyes. Her cheeks were flushed but I didn't know then if it was annoyance or arousal. But I did know she had obeyed me.

I was in no hurry: I wanted to savour the moment. I had just ordered my best friend to hurt herself, and she had done exactly as I wanted. Kerry said something about finding a dock leaf, because that was what she had used on nettle stings when a child. That made me smile. Would we really find another weed in her perfect garden? Anyway, we weren't going to look for one. I had no wish for her to stop suffering then and deep down I think she knew that.

I said we should go to the little summer house she had erected at the far corner of the garden. Kez's retreat, she called it, from when the family were making demands. It wasn't much more than a large shed, but she kept it tidy with a large but comfortable garden seat on a small verandah. Hidden from the house by evergreen bushes. I went first and she followed, still with the nettle in her open hand. I hadn't even said anything being careful not to drop it but she was careful. Respectful, I suppose, as it had hurt her.

In the summer house I sat on the chair and she stood with the source of her pain, motionless in front of me. I took my time, letting her watch me, as I brushed an imaginary insect or small leaf off my skirt. I even pretended I had found a seed of something on me and examined this mystery between fingertip and thumb. Then when I was ready I told her then what I had been wanting to tell her for ages, that as far as I was concerned this was how it should be between us. That I would have to see her hurt more, because I loved her.

Poor Kerry. She looked just as startled as when she grasped the nettle. But to her credit she didn't move, or object, though I recall her saying something about not being like that.

Like what? She didn't know.

I said we were like us, two ordinary women – wives, mothers, workers – who had feelings for each other. Strong, unspoken feelings that had drained through the soil of our cultivated lives, down into a deep underground pool. But we had never explored these feelings, never tried to unearth the dark waters of the real us.

Perhaps we had never wanted to upset the status quo, or possibly we were frightened of our inner lives being changed. I told her that now this doubt was over. We were us from now on because we were right for each other, her and me.

One on top, the other on the bottom. Me and her.

She looked a little confused as if women shouldn't express such thoughts between them, have such a relationship. She started to open her mouth to offer an argument but maybe I frowned, or maybe Kerry thought better of it as a bottom should do, and she bit her lip instead. I asked if she understood, and the woman nodded.

I was silent as I knew she needed to let all this sink in, but then I wanted to know if she was ready for her next pain.

I will never forget how she took a deep breath, flushed pink with anxiety and arousal, and nodded.

Good, I said as I stood, took a tissue from my skirt pocket and carefully grasped the end of the nettle in her hand. I grinned: after all, I didn't want to be stung, did I? She seemed to understand the hurting was for her, not me. I took the nettle and held it up in front of Kerry. As I looked into her hazel eyes she nodded because she knew I was in charge. My friend knew I held the source of her pain, and her final freedom.

She asked me if she could ask a question. I said yes, but be quick. She asked me if I would kiss her.

I said we could kiss only when I had hurt her a little more and she seemed relieved. I suspect Kerry thought I wouldn't give her any solace, I might cruelly deny her any comfort. Perhaps she feared there would be no reward for being so willing. But I told her that while the flowers among the thorns were important to me too, the honey could only be discovered between the stings.

She did what I told her to do, rolling up her pale lilac top to show me her breasts. She has a bigger bust than me and her boobs were cradled perfectly in her plunge bra. It made me smile a little as her chest came into full view, thinking that perhaps she had selected this daring bra that morning, knowing I was coming to her house, knowing something would happen between us. Finally.

Without a word she put her hands behind her, pushing her chest forward invitingly and slowly I drew the stinging nettle over her vulnerable breasts. The rash on those pale orbs was instant and her stifled cry little more than a gasp of exhaled air.

I drew the nettle across twice, once each way, and then down between her breasts bringing a renewed gasp from my friend – my pain lover – each time.

I asked if she wanted more, and she nodded, trying not to cry. Striving to be quiet, hands clamped behind her, knuckles white as she fought the new agony consuming her senses.

Kerry followed her next instructions perfectly, undoing her jeans and letting them fall, easing her plain white cotton pants to halfway down her thighs with legs slightly apart. I placed the nettle, not so dangerous now but still with a bite, on the crotch fabric of her pants. Damp, I noticed, as they should be. I could see her trimmed pubic hair with a little moisture glistening on it. Tiny dew drops, you could say. Dear Kerry, who moaned slightly as I put my face close to her sex as I breathed in the muskiness of her arousal. I knew what she wanted and she knew it too.

She also knew what was to come. How much it would hurt, and she was patient because she loved me. I motioned she should pull her cotton pants up, crushing the last of the nettle's venom against her pussy. At last as the nettle made contact with her puffy nether lips, brushed up against her engorged clit, she gave a small scream. It hurt and her hands clenched, knuckles whiter than before. Above me, I could hear her sobbing, aware her body was shaking.

A tear fell past me.

Kerry was crying and moaning now and I stood, told her I loved her and for the first time kissed Kez like a lover, not a friend. Between the sobs she accepted my deep and searching kiss, my tongue in her mouth. I broke the kiss, put my left hand over her mouth and with my right hand I slowly pressed the crotch of her pants up, crushing the nettle's leaves even more into the folds of Kerry's inflamed sex.

I told her I loved her deeply as I worked my fingers against Kerry's swollen, wet pussy, the venom of the crushed leaves burning into her. Just as I wanted my love to burn into her.

That was when the woman came. The first time at my hands. When she had stopped trying to scream, I took my hands away and kissed her deeply again. A reward she had longed for.

It would be perfect to say that at that moment, a butterfly – a delicate and pretty creature she had always wanted more of in her beautiful garden – had alighted on my friend. A symbol of our new found love. But nature isn't quite like that.

The insect that landed on her was a wasp, and she flinched as it crawled over her naked, quivering breast. Kerry, hands behind back still, didn't move but she was terrified. My friend, my lover, looked at me imploringly. She didn't utter the words but I could tell what she was thinking, what she wanted to say: please, not this.

I said, my darling, we have to have pain and pleasure, don't we? Sharp edges in the softness, cruelty in the midst of joy. Crush the wasp to your breast, I told her, and we will make each other come with our tongues.

And we did in the peace and quiet of Kez's retreat, hidden from the world, when she had stopped crying.

Tess of the Suburb's Bills

H. L. Berry

"You missed a fantastic Sociology lecture today," said Helen.

"Really?" Abigail Valling looked up from her work at the kitchen table.

"Yes, really. Lady Chatterbox was on top form."

"Was she talking about the impact of prostitution on the post-war British middle classes?"

"Abby, as I've told you on numerous occasions, Lady Chatterbox is not running a brothel."

"Well no, of course she's not now, because I shut her down."

"She was helping students with their coursework."

Abigail laughed. "Is that what they call it these days? Well, all I can say is that it's a pretty lame metamorphism."

"I think you mean metaphor. And . . . oh, never mind. She was asking after you."

"She wanted to know whether I'm still keeping an eye on her, no doubt." Abigail folded her arms and smirked.

"No, actually, she was asking when you might be likely to hand in your assignment."

"Pah! Lecturers ask that all the time."

"They only ever ask that about you, Abby, because you never hand in your bloody assignments. If you're not careful, you're going to fail the course."

"I don't care about that. I'm following a higher calling now."

"Oh, Abby." Helen put her hands on her friend's shoulders. "Even if you don't grow out of this silly Nightgirl thing, how will you fund her without a job?"

"It's not silly, Helen." Abigail tilted her head to one side. "But I do see your point. Perhaps I'll get Brendan to hack into the university computer and adjust my grades."

"Abby! You can't do that!"

"No, you're right," said Abby. "His kid sister Georgina would be even better. She managed to get into the Government gateway site."

"That's a public site. Anyone can get into it."

"Sure they can." Abigail winked.

Helen changed the subject. "I was chatting with Tess over lunch."

"Tess?"

"Tess Carlin. You remember? She used to live on the floor above, but moved to that house in the suburbs with a bunch of other students."

"Oh, yes. Blonde hair, green eyes, a bit dim."

"Pot," muttered Helen. "Yes, that's her."

"How's she doing?"

"Fine, except she's finding the bills a lot to cope with."

"I thought she lived with Anna, John, Simon and Dave. When did the Bills move in?"

"No, you muppet. The phone bill. The electricity bill. Food bills. She's struggling to make ends meet."

"But she's studying accountancy, Helen. I remember she produced a sixteen-page spreadsheet before she moved, setting out her budget for the next three years."

"Well, she must have made some errors."

"More likely one of her housemates is spending more than his fair share." Abigail looked up and grinned. "You know what this means, don't you?"

Helen's shoulders slumped. "No, Abby, please. No."

"Yes! This is definitely a job for Nightgirl!"

It was drizzling, and the tarmac surface of the deserted car park was wet. The puddles reflected the orange light of the few working streetlamps. A lone pigeon walked carefully around the edge. It stopped and cocked its head to one side as though listening. With an explosive burst of sound and light, the Night Car barrelled down the street opposite and shot through the car park entrance, fishtailing wildly. The pigeon scrambled into the air, leaving a few feathers behind. Abigail, dressed in her spandex Nightgirl costume, yanked at the steering wheel. The car pirouetted through three hundred and sixty degrees and slithered to a halt. A blue glow lit the underside, and in the bonnet a red light oscillated back and forth.

Abigail climbed out and shut the door. She pointed a remote control at her car and clicked a button. The locks clunked and the lights faded. Abigail looked around and strode across the car park towards a row of semi-detached houses. Her red cape flapped behind her. She reached for the set of lock picks in her belt and headed for number 27.

The lock was old-fashioned and no match even for Abigail's limited skills. She punched the air in delight and put the picks back in the pouch on her belt. Inside, the hallway was dark. Abigail headed for the stairs. Flat E was at the top of the house, spread across the generous loft. She knocked at the door.

"Hello?" Tess peered through a gap in the door.

"Hi!" Abigail grinned. "I've come to help you."

"Who are you?" Tess opened the door fully and peered closely. "Abigail? Abigail Valling? Is that you? What are you doing here, and why are you wearing a mask?"

Abigail drew herself to her full height. "I'm Nightgirl, crime-fighting super heroine, and I'm here to help you with your bills."

"Nightgirl? But you're Abigail Valling. I sit next to you in our Organizational Analysis classes."

"Well yes, that's my secret identity, but after dark I'm Nightgirl, the Dim Defender. How come you recognized me? That never happens to Superman or Batman."

"I knew your voice. And your eyes." Tess looked up and down Abigail's body and grinned. "Look at you, girl! You look fantastic."

Abigail grinned back, and twirled. "Do you think so? I've always worried that it makes my bum look big."

"Are you kidding? Your bum looks perfect, and so does the rest of you. Hell, I wish my stomach was that flat." Tess reached out and ran her hand around Abigail's waist. "Wow! The material feels amazing, doesn't it?" She let her hand slip down over Abigail's hip and bottom. "What are these knickers made from, PVC?"

"That's right."

"And why are they on the outside?'

Abigail giggled. "I'll show you. Look!"

She peeled the panties down a couple of inches to reveal a chrome zip. "That goes right down between my legs!"

"Really? Can I feel?" Tess didn't wait for a reply. She ran her fingers down the zip and inside Abigail's red PVC panties.

Abigail wiggled her hips. "Blimey. I can see why you'd want to keep that hidden. Why did you get trousers like that?"

"At first they were the only ones I could find on eBay, but now I find them quite convenient, actually."

Tess winked. "I bet you do, honey. Anyway, look at me, being all rude. I haven't invited you in."

She held the door open and Abigail stepped into the flat. She looked around the large, open space. "This is nice, Tess."

"Yes, it's not bad. I share a kitchen downstairs, but I'm lucky that this flat has its own ensuite shower room. The others have one between the three of them. You should hear them in the mornings."

"Helen said you'd been having trouble with your bills."

Tess frowned. "Yeah. I can't understand it. I worked it all out so carefully, but the phone bill is about three times what I'd expected. The electricity is a bit high too, and I'm even spending more on food than I thought. I seem to go through a box of cereal a week."

"Don't you split the bills?"

"No. I rent the house and sublet rooms to the other three. They pay me a fixed amount each month. I had hoped it would cover some of my own costs, but it's not even close at the moment."

Abigail gave Tess a solemn look. "Tess, I'm sorry to tell you this, but there's a high possibility that at least one of your housemates is ripping you off."

"Oh!" Tess put a hand up to her mouth. "But they're so nice. They wouldn't do that, would they? How can you be so sure?"

Abigail clenched her fist. "It wouldn't be obvious to someone like you, Tess, but to a trained and experienced crime fighter like myself, it sticks out like a sore thumb. Someone is abusing the trust you have placed in them."

"But what can I do about it?"

"Don't worry. Now I'm here, we'll soon get to the bottom of this evil plot. The first thing we need to do is commence a surveillance operation."

"You mean spy on them?"

"Yes. We'll start with the guys, because in my experience, only one in . . ." Abigail silently ticked off her fingers. Her lips moved slowly ". . . eight villains is female."

"Okay. John is in room C and Dave is in D. They're both on the floor below. Simon is on the ground floor in room A."

"We'll spy on Simon first, then, because he will be the easiest. Looking through first-floor windows is tricky unless there's a tree opposite." Abigail looked hopefully at Tess. "There isn't one, is there?"

Tess shook her head.

"Never mind. I'll go and see if I can see what Simon is up to." Abby unclipped a case from her belt.

"What's that?"

"It's an extendable periscope. I'll crouch outside his window and use this to look inside."

"What if his curtains are drawn?"

"Villains never draw their curtains."

"Why?"

"Because it makes them look suspicious."

"But if you can look in and see what they're up to, doesn't that make them even more suspicious?"

"Well, yes, but – never mind. You wait here."

"Can't I come with you?"

"Not yet." Abigail pointed at Tess's white blouse. "You're not dressed right."

She crept downstairs and out of the front door. There was only one window on the ground floor, to the left of the door. Abby crawled along in the shadows until she was underneath it. She extended her periscope and smiled. The curtains were drawn, but they didn't quite meet in the middle. Abigail peered through the gap.

Simon was lying on his bed in jeans and a T-shirt, watching a small portable television. A cup of coffee steamed on a bedside table. As she watched, he picked it up and took a sip. He looked back at the television and chuckled.

Abigail was just shifting position, trying to get comfortable, when she heard the front door open and close. She froze. Footsteps scrunched on the gravel path. Abigail had to bite back a scream when someone sat down beside her.

"Hi, Abby," said Tess. "I got changed into some dark clothes. Is this better?"

Abigail's heart was still pounding. "Golly, you gave me a fright."

She looked at Tess, who was wearing black slacks and a black polo neck sweater. "Well, your clothes are better, but the blonde hair is a bit of a giveaway. You could do with a hat."

Tess nodded. "Good point. Don't you have a spare hood or something?"

"I'll bring one tomorrow. Now hush. He's just getting up."

"Let me see."

"Not yet. Just sit there for a moment. And stop fondling my bottom."

"I'm sorry. I can't help it. Your outfit feels so nice."

"Well, stop it. It's distracting. He's left his room."

"Oh, no! Is he coming out?"

"I doubt it. He was barefoot. Look, he's back. Now that is interesting."

"What? What?"

"He's got a chocolate digestive biscuit and a cordless phone."

"But I'm the only one who buys chocolate digestives! He usually gets Kitkats."

"Told you so. He's pinching your food. They're probably all at it. What about the phone?"

"Well, I got cordless so they wouldn't have to sit in the hall and make calls. They just have to replace it afterwards."

"Damn! He's got into bed. Now I can't see what he's doing. He's definitely on the phone, though."

"How will we find out where he's ringing?"

"Easy. We'll wait until he puts the phone back and press redial."

"Wow. You really are good at this."

"Thanks. Do you have to sit so close? Your hand is rubbing against my nipple and it's getting a little stiff."

"Sorry."

It was over half an hour before Simon replaced the telephone. Abigail jumped to her feet and entered the house. She picked up the handset. It was still warm. She pressed the redial button.

"Damn! I think he must be onto us. He's cunning, I'll give him that."

"What?" asked Tess. She shut the front door. Abigail held the phone out. Tess took it and listened.

"At the third stroke, the time will be eight fifteen precisely," said a well-spoken female voice.

Tess looked puzzled. "The speaking clock? How could he have spent forty minutes talking to the speaking clock?"

"He didn't," said Abigail. "He rang it just before he put the phone back so no one could find out who he'd been ringing."

"Gosh. That is cunning. What will we do?"

"What time does he usually get back in the evening?"

"About six o'clock. Why?"

"I'll be here at half-past five. I'll break into his room and hide under the bed. Once he's got the phone and I know whom he's ringing, I'll signal you. Then you can distract him for long enough for me to sneak out."

"That's a great plan."

"See you tomorrow, then."

"I hear you're going round to see Tess again tonight," said Helen.

Abigail frowned. "That was supposed to be a secret."

"She's very excited about it. I think she's rather taken with you. God knows why."

"Maybe she thinks I'm someone to look up to."

Helen coughed, and swallowed hard. "Yes, that must be it."

Abigail folded her arms. "If you've quite finished, Helen, some of us have crime to fight."

She sniffed and walked out.

Abigail stood outside flat A and brandished her lock picks.

"Abby, wait!" called Tess from the top of the stairs.

"Shhhh!" hissed Abby with a finger to her lips. "Do you want everyone to know we're here? And try to remember that my name is 'Nightgirl', not Abby."

"There's no one else in, Abby. Anyway, I thought you'd like to know that I have a master key. It might be easier than picking the lock."

"Yes, well, that seems like a very amateur way of going about things, but as you're here, you might as well open it."

Tess unlocked the door and held it open. Abby stepped into the room. She reached up to her throat and unfastened her red cape.

"Tess, would you look after this for me? If I need to make a quick getaway, it might hinder me."

Tess looked as though she'd been given the crown jewels to look after.

"Wow, thanks, Abby! You can rely on me. I won't let you down."

"Good. Now scoot, quickly, before he gets back."

"Bye!" Tess skipped upstairs.

Abigail closed the door and walked over to the double bed. She knelt down and peered underneath it. Seeing nothing but a couple of boxes, she lay on her stomach and slithered into the gap. She looked at her watch. Ten minutes to go.

The door opened. She heard a footstep, and a click as the person pushed the door shut. Abby shifted position and was surprised to see a pair of stiletto heels. She gulped as the figure knelt in front of the bed and slowly lowered its head.

"Hi, Abby!"

Abigail looked away and banged her head on the floor. "Tess. What are you doing here?"

"I couldn't stay in my room, Abby. I was too excited." Tess flattened herself and shuffled sideways. "Come on, budge up."

"Tess, you can't get under here! What about distracting him so I can get out?"

"Oh, I've thought of that. I rang Helen. She's going to come round at about half past eight to discuss an assignment with him."

"Helen agreed to do that?"

"Yes. She wasn't too happy about it, mind you. Muttered something about how you'd probably enjoy getting tied up again. Gosh, it's cosy under here, isn't it?"

Abigail jerked up and banged her head on the underside of the bed. "Ow! Would you stop that?"

"What?"

"You touched my bottom again."

"I didn't!"

"You did, too. There! You're doing it again!"

"Oh. Sorry."

"Tess, I don't think this is going to work. You'd better go back to your room."

The front door of the house banged.

"Too late," whispered Tess. "I think he's back."

A key slid into the lock with a scrape of metal. The tumblers clicked as it turned. The door gave a faint creak. Abigail held her breath. Behind her, Tess snuggled closer. A pair of black boots stepped into view. The girls heard a rustle of material, and a faded leather jacket landed on the armchair at the other side of the room. The television burst into life.

"This is the six o'clock news, from the BBC. In the headlines tonight, the Government proposes sweeping changes to the education system. There's confusion in America when the president fails to recognize his own Chief of Staff, and in sport, despair for giant-killing minnows Millington Town as they are knocked out of the FA Cup quarter finals by Chelsea."

"Bastards," said a voice. The bed creaked when Simon threw himself on top of it.

Abigail shifted. Tess was very close, and had slipped an arm around her. She could feel Tess's breasts pressing into her back. She tried to slide forwards. Tess clung tighter.

The bed shifted again. Simon sat up, his feet inches from Abigail's nose. He walked to the door and opened it. As soon as he left, Abigail rolled over to face Tess.

"Come on. This is your chance."

"Chance for what?"

"To get out of here and go back to your room. It's too distracting, having you here."

"But I like it!"

Abigail looked down at Tess's hand, which was stroking her breasts through the spandex costume. Tess froze.

"Oh. Sorry. I didn't even realize I was doing it."

"Well, I wish you wouldn't. You're making my nipples go all hard again, and it's difficult to concentrate. Please, go back to your room."

"I can't, Abby. Listen." Tess cocked her head to one side. "He's only in the kitchen. He can see right down the corridor. If I go, he'll see me."

"Bugger," said Abigail. She rolled over. Tess snuggled into her back again. Her hips pushed into Abigail's bottom.

The door banged shut and Simon sat back on the bed. He set a cup of coffee on the table beside his bed. The smell drifted down and tantalized Abigail's nose. She sighed and rolled onto her back. Simon had been flicking through the channels on his television, and had settled on *Witch Babes*, a loud US import whose stars regularly appeared in tight, black PVC costumes. Abigail rolled her eyes at Tess.

A few minutes later she felt a hand on her stomach. She looked over at Tess, who was smiling. The hand circled around and crept lower. Abigail took a firm hold and placed it back on the floor between them. Tess pouted.

"I'm bored," she mouthed.

Her hand drifted back to Abigail's tummy and moved down over her slick panties. Once again, Abigail removed it. Tess batted her eyelashes. Abigail gave her a very stern look and wagged her finger. She held it up to her lips.

"Behave yourself," she muttered.

Tess stayed still for a few minutes. Her hand slipped inside her trousers. Simon slurped at his coffee. When Tess's damp finger brushed against Abigail's lips, she only just managed to stop herself sitting up and banging her head on the underside of the bed.

At that moment, *Witch Babes* finished, and the heavy rock theme tune filled the room. Simon got up and went out, leaving the door wide open.

"You're making this really difficult, Tess," whispered Abigail, removing Tess's hand from between her legs.

"Sorry, Abby. I'll try not to do it again."

"Shh. He's coming back."

Simon closed the door and drew his curtains. He lay on the bed above them, and they both heard the distinctive beeping of a telephone keypad. Abigail grinned at Tess and gave her a thumbs-up sign.

"Hello?" said Simon. "Is that Miss de Meanour, the Horny School Mistress?"

He listened for a moment. "Yes, I've been a very bad boy, and I think I deserve to be punished."

His zip made a scraping noise. The bed squeaked.

"Yes, Mistress," said Simon. "I've dropped my trousers. Do you want me to take down my underpants as well?"

He shifted positions. "Oh, yes. Oh, that feels good. Spank me hard, Mistress."

Abigail jumped at the sound of a hand hitting flesh. She looked at Tess, her eyes wide. Tess wasn't looking anywhere. Her eyes were closed, and her hand was deep between her thighs.

Simon continued to spank his own bottom, groaning down the phone all the while.

"Thank you, Mistress. Smack me again."

Finally he stopped. The mattress bowed as he slumped onto his back.

"Thank you, Mistress. Please may I sniff your panties?"

Abigail bit her hand to stop herself from laughing out loud.

"Yes, Mistress. I'd love to play with myself."

The mattress started to bounce. The springs creaked rhythmically. The noise drowned the slight squelching that Tess was making.

"Oh, yes! Oh, yes! I'm going to come, Mistress. I need to come. May I come, please?"

"Just come, already," muttered Abigail.

Tess gasped. Her body went rigid. Above her Simon let out a long groan. His movements slowed, then stopped.

"Thank you, Mistress. Thank you. Good night."

The phone beeped. Simon dialled another number.

"Twenty past eight. Cool."

Abigail flinched when a scrunched up piece of tissue paper landed on the floor in front of her. It looked wet. Simon's feet appeared beside it, his trousers around his ankles. He bent down and pulled them up. Right on cue, the doorbell rang.

Abigail and Tess heard Simon walk out and open the door.

"Oh, hi, Helen," he said.

"Hello, Simon," replied Helen. Abigail grinned. "I've been having a few problems with this assignment, and I was wondering if you'd like to discuss it over a quick drink."

"Sure! I'd love to. Just let me grab my shoes."

Simon rushed back into his room. He pulled on his shoes and grabbed his leather jacket. He paused briefly.

"Shit," he said, and fastened the zip of his trousers. The door banged shut.

"Thank goodness for that," said Abigail. She dragged herself out from under the bed, followed by Tess. "Well, now we know why your phone bills are so high."

"Yeah," replied Tess. "The dirty little bugger. So what happens now?"

"We wait until he comes back, and confront him."

"And what will he do?"

"Probably he'll tie me to the bed and confess everything before having sex with me."

"That really happens, does it?"

"Oh, yes." Abigail puffed out her chest. "Five times, so far."

"How do they tie you? Could you show me?"

"Of course. Let's get back to your room."

They walked upstairs to Tess's flat. Abigail threw herself on the bed and stretched out her arms and legs.

"Generally, they tie me like this."

"What do they use?"

"All sorts of things. Neck ties, rope, cuffs."

"What about these?" Tess held up a pair of long straps, each with Velcro cuffs at both ends.

"Gosh. You just happened to have those handy, did you? Well, yes, I guess they would do."

Tess attached a cuff to Abigail's wrist. She ran the strap

around the top of the bed and cuffed her other wrist. The second strap held her ankles wide apart.

"How's that?" asked Tess.

Abigail pulled at the straps. "Pretty firm, yes. Where did you get them from?"

"Jan Winters. So, if I were a villain, what would I do next?"

"Well, you'd probably roll my top up and play with my tits. If you were really evil, you'd cut off my panties and undo my crotch zip."

"Mmmm," said Tess. She reached down and pulled Abigail's top up, exposing her breasts.

"Tess, what are you doing? You're not a villain."

"I don't know about that," said Tess, with a wink. "I'm feeling pretty wicked right now."

"But this was supposed to be a demonstr— Oh!"

Tess tweaked Abigail's nipples, gripping them firmly between her thumbs and forefingers. She lowered her head and ran her tongue over the little pink buds.

"Very nice. Now, about those panties . . ."

She walked into her lounge area and returned with a pair of scissors.

"No!" moaned Abigail. "I've only got two pairs left."

"I'll buy you more," said Tess. She snipped the panties up both sides and pulled them away. "This zip does go a long way back, doesn't it?"

She reached under Abigail's bottom. The zip clicked forward and the spandex on either side parted, exposing the pink flesh underneath.

"Wow, Abby, you shave!"

"Actually, I've started having it waxed. It hurts like hell, but it lasts longer."

"It looks yummy," said Tess, licking her lips. "Are you ready?"

"Ready for what?"

"This." Tess lay between Abigail's legs and ran her tongue along her pussy.

"Ooooooh!" Abigail jerked. "Oh, gosh! Stop it! Ooooooh!"

Tess found her clit and wrapped her lips around it. Slowly she sucked the little button into her mouth. Abigail squealed. "Oh, God! Stop! Oh! That's . . . um . . . nice!"

Tess flicked with her tongue. She slid two fingers along Abigail's pussy and pushed them inside her. Her captive bucked and pulled against the straps. Tess hummed, sending vibrations through Abigail's clit.

"Bloody hell! Oh! Do that again!" Abigail arched her back off the bed. "Oooooh!"

Tess pumped her fingers in and out of Abigail's pussy. Her tongue circled above it, each pass drawing another gasp from Abigail's lips.

"Oh, God! I'm going to come!" She pulled the straps taut and threw her head back against the pillows. Tess shook her head from side to side. Abigail jerked three times, let out a long groan and collapsed. Tess gave her a last, lingering kiss on the pussy and sat up. She leaned forward and kissed Abigail's mouth.

"You taste good, don't you?"

Abigail's eyes flickered open. "Golly. That's never happened to me before."

"What? A woman making you come?"

"No." Abigail thought for a moment. "Well, yes, that too, but I meant I've never been captured by one of the good guys before."

Tess chuckled. "There's a first time for everything, honey."

Later that evening, Abigail and Helen sat in their flat, drinking wine.

"So then, after tying me up and doing all sorts of things to me, she says she thinks that she's a bicycle!" Abigail looked at Helen and shrugged. "I mean, I like my bike, especially when I ride it down the cobbled street across town, but it never does stuff like that to me."

Helen stifled a laugh. "I think she might have said that she was bisexual."

"Bisexual?" Abigail shook her head. "That can't be right. She didn't pay me anything."

"Not 'buy'. 'Bi'. B-I. It means she likes girls as well as boys."

"Nooo! Really?"

"Yes!" Helen nodded. "She's had the hots for you for ages. Don't tell me you didn't realize."

"Gosh, no. I thought she just wanted to be my sidekick."

"Did she say what she was going to do about Simon?"

"I think she's going to go on a date with him."

"What? Why?"

Abigail took a sip of wine and looked at Helen over the top of her glass. "I may have inadvertently planted the idea in her mind."

"Oh, boy. How?"

"I just said that if Simon had been watching what she did to me, he wouldn't have needed to call those dirty phone numbers."

Helen snorted with laughter. "Too right he wouldn't. So she's going to go out with him?"

"Well," said Abigail, "What she actually said was that she'd ask him if he was interested in a threesome. I wonder who else she has in mind?"

Opposites Attract

Nicky B.

Freddy Deadbeat leaned forward into his microphone, his huge shades covering his eyes; he had long curly dark hair and a thick moustache that made him look like a seventies cliché.

He was a late night radio host and spoke in a New York accent to the thousands listening, and most of them never asked if he really was American.

The truth was, he was from Bristol and he never advertised the fact; he had an image to keep up in order to get the girls, after all.

The show was low on listeners so management had turned to controversial guests to boost the figures a little.

Freddy was desperate to get it going so he could play music and leave the building for a cigarette.

"Good evening, all you cats out there. Tonight we have two guests who are here to slug it out on the air: Angie and Rebecca! Welcome to the show, ladies!"

Angie had dark straight shoulder-length hair, was of petite build and had large breasts that spilled out of a tight vest top. Her leather mini skirt was virtually non-existent, with two immaculate legs protruding from it.

The two women nodded at the presenter through the thick glass partition; they could barely make him out in the dark studio but he was larger than life in their headphones.

Then they realized that they had to reply through the microphones in front of them.

"Good evening!" they said in unison.

"Angie, you have a doctorate in metaphysics and scored high marks – so why did you become a porn star?" said the almost hidden figure in the adjacent room.

"Well, it pays well and the hours are not too long. And I get to fuck lots of really hot men and women."

"Whoa!" yelled Freddy, "No bad language on the air, please! Sorry, listeners!"

Angie gave an embarrassed smile. "Sorry guys!" she said through gritted teeth.

Freddy continued, "So how did you get into it in the first place?"

"I was short of money when I was studying and a photographer approached me. He got me lots of work and it just seemed to progress into low-budget porno and then to where I am now!" She had a quiet voice and a smile that could melt chocolate at ten paces.

The other woman was a stark contrast to her.

"So, Rebecca, you are a lawyer and a campaigner against pornography. What do you think of Angie's profession?"

Rebecca had short blonde hair and was dressed very conservatively. She was thick-set and tall with a look about her that would make a headmaster shrink.

"I think she's trash and a victim of exploitation in modern society!" Her expression never changed on her chiselled features.

Angie spoke up quickly. "Modern society? But pornography has been around for thousands of years! Look at the pots found that were produced by the Egyptians. Since the camera first captured a still or moving image, it has been used to produce nudity and sexual imagery – pornography!"

Rebecca suddenly realized that she was not up against some dumb bimbo and it infuriated her. "Men use these women like pieces of meat for their own enjoyment!"

"But most of my movies are written, produced and filmed by women!" She pointed up to the air conditioning unit in the ceiling. "Look! There goes another of your pointless theories, and you a lawyer? Listen, honey – I fuck people for money and you fuck people for money so that makes us even, right?"

The veins on Rebecca's fore head were beginning to show as she scowled at Angie.

"This isn't the eighteenth century any more, so do us all a favour and get yourself laid once in a while. A good orgasm now and again will lower your blood pressure." Angie wore a smug look on her face.

Freddy was lapping it all up, for this was quality radio: Beauty and the Beast, and the Beast was losing!

You could almost feel the rumble as Rebecca's blood boiled.

There was an awkward silence in the room, so Freddy decided to break it. "Okay, let's take a break for some music now. Catch you cats in just a minute, so do not touch that dial!" And finally he put a music track on.

"I'm out of here. I need the toilet," said Angie as she stood up and clicked across the room in her high heels.

Rebecca looked her up and down contemptuously as she left.

". . . Oh, yes, and you should have seen the look on the frigid bitch's face! Anyway, I'd better get back before the track finishes. Ciao!" Angie's mobile phone blipped as she closed it and she stood up in the small toilet cubicle.

She opened the door to find herself face to face with Rebecca, who did not look too happy.

"Frigid bitch, eh? Well, that shows just how little you know about me, doesn't it?"

Even with her high heels on, Angie was still nowhere near Rebecca's height; she was suddenly feeling a little vulnerable all of a sudden.

"You, little lady, are a menace and should be punished!" Rebecca took a step towards her.

"Uh, how?"

Rebecca looked around the washroom.

"Go and lean over that sink. Now!"

Angie obeyed with a half smile on her face.

She leant over the sink and took hold of the taps; Rebecca came up behind her and took hold of her hips.

She pulled them sharply so Angie had to take small urgent steps backwards; she was bending over now and her buttocks were tight against Rebecca's midriff. Angie looked at the spectacle in the mirror.

"If I had a strap-on, I'd fuck the intelligence out of you!" Rebecca smiled for the first time. Angie looked up at her eyes in the reflection.

"You must get it every day, then?" The smile quickly vanished and she stood aside.

She lifted up Angie's tight skirt to reveal her naked flesh; her tight little buttocks were perfect and she wore no underwear.

Rebecca rested her left hand on the small of Angie's back and brought her right one sharply down to her left cheek. She smacked it so hard that it echoed around the tiled room.

"Mmm!" Angie purred, and then her right cheek was struck just as hard.

"Oh, God yes!" Her hand massaged Angie's cheeks in turn and then Rebecca brought her hand down sharply again – once for each side.

"Ooh!" Rebecca brought down both hands at once, and then she did it again.

The pert little cheeks that had made Angie's first million were beginning to go red; her mouth was wide open as she watched her own reflection in the large mirror before her.

Rebecca got down onto her knees and ran her tongue over the smarting areas of the cheeks and felt the heat from them. She took hold of Angie's ankles and pulled them further apart; Angie's heels slid across the carpet and made her unsteady for a second. Her pert little cheeks wiggled in the process.

Rebecca stood up again and placed a hand inside Angie's thighs, they made eye contact and shared a smile. Angie's smile changed to a gasp as a hand was brought down against her cheek again; Rebecca's other hand slowly slid upwards until it was next to an already drenched pussy.

The palm of her hand pressed against it and began to massage the wetness.

"Ooooh, my God!" Angie moaned as her pussy was tended to with an expert touch.

Rebecca moved her hand back and forth and then curled up her middle finger, it slid into Angie's pussy with ease and she started to stir it around inside her.

Angie gripped harder onto the taps and rested her head onto her right arm; her eyes were tightly shut and mouth wide open, giving out short pants of breath.

Rebecca was massaging her own breast through her top; her nipples had become prominent through the thick material and she too was breathing deeper than ever.

Freddie was tearing his hair out; his girl who answered the phones was missing, as were his guests, and any minute the station manager could be on the phone asking questions.

"Hey cats, we seem to have a little glitch with the microphones so our guests can't be heard right now, but they are still in discussion and they will give an outcome when we are back in business. Stay right there, folks."

*   *   *

Rebecca hitched up her skirt and got down onto her knees. Angie looked up to see what she was doing and why she had stopped.

Before she knew it, she had a tongue flicking against her wet pussy lips.

"Mmm!" She couldn't believe what was happening.

Rebecca was parting the wet lips with her tongue while stroking her own pussy; it slid in as she pressed lightly against her clit.

Angie could feel Rebecca's tongue against her pussy walls; she explored inside with her mouth pressed hard against the soft shaven skin while gripping her thighs.

Rebecca's tongue moved a little faster as it glided in and out of Angie, whose body convulsed as she was mouth-fucked by Rebecca. She felt a climax was near.

With her free hand, Rebecca undid her top to reveal her bra. As Angie turned to look, she slid it up to reveal a huge breast with a rock-hard nipple.

As Rebecca squeezed her own breast, Angie watched and could hold back no more.

"Arghhhhhhhh!" Angie came hard into Rebecca's mouth and her whole body shook; the mirror had frosted over with her breath.

Rebecca stopped and stood up; she took Angie's arm and pulled her back upright.

She was spun around on her heels and embraced tightly; before she knew it, Rebecca was kissing her deeply and passionately. Numb with disbelief, Angie accepted a long tongue deep within her mouth and followed suit.

When they broke contact, Rebecca stood back and undid her top completely; she lifted out her remaining breast, held both up and looked at Angie. Angie didn't need telling and walked forward to take a nipple into her mouth.

She sucked it and then rolled her tongue around it; Rebecca's jaw fell open as she watched in the mirror. She held a pained expression but it was really ecstasy; her eyes snapped shut as Angie gave a light bite of her nipple.

"Ooh!" She stroked Angie's neck as her stiff nipple vanished in and out of soft lips and she pinched the remaining one with her fingers.

She looked down and watched the pretty little face lovingly lick and suck her formidable breasts. It was time for more, though.

She took Angie's chin and lifted her head up to make eye contact.

"I'm not finished, yet. Get on your knees. For now you are my toy and it's playtime!"

Angie obeyed with a big smile and Rebecca lifted her skirt right up, placed a foot onto the sink edge and slid her panties aside to reveal a trimmed pussy that was glistening in the artificial light.

She parted the lips with two fingers and played with her left breast with the other.

Angie reached around and gently scraped her nails over the backs of Rebecca's thighs. She licked each side of the pussy lips in turn her tongue slid up and down a few times before resting in the middle.

"Mmm!" Rebecca pursed her lips and then parted in a loud gasp as Angie's tongue slid slowly inside her pussy.

"Aah!" she squealed and moved her hips forwards rhythmically.

Angie grabbed her buttocks and held tight as her tongue twirled around inside.

Rebecca began to scream as every inch of her pussy was explored inside and her juices streamed into Angie's mouth. She thrust her hips forward, causing Angie to jolt back but she dug her nails into her cheeks to maintain contact. Rebecca pinched both her nipples tight and screamed again as a climax started to take hold. Angie tongue-fucked her as deep as she could and felt the pussy wall pulsate over her tongue.

"Oh! Yes, yes! Argh!" Rebecca was struggling to stand on one leg as her whole body replicated what her pussy was doing.

She shook for a second and another peak swept through her.

"Mmm!" Her face was drenched in sweat as she gently pushed Angie away; Angie had to support Rebecca as she lowered her leg back down.

Taking hold of each other tightly, they kissed deeply and fed off the taste of each other's pussies.

They broke contact and smiled at each other.

"Maybe we should go back to the radio show now?" Angie said breathlessly.

"My God! I had forgotten about that!" said Rebecca and looked horrified.

She gave Angie a final tender kiss on the lips and they both checked their reflections in the mirrors before leaving.

The door shut behind them and the toilet was quiet again.

This seemed like a good time for the phone girl to leave her cubicle after waiting red-faced in silence for the two ladies to finish and leave.

Angie and Rebecca were sitting back down in front of the presenter again. He didn't want to get too annoyed because the lawyer lady scared him and he wanted to get into the pants of the porn star.

"Okay, we are on the air in five seconds!" He counted down with his fingers and pointed to the ladies on zero.

"So, ladies, where do you go from here?" he said eyeing Angie's cleavage.

"Well, I'm going home with Rebecca. We're going to take out her video camera and film me fucking her with a strap-on dildo!" Angie smiled sweetly at Freddy and then at Rebecca, who was grinning through smeared lipstick.

Freddie felt a mixture of rejection and frustration.

"Why does everyone have to swear on my fucking show?" he shouted.

Both ladies looked at him as if he was a naughty schoolboy.

"I need a smoke!" he said as he started up some music quickly.

The studio phone lit up, the indicator signified that it was from the station manager.

"Oh, shit!"

Car Bomb

Maggie Kinsella

Nell waits in her car outside Alex's workplace. Past seven on a Dublin winter night and Nell's car is one of only a few in the car park. The rain streams down the windscreen and she flicks the wipers. It makes no difference; there's nothing to see except blurred waterlogged shapes.

She's been here twenty minutes, and there's no sign of her lover. Nell peers through the downpour up to the third-floor window, where a cocoon of light makes a weak attempt to push back the darkness. They never turn the bloody lights off. Alex could have left already, except Nell knows she'll still be sitting there, hunched over her computer, absorbed by the formulas on her screen. No doubt, she's already forgotten she asked Nell to collect her. Nell curses the flat battery on the mobile phone which means she can't call her, and double curses the security at Alex's workplace. When Dervla the receptionist goes home at 5:30, picking up her bag and scurrying out for a reviving drink in Maguire's, there's no chance of walking in. Not without a staff card, security clearance, and knowledge of the door code. No, Nell simply has to wait, willing Alex to unwind her brain for long enough to remember the time, look out of the window and see the Peugeot squatting there in the rain.

Nell sighs and squirms against the door. She tries not to think of the casserole sitting on the bench in their tiny galley kitchen – it needs an hour and a half in a slow oven to make the cheap cut edible. She tries not to think of her own computer screen, still powered on, and filled with the words that were only starting to flow when she realized the time and raced out the door. She hopes the rain doesn't turn to a thunderstorm. Now is not a good time to remember she never replaced the broken surge protector. Nell closes her eyes and tries to recapture the mood that had the words tumbling out to fill the screen. It was hard enough to get excited about advertising copy for porridge oats; now the elusive words flicker and dance out of reach, spinning away like the raindrops down her windscreen.

The glowing clock on the dash tells her it's now seven-thirty. Thirty minutes of wasted time, when she could be home in their flat, surrounded by cooking warmth and written words. Her fingers drum on the steering wheel as she leans forward to peer through narrowed eyes up to Alex's office.

Goddammit! Why can't she remember for once? Nell's lips crunch to a thin, white line. It's not as if her job as a research scientist is that important; it's only numbers and Petri dishes and damn bacteria. Suddenly determined, she rummages around in the glove box. She'll leave a note for Alex under the wiper and go down to Maguire's for a pint. Maybe Dervla will still be there and they can natter over a couple of jars. And Alex can damn well wait for her for a change! But as her fingers close on a pen, the downpour intensifies and rain and hail lash the roof.

Nell drops the pen and closes her eyes in resignation. She'd drown before she got more than a dozen steps from the car. She'd be sitting in Maguire's steaming in front of the fire – assuming they'd even lit one on a quiet Wednesday night. No, she's stuck here, waiting for Alex to remember that patient old Nell is waiting outside.

Seven forty. Nell finds a crumpled parking ticket – unpaid, she notices with a guilty start, and more than two months overdue. Gripping the pen, she twists to rest the ticket on the dash and capture those magical words about porridge oats; words that will make the product leap off the supermarket shelves into shoppers' trolleys, and make her boss send more work her way. But the words have slid out of her head, out through the ventilation and down the wet cobbled street, down to the Liffey and out to the Irish Sea.

Bitterness rises, seeping thick and black into her chest. She's a supportive partner, always there for Alex, understanding when she disappears after dinner to read a research paper before bed. Uncomplaining when Alex's gaze morphs to an unfocussed stare, and Nell has to repeat everything three times. Alex is undeniably brilliant, but that doesn't excuse her selfishness. Nell's fist crashes down on the dash, and the radio announcer stops in mid sentence. The last thing she needs; now she'll have to dismantle the dash to fix it. Her simmering discontent boils over in a froth of white rage.

Well, feck Alex and feck the rain. She'll go to Maguire's even if she crawls in as sodden as a mop head. Grabbing her purse and keys, she scrambles out into the night, and the rain instantly slicks her hair to her forehead. Locking the car, she stomps off in the direction of Maguire's.

After ten paces, she hears a shout over the rage clattering in her head, over the pounding of rain.

"Hey, Nell! Wait!"

She turns, and Alex is running toward her. Her dark curls bounce in disordered array, raindrops clinging to their wiry tumble.

Alex pants to a stop in front of her. "Sorry, sorry," she says. "I forgot the time, and I had to let the computer finish generating the report. I only saw the car when I looked out of the window a minute ago. Why didn't you call me?"

"Mobile's flat," says Nell shortly. "I'm going to Maguire's."

Alex's face is open, bewildered. "Why? You're drenched! Let's go home . . . I'm starving."

Nell rounds on her, and snarls, "Then I suggest you find a chipper. There's no dinner, and I'm sick, sick, of waiting around until you deign to remember I'm here." Her voice rises, spills over in a tirade of wounded, forgotten misery.

A woman scuttles past, huddled under an umbrella, and eyes her apprehensively. Alex darts her a sideways glance and grabs Nell's arm, steering her back to the car. "If you want to fight with me, fine, but do it in the car, not the street."

Nell grunts and shakes her hand off, but stalks back to the car. Wounded pride, affront, and anger simmer in the moist air.

Inside the car the words lash like tentacles. "Forty feckin' minutes I was waiting. Inconsiderate doesn't even begin to describe it! You don't need a lover; you need a chauffeur, a cook, a cleaner—"

"I already apologized! For feck's sake, Nell, do I have to grovel? And that's why we have a mobile phone, so we can call each other! It's not just a pretty paperweight to cart around."

"Oh, so I'm now responsible for charging it, as well as everything else around here? I might as well be your slave for all you notice me!" Alex's face spurs her on; it's bewildered but an edge of irritation shows around her eyes. "When was the last time you did anything for me?"

"Stop playing the martyr. You know it's not like that."

"Well, it feels like that!" She goes to jerk the ignition, but Alex's hand on her leg stops her.

"I'm sorry," she says, quietly. "I should have noticed the time."

Nell stares stonily ahead. "It's not the first time."

"No, it's not." Alex hesitates, and her palm smoothes over the inner seam of Nell's jeans. "I am so lucky," she says. "To have you in my life."

The heat of Alex's hand warms her through the rain-sodden denim. "Fine words," she says. "They're easy, aren't they? Words. You string them on a page, one after the other. You must think that. Words aren't as important as what you do."

"Is that what you think?"

"Isn't it true?"

"No." The word is low and forceful, and Alex's fingers bite into Nell's thigh. "You do wonderful things. You make words fly off the page and into my head. You have a gift for that." She laughs. "I'm sure you could even make me want to eat porridge oats."

Nell's surprise tumbles out. "I didn't think you even knew what I was working on."

Alex smiles and her hand rises to cup Nell's cheek. "Of course I know. I hear you talking, even if sometimes I don't always reply. I love you, Nellie."

The edges of bitter, dark anger melt away, dissolving into the evening rain. Nell swallows, and her fingers find Alex's, curling over her hand to clasp them tightly. She leans her face into Alex's palm, and her breath hitches in her chest at the touch. So sweet, so hot.

Alex sees her forgiveness and leans forward seeking her lips. The kiss is intoxicating; a meshing of breath, of lips, of tongues. It escalates, swelling into something that takes Nell away from her sodden clothes, and the cold car. Alex's fingers trail down Nell's cheek, matching the fire her lips are creating.

It's urgent and it's frantic, this kiss, taking Nell back to the earliest days of dating. When they were so consumed by their need for each other that any dark corner, any small time alone, was a chance to caress. She drowns in the kiss, allowing the spark to ignite to flame. It's incandescent, escalating until the desire coiled in her belly streaks lower. Nell's fingers clench in Alex's hair, twining the dark strands around and around her fingers, binding them with silken ropes.

The car is dim, but Nell sees Alex's eyes glittering in the orange glow of the street lamp. Her breathing labours and her heart skitters in her chest.

"Let me show you just how much I love you," Alex says, and her fingers reach purposefully for the snap on Nell's jeans.

Nell bats feebly at those insistent fingers. "Not here," she says, but it's as if the voice is someone else's; it's weak and slides away unheard. She darts an anxious glance out of the car window, but there's nobody there. No one to notice. She and Alex are cocooned in their own world with walls of steamy glass and worn upholstery. It's the two of them, together, as they were meant to be. She lets Alex's fingers snap the buttons loose and delve inside, down between her thighs, down to the moist, dark places.

One part of her mind wonders at herself; making out in a car park, in the orange streetlamp's glow, but that fleeting thought spirals off into the rain as Alex's fingers tread familiar pathways. The hard kernel of hurt and anger transmutes to the aggression of passion. She spreads her thighs as far as the tight jeans allow.

Alex curls a probing finger around, up into Nell's cunt, sliding easily in the slickness, wet like the Dublin night, instantly sodden. A second finger joins the first, and Alex twists so that her thumb rubs steadily on Nell's clit. It's as if there's a thread connecting her pleasure points. Each tender stroke over her clit makes her burningly aware of her nipples peaked against her bra. Her lips tingle with the remembrance of Alex's kisses. Her body pulses with anticipation.

Nell bites her lip, concentrating on the implosion. Alex's done this so often, but each time feels vibrant and new, especially here, away from the comfort zone of their bedroom.

"Are you still mad at me?" Alex's voice penetrates the ripples of impending orgasm.

"No."

"Do you love me?"

"Yes . . ." Nell's back arches, away from the seat, and her fingers curl around the door handle. The rigid plastic bites into her palm.

"Tell me how much."

"I love you, oh, God, Alex . . ."

Alex's fingers thrust, filling her easily and her thumb plays steady rhythms on her clit. Nell bites her lip, concentrating on the way the ripples expand from her cunt to her belly, her belly to her breasts, her breasts on, outward until her whole body is awash with one long paean of pleasure. She closes her eyes and visualizes Alex's fingers, and the journey they are taking.

A car passes down the street and its headlights sweep across her closed eyelids, blinding white.

She shouts as she comes, an involuntary rush of noise, as she clenches down on Alex's fingers. Her tension blows out the window in a wild, white-heat explosion. And after pleasure's peak, the sweetness and mumbles of love and warmth.

When she opens her eyes, Alex is smiling gently and her fingers wipe away moisture from Nell's eyes – tears she didn't remember shedding either in anger or in passion. Deliberately Alex holds her gaze as she licks her fingers clean, tasting salt from different places

Nell draws a shuddering breath and releases her grip on the steering wheel one finger at a time. Her focus shifts to outside her body, to the drumming of the rain on the roof, and clammy denim around her thighs. There's blood in her mouth, coppery hot, where she's bitten her lip. Her thighs relax and she realizes she's been arched over the seat.

Alex watches her with a small smile, but there's a hint of insecurity in the frown creased between her eyes.

The pieces of her life settle around Nell, meshing themselves back together: the words she tries to write, their home, Alex's job, and Alex herself. The roles they play and how they fit together. The important things shine through the clear air between them.

She reaches over and takes Alex's lips in a soft kiss, resting her forehead against her lover's, enjoying the closeness.

"There's no dinner," she says, as her stomach rumbles an accompaniment to her words.

Alex shakes her head, "It doesn't matter. I'm not—"

Nell stops her word with another soft kiss. "Let's get fish and chips and take them down to Dollymount Strand. It'll be quiet there. *Very* quiet. And after we've eaten, I'll show you how much I love you."

Erotic Fantasy

Susan Wallace

She stepped into the dark hotel room with trepidation. The door clicked shut behind her. She could hear her own breathing and feel her heart thundering in her chest.

"Are you here?" she asked in a whisper, voice wavering, revealing her nervousness.

"I've been waiting," came the reply, the older woman's voice husky.

"Can I put the light on?" Amy wiped sweaty palms on her black skirt.

"No!" The reply was stern and immediate.

From the concealing darkness came the sound of movement. Bare feet padded on a thick carpet, coming closer.

Silence returned.

Amy couldn't see anything. There was no light from even the faintest source. She swallowed hard.

The touch of fingertips on her right thigh made her jump. She gasped in surprise and tried to make out the woman she knew was before her, but she was hidden in the darkness.

The fingertips stroked her skin, moving to the damp crotch of her pale panties.

Amy took a deep breath. She shivered involuntarily as her knickers were slowly moved aside. A fingernail moved along her lips from bottom to top, pausing at her hooded clitoris for the merest instant.

A hint of warm breath brushed against her legs. She felt her skirt being raised and a strange kind of helplessness in the darkness.

The finger moved between her lips with a gentle pressure. They held it in their weak, moist grasp and Amy caught her scent rising. The finger pushed deeper. It slid inside and she leant against the door, finding comfort in its solidity.

Her breathing became heavier as the finger began to explore. The blackness of the room increased the sense of its presence, heightened its movements so they became all consuming. The sensations took over. In those moments her vagina was the centre of her existence.

A second finger entered. She inhaled with pleasure and licked her lips. The hairs on her bare arms rose. She tingled. Then the touch of a tongue upon her thigh made her . . .

There was a knock on the lecture room door and Miss Spencer quickly turned over the story she'd been reading at her desk. Wendy walked in without waiting for a reply, displaying her usual confidence, something afforded her partly by the fact she was a mature student of thirty-eight, ten years the senior of Miss Spencer, her tutor.

"Did you like my work?" asked Wendy as she strode over to the desk in a pale blue summer dress, its hem not far below her waist.

Miss Spencer took in the bright and breezy creative writing student, gaze lingering on her shapely legs and the soft bounce of her large breasts, which were unsupported as usual. "It was . . ." She searched for suitable words as she felt herself blush, running a hand through her shoulder length, dark hair.

"Yes?" responded Wendy expectantly as she perched on the corner of the desk, her dress rising slightly.

Miss Spencer noted the wisp of black pubes which were visible and could see that it wasn't just bras that her student didn't wear. She averted her gaze, looking up to see that Wendy had noticed, a wry grin on her dark face, which was framed by tumbling ringlets.

"I haven't finished reading it yet," said the tutor after a pause, wanting to avoid talking about the piece of erotic fiction which had so unbalanced her. There had never been a student who'd written erotica before. It wasn't that she didn't think it had its merit, it was just such a surprise, as was its content.

"What do you think of it so far?" There was a mischievous sparkle in Wendy's brown eyes as she regarded Miss Spencer, catching the scent of her mild arousal as it drifted from beneath her dress, the sight of her tutor looking between her legs having sent a small shiver of delight through her.

"It's well written," conceded Miss Spencer.

"Did it turn you on?" Wendy fixed the other woman with her gaze.

"I hardly think . . ." began Miss Spencer defensively. "Only, there's not really much point writing erotica if it doesn't turn on its readers."

Miss Spencer felt her cheeks flush again. She had to admit the story had made her excited and she could still feel the heat between her legs.

Wendy's grin grew. "I can see from your expression it did have an effect." She slid forward a little on the corner of the desk, her dress riding higher, revealing more, her fleshy lips apparent amidst the dark pubes.

Miss Spencer glanced at them and felt her heat grow.

"Do you like what you see?"

"I . . ." The tutor was at a loss for words.

The door to the lecture room burst open and a knot of students bustled in, barely noticing the two women at the front desk as they playfully jostled, laughed and joked with each other while going to their usual seats.

"I'll speak to you after class," said Wendy, reaching out and squeezing Miss Spencer's left hand with a show of affection, which made the tutor curiously excited. It held a potential, a promise for the future, which she hoped, would bear fruit.

Other students filed into the room, most in their late teens and early twenties. Wendy slipped from the desk and walked to one of the seats at the front of the room. She took out a writing pad and a pen, smiling at Miss Spencer.

After the final stragglers had arrived, Miss Spencer stood before the students and began to talk about the exercise she wanted them to begin during the two-hour class, an autobiographical piece which featured an event that had changed them forever. Once she'd given her instructions Miss Spencer sat back at the front desk and turned her attention to the stories she had yet to mark, well aware which one she'd last been reading. She turned the sheets of paper over and continued to read Wendy's piece of erotic fiction, the heat in her vagina growing once more and her nipples straining against her bra beneath the cream top she was wearing.

When she looked up she saw Wendy looking at her. Miss Spencer's eyes drifted to the view beneath the table. The thirty-eight-year-old student's legs were open, the hem of her dress at her wide hips. Her index finger glistened as it pushed in and out of her vagina.

Miss Spencer could hardly believe what she was seeing and couldn't tear her gaze from the seductive sight. She stared at the rhythmic movements of the finger as it plunged inside and then slid out, its pace and vigour increasing now she was watching.

Wendy savoured the small, discreet audience, kept her eyes open and firmly fixed on her tutor. Her pulse raced as she masturbated for their mutual enjoyment. The orgasm came closer, her finger's movement quickening further.

Miss Spencer could feel the wetness between her legs. She longed to stand, to cross the small distance between her desk and the student before her. The story Wendy had written had stirred her, awoken feelings, given her a desire for fulfilment.

Wendy's dark legs spread wider as two fingers entered and her thumb rubbed at her clitoris. A redness touched her cheeks as her body tensed, her eyes narrowing and mouth slightly open.

Miss Spencer watched as Wendy trembled, knew the wonderful pleasure that was spreading from the epicentre between her legs.

The sound of chair legs scraping on the floor gave Miss Spencer a start. Flustered, she looked towards the back of the room as Robert, one of her less gifted students, rose from his seat.

As Wendy pulled her dress down to cover herself, he walked to the front of the class and placed a single sheet of paper on Miss Spencer's desk, only half a side actually having been written upon.

"I've finished," he announced. "Is it all right if I go now?"

Miss Spencer tried to compose herself. "Erm . . . Well, it's supposed to be typed up and handed in next week, but I suppose, as it's such a short piece, I can make an exception."

Robert trooped out of the room with his rucksack slung over his shoulder. Miss Spencer turned back to Wendy, who raised her fingers to her lips and sucked them with slow deliberation, holding her tutor's gaze meaningfully.

At the end of the class the other students left for their lunch, hurrying from the lecture room. When everyone else had left Wendy slowly approached her tutor. She stood before the petite woman who she lusted after and smiled down at her.

"Would you like to come to mine tomorrow afternoon?"

Miss Spencer stared into her eyes and hesitated.

"Please," added Wendy. "Maybe we can try a little role-reversal."

"Yes," replied Miss Spencer in a whisper, surprising herself with her answer.

"Here's my address." Wendy placed a piece of paper on the desk.

The door opened and Mr Woods, the media lecturer, put his head into the room. "Are you ready for some lunch?" he asked.

Miss Spencer looked into Wendy's eyes and then turned to her colleague, who had been unsuccessfully pursuing her for months. "Okay," she replied, standing and collecting her papers together.

"See you tomorrow," said Wendy as she walked to the door, Mr Woods holding it open so she could exit.

Those three words filled Miss Spencer with excitement as she looked up at her student and smiled before Wendy disappeared from view.

Miss Spencer's heart began to flutter, its pace increasing as she turned onto the street where Wendy lived. Not far now, she thought, feeling incredibly nervous.

Soon she was standing before a blue front door. She stared at the paint and took a deep breath. Beyond it lay the realm of the unknown, of a future yet to take shape. Beyond the door was Wendy.

She smoothed the blue skirt over her slim hips and brushed the collar of her dark coat, flicking back her long, black hair. Her right hand rose slowly and she knocked three times. Stepping back, she took a couple more deep breaths in a futile attempt to calm herself.

A few moments passed and her nervousness increased. Then she heard footsteps from within and the handle turned. Wendy's smiling face greeted her as the door swung open to reveal a long hallway decorated in soft, pastel colours with a fawn carpet and stairs rising to the left.

Wendy's gaze took her in, moved down and then back up her body. Miss Spencer tingled, as if the appreciative look had somehow caressed her.

"Come in." Wendy stepped away from the doorway in her thin and scanty yellow dress.

"Thanks," she responded, walking passed her host, heart rate increasing when she heard the door closing behind her. Now it was too late for second thoughts. The teacher–pupil relationship was soon to change forever, a change that would be for the better.

"Lets go through to the sitting room," said Wendy, indicating a door to the right with an outstretched hand.

Miss Spencer went into the large room. A pale, mauve three piece was placed around the room and there were framed prints of sunsets on the walls.

"Do you want anything to drink?" Wendy asked from behind her, making her tutor jump slightly, her attention having been concentrated on the bookshelf on the opposite side of the room.

"No. I'm fine thank you."

"Did you get to finish reading my story?" Wendy moved past her and then turned to look into her eyes.

"Yes," replied Miss Spencer.

"And?"

"On second thoughts, maybe I will have a drink. Have you got any red wine?" asked the tutor, needing something to bolster her courage.

Wendy smiled and nodded. "I'll go and get us both a glass and then you can tell me what you thought. Make yourself comfortable."

She left the room, Miss Spencer catching the soft scent of her mild, musky perfume. The tutor looked around the room and then sat on the cream coloured settee which was placed before the large front window, sun pouring into the room.

She listened to the chink of glasses that drifted from the kitchen down the hall. There soon followed the sound of a bottle being uncorked and Miss Spencer felt her heartbeat increase as her student's return became imminent.

Wendy breezed into the sitting room with a full glass of wine in each hand. "It's sweet and fruity, like me," she said with a disarming grin as she held one out to her guest, fully aware of Miss Spencer's nervousness.

"Thanks." The younger woman took the offered drink and immediately took a sip, hoping it would calm her down, though she thought it would probably take a few bottles to manage that.

"So, what about my story?" asked Wendy as she sat in the armchair opposite, crossing her smooth legs. She was aroused by the presence of her tutor in her home and by the fact that the two of them were alone and beyond any disturbances.

"Well," began Miss Spencer, taking another sip to wet her dry mouth. "I have to admit it came as a bit of a surprise."

"The fact that it's erotica or that the characters were based on me and you . . . Amy?"

"Both," admitted the tutor, a tingle running down her spine after hearing her first name uttered by Wendy's smooth and rich voice.

"But did you like it? Did you like what our characters did?" She looked at the woman opposite her expectantly.

Amy hesitated. "Yes," she whispered after a moment.

Wendy's smile grew wider. "I'm glad."

There was a moment of silence and then Wendy put her glass down on a low coffee table beside her, stood, and stepped towards the younger woman. With the immediacy of the situation making her nervousness increase dramatically, Amy quickly stood and walked over to the bookshelf on the far side of the room. Trying to appear as natural and nonchalant as possible.

She put her glass down and began to study the spines of the works gathered there, noting the slight trembling of her hands. She ran fingers through her long hair as she tried to think of something to say.

Then Amy heard soft footsteps drawing close. She could feel Wendy move to stand just behind her. The slight pressure of a hand on her right shoulder made her start a little, heart missing a beat.

"Do you see anything you like?" The words were almost a whisper, Wendy's mouth beside her left ear, the hairs on Amy's neck brushed by soft breathing and sending shivers down her spine.

"Well . . ." Amy's fingertips stroked the spines of the books on the third shelf down.

"You're trembling," observed Wendy. "Will this be your first time with another woman?"

The motion of her hand halted immediately.

"Yes." Amy's eyes closed temporarily as breath caressed her neck once more. Then she looked at the books where her fingers had stilled and found that they were all works of erotica.

"Why don't you have a look at one of those books?" The hand resting on her shoulder began to move down her back.

Amy slid one of the volumes from amongst the others. In unsteady hands she held it before her, two entwined woman portrayed on the front cover, their clothes extremely revealing.

"Check out the second piece of fiction," Wendy said at her shoulder, hand at the small of her back, pressing lightly, moving slowly to the top of her firm backside.

With nervous fingers, Amy awkwardly opened the front cover and checked the index. She flicked to the relevant page. "Red Wine, by . . ." Her words trailed off as the sensation of Wendy's lips upon her neck almost made her drop the book. The older woman's hand moved to her backside and groped her buttocks. She sighed, head rolling back as her eyes closed.

Wendy raised her skirt with her right hand. She felt the warm air of the house against her bare legs, followed by the student's touch upon her inner thighs.

Wendy's arms reached round her, hands at the buttons of her navy shirt. Amy felt it loosen as her bra and smooth, pale stomach were revealed.

With a couple of tugs, Wendy pulled the shirt from her gently curved shoulders and started to kiss them. Her hands ran across Amy's belly, traced circles and lines across it, up it, along her sides, moving to her upper chest and the slopes of her breasts, held firmly in a black bra.

Amy dropped the book onto the edge of the bookshelf, her eyes tightly shut. Her hands moved to Wendy's black ringlets, fingers grasping as her pleasure built. She longed to feel her fingers and her tongue inside her. The lust was almost overpowering.

The straps of the bra were slowly slid along her arms and then it fell away. Then the zip of the skirt was pulled down and it dropped to the floor as she slipped off her shoes.

Amy now stood before the bookshelf wearing only a pair of black knickers, damp with her rising excitement. She could smell herself as Wendy's hands grasped her breasts, squeezed hard and then gently. A fingertip then circled each nipple, barely touching the skin, leaving a tingling in their wake, as if charged with electricity.

Her right hand moved from Wendy's hair and she went between the legs. Pushing down on the crotch of the yellow dress, she felt the moisture of the older woman's vagina seep through. Like the previous day, Wendy wasn't wearing any knickers and Amy prickled with pleasure of touching the softness of her hidden lips for the first time. The feeling of another woman's privates was such a sensuous thing and more erotic than she could have imagined.

She turned in Wendy's arms and lifted her face. Their lips pressed together. The older woman's hands stroked down her spine and tucked inside her knickers. Their tongues met and even as Wendy pulled her mouth away from Amy's they continued to wind about each other until the distance grew too great.

Crouching before her, Wendy pulled the panties down her legs and Amy stepped out of them. The tight curls of her dark triangle were in front of the student's face. The scent of Amy's desire was strong as Wendy's hands gripped her buttocks. She ran nails over them and down the outside of her legs. The creative writing tutor shivered and groaned as they ran down to her ankles and then began to rise up the inside.

Leaning forward, Wendy placed her lips just above the dark pubes and kissed the soft skin. Then her tongue ran upward, circled Amy's navel and then descended to run alongside the hair and the top of her inner thighs.

Wendy's fingers stroked the length of the pink, fleshy lips that glistened with moisture. Amy groaned, pushing her crotch towards the other woman with increasing urgency as she felt the climax building. Wendy's index and forefingers held her open. Her thumb began to rub Amy's clitoris with a growing pressure. She licked it and then wiggled her tongue in the hole revealed by the spreading fingers.

Wendy's thumb gently flicked her clitoris as her tongue darted in and out of her. Amy's breathing was heavy as her hands grasped the older woman's head, held her hair. Her mouth was open as the orgasm built. She began to writhe with the pleasure of the attentions and gasped as two fingers entered her.

The thought that this was one of her students added to her sexual excitement. Further adding to her pleasure was the newness of another woman giving her such sweet sensations. She'd always known she had the potential to find fulfilment in this way, but had never had the courage to instigate such a rendezvous. Thankfully Wendy had instigated it for her and she glad the mature student had the confidence to do so.

Wendy's tongue was working a special kind of magic along with her fingers as they pulled out and pushed into Amy. The tutor's muscles were filled with tremors as she tried to remain standing. Her legs threatened to buckle as the orgasm drew ever closer and then suddenly cascaded through her body and mind. Wendy felt the added wetness and saw the tension and then release of Amy's body, slowing the rhythm of her fingers and tongue.

Pulling her head away from Amy, licking the tutor's juices from her lips, Wendy continued to stroke her clitoris. Amy slowly sank to her knees and let out a long, satisfied sigh. Wendy kissed her and she tasted herself.

"Stay right here. There's still a lot I want to teach you," said the mature student with a large grin on her dark face.

Amy simply smiled in response as the afterglow of the orgasm continued to make her body tremble and its warmth remained centred in her vagina.

The older woman left the room and Amy heard her ascend the stairs. There were sounds of movement from above, the floorboards creaking slightly. Then there was a moment of silence before Amy heard her host returning.

Her eyes widened as Wendy walked back into the sitting room. She was naked. The tutor's gaze took in her large breasts, the nipple on the left pierced, the silver bar glinting. Her body was curvaceous, dark skin silky and smooth.

Amy started to rise, wanted to go to the other woman and explore her nakedness.

"No. Stay there." Wendy took her hands from behind her back and Amy saw that she was holding a red silk scarf and a couple of pieces of white cord.

Expectation built within the tutor as her eyes widened and her arousal grew quickly.

Wendy walked to where Amy knelt. "Don't move, just let me guide you," said the older woman, feeling a glorious and sensual freedom as she tingled beneath the other woman's gaze.

She gently took hold of Amy's wrists and tied her hands behind her back. The tutor shuddered with pleasure as Wendy kissed her shoulder blades while fastening the cord.

"Stand," whispered the older woman.

Amy rose unsteadily and stood naked beside the bookshelf, keenly feeling Wendy's eyes upon her, finding a thrill in the simplicity of her nudity for the first time in years. Wendy's closeness and nakedness filled her mind, along with the continuing kisses, now moving down the left side of her body. The older woman's lips kissed each rib in turn, moved to her hip, and then down her leg.

The second cord was tied about her ankles, not tight, but allowing circulation and her legs to part a little. Wendy rose behind her. The mature student touched her buttocks, cupped them in her hands and kneaded them with obvious enjoyment.

Then a finger stroked between their curved sensuality and along the bottom of the tutor's back, sending a shiver down her spine.

Wendy removed her hands and the soft luxury of the cool, silk scarf slid across Amy's pale throat. It rose smoothly over her chin and brushed against her lips. Then it moved over her petite nose and high cheekbones, finally coming to rest over her eyes. The scarf was tied behind her head, knot against her dark hair. She was left without sight, blind to the actions of her new lover.

Wendy moved away from her naked captive, who heard her retrieve something from the bookshelf. The sound of rushing blood roared in Amy's ears as she came up behind her. The older woman's breath settled between her shoulder blades and sent yet another shiver down her spine. She felt her hands move to either side of her head. Then Wendy inserted two spongy earplugs and Amy was left with only the sound of her heart and desperate blood. Every part of her body prickled as she suffered the sensory deprivation. Her skin tingled in expectancy as she waited for Wendy's touch.

One of the student's fingers ran across Amy's glossed lips, which tingled with sensitivity as it then moved across her cheek and traced lines down her neck. Wendy's tongue ran across her back, licked down her spine. It ran over her buttocks, followed their tight curves inward. Then it entered her from behind as the older woman's nails ran delicately over her hips, through her pubes, into the wetness that awaited as a new orgasm beckoned.

Then, suddenly, all physical contact was ended. She could still feel Wendy's closeness, but the tempting touches and kisses were gone. In her world without sight or sound she relied on some primal sense of her presence. It made the hairs on the back of her neck and arms stand on end as she waited for the next caress.

Amy sensed Wendy move in front of her. She exhaled sharply through the silk covering her mouth as hands took hold of her breasts and played with them roughly. Her breathing was heavy as her second orgasm continued to build.

Wendy's hand pushed between her legs, rubbed against her hidden lips, made her hotter than she'd ever been before as she stood bound and blindfolded, without anything but interior sounds and sensations. The mature student's body was pressed to her, the two women's breasts pushed against each other, Amy feeling the initial coldness of the nipple piercing, its touch adding to the pleasure of the moment. Their nakedness, their sensual union, was intensified by the tutor's helplessness. The orgasm drew closer.

Wendy's left hand went to her arse, groped it and pulled her onto her other hand as the older woman's fingers moved inside. Amy could feel every motion of those fingers, however slight. Without her sight or hearing all that was left was the warm body against hers and the writhing, plunging fingers filling her with erotic fire.

The orgasm exploded through her. If Wendy hadn't held her on her feet Amy would have collapsed. She felt weak, every muscle trembling and without energy. The orgasm consumed her. There was nothing else as she sighed and hung limply in her arms.

Wendy moved her fingers with decreasing speed, keeping them inside the tutor, adding gentler motions to enhance the strong echoes of orgasm's flush. They sank to the carpet together and lay there for a few moments, Wendy's hands then reaching behind Amy and undoing the bonds that held hers together.

Amy put her arms around the woman who had now taught her a new dimension in the pleasure her body could bring. They kissed as Wendy pulled the blindfold over and off her head and then took out the earplugs.

"Did you enjoy your first time?" asked the older woman.

"I loved it. You're a great teacher and if that's the way you teach then you can put me down for the entire course." Amy smiled.

"In that case I'll always teach you like this." Wendy paused. "You've taught me a lot as well, you know." A grin spread across her face as she looked at Amy's glowing features.

Wendy rose and stepped over to the bookshelf. She selected one of the books, another collection of erotic stories, and took it from the shelf.

"This has only recently been published," she commented while settling back beside Amy, who undid the bonds about her ankles.

Wendy flicked to a specific page, looked at the younger woman with a mischievous glimmer in her eyes, and then passed her the book. "My writing has come on in leaps and bounds thanks to you, and my confidence in it has grown too." She smiled. "I sent a couple of pieces off and . . ." Wendy nodded towards the open book that Amy was holding.

The creative writing tutor looked down and began to read aloud. " 'Erotic Fantasy' by Wendy Stone." Her eyes widened. ". . . Miss Spencer's heart began to flutter, its pace increasing as she turned onto the street where Wendy lived."

Amy looked at the other woman in surprise.

"I've been fantasizing about what's just happened since I first laid eyes on you," explained Wendy. "It's like the other erotic story I wrote using us as the characters, apart from the fact I always hoped this one would come true."

"I'm glad it did," replied Amy. "And maybe we can make the other story became a reality too."

Wendy nodded. "I'd like that."

"So would I," said Amy, taking Wendy into her arms.

The women kissed, eyes closing as they savoured the sensations of their entwined nakedness, fiction having become truth in the narrative of their lives.

My Room with a View

Janey Maurice

Whoever decided exams should be sat in the summer needs shooting. Being banished to my room in the attic whilst the rest of the family lounged around the house and garden without a care or commitment, made me want to scream. But if I did, no one would hear me. I longed to be splashing in the paddling pool with my kid sisters; I'd even endure sitting with my mother, helping her write her weekly column for the Gazette rather than list the arguments for and against religion in the 21st century for my Sociology paper.

The slightest diversion fascinated me and recently I'd found the most compelling distraction of all. Trying to let some air into my stuffy garret, I'd been leaning out of the roof top window when I found the perfect view of a piece of our neighbour's garden which had previously been totally unexposed. She obviously thought it was private as she lay in the nude trying to get an all-over tan.

This neighbour hadn't really interested me before. If asked to describe her, I'd have found it difficult. She was that sort of age which isn't relevant to an eighteen-year-old: too old to be my friend and too young to be my mother's friend. Her hair was the proverbial mousy brown and her clothes a bit school teacherish, if I was honest. I think we'd probably spoken to each other all of three or four times. Words, such as, "Cold, isn't it?" or "Have they put my newspaper through your door?"

But there was something very appealing about her nakedness. Maybe it was because she didn't know I was seeing her like that. The secretiveness excited me. I'd never seen anyone outside our family without their clothes before and I have to say she looked far better out of hers than in them. She was much slimmer than I'd have thought, almost boy-like. She certainly didn't have what my father would call "child-bearing hips", but that was probably because she didn't have any children. Her tummy was totally flat – even when she wasn't lying down on her sun bed – and her breasts were small but with amazingly long, dark nipples. The first time I'd spotted her, she'd been rubbing sun cream over them and even from my far-off viewpoint, way up in the loft, I'd been fascinated by how they'd seemed to grow as she massaged the cream into her skin.

I felt stirrings in my crotch as I waited eagerly to see what would happen next but nothing did. After about ten minutes she turned over and then she fell asleep. Grumpily, I went back to my books but I couldn't get the image of her nipples out of my mind.

Did I have lesbian tendencies? I asked myself. It wasn't a question I've ever contemplated before. I'd had a crush on Gemma Cotton, a Year 11 girl, when I'd started at the High, but then I'd also fancied several boys, too. And I'd definitely lusted after Leonardo di Caprio in *Titanic*, Kate Winslet leaving me cold. However, from then on the first thing I'd do on entering my room would be to open the window to see if she was lying in the sun. I'd get quite moody if it was an overcast day.

It didn't occur to me that my neighbour might be a lesbian. I'd never seen her with a partner, man or woman, so it was quite a find on the Sunday before my calculus paper when I leaned out the window and saw a female friend sitting on the lawn next to the sun bed. I couldn't hear what they were saying but they were chatting together and occasionally they'd laugh. They were drinking something alcoholic and chilled; I'd seen them emptying an ice tray into a jug of what looked as if it might be Pimms. My neighbour was semi-clad in knickers and a pair of flip-flops. Her friend was wearing a skimpy sundress.

I knew I must revise, so I'd make myself do a page then treat myself to a glimpse at the window. It was after my third page that the calculus completely disappeared from my mind. My neighbour was lying face down on her sun bed and her friend was rubbing sun cream into her back and shoulders. She then picked up each of her feet and massaged it onto her soles and in between each toe, taking such care, as if she'd be sacked from her job if she missed a fraction of skin. Next she worked her way up the calves and thighs. I was willing her to turn my neighbour over because I really wanted to see her rubbing the cream into her tits, when something even more interesting happened.

She pulled her knickers off and I watched her begin to stroke her bum cheeks with the lotion. And then she started kneading the cheeks quite hard by the look of it and I could see my neighbour raising her bum up and then pushing it down as if she was grinding into the cushion. I wished I could see more clearly – it looked as if her friend's fingers were pushing between her bum crack and up into her fanny – but as I leaned as far as I dared out of the window they both got up from the bed and lawn and went indoors.

My whole body was on fire. I pulled my dress off and stared at myself in the mirror to see if I was as flushed as I felt. What I did see was a pair of soaking wet knickers. I put my hand to the sticky material and pressed it to my mound and immediately felt a small shudder. I'd never watched myself have an orgasm before. I slipped my hand inside my soaking pants and felt for my clitoris that was fully engorged and poking through my pubic hair. It felt as big as my neighbour's nipple and, as I rubbed it, I imagined I had her nipple in my fingers. I watched as my face contorted into a strange expression of pain and pleasure.

From that moment onwards I knew I had to have sex with this woman and I spent every waking minute playing out various scenarios in which we would meet up and she'd seduce me. When it did actually happen it wasn't at all as I'd planned and it began with what could only be called a disaster.

I'd had a grotty day at college and an even grottier journey home. I'd narrowly missed my train and when I eventually caught the next one it was full of commuters. I'd had to stand all the way, sandwiched between two pinstripes who obviously hadn't bathed for a week. I was desperate for a wee but couldn't even begin to push my way through the packed corridor to find a vacant loo and at the station the toilets were closed for cleaning. When I got home, I couldn't find my key and no one was there to let me in. Tears of frustration were in my eyes as I went to my neighbour's house and rang her bell. These soon turned to real tears as she didn't answer. Standing there, wondering what to do, I pushed my fist hard against my mound, willing myself not to wet myself.

I could feel the pee start its first warm trickle as I took a step away from the door when she finally opened it. So there we were; our first meeting of any importance, and she was standing looking cross because she'd obviously had to hurriedly put clothes on to come in from the garden to answer the bell. And I was standing facing her on her doorstep with pee gushing all over it. There was nothing I could do to stop myself.

Neither of us spoke till I'd finished and then I started babbling about the train and she smiled and said, "You'd better come in," and there I was dripping onto her hall floor. She made me take my knickers off and then she saw how wet my skirt was so that came off too and then we were in her kitchen with her loading her washing machine and me standing there, thinking, this isn't how I planned it. She got a towel and offered it to me so I could dry myself and I wanted to ask her to do it for me but, of course, I didn't dare. She lent me a pair of her pants and a wrap-around skirt; we had a cup of tea. I heard myself saying my mum should be home by now and then I was back in my attic room, so angry with myself for messing up such a perfect opportunity.

What I didn't know at that point was how turned-on my neighbour had been by the whole situation and how she'd had to force herself to be the responsible adult and not throw my piss-saturated body to the floor and clean it with her tongue. That came later!

Later – much later – she told me how she'd taken my wet knickers from her washing machine and worn them. She'd pressed the damp material against her clit and masturbated, pushing as hard as she could so that she'd filled as much of her vagina with the sodden material as possible. And at the same time I'd been in my room, rubbing myself with my still pissy fingers, totally unaware of what was happening next door.

Two days later I plucked up the courage to go and ring on her bell again. I apologized and said I'd come to collect my clothes. She was fully dressed this time, in the boring clothes I'd seen her wear in the street. Everything seemed very normal. We drank more tea, I told her all about the subjects I was studying. She told me about her job; she worked in a law firm and then I went home – and straight up to my attic window, willing her to come into her garden. She didn't.

Each day, I'd come in from college and go to my window. Every day I was disappointed. It was irritatingly cloudy. I flicked from channel to channel on the TV looking at every weather station, willing heat waves.

I was rewarded on the Thursday. The sun was out and so was my neighbour. She'd pushed the lounger against the wall and was sitting upright, reading. I was so pleased to see her that I didn't mind whether she was clothed or unclothed. I didn't care whether she sun-creamed herself or not. I just needed to feast my eyes on her.

I tried to make out what she was reading but it was impossible. All I could see was the book masking her upper torso, leaving her crotch and legs revealed. She was sitting upright, cross-legged. The windowsill was digging into me but I couldn't bear to leave what felt like my perfectly positioned theatre seat. It was worth the discomfort. As her right hand held the book, her left hand fell to her gusset. One finger moved ever so slightly outside the fabric of her pants, stroking horizontally and then vertically. There was no pattern or rhythm. I ached for some sort of consistency but it was as if the pages she was reading jumped from erotica to the life story of the earthworm – or something as equally unerotic as that! Her hand wavered from titillating herself to gripping the book so tightly as if she feared she'd lose not only her place but also the entire storyline.

It was only later when I'd laid on her silk sheets and described my peeping-Tom habits to her that she admitted she'd been reading a law text book whose words had whirled around her head as she'd tried to concentrate, whilst all the time she'd been thinking of me, standing on her doorstep with piss gushing through my hand-clenched knickers.

So, there she'd been, trying to take in the legalities of business management and her mind kept jumping to me. Her fingers fondled the silky material of her bikini bottoms and I was watching avidly, my own fingers emulating hers inside my own pants. When she put her book down and stood on the lawn, letting her wee stream down her legs, my whole body ached. She weed and rocked as she came and I came, too.

At the weekend, I was walking back from town and she was working in her front garden. She told me later she'd been there all morning looking out for me especially. "You look hot," she said. "Come in and have a glass of orange." Of course, I accepted her invitation without any hesitation. She then asked me out into her back garden where we sat on the lawn. I wondered if it was the patch I'd seen her wet only a couple of days earlier. I couldn't help peeking up to my attic window to see if she'd be able to see my spy hole but it wasn't obvious.

We made loads of meaningless banter when really all we both wanted to do was leap on each other. Eventually, she asked if I'd mind if she took her top off as it was so hot and she loved to do nude sunbathing. She looked so anxious as if she'd hate to offend me. If only she could have read my mind, she'd have known I was begging her to do just that. "You can join me, if you like." So I did just that.

"Oh, you are lucky," she said. "Your body's so young and smooth. Mine feels so old in comparison."

"It looks good to me," I said and she smiled.

"I have to keep it well creamed," she said. "I don't want to shrivel into a prune if I can help it." And I wondered if she'd used those same words to the friend I saw rubbing in the lotion when I'd seen her. I was just going to offer to rub the cream in for her when she asked me if I'd like her to put some on me.

The only person I can remember applying sun cream to my skin was my Mum on family holidays. I'd be in a hurry to get into the sea and reluctantly squirm as she'd dab the stuff at my retreating limbs. This was absolutely nothing like that. I purposefully lay on my back because I wanted to know what it would feel like having a woman touch my breasts. She purposefully left those till last but the waiting was exquisite. Every single part of my body, bar the triangle my thong was covering, had been touched by her fingers, which felt so silky. As she rubbed my upper chest she let her fingertips move lower and lower, tantalizing me. I felt so hot I was surprised her hands and the cream weren't sizzling. All the time she massaged my breasts she avoided the actual nipples, which by now were so erect, I thought they might ejaculate like mini penises. I was silently begging her fingers to close in on them and arched my back so that they almost touched her face. She got the message.

As her lips gave each nipple a gentle kiss a shiver went through my entire body. She then let her tongue run over them and alternated between kisses and wet licks, leaving pauses in between so that when each touch eventually came the pleasure was heightened more and more and more until I came. It was the first time I had ever experienced an orgasm without my pussy being touched.

Goodness knows how I ever managed to pass my exams that summer. If there'd been a paper on lesbian love I'd have got an A*. However, I managed to get good grades in the more mundane subjects of life and I'm off to university in September. Sadly, it's at the other side of the country, so I shall only be able to see my neighbour in the holidays.

I wonder what sort of a view I'll have from the room in my student lodgings. It's the first thing I'll look at when I arrive.

Nina, My Love

Tamara

I was horny the night I met Nina, and that made it easier for me to do what had to be done to interest her. Nina is one of the most desirable women I have ever known. Young, with soft round tits that are delicious to suck, and an ass that drives men and women wild.

The party was in full swing when I first saw her. She was on the arm of a young man – good-looking if you care about that sort of thing. But the look in her eye told me that she was not really interested in him. She was still "in the closet", and going through the motions of being straight. She had the figure for it. She reeked femininity. And the figure-hugging gown, low-cut with a slit up the thigh that showed most of her gorgeous legs, drew stares of appreciation from the men in the room.

I wanted her as soon as I saw her. Ordinarily it would have gone no further. But I had broken up with Melissa a month before and was starved for affection. Bringing pleasure to myself, writhing and moaning under my own touch, was my only release. I needed more. And I was certain that Nina would be willing to share my bed. Don't ask me how I knew. An instinct develops when you are gay and not able to freely express your desires, an aura that is only sensed by another of the same persuasion. I sensed it in Nina.

I made my way across the room until I was a few feet away from her. We made eye contact after a few minutes. It was electric. She smiled at me briefly, her perfect white teeth flashing in a luscious mouth. Then she looked away. I went to the bar, looking over my shoulder at her as I walked away. Her eyes followed me.

I ordered a glass of white wine, took a sip, and turned to lean against the bar in what I hoped was a provocative pose. I have an attractive figure, if not as lovely as Nina's. My low-cut dress showed off my own tits which have drawn the attention of many men. I was hoping at the moment that Nina would find them desirable as well.

I watched as she broke away from her escort and glided across the room. She came up to the bar a few feet away. The smile she had flashed earlier returned as she looked at the bartender.

"Chardonnay," she said in a low sultry voice that sent a stir through my loins.

I picked up my glass and moved over next to her. She glanced at me, turned back to the bartender and took the Chardonnay from him.

"Nice party," I said. Not much of a pickup line, but I needed something to break the ice. Besides I knew she was interested as soon as she came to the bar. And she knew that I was interested as well, I'm certain.

"Yes," she replied. "Are you a friend of Bill's? Or Mary?"

"Both," I said. Bill and Mary were business partners. I knew them both. They were hosting the party for their friends and employees. I was in the former category.

"Do you work for them?" I asked.

She shook her head. "I'm a friend of a friend," she said, nodding toward her escort who was engaged in conversation with a statuesque blonde and hardly aware that Nina had left.

"Men," I said with just enough inflection to give her the idea. The inflection wasn't lost on her.

She made a face. "I can take them or leave them," she said.

I held out my hand. "I'm Tamara," I said.

She took my hand in her own. "Nina." She started to take her hand away, but I squeezed it before releasing my grip. The gesture wasn't lost on her. I felt a slight squeeze of her hand before she took it away.

The wine was taking effect. I felt a warm glow come over me. I leaned over and put my mouth close to Nina's ear.

"Excuse me. I'm going upstairs. Are you interested?"

She searched my face with a trace of a smile on her lips. Then, turning away, she placed her hand on mine. "Give me five minutes."

The promise in her statement sent a wave of warmth through me, and I walked away unsteadily. The anticipation of a round of lovemaking with this desirable creature made me weak.

I found the bedroom at the head of the stairs and left the door ajar. I loosened the top buttons at the back of my dress and sat down on the bed. My heart was beating hard. I felt like I was on my first date. A little lightheaded and burning with desire.

Nina tapped gently on the door, then entered and closed it behind her. She turned the lock, giving me a conspiratorial smile as she did so. I smiled back.

I stood up and crossed over to her. Wordlessly I searched her beautiful face. She licked her lips and lowered her eyes in a silent invitation.

I kissed her, lightly at first, then harder. My tongue caressed her lips and her sharp intake of breath at my touch heightened my desire. She parted her lips allowing my tongue to probe her delicious mouth, then she returned the kiss, pushing her tongue into me.

I encircled her in my arms, and undid the clasp of her gown. Breaking our kiss, she stood back, undid the other clasps and let her gown fall away. The silky bra did little to hide her round firm breasts and the delicious pink nipples. I massaged the nipples with both hands, delighting in her almost inaudible moans of pleasure. Then I took one in my mouth and let my tongue search the nipple and the firm round mound. She let out a muffled scream and drew me to her.

I dropped to my knees and pulled her lacy panties off. The downy patch of hair between her legs made me dizzy with delight. I leaned back to better see the pleasure spot, soft burnished hair that hid her treasure box. How many men had buried themselves in it? I wondered. And how many women like me had tasted it? I buried my face in her womanhood, delighting in the slightly pungent smell of her juices. I found her clit with my tongue and teased it.

Together we made our way to the bed and fell on it. I was on top, kissing her hard with teeth and tongue. She pulled at my dress, finally working it off.

"Stand up," she said.

I did as she asked, shedding my bra and panties. Standing naked in front of her I watched with pleasure as she took in my body, her tongue licking her lips in anticipation and growing desire. She had a hand between her legs, gently working up and down, her eyes bright with lust.

Falling on the bed, I took her in my arms and rubbed my body over hers. I kissed her mouth, her nipples, her stomach. Then I put my mouth on her soft hot womanhood.

I drank the juices from deep within her pussy. Her hand

found mine and she pushed hard against my clit. Without removing my mouth from her delicious cunt I moved around until my pussy was on her mouth. She bit it gently, then let her tongue explore the inner lips with a frenzy that sent me to a new height. I probed with my tongue working in and out, thrilling at the feel of her soft wet walls against my tongue.

"God, that's so good," she moaned. "Don't stop."

Her impassioned words, uttered in her sultry indescribably sensuous voice, aroused me to the point of climax. I probed harder, glorying in the feel of her tongue inside me and my mouth covering her pussy.

I pulled away, stood up and looked at her with burning eyes.

"Spread your legs," I said.

She spread her legs slowly, revealing the pink juicy bed of sexual promise. I drank in the sight while my hand sought my clit and I massaged it. Then I covered her pussy with my hand and probed her with two fingers.

"Good," she moaned. "So good. Better than a cock. Oh, yes."

Suddenly her body stiffened and she moaned loudly in the height of arousal. She collapsed in an ecstatic orgasm that that aroused me further. I covered her hand with my own and helped her massage my cunt until I reached the heights and exploded in a glorious cum that made me shudder uncontrollably. My clit was on fire. The freedom of sexual release made me giddy, and I moaned with a pleasure that I hadn't felt in months.

She gave a throaty laugh, laid back on the bed and sighed. I lay next to her, one hand on her thigh, the other behind my head. We shared each other silently for several minutes. The sound of her soft breathing thrilled me. I wanted this to last forever.

Finally I sat up, found my bra and put it on. Nina watched sleepily, her face showing a serenity that made me feel good. I leaned over and kissed her lightly on the lips. She responded with the tip of her tongue. It was a gentle but thrilling touch. Nina knew all the right things to do. I wondered if she had ever shared her incredible sexuality with men as well. I decided to find out.

"Have you ever fucked a man?" I asked.

Her eyes widened at the question and she sat up, her back against the headboard. "Yes. Before I realized how much more pleasurable a woman was. Before I fully realized that I was a lesbian."

"Did you like it?"

She made a face. "I hated it." She sighed and lay down again. "How about you?"

"No. I never had the desire. But I dated a guy in college and he wanted to fuck me in the worst way. He was so horny I was afraid he would rape me. So I sucked him off instead."

She laughed. "How did it taste? His come?"

I made a face. "Not like yours," I said. "Yours is like honey. Oh, God, but you're beautiful." I leaned over and kissed her passionately. She returned my kiss, her hand between my legs. I felt the stirrings of sexual arousal returning and found her cunt with my hand. Her hand worked against my clit, sending me soaring to new heights.

I had never had two climaxes in one session before in my life. It was exquisite. I lay back, exhausted but giddy with satisfaction.

Nina sat up suddenly. "We'd better get back to the party," she said, reaching for her bra. "David will be looking for me."

"Is he the man you fucked?" I asked.

Nina laughed. "No. He's my brother." She put a finger to her mouth. "But don't tell anyone. I have to give the appearance of being straight. My job depends on it." She ran her fingers through her hair. "I am 'eye candy' to the male clientele where I work. They fuck me with their eyes every day. If they knew I was gay – well. I'm good for business as long as I stay in the closet. I hate it. But that's the way it is."

"Does your brother know?"

"Yes. My secret is safe with him." She rose and crossed to the door.

"When can we see each other again?" I asked.

Nina paused with her hand on the doorknob.

I felt a surge of panic in my throat. Had this just been a diversion for Nina? Surely she had enjoyed it as much as I?

"We *will* see each other again, won't we?" I asked, struggling to keep my voice steady.

For an eternity of seconds she said nothing. Then she turned and looked at me with those enchanting brown eyes.

"It's not that simple," she said.

"What do you mean?"

I waited for her to speak, desperately hoping she would tell me she wanted to see me again, to kiss me, fondle me, send me to the moon with her tongue and fingers. She lowered her eyes and played with the top button of her gown.

"This never should have happened," she said.

"I . . ." I started, but she hushed me with a wave of her hand.

"Don't misunderstand me. It was great. In fact it was fantastic. But."

"But?" I repeated. "But what?"

Nina expelled a sigh, came back to the bed and sat down. Her hand worked nervously in her lap.

"Margie," she said. "Margie is my lover."

I recoiled at the word. Nina had a lover? Of course she did. This desirable, beautiful woman had both men and women lusting after her. I had to face that fact. But I never considered that she had a lasting relationship with someone.

"I never cheated on her before," she went on. "And I don't want to hurt her."

"What about me?" I said. "You're hurting me."

She placed a sympathetic hand on my thigh. "I'm sorry. But you must understand. It's not your fault. I never should have come up here. But you brought out the adventurous side of me. When you first looked at me you sent chills down my spine. I knew you wanted me, and I couldn't help wanting you. I got reckless. I guess it's no different from a straight man or woman having an affair. But I can't continue."

I watched in growing despair as she crossed to the door and stepped out into the hall. She turned, blew me a kiss and shut the door.

Nina. Sweet Nina. I dreamt about her, made passionate love to her in my dreams. I drank her sexual juices, probed her with my tongue and fingers, kissed her with a passion I could never describe.

Waking hours were different. I spent a few evenings a week in a gay bar, occasionally making it with someone. But the experience always left me vaguely unsatisfied. No one could compare to Nina.

I knew I had to get over her, let her go. But I needed help. I needed to do something new. The trouble was, I had no idea what it would be.

Then it happened. I was sitting at the bar in my favourite club, nursing a glass of wine and watching the other patrons with a detached amusement. Two girls, young and beautiful, were sitting in the booth by the bar. From where I sat I could see them both clearly. One girl had her hand on the other girl's thigh and was stroking it gently as they talked. They kissed, a gentle friendly kiss. Then one of the girls looked at me, leaned over and whispered in the other girl's ear. They both giggled. The first girl slid out of the booth and came over to me. Sitting on the stool next to mine, she drew a line on the polished surface of the bar.

"Interested in a threesome?" She said finally. She smiled coyly, her eyes searching mine.

I was surprised at the question, and my first reaction was to send her away. But the look in her eye, the curve of her tits and the promise of young tender flesh – two bodies – was intriguing. I had never had multiple partners. I had seen films, watched them with more than a little interest. But the opportunity had never presented itself. It had been weeks since my last bit of lovemaking, an unsatisfying experience that left me depressed for several days.

"You and your friend?" I asked, nodding toward the booth.

"Yes." She smiled. "I'm Beth." She nodded to her friend. "That's Mary Ann."

"Tamara," I said. I slid off the stool. "It sounds like fun."

"Good," Beth said. She led me to the booth, introduced me to Mary Ann, and invited me to sit down.

"My pussy is throbbing just thinking about it," Mary Ann said.

Beth reached over and put her hand between Mary Ann's leg. "I can feel it," she said. "Let's get out of here."

We drove to Beth's house a few miles away from the bar. Getting out of the car, I grew hot with anticipation of a new experience, and viewed Beth's firm young ass with a growing lust. Mary Ann had tits that filled her flimsy blouse to over-flowing. I wanted to take them in my mouth. Juices were flowing from my pussy as we went inside and into the bed-room.

Beth had Mary Ann and me sit on the bed while she slowly stripped. She was even more beautiful than I realized. She ran her hand down over her firm nipples and between her legs. She threw her head back and licked her lips as she stroked her clit. Mary Ann stood up and went over to Beth, falling on her knees and burying her head in Beth's pussy. Beth tugged at Mary Ann's blouse until it came free and dropped to the floor. Looking at me, she laughed through her gasps of pleasure.

"Take off your clothes. Get over here and play with us."

I quickly stripped and joined them. Beth put her arms around my neck and pulled me to her. Her hot sweet mouth covered mine and together we fell to the floor. Mary Ann fell on top of us, her tits tickling my face. I took a nipple in my mouth and ran my tongue over it. I felt a hand on my cunt, a finger inside, and I sucked harder.

While I kissed Beth, Mary Ann licked my clit with a soft hot tongue. Beth was squeezing Mary Ann's nipple while her tongue searched my mouth like a miniature cock. I thrust my hips up and down, meeting Mary Ann's probing tongue.

Mary Ann stood up, spread her legs over my head and stroked her clit, her breathing becoming heavier and louder.

"Ooh," she moaned. "I'm going to come." She sat on me, her hot cunt over my mouth. "Fuck me with your tongue, Tamara. Make me come."

I flicked my tongue over her clit while Beth sucked my nipples. Her hand found my pussy and she thrust a finger inside, back and forth until I felt the exquisite sensation of rising passion.

Mary Ann moaned loudly, exploded in a rush of sexual release, and collapsed on the floor next to me. Beth was now lying on top of me, her hot mouth on mine, her hand stroking my clit with a growing frenzy. I found her pussy with my hand and fucked it with two fingers.

We came together, Beth writhing in ecstasy as I felt my own pussy grow wetter and hotter. Mary Ann, having recovered from her climax, put her mouth on my pussy and drank the juice. I writhed with delight at the feel of her tongue.

The three of us lay together one the floor, silent and satisfied. After several minutes, Beth sat up and brushed the hair from her eyes.

"First time?" she asked me.

"Yes."

"Did you enjoy yourself?"

I nodded.

"Next week?" she asked.

I didn't say anything. As pleasing as it was, it wasn't what I was looking for. I wanted a mate. Like Nina. My envy of Margie engulfed me in a rush and I stood up.

"I don't know," I said.

Beth came over to me and took me in a hug, her hips pressing against me, her mouth close to mine.

"Next time we'll make it a foursome."

"Are you serious?" I said.

"There's a hot number I've had my eye on for a couple of weeks now," Beth said. "I want her. Bad. But I'm afraid she'd turn me down. Maybe she'd be agreeable to a group session." She smiled naughtily. "You were."

I thought for a few minutes. I had to admit that I had been more than happy with Beth and Mary Ann. And anything was worth a try.

"OK," I said. "I'll be here."

"Good," Beth said. "Three o'clock. Right here."

By Saturday I was regretting my decision. Group sex was fun, yes. But I wanted a relationship, and if it couldn't be with Nina it would have to be with someone else.

Unfortunately, I didn't have Beth's phone number and couldn't call her to cancel. I would go through with it. But after that . . .

Beth and Mary Ann were already at the house when I arrived. Beth, dressed in the briefest of bra and panties, was already flushed with excitement. Mary Ann had on a filmy negligee with nothing underneath. Her nipples and brown pubic hair were visible. I felt myself getting wet with anticipation.

I looked around the room. "Where's the fourth?"

Beth shrugged. "She'll be along. Why don't you slip out of those clothes?" She smiled at me, put her hand under her panties and rubbed herself, her eyes rolling back in sexual arousal.

I slipped off my blouse and skirt. Kicking off my shoes, I sat on the bed, unsnapped my bra and leaned back. Mary Ann watched with growing desire, crossed over and kissed me hard on the mouth, her hand stroking my nipple. Pulling away she sat next to me on the bed.

"That will have to do until we're all here," she said.

As if on cue the doorbell rang. Beth opened it. Squinting into the bright light, I could only see the silhouette of the woman. Shapely, with a full head of hair, and tall. From what I could see, I was pleased.

She stepped into the room and shut the door behind her. She turned to face us, a bright smile on a beautiful face. I took a sharp breath when I saw her.

Nina!

"Hello," she said, looking at me hungrily. "What a pleasant surprise."

Beth looked from her to me and back again. "Do you two know each other?"

"Yes," Nina said with amusement in her voice. "We know each other quite well."

She walked over and kissed me on the mouth, running her tongue over my lips.

"I've missed that," she said, kissing me again. I returned the kiss fervently, reaching up under her short skirt to find her delicious cunt, hot and moist through her thin panties. Beth and Mary Ann watched in fascination.

"I wanted to do that ever since the last time we made love," she said.

"What about Margie?" I asked.

Nina gave a harsh laugh. "She's history," she said. "I came home early and found her in bed – with a man." She laughed again. "I know I cheated on her, but that was more than I can handle." She looked from me to the others. "Can you imagine? Fucking a man? Just thinking about having that hard cock in my pussy makes me sick."

"Oh, God, Nina, I'm sorry," I said. Then quickly, I added, "No. I'm not sorry. It means you're free."

"Yes," she said. She slipped out of her dress and undid her bra. Her fantastic tits beckoned to me. Completely unaware that Beth and Mary Jane were watching, I dropped to my knees and took her in my mouth. She moaned, grabbed my hair and pulled it.

"Yes, Tamara. Oh, yes. Go down on me. Fuck me with your tongue."

I pulled at her panties, found her clit and licked it hard. Suddenly I felt a hand on my cunt. Beth.

Mary Ann, hot beyond words, joined us on the bed, kissing and fondling Beth while Nina put her fingers in Mary Ann's throbbing pussy.

Beth and Mary Jane soon found one another and fell to the floor in a frenzied embrace, their mouths and tongues intermingling while they thrust against each other in growing ec- stasy. Nina and I fondled each other as we watched. Then, aroused by their lovemaking and desiring each other so much it was almost unbearable, we lay on the bed in each others arms.

Nina was everything I remembered. Soft. Sweet. Hot with lust. We thrilled to each others touch, kissed and fucked with a passion I had not felt since the last time we were together. There was no one like Nina.

The rolling, passionate love play left us all weak with pleasure and sexual satisfaction. Beth and Jane lay on the floor, drowsy and smiling. Nina rose and stood in front of me. I stood up. Taking her in my arms, I turned her around until her back was against me. I stroked her softly, neck, breasts, stomach and pussy. She moaned with pleasure.

"Nina. Now that we have found each other again, let's be lovers."

"Yes," she said. She turned and kissed me hard, her moist lips, soft warm tongue and sweet breath sending me to a new height. I was drunk with happiness.

"Let's go home," she said.

"Your place, or mine?" I asked.

"Ours," she replied, linking her arm into mine

Saying goodbye to Beth and Mary Jane, we left the house together.

A Feast of Cousins

Beth Bernobich

Consanguinity was Cousin Tessa's new favorite word. The one she whispered to me last week, when we made sticky, bone-crunching love in her bedroom. Tess collected words like pennies, snatching them up from wherever, setting them sideways and spinning them around, before she lost interest and tossed them aside for a newer, shinier word. She did the same with lovers.

Okay, that's not fair. But as Aunt Louisa would say, it's true.

Back to *consanguinity*. Of course Tess knew what it meant. Family. The thicker-than-water blood. She had a point, I guess, because our family does stick close. Thanksgiving. Easter. Baby showers. (Even the Our Lady of Polenta Feast, as my brother Eugene says.) Two things I know. That we're always celebrating something, and Great-Aunt Gabriella is always cooking an enormous family dinner.

"Christmas Eve, my favorite," Uncle Teo said to me, pouring out the white wine. "Come, I hope you're hungry, Maura."

I smiled and took the glass he offered, looked around for a seat. Christmas, and Christmas Eve, meant a stuffed and over-heated dining room, long loud conversations that unraveled and rewove themselves, and a gorgeous soup of smells – cinnamon and baked apples, tangy pine and crushed peppermint. And tonight, the fresh baked haddock and breaded flounder, shrimp with hot sauce, and more. Always more.

Spotting an empty chair, I squeezed in between my brother Eugene and my cousin Donny. Uncle Sal was passing around the dishes of noodles and anchovies. Across the table, Aunt Delores and Aunt Louisa bent close, plunged into talk about their kids, while Great-Uncle Umberto argued politics with my father. It was like fireworks and cannons, the noise, but some-how we all managed to keep talking and eating, eating and talking.

Eugene snagged a handful of shrimp and popped them into his mouth. "Hey, sis."

"Hey, yourself."

A shriek directly behind my chair made me jump. "Antonio!" My cousin Lia scooped up my nephew Antonio and deftly removed the fork from his grubby hands. "You nutty kid. You might stab someone with that."

Little Antonio screamed happily and squeezed his aunt, who carried him back to the kids' table, singing a nonsense song. I thought she hadn't seen me, but she gave me a passing wave before turning her attention back to Antonio.

Good, capable, dutiful Cousin Lia. None of the kids were hers, but she always ended up watching over the children at these things. Just as Aunt Juliette helped in the kitchen. Just as Uncle Sal always vidded the whole evening. Tradition, Sal called it. Like a thick knitted muffler that kept you warm, and sometimes made it hard to breathe.

And here came Sal, with a tiny new vidcorder in his meaty fist, swooping in between the tables. "Formaggio," he cried. "Say cheese, Antonio. Oh my god, the kid's gonna burp anchovies. Hey, Teo, did I tell you how these new vidcorders pick up smells, too?"

". . . he's shipping out next week, Delores . . ."

". . . hear about Pauly and Anita getting back together . . ."

". . . have some more noodles . . ."

". . . I think I'll have some salad . . ."

". . . no more room on the table . . ."

". . . always more room . . ."

More wine appeared in my glass, even though I didn't ask for it. Cousin Donny winked at me. "Cheers, cuz."

His face was sweatier than usual, and his muskrat aftershave made me gag when he leaned too close. I mumbled a hello-and-thanks and turned to Eugene. "So, how's the new job?"

"Good enough. What about you?"

I shrugged. "Same as usual. Hey, do you know if Tess will show up tonight?"

Before my brother could answer, Donny leaned in. "Yeah, she's coming tonight. She emailed Grandma about half an hour ago to say she'd be late. At least, I think she did. I was kinda busy."

He leered at me, and I shifted my chair a couple inches back and away. That's when I noticed the mesh glove on Donny's left hand. "What the hell is that?"

Another leer. "Early Christmas present. Watch."

He wriggled his fingers, and a funny look came over his face. Good god, I thought yanking my gaze away. I'd heard about those things, advertised on lurid X-rated websites. Cousin Donny hadn't changed since we were eight and he tried to catch me naked in my bath on his camera-phone. Only now he'd figured out how to jerk off in public and not get arrested.

A loud popping noise caught everyone's attention. "Umberto!" came a cry from the kitchen. The next minute, my Great-Aunt Gabriella staggered through the doorway, wreathed in clouds of acrid smoke. "System crash!" she wailed.

I sighed. Last month, Great-Uncle Umberto had replaced all the kitchen appliances with the latest stainless steel AI models. Everything had sensors and links and touchpads and programmable features. It was all supposed to making cooking easier, but it turned out that the new AIs had a few bugs.

Cousin Nicci wiped her mouth with a napkin and slid from her seat. "No problem, Aunty. I know how to jig the system."

Nicci, Gabriella, and Juliette vanished into the kitchen. The roar of conversation swelled up in their wake.

"Good thing Nicci knows her hardware," Donny said. He was busy stuffing his face, using only one hand.

"Not like some," Eugene said with a grin.

Donny had just opened his mouth to toss back an insult when the front door banged open. Tessa ran through, laughing and chattering, and exclaiming how cold it was outside. Her cheeks were ruddy, her black eyes bright with mischief. Dark hair tumbled from underneath her knitted cap, which sparkled with miniature Christmas lights. Oh, yes. Already my mood got better. I lifted my hand to wave, when I saw Cousin Lucia.

Lovely Lucia, who wore a bright red cashmere dress that barely covered her thighs. Uncle Teo called her the family angel, but seeing her slip an arm around Tessa's waist, I thought she looked more like an imp.

Not fair. Not even really true.

"What's the word, Tess?" someone called out.

"Serendipitous!" Tess replied with a laugh.

I closed my eyes, feeling sick. Oh yes. I could just imagine how Tess picked *that* particular word. Next to me, Eugene muttered something about some cousins being idiots, but I ignored him. He knew about me and Tess. Everyone did. But the last thing I wanted right now was pity.

One good thing about family dinners: you eat. And if you eat, no one bothers you. So I loaded up my plate with the baked flounder and noodles with cheese and spinach bread, and with my aunts and uncles and cousins and parents all chattering over and around me, I ate. But all that time, I could see Tess and Lucia flirting with each other, bumping shoulders and giggling and who knows what else.

Just like Tess and me at Thanksgiving. Or my parents' anniversary celebration last week. Or . . .

. . . or that lovely luscious first time. Through a bright haze of tears, I could see the images, like ghosts over today's feast.

Tess giving me secretive smiles all through the Labor Day picnic. Tess cornering me in the second-floor guest room, after Aunt Juliette's birthday party, where I went to fetch my jacket. Hey, she whispered. Don't leave yet. I have a present for you, too. And before I knew it, we were wrapped up in each other, Tess giving me nibble-kisses over my cheeks and lips and throat, until my knees turned into water and we both fell over into a pile of leather and wool coats . . .

"Presents!" called out Uncle Teo. "Time for the gift exchange!"

Shrieking even louder, the littler cousins thundered into the living room. My mother and Aunt Juliette and Lia stayed behind to clear the tables, while Uncle Teo took charge of handing out gaudily wrapped packages, some of them smothered in ribbons, and Aunt Delores trailed after him, picking up discarded wrapping paper, and writing down who gave what.

Nothing ever changed, I thought, rubbing my forehead, which ached from the heat and the noise. Cousins yelling and laughing. Cousins drinking too much. Cousins pretending that tonight was the best night of the year. Part of me wanted to see where Tess and Lucia had gone. Part of me knew better.

A whiff of roses wafted past, sweet and soft. "Hey," murmured a voice in my ear.

Cousin Lia knelt beside me, a tumbler of water in one hand. "You look like you could use some aspirin," she said.

I shook my head. A mistake, because my headache-addled stomach gave a lurch. Without saying anything, Lia wrapped my hands around the tumbler. For a moment, our hands made layers, mine cold, her warm and soft and strong.

"You filled up my hands," I said, stupidly.

"So open up." She popped two aspirin deftly into my mouth. "Now drink the whole glass full. Want some coffee, too?"

"No, thanks."

When I finished off the water, she took the glass, but lingered a few moments. She wore her dark brown hair coiled around her head, but a few strands had worked loose – tugged free by the irrepressible Antonio, no doubt. Lia tucked one curl behind her ear. "So. Any good presents?" she asked me.

I shrugged. "A couple. The usual."

Lia gave me a crooked smile. "Nothing ever changes. Sometimes that's a good thing. Sometimes . . ."

"Yeah," I said, standing up. This time, my stomach didn't protest the sudden movement. "Well, I think I'll go home."

She said nothing more, but when I came back with my coat, I found all my presents neatly packaged into one, easy-to-carry bag. Lia herself had vanished.

Soft brown shadows, threaded with light. Rippling, as though stirred by a woman's quick breath. Soft lips grazed my cheeks and throat and breasts. The spicy scent, warmed by skin and sweat, filled the air. Maura, Maura, Maura, oh, yes, that's exactly where . . .

I woke late and miserable. A sour taste coated my tongue. That would be from the glass of straight bourbon I drank after I got home. A headache lurked behind my eyes, which felt grainy from the wrong kind of sleep.

No wonder I had such bad dreams.

Remnants of those dreams flickered in and out of recall, along with little flames of warmth that teased me in all the wrong places. I groaned. *Cousins. I'm sick of them.*

And there would be more cousins today. More aunts and uncles and gossip. Great-Aunt Gabrielle and Juliette would have had started cooking at dawn for the Christmas Day feast. There would be gnocchi, of course. And roast turkey. Asparagus drowning in a buttery death. Not to mention Aunt Louisa's fabulous apple pies.

My stomach ached just thinking about all that food. First the Tums, I decided. Then aspirin and warm ginger ale, followed by coffee. Neck and shoulders creaking, I levered myself upright. For a hideous moment, my balance tilted, as though I were navigating the world underwater. No more bourbon, I swore. Especially not after white wine.

A needle-hot shower helped ease the stiffness, and the medicine settled my stomach well enough that I could face the morning. Coffee mug in hand, I shuffled into my living room, where I checked my v-phone, skimming through the voice and text messages left by half a dozen relatives. When I came to the end, I leaned back in my chair and closed my eyes.

You expected a call, didn't you? Idiot.

No, I expected – a good-bye, perhaps.

I sighed and let my face soak in the scent and warmth from my steaming coffee. Maybe, just maybe I could skip Christmas dinner this year. No. Bad idea. Aunt Delores the human vidmachine would never let me forget. Besides, Grandma Rosalie looked awful frail the night before. I didn't want to miss any time with her.

Another mug of coffee. A leftover raisin bagel steamed into life. (Like me, I thought, inhaling the coffee.) I rifled through the bag with my gifts, the one Lia had so thoughtfully packed for me, and started making my own notes for thank-you cards. Three identical gift cards to BooksNBytes. (Those from my brother.) A thermal scarf with solar heating threads woven into the yarn. (That from my Aunt Carlotta.) A mini vid-card with a flash of my youngest niece laughing. A bottle of cheap air freshener from Donny. (Idiot, I thought.) DVDs. Movie tickets. Refrigerator magnets. A bottle of my favourite perfume.

Then, at the bottom, underneath a layer of green tissue paper, I found a square black envelope. Hmmmm. No name. No imprint. How odd.

I sliced the flap open and pulled out a thick rectangular card, glossy and black, with a wafer-thin connector port around the edge. As I tilted the card back and forth, silvery dots coalesced into letters that glided across its surface, only to dissolve as they slipped over the edge.

Je Ne Sais Quoi.

Joyeux Noël.

Choissisez nous pour le ravissement.

I parsed the first message. "*I know not what*" Huh? What was that supposed to mean? Some sort of joke? No, wait. That had to be the name or catchphrase for the . . . the whatever this card was for. And Merry Christmas was obvious. The third one, I had to struggle with, and finally retrieved my dog-eared French dictionary from college.

Choose us for . . .

My throat squeezed shut. That last word meant delight, or ravishment, or seduction. *Tess*, I thought. *Tess* making a very bad joke. What was she thinking? Or was this her idea for a good-bye present?

I flung the card into the wastebasket and went back to my thank-you notes, but my hands shook so badly, I had to rewrite three cards. And typing emails was not an option. Not in our family.

Finally I gave up and pressed both hands against my eyes, listening to my pulse beat a tired tattoo.

I'm lonely.

Of course. It was Christmas. Tess had taken up a new lover. And here I sat, in my tiny apartment, where every metal-framed designer print, every muted colour and expanse of polished wood suddenly felt like an anti-choice. No wonder I felt an odd vertigo going between here and Great-Aunt Gabriella's house crammed with knick-knacks from the 20th century.

Vertigo. Another of Tess's recent favourites.

I sighed again. Another four or five hours, and I would be immersed in that old-fashioned world again. Facing Tess and Lucia. Maybe it was a kind of good-bye present, but there was only one way to find out.

I flipped open my cell and dialed the familiar number. One chime, two, three. Maybe Tess wasn't even home.

"Hello?" said Lucia.

I took a deep breath. "Hey, Lucia. It's Maura. Is Tess awake yet?"

"Um, yeah. Are you mad?"

"Maybe. But that's not why I called."

"Then why – Oh, never mind. Hold on a minute."

A muffled conversation followed between Lucia and Tess. Before I could lose my nerve, the cell changed hands. "Hey," Tess said. She sounded wary.

"Merry Christmas," I said. "Yes, I'm unhappy. No, that's not why I called. This might sound stupid, but did you sneak a gift card into my bag last night?"

There was a moment's puzzled silence, then, "Oh no! I forgot to bring yours. No, God, I . . . I got you a book. I'll bring it tonight. Really. Um, what kind of gift card?"

I clapped a hand over my mouth and shook with silent laughter. Tess. Dear, forgetful, eternally curious Tess. "Something from a place called *Je Ne Sais Quoi*," I told her.

"*Je Ne Sais Quoi?*" Her voice scaled up. "Oh. My. God. Someone loves *you*, Maura. That's the spiff new techno-spa that just opened last month. *Très* expensive. Hey, maybe Donny gave you the card."

I shuddered. "What a horrible thought. Thank you for mentioning that possibility."

"You're welcome," she said brightly. "See you tonight."

Cousins, I thought, as I clicked off the phone. Still shaking my head over Tess, I fished the gift card from the wastebasket. This time, when I tilted it just right, a cell number appeared, shimmering like raindrops against the black surface. So. A treat with no name, and therefore no strings attached. And just for me. Did it really matter who the giver was?

Still not certain, I called the number. Amazingly, they were open, and when I described the card, the woman gave a soft laugh. "Ah, yes. Our Christmas treats are quite popular. You might even come today if you like," she said with a velvety-dark purr. "You will need one hour, no more. We guarantee total relaxation."

Good God, I thought. But curiosity ran all through our family, and one hour gave me plenty of time before Christmas dinner. Better than staying here and feeling sorry for myself.

I brushed my hair, changed into better clothes. Then, armed with directions from MapQuest, I drove to the new Ninth Square project downtown, where a cluster of boutiques and expensive restaurants had appeared during the summer. Parking, usually nonexistent, was no problem today.

And there, between a coffee shop and a chocolatière, I saw a discreet illuminated sign that said *Je Ne Sais Quoi*.

The front door hissed open as I approached. Oh very nice, I thought, noting the fresh orchids in the windows, the chocolate-brown carpets, the tasteful photographs of landscape stills from all over the world. There was no particular scent in the air, just a fresh clean aroma that made my skin prickle with energy.

"Good morning, cousin."

I jumped. Behind the reception desk sat my cousin Lia, dressed in dark blue wool trousers and a darker blue silk shirt, and with her hair pulled back in a shining brown cascade.

"What are you doing here?" I demanded.

She laughed. "Working between semesters. Didn't Aunt Delores tell you? Oh that's right. You left before she started her recital of who did what and when. So what are *you* doing here?"

I hemmed a bit, sounding like Tess. "Um, mystery present."

She grinned. "Those are the best kind. May I have the card please?"

I handed it over. Lia inserted the gift card into a slot on her desk. Her eyes widened slightly. "Here," she slid a clipboard with a pen over the desk, "fill these out while I check the equipment."

Equipment?

But Lia had disappeared through an arched doorway. I skimmed over the form's questions. *Name, address, profession, classical or jazz or other, favourite books . . .*

I jotted down the answers, wondering if I could answer these same questions for Tess. Or if she could do the same for me. Families. We hardly knew each other, in spite of crowding together every week or two. My cousin Lia, for example. At family dinners, she tended kids and acted the good niece. It was easy to forget she went to grad school for microbiology, and was heading for a research job. Then again, we all slid into different skins at those affairs. Me. Lia. Eugene. Even Donny, in his own weird way.

Lia reappeared and took the clipboard from me. "Go through here," she said, pointing to a doorway on my left, "and into dressing room number three. You'll find robes and slippers, if you want them. Remember to put the mesh suit on first if you want the light massage."

Mesh suit? Light massage?

Puzzled, I went through the doorway Lia indicated, and down a short hallway, which ended in a plain octagonal room. Four white doors faced me, all of them closed. The dressing rooms, obviously.

I opened the door labelled "three."

Oh, my.

No wonder Tess had squeaked. Antique prints hung on creamy beige walls, polished wood edged the ceiling and doors, and when I stepped inside, a dusky rose-coloured carpet cushioned my footsteps. But it was definitely a dressing room, with a shower stall, locker, hooks for my clothes, and a padded bench before a table stocked with brushes and combs and other toiletries.

The door swung shut behind me, and a woman's voice said, "If you wish to use the locker, touch the fingerprint pad with your index finger and thumb. This will key the lock for your visit."

The woman's voice sounded low and soft, but with a faint blur that made me think this was a real voice filtered through electronics. They do it with motion detectors, I told myself. And heat sensors. And pre-recorded instructions. Still, my mouth turned dry at the thought of someone observing my movements. I swallowed and touched the keypad.

The locker clicked open. Inside I found a soft cotton robe, which smelled of fresh soap, and the suit Lia mentioned, which turned out to be a full-body leotard made from a stretchy material. There were even fingers and toes and a hood. Curious, I ran my fingers over the silky mesh.

After another glance around, I changed from my clothes into the leotard. It fit me perfectly, and the material clung to my skin as I stretched and twisted, testing its comfort. "When you are ready, please go through the next door and lie down."

I twitched, then scowled. Resisted the urge to make rude signals to the invisible camera. Was that faint laughter, or the ventilation system? Whichever, I ignored it, pulled on a robe and stacked my clothes and purse in the locker. Another touch of my fingers to the lock, and the door clicked shut. At the same moment, the second door swung open on its own.

Motion detectors, I repeated to myself, but my nerves were jumping as I peered into the massage room.

It was empty, except for a long padded bench with a pillow at one end. Stepping inside, I had the sense of floating through an ocean. Floor, ceiling, walls were painted in shades of green, rippling from pale green to streaks of emerald. The bench itself was covered in soft black leather, making an anchor point in that unsettling room.

"Take off your robe and lie down, please."

Again, that contralto voice.

I let the robe drop onto the floor and stretched out face-down on the bench. The leather was softer and warmer than I expected, and had the faintest scent of roses, which I found soothing. No sooner was I comfortable than music started to play from unseen speakers – a slow, contemplative piano piece. Modern, but I couldn't recognize the composer. Between the soft perfume, the lighting, and the music, it would be easy to fall asleep, but I doubted that was the point of this mystery gift. Hopefully the attendant would arrive soon.

Somewhere, an unseen machine whirred into life. A moment later, warmth rippled down the length of my body. Startled, I jerked my head up.

"Hush," said the voice. "This is the light massage."

Still unnerved, I rested my head on the pillow. Now the music changed slightly – a clarinet joined the piano, weaving a counter-melody – and the light dimmed, making the walls look even more watery. Another ripple of warmth circled my legs, merged, then divided to travel down both arms and brush my palms.

A cello sounded a rising arc of notes. The piano answered with a brighter trill, joined by the clarinet's throaty voice, which reminded me of the invisible woman, and lights flickered over me, echoing the path of warmth that touched and teased my skin. Like whisper soft feathers, stroking my body. Like silk-soft hair brushing over my skin.

It shouldn't be this easy, I thought. *That's what happened with Tess. That's why it hurts so much.*

"Are you crying?" said the voice.

"I can't help it," I whispered.

"Then let me help," came the answer.

Tiny electric pulses, counterpoints in sensation, just like the counterpoints of the music, tickled my cheek where it rested against my arms. Tiny kisses nibbled my throat, my fingers. I wanted to protest, to say this was no massage – not alone, watched by a stranger – but my greedy body refused to obey.

The pinpricks came faster now, spiraling outward from my belly toward my breasts and thighs, light stings that sparked a flame in my belly. Fire kisses running from my scalp to my toes, dancing over my skin and drawing my nipples to hard points. Another moment and I would reach a climax.

What if I electrocute myself? I thought hazily.

Soft laughter sounded in my ear. Or was it the music, which had quickened its tempo? Flutes and piccolos trilled brightly, the piano thundered now, and the violins and cellos cried, while the suit flexed and contracted, as though an enormous hand caressed me. Sweet, soft, hard, and sure. This lover's hand knew me. I was sobbing and crying out, beyond caring who watched. Again, and again, the heat flashed over my body. The mesh rippled like fingers from an invisible lover, squeezing my breasts, diving between my legs, and licking me with fire, then plunging into my vagina – though surely that was not possible –

once and twice and more, until that last delicious explosion that left me limp and sprawled on the bench.

And with the tide receding, so too the music and the warmth; the flutes and piccolos danced away, next the violins and cellos, leaving only the piano in a soft slow melody, while the suit clasped me loosely.

I lay there, breathing in the sweat and satisfaction.

"Lovely," I murmured.

"Satisfied?" said the invisible woman.

"Oh yes," I breathed. "Thank you."

"The gift is mine."

She did not speak again. For a while, I did nothing but stare off to one side, until the last few sparkles and ripples of passion faded away. Only then could I coax my body to stand and walk the few steps to the dressing room.

A brisk shower woke me up. I dressed, dried my hair, and returned to the reception area. Lia waited behind the desk, a curious smile on her face.

"Did you like the gift?" she asked.

Still unable to talk, I nodded.

Lia's smile dimpled her cheeks. "You look thirsty. Would you like some water?"

Barely waiting for my nod, she disappeared a moment and returned with a large tumbler of sweet, cool water. Her hands wrapped around mine to steady the glass, reminding me of the night before. This close, I could easily smell her perfume.

. . . the scent of roses. A woman's soft low voice . . .

All the clues shifted into place.

"You," I whispered.

Lia went very still. Her friendly smile had vanished, replaced by a cautious look. "What about me?"

Even so, I noticed she had not removed her hands from mine. "You gave me the gift card, didn't you? You set up this appointment."

A long silence. Her answer, when it came, was like a sigh. "Yes."

"But why?"

Please, not because you felt sorry for me. Please, not that.

A faint blush edged her cheeks. Lia dropped her hands and turned away. "Do I really need to say why?"

A wisp of hair had escaped her hair clips. I set the glass aside and brushed the wisp back into place. Her blush deepened.

"No," I said softly. "You don't need to say why. But were you going to keep this a secret? The gift, I mean."

Her gaze flicked toward me, then to the floor. "Oh. Well. It all depended on you. Before last night . . ." She drew a deep breath. "Before, I didn't think I had a chance. But I wanted to give you something special. Just because."

I laughed shakily. "You certainly did that."

Silence. We were both embarrassed, I guessed. Both unsure what to do next.

"How late are you working tonight?" I asked.

Lia gave me a faint smile. "You were the last appointment."

"The last one, or the only one?"

She laughed and shook her head. Was that a *yes* or *no*? Hardly daring to breathe, I leaned forward to kiss her. A nibble-kiss, just at the edge of her mouth. It didn't matter, her watching me before. This was new. This was, I thought, a little bit scary.

Lia slid her arms around my waist. Kissed me back. Tiny soft kisses that made my pulse flutter. "So," she said, her breath tickling my face. "Are you going to the Christmas dinner?"

Not the question I expected. I drew back, uncertain. "Are you?"

"Of course. Aunt Delores would kill me if I wasn't there to help with the kids." She reached up and cupped my cheek in her warm palm, studied me with bright dark eyes. "But this year, I think I'm going to be very, very late."

Laughing, I pulled her close and kissed her again.

Sexual Healing

Helen Highwater

Tia was abruptly ordered to sit when she entered the shrink's office. Dr Kismet didn't stand up or even greet her; she just looked at her over the top of her glasses and said "Sit down," no "please", not even a welcoming smile. Kismet read the case notes, with the air of someone who did not want to be disturbed. Not even daring to speak, Tia felt like a schoolgirl who had been sent to the headmistress for six full strokes of the cane.

Eventually, Kismet looked up. A petite but confident brunette, elegantly dressed in a gray business suit with a knee-length skirt, she presented a stark, harsh image to Tia. Nevertheless, there was something mesmeric and beautiful about her.

"You were referred to me by Dr Everett," the doctor said at last. "She says here that you are a sex addict. Is that correct?"

"Yes," Tia confirmed.

Kismet stared at her for a long, uncomfortable time. Tia's cheeks burned. It wasn't simply that she was ashamed of her condition; it was the doctor's icy, impassive stare. It seemed rude and invasive, as if she were undressing every aspect of her mind and body and looking at her darkest secrets with a magnifying glass.

"And yet you're only seventeen?" the doctor asked, as if suggesting she were somehow dirty and repugnant.

"Yes," said Tia, lowering her head, both as a gesture of passivity and also with the intention of covering her blushes.

The doctor read on.

"According to this, you have never actually had sexual congress," said the doctor "You're a virgin?"

The question felt more like an insult. Tia nodded shyly.

"I see," said Kismet, continuing to read on "you masturbate. On average seven times a day, according to what you told Dr Everett."

The doctor put her file down neatly on the desk and walked around behind Tia's seat.

"Do you feel dirty and shameful?" she asked.

Tia turned around and opened her mouth to retort. Doctor Kismet told her firmly to face the front and answer yes or no. She answered in the affirmative.

"Yes?" chided the doctor. "Yes what?"

"Excuse me?" Tia queried anxiously, turning in her chair.

"Don't turn around. Yes, I feel . . ." Dr Kismet promted.

"Yes, I feel . . . dirty and – and shameful." Tia managed.

The doctor congratulated her:

"Good!" She said simply. Not "Good! I know how hard that was for you", just an economical (though ambiguous) "Good!"

Tia felt Kismet's hair on her neck, leaning over her from behind.

"Would you like to tell me what you fantasize about?" she asked.

Tia blushed even deeper and lowered her head.

"It's all in Dr Ev—"

The doctor interrupted her coldly.

"Tell me what you fantasize about, during these seven-a-day masturbation sessions of yours," she commanded.

Tia breathed in deeply to calm herself. The hairs on the back of her neck were standing on end and she was beginning to realize that coming here had been a bad idea. The relationship with her counsellor was evidently not going to work.

"I'm sorry, Doctor, I have to go," she said politely, placing her hands on the arms of the chair to raise herself out of it.

"You're not going anywhere," observed Kismet, confidently. "Sit down and answer my question, please."

Tia sat involuntarily. She was taken aback by the word "please". Steadying her nerves, she braced herself to answer the question.

"Facesitting," she answered. She tried to let the word slip out matter-of-factly, as though it were as humdrum as the word "knitting".

She sat facing forward, not daring to turn around. The shrink was silent. Was she even in the room?

Tia's heart raced, but she calmed a little when at last she heard the doctor's footsteps pacing the floor behind her.

"Facesitting?" Kismet mused. "Is that actually a word?"

"On the web search, it is," Tia offered, meekly.

A hand came over her shoulder, holding a copy of the Webster's dictionary.

"And what about in here?"

Tia flicked through.

"No," she muttered at last.

"And what about you, are you a facesittee?" the doctor pressed.

Tia shook her head.

"What is the website called?" Kismet demanded.

"There's a few of them: uh – butt munchers, ass . . ."

"So you're a butt muncher?"

Tia bristled angrily at the intrusive and insulting nature of the question, but her will was already broken and she felt she had to nod anyway. The doctor was close now; she could smell her perfume strongly and hear the scratch of her pen on her notepad.

Dr Kismet returned to her seat and sat daintily upon it. She leaned on her hands upon the desk, staring deep into Tia's eyes. Tia became lost in the deep brown eyes that fixated her so icily. The doctor's expression remained calm, commanding and unchanging until at last she raised an eyebrow.

"When did you first discover that you were a lesbian?" Kismet asked.

Tia had only recently discovered that the sight of a slender ankle, a classical, poised breast, the ball of a beautifully rounded bottom all turned her on. The term lesbian offended her when applied to her own desires; these were visual, sensual images. To appreciate a sculpted sort of feminine grace was not necessarily homosexual. However, she did not appreciate the leering attentions of the guys in high school. Little boys, she would often think. And to crave the attentions of more mature and sophisticated girls and to yearn for them to tie her down with skipping ropes in the change room . . . well, perhaps this was little more than a fantasy. And fantasies can change as time goes by.

"I'm not . . ." she started, but the doctor killed her denial with a sharp look, "I – I started, I guess, a year ago."

She thought for a moment and was about to supply more information when the doctor broke the silence.

"How did it make you feel?" she asked. "Were you sad? Happy?"

This was more how Tia had imagined the counselling to be, and she welcomed the chance to talk. "I was depressed. I still get a little depressed. Sometimes."

"That's not uncommon. Are you scared that other people might find out?"

Tia nodded. "And scared of living a lie. If this isn't just a phase, I mean."

"Again, not uncommon." Kismet reassured her. "You have heard the word used as a schoolyard taunt, no doubt."

"Uh-huh."

"You are nearly a woman, Miss Rodriguez. Your friends have grown up. Do you really think they will treat you that way if you tell them the truth?"

Tia smiled shyly, brightening up. "I'm not ready to tell them, just yet."

The doctor smiled supportively at her. She had gone as far as she needed to with this line of questioning; she stood up and resumed pacing the floor behind Tia.

"So, supposing I were to sit on your face," conjectured Dr Kismet. "Supposing you were to 'munch my butt', so to speak . . . take me through it. What would happen?"

Tia was a little surprised at the sudden reversion of the psychoanalyst to her former coldness. "Well, I really think you're personalizing it." Tia protested.

"Just describe what I would do to you," came the sharp rejoinder.

Tia shivered and tried to recount her fantasy as best she could. "Well, you would drag me by the hair into a small room and lock the door," she said, to the doctor's evident approval, "then you would throw me to the floor at your feet, where you would taunt me for a while . . ."

"Would I bend you over and spank you with a hair brush?" inquired the doctor, interrupting.

Tia was puzzled. She wondered where this line of questioning was leading.

"Wh- uh- no. I never thought about it," she said. "I probably will from now on though, I guess."

"And then . . ." prompted Dr Kismet.

Tia thought for a moment before continuing. "And then," she said, "you would order me to lie down on a table, and bind my hands. Then you would squat over me and gently lower your ass down over my face."

"And you would lick my anus, yes?" asked Kismet very matter-of-factly.

Tia nodded her head in shame. She continued facing forwards and listened to the doctor writing her notes.

"Turn around," Dr Kismet instructed.

Tia turned around and instinctively pushed her chair backwards, on seeing her analyst. The psychiatrist was standing very close to her, with her back turned. Tia followed her calf up to her thigh and on up to her pert buttocks.

"I told you to turn around," said the shrink angrily. "I didn't tell you to move away. Move further forward."

Reluctantly, Tia moved her chair back to where it had been. She felt nervous, yet excited; the hem of Dr Kismet's skirt was practically brushing against her face.

"Now," said Dr Kismet authoritatively, "describe what you find so attractive about my bottom."

Tia stared at it.

"Its . . . its shape . . . so elegant and-and firm, but soft. Like the flesh of a peach."

The doctor turned her upper body so that she could look down on Tia. "Good!" she congratulated, before turning back around and bending over, such that her dark brown hair touched the floor. "And now?"

Tia jerked backwards in her seat, but the doctor reprimanded her sternly. She sat up straight and looked. "It's so perfectly curved," she said. "So powerful, like a thoroughbred race horse."

Dr Kismet stood up and turned to her. "So, at the root of your fantasy, there is something much more childlike and innocent," she suggested kindly. "After all, what little girl doesn't want a pony?"

Tia considered this. Her feelings of shame started to dissipate. She thanked the doctor and stood up, sensing that the appointment was finished. But Dr Kismet had something more to say. She told Tia that she would need to see her again, to check her progress. She explained that this next visit would be quick and that she should come around to her house in the evening, rather than bothering to reserve an appointment with the surgery.

Dr Kismet lived out in the sticks; she owned a big ranch out in the country. Tia was looking forward to meeting her again as she walked up the driveway. Seeing the front door was open, she walked on in. There was a rudimentary reception desk in the entrance hall, manned by a dark-haired older lady. Tia looked down at the upturned hatful of twenty-dollar bills on the desk as she told the lady her name. The lady studied her list and instructed Tia to go through the second door on the left.

As Tia entered the room, the light was switched off and she was grabbed and manhandled in the darkness. When the light came back on, she found she was on her knees, tightly bound and gagged at the back of the room. She heard a voice from over near the door, and although she could not see who it was through the forest of legs, she instantly recognized that it was Dr Kismet.

"Ladies," said Kismet, "welcome. You should all have her likes and dislikes in your brochures, but feel free to use her as you wish. Do not allow your faces to be shown in any of the photographs; I don't want the cops busting down my door in the middle of night, thank you. If you do take any photographs, you should find her address in your brochures; she is deeply ashamed of her filthy desires, so if you threaten to post them up around her neighborhood, I'm sure she will accommodate any desires you may have in order to avoid disclosure. She is a very dirty girl but, should she refuse any reasonable request, write it down . . . she will be dealing with me later. But for now, feast yourselves, ladies. Enjoy."

The ladies turned around one by one to face Tia. They unclipped her ball gag and dragged her onto the psychiatrist's couch. At the head of the mob was a lady whom Tia recognized. She was dressed as a nasty blonde cheerleader.

"All right!" she exclaimed. "Let's get this little slut warmed up."

"Dr Everett!" exclaimed Tia reproachfully.

"So bite me, bitch!" said Dr Everett, nimbly straddling Tia's face and pinning her shoulders down firmly with her knees. "I have needs!"

And then the lights went out.

The Goddess Within

Catherine Lundoff

Kerry looked over the ingredients for the love spell again. Two red candles, check. One sachet of lavender, check. Weird little packet of dried herbs that came with the "Embrace Your Inner Love Goddess" kit that she bought last weekend, check.

She took a deep breath and picked up the directions, part of her not believing that she was even thinking about doing this. But she'd tried everything else: potlucks, singles mixers, blind dates, being friends first. Nothing seemed to work; none of the other women that she met were as beautiful as Lena. Or as funny and smart. But it had been two years now and Lena still just thought of her as one of her best customers at her tea shop/brew pub, the Lavender Steep and Brew. Kerry was getting desperate and that was all there was to it.

She imagined kissing Lena, feeling her warm lips open under her own. She could almost feel Lena's big soft breasts pressed against hers. A trickle of wet warmth touched her thigh and a pleasant ache spread itself below her belly at the thought. Not that there wasn't a lot more to Lena than that, she reminded herself sternly, but today that was all she seemed to be able to think about.

She dragged herself back to reading the directions. Well, skimming them, really. Her eyes were drawn to the new vibrator that she'd picked up at the same store where she got the kit. Maybe she should just take a little of the edge off before she got started. Wouldn't want to give the whole thing too much of a kick, after all.

But the directions in the little pamphlet said, "Be sure and work your magic when your desire is clearest in your mind. This will give your spell extra potency." Well, she needed all the potency she could get, judging by how far she'd gotten with Lena on her own.

So she thought hard about Lena instead and Lena's beautiful, full breasts, while she lit the candles. She closed her eyes and pictured a hardened nipple in her mouth while her hips squirmed against the chair. She opened her eyes and sprinkled the herbs in a circle around the candle, then put the big quartz crystal in the middle for better focus.

She took a deep breath, trying to get in touch with her inner love goddess, the one who would be unleashed when she was done casting the spell. She tried putting the faces of various women onto the mental picture that she had formed, but the goddess kept turning into Lena. Come to think of it, the teashop owner would make a fabulous earth mother type goddess. Kerry gave a rueful smile down at the crystal; she had it bad.

Let's get this done already, she admonished herself. She looked at the chant in the booklet and mumbled the words a bit cautiously: "Holy Aphrodite, help me to be the goddess I know I am. Help me to find and keep love in my life. Let the love in my bosom find its way out to bring my love to me."

The "love in my bosom?" Really? It had to be some kind of mistranslation or a printing error or something. Shouldn't it be "love in my heart" or something like that? That would make more sense, at least to her non-goddessy way of thinking. It certainly didn't seem to be working the way it was written, at least not as far as she could tell. She read it aloud a few more times, sometimes substituting "heart" for "bosom" in case it helped.

But thirty minutes later she was feeling cranky and tired and not a bit like a goddess. Maybe it was her Presbyterian upbringing that made her too strait-laced for this sort of New Age thing. She blew out the candle, ignoring the part in the directions where it said to let it burn itself out in a fireproof container. She swept the herbs into the trash and very nearly sent the crystal with them. But it was too pretty to just toss away so she put it on the bookshelf instead.

Then she washed her hands and went out to go shopping. Sort of. She did manage to buy some groceries before her steps led her past the teashop. She just lingered on the sidewalk outside though instead of going in to drink a half dozen cups of tea like she usually did on Saturdays. The thought of Lena in all of her unattainable glory was too much to bear today. She made herself walk away after one longing glance or two.

By the time she got home, she wasn't feeling very good. In

fact, she could barely keep her eyes open. Maybe her inner goddess was a germ pool. She grimaced at the thought as she took a hot bath. But even that didn't help much. Finally, she gave up and went to bed early.

Once her head hit the pillow, she was out like a light. Her dreams were strange, filled with visions of an ancient temple and dancing acolytes. She even danced with them, at least at first. Then the temple priestesses showed up and started dancing, each movement slow and sensuous and erotic beyond words. At some point in the dance, each priestess embraced a worshipper and Kerry's dream got a lot hotter and wilder.

She thought about joining in and finding comfort and release with a cute priestess on one of the reclining couch-like things that lined the room. But something turned her away to look at the big statue in the middle of the temple instead. It was a goddess, her face serene and powerful. There was something odd about her body, though, and Kerry stepped closer to try and figure out what it was. At that moment, the statue turned and looked at her, stone lips parting in a big smile and a peal of laughter that echoed like thunder through Kerry's head.

The sound rolled her out of that dream and into another. Now she was dancing for Lena and taking her clothes off slowly, just like one of the temple priestesses. First she dropped her skirt, then she started unbuttoning her blouse, her movements slow and sure and sensual. Her shirt dropped away and she went to unfasten her bra, only to find that she wasn't wearing one. Instead her hands felt glorious handfuls of sensitive flesh as she caressed her rib cage.

Clearly it was too much for Lena, at least in her imagination, and she stood up, tugging her own clothes off impatiently. Her beautiful breasts spilled out and Kerry danced up to her to cup them in eager hands and searching mouth. Lena's hands caressed her, moving swift and sure over her body, igniting her nerve endings with every movement.

That was when Kerry glanced down and realized that something had changed. Her small breasts were right where they should be, but they had company. Trailing down her torso and even her back as she glanced around in amazement, were breasts of all sizes and colors. There were breasts with big nipples and breasts with tiny ones. Large and small, perky and droopy, each one sang to Lena's touch until Kerry thought she'd faint.

That was enough to propel her awake, the wet space between

her legs aching for release. She stuck her hand down into her pajamas, manoeuvering around the blanket which seemed to have gotten fuller and downier since the night before. Her restless fingers found her clit and she rubbed hard, dragging the little bundle of nerve endings around in a tiny circle for a moment or two before she found fiercely bucking release.

She lay there gasping, eyes still closed for a moment. Then she pulled her hand from between her legs and stretched her arm out with a big yawn. She shook a little from post-orgasm tremors, the sensation making her smile. And the memory of her dreams made her smile even more.

She opened her eyes and reached over to turn the alarm clock so she could see the time. It was still too early to get up so she decided to lay around for a while longer. But her back ached for some reason. She arched herself up against the bed, trying to stretch out, but it wasn't helping. That was odd. She stretched a slow lazy hand around to reach beneath her and feel the mattress. Her back felt . . . weird, through her pajamas.

Alarmed, she shoved her hand up her top, connected with something soft and sensitive, and yelped as a quick pain filled her. She yanked her hand out and sat up, trembling fingers undoing her buttons. Even sitting up felt strange, like there was more of her body than there should be. Maybe she'd been sleep-eating, she thought hopefully.

The last button opened and her top flopped loose as she stared downward in disbelief. Her torso was covered in breasts, just like in her dream. She got slowly out of bed and walked over to the full-length mirror on the closet door. Her hand fumbled for the switch as she dropped her pajama top to the floor.

They were all still there, cascading from just under her shoulders down to her waist. She turned slowly and they swung gently with her movements. Her back was covered as well: small and large, triangular and conical, nipples tiny and huge. Some were gold-toned, others blue-black, while the rest were in shades of brown and beige and pink.

She touched all the ones she could reach, fingers moving slowly and carefully over them all, her brain spinning in disbelief. How could this have happened to her? She must be still dreaming, that was it. And if she wasn't, she needed help and lots of it.

She stepped up closer to the mirror and examined her face, looking for some sign that she was still asleep. But she looked normal, in a serene goddessy sort of way. She wondered why she looked serene. This was insane. It just wasn't normal to wake up and find out that you'd turned into . . . whatever she had turned into. She reached into the bookcase for a book on women's spirituality that she had left over from a long-ago class. She'd never bothered to open it before but if there was ever a time to learn more about goddesses, this was it.

It took a few minutes until she found what she thought she might be looking for when she ran across the photo. A familiar stone goddess stared back up at her, breasts or something like them adorning her entire torso. She looked at the caption: "Artemis of Ephesus". But wasn't Artemis supposed to be all virginal, at least as far as guys went? There was an echo of laughter from somewhere that faded away as soon as she tried to listen for it. She remembered her dream about the temple and her pussy clenched just a little more.

Still, she forced herself to try and ignore it while she went on skimming the book. But it was no use. It was as if some force greater than herself was taking over her body, humming a siren song of lust and desire that made her bones vibrate. She wanted sex and lots of it.

By the time she flipped the page to the section on the cult of Cybele and her sacred prostitutes, she was ready to take on all worshippers, her thighs slick with wanting. She dropped the book and stared at herself in the mirror. After all, she was beautiful now. She just had to see her new body the right way. She stretched out, hands high over her head and all of her new appendages swayed slowly with her.

The feeling was unbelievable. She lowered her hands and brushed her palms over what seemed like acres of nipples that hardened under her touch. Her desire was manifesting in a small stream down her thighs as she gave her reflection a voluptuous smile. Her fingers pinched a mismatched set of breasts, sending a light pang through her that had her reaching for her vibrator.

It hummed on and she smiled at herself. Of course, she had to be imagining all of this, but why not have fun with it before she had to go back to real life? She ran it on low over a few of her breasts and found herself with hips spread wide and pussy thrust out at her reflection. Her back arched and she ran the vibrator lower and lower until she had it between her thighs.

Then she turned it on high and pressed it to her clit. The first orgasm shot through her and her knees buckled, sending her to the carpet with a muted yell. She grinned at herself as she slipped the vibrator inside her, sending tremors up through every nerve ending she possessed, new and old. She watched her reflection as the next orgasm built inside her and wished for a moment that she'd grown a few extra arms to play with her body. Her new breasts swayed slowly and sensuously with her movements, brushing up against each other until she came again, collapsing on the carpet as her trembling legs gave out.

When she could stand up again, she raised her arms above her head and twisted them in a sinuous snakelike movement. Her hips swung around, rocking like a bellydancer's, even though she'd never learned how to bellydance. She began to dance, feet gliding over the carpet and movements sure and slow and unbearably sexy.

As she drew in a deep breath, she imagined that she could feel the world around her, the other tenants in their apartment building, the animals in the park down the block. All of them were rutting and lusting and humping. The wave of pure desire and sensation swept over her, filling her.

Best to go and find Lena and do what she'd wanted to do since she'd first seen her two years ago. For a moment, she almost turned and walked out the door just as she was. She felt so powerful that she could only imagine that everyone who saw her would simply worship her with whatever celebration of desire they wished. Her mind filled with a picture of city streets filled with naked, writhing bodies, of trees filled with copulating birds and beasts. It was intoxicating.

But some little part of her was jumping up and down to get her attention and turning her toward the closet instead of the door. *You'll get arrested,* said the voice of non-goddessy Kerry. Maybe she had a point. For all that she felt powerful, she wasn't sure that she could do anything more than enjoy sex more than usual and imagine others doing the same. It probably wouldn't cut it with the police.

She stared mournfully at her wardrobe, feeling less powerful by the minute as she wondered what if anything, she owned could possibly cover all of her new body. A bra was out, clearly. She'd never been one for baggy shirts so it took some digging back into the soon-to-be-discarded sections of her clothes to find something that came close to fitting.

As it happened the poet's shirt she found was ample and flowing and silky. She slid it on over her head and let the fabric caress her skin. In a minute, she was wet and aching as if she hadn't already come several times this morning already. She made herself pull out a pair of loose-fitting pants instead of going back to bed. Who knew how long this would last? She'd better go see Lena now before it all faded away.

She gave one last spin in the mirror, checking to see if her breasts were too obvious. Fortunately, they packed together well under the shirt, making her look globular rather than lumpy. She smiled at her reflection and it smiled back, its expression a faint echo of the temple statue's. It would all be all right.

With that thought uppermost in her mind, she swept out of her bedroom, only just remembering to put on shoes and a light jacket. Then the city outside hit her hard, overwhelming her for the first few moments that she stood on her doorstep.

Her mind was filled with the sensation of cold hard brick and stone, the rush of cars, the angry speed of the streets. She forced herself to walk down her steps and place her hand on the skinny tree in front of her apartment building. Then she closed her eyes, trying to find the same sensation of power and connection that she'd experienced in her room.

After a moment, it was back: the rutting desire of a city filled with want and passion. She smiled to herself and began walking down the street, her steps leading her to Lena's. Behind her the tree grew several feet upward, its trunk thickening perceptibly and buds sprouting on its new branches.

Kerry walked on, riding the power that she felt building around her. A man and a woman in a parked car, arguing a moment before she passed by, kissed each other passionately as she looked their way. A group of tough-looking young men across the street made a few catcalls in her direction before beginning to eye each other. Two women walked past her, bodies held carefully just outside of accidental touching range. She felt rather than saw them vanish down an alleyway behind her, mouths and hands frantically scrambling with each other's clothes.

All of it made her feel like dancing down the sidewalk. She touched the trees as she passed, let her feet graze the little grass patches around them. Bushes blossomed and flowers budded in the early spring of her touch. Birds sang mating songs and, above it all, her breasts swayed slowly together, rubbing and caressing until it was all she could do not to pleasure herself on the street.

She settled for swinging her hips just a bit more, tugging her pants upward so they rubbed against her the right way. The seam caught itself between her labia, sending a shockwave through her. It made her feel full and empty all at once. Somehow, she kept walking through the cloud of sensation, her feet unerringly guiding themselves of their own accord toward Lena.

When she finally arrived, she wasn't sure when she got there or how long she stood staring at the door to Lena's apartment. A neighbour going out to walk her dog let her into the building after making eye contact and blushing profusely. So now that she was here, why was she hesitating? She took a deep breath and let the energy of the city fill her as she rang the bell.

Minutes passed and her sense of being both desirable and powerful ebbed slightly as she thought that maybe Lena had gone out. Or perhaps was sleeping in with some girlfriend that she hadn't known about. Or else she just didn't answer the door at the crack of dawn. Kerry pressed the bell again, sending every bit of the molten wave that had carried her here along with it.

The door opened. Lena looked out, a confused expression on her round face. "Hi, Kerry. What are you doing here?"

By way of answer, Kerry slipped her jacket off, dropping it to her feet. She kicked her shoes off and let her feet find the serpentine rhythm they'd held in her room. She swayed seductively, her fingers finding each button in turn on the silky shirt. Through it all, Lena looked first baffled, then stunned and finally something that Kerry couldn't quite read. Clearly she wanted the crazy woman at the door but something made her hesitate.

"Who is it, baby?" The other woman appeared at Lena's side just as Kerry's shirt dropped open, exposing her breasts. "Holy shit," the woman breathed, almost a prayer.

Lena reached out and grabbed Kerry's arm, pulling her inside. The other woman scooped up her jacket and shoes and dropped them on the apartment rug as the door closed. A pang shot through Kerry's entire body as she looked from Lena to the other woman and back again. So Lena had a girlfriend already. She might have known. So much for the love in her bosom finding its way out to bring love to her.

But that was pre-love spell Kerry talking, her uncertainty spinning under in the whirlpool of this new and unbelievably sexy Kerry. That Kerry raised her hands above her head and began to dance, shedding her clothes as she went spinning and twirling through the living room. She could feel the other two women watching and wanting her. She reveled in what she could feel and smell of their desires before she pulled them into the dance with her.

Together the three of them writhed and spun and gyrated to an ancient imagined music. Lena and her girlfriend shed their clothes, their hands somehow always touching Kerry, themselves and each other. Soon their mouths followed and the dancing slowed until Kerry was only twisting slightly as the other women hungrily tasted her skin and sucked on her breasts.

Her own hands were full of Lena's breasts one moment and buried in her girlfriend's soaking wet pussy the next. She threw back her head and gave an earth-shattering moan as Lena's mouth closed over one of her smaller breasts. Her eyes were closed as all three of them sank slowly to the floor, rolling into the softness of the carpet.

Someone was between her legs, hungry mouth searching for, then finding the red-hot nub of her clit. Her pussy stretched itself joyously open to admit an entire hand. She rode it fiercely, her hips rocking up to find their own rhythm with the hand and tongue. More hands and another mouth were exploring her breasts, sucking and biting and stroking and pinching until she came with a shout, body shaken to its core.

Someone straddled her face now, moist slit pressed to her mouth. She raised her head and licked furiously until she found the other woman's clit buried in her soft fur. A cloud of musky scent filled her nose and mouth until it was all she could breathe and she inhaled deeply, pulling it into herself until it etched itself on her memory.

Between her legs, she could feel a finger being worked slowly and carefully up her ass. The hungry mouth hadn't left her clit and those fingers were still there driving themselves in and out of her aching wetness. At the same time, the woman whose clit she was sucking came with a soft howl, thighs shaking around Kerry's ears.

As the other women's bodies pressed into her, sucking and tasting and possessing, Kerry knew what it was to be worshipped. She revelled in the feelings, even casting some of the power she found inside her outward just a little. She could almost feel it flow through the building and out into the city and she knew that while earlier she felt the desire that was already there, now she was creating it on her own. A voice, not her own, murmured something through her lips about multiplying and worship. Then it laughed, a triumphant sound that made Kerry shiver all over.

That brought her back to herself in a hurry. She tried to wrap the tendrils of power around herself like a blanket, pulling them all back into herself. But that was when her nerve endings crescendoed. It was as though every muscle in her body shuddered its way to release all at once in the most intense orgasm of her life.

All the power she'd pulled back in washed out of her in a giant flood as she sank back into the carpet. But a moment later, she couldn't remember why. There was Lena and her girlfriend, Jan, and soft warm female flesh to explore. She lost herself as the three of them tried new positions, new angles. Sex toys appeared or objects became sex toys as the need arose. They ate breakfast, then lunch from each other's bodies and Kerry learned the exquisite joy of savouring pussy-flavored eggs. They took a shower, then a bath together, bodies becoming one as they entwined. Then, finally sated, they all climbed into the big bed that Lena and her girlfriend shared and slept, their dreams still gently sensuous.

It was the vine tickling her nose that first woke Kerry. She blinked at it in the early morning light, trying to remember what day it was and where she was. Lena let out a gentle snore from the pillow next to her and Kerry gave her sleeping face a giant grin. It lasted until someone else's arm dropped over her waist and she remembered Jan. But then again, after yesterday, sharing Lena might not be so bad. A slight throb went through her at the thought.

Then she realized that there hadn't been any vines in the bedroom when they'd gone to bed. At least, not coming down from the ceiling. She sat up slowly, hands going instinctively to her ribs. Her multiple breasts were gone. The spell must've worn off. She sighed, at once disappointed and relieved. It wasn't like they would have been convenient to keep.

At the same time, her eyes tracked the new vegetation growing over the ceiling and the walls. And the floor when she looked down. She clambered out of the bed as carefully as possible so as not to wake the others and looked out the window. The city was green as far as she could see and nearby buildings were a riot of vines and flowers. Trees and bushes burst through the sidewalk. Already they were too thick for cars to travel on the street below.

She could see naked bodies in the lush green jungle too. Bodies of all shapes and sizes and genders in all sorts of combinations, all of them waking puzzled and confused and sated to the new green jungle around them. Kerry pressed her hands to her cheeks in shock. "Did I do this?" she mumbled at last.

"Hmm?" Lena gave a questioning, waking sound from the bed.

Kerry turned around to find two sets of eyes squinting into the morning, glancing from her to the vines hanging from the ceiling. She looked back out the window, still not quite believing her eyes. She couldn't have done all this with her simple love spell, could she? No, it was impossible. Just like growing then losing multiple breasts overnight.

Lena's girlfriend came over to stand next to her. Jan was clearly occupied with the changes outside. Her mouth hung slightly open as she stared around. There was a long pause before she turned back to Kerry. "Hey, you've got the usual number of boobs!" She said in a slightly accusing tone. There was a short pause before she reached up and pulled at one of the vines. "Is all this related, somehow? Did you do something?"

"I'm not sure," Kerry muttered, hoping that it wouldn't be that obvious.

"Lena, come look at this," Jan ordered over her shoulder. "I think your friend got a little carried away with the whole love goddess thing she pulled yesterday."

Lena rolled out of bed and came over to stare out the window with them. "She was your friend yesterday too," she reminded Jan.

"Yeah, well that was before she probably put me out of work. Not much need for a road crew out there," Jan gestured outside with a look of disgust.

"I'm sorry," Kerry murmured, giving Jan an apologetic look.

"I'm not sure you should be." Lena wore a big grin and nothing else, which made Kerry stare longingly at her lush curves despite her fears.

Jan made an angry noise and stomped away toward the bathroom. Lena and Kerry kept looking out the window, digging their toes into the moss growing under their feet. "Should I try and reverse all this?" Kerry asked in a doubtful tone.

"Do you really think you could?" Lena asked quietly. "You did this for me, didn't you?"

Kerry blushed and hung her head, then nodded. Whatever had been inside her yesterday was completely gone, taking the city as its vessel instead. Instinctively, she knew that she wouldn't be able to stop it; it was much bigger than just her now. So that just left her on her own once more. She turned to leave, eyes not meeting Lena's.

Lena reached out and grabbed her hand. "Let's go check out our brave new world. No one's ever reversed Western civilization for me before. I think I'm flattered." Kerry looked up into her glowing smile and returned it with interest. Then, hand in hand, they walked out to explore the city.

Hanging in Suspense

Shaunda Randleman

I kneeled on the floor of the darkened, empty room, naked except for the chain clasped with a lock around my neck. I was on my hands and knees with my thighs spread and my ass as high in the air as I could hold it. My face was near enough to the floor that I could feel my warm breath deflected back at me. This was one of her favourite ways to see me, and I knew she would see it as a gift from me. I had no idea exactly how long I had been there, if it had been minutes or hours; my mind had raced though so many thoughts swirling in my head, so many possible scenarios, that I had lost track of everything except for my desire to please her. She is many things to me; she is a mistress, a master, my rope loving life partner, at times she is my devious and torturous captor. But I don't call her any of these things. To me she is everything; no word can describe that, so I don't even try.

Right now, all that separated us was one door. But she needed me to wait, she was busy, she had many things to do before she could attend to me. She told me earlier that today would be very satisfying for me, if I did as she instructed. I trust her, and I had no intention of disobeying. Now she was on the other side of that door, readying herself for me, taking her time to get into the right mood and mindset, while I was to wait out here. Before assuming this position of patience and waiting for her, I had taken some time to ready the room, setting the mood, trying to make it as pleasing to her as possible so she could see how much I wanted to please her. It was slightly cool in the room; just cool enough to keep my nipples hard. The air smelled of cinnamon from the flickering candles I had lit.

Finally the door opened and she walked in, radiant in her black satin. She stood above me, and though I dared not look at her, I knew she was visually inspecting me and the scene I had set. She walked around me slowly, stopping when she got behind me to look at my vulnerable ass. She liked it when I put myself in such compromising positions for her, making myself as exposed and open to violation as possible. She gave my ass a few light whacks, making me moan softly and push my ass further out toward her. She reached to my head, grabbed my hair, and pulled my head up from the floor. I instantly and instinctively opened my mouth for her; I knew very well that I was to keep my lips parted at all times. I silently hoped that she hadn't noticed that my mouth had been very much closed while my head was down.

She sat down in the only chair that occupied the room and gazed at me. I held my position, loving the way she looked at me, knowing that she was thinking about so many degrading things she could do to me. I looked longingly at a box that was situated by itself in the corner of the room in front of me. She noticed my look, and asked me what I was looking at. I dropped my eyes immediately; it made me feel naughty, as if I had been caught thinking dirty thoughts or something. She laughed darkly and stood. Walking to my ass again, she spanked me one more time on each cheek, just to tease and chastise me, but doing so hard enough to leave her handprint. She then walked away for a moment, going to the corner of the room to retrieve the box that had already caught my eye.

Moving with burning intensity and purpose, she sat the box down beside me and opened it, taking from it a coil of dark blue hemp rope; so dark it was almost actually purple. As the rope uncoiled, she let it fall on my lower back and ass. It felt amazing, sliding softly over my tender skin. Quickly finding the middle point of the rope, she pulled me upright and left me sitting on my knees. She dropped to her knees and teased my nipples with her fingers for a while, pinching and caressing, sometimes brushing my nipples with the soft rope, grass scented rope. Then she began wrapping her ropes around my body, and I could feel the ropes caressing my skin, like her hands had just been, and her hands still wanted to be as they kept stopping to pinch and tease my nipples. I could feel the ropes taking hold of my mind, driving me into a place of mental submission, where my bound mind would soon match my bound body.

As she wrapped the blue rope around my chest, over and under my breasts, over my shoulders, I simply sat there and swayed gently as her ropes tightened around me, holding me as a lover would. When she finished her work the chest harness she had fashioned looked beautiful, accentuating my breasts and the curves of my upper body. She leaned me back against her so she could caress my own rope-clad body; I laid my head back against her shoulder, breathing harder now through my open lips and I spread my knees for her, placing my palms face up, so I could more fully show her my submission. I knew instantly that she noticed this slight change in my posture, because I could hear it in the way her breathing hitched momentarily, betraying her excitement.

She nipped at my neck and shoulders, stinging hard little bites that almost made me cry out. Choosing a particularly delicious part of my neck, she kissed the spot deeply, sucking hard which created a feeling much like that of the dark embrace of a vampire. I swooned; my eyelids fluttered, and I felt the temperature of the room rising in great leaps and bounds. I became light-headed and my body sagged against hers. She pulled away from my neck, and instead began to kiss my open lips. This brought me back into myself, and I returned the kiss for a few blissful moments before she abruptly stood up, and pulled me to my feet as well.

Grasping the few feet of rope hanging from my completed chest harness, she pulled my hands behind my back and firmly tied them there, thrusting my breasts out further. As I stood there, trembling with excitement, she ran her hands, her wonderfully deft fingers, over my chest, touching my breasts, my shoulders, my back; sometimes tugging the ropes that now covered my skin maybe to adjust a rope or maybe just to watch me sway gently as she tugged. Though the room had been cool to begin with, I was now rather hot; the instant she had started tying me it felt warmer to me, as if the rope was a warm blanket that enveloped my body. She looked at me, drinking in the vision of me before her, adorned in her ropes and hungry for violation, her blue eyes burning in the flickering candlelight.

She picked up the box that contained her rope and, pulling me obediently along behind her by my chest harness, she walked out of the room. I followed her throughout the house until we reached our destination. She opened a glass door that opened onto a large room with three walls of brick and one of glass. There were many large and looming, ominous yet sexy looking objects in the room, a spanking bench and a St Andrew's cross, among others, but it wasn't these objects that we approached.

Instead she walked me toward the single largest thing occupying the room, a beautiful golden wood spiral staircase.

She had set the scene in this room; I had had nothing at all to do with it. Lights were strung around the stairs, giving off a subtle glow similar to the candlelight that we had just left, but bright enough to illuminate the entire scene clearly. On our way to the stairs, we passed a metal clothing rack, but it held nothing as innocent as clothes. Instead, hanging from hangers and hooks were a wide variety of paddles and floggers, slappers and crops, pretty much every kind of striking implement one could desire, creating a raging fire of excitement and anxious anticipation inside of me. I knew that anything was possible; I knew that I was in her world now, and unmistakably and completely vulnerable to her whims, however devious they might turn out to be.

She stopped me directly underneath the spiral stairs, so the largest central post was to my right and the stairs curled lazily above my head. I was looking out the two-story wall of windows into a land of deserted wooded wilderness. It was dusk, and the dark purple glow of the sky was entrancing; a beautiful shade that was so similar to the dark blue hemp ropes encircling my small breasts. As I stood there, my body shivering with anxiousness and longing, she placed her box of rope down on the ground, opened it again and pulled out another tight coil of blue hemp rope. She whipped this piece of rope around my hips skillfully, making a sort of belt around my midsection, and tying it off with much rope remaining, which she let fall graciously around my feet.

She then securely attached another piece of rope to the back of the chest harness she had finished and, throwing the remaining rope over one of the steps above our heads, she grasped the rope and pulled it taut. At her direction, I bent forward at the hips and I felt a tightening of the ropes around my chest as she began to tie, finishing it off with a beautiful coil. Then she took the rope that remained from the tie around my midsection, and did the same thing with it, throwing it over another step and pulling it taut as well. When she pulled this rope, my hips lifted and my entire body was straining to hold itself somehow, fully bent at the hips, ass exposed, my toes barely touching the floor anymore yet still trying to hold me still.

My breathing began to grow faster and harder, partially from the excitement and partially from the physical strain as well. I didn't know what else she could do, what else she had planned. She stepped away from me for a second, just to watch me struggle in my predicament. I couldn't see her, not even her reflection in the glass, but I knew that she was still there, watching. After a few moments of my struggle, holding myself for a moment with my toes before losing my balance and swinging forward or backward a few inches and catching myself again, she came to me and steadied me with her hand. She ran her hands over my exposed ass, down my quivering thighs, and to calves that were tightly flexed.

She began spanking my ass, slapping gently with her hands, side to side, growing harder and harder with each blow. I moaned from the sensation of her slapping hands, thinking I could endure it forever with no problem. But she kept going and it seemed as if she would never stop; the spanking got more painful, my ass burning as time went on, my left leg growing weaker and weaker as I tried to keep my balance and hold myself there. I began whimpering and wiggling under her hand. After what seemed like forever, she stopped, and I am sure that by this time, my ass was quite a dark pink for her.

She went to the metal rack holding her various tools of delicious torture, and she chose a large paddle in the shape of a coffin, one side covered in purple suede and the other side in black patent leather with the shape of a cross emblazoned in round metal studs. With care she rubbed the soft cool suede leather on my burning red ass, comforting my cheeks immensely, before pulling back and smacking them with the soft suede, showing me that it doesn't have to feel good.

She worked long and hard with that paddle, working my ass over, spanking me hard with the suede side, the caressing sweetly for a few moments. She turned it over and caressed my ass with the studded patent side as well, and it took me by surprise, the coldness of it and its studs, I deeply drew in a breath and pressed my ass out toward her further, causing me to lose my already unsteady balance. I swayed, but she caught me, then smacked my ass with that vicious black studded side as well, softly and gently at first, but gaining in intensity as she had proven herself so good at doing. Then she played for a while switching sides of the paddle and switching sides of my ass as well, until I was moaning and crying out, my ass ablaze with her dark red markings.

Returning the paddle to its place on the rack, she picked up a new coil of rope and unwrapped it. With this unused piece of rope draped over her shoulder, she took a hold of my ankle and pulled it up, folding my leg back at the knee and pressing my heel snugly against my ass. She began to wrap my leg in this position, moving so quickly and easily that before I realized what had happened she had finished wrapping that leg, and had pulled the rope over a step and tied it as she had the ropes before it. I was now precariously dangling in the air with one leg still desperately reaching for the ground. The quickly darkening windows reflected a sea of coiled ropes around my body, reaching this way and that, holding and supporting my various body parts. Without sparing another thought, she grabbed another rope, reached for my left leg and lifted it into the same position as the other and began wrapping and tying it the same way.

Now fully suspended in ropes, my body no longer under my own control and completely helpless, she let go of the ropes holding me and I swung forward towards the glass, rushing at my own reflection. As I swung back to her, she grabbed my hips and stopped me from flying forward again, letting me know that she was in full control. I could feel the ropes as they caressed me all over my body, but these were not typical caresses. The caress of rope is different, especially when the rope in question holds my full body weight in the air, feet above the ground. Rope holds the body tightly, forcefully, like a strong and determined passionate lover, and the rope is not afraid to bite into tender skin.

I felt every particle of my body; each and every nerve was singing with sensation. My heart was pounding and I could feel the blood as it flowed through every artery and every vein. My breath was quick and ragged, and my chest burned every time I inhaled, constricted by the secure grip of the ropes. The way my legs were tied my thighs were forced apart, rendering me utterly unable to hide my pussy, which was now undoubtedly drenched. Even trying to close my thighs an inch made me swing madly from side to side. I knew that she was enjoying the sight of me like this, thinking about how I always liked to be so in control of everything; control was now nothing but a vague concept to me, a fleeting idea that had no reality in my world any more. The only things that were real to me now were my body, the ropes, and her.

As I hung there swinging through the air, I felt her hands fall away from my body and the ropes holding me. I heard a familiar click, the lube being opened, but I could not see what was receiving the lube, if it were a toy or her fingers. She had yet to touch my pussy, and being ignored had so far succeeded in making my pussy extremely wet. But it wasn't my pussy she had in mind. I felt a gentle pressure around my asshole, and it opened up easily with the assistance of the lube, allowing in a small yet wicked butt plug. Every last nerve in my ass burned with delight, craving to be fucked, but she stopped after inserting the butt plug. She simply allowed it to remain there, holding my tight hole open, giving me the feeling of being fucked motionlessly. She disappeared from my sight again and I soon lost all sense of where she had gone. Muscles all over my body were still straining, quickly becoming exhausted as they struggled to regain the slightest illusion of control. I closed my eyes as I swung, letting my mind drift through this space, feeling the wonderful sensations from my ass and breathing deeply through the exquisite pain that throbbed in my tiring muscles.

I opened my eyes abruptly as a hand, her hand, roughly grasped the hair on the back of my head and forced my head down until my parted lips met a hard spear of purple silicone. She had slipped on her strap-on, what she called her butchcock, as she had stood in the shadows watching my body writhe and swing in the prison of ropes she had made for me. It fit her well as it always did; the five-inch cock just right for a dyke of her size, barely 5 feet 3 inches and a muscular physique. I loved the way the black straps wrapped around her body, offset beautifully by her milky white skin. The thought that beneath that cock was a throbbing clit made my pussy drip with desire.

My mouth opened fully to take her butchcock in. She kept her hand on the back of my head, guiding my swinging body to meet hers. Her butchcock hit the back of my throat time and time again, a good two inches still outside my lips. She thrust her hips forward and shoved my mouth farther down the shaft of her butchcock, making me gag as my throat opened up to allow the full length. Her free hand fumbled to grab the stairs above my head in an attempt to hold her body steady as she fucked my mouth harder, becoming more and more aroused as she did. Her eyes were open, watching and enjoying every tiny detail of her oral assault on me. Every time her butchcock would hit the back of my throat, she would force herself past, ignoring the sounds of my gag reflex and the hot tears that had begun to stream freely down my face. Letting go of the step, she grabbed my head with both hands, and thrust deeply into my throat. I could tell that she had come in my mouth by the way her body was convulsing and by the fact that she had allowed a long low moan to escape her lips.

Her body gleamed with sweat and she began to back away, pulling her butchcock almost all the way out of my drooling mouth, but I caught it with my lips and began licking and sucking again with fervour. I looked up at her, my cheeks hot and wet and my eyes still swimming with tears, with a ravished look that showed her just how much I had enjoyed what she had just done to me. I let her butchcock bob out of my mouth and straining to get my lips close to the base, close to the leather that barely hid her female sex underneath the purple cock, I licked shamelessly up the quivering shaft and kissed the gleaming purple head.

With this, she pulled away from my mouth; a thin string of saliva still connected us for a moment, and then broke, swinging back to dangle from my open lips. She caressed my body as she walked behind me, trailing her fingers lightly over my sweaty, flushed skin. She stood directly behind me, facing my deviously tied and parted thighs, her butchcock still sparkling with wetness from my mouth. I dropped my head, trying to see what was coming next. I could see my tightly wrapped body, the blue ropes of the chest harness and the white ropes everywhere else. There was a long, unbroken ribbon of come dripping down from my cunt into a small puddle already formed on the floor below.

She stepped in between my helplessly tied legs and drove her butchcock into my waiting, wanting pussy, and as she did I felt the butt plug in my ass even more than before. I felt totally and completely full, as well as totally and completely helpless. Flying through the air, I was vulnerable to so much. She fucked me like this for quite a long time; occasionally I tried to fight against the ropes that bound me and thrust my body against hers, but to no avail. I was being fucked and in control of nothing, so I gave up and simply went limp in the ropes, which she grabbed, pulling me hard onto her butchcock, using my swinging body for her benefit. I moaned and cried out, loving the way my body was being used for her pleasure, and she relentlessly fucked my cunt until she was on the very verge of orgasm again.

She withdrew her butchcock from my pussy, which was still dripping long strands of come into the growing puddle on the floor. For a moment I was sad, wishing she had kept fucking me until I came, and missing the fullness in my cunt. When she pulled her butchcock out of my pussy I was already on the edge of such orgasmic bliss, I had no thoughts of what could possibly come next. She took my chin in her hand, turned my head, and pushed her butchcock deep into my mouth again, this time deliciously covered in my own come. It was such a hot, sexy, degrading, and submissive violation, it made me come a bit; I could feel the hot come dripping out of me, like liquid fire. She thrust deep into my mouth, parting my lips farther, making sure I took every last centimetre, and making me choke as her come-soaked butchcock hit the back of my throat. I could taste myself on her. My eyes were wet with tears again, and they overflowed, staining my pink cheeks with little salty trails that dripped from my chin.

She pulled her butchcock out of my defiled mouth again and quickly walked back behind me, to my already spread, already fucked cunt. Ignoring my throbbing and dripping cunt, she pulled on the butt plug gently and began thrusting it back and forth, fucking my asshole with it. Slowly, she pulled it out of me, and for a moment I was completely empty. Then I felt her press her come- and saliva-drenched butchcock against my now very wet asshole. Despite already having been stretched open around the butt plug, my tight asshole didn't want to spread open for this large and imposing butchcock at first, but she pressed on, harder, and finally my ass opened up for her, taking in all of her butchcock. She just stayed there for a moment, deep inside of my ass, completely motionless. Then she began rocking, holding the ropes above my limp, hanging body for support while driving inside me, from deep inside my ass to the very brink of pulling out completely, over and over. I know I cried out for her many times, screaming and moaning, pleasure and pain interpreted by my body as one in the same. It felt amazing!

She pulled back on my chest harness, swinging my body towards her, and bounced against my ass. All this time I was still held securely in the ropes, drenching them with sweat, though their tight caress remained unchanged. I lost track of everything, I don't know how long she fucked me like this; I could see nothing, yet I could feel everything. The air rushed against my face as I swung back and forth through the air being impaled time and time again on her butchcock. I felt the orgasm growing inside me like a wildfire! I arched my back and raised my head up as far as possible, she reached forward and grabbed my chest harness, holding me up and back within my ropes, as she rocked with me, knowing that I was coming, and coming with me, inside of my tight ass!

Delicately, she removed herself from my ass, and came around to face me. She dropped to her knees and pressed her lips to mine, kissing me as if it had been the one thing on her mind she had yet to do. Her lips tasted of salt from her sweat, or maybe it was from my tears. She indulged in one long, lingering kiss before she stood and walked to my right side, and taking hold of my leg, still tightly wrapped holding my heel to my ass, she began the process of letting me down. She untied the ropes that held this leg in the air, and then began unwrapping it, removing coil after coil from my leg, revealing deeply imprinted rope marks. She helped me straighten my leg, and gingerly lower it to meet the ground. She did the same thing for the left leg, unwrapping it and helping me lower and finally place weight upon it. She removed the rope around my waist, and untied the rope attached to the chest harness, finally freeing me to stand fully.

I stood there, naked except for the blue chest harness, my body quivering from head to toe, partially from my strained muscles and also because I was cold now that I had been released from the majority of the ropes, thought it wasn't particularly cool in the room. She held me tightly and kissed me again. Locked in this embrace, we sank to the floor together. I could tell that she had anticipated us not making it out of this room after a full body flight like such as this one, by the way she had laid out a very large, soft pad over most of the floor, including underneath the spiral staircase where I had been suspended. She loosened the straps that held her butchcock so tightly against her, and slid it off smoothly, then reached behind me and freed my wrists. Slowly, she removed the chest harness that had held me so carefully for so long. She was very tender as she lifted the ropes from my skin, placing soft kisses upon the rope marks deeply etched all around my breasts, and tracing them with her fingertips which made delectable shivers run down my spine.

We kissed passionately and lay back upon the soft padding, and we began to make love to each other and our up-until-now ignored clits! Our clits were so engorged with blood I could feel the blood as it pounded; her clit throbbed under my finger, and I could feel my own clit throbbing under hers. I kept my lips parted for her, so that she could look at me, my open mouth, and easily see my total submission, my hunger to please her. She put her hand over my open mouth, and covered my nose as well, controlling my access to air. My eyes sprang open wide with excitement and immediately I thought I would come. But not quite, not right then; she didn't allow me another orgasm quite so soon. She removed her hand and I breathed in, gratefully filling my lungs with air.

Each of us focused on nothing other than the wonderful pleasure centres located between our legs, and together we drove each other almost to the point of orgasm countless times, with her always firmly telling me "No!" Finally, I knew I had her and her clit at the point of no return, and I breathlessly asked her, "Can I come with you?" and she moaned, a yes. And again, she covered my nose and mouth, and fucked me hard until I came again, screaming into her left hand, and gushing hot come into her right. She came with me, rocking her hot, sweaty body against me, until we just lay there shaking and moaning.

We lay together; holding each other in silence for what seemed like hours, almost drifting to sleep, enjoying the after-glow of a high that can be matched by nothing else in this world.

Eventually she sat up and stroked my hair, and said to me, "You looked beautiful tonight as you flew, and you made me very proud as you took everything I gave you without protest. Thank you for trusting me. Now . . . Let's get you cleaned up."

I smiled sleepily up at her, already thinking of my body sinking under the warm bubble-filled water, and whispered, "I love you."

If the Shoe Fits

Susan Wallace

Jayne wandered into the shoe shop as nonchalantly as she could. Her hands were buried deep in the pockets of her black trousers and she was wearing a long, grey raincoat. This was the third visit she'd made during the past week and today she intended to speak to Sarah, the manager, who had a bob of deep ginger hair and eyes the colour of orange marmalade, the kind of colour only women with ginger hair can possess. Then she'd have to go to the shopping centre's lost property to see if her handbag had been handed in.

She spied Sarah immediately, her attentive face turned to an elderly woman as they discussed suitable winter footwear. The smell of leather filled her nose and she took a deep breath of the familiar scent, her spine tingling a little.

Jayne walked casually over to the high-heeled shoes on the right of the small shop, the sunlight streaming in through the window beside her. She absentmindedly picked up a black, strappy shoe and looked at it, turning slightly so she could glance at Sarah as she bent down, the old woman now seated, her stockinged feet waiting for the attentions of the manager.

Jayne's gaze briefly lingered on Sarah's backside, black trousers tight around her cheeks and no visible panty line. She imagined them bare, the thin, black line of a thong disappearing seductively between her pale, rounded buttocks. The fingers of her right hand pushed deeper into the trouser pocket and she rubbed at the top of her vulva gently beneath the concealment of her coat. The hairs on the nape of her neck rising, she felt weakness in her knees as she imagined stroking and kissing Sarah's rounded buttocks with a tenderness wrought of sweet anticipation.

"Can I help you?" came a gentle female voice, making Jayne jump.

Slightly flustered, she turned to the young shop assistant whose face was thick with powder which accentuated rather than hid her mild case of acne. "Just looking," she replied with a forced smile, her hand stilled beneath the long coat, the crotch of her knickers damp and sticking to her hidden lips.

The assistant turned to go and answer the phone which had just started ringing beside the pale counter to the rear. Jayne glanced over at Sarah and felt more heat rising between her legs as the object of her desire crouched before the old woman in a servile position, one which she'd imagined her taking on numerous occasions.

Sarah knew she'd come into the shop. She felt the woman's gaze upon her and the stiffness of her nipples as they rubbed against her black polo shirt. She'd been coming in regularly that week, presumably on lunch breaks, always immaculate in her suit, long, black hair trailing to her shoulders, curling slightly about her pale neck. She judged the woman to be in her mid-thirties, a few years younger than she was.

She wanted her and yet she didn't even know her name. She'd served the stranger the first time she'd come in, but their effort at conversation had been a stumbling affair filled with awkwardness. "I should make an effort to talk to her today," she thought as she crouched before the old lady whose bridge of upper front teeth kept coming loose as she spoke, a gentle sucking sound just audible as she pushed the line of four ivories back into place with her podgy thumb.

The young shop assistant approached Sarah. "That was Head Office checking to see if the new area manager has been in to see us yet," she informed her boss with a frown.

"Thanks, Vicky," responded Sarah.

The assistant nodded and walked over to a mother and daughter who had just entered. "May I help you?" she said with a smile.

Sarah turned her attention back to the lady seated before her as Jayne waited, loitering by the dress shoes and handling them with disinterest. She glanced over at the counter to the rear of the shop and their eyes met, the gaze held for an instant longer than was normal, a tell-tale sign of mutual interest.

After making the sale to her customer, Sarah walked slowly around the white counter and headed over to the woman, smile betraying the nervousness she was feeling; tight lipped and tentative. "Would you like to try on a pair of those?" she asked in her rich, smooth voice as she straightened her name badge, "Sarah" written black on gold.

Jayne hesitated, gaze moving briefly to the other woman's lips, imagining them upon her skin, gently caressing her neck, Sarah's breath making her tingle. "Yes, thank you," replied Jayne, holding out the red shoe that happened to be in her hand.

"Size six, isn't it?" Her eyes sparkled.

Jayne nodded. "That's right," she replied, happy that the other woman had remembered.

As Sarah went to the back of the shop and descended the stairs to the store room, Jayne seated herself on one of the green cushioned stools and slowly slid off her shoes, enjoying the gentle sensation. She caught sight of her reflection in the tall mirror against the wall opposite and ran a hand through her dark hair, feeling a prickle of excitement, still aware of the moisture between her legs as her pulse quickened.

The manager soon returned with a black shoebox and crouched at her feet with head slightly bowed. The open collar of her blouse revealed the alluring upper curves of Sarah's breasts; pale like snow and smooth like silk. Jayne longed to reach out and stroke them, but resisted the temptation as the manager opened the shoe box. She slowly took out the pair of red shoes and removed the crumpled paper from within them.

Jayne's eyes moved to the slightly pouting lips of the other woman, a sensuousness to their enticing fullness. Sarah looked up at the woman whose feet she obediently crouched before, aware of the appreciative gaze which had been studying her carefully.

"Lift up your right foot, please," she requested softly, Jayne taking in every movement of her glistening lips, which were touched with the merest hint of deep red.

Jayne did as asked as Sarah held the shoes at the ready, her index fingers stroking the leather subconsciously as she looked at the tightness of Jayne's trousers about her thighs and crotch, the rain coat falling open with the customer's movement. She could make out the slight indent between the woman's legs and the raised flesh to either side pressed tightly against the cotton.

The shoe was slipped on with a delicious slowness, the tips of Sarah's fingers brushing against Jayne's instep, ankle, and the top of her foot. Her eyes closed temporarily in pleasure and her legs came together slightly in an automatic response to the small tremor of delight that filled her vagina and made her tingle.

When Jayne opened her eyes again she found Sarah quickly looking away, a smile and a flush upon her face as she took the left shoe and prepared to place it on the other foot with the same gentle ease that made Jayne melt.

Then Sarah sat submissively at her feet, ready to assist in any way she could. The sight of her so willing and waiting, so ready to serve, turned Jayne on and she could feel the heat between her legs rising further in reaction to the manager's subservient position on the floor.

Sarah saw the craving in the other woman's eyes and felt herself become wet, the way she was sitting helping to accentuate the presence of her thong as it became damp and pressed against her, parting her lips with a hidden deliciousness.

She shifted, feeling the thong tighten further, enjoying the secret sensations as the woman before her looked around the shop in a desperate attempt to distract herself, to calm the lust she was clearly feeling.

Sarah took a deep breath and then took the plunge. "What's your name?" she asked in a whisper, their eyes meeting and the electricity of lust passing between them with a surprising strength.

"Jayne," she responded.

"What are you doing after work?"

Jayne's heart fluttered now she knew the feelings of attraction were mutual. "Nothing," she replied, swallowing hard, wanting her desire to be fulfilled, wishing Sarah would reach out and touch the centre of her growing heat.

"Meet me here," the manager instructed simply.

"Okay." Jayne nodded and took a steadying breath as Sarah leant forward to remove the shoes.

She slowly took them off one at a time, making sure her fingers brushed Jayne's skin, invisible sparks crackling, the contact intense despite its apparent triviality. Both women's physical awareness was heightened in their close proximity, both finding the touch of skin on skin almost overpowering.

Sarah packed the shoes back into the black box as her heart pounded. "You didn't really want these, did you?" she asked with a smile, delicately curved, ginger lashes batting as she blinked, pupils dilated as she continued to feel the warm pleasure between her legs.

Jayne shook her head. "No, not really," she admitted, a thin smile on her lips as she licked them, the movement of her tongue slow and measured, Sarah watching it, imagining it playing across her stomach, making the muscles jump and skip with its considered touch as she moved to explore lower.

There was a moment of silence and then Sarah rose to her feet. "I'll see you later," she whispered as they reluctantly parted.

Jayne nodded again and waited for a few moments before standing and exiting the shop, her gaze taking in the generous curves of Sarah's figure as the assistant who'd first approached her smiled sweetly as she left and a tall, serious looking man in a pin-stripe suit peered into the shop.

Sarah walked to the stairs at the back of the shop and stopped on the landing halfway down. Putting the shoebox on the floor, she unlocked the red door beside her and stepped out into the cool freshness of the small yard which belonged to the shop and served as a suntrap in the summer months.

Locking the door behind her, she moved over to the white, plastic garden table and three matching chairs, seating herself on the nearest one. With her right hand, Sarah undid the clasp of her trousers and then gently pulled the zip down, closing her eyes, listening to the soft sound and letting the expectation of what was to come fill her, images of Jayne seated before her in her mind's eye.

Enclosed by four brick walls, Sarah sat in the yard and pushed her hand inside her trousers. She gradually pulled the thong aside, enjoying its movement against her eager vulva as it rubbed her slightly protruding lips. Sarah sighed as her middle finger ran the length of her vagina, slid in the wetness and heat which had been building. It moved to her clitoris, rubbing gently, the pulses of electricity it radiated making her gasp each time they jolted through her nerves. She imagined Jayne's tongue there, her head buried between her legs as she licked and held her open with her hands, exposing her.

Using her index finger to massage her clitoris, Sarah slipped the tip of her middle finger inside slowly. She moved it with increasing quickness as her clitoris continued to send spine melting sensations through her body and she imagined Jayne's tongue delving within. In her mind she ran her hands through the other woman's long, dark hair, pulling her tongue closer, feeling it enter and explore her. She imagined hot breath upon her skin, her body alive with the thrill of Jayne's touch.

The sudden knock on the red door made Sarah jump.

"Sarah, are you out there?" It was Vicky's voice.

"Yes," she replied croakily before clearing her throat, her fingers stilled, but pulse still racing.

"I think the area manager is here," said the young shop assistant.

Sarah sighed. "Perfect timing," she mumbled sarcastically as she quickly withdrew her hand and did up her trousers. "I'll be there in a minute," she called back to the girl.

She stood and took the key from her pocket. Adjusting her thong and taking a few deep breaths, she glanced up at the cloudy sky before stepping over to the door, feeling very unenthusiastic about meeting the new area manager.

When Jayne left the shop she'd completely forgotten about her lost handbag. Her mind was filled with a maelstrom of thought which whirled around Sarah and the meeting that was promised for later in the day. Her legs were a little weak as she headed for the shopping centre's car park, her pace quick as she longed to relieve her sexual tension.

The sound of her heels echoed as she walked up to her silver hatchback on level three. The indicators flashed as she disabled the alarm and put the key in the door.

Once inside she took a deep breath and then stared ahead at the brick wall in front of the car. Her vagina throbbed as she thought about Sarah's lips, her eyes, her attentiveness as she crouched before her in the shop. Jayne recalled the touch of her fingertips and closed her eyes, mouth opening slightly as she slid her hand under the rain coat and rubbed herself.

The movement of her hand was slow at first, but the rhythm increased steadily with the pressure she applied. Regularly glancing in her mirrors to make sure no one had noticed her activity, she slipped her hand inside her trousers and immediately pushed a finger into herself, overcome with urgency.

The finger delved, pushed, writhed, brought her ever closer to climax. Her breathing became heavy and her eyes remained tightly closed, Jayne forgetting where she was as she thought about the manager of the shoe shop.

The orgasm rushed through her and she stifled a small yell as her legs trembled violently, feet involuntarily kicking out against the pedals. With teeth gritted, she took deep breaths, the tension which had arisen in her muscles fading and being replaced by a deep sense of calm.

Her eyes snapped open when she heard the sound of footsteps

approaching. Looking in her driver's side mirror she saw one of the car park security guards coming towards the car with a serious expression on his young face.

Jayne quickly put the key in the ignition as the stocky man walked alongside the hatchback. He knocked on the driver's window and she pressed the button for it to descend.

"Hello, officer. Can I help you?" she asked with as much innocence as she could muster, well aware that her cheeks were flushed and there was a slight sheen of sweat on her forehead.

"Is everything all right?" he enquired, bowing slightly so that he could peer into the car's interior.

"Yes, everything's fine, thank you." Jayne smiled at him and started the engine.

The officer looked at her with a frown as she put the hatchback in reverse and carefully pulled out of the parking space. With a quick look into her rear-view mirror to confirm he was still watching, Jayne drove towards the exit, a little disappointed she hadn't been able to enjoy the fullness of her orgasm, the feelings now only faint as she concentrated on driving.

Still, hopefully this evening will be better, she thought as she smiled at herself and left the car park.

By the time Jayne saw her reflection in the glass of the shoe shop's door she was feeling a heady mixture of excitement and nervous tension. The steel shutters were already lowered over the windows and all the lights were turned off inside. She raised her hand to shield her eyes and peered in, but there was no sign of Sarah.

With hands trembling, Jayne knocked gently and the door rattled slightly.

She waited, but there was no response.

Looking both ways along the street, Jayne then took a deep breath and tried the handle, her mouth dry. The door opened silently and she quickly stepped in, not wishing to be seen entering the apparently closed establishment.

"Sarah?" she called apprehensively. "Are you there?"

"Lock the door," came Sarah's instruction from somewhere in the darkness at the back of the shop.

Jayne tried to make her out in the gloomy interior, but could see nothing. She turned and found a bunch of keys dangling from the lock and did as she'd been told, the latch clicking shut.

"Take a seat," said the manager from her hiding place.

Jayne breathed in the strong smell of leather and walked over to the cushioned stool where she'd sat earlier that day, beyond the view through the glass of the front door. As she sat down she heard Sarah's steps on the stairs and turned to the sound. Somewhere in the darkness the manager flicked a switch and a light came on in the display of shoes before Jayne. Sarah calmly stepped from behind the counter, a large grin on her lightly freckled face.

Jayne's eyes widened as she took in the fantastically erotic sight. Sarah stood near the counter completely naked bar a pair of black knee-high boots. She looked ghostly, her skin as pale as snowdrops in early spring in contrast with the leather.

Sarah felt her heat grow as the other woman's gaze drank in her nudity appreciatively. She walked slowly towards her, arms loose at her sides, wrists rubbing gently against the curves of her hips as she caught the faint scent of her arousal and felt the downy hairs on her inner thighs brushing together with a sensual subtlety.

Coming to a halt before the other woman, Sarah smiled down, her nakedness accentuated by the single light shining nearby and their aloneness in the silence of the shop. Jayne's gaze roved up and down her bare flesh, pausing at her large breasts with their pale nipples and again at the rise of deep ginger pubes between her curvaceous legs.

"Touch me," whispered Sarah, her exposure turning her on as Jayne sat before her, their roles reversed from earlier that day; Sarah now in the position of power.

Jayne hesitated and then raised her hands to Sarah's stomach, fingertips touching the warmth of her pale skin and stroking the gentle curve of her slightly rounded belly. Her hands slid over Sarah's hips and round to her buttocks, the manager taking a step closer as Jayne watched her fingers on the silken skin in the mirror opposite them. Sarah's scent wafted to her as she raised her hands to the other woman's soft breasts. She followed their curves and circled the erect nipples slowly.

"Pinch them," said Sarah huskily.

Jayne did as she was told, taking the firm nipples between her thumbs and forefingers, rolling them carefully and then applying more pressure. Her palms pressed against the warm skin of the manager's breasts, felt their malleable softness.

Sarah took another small step closer, her ginger pubes now right in front of Jayne's face, a heady mix of leather and the scent of her sex filling her nostrils.

"Use your tongue," said Sarah, laying her right hand on the back of Jayne's head and pulling her closer, legs parting slightly.

Jayne saw the pink lips peeking from between mounds of flesh which contained her desire. Leaning forward, she kissed Sarah's abdomen, the muscles quivering beneath her skin. Then Jayne ran her tongue down the inside of the manager's left thigh, eyes closing, lust filling her as she gently licked at the exposed lips, barely touching them at first.

Sarah felt the brush of the other woman's tongue between her legs and sighed. Hot breath caressed her thighs as Jayne's tongue pushed harder against her, parted her as hands still toyed with her breasts, squeezing them and rubbing the stiff nipples.

Jayne moved her left hand down Sarah's smooth belly and opened the manager wide with her fingers. Her tongue delved deeper, circled the edge of the wet entrance and then slid inside to explore within.

Sarah grasped the hair of the woman seated before her and moaned aloud, feeling exposed and aroused by her attentions. "Deeper," she said with a sense of urgency.

Jayne's tongue moved further within, curling and wiggling with a deliberate slowness that made Sarah want her more with every passing moment. Her thumb massaged the clitoris, sent little sparks of delight flashing through her, legs trembling a little and feeling weak.

Suddenly Jayne stopped, slowly withdrew her tongue and hands.

Sarah's eyes opened and she looked down. "Don't stop," she said with cheeks flushed. "Please, don't stop."

Jayne simply smiled up, ginger pubes glistening in front of her face. She pulled back further and then stood, Sarah stepping back in her knee-high boots, the leather creaking softly.

Jayne quickly undid her smart black trousers and pulled them down with her white knickers in one, fluid motion. The dark triangle was revealed between her legs and Sarah grinned.

Sitting back down, Jayne reached for the manager's hands and pulled Sarah towards her.

She resisted. "No. I want to see everything," she said, pulling her hands free.

Sarah knelt on the deep blue carpet with her vulva towards the mirror, her body angled so she could look over her shoulder at its reflection. Turning to Jayne, she smiled. "I want to see your tongue parting me as I feel your hot breath on my skin.''

Jayne nodded, her body tingling with expectation. Standing up again, she removed her white shirt and bra, laying them over the seat. Then she manoeuvred herself beneath the ginger-haired shop manager. She felt a deep sense of excitement as she thought about Sarah's face only a few inches from her sex, which ached to feel the sensations of the other woman's tongue upon it.

Looking up, Jayne slowly raised her head towards the glistening lips before her, slightly parted as if to invite her attentions. She glanced at the mirror and saw Sarah watching intently as her tongue slipped out and made gentle contact with the warmth between the other woman's pale legs, the sight of the spectator turning her on even more.

Jayne closed her eyes, her nostrils filled with the erotically charged scent of Sarah's sex. She reached round and sucked her right index finger before carefully inserting it into Sarah's anus. She moved it with calm deliberation as her tongue pushed between the fleshy lips and the fingers of her left hand parted them further, Sarah letting out a groan as her body quivered.

The sensation of Sarah's lips upon her inner thigh made Jayne pause momentarily as the other woman began to caress her with obvious purpose, her kisses leading slowly towards the centre of desire. Jayne tried to concentrate on the movement of her index finger and tongue as the manager ran her nails along her lower stomach, brushing the dark pubes and making Jayne tingle.

Lust took over where thought could not go, the feelings of pleasure and flames of desire so strong as the two women abandoned themselves to the moment. Jayne's tongue moved inside, writhed in the wet confines, Sarah's taste adding to the intensity. The manager slid two fingers into Jayne. They explored her, found the spot within which caused the fire to burn with such fierce brightness. Their nerves were alive with powerful sensations as tongues and fingers brought them towards the pinnacle of pure ecstasy.

Their breathing was heavy as their bodies writhed, desperate for the other's attentions, wanting more, needing more, longing for the release of the molten glow within.

Jayne's tongue darted in and out of Sarah, her fingers now flicking the other woman's clitoris. In turn the manager sunk her fingers into Jayne as she kissed her thighs, bit them, ran her tongue along them. She had never wanted anyone more, was overcome with such lustfulness. She thrust into Jayne's vagina with increasing pressure and speed, reached between them and grasped one of the other woman's firm breasts as she leant forward and tasted her again.

Jayne let out a scream of pure, erotic pleasure as her nails dug into Sarah's buttocks, the world shrinking into a ball of white light centred in her womb and then exploding, sending its warmth throughout her body.

"A little more," said Sarah, urging Jayne to continue.

Jayne's tongue moved with a quick rhythm as she breathed heavily, a finger entering with it as her thumb rubbed the manager's clitoris. Her jaw ached from the effort as Sarah finally bucked and trembled, collapsing onto her as the rush of orgasm filled her every nerve.

After a few moments of succulent silence, their skin flushed and bodies close, Sarah moved from on top of Jayne and changed positions so they were lying face to face. They grinned at each other like Cheshire cats as the feelings of ecstasy lingered, pulses of warmth rolling out through their bodies.

Jayne stared into Sarah's eyes as she reached out and stroked her cheek affectionately. "I'm the new area manager," she said quietly.

Sarah looked at her, recalling the false alarm earlier when Vicky had mistaken a bank manager for the anticipated visitor.

Jayne's fingers ran through Sarah's ginger hair. "I always pose as a customer the first couple of visits to get a feel for the shop and its staff. But don't worry . . ." She smiled at Sarah disarmingly. "You've got a lot more than just great managerial skills."

Sarah grinned. "I knew who you were all along," she admitted. "You left your handbag here when you came in on Monday and it had the shop's address in it, along with directions so you could find your way. When I heard the area manager was due I put two and two together."

"You really knew?" Jayne was clearly surprised.

Sarah nodded and took hold of Jayne's hand, giving it a gentle squeeze. She leant forward and they kissed softly in the warm afterglow of pleasure's promise.

New Beginning

Melissa Fawcett

Terri had always hated motorway driving, especially at night; the small area of visibility and the speed unnerved her. An argument at the same time was more than she could cope with, especially when the argument was with Marilyn. One of the reasons she didn't want to argue with Marilyn at the moment was because they were going on holiday, but also it was because of what arguing with Marilyn did to her. She didn't understand why but arguing with Marilyn never failed to arouse her sexually – and she couldn't afford to get aroused while she was driving on the motorway.

"I don't know what possessed me to agree to coming away," Marilyn said. "You know I don't get on with your friend."

"You couldn't wish to meet a nicer woman than Annie, and after the last time I would have thought you'd want show yourself to be a bit nicer as well."

"You thought wrong."

Terri dug her fingers into the leather covering of the steering wheel. She had gone to a lot of trouble to arrange for them to stay in a cottage next door to her friend Annie. And although she was looking forward to the holiday – to seeing Annie and to spending time with Marilyn – she was nervous about those two meeting again; it had been such a disaster the first time. Unless Marilyn's mood improved before they arrived it would be equally bad this time. Marilyn had been behaving like a spoilt brat ever since they had set out. And just to confuse everything, arguing with her was making Terri feel damp.

"You know how much my back hurts without my cushion," Marilyn continued. "You've no consideration, that's your trouble."

Terri couldn't believe that, after all she had done to put the holiday together, Marilyn was bitching about a cushion. A bloody cushion! She told her that if the cushion was so important she should have put it in the car herself, instead of leaving everything to her. But although she was furious at Marilyn for complaining, her fingers were digging into the steering wheel as much in an attempt to control the unwanted sexual arousal as much as her anger.

"It wouldn't have been difficult to put it in the car with everything else. Or maybe you like the idea of me being in pain? Maybe it satisfies some sadistic urge in you, is that it?"

"For God's sake, Lyn, I forgot your stupid cushion. It's not the end of the world."

"Well, thank you for caring."

Terri glanced sideways and saw that Marilyn's pretty face was distorted by her petulance. She felt like pushing her out of the car. All she had to do was lean over and open the door, depress the catch on Marilyn's seat belt and give her a shove. She could tell the police that Marilyn had committed suicide while the balance of her mind was disturbed by a cushion. She couldn't help smiling at the thought.

"Oh, so now you think it's funny?" Marilyn snapped.

"No, of course not. Please, Lyn, let's not have an argument."

"It's a bit late for that. It's no use going out of your way to upset me and then saying let's not have an argument. Pull into the next service area, I need a cigarette."

"I thought you'd agreed to stop."

"If you didn't make my life so stressful I might have half a chance."

"Come on, you can't give up at the first hurdle."

"Just pull in at the next service area and stop disagreeing with everything I say."

Terri half-wanted to say something to ease the tension; but at the same time she didn't see why she should. She wasn't the one who was in a foul mood.

"Okay, buy some bloody cigarettes, see if I care. Have stinking breath and diseased lungs, it's your choice. I'm not going to argue."

She immediately regretted having said that. She wondered whether she was deliberately trying to provoke and prolong the argument so that she would get aroused? No, she couldn't believe that. Why was she even thinking it? It was Marilyn, not her – Marilyn was the one who was being difficult.

At the start of their relationship, Terri had been impressed by

Marilyn's cool independence – Terri was of an age when she no longer wanted a partner who would cling – but the cool independence seemed to have turned into selfishness.

"Oh, no, of course, it's never you, is it? You're not the one who argues? It's always my fault!"

Terri refused to respond. She tried to distance herself from the bad vibrations in the car by recalling earlier, more pleasant days.

It was less than six months ago that she had picked Marilyn up at an exhibition of erotic art. She had noticed Marilyn's pale pretty face from the other side of the room. Dressed in a leather mini-skirt and tight top, Marilyn had looked incredibly desirable. She had been standing in front of a Gustave Coubet painting of two naked women lying on a bed, supposedly sleeping but wrapped around each other and entwined in a highly suggestive manner. One of the women's lips were close to the other's breast. Marilyn was smiling to herself and probably showing her thoughts more blatantly than she intended. Terri had gone up beside her and said, "Does that appeal to you?"

"What d'you mean?" Marilyn had asked, a little flustered. "The painting or the act?"

Terri had laughed and Marilyn had blushed. Terri had suggested a drink. Marilyn hesitated, but when Terri had asked her again she had finally agreed. Marilyn was not as diffident as she at first seemed. In fact she was quite argumentative. While having the drink, she had been surprisingly rude by contradicting everything Terri said and had started an argument which had become heated on both sides. That was the first time Terri had ever been aroused by an argument. She couldn't wait to get her hands and mouth on the girl. She persuaded her to come back to her flat, where they had re-enacted the modeling of Courbet's painting.

Terri couldn't remember when she had had such wonderful sex. Marilyn's skin was gorgeously soft, her breasts firmer than any she had caressed in a long time, her bottom deliciously kissable and her vagina so young and tight that Terri's tongue almost had to force its way in. And Marilyn's muscles made Terri feel that her tongue was being pulled right up into her vagina. Terri had never thrilled at soixante-neuf so much as with Marilyn. She would happily have stayed in that position for hours, giving Marilyn pleasure and tasting her sweet juices while encouraging Marilyn to do the same to her.

Just thinking about how wonderful it had been that first night softened her towards Marilyn. But it also made her even more aware of the dampness between her legs.

"Maybe when we get to the service station we could find a dark corner and get in the back of the car for a little while?" she suggested.

"Are you kidding? After being so horrible to me, you expect to eat pussy? You've got a bloody nerve. You're always the same. You deliberately start an argument and then you expect sex afterwards!"

"Please, Lyn, I need something, even if it's only a loving finger."

"No way!"

She had not told Marilyn how their arguments aroused her; she had always felt slightly ashamed of the fact. In all her forty years, Terri had never experienced such strange emotions before and she was confused by them. Marilyn was nearly twenty years younger than her and was undeniably difficult but Terri knew that the arguments were her own fault as well. Although she didn't want to admit it, she seemed to need them.

Initially, she had thought she was in love with Marilyn, and she had wanted her to move in with her, but Marilyn wouldn't; she had said she wanted to retain her independence. And after a while Terri was glad of that. She realised that what she had taken for love had in fact been lust. She didn't mind – she was still having sex with someone twenty years younger than she was – but she knew it couldn't last. And the arguments worried her; it didn't seem right to be aroused by arguments.

"You'll do something else to start an argument before long, I know you will. You always do! I wouldn't mind betting you've even brought that stupid flute with you."

Despite herself, Terri smiled. There was no denying that she had provoked that particular argument. It had been a Sunday afternoon. They had been out for a lunchtime drink. Terri had wanted Marilyn to go to bed with her but Marilyn had gone into the living room to practise her yoga. Terri sat on the bed and began playing her recently acquired flute – even though she knew Marilyn hated the noise it made.

"What d'you think you're doing?" Marilyn said, coming into the bedroom.

"I'm playing my flute." She smiled. "Why?"

"Why? Because I'm trying to relax, that's why. How can I do

my yoga when you're making that horrible noise? I'm trying to concentrate."

Marilyn's anger had made Terri want her more than ever.

"Why don't you concentrate on me instead? Come on, come and have sex with me and I'll leave you alone to practise your yoga afterwards."

"No!"

"All right, I'll carry on playing, then."

"Oh, for God's sake, don't be stupid."

Terri had resumed playing. Marilyn had tried to snatch the flute away. Terri had then began shouting at her for damaging the flute and the argument had raged. Eventually, Marilyn had flopped reluctantly yet submissively onto the bed, where she had tried to stay aloof to show her irritation But Terri went down on her and soon got her excited and involved. Terri knew that no woman was going to stay aloof with her tongue working between their legs.

Although Marilyn had refused to move in with her, she stayed with Terri most nights. It was six weeks after they had met that Annie, Terri's best and oldest friend, was passing through town and came over for a meal.. Terri cooked for the three of them. She had always got on exceptionally well with Annie and she was delighted that she was meeting her other favourite person. Unfortunately, Marilyn was in one of her petulant moods and at ten o'clock she went upstairs to practise her yoga. Annie and Terri stayed down in the kitchen to talk and laugh and to remember old times. Fifteen minutes later, Marilyn reappeared.

"Are you two planning on keeping up this noise for long?"

"What noise? We're only talking," Terri said

"Talking? You sound like a couple of braying donkeys. If you're going to make this sort of noise, I'm not going to stay here in future! You shouldn't have friends here when I'm here."

Annie said she'd leave. Terri was mortified. She followed Annie to the door in an embarrassed silence and then went upstairs to have a blazing row with Marilyn. She told her never to dare be so rude to one of her friends again. Terri couldn't remember ever having been so angry. But Marilyn was equal to her, insisting that Terri had ignored her all evening in favour of Annie. They were both shouting and screaming at each other and in the middle of all the noise Terri's whole body was aching for sex. That evening their sexual endeavours reached new heights. They had been locked so hard in their favourite soixante-neuf position that Terri felt they had become a single entity. By the time they finished, Terri's face was drenched with Marilyn's sweet juices.

Now Terri felt wet at the thought of that night. Then she looked sideways at Marilyn's stony face.

The service area was ahead.

"You should be in the nearside lane," Marilyn said.

Terri signalled and pulled off the motorway.

"I'm going to have a coffee with my cigarette," Marilyn said, getting out at the service area.

"Okay. I'll go and fill up. I'll see you back here when you're ready."

She watched Marilyn walking to the shop in her high heels and she smiled wearily at the movement it created in Marilyn's lovely little bottom.

After two hours of argument and arousal without any satisfaction, Terri was suddenly exhausted; she felt as though she'd been on a sexual helter-skelter. She could see Marilyn in the shop; she looked as though she were arguing with the shop girl. Terri smiled again. It made her feel better to see Marilyn in a bad mood with someone else.

Terri drove to the petrol pumps, but while she was filling up with petrol, in her mind she began another argument with Marilyn. She often found herself having pretend arguments with her these days. It was either sex or arguments, real or pretend, there didn't seem to be anything normal in their relationship. Sometimes, she even imagined herself having an argument during sex; even with her head between Marilyn's legs and while she was teasing her clitoris with the tip of her tongue she would imagine herself arguing. Once she had got so carried away with a pretend argument that she had bitten the inside of Marilyn's thigh in her anger. It was almost as though sex stimulated the arguments as well as the arguments stimulating the sex. She wished it wasn't so.

Right now she was defending herself and attacking Marilyn even more vociferously than in one of their real arguments. She was telling her that things could not go on as they were and that she was thinking of ending it. Marilyn said she didn't care because she'd never liked her anyway.

By the time Terri got back in the car, the argument was raging furiously inside her head. But also she was sexually aroused. She couldn't believe how much the make-believe argument was arousing her. She had to undo her jeans and put her fingers in to her vagina. She was having difficulty not vocalizing her anger. She continued playing with herself. This was just the relief that needed.

She was still arguing as she had an orgasm. She collapsed onto the steering wheel. After a moment, she started the engine and put the car into gear. Without thinking what she was doing, she found herself driving back onto the motorway. Only when she was filtering into the main stream of traffic did she realize what she had done.

"Oh God. Marilyn!"

She felt a moment of panic. Then she laughed. What an idiot she was. She wondered if Marilyn would see the funny side of it. Would she tell her about the argument, the sex or just the forgetfulness? Maybe just the forgetfulness. She didn't know how long it would take to get back to the service station. It would probably be half an hour or so. Marilyn would have long since finished her cigarette and be searching for her. She would probably think she had done it deliberately. She'd be really pissed off. Did that mean she would start an argument?

She put the radio on to relax. She was thinking about Annie, about the long friendly relationship that they had had and the other relationship that they had never. She wondered why they had never crossed from friends into lovers. They had always got on so well and Terri was excited about seeing her and spending time with her. The only problem was Marilyn. Terri almost wished she was going to see Annie on her own.

Fifteen minutes later, Terri came to an exit and indicated that she was going to pull off the motorway. There was no one behind her to see the signal; so she switched the indicator off again. And once she had done that she realized there was no reason to pull off the motorway. She felt quite light-headed at the thought. She wasn't going back. It was over. The feeling of relief caused her to laugh.

College Grind

Courtney Bee

Violet liked to joke that I had only been a "kinda" lesbian until college – until the frat parties. Watching all the beer-guzzling jocks hoot and holler like apes, slurring obscenities and dripping sweat, certainly didn't enhance my appreciation of the male specimen. Although watching a snot rocket contest from across a crowded room may have reaffirmed my sexuality a bit, I had always been gay. I remember being on the cheerleading squad in high school, continually volunteering to be on the bottom of the pyramid so that I could feel the other girls' sweat-slicked bodies pressing down on me. If I timed it just right I was able to tilt my head as the top rows climbed down, catching flashes of white panties as their skirts swished about their hips.

Sophomore year of college, my little goddess appeared, smiling at me at our sorority initiation from across the room. She wore a red headband and a simple white sweater that hugged her high, rounded breasts so lovingly that I was instantly jealous; her skirt was just short enough to make me break out in a mild sweat. When she turned her head and caught me staring she gave me a look that said she knew exactly what I was thinking – and liked it.

Fast forward eight months: we're so close you'd have to pry us apart with a crowbar if you wanted to talk with one of us alone. The fact that we live in the same sorority house is great – we get to share a room and live in pre-marital sin on the university's dime. For a while we had a third girl sharing our room, but one night she saw our hips gyrating beneath the covers and the little whistle-blower ran down the hallway and cried "lesbian". Well of course Tiffany and Cindy and Candy and all those other little bitches threw a hissy fit and immediately tried to get us thrown out, but the dean gave them a long speech on discrimination and we got to stay.

Most of the girls stopped talking to us, and one handed Violet a bible and tried to get us to go to her youth group. Some were outright malicious, like Mindy, calling us gross and weird and whatever other small, uncomplicated words her Communications Major brain could concoct. She happened to inhabit the room next to us, so one night after Violet overheard her telling one of the other girls that the sorority should try harder to make us feel unwanted so that we'd leave, we had our loudest evening of sex yet, banging the headboard against the wall and letting our groans send her to sleep. Little Miss Mindy went to the dean again, and this time her complaint didn't fall upon deaf ears. Violet received a letter informing us our "case" was under consideration and it was possible we might be evicted from the sorority, as we had now been accused of reckless and inappropriate conduct. We shrugged and figured if there was a chance we'd have to leave the house, we might as well savour our current living arrangements as much as we could. The volume of our nightly groans tripled.

I couldn't have cared less about the sorority and fraternity party scene, but Violet loved it, so for her sake we went to many a drunken beerfest. By now everyone knew we were dating, and whenever we walked through the threshold of a big bash the girls would whisper or roll their eyes. The guys, however, had a rather different reaction. They would see us holding hands, navigating our way through the crowd, and they'd stand at full attention, craning their necks to get a better look. "It's 'cause we're both hot," Violet liked to say. "If we were wearing flannel and penny loafers they'd be burning crosses."

The jocks had taken to calling us Betty and Veronica on account of our contrasting features. Violet had buttery blonde curls and soft grey eyes, while my hair was jet-black, my eyes a deep shade of green. I knew exactly what they were picturing when they stared at us. I usually responded to their leers with an annoyed glare, but Violet was a bit kinder, smiling and waving diplomatically. The only pleasure I got out of these outings was seeing Mindy's look of abhorrence when we entered the room. She'd usually be clinging to her jock boyfriend, her little squeak of a laugh piercing through the room. Her eyes would quickly narrow as we flashed her our best sickly-sweet smiles. Meanwhile, her ape of a boyfriend Steve would gawk at us so bluntly that Mindy would immediately tighten her grip on his arm. Normally I didn't care, but tonight her look was so spiteful that it churned my stomach. Her eyes were gloating, and I could practically hear her thoughts: Soon you freaks are outta here. Enjoy this while you can!

"Come on," Violet whispered. "Let's go rustle up some booze."

We downed a couple drinks, glancing over our shoulders every so often to see Mindy glaring at the back of our heads.

"It's not fair," said Violet. "I really liked living in the sorority house. I liked having our own room. And I know you hate this, but I'm actually going to miss these stupid parties."

I grabbed her hand, running my fingers over her palm. "This isn't for sure yet. The dean hasn't said—"

"Oh, come on, Anne." She rolled her eyes. "He wanted to kick us out the moment he heard about our situation – you know how diehard Republican the guy is. He was just waiting for an excuse that looked legitimate, and thanks to Mindy he's got one. We'll be out on our asses by the end of the week."

I thought for a long moment. "You know Mindy's little boy toy over there is related to Dean Mason?"

"That right?"

I nodded. "Nephew, I think."

We both turned to look at Steve, who appeared to be en-thralling Mindy and a couple of his football buddies with one of his harrowing sports tales. Their "huh, huh, huh" laughs blended together in a far-reaching Cro-Magnon chorus.

"You know," said Violet. "Steve actually asked me out during rush week."

I raised an eyebrow. "You too? I caught the jerk trying to look up my skirt three weeks ago. He said he wanted to make sure I was a thong girl before he asked me out!"

Violet's fingers tightened around the little plastic cup. "That son of a . . ." She raised her head sharply. "And he's the dean's nephew?"

"Pretty sure."

"You know," she said brightly. "This could work! This could actually work!"

"Baby, what are you—"

"Okay," she said, clasping her hands together. "Steve's made no secret that he wants to see us get it on together."

"Tell me about it," I grumbled. "I heard the lacrosse team was putting together a pool to try and get us to Jell-O wrestle."

"W-well," she stammered. "You know how you said you were curious about exhibitionism?"

"Uh-huh . . ." I saw the wheels churning and suddenly I didn't like where the ride was taking me.

"He's related to the dean," she said, her voice taking on the tone of a plea. "He can help us."

"Uh-huh . . ."

"Maybe if we put on a little show for him, he'd convince the dean to let us stay in the—"

"A little show?" I croaked. "What, you want to give the biggest jerk on campus a free peep show?"

Violet stared at the ground. "Well, we wouldn't let him join in or anything. I know he'd agree to it, Anne. You know he would."

I couldn't believe what my girlfriend was suggesting.

"You know –" I glared. "– I always thought that the element that made our sex so hot was, oh, the absence of boys!"

"We're only going to let him watch!" she implored. "Just this one time – please, Anne!"

"Why don't you chug down another beer," I said. "Maybe if you get a little more inebriated you'll have an even more brilliant idea – like blowdrying your hair while you're still in the bathtub to save time."

"All right!" she yelled, slamming her cup onto the table. "Fine. I was just thinking about how much I loved you – how I couldn't bear the thought of us living in separate apartments after we've been so happy living together. If the dean throws us out of college housing everyone will know why. The school will tell our parents, and I don't know about you, but mine will try and keep me as far away from you as possible."

Her eyes were glossy with tears. I felt myself softening, smoothing her hair with my palm.

"I'm sorry," I said. "I didn't think of it like that."

Her face was so pained that I felt my resolve melting, even as my fists remained clenched.

"I'll do it," I blurted. "Tonight, while there's still enough alcohol in me to make me overlook the fact that this is insane."

"Oh, Annie!" She gave me a soft peck on the lips, causing every male within a twenty yard radius to snap their heads in our direction.

"I can't believe I'm going to – to—"

"Hey, you hate Mindy, right?" Violet's face broke out in a wicked grin.

"I wish I could wrap her extensions around the wheels of a city bus."

"Well," Violet beamed. "How would you like to watch her boyfriend cast his relationship aside to watch two girls get it on?"

Actually, I did like that thought. Very much.

"Follow my lead, baby."

Taking one last deep, courageous breath, I took Violet's hand and we marched brazenly to the corner of the room where Steve and his football pals were chatting. Mindy stared at us incredulously, as if she was unable to believe that the lowly lesbians would be so bold as to attempt to converse with them.

I forced my lips into a flirtatious smile while Violet batted her eyelashes.

"Hiya, Steve," I purred. "My girlfriend and I were just talking about a little fantasy we've been having lately."

The guys quickly leaned forward. Steve raised an eyebrow.

"Um, excuse me," Mindy glowered. "But what makes you think we have any interest in interacting with you?"

"Do you mind? I'm talking to my friend Steve."

Ignoring her, I stepped forward, running a finger down Steve's chest. I felt his heart beating in rapid little thumps beneath his shirt. Violet dutifully slipped beside him, rubbing his shoulder with slow, enticing strokes. Steve's mouth dangled open; his friends watched in disbelief as we pressed our bodies close.

"Steve," I whispered, letting my breath waft across his neck. "Do you want to know what our fantasy is?"

He answered so quickly the word made a little whistle as it flew from his lips. "Yes."

"Get lost," Mindy chirped. "Nobody cares about your—"

"Shut up," two of the guys hissed in unison. Mindy glared indignantly.

"You see," I continued, my eyes burning into his. "Violet and I have decided it would really turn us on to have someone watch us."

"W-watch you?" he gulped. "Like . . . like watch you guys—"

"Screw."

His hands tightened around his beer; the can made a crunching noise as it imploded.

"We wanted it to be someone who would really appreciate it," Violet murmured. "And we thought of you."

Mindy opened her mouth to say something, but Steve interrupted. "Are you joshing me?"

"We only have one condition," I smiled. "We want you to persuade your uncle to let us stay in the sorority house."

As Violet let her hair sweep across his arm, stirring his flesh into goosebumps, I could taste victory.

"That's it?" Steve said. "You guys'll get it on in front of me if I tell my uncle not to kick you out?"

"Tonight. Right now."

I saw the yes about to fall from his lips and suddenly I got greedy.

"And," I said. "I want you to tell him that Mindy made the whole thing up. She's on drugs, you see, and rather prone to delusions."

"You bitch!" Mindy shrieked. "Get the hell out of—"

"Done," Steve said.

Mindy let out a horrified screech.

"You all heard it," I grinned. "Steve Anderson has promised, with his closest friends as witnesses, to make sure we aren't evicted from our dorm. Now, gentlemen . . ." I stared at Mindy. "And shrew, if you'll excuse us, Violet and I are going to take this lucky boy upstairs and give him sweet dreams for life."

With a squeal of glee Steve pushed Mindy aside and Violet and I each took an arm. We led him to the staircase, Mindy's wails a symphony to my ears as we ascended the stairs. He waved one last time to his friends, who were cheering like monkeys, as we disappeared into the nearest bedroom. Violet brushed the curtain from the window, letting the moonlight flood the room. As I turned to address Steve I saw his hands lunging for my ass and I quickly darted away.

"Nuh – uh," I said firmly. "You watch. We play. Got it?"

He mumbled something beneath his breath and sat on the bed. I shut the door, clicking the lock.

"Fully nude," he blurted. "I wanna see tits and ass."

"We have a lot in common."

I approached Violet, blocking out Steve's eager grunts. She glanced shyly at him, then at me.

"Come on, baby," I whispered. "Pretend it's just you and me." I turned to glare sharply at Steve. "And no punching the munchkin, understand?"

He nodded, grumbling.

My hands circled her hips, drawing her to me. With a smile I leaned forward and traced the pillowy outline of her lips with my tongue. Her jaw was tense; she was still a little nervous. I probed her lips with my tongue, parting them gently. I felt her face relax as we began to kiss.

From several feet away Steve's voice vibrated the walls. "Holy shit!"

Violet flinched at his voice until I coaxed her back into a long, wet kiss. Her arms went lax as I probed deeper, reassuring her with each hot breath. When I finally pulled away her eyes were sparkling.

"All right?" I asked.

"Y-yes."

"Just you and me, baby."

She nodded. Slowly, gently, I peeled her tank top over her head, revealing the soft breasts beneath. As Steve's breath caught in his throat I felt momentarily sick exposing the girl I loved, unwrapping her like a present for a slobbering stranger. Then Mindy's outraged screech rang through my head, giving me the boost I needed to continue. I smothered her breast with my lips, nibbling and sucking until she was forced to let out a low groan.

From across the room I heard Steve muttering a steady stream of "oh, Gods". I tuned out his voice, focusing on the little pink nipple that was growing hard beneath my tongue. Violet began to make the soft whimpering noise I loved so much, her chest shaking in little heaves. I felt her hands fumbling with my blouse, twisting the buttons until it fell silently to the floor. Steve's eyes glinted from across the room, his breathing so shallow that he sounded like a rabbit.

When I looked up to assess Violet's comfort I was surprised to see her eyes dancing playfully. Her hips were rocking from side to side; she ran a hand coyly through her long blonde hair. The little showboat – she was playing it up! She was like a little kid in front of a video camera. And I had to admit that I was feeling a bit of a thrill myself – knowing that someone's eyes were combing our bodies and watching our every move was more titillating than I had imagined, even if the voyeur was an undeserving prick. But the fact that Steve was of no sexual interest to either of us, coupled with the fact that his persona made me queasy, propelled me to flaunt the situation – torture him a bit.

Violet seemed to be having just as much fun. She pushed her chest forward, letting the tip of her nipple graze the outline of my breast. I let out an exaggerated moan, arching my back so that our breasts smashed together. Steve groaned. I flashed him a smile with a hint of sadism.

As our hips came together, rocking slowly, rhythmically, I slid my hand up Violet's thigh, feeling for the damp cotton panties. I tugged them down to her knees. Her eyes became nervous again, darting to Steve, then back to me.

"I don't think . . ."

"Come on, baby," I smiled. "You're halfway there. Besides – you're wet."

And she was. A single drop of moisture was gliding down her leg. I leaned forward, stroking her flesh with my tongue, lapping up the warm fluid, moving steadily upward until my lips were inches from the soft pink folds tucked between her thighs. Out of the corner of my eye I saw Steve running his hand over his crotch, a firm bulge beneath his jeans. With a grunt of satisfaction I yanked Violet's skirt to the floor and buried my lips between her legs, running my tongue over every delicate contour. Her hands gripped my shoulders to steady herself as I began to tease her into a wet frenzy. She went crazy whenever I let just the tip of my tongue glide inside her, but tonight I probed her so forcefully she began to squirm with shock. My hands gripped her ass, driving her hips forward so that I could taste her deeply.

I pulled away and rose so that I could read her face. Every last trace of fear had vanished; her eyes were dizzy with lust. The man in the corner of the room had disappeared as far as we were concerned. It was just us. And we were very, very horny.

I kissed her, letting her drink deeply from my lips, the sweet taste of her own juices still clinging to my tongue. Her fingers slipped around my waist, tugging at my jeans until they glided down my legs. She slid the black thong aside and let her hand roam the soft triangle below my navel. I tilted my head back, enjoying the way her fingernails brushed against my skin. As I felt my hair tickling the arch of my back I turned my head, catching Steve's tortured expression. I felt a little smirk of satisfaction. Before I knew it I was batting Violet's hand away and digging my pelvis into hers. She loved it when we came that

way, grinding and squirming against each other until our thighs
were soaking wet. Violet came so easily like that, but would she
come quickly, breathlessly, while a practical stranger watched?

As our bodies rubbed together Violet suddenly stuttered, "I
d-don't know if I can c-come with him watching."

I ran my hand through her hair and gave her a reassuring
smile.

Steve's voice was so high it sounded like he was going through
puberty. "You both have to come or the deal's off."

I flashed Steve an annoyed look before turning back to Violet.
"You can do it. Close your eyes, baby . . ."

I took her hands and gently guided her to the floor. Silently I
laid her across the carpet, my hips gliding on top of hers. I
straddled her, staring at her for a long time before I saw the
reluctance melt from her face. With a wink I began rocking back
and forth, the wetness between my thighs gliding over her clit,
coating it with heat. Her legs parted wider.

I barely heard the creak of the bed as Steve leaned forward,
his eyes like a laser beam on our grinding bodies – Violet's voice
was smothering the room, an avalanche of whimpers and guttural moans. As I slid up and down, teasing her clit with my
wetness, my warmth, the softness of my triangle, she broke into
a fevered panting that only meant one thing – she was coming.
Violet was going to come in front of a stranger whether she liked
it or not. She bit her lip as the first wave came, her body going
slack against the carpet. She winced. A stream of whimpers
cascaded from her lips. I leaned down and kissed her, savouring
her rapid gasps as the shockwaves began to ebb.

I looked up to see Steve wide-eyed and unblinking.

"I . . . oh, my God . . ."

I kissed Violet's cheek. Her chest was rising and falling in
deep, ragged breaths. Her eyes were soft when she tilted her
head to smile at me. I lowered my head to give her another kiss,
but Steve's voice made me pause.

"You both have to come." He grinned.

"Well," I said sweetly. "Why don't you come over here and
help me out?"

He jumped straight into the air.

I glared. "Sit down, jockstrap."

He fell back onto the bed, glowering.

Violet had already sprung into action. She knew exactly
what to do to send me over the edge – and no one had a more

capable tongue. I stood up as she kneeled on the floor, her head tilted upward, ready to lap between my thighs like a kitten laps at milk. I cradled her head with my palm as her tongue glided over my pussy, swirling in urgent circles around my clit. I felt her finger glide inside me, rubbing in harmony with her tongue. She made a little moan of determination, pressing hard, until I felt my mouth contorting into an o. The wetness of my orgasm flooded her lips, trickling across her cheek in a warm flood. My fingers wrapped around her hair, pulling it tightly.

Her lips brushed against my clit until the last spasm. When she finally pulled away a mischievous smile was on her lips. I ran my finger down her cheek, unable to suppress a giggle. She flashed me an amazed look that said, I can't believe we just did this! I'm pretty sure my expression was the same.

I ran my hands over her shoulders, frowning at the goose-bumps that covered her body; without the heat of arousal the room was rather cold. Silently I began to dress her. I pulled on my pants, my blouse, my shoes. When we were clothed we stood for a moment in a daze, surprised by the thrill of what we had just done.

Steve sat rigidly on the bed, staring at us as if we were the angel Gabriel himself. I noted the dark wet spot on his crotch, smiling with satisfaction. Steve shifted quickly so that the evidence of his pleasure was tucked between his crossed legs.

Without groans and pants to fill the silence an awkwardness washed over the room. No one knew what to say now that our clothes were on.

Steve was the first to speak, standing clumsily. "Er, uh – very nice. Beyond expectation."

He leaned forward, shaking our hands politely. Violet and I giggled. Had we just given a PowerPoint presentation?

"And you'll keep up your end of our agreement?" I said.

"Of course."

"Good." I smiled. "Because if you don't I'm going to tell everyone that you came up here to have a hands-on threesome with us and couldn't get it up. Good day, Steven."

Steve kept up his side of the bargain and no one ever questioned his erectile abilities. Much to our beloved sorority sisters' dismay, we continued to live in sin amongst them, spending our evenings studying for exams, watching *The Daily Show*, and playing poker . . . naked.

As for Mindy, a series of tragic circumstances led to her eviction from the sorority house. Her parents demanded she live under their roof for the remainder of college after some very unsettling rumors fell directly upon the dean's ears. It appears the stories about Violet and I performing lewd acts while living in the sorority house were simply wild accusations Mindy had made while not in a normal state of mind – she was on drugs, you see. Heroin apparently. Nice, Steve. Nice.